UFSD 71

A School Novel

by
Joseph E. Scalia

Tawny Girl Press
Farmingdale, New York

ISBN-13: 978-0692999752
ISBN: 0692999752
ASIN: B078R6HHHD

Dedication

For Ginny with love
who put up with me
all those years. Always #1

Terry Rowan
so much of this book is you, my friend

The teachers and staff
and students of
Hicksville Junior and Senior High Schools –
my inspiration,
my lifelong friends, my family

INTRODUCTION

UFSD stands for Union Free School District, which is how independent school districts across Long Island are identified, not because there are no unions, but because they are not combined with other LI school districts. *UFSD 71* is an "old-school" novel set in a suburban high school during the 1971-72 school year. But it's not just a book about school. It may be set in a school and the characters work in a school, but even if you haven't been in or thought about school since graduation, you will recognize my characters no matter where you work.

I like to think of *UFSD 71* as *Catch 22 Goes Up the Down Staircase,* and I am hoping reviewers will too. If you don't know those two books, you should–so I'll wait while you go read them and come back.

I started writing the book in 1971, the year I took a sabbatical leave after seven years teaching English to junior high-school kids. I was young and naïve, and teaching was just "a temporary job." My plan was to get tenure, then like Joseph Heller (see *Catch 22*) write a best selling novel that would point out all the fools and foolishness I had come to know during my seven years as a teacher, and "blow the lid off the teaching game"! I'd get rich and famous, drive a Porsche 911, become the darling of the talk show circuit, get a seat on the *Tonight Show* couch between Johnny and Ed–and I'd never again have to go back to reading Robert Trumbull's *The Raft* five times a day with bored seventh-graders! But alas, the best laid plans, as the saying goes....

Though there are many drafts of the manuscript, I finally finished writing *UFSD 71* in my twentieth year of retirement and after a thirty-three-year mediocre career making red marks on essay papers. I may have been an English teacher, but my math is good enough to know that *UFSD 71* was forty-five years in the making! That will either look great on the dust jacket of the book, or pretty lame. I can see and hear the comments: "It took him forty-five years to write? So it must be an amazing book!" or "Forty-five years? That sure was a lot of wasted time!"

Over those years of numerous rewrites many things changed–my original story, the characters, the world, and especially me. Johnny and Ed are dead and I never could afford a Porsche 911, let alone fit into one today! But more than anything my feelings about teaching changed.

In the final rewrite, thanks to Patricia Ruggero for the suggestion, I connected real world events in that turbulent time during the reign of Richard Nixon with my fiction by adding "In the News" at the beginning of each month as an anchor.

Looking back I'm glad I didn't become rich and famous and leave the classroom. In my thirty-three years so many wonderful people, teachers and students, have filled my life, have become my lifelong friends–my extended family. After more than twenty years out of the classroom we are still connected and they are still major part of my life. To them I say thank you for your love, inspiration and support. This book couldn't have happened without you. I am sure you will recognize many of the characters between the covers of *UFSD 71* and recall the real stories behind the fiction.

Two final acknowledgements to Rob Dircks and Martha Trachtenberg. Rob is a former student and now accomplished author, the first person other than me to read my manuscript and encourage me to finish it. Martha was the second to read it. She proofread and corrected my mistakes. It's a very long book and I am sure there are still some things that slipped by. If you do find any between the covers let me know and I'll correct them in the sequel!

All that being said, I hope you enjoy reading the book. And I hope it doesn't take you as long to finish as it took me to write.

Joseph E. Scalia
January 2018

PREAMBLE

The following pages provide a brief history of the founding of the town of Farmington, New York, in the central portion of Nassau County, Long Island. It details the decades of construction of what would one day become Rosencrantz and Guildenstern Memorial High School, the jewel in the crown of Farmington Union Free School District 71, and it provides insight into three generations of Klaus Brinkers who designed, planned and oversaw the three separate stages of construction from 1941 to 1960.

I
A BRIEF HISTORY OF THE FOUNDING OF THE TOWN:

Hicklerville was built on shit and founded by mistake by Ephram Hickler, a Bavarian blacksmith war criminal and fugitive. In October 1914, after bribing guards at the prison where he was awaiting execution for war profiteering selling inferior goods to Kaiser Wilhelm, Hickler and his supporters escaped to *the port of* Bremerhaven. From there they steamed on the Norddeutsche Lloyd ship *Eisenach* destined for Brazil. When the ship's crew mutinied mid-Atlantic they steamed instead to Hoboken, New Jersey, where the Hickler band jumped ship and fled across the Hudson River to New York City, east across the Brooklyn marshes into the soft underbelly of the fish that is Long Island. Stopping somewhere well below the fish's heart, they settled closer to its anus on a tract of soil blackened from New York City sewage that had been dumped on the site for decades. There Hickler and his inexperienced followers established "The Great Northern American Cotton Belt." A ten-mile-long bicycle caravan carried the delicate cotton plants from Georgia to Long Island to get them into the ground by late spring. "The Cotton Pony Express," as historians would later call the caravan, arrived too late and an especially severe winter killed all of the plants.

A week before President Woodrow Wilson declared war on Germany on April 2, 1917, the newly established Hickler Scrap and Salvage Company contracted to ship scrap iron to the Fatherland, but the cargo was intercepted at sea and confiscated by the destroyer *U.S.S. Looney.* Hickler was found not guilty on a technicality in December 1919, and was free to undertake his next venture distilling alcohol. On January 2, 1920, the Hickler Distillery and Brewing Company opened its doors for a little more than two weeks before the 18th Amendment "Prohibition Act" went into effect drying up America and bankrupting Hicklerville, as the town had been named. Once again they were on the wrong side of history. When New York and New Jersey mobsters enlisted Hickler and his resources for their lucrative bootlegging enterprise, it looked to be the beginning of a beautiful and lucrative friendship, until Chicago's Al Capone muscled in. At their face-to-face meeting Hickler, always a stubborn and defiant man, unfortunately called Capone "Scar Face" to his scarred face and refused an offer he shouldn't have. Two weeks later Ephram Hickler, founder of Hicklerville, was gunned down in an open-car motorcade through town during the annual Founder's Day Parade. The shooter, Hickler's nephew Ludwig, the driver of the car, claimed his pistol accidentally discharged five times. Police suspected Capone was behind the hit, but shortly after Ludwig Hickler disappeared the case was closed.

Two years after Ephram Hickler's death, Italian immigrants and Irish potato farmers joined forces and wrested political power from the few remaining Hicklerites. Their first official act after they took control was to change its name to Farmington, which it is still called today.

II
ROSENCRANTZ AND GUILDENSTERN MEMORIAL HIGH SCHOOL: BUILDING ORDER OUT OF CHAOS

From the outset Farmington's high school was plagued by controversy, scandal and a family feud. Board President Wilbur Vecht approved construction plans submitted by local architect Klaus Brinker Sr. at an unprecedented Sunday meeting on December 7, 1941. At exactly 1:55 p.m. Zachariah "Zak" Change, Exultant Chancellor of the town's chapter of the Invisible Empire of the Knights of the Christian Coalition, burst into the meeting minutes too late to put an end to what he called "an unnecessary taxpayer expense for an unnecessary school when the old one was doing just fine." When President Vecht called for Zak Change to be removed by the sergeant at arms, the Exultant Chancellor produced a large pistol from under his KCC robes and fired several shots. One went into the ceiling, one through the window and one removed the greater portion of President Vecht's right ear before the gun was wrestled from Change's hands. From his position on the floor amid the fallen plaster and his own blood, Vecht shouted over the panicked crowd that the motion to build a new high school was passed before he passed out. He was later quoted in the Mid-Island *Clarion-Herold-Sun-Times:* "The citizens of Farmington deserve what they get and they will get what they deserve. A new high school *will* be built now and without delay, even if we have to use substandard materials." So on December 8, while the rest of America mobilized for war with the Japs, Farmington rushed to begin construction on its new high school, where President Vecht's immortal words would be forever inscribed on the building's cornerstone.

Klaus Brinker Sr. oversaw the beginning phase of construction, but was too old and feeble to see it through to completion. Klaus Jr., himself ailing from the yellow fever he had contracted while working on the Panama Canal, took over for his father. Headaches, fever and muscle pain, jaundice, thirst and black vomit caused by occasional internal hemorrhaging caused Junior to rely on his only child, Klaus III, or Trey as he was known.

Construction was slowed by the war, the shortage of workers, the high cost of materials and additional modifications to the original plans. The first added the clock tower originally designed for the railroad station and the second consisted of eight large columns, four per side, to support the two peaked roofs were extended beyond the original bare facade to give purpose to the columns, creating a decided Southern antebellum look. It was Trey's contribution after he read an account of Ephram Hickler's unsuccessful attempt to grow cotton decades before, published in the *Clarion-Herold-Sun-Times,* and saw Tara in the movie *Gone With the Wind.*

A month before the scheduled opening of the building the Board sponsored a contest to name the school. It was won by Helene Hunt, wife of the town's Volunteer Fire Commissioner. "Moved to tears by the off-Broadway performance of *Hamlet* and the tragedy of those two fine men Rosencrantz and Guildenstern," she said on the entry form, later published in the newspaper, "there can be no more fitting tribute or lasting monument to two such great, but unfortunate, men of history and literature than naming the new school building after them."

Rosencrantz and Guildenstern Memorial High School opened its doors in 1945. A showplace, it drew spectators from miles around who came to see the graceful Southern columns, the steeply pitched roofs and the clock tower. There were also some flaws. Most obvious was the clock tower. Money raised for the imported Swiss mechanism to drive the large clock mysteriously disappeared and the town voted down a bond issue for additional funds. So the tower remained empty and the clock never moved. "It will be right twice a day," President Vecht said. And the people of Farmington quickly grew accustomed to a clock whose hands were perpetually frozen at seventeen minutes past nine. In fact, they came to enjoy the security of time standing still in their little town.

The postwar growth, returning war veterans who moved east from the city eager to start families and "own a home in the country with a little piece of grass" and booming babies made it evident that R and G would soon become too small for its swelling student population. Town planners again looked to the two remaining Brinkers for help, unaware of a rift between father and son. Legal papers filed by Junior Brinker, who sought to disown and disinherit his son, cited Trey's "flamboyant lifestyle and ambiguous-gender cross-dressing."

All communication between them ended, so the expansion project was done in total silence. Weeks before completion it was discovered too late that their failure to communicate alterations to the blueprints caused large gaps in the construction, missing walls, windowless rooms, stairways that led nowhere and floors that did not connect exactly. But the work had progressed beyond the point of no return and the gaffs were hastily corrected or covered up. "The students of Rosencrantz and Guildenstern Memorial High School will just have to learn to live with our mistakes," President Vecht proclaimed. His words were inscribed on the cornerstone of the new Klaus Brinker Sr. Annex at the dedication ceremony.

1960 brought the final addition when the District purchased surplus prefabricated wooden and corrugated tin shells used by U.S. "peacekeeping" troops in Korea. "They are cheap and easy to install," said the new board president and they were erected virtually overnight to provide additional room for the still-growing student population. Though intended to be temporary structures until the taxpayers of Farmington voted to fund a more substantial structure, the chilly, drafty, noisy and substandard additions, christened the "Klaus Brinker Jr. Temporary Wing," remained as erected, untouched and unimproved for more than a decade. That was the last construction until the expanded Administrative Parking Lot and the new cesspools that came to Farmington after the arrival of Dr. Donald F. Flackett, the new superintendent of schools in 1967.

In the News
September 1971

September 3
What would later be known as "The Watergate team" breaks into Daniel Ellsberg's psychiatrist's office.
September 8
Nixon tells John Ehrlichman, Assistant to the President for Domestic Affairs and White House Counsel, to investigate the tax returns of rich Jews contributing to the democratic campaigns of Humphrey and Muskie.
September 9
John Lennon releases his megahit *Imagine* album in the U.S.
Nixon's "Enemies List" is compiled by Special Counsel to the White House Charles Colson, written by George T. Bell, assistant to Colson, is sent in memo form to White House Counsel John Dean.
A thousand prisoners seize control of the maximum-security Attica Correctional Facility near Buffalo, NY.
September 10
Nixon is informed of and approves John Ehrlichman's plan to steal Vietnam War records from the National Archives building.
September 11
Former Soviet leader Nikita Khrushchev dies at age seventy-seven.
September 13
New York State troopers and prison guards storm Attica Correctional Facility to end the four-day inmates' rebellion over poor living conditions. Forty-three lives are lost, eleven guards and thirty-two prisoners.
September 17
U.S. Supreme Court Justice Hugo Black retires after serving thirty-four years.
September 25
Retired U.S. Supreme Court Justice Hugo Black dies.

It was a good summer, but not a *great* summer.

"Nothing's the same!" Jesse's grandfather had told him earlier that morning during one of the old man's more lucid moments. "Summers too hot. Winters too cold. Foods don't taste the same. Ever since the Russians landed men on the Moon."

"We landed them on the Moon, not the Russians. The Russians sent up Sputnik," Jesse had replied.

But the old man wasn't listening or not remembering what he'd said. "What?"

"Never mind. Please get out of the bathroom, Pop. I'm going to be late for my first day of school."

"You're too old for school," the old man said. "You should get a job."

"I got a job–at a school. I'm a teacher."

The summer had been exceptionally hot, but with entirely too much rain and Labor Day came early. On a scale of one to ten, as summers went, this one, Jesse's *last* summer, was a seven... at best a seven and a half... but certainly not an eight. If he were still using the "Helen of Troy–Face That Launched a Thousand Ships" scale he developed after reading Homer in Ancient Greek Literature, it would have been about a 750-ship-launch summer. But a thousand was too unwieldy, so he reduced everything in his life–food, movies, girls, summers–to a number somewhere in that simplified one-to-ten range and now life could be reduced to its lowest terms.

Two hours later Jesse's old Mercury wheezed and farted to a stop at the curb in front of Rosencrantz and Guildenstern Memorial High School. He looked across the newly mowed lawn and his entire brief life flashed in front of his eyes like a drowning man's. All twenty-one years four months ran through in one quick montage of silent single frames.

He clicked off the ignition and just like that it was behind him, college, the "best years of his life" and this seven-and-a-half summer, his final summer. Ahead of him loomed the building that would be his workplace, his home away from home, his prison for the next one hundred and eighty-two school days, adulthood and the specter of death.

He didn't feel like an adult. He felt uncomfortable straddling two worlds, and even more uncomfortable in the suit pants that his mother bought for him the week before. They were too tight, but not at all in a good way like the jeans that were his second skin, his uniform in the old life. His face burned from scraping clean the beard he had cultivated while he was away at college. He had shaved the night before and let his father cut his hair because Jesse knew that a beard and long hair would make a bad first impression. He certainly didn't want anyone to think he was a hippie, one of the great unwashed of the Woodstock Generation, now that he was a teacher. His feet already hurt in the unforgiving stiff leather shoes that cut across his instep and pinched his toes.

Inside the car Jesse shook from nervousness and he wiped the sweat from his forehead. He stared through the dirty windshield and the building shivered in waves of the early morning heat. It was going to be a scorcher. He could feel the mounting hysteria gathering just below the surface into a sour ball in his stomach, threatening to explode onto the dashboard in the form of partially digested scrambled eggs and buttered toast that his mother had insisted he eat for breakfast. "You can't begin the first day of your teaching career on an empty stomach. Eat," she said, spooning more runny eggs onto his plate.

Ever since kindergarten, the first day of school had been difficult for him. It meant a week of lost sleep, fits of crying, stomach cramps and diarrhea. And now, after all those years of first days from kindergarten through college, nothing had changed. His insides rumbled and percolated and Jesse felt like he was going to explode.

"You're too intense," his father said the night before. "You have to learn how to relax."

"That's easy for you to say." He rushed around his grandfather who was blocking his path to the bathroom. The old man's dementia was worse and he spent much of his time wandering back and forth between the trenches in France and the single bathroom in their Brooklyn house.

"It's a job," his father tried to assure him. "Do your best. That's all you can do. They can't expect more than that."

"It's more than just a job, it's a profession. It's a career," Jesse called from behind the closed door. "A responsibility. Why, probably for the rest of my life–" His words were garbled by the flushing toilet. The door opened and Jesse, his face drawn and pale, looked sheepishly at his father. There was perspiration on his forehead and his eyes were red and watery from lack of sleep.

"What?"

"I said, in ten years what if one of those kids can't get a job because of some mistake I make? Because of some failure on my part? Because they don't know their personal pronouns?"

His father smiled and shook his head. "Life isn't like that. You went to school, studied, learned and became a teacher. What are you worried about? I never went to college. I didn't even graduate high school, but I know that things have a way of working out. Life has a way of happening when you aren't paying attention, and it doesn't rise or fall on personal pronouns whatever they are. You're too intense. You have to learn how to relax."

Jesse turned away abruptly and walked, head down, into his bedroom. His father followed. "You see these," Jesse pointed to the books lining the shelves along the wall. "I read every one of them in the last sixteen years. I have a B.A. in English. I graduated *cum laude,* but I don't know *anything.*"

His father put his hand on Jesse's shoulder. "I remember when you thought you knew it all. I remember when *I* thought I knew it all." But his attempt at humor was lost on his son.

"Now I don't know the difference between Romanticism and the writers of the twentieth century. I don't remember the name of *one* Naturalist writer. What if somebody asks me something and I don't know the answer? What then?"

His father looked at him with love and smiled. "You tell them you don't know and you'll look it up."

"You just don't understand. This isn't being a barber. I'm a *teacher*," he said. It was an unkind cut his father didn't deserve and he regretted it as soon as he said it.

"Well, by tomorrow at this time one day will be over and you'll feel better. Come on, it's supper time."

"I can't eat. I feel sick." The smell of his mother's pot roast filled the house. She made it because it was his favorite. The condemned man's final request. "Tell Mom I can't eat." He took a book from the shelf, *Comparative Literature, Romanticism to the 20th Century*. He chased his grandfather out of the bathroom again and locked the door behind him.

"You're too intense. You have to learn to relax," Jesse said to himself. His new gray sharkskin suit jacket was limp and wrinkled after the forty-two-mile ride on the Southern State Parkway. He pulled it on and buttoned the collar of his sweaty shirt; his perspiration had wilted the starch and the collar ends curled up under his chin. He slipped up the tie knot and had one last look around his old car, his old life. He pushed open the car door and his childhood, his adolescence were over as simply as that.

Thoughts ricocheted around his brain like bullets in a flowing stream of consciousness, a disjointed soliloquy like Molly Bloom's in James Joyce's *Ulysses*. Ugh! The thought of the novel that had made his life hell for a semester caused an additional stab in his stomach. But gladly, he thought, would he trade this new hell for old Molly Bloom.

One hundred eighty-two school days only six months laid back to back no Saturdays Sundays or holidays twenty-year retirement Do teachers retire after twenty years maybe forty years and I'll be sixty-two God forty years times one hundred eighty-two days makes only seven thousand two hundred eighty days until retirement no Saturdays, Sundays or holidays. He turned up the cement walk that led to the center doors of the school and felt inside his jacket to be sure he had remembered a pen.

The mark of a good teacher is always be prepared like the Marines or is it the Boy Scouts and never lose control control Thorndike page fifty-six in the upper right hand corner control begins with the establishment of a logical and consistent system in the classroom from the first day's lesson plans The eight parts of speech punctuation including the apostrophe on the first two days leaves only one hundred and eighty more days to fill Shit. The sound of his leather heels on the walk reverberated off the building, broadcasting across the lawn a warning of his approach to some seagulls feeding on bits of garbage in the grass. They complained and scattered, wheeling suddenly into the air in noisy flight that startled him.

Discipline establish control from the first day the first second stay in your seat desks in straight rows no papers on the floor no talking no calling out raise your hand before you speak. The segment of a recurring nightmare exploded into his consciousness. Three times in the last week the same dark dream had shaken him awake in a cold sweat. Thirty kids flying paper airplanes, standing on their desks calling out answers without raising their hands, throwing garbage on the floor. Backed into a corner by their savage smiling faces like a scene from the novel *The Lord of the Flies,* he was bombarded with balled-up aluminum foil, lunch bags, pieces of stale bread, smelly tuna fish sandwiches, chalk erasers, rocks, stones, desks and chairs. A bang, a flash, a silver bullet in slow motion getting bigger and closer until he could read his name written across it–JESSE TIETJEN! That was always when he woke up. He shivered involuntarily and groaned audibly. He was sweating tiny rivulets that ran down his back and under the waistband of the new underwear his mother had also bought him, down his legs and into his new socks.

The best schools have the least kids in the hall Keep them in their seats in the room for fuck's sake What if I fuck up Can't say fuck Can't think fuck Erase fuck from my mind No more fucks FUCK.

"Fuck!" he said out loud and recoiled when he heard it reverberate off the facade of the building. He thought about cutting across the grass, but stayed instead on the winding cement path that first curved away from the entrance before it turned back.

Keep off the grass Keep off Don't don't don't. He mopped his face with his damp handkerchief and glanced at the clock tower above the center of the school. The black hands indicated it was seventeen minutes after nine. *Seventeen after nine Christ I'm late on the first goddamned day the first goddamned day impossible Fuck!*

He was such an over-preparer he had left a whole forty-five minutes extra for travel, even set his watch ahead ten minutes so he'd have extra extra time. He looked at his wristwatch, the new Benrus, a graduation gift from his parents. Eight thirty-two. He checked the second hand and listened for the tick. "Yes, ladies and gentlemen, Benrus takes a lickin' and keeps on tickin'!" he said out loud. *Or is that Timex even after the most grueling test of all strapped to the wrist of a suburban high school teacher for one hundred and eighty-two days no Saturdays Sundays or holidays.* He felt foolish and looked around to see if anyone had overheard him. *No jokes Teaching is a serious job a serious business a serious profession the world's oldest profession or is that prostitution Then what's the world's second oldest profession.* He reached the main entrance. It was ugly and drab. The cramps in his lower tract told him in no uncertain terms that he had to find a bathroom immediately.

The word is defecate no shits no fucks no errors no jokes Christ I wish I was back in college Were back in college subjunctive mood I never understood subjunctive but I can't say I was absent the day they taught it Note to me Look up subjunctive as soon as I get home Can't mess up the kids eager yearning faces ready to suck up knowledge like thirsty sponges kids expecting the very best deserving what they expect. He climbed the steps and except for the rumble in his stomach he felt that he was almost in control. *No matter what I can do it I will do it I'll be the best teacher in the school teacher of the year the decade the century best in the whole country in the world dedicated hard working sincere honest human the best not just an eight or a nine but a perfect ten.*

He put his hand on the doorknob. Something written on the wall near the door caught his eye. It was scrawled in small block letters, crudely printed in black paint or marker. He leaned closer to read the five cryptic words that might be an omen, an inspiration, like a good luck message in a Chinese fortune cookie.

"THIS SCHOOL SUKS BIG DICK."

Jesse made another note that he would have to review spelling with his classes.

* * *

The most striking thing about the inside corridor of Rosencrantz and Guildenstern Memorial High School was the absence of striking things. It was drab, downright dismal. The worn floor tiles were a random checkered pattern of maroon and brown, the school colors Jesse would later learn, and where the original tiles had been removed by the ages or the vandals, newer, mismatched tiles further added to the randomness. The ceiling and walls were institutional gray, painted down to a point about shoulder height, where the lower section was a mess of brown, black and tan paint strings spit-sprayed randomly over a beige background, like a terminally ill Jackson Pollock. Two large varnished doors were open in front of him, a gaping maw threatening to devour anyone who came too close, and the rest of the hall a long dark tunnel that curved out of sight. The plywood sign above the doors cautioned "Silence Area!" Jesse put his leather heels down quietly.

An arrow drawn on a curled piece of ditto paper taped to the closed Main Office doors pointed the direction to the Bernard H. Prahl Memorial Auditorium. Jesse pulled from his damp pocket the wilted postcard he had received weeks before announcing the opening day schedule. It came the same day he got two recruiting letters from the Farmington Teachers' Association, FT ASS, and the Farmington Union Local # 2, FU-2, both with the news there was still no teacher contract and the district was once again on austerity budget. He read the postcard for the hundredth time. "To all faculty and staff of UFSD 71–Greetings! General Meeting, Tuesday, September 7,

1971, in the Bernard H. Prahl Memorial Auditorium 9:00 a.m. Welcome back. Be prompt. **ATTENDANCE WILL BE TAKEN!**" He was in the right place.

Jesse proceeded toward the auditorium, slowing to look at the display cases lining the corridor. The first contained a miniature model of Farmington, complete with tiny buildings, cars and people that reminded him of his model train layout. The second was a detailed reproduction of the high school. "Assembled by the Industrial Arts Honor Society" the plaque said, "under the supervision of–" Jesse couldn't read the name because someone had scratched "BOOK YOU" into the brass plate, making the name illegible. It depicted the various stages of the school's construction from 1941 to 1960.

Dr. Donald F. Flackett, the current Superintendent of UFSD 71, would have loved it if Rosencrantz and Guildenstern Memorial High School were nestled in a picturesque valley amid green rolling hills and tree-lined rises for the publicity pictures that were printed in the district newsletter and sent to the taxpayers every year when the annual budget came up for a vote. It might have encouraged the tightfisted citizens of Farmington to pass the school budget occasionally, instead of voting it down nearly every year. But the reality was there are no mountains on Long Island and few rolling hills. So the school squatted just off a busy county road in an industrial area just under the flight path of the town's aviation factory, between the railroad station and the Long Island Expressway. And the district was starting yet another school year on austerity.

The reason Jesse knew about the job opening and applied for the teaching position was because of his mother's sister, Aunt Dimitra, nicknamed Dimmy, who had traded in her Brooklyn apartment for a small house in Farmington five years before, and sent him a Mid-Island *Clarion-Herald-Sun-Times* clipping. "ARRESTED HIGH SCHOOL TEACHER SENTENCED! Thomas Keller, a Rosencrantz and Guildenstern Memorial High School English teacher was surprised by a Nassau County police officer returning home early to find Keller in bed with the officer's wife. The fleeing

Keller was shot once in the buttocks trying to escape through the bedroom window. Not seriously wounded, Keller was apprehended when he showed up at the Nassau County Medical Center Emergency Room for treatment. Keller pleaded not guilty to the charges of breaking and entering and attempted rape filed by the wife of the police officer, both of whose names were withheld to protect the woman's anonymity. At his trial Keller told the judge that it had all been a terrible mistake, that he shares a house in town with two other renters and admitted he had been out drinking. 'I became disoriented and wandered into the wrong house on the wrong street. All these Levitt houses look alike,' Keller testified. 'I thought the woman in bed next to me was somebody else's wife." Keller was found guilty of the lesser charges of trespassing, drunkenness and public indecency. He was sentenced to two years in the county jail and will be required to register as a sex offender. Additionally, he was suspended by the school district without pay pending a 30-20A tenure hearing after his release." His aunt had attached a note to the article. "I think there's an English position open in the high school."

Beside the building models in the case there were old photos and other memorabilia: bricks from the earliest school construction, a pile of something dark and hardened that Jesse assumed was cement, but would have avoided if he passed it on the street, a rusted trowel, roofing materials and corrugated tin. One of the faded images showed a man with his head bandaged like a mummy beside a well-dressed smiling, perfectly proportioned miniature man. Both were lifting shovels full of dirt. The caption read: "President Wilbur Vecht and Principal Bernard H. Prahl break ground for the new high school— December 8, 1941." There were images of work crews at various stages of construction, shoveling, cementing and many just pointing. A yellowed photo of a very old man supported under each arm by two almost identical younger men who were peering into a huge hole was labeled, "Architects Klaus Brinker Sr., son Klaus Jr., and grandson Klaus III at the 'digs.'"

Jesse passed posters that were taped to the walls along the way in a frantic, graphic attempt to grab the attention of the returning teachers.

"The Partnership of Parents and Teachers in Association–Harriet Stegle, President and Founder, welcomes you." A smiling woman thirty-five or fifty-three with red hair sculpted like a helmet stared out. Her eyes behind tapered glass frames followed Jesse as he passed. "Join the P–PTA today and support excellence in education."

"Become part of The Farmington Teachers' Ass.," another sign with an "Uncle Sam Wants You" picture invited, "and support *yourself* where it counts. FT Ass. Wants You to JOIN US for a Gala Social, Friday, September 10th at Fred's Happy Hour Bar and Grill beginning at 3:15. Free admission, drinks, dancing and hot hors d'oeuvres. Get the latest news concerning contract negotiations!" Someone had scribbled across the poster in black marker, "Scab company union!"

Further along the wall was a third sign that seemed hastily printed in red marker on a torn sheet of ditto paper. The small and uneven letters were hard to read. "FU–2! NO CONTRACT! NO WORK! The Farmington Union Local #2 is supporting *you* so join and let us be your truss. Beer Blast. All you can drink $1.00. The Stikitt Inn, Friday 3:14!"

A small crowd was collecting beyond the trophy cases in front of the four large auditorium doors at the far end of the corridor. Jesse's liquid insides grumbled and a taste of bad eggs rose in his throat. He was desperate for a bathroom. He crossed an open area that was the hub of three connecting corridors. A sign on the wall noted that it was called "The Hub." There were more cases, more trophies, semi-naked bronze and silver men and women piled against each other reaching for footballs or basketballs, and in a dark recess between two cases he saw a door marked "Boys."

He pushed it open and was assaulted by the accumulated smell of years of old urine and Pine-Sol. He pushed the door of the first stall that opened with a farting squeak. The cubicle was damp and the runny toilet wet from the summer's last heat on the stained porcelain. He turned the lock and read a note carved into the thick paint on the back of the door: "MILLIE SADOWSKI HAS BIG PITS." There wasn't any paper in the dispenser so he hitched up his pants and hobbled into the center stall. "MILLIE SADOWSKI SOCKS BIG COOK." The paper dispenser was empty. He made a tiny whimpering noise deep inside and went into the last stall. "MILLIE SADOWSKI BOOKS LIKE A BUNNY." No toilet paper.

Jesse struggled to tighten his sphincter. "Why me, God?" he whispered. "What did I do?" Then he remembered the small notebook in his jacket pocket. "Hold on! Hold on!"

In a few minutes he was out of the stall washing his hands and face at the sink. "BOOK YOU," the message at eye level said. He felt for a paper towel, but the dispenser was empty. "Jesus Christ!" he muttered and his voice cracked a little. He took his already sodden handkerchief from his pocket and tried to dry his hands. In the empty chrome towel dispenser Jesse examined his image, distorted as in a fun house mirror. There were dark circles under his eyes, and the beginning of a fever sore on his lip. Nerves always made him break out. He had a pounding headache and he felt nauseous. He took a deep breath and looked at his watch. There were nine minutes until the start of the General Meeting.

Like an amorphous living organism, a giant amoeba, the crowd had quadrupled outside the auditorium, pulsating around the open doors but not entering. The blob swallowed and digested anyone who came too close. Jesse didn't see a familiar or friendly face in the crowd. He felt so alone. He tried to hang back, but he was pulled slowly by the flow and sucked into the vortex, like a tiny speck of protoplasm in the belly of the beast, being digested alive. He was drowning in the scent of exotic perfumes mingled with perspiration, sun tan oil and cigarettes. The indistinct voices were like the hum from a beehive. He overheard snatches of meaningless conversations.

"–Europe," a suntanned woman in summer-yellow sing-songed. "Harold and I did a charter again this year and spent a month on the continent."

Jesse bumped into the back of a man in a rumpled plaid jacket and white straw shoes. "Excuse me," he said timidly.

"Vacation?" the man said to someone. "I spent the summer working in the shoe store in the South Bronx–"

Jesse eased by and stepped on another woman's foot. She stopped talking long enough to register her annoyance, examine her thick ankle and her shoe for damages.

"I'm terribly sorry–"

She turned away brusquely and continued. "She's not coming back. Personally," she whispered, "I think the poor thing has cancer. Lost forty pounds since the last time I saw her in June, and complaining about severe abdominal pains. The surgeon removed both her–"

"–dirty spark plugs. So I couldn't start my car and I had to take the LIRR and then a subway all the way up to the South Bronx. It looks like Vietnam–"

"–I was in misery," another woman's nasal voice complained. "The worst summer of my life. First the flu in June, then two severely sprained ankles. I spent a week flat on my back in bed with my legs in the air–"

"–it was a *marvelous* honeymoon!" An attractive young woman flashed her matching engagement ring and wedding band to admirers. "Paul's an animal and I got a yeast infection–"

"–baking cookies I burned my hand. So my sister-in-law came with her four kids who gave me the chickenpox. That was another week in bed–"

"–I was unable to pee without it burning and a discharge–"

"–of course the doctors didn't come right out and say it was terminal. They didn't know what it was, but I'm telling you, all shriveled up like that, it looked just like–"

"–leather goods from Madrid. You wouldn't believe the bargains in Spain. Cheap labor. Harold bought himself a long leather coat, and I spent–"

"–hours on my hands and knees and ended up with rub burns–"

"Stooped over like that I worked harder in the shoe store than I do here and I made a lot more money. Sometimes I'd get really lucky and see a little beaver. A lot of Bronx women don't wear panties. And sometimes I'd really get a jolt like–"

"–an electrical fire! Ironically the poor man was installing a smoke detector. Lost everything. Second-degree burns over ninety percent of his body. He's not coming back either. Oh well. And the house still smells like smoke and–"

"–diarrhea–"

"–I picked it up in gay *Pa–ree*. And the most adorable handmade sweaters we practically stole in Ireland. Harold and I went through Customs we were so nervous. I nearly died–"

"–dead as a doornail. Lost her mother and her father in a car accident, the poor woman. So I doubt if she'll be coming back, for a while at least."

"–Paul wanted a quiet wedding with a few intimate friends, but since Daddy paid for *everything,* we had–"

"–cat scratch fever from–"

"–pussy. Even a pet store owner doesn't see as much pussy as I saw. And for an 'extra discount' we'd go into the back room and she'd let me play with her–"

"–hysterectomy. She won't be back for a month at least–"

"Paul said we couldn't afford it, but Daddy has a friend in South Africa who gets diamonds cheap, so this one is just a shade under two and a half carats, and perfect blue-white–"

"–self-winding and waterproof. And our camera was the perfect place to hide them from Customs. Who would ever think of opening it up–"

"–but when they finally did open him up, the poor man, it had spread through his entire system. So they sewed him up immediately and now he's getting cobalt treatments. But if you ask me I don't think it'll do any good. Too far gone. You can bet he's never coming back."

"That's nice."

"What did it cost?"

"–another week on my back in bed–"

"–coming–"

"–and going without stop. Like those African babies with flies in their eyes you see on TV–"

"–watching porn and having drinks with the divorcée next door during the week while my wife and kids were on vacation in the mountains. It nearly killed me."

"–died in bed you know. Left a wife and two kids nearly destitute because he had no insurance. And never sick a day in his life. He started teaching the same year I did. The poor man went just like that–"

"–but before we returned we picked up some stereo equipment in Germany, and some adorable music boxes in Switzerland."

Jesse was almost inside, past the knot of them.

"–Paul wanted a quiet honeymoon at Niagara Falls, but Daddy has a friend with a yacht, so we spent a month cruising the Caribbean. Paul was so seasick he spent the last week–"

"–sleeping on a Trailways bus. I went up Friday nights to put in time with the wife and kids in the Catskills. Then I rushed back Sunday early enough to see the divorcée. All that travel and sex almost killed me–"

"–suicide. And only thirty-seven, the poor thing."

"–vaginitis–"

"–prostate cancer. He's not coming back. And his medical bill is so big–"

"–Daddy paid for it–"

"–we saw the Pope–"

"–another pain in the ass–"

"–cancer of the colon–"

"–that's very nice. What did it cost?"

"–a double mastectomy–"

"Paul likes big ones–"

"–she's *definitely* not coming back!"

Jesse was almost inside the auditorium. He was dizzy and felt like he was going to throw up. Just outside the doorway he stopped to steady himself and he read the bronze plaque and inscription posted there. "In loving memory of Bernard H. Prahl, first principal of Rosencrantz and

Guildenstern Memorial High School 1945–1964. He may have been a *little* man, but he did a very *big* job." Below that was a quote from the principal. "In the education of children, better something *imperfect* than nothing at all."

Jesse slipped through the doors into the hot auditorium that was still relatively empty. The people outside outnumbered those already seated, and those in the seats were mostly near the exits. Occasionally the sounds of music from the student orchestra up front welled up over the louder voices. Both audience and musicians seemed to be doing an effective job of ignoring each other.

The music conductor stood in the pit below the stage. His sweating, bald head bobbed and nodded, reflecting the light like a mirror as he waved his arms in a frantic attempt to keep up with the musicians. He turned occasionally to silence the noisy, slowly growing crowd and when the orchestra ended the piece, not quite together, there was a smattering of unenthusiastic applause. The conductor mopped his forehead with a balled tissue that left remnants on his head before he unintelligibly announced the next selection. Jesse recognized the tune from a TV ad in which quantities of puffed rice cereal were shot from giant cannons. He slipped into a broken seat three-quarters of the way down the center aisle and picked up a mimeographed program from the number that had been dropped on the floor.

The Farmington Public Schools–UFSD 71
General Meeting Bernard H. Prahl Memorial Auditorium
(Attendance will be taken!)

Processional Selections "B" Orchestra–Herbert Gateway, Conductor
Opening Remarks M. Seymour Baltz, Principal R&GMHS
First Attendance
Welcoming Address Harriet Stegle, President and Founder P–PTA

Keynote Address "Individual Differences, Sensitivity and the Melting Pot of Education" Dr. Donald F. Flackett, Supt. of Schools

Additional Comments "Athletics on an Austerity Budget" Edward "Birdie" Boid, Acting Dir. of Phys Ed

Closing Remarks M. Seymour Baltz, Principal R&G MHS

Second Attendance

Flag Salute Assembled Multitude

National Anthem "B" Orchestra

Final Attendance

Recessional March "B" Orchestra

Dismissal to Home Schools

(Special thanks to Mr. Sussman and the "G" kids in the Print Shop whose motto is: "Printing done cheep")

"B" Orchestra completed the selection and a dark-haired man with a trimmed mustache and a striking resemblance to Richard Nixon stepped up leisurely to the podium. He smiled and shot acknowledgments to people with the cocked fingers of both hands and waved to others in the crowd. He tapped his fingers on the microphone and waited for a break in the conversations that didn't come.

"Ladies and gent–" The public address system crackled, sputtered and died.

Four students in brown shirts and AV/CM armbands with lightning bolts between the letters moved with precision onto the stage. Two checked the wire connections and two worked on the microphone. "Test, test, test." The microphone came to life again.

"Ladies and–" he began again. Loud electronic feedback silenced the crowd and made them cover their ears. A single AV/CM member reappeared and reset the microphone.

The silence in the auditorium was only momentary and the muffled voices, like the sound inside a seashell, grew and intensified. Even those sitting on the dais resumed their interrupted chatting.

"The longer *I* wait," he said sounding like every teacher Jesse ever had, "the longer *you* wait. It's your time, people." He

28

paused and scowled and when there was enough quiet the scowl turned to an automatic smile, like a car shifting gears, and he began his third attempt at opening the formal proceedings. "For those of you who don't know me, I'm Seymour Baltz, principal of the high school, and I would sincerely like to welcome all of you back for what will be, I'm sure, another successful school year. I hope that you all had a pleasant summer, are well-rested and ready to shake the cobwebs and get back to work–"

A long, resounding "Faaaarrrt!" came from somewhere in the back of the auditorium. It reverberated off the cement walls and spread across the hall. The explosion unleashed a titter of laughter behind Jesse that grew. People turned and strained to see who had done it. Mr. Baltz's smile disappeared. He pursed his lips and tucked his chin deep into his neck, creating a folded ridge from ear to ear. His dark eyes darted around the assembly for the offender.

"I direct your attention," he went on pretending to ignore the offense, but there was anger in his voice, "to the Official First Day Attendance Sheets." He held up a number of yellow pages. "All teachers must sign in, in three places, on the left side now, in the middle at your individual building meetings and again on the right at the meeting before dismissal this afternoon. If you expect to be paid for the day be sure to write legibly in your own script. Do *not* print and do *not* sign anyone else's name. All signatures will be verified. If you do not sign in three places or if the secretaries can not read your writing, you will not be paid for –"

The microphone popped and whistled again and there was a loud cheer from the crowd until the PA system came back to life.

"–It is my *sincere* pleasure to introduce you to someone who needs no introduction." Mr. Baltz was smiling again. "Mrs. Harriet Stegle, the president and founder of the P-PTA."

It was the woman Jesse saw on the poster in the corridor. She walked stiffly to the microphone, smiling at the indifferent crowd. She looked down at the index cards that were curled in her hands.

"Tha-thank you, Mr. Baltz," she stuttered painfully. "Sup-superintendent Flackett, administrators, Coach Boi-Boid, staff and tea-tea-teachers." It was painful. "It is my ple-pleasure to welcome you." She turned her arms in an all-encompassing motion and her index cards flew into the orchestra pit. Jesse saw the fear in her eyes. She plunged on unaided. "We are embark-bark-barking on a new year, a new pa-page in a book fre-fresh and ready to be written in. September is always so exciting a ti-time for me. The beginning of new frien-friendships and new cha-cha-challenges–"

Someone snored behind Jesse and he turned to see the man with the straw shoes fast asleep, his mouth hanging open.

After the woman had droned on about cookie sales, count the jelly beans contests, doughnuts on Parents Night and other P-PTA-sponsored events they could look forward to in the coming school year, Mr. Baltz took the podium again. "Thank you, Mrs. Stegle."

Teachers who had been in the lobby entered the back of the auditorium and the sleeping man behind Jesse snored and slipped off his seat.

"And now it is my pleasure to introduce to you a man who is no stranger to the faculty and staff of Farmington Schools, a man responsible for making UFSD 71 what it is today, Superintendent of Schools Dr. Donald F. Flackett, who will speak about sensitivity to individual differences in our schools." Mr. Baltz halfheartedly began the halfhearted applause and returned to his seat.

A weaselly looking man with a bad toupee, Dr. Flackett adjusted the microphone, removed a piece of folded paper from his jacket and pressed it down on the stand. He swept the front of the auditorium looking for a friendly face and stopped on Jesse. Slowly, uncomfortably, he sank lower in his seat just as the man at the end of the row got up and handed Jesse an Official First Day Attendance Sheet. He sat up straight and scanned the sixty or so names that were on the page, many printed despite Mr. Baltz's warning. More were illegible. Mickey Mouse, Dick Hertz, Mike Hunt, Harry Ballsack and

Jesus H. Christ were the ones he could read. At the very bottom of the page under the words "Break Baltz!" and "The Phantom" boldly lettered in red felt marker, Jesse carefully and legibly wrote his name in script before he woke the man behind him and passed him the sheet.

"A funny thing happened on the way to the assembly this morning," Dr. Flackett was saying. "I passed a construction site where I noticed a group of men, ditch-digging laborers, their foreman in an open-collared blue shirt and the owner in a silk suit and tie with diamond cufflinks, a gold Seiko watch and shined shoes." He stopped and looked up from his paper. "I'm not much for dialects, but it's important in understanding my point. One ditchdigger asked, 'Hey Latrel, how comea we worka in thisa ditch when the foreman O'Hara anda the bossman Mr. Silverstein are uppa there ina clean shirt anda suit?' 'Beats the crap outta me, Tony. Why doan you go aix?' the other ditchdigger said. So Tony climbed up and went directly to the foreman to asked. 'Well now, *paisano,* go ask Mr. Silverstein.'" Dr. Flackett paused and looked up from the paper. "To make a long story short, the ditchdigger repeated his question to the owner. 'Because I'm smart. O'Hara's not quite as smart, that's why he's just the foreman and why you dig ditches. Let me demonstrate how smart I am.' Mr. Silverstein put his hand against a brick wall. 'Try to punch my hand.' Tony balled his fist and took a swing." Dr. Flackett demonstrated. "Just as his fist was about to connect, Mr. Silverstein moved his hand and Tony punched the brick wall and howled. 'See,' he said, 'that's smart.'" There were some snickers. "Wait," Dr. Flackett said, "I'm not finished. So Tony went back into his hole. 'He'sa smart.' he explained to Latrel. 'Wut chew mean smart?' Latrel asked. 'I show you. Try to hita my handa.' Tony said and he put his hand in front of his own face!" Dr. Flackett convulsed with laughter.

The audience was still.

From the back of the auditorium someone yelled, "Bastard!" The auditorium erupted in cheers.

"That little story brings me to my point. Public education is truly the melting pot, reducing everything to the most common denominator. The buzzwords for this school year in your classrooms on every level are 'Individual Differences' and 'Sensitivity,' though the first word is actually two words. Our student body is diverse, sort of like my little story. Germans, Irish, Italians, Polacks, and still a smattering of Jews who haven't yet fled to wealthier school districts. And this year it's my understanding there actually may be a few coloreds running around our corridors. Unless, of course, somebody tampers with the school buses like they did in past years." He looked pensive. "As for sensitivity, you all must be aware of the differences that exist in the children in your classrooms tomorrow and you must provide for those differences." He took a long breath. "All men may have been created equal according to our Declaration of Independence, but not in Farmington Schools. We *know* better. There are different jobs in America and different types of people to fill them. As educators it is imperative that we early on identify the ditch diggers and the doctors, the manual laborers and the executives, the teachers and the administrators. We do this through exhaustive testing, then classify each child and put them in an educational track that will point them toward their particular future roles in society. The aware teacher can look at the kids in class on the first day and know who will fail in June, who will fail in life. The Tracking System in Farmington drives a wedge, so to speak, between the social and ethnic strata, insuring that tomorrow's America will have no shortage of ditchdiggers, garbagemen, auto mechanics and shoe salesmen." Dr. Flackett trailed off and the man behind Jesse stirred. "So much for that. Now I have a few practical words about the school budget." He changed his tone. "As you know, the taxpayers have once again failed to pass a working school and library budget after three separate votes, so this will be another school year that we begin on an austerity budget."

There was an audible groan from those in the crowd who knew what austerity meant.

"Contract!" someone yelled from the back.

"Contract! Contract!" Others picked up the chant.

Jesse looked around.

"That's another matter altogether." Flackett held up his hands. "But we all know austerity is just a temporary problem. A minor speed bump. The administrative staff, learning from past experiences, worked hard over the summer while most of you were on vacation, to develop a system that will pressure parents to get off their butts and pass a school budget. An envelope explaining the details of the master plan is in your mailboxes at your home schools, but here are the basics for you to digest." He removed a folded paper from his jacket. "Students once again will be required to rent their required textbooks. The District will provide no supplies, zilch, zero, *nada*. Parents will have to buy all necessary classroom materials, including chalk, one box per student, ditto paper, one ream, notepad and three-hole looseleaf one package each, and one pack each of three-by-five and four-by-six-inch index cards. That is in addition to the notebooks you may require for your classes. The average cost per student at the secondary level for each family comes to more than that of the proposed budget increase that they rejected. The expense at the primary level is just as substantial." He smiled. "To paraphrase the words of our beloved president, it will really sock it to them! With regards to the buildings, all schools will open five minutes before classes begin and close promptly five minutes after dismissal. So get those little beauties out the doors as quickly as possible. Of course teachers will still be required to report at the usual time and remain on post for an additional half hour." There was a smattering of boos. "And there will be no extracurricular activities during austerity." He paused. "This is where it gets good. Student supplies already purchased last year have been gathered up and put under lock and key. That includes paper towels and toilet tissue in all student bathrooms. Be sure to advise your students that if they expect to go at any point while we are on austerity, they should carry a supply of toilet paper and paper towels with them." He smiled. "That's a new wrinkle this year. I'm sure with this extra little push, if we can harass and inconvenience the kids enough, the next budget vote will be successful, and then we can get on with the task of giving these wonderful youngsters the education they deserve."

He waited for applause, but there was none. "To head off any complaints from the community and in the name of justice and fair play, all bathroom supplies have also been removed from the faculty toilets. I'm sure all of you will be able to circumvent any minor personal inconvenience by carrying your own packets of papers... toilet papers, I mean, not rolling papers." His smile broadened. "Thank you. And again, I wish you all the success of a great school new year."

Silence.

Mr. Baltz went to the podium and when he attempted to readjust the microphone an electrical spark arced to his wedding band. He pulled away and sent the microphone into convulsions that continued until an AV/CM member set things right.

"–and last on our agenda," Mr. Baltz said over the wild cheers from the back of the auditorium, "to speak about athletics on an austerity budget, the Acting Director of Phys Ed, Coach Edward 'Birdie' Boid–"

Coach Boid, a stocky man with a gray crew cut and sweats, walked to the microphone. He smiled and clasped his hands over his head as the crowd exploded. "Yahoo!" "Bird-ie! Bird-ie!" And when there was no letup, he pulled the chrome whistle hanging from the lanyard around his neck and blew directly into the microphone.

"Now hear this," he shouted. "The Phys Ed Department is doing its part to help pass the budget. No budget, no atletics! No atletics, no sports, no sports, no sports scholarships!" He turned and bounded back to his seat to the deafening noise of the crowd.

Caught by surprise at Coach Boid's brevity, Mr. Baltz ran back to the microphone. "Dismissal to home schools will take place–" The microphone crackled and echoed. "–all Official Attendance Sheets must be properly–"

But no one was listening. Teachers were already on their feet and rushing out the exits, headed to their home schools.

"–no one will be paid unless–"

Silence.

Someone in the wings pulled a rope and the stage curtains shut with a sudden swoosh. The impact scattered the papers that were on the podium and trapped Mr. Baltz in the surging material like a swimmer caught in a breaking wave. He grappled with the heavy curtain in an attempt to find the opening. The closed curtains were a cue for the AV/CM members to march out and begin disassembling the equipment. And the orchestra leader, who had been reading over the score, signaled "B" Orchestra to begin the recessional tune. But since "The National Anthem" was scheduled next in the program after the "Pledge of Allegiance" that had been omitted in the confusion, half the orchestra began the wrong piece, which was actually the correct piece, and half began the recessional selection. The musicians battled each other, playing two pieces equally unrecognizable until the entire orchestra finally reached a consensus and played "Onward Christian Soldiers Marching as to War."

Mr. Baltz's disembodied voice crackled from the speakers. "–all teachers report... directly... home schools. Senior High... here in fifteen... staff punch in... Main Off–"

One AV/CM member pulled the electrical cord from the socket and rolled it up, another pushed the portable podium from the stage and the General Meeting was over.

* * *

The crowd at the back struggled to escape. In his seat Jesse felt overwhelmed and the day had barely begun. He wanted to get up and run through the doors out into the summer daylight to his car and drive back home. But he just sat, pinned to his seat by an invisible force. An angry Mr. Baltz rushed up the aisle past him yelling at a man following sheepishly behind with his head down. From the bits of the monologue Jesse heard the man was the AV/CM Coordinator, a fatherless bastard and an incompetent son of a bitch.

He waited until "B" Orchestra left the pit with their instruments and the AV/CM Squad began resetting up for the building meeting. He made a mental note of his seat location and hiked uphill toward the back where the last of the elementary and junior high teachers were leaving for their home buildings. He was already exhausted and it was only 10:17. Slowly he moved down the hall toward the mob bunched in front of the Main Office.

"Excuse me," he asked one of the blue-shirted custodians changing fluorescent bulbs in the corridor. "Is there a faculty bathroom I could use?"

The custodian removed the pipe he was holding in his clenched teeth and vaguely pointed with it. "Second floor," he said. "But there's no toilet paper."

* * *

Mr. Baltz scrambled past the busy secretaries in the Main Office with Harry Dexter close behind, sucked along in the jet stream. Even before his door slammed closed he snarled, "Look at me, you bastard." Dexter's head hung low like a kid in the principal's office. "My sister says, 'Seymour, Harry needs a job. Take him into the business–as a favor.' And for her sake I make the arrangements. Calls. Pull some strings. I do what has to be done. And what do I get? You!"

"But I–"

"More like butt *head*!" He walked to the window and turned up the air conditioner to high. The fan complained audibly. "Do you want *my* job now? Are you conspiring to sabotage me?"

"Uncle Seymour–"

"*Never* call me that, you *putz*!"

"I'm sorry, Mr. Baltz–"

He sat in his chair and lit an unfiltered Lucky Strike, took a deep drag and blew out a stream of blue smoke that was dissipated by the air conditioner. "I didn't like you even when you were a kid, but I called in a few favors for my sister. And you skated right past all those others. No background check. No degree. No transcripts. No qualifications. And after Don Cooley's accident you jumped into his seat before his body was even chilled in his grave. Remember that shocked look on Cooley's electrocuted face, Harry? Keep it in your mind." An image of the former AV/CM Coordinator's face flashed in

Dexter's mind. "One more snap, crackle or popping speaker... one more sparking microphone and..." He fished for something appropriate. "...what I have in mind for you will make five classes of Track IIIs and Cafeteria Duty seem like a plum."

"It won't happen again, Mr. Baltz," he said finally.

* * *

Teachers lined up in the Main Office waiting to punch in at the old time clock. Some rummaged through the mailbox cubbies that lined the wall. It was hot. The old window fan made more noise than it moved air. The line shuffled along until Jesse stood face-to-face with the clock. He looked for his card–TIETJEN, JESSE. He read the posted notice: "Punch in fifteen minutes before morning Homeroom and punch out thirty minutes after the end of the school day." He pulled his card from the right and slipped it into the slot until it stamped and he flinched. Before he placed it on the left side he looked at the time and date, the first of one hundred and eighty-two sign-ins. When he punched out in the afternoon he would replace it on the right.

He found his name printed on a piece of red adhesive plastic stuck over his mailbox cubby between Taylor and Trikamenis, under Scapelli and over Zaza. It was overflowing. He pulled out a stack of program cards, IBM green bar class roster sheets, IBM brown bar lists of students who had been added to or dropped from the green bars. He sifted through the list of required textbooks and school supplies, dittos from the Farmington Teachers' Ass. and FU-2, a "Welcome back for another year..." message from Mr. Baltz and his staff, a P-PTA membership envelope and he still hadn't made a dent in the paper jam. A "Retirement, Accident, Dismemberment and Death Benefits" folder and several large manila envelopes jammed the slot. The envelope with Dr. Flackett's austerity information slid out, but the other was stuck. Something inside the envelope was holding it. He pulled hard and it came loose and he dropped the class rosters. Inside his box the only thing that remained far in the back was half of an old bologna sandwich there since June. He stooped to retrieve the papers he'd dropped when the woman with thick ankles he recognized kicked them under the counter below the mailboxes. Jesse got down on his knees. He saw them far in back just out of his reach.

The principal was still deep in conversation when he rounded the front counter with Harry Dexter. He never saw Jesse on the floor until the impact. He toppled over Jesse and banged his face into the mailboxes.

Jesse tried to get to his feet. "I'm so… sorry... I... my class list... Are you okay?"

Mr. Baltz held his nose and glared at Jesse through watery eyes. "Who *are* you?" he demanded.

"Me?" Jesse panicked. "I think you're bleeding, Mr. Baltz," he said and pulled his wadded damp handkerchief from his pocket **and** tried to blot the blood. "It was an accident…"

Mr. Baltz pressed his own clean white handkerchief to the bridge of his nose. "What the hell is your name?"

"Jesse Tietjen, Mr. Baltz. English. First year. It really was an accident... my class list... some other teacher kicked it... I didn't know...."

"Tejent. I'll remember that." Jesse didn't feel the need to correct him.

Mr. Baltz turned and collided with Harry Dexter, who was grinning. "Get the hell out of my way, Dexter!" He stormed out of the office holding his nose.

"Nice first impression, kiddo," Dexter said. "You know that's going to cost you. He doesn't forget anything." He turned for the auditorium.

Jesse wanted to cry. He picked up his scattered papers while the teachers and secretaries watched him silently. He was numb and before he realized it he was back in the auditorium sitting in his same seat holding the "FIRST DAY PROCEDURE AND OFFICIAL AV/CM KIT" envelope so tightly his hand hurt. It contained a plan book, grade book, teacher's handbook with an attached dress code, a floor map of the building and a red felt marker pen clipped to a number of AV/CM requisition forms. An electric plug and socket labeled "male" and "female" protruded from the torn envelope. That was what had been stuck in his mailbox and caused his fiasco in the Main Office.

The young woman he had noticed in the corridor before the General Meeting sat in the end seat of his row. Despite everything that he had been through and based only on that one quick glance, Jesse rated her a definite eight and a half. But he didn't dare turn to face her, though he felt her staring at him. He began to perspire heavily again. When he dared to sneak a peek she caught him and he was trapped. "Uh, you teach here?" He sounded so stupid.

"Uh… no," she mocked, looking beyond him, "I just come here to read the magazines while I'm waiting for the bus."

"Oh." Teacher sarcasm. It was painful. He felt stupid and hurt. His face flushed redder and the perspiration rolled down his neck. He pretended to dive back into the envelope and rummaged through his papers with feigned interest.

"Let me guess, first teaching job, right?" she asked.

Jesse didn't know she was talking to him so he didn't answer.

"Hello?"

He looked up. "Me? Uh… huh? Yeah, uh… yes, uh… my first. Does it show?"

"You had me fooled. I really couldn't tell." More sarcasm. "You seem to have it all under control." She looked inside her envelope. "I caught your little encounter in the Main Office." Jesse shriveled like a raisin. She moved down the row closer to him. "It was very funny. The look on your face. Baltz was ready to explode. What are you planning for lunchtime?"

He just stared into his envelope, feeling petulant. He didn't respond.

"Sue Wellen, History," she said. "Sue Ellen Wellen, actually. My parents had a sense of humor. And your name?"

"I thought everybody knew it by now," he said. "Jesse Tietjen. English, if I still have a job." He considered dropping her down to a seven for being such a bitchy smart-ass. But then she smiled a genuine smile and he changed his mind.

"Just relax, Jesse. The school year hasn't started yet."

"This can't be your first year?"

"Three years and one day. I just got tenure today. So now the pressure is off and I can stop teaching, just sit back, read the newspaper and collect a big fat check, if we ever get a contract." He stared at her. More teacher wit? "You do know the hardest part of teaching actually starts after tenure when you really learn *how* to teach without worrying about all the other stuff."

He exhaled. "I don't think I'll last long enough to get tenure."

"Wipe your face," she said. "You're really sweating."

Jesse grabbed for his handkerchief and he was embarrassed by it. "There wasn't any paper in the bathroom so I had to use this."

"Ewwww!"

"I mean to dry my hands." He wiped his face.

She turned toward the back of the auditorium. "Have you met Terry Scapelli yet? He's in your department."

Jesse recognized the name. "I read his mailbox. I mean, I read his name *on* his mailbox. It's over mine."

"What's your schedule?"

"Nobody told me."

She reached across the empty seat between them and took his folder. "It's in this specially sealed, Top Secret envelope. They don't want the teachers to know each other's assignments, to cut down on complaints." She removed from the inside cover of his Plan Book an attached, officially sealed business envelope with the letter "B" pressed into a circle of wax on the back. She broke the seal with her thumbnail and took out the index card. "And the winner is... Homeroom 234. First Period, English 11 Regents Track II Room 235. Second Period, English 10 Basic Track III. The 'Duh Kids.' At least it's early in the day and most of them will be late, asleep or at their parole officer. Prep third, fourth lunch, the Breakfast Club eats at eleven twenty-three." Jesse looked at the card. "Fifth, sixth and seventh more English 11 Regents Room 201 and PB Patrol eighth. I guess we won't be seeing much of each other until June."

Jesse nodded as though he followed what she was saying.

"You didn't get Cafeteria Duty. That's the worst. They do that sometimes to first-year teachers to weed out the weak. But who knows, after you attacked Baltz, he just may switch you." She smiled. "You only have one Basics, but you have three in a row at the end of the day and that's tough."

"What's PB Duty?"

"The Doody Duty. Potty Patrol. Toilet check. They'll tell you all about it at the duty meeting after this meeting and before the department meetings. There are meetings all day long to fill up the time. They wouldn't want us to have an opportunity to prepare for tomorrow's onslaught, or, perish the thought, send us home early." She sat up a little on her seat. "Terry," she called over him and waved.

A long-haired scruffy-bearded man was shaking hands and hugging his way down the aisle with a confidence that Jesse envied. His smile widened when he saw Sue Wellen and he hurried across the long row of empty seats. Close up Jesse saw he was wearing jeans, a wrinkled shirt and love beads. He stepped over Jesse with a tacit "Excuse me" and slipped into the seat between them. "How was your summer?" he asked.

"Short. I didn't see you at the General Meeting."

"I came in late. Went out for breakfast instead. Thought it would be more productive. I came in for Mr. Sensitivity's punch line." He looked around the auditorium. "Lots of fresh meat, I see."

"Speaking of which"—she pointed to Jesse—"the one you stepped over is a first-year virgin in your department. Jesse Tietjen, Terry Scapelli."

Terry nodded. "Greetings, comrade. I guess you got Tom Keller's job." He turned back to Sue. "The poor bastard took a plea bargain and is in the Nassau County jail until he's transferred upstate. He got a year, but with good behavior will probably only do nine months. Free love isn't really free."

The seats in the back half of the auditorium began filling up while Mr. Baltz stood at the podium with his hand over the microphone talking to a nodding Harry Dexter. Three men and a pigeon-looking round-breasted woman walked onto the stage and took the seats behind him.

"Heil, heil the gang's all here! The *junta* has arrived, let the festivities begin," Terry said loud enough for those around him to hear. "The four Stooges and *der Führer*." He clicked the heels of his tennis sneakers with a rubbery clump.

Jesse slouched deeper in his seat.

Mr. Baltz tapped on the microphone and there was no whistle, hum or electric shock. Harry Dexter looked relieved.

"Who *is* that man?" Jesse asked Sue.

"Harry Dexter. He's the Audio Visual and Curriculum Material Coordinator."

"Is he important?"

"In his own mind," Terry said.

"But you don't want to get on his bad side if you ever want to show a film or play a record," she added.

"And even if you're on his good side you may not. Ah, young Jesse, there is so much they didn't teach you in all those Education courses," Terry said cynically. "Like how school actually works." His attitude annoyed Jesse. "You probably think the most important person in a school is the principal, but it isn't. It's the custodian. And Stash Polakas is the head custodian at R and G, so make friends with him ASAP. Tip? Some cherry blend pipe tobacco will go a long way if you need anything fixed, moved, delivered or a body disposed of. The secretaries are a close second, maybe even tied. They actually run the building and keep it running. They know everything. When things are due and who's doing who. Phyllis Lind, Baltz's personal secretary, is the go-to person. She remembers everything and keeps it filed in her vault." He tapped his head. "Don't piss off the cafeteria ladies and they won't spit in your food. Doris Carter, the head of Transportation at Central, is your only chance to get out of town and go on a field trip. Not that you'll do much of that in your first year if you're smart.

Then come the administrators, Baltz, the APs and Harry Dexter, 'Prince of Projectors.'"

"Attention please," Mr. Baltz began. He tapped the microphone again, but nothing happened. "Attention without the please!" The auditorium quieted.

From his seat Jesse saw the large red welt he had inflicted on the bridge of the principal's nose.

"We have lots to do today so let's get to it."

Terry made a loud snoring noise without moving or changing expression, then turned as if the culprit were behind him. The teachers sitting around him lowered their heads and covered their laughing faces. The assistant principals stood and scanned the auditorium. Mr. Baltz's eyes grew cold and hard and shifted rapidly. Jesse sank lower in his seat.

"Teachers are the worst audience," Terry said. "They never listen because they have more important things to do. Just look around."

Jesse did. They were talking, reading newspapers, writing, doing crossword puzzles. Teachers would never tolerate that behavior from the kids, he thought.

"Here's another bit of advice for you." He turned and faced Jesse. "When they give you a shitty job, and they always do, don't be too good at it. Just screw it up the first time because competence is always punished and they'll give you the same shit every year."

"I guess that means you got Cafeteria Duty again," Sue said.

"Three years in a row coming off two years of In-School Detention!" he said with mock pride.

"ISD is even worse than cafeteria," she said to Jesse. "Like being a prison guard."

"Don't be good at what you do," he said loud enough for those around him to hear, "and you too can become an assistant principal." The laughter around them got louder.

The queasy feeling that had never quite left was back with a vengeance in Jesse's stomach. Already he had one run-in with the principal and didn't want another. He thought about changing his seat. He didn't want to tell his parents he got fired on his first day.

"–and for the benefit of those of you who are new to the district I would like to introduce you to–" Mr. Baltz was saying.

"The goon squad," Terry said out of the corner of his mouth in a well-timed running banter.

"–the four assistant principals who help me keep the building running smoothly–"

"Our weakest link, the Silver Fox–"

"–Noah Lewis, Senior Assistant Principal."

A tall man with silvery hair stood up, grinned, waved and took a bow. Terry put two fingers to his mouth and whistled. Others applauded and cheered and stomped their feet.

"–Mr. Willy Zwill is Number Two."

"Number two is exactly what he is, but in other words."

A thin nervous man with large bags under his eyes stood up partially and sat down quickly.

"Next is the ever unpopular slick and slippery, pointy-shoed Sicilian, the inspiration for Mario Puzo's best-selling book, soon to be a major motion picture, our very own Mini Mussolini–"

"–Mario Giovanni, my right-hand man, even though he's a lefty–though not in his politics." Mr. Baltz chuckled at his little joke.

A dark little man in a black pinstripe suit with a pink carnation in the lapel stood up.

"And last but by no means least, that lovely star of stage, screen and eight-millimeter porn films. She's the one who wears the false mustache–" Terry's voice rose as more people turned and reacted.

"–looking fresh, rested and lovely, Helen O'Dell–"

The pigeon-breasted woman in a blazer and skirt stood.

"And I am"–Mr. Baltz said, and his face radiated a smile–"Principal M. Seymour Baltz. Thank you." He smoothed his mustache with his fingers.

"The M stands for 'May God help us,' Mr. Warmth. Mr. Charm, the Richard M. Nixon of Rosencrantz and Guildenstern Memorial High School."

"I now direct you, especially the new ones on staff, to refer to the materials in your First Day envelopes. There have been some changes since last year, so be sure to familiarize yourself with them. A smooth opening is the key to a successful school year."

Terry turned to Sue. "How's your opening? Smooth?"

"Wouldn't *you* like to know?"

Jesse turned crimson. He began taking notes about things to be done in the next weeks and months, lists to be made, phone numbers for the Snow Chain if school was closed in an emergency, things to be handed in to Guidance, the Main Office, Central Administration, things to be held on to, forms to be filled in and filed, medical insurance, retirement funds, important days, dates and times for Parents' Night, the end of each quarter report cards, midterms and final exams.

"Can I have your attention, people?" said Acting Guidance Chair, Rory Aaron. No one was listening, but he talked anyway about new Homeroom procedures, new IBM yellow bar sheets to record student attendance, lateness and absence. "Those new forms are going to make life so much easier for us. I mean for you, as well as Guidance. So listen up, people. The forms aren't ready yet, but as soon as we get them in Guidance we'll stick them in your boxes. Can I please have your attention, people. People, this is important, so listen. Meanwhile, for the next month or so until those IBM forms are in and the new program is activated, just continue with the *old* way of doing things. Record all the information by hand, but be sure to be accurate because you will have to transfer everything onto the new IBM forms when they finally arrive. People." But nobody listened.

"Teacher, auh, room keys," Noah Lewis announced in halting English, "will be distributed in my, auh, office along with student locker lists, student, auh, padlocks and all other teacher keys, filing cabinet keys and whatever after, auh, lunch."

"What?"

"Don't worry. You'll learn to speed listen and pick out the important things. But generally there isn't too much that's important," Sue said.

"Mr. Lewis is smart," she went on. "Just in the time I've been here his administrative duties have become less. Now he's only responsible for, auh, locks and, auh, keys."

"But since no one ever turns in their *real* room keys in June," Terry said, "he really has nothing to do in September except redistribute the ones that don't open anything. We all know it, but nobody cares."

Willy Zwill sidled up on the microphone and spoke quickly about student discipline. He said something about his years as morale officer in a Japanese POW camp in the Pacific during World War II preparing him for this job, with a wink and a smile, which Jesse realized was actually a twitch. He ended with, "Remember, it's us against them and when things get out of hand you can always count on Willy Zwill if you need backup or a witness." He twitched or actually winked and slid back to his seat.

Mario Giovanni talked about the bathrooms, student and faculty. And then Helen O'Dell announced new procedures for teachers to call in sick.

"There's a new automated sick number for calling in and arranging for a sub to cover your classes instead of teachers having to do it during prep periods like last year, which was a nightmare," she said. "The system isn't operating yet, and because of austerity there is no money to hire subs, so nothing's changed. Before you punch out today be sure to update your contact information with Phyllis Lind for the Snow List. New teachers, this is vital or you won't get a call if it snows and school is closed. Last year we had teachers not on the list who came in during a blizzard when school was closed."

Chants of "Stan-ley, Stan-ley, Stan-ley!" and "Far-ley, Far-ley, Far-ley!" resonated around the auditorium.

Then Noah Lewis's halting voice came out over the speakers again. "All, auh, teachers who have the following duties, auh, cafeteria, study hall, hall patrol and PB, report to their, auh, duty meetings in the following rooms 305, auh, 211, Library and, auh, 234."

Jesse's brain was going to explode. "I missed it. What did he say? What room number? When did she say that the Snow List is due? Did you get it?" He was in a panic. Sue was filing her nails and Terry had his head back and his eyes closed.

"Are you always this intense?" Sue asked. "They'll send you plenty of memos when things are due."

"And if they *really* want something bad enough," Terry said without opening his eyes, "you'll get a personal call from one of the secretaries. And if it's more important than really important, Phyllis will come to your classroom to collect whatever it is they need."

"When today's crap is over," Sue said, "life returns to normal and things go back to the way they have always been. Believe me, in my three years and a day I learned that it all works out… eventually."

It was the closest thing to encouragement Jesse had heard all day.

"Just keep telling yourself, as bad as this may seem," Terry added, "it's better than the rice paddies in Vietnam."

"After the Duty meetings," Mr. Baltz said to end the building meeting, "lunch will be announced later over the P.A. Department meetings begin promptly after lunch. Check with your department chair for the rooms. Then there will be a brief meeting here for attendance before sign out and dismissal." There was a smattering of boos. "We have a long and busy day, so let's get started." He turned for the exit followed by the APs, who marched out of step behind him, except for Willy Zwill.

"Meet you in the Main Office for lunch." Terry bounded up the aisle. Sue nodded.

Jesse didn't know if he was included in the lunch invitation or if he even wanted to eat with them. "Is he always so negative?"

"He really helped me. You'll learn a lot from him, just don't take everything you hear so seriously." She got up. "Your PB meeting is in 234. That's your Homeroom and first period classroom too. I'm in the Library so I can show you the way. The building's tricky. Floors don't exactly match up and in places you have to walk down from the second floor to get to the second floor, but you'll to get used to it. Let me see your schedule again." Jesse had packed everything together. He found it and handed it over. "Room 234 is in the New Wing, even though it's old. 235 is in the Old Building on the other side from 234. It's a trip to get to. 201 is on Second Floor B, which is really part of the third floor. You'll be fine. Relax. But wipe yourself again. You're sweating."

They walked up the aisle through the exit and scattered with the other teachers looking for their meetings or a place to play cards before lunch was called.

* * *

Mario Giovanni was already seated behind the big desk when Jesse looked into Room 234. There were a dozen bored teachers in the student desks. Although the windows were wide open the room was stifling. "You're late."

"Sorry. I got lost."

"Take a seat," he said brusquely.

Jesse walked slowly to the back of the room and sat in an empty place. He felt their eyes following him.

"Move up closer so I don't have to yell," the AP said, pointing out an empty seat in the front row. Jesse got up and did what he was told. "As I was saying," he began again with a slight *Casablanca* Humphrey Bogart lisp, his lips back over his teeth, "–before the interruption." Mr. Giovanni's black eyes glinted under the fluorescent lights. He sounded like Bogart, but he looked like John Garfield, another dead actor Jesse knew from old black-and-white movies he'd seen on TV. He was meticulously dressed, with a naturally dark complexion made darker by summer, accenting the little scar on his cheek that a century before might have been from dueling. His pinstripe suit was pressed and crisp despite the heat and the pink carnation in his lapel wasn't even a little wilted. "You old-timers know what this is all about. You new people"–he looked directly at Jesse–"might be a little confused." He twisted his neck from side to side and it cracked. It was a habit he'd developed when someone told him that stretching his neck would make him taller. It hadn't. "PB Patrol stands for Police Bathrooms Patrol, though you **may** call it other things." They laughed. "Doody Duty, Shit Detail or Potty Book." He smirked. "Bathrooms make up a major part of my duties, so it's important to me that you take your job seriously. Patrol the bathrooms. No short cuts. Circulate from bathroom to bathroom on all the floors during your rounds."

He handed papers to Jesse who took one and passed the rest behind him.

"Inspect passes carefully. There may still be some counterfeits around from last year's heist. The new legitimate passes are a slightly different shade of yellow. Check for smokers. Examine each stall and, if necessary, give the bowl a flush. That's new this year since there's no toilet paper. Be sure whoever is there is there to take care of business. Not that you want to wait too long, but a little pressure goes a long way in moving things along. Male teachers please remember to stay out of the girls' bathroom no matter what sounds you hear coming from there. We don't want another lawsuit." He stood up. "Again your biggest focus will be the graffiti, especially the obscenities. The objective is to neutralize anything offensive and make it not-offensive. This summer I've expanded the word list and those dittos now contains forty obscene words and expressions with suggested alternatives. On the left is the original word or phrase, on the right how it's been effectively altered rendering it not-offensive. In some cases there's more than one alternative."

Jesse looked at the words on both sides of the list. Of course! BOOK YOU and MILLIE SADOWSKI's BIG PITS now made perfect sense.

"Some of you were very creative in the past and I don't want this list to stifle that creativity. But if you're unsure or need some help, carry this with you until you have the knack."

Some of the teachers started to get up.

"Before you head for the card games, the good news is that because of austerity and no paper in any of the student bathrooms, you will *not* be required to leave me your lists of bathrooms low on supplies until the budget is passed. Now if there are no questions–"

There was a scramble for the doors.

Mr. Giovanni stretched his neck, fixed Jesse with a John Garfield look. "I heard about you," he said when they were alone. He pulled his lips back tight over his lips. "And I'll be watching you." He got up, adjusted the seat of his pants, fingered his carnation and left Jesse alone to consider the threat.

He waited to get up from the desk. According to the clock on the wall it was only eleven thirty. He had been a teacher for three hours and he wanted to quit. He took a good look around what was to be his room for at least one of his classes. It wasn't what he expected. Nothing was. It was small and dark and hot and it smelled like old gym socks and tuna fish sandwiches. He walked to the front and tried to imagine himself writing on the chalkboard that wasn't black or even real slate, but a wood composition that was painted over with a shiny green paint. The surface was slick and there were places where chunks had been knocked or carved out and he could see the cinderblock wall behind it.

He sat in the chair behind the old wooden desk and immediately he caught his new pants on a sliver of wood inside the leg well. "Shit!" He examined the snag it caused. "Shit!" He cautiously poked through the drawers and discovered a trove of daily student attendance lists from June past, names of people getting ready for summer vacation. He sighed. Next June was a hundred and eighty-two school days away. He leafed through a pile of faded ditto notes and a bunch of unmarked final exam papers. In one of the side drawers he found a package of Saltine Crackers wrapped in wax paper taped closed, a half bottle of store-brand pink liquid antacid, a tin of Extra Strength Excedrin and a water pistol.

His pants caught again so he ducked under the desk to find the offending splinter. "I'm not taking any shit from you!" he said and was aware that someone had walked into the room. He looked around the corner of the desk and saw a pair of scuffed white bucks, shoes he hadn't seen since the Pat Boone years.

"You're the new English guy, right, who came late to the PB meeting?"

Jesse lifted his head and banged it on the inside edge of the desk. The white bucks were attached to one red and one blue sock under a pair of chalky chinos over a round body. The shirttail hung out of the man's pants and the shirt gaped open slightly. Jesse stared into a tuft of red body hair and a belly button.

"Can always tell the fresh meat by the green color and the deer caught in the headlights expression! Red Farley, Math," he said and turned and looked around the room. His hair was a flattop crew cut, an anachronism that matched the shoes. "You got Crazy Keller's room. Now that was a strange guy. English Department is all a little weird if you ask me. But they locked Keller's ass in jail. No loss. Deserved it. I never really liked him." He stopped walking around and looked at Jesse. "Christ, you look lousy, kid!" He shook his head. "Scared, right! Well, you should be. More than fifty percent of first-year teachers don't make it through the year. And thirty percent of those that do don't come back the second year." He came around the desk. "Who you talking to under the desk? A midget?" He pulled some slips of paper from his pocket. "Wanna buy a ticket for the pool?"

"Just a damn minute," Jesse snapped. It was the last straw. "I might be a little green and maybe a lot naïve, but I'm not *stupid*. Not *that* stupid anyway. And I resent you trying to take advantage of me!"

Red rubbed his belly. "Huh? This room must attract the crazies, like a flame attracts flies. You got something against pools?"

"No. I was actually on my high school Swim Team. But there probably isn't any pool here and if there is, I'm sure it's free." Jesse was wound up. "I can't believe the insensitivity of everybody I've met in this place since I walked in the front door this morning. I'm sick and tired of being laughed at and the butt of jokes. And there's no toilet paper in any of the toilets for chrisakes!"

"Austerity, kid. Get used to it. You got something against baseball?"

"Baseball?"

"The national pastime. And you opposed to baseball pools."

"You're talking about a baseball pool?"

"What kind of pool did you think?"

"A *swimming* pool. I thought you were trying to sell me a ticket–"

"What swimming pool? We don't *have* a swimming pool. So why would I sell you a ticket to a pool we don't have?" He blinked. "Stupid. Dishonest. Illegal. This is just a little gambling pool." He frowned. "Where'd you go to school? Columbia? NYU? Berkley? You weren't hit on your head during some student demonstration were you? Or gassed? You don't smoke pot, do you? Baseball pool. That's what I said."

Jesse lowered his voice. "I'm sorry. I just thought–"

"And I thought Keller was nuts. Get rid of one and hire another!"

"I just misunderstood. I'm sorry. I'm a wreck. I'm so nervous and I'm not prepared–"

"You want some free advice, kid? Don't say that too loud around here. And whatever you do, don't ever let *them* know it." He pointed to the student desks. "The little bastards can smell fear and if they do they'll go right for your throat. Teaching is warfare, mostly psychological. You have to outthink the little shits. Find their weakest link and exploit it. Divide and conquer. If you let them get the upper hand you're finished." He leaned in closer to Jesse. "If you want to survive as long as I have, kid, you have to keep them off balance." He bobbed and weaved and jabbed awkwardly. "Don't believe anything the little bastards say. They're all liars, especially the girls. The girls are the worst with their perfume and open buttons." He leaned both fists on Jesse's desk like a silverback gorilla. "Tomorrow when the bell rings, wait in the hall until they're in their seats. Then walk in, slam the door hard, sneer, throw your books on the desk." He banged the desk. "That'll give them something to think about. Then you hit them with the class rules, all the things they *can't* do, all the things they *have* to do. And whatever you do, don't smile, at least until November, the whole year if you can. I usually make it through April or May. Otherwise they will eat you alive!"

"But all the Ed classes–"

"All bullshit, kid. And one other thing. You may want to single out a kid tomorrow and make an example of him. But don't pick a girl and don't pick the wrong kid who'll go running home to Mommy. A tough looking kid, but not too tough. You wouldn't want to get your ass kicked on the first day. You can't hit them anymore, but you can humiliate them. That's my advice. Take it or leave it. Now do you want a ticket for the pool or not?"

"No," Jesse said finally. "No... thanks."

He shook his head and walked out of the room. "Another English Department asshole!" he muttered audibly under his breath.

* * *

The door to the Principal's Office was closed, so Noah Lewis knocked before he turned the knob and walked in. The other three APs were already gathered around the desk. No one turned around.

"Sit, Noah." Mr. Baltz watched him settle into the high back chair in the corner of the room away from the others.

"Nobody, auh, told me we were having a meeting. I was down in the, auh, cafeteria. The walk from there seems to get longer, auh, every year."

Mr. Baltz continued. "The Phantom already made an appearance!" He held up the official sign-in sheets with "THE PHANTOM" printed in red block lettering in several places. "Dexter suspects someone sabotaged the AV equipment before the General Meeting." He touched the bruise on his nose where the swelling had puffed up his eyes. "And I was assaulted by that new teacher... what's his name... Tejent...?"

"Tietjen," Mario Giovanni corrected. "He was at my PB meeting. I doubt it was intentional. He looked so scared I thought he was going to cry."

"All I know is I just don't want a repeat of last year. The shotgun approach proved to be ineffectual." He stood at the portable chalkboard where "Operation Flush" was printed in neat letters and their names below that. "Mario and I met during the summer to set up a more focused campaign. I want to know *everything* that goes on in this building, so in addition to your regular AP duties, each of you will be assigned covert jobs to gather intelligence and tighten control. A good administrator has his finger on the pulse of his faculty, a great administrator has a stranglehold on their throats."

They all nodded, except for Noah Lewis who was digging through his pockets for a candy he unwrapped noisily and popped in his mouth. Mr. Baltz frowned. "O'Dell, besides the information that you've been picking up in overheard conversations, I want you to be more aggressive this year and conduct regular daily inspections of the teachers' desks, file cabinets and contents of their wastepaper baskets. Dig up what you can from the classrooms. Be creative. Improvise. Your WAC training should come in handy here. Arrange your own time schedule in the early morning before Homeroom and after school. Be thorough, discrete and undetected."

"Keys?" she asked. "I have a passkey for the rooms, but I'll need them for desks, file cabinets and closets."

"You'll see to that, Noah?"

"Auh?" He was looking out the window into the courtyard and turned when he heard his name. "Keys after lunch. Did you, auh, say it was lunchtime?" He started to get up from his chair.

"Soon, Noah. I was just telling O'Dell–" He turned to her. "On second thought, Helen, see Phyllis about that as soon as possible. Start tomorrow. Every room, every basket, every day."

She made a notation on the pad that she kept tucked in the front of her jacket.

"Willy." The AP sat up straight in his seat and his face twitched rapidly. "Again, you're my 'inside man.' Most of the teachers and chairs underestimate you and are likely to say things because you tend to be–"

"Invisible?"

"–not all there. Keep your eyes and ears open and your mouth shut. Mingle. Insert yourself. And keep a running account of everything you hear. It's basic intelligence work."

"Like when I was in the camp. I–"

"Exactly," Mr. Baltz cut him off before he could launch into another account of his prisoner of war days. He turned to Mario Giovanni. "Mario, you'll have the hottest spot again, the faculty toilets where problems with the Phantom began and where most of the activity is centered. Concentrate your energy there. Pop in and out of the faculty toilets at random times. Vary your schedule so no one knows when you might show up."

He nodded and stretched his neck. His John Garfield gaze rested on Helen O'Dell's round chest.

"Noah–"

He was rustling a wax paper-wrapped sandwich. The others turned to see what he was doing. "Sorry," he said. "I, auh, forgot what I brought for lunch." The smell indicated egg salad. He rested it on his lap and looked up.

"–why don't you go down and scout out the cafeteria while we finish up here. You can get a head start before lunch."

He rewrapped the sandwich and put it back into the bag and into his jacket pocket. "Right. So it's, auh, lunch then?" He looked at his wristwatch. It was almost noon. "I'll, auh, go ahead then." He left the room.

"For the record, 'Operation Flush' is a covert operation, on the need-to-know basis, and nobody outside this room needs to know." They nodded. "You two can go. Mario, you stick around."

He pulled out a Lucky from the open pack with his lips and lit it when they were alone. He threw the pack to his AP, who took one and let the unlit cigarette dangle at the corner of his lips while he practiced a Garfield squint.

"I checked the faculty toilets twice already and the walls are clean."

"And that new kid Tejent who was sitting next to Scapelli?"

"Tietjen," he corrected.

"You don't think there's a connection there? With Keller gone, we don't need another troublemaker in the English Department."

"The kid's terrified. You can smell it on him. But I warned him. Told him that I had my eye on him. He looked sick. I was afraid he was going to throw up." He cracked his neck.

"Keep an eye on him and keep him away from Scapelli."

* * *

"You little shits! How dare you?" The four members of the AV/CM Squad stood in front of Harry Dexter at rigid attention with textbooks supported in both of their outstretched arms. "This is my domain. If a microphone isn't supposed to work, I'll tell you it isn't supposed to work. Your job is to follow my orders."

He walked up close to the squad leader, a wiry blond kid wearing a captain's insignia. "Your actions today embarrassed me!" He tore the rank insignia from his shoulder and threw it to the floor. The boy didn't flinch and continued to hold the textbooks out at smart right angles. Dexter turned his back on them. "Tomorrow, seven thirty sharp before the regular school day starts. Full AV/CM dress uniforms and packs." He turned on his heel. "Dismissed." They put down the books, right-faced and marched out of the office.

When he was alone Dexter walked to the cabinet where he kept his files. He carefully selected the right key from the ring and opened the drawer. He removed an index card marked Baltz, Seymour. On a new line under the last entry he wrote the time and date and on the next, "Threatened me with death." He wrote a brief description of the events of the General Meeting and then he replaced the card among all the others and locked the cabinet.

* * *

Phyllis Lind announced lunch at 12:17 over the PA System. Jesse heard it, but he didn't move. He was seated at the desk when Sue Wellen looked in.

"Lunch?" she asked. "We only have until one o'clock." Jesse didn't even look up. "Hello? Anybody home in there? Are you going out for lunch? We have to move because we only have forty-five minutes."

He looked at her as in a dream. "I don't think so. I have a lot to do. And I really couldn't eat anything."

"Suit yourself," she said and disappeared from the doorway. "See you tomorrow."

Jesse hardly moved for fifteen minutes. Then he took out the new notebook he had bought with so much hope and promise the week before. The first pages were filled with the lesson plans he had hastily scribbled. The next pages were all the notes from the day's meetings. He turned to a fresh page and left the book open on the desk. He took out the gold Cross pen, a graduation gift from his sister and brother–in–law. "For your new career as a teacher," she said.

He thought for a second and then he began to write. "Dear to whom it may concern." He changed it to "Dear Sir" and finally settled on "Dear Mr. Baltz." That effort was so great he stopped, put his pen down and rested his head in his hands on the desk. For the first time he realized along with everything else how exhausted he was. When he recovered, he quickly scribbled out the lines of the letter he had been considering, closed the notebook and put his pen away. The rest of his lunch hour he sat with his head resting in his arms on the desk.

The Department Meeting after lunch was a blur. Dick Janus, the chain-smoking English Chairman, introduced Jesse to the rest of the English Department. He avoided Terry Scapelli, who was too busy working the room to notice, and he sat alone in the back collecting more dittos, lists and schedules. Mr. Janus discussed text book lists, required reading lists, and he learned that the money raised by the faculty for the Tom Keller Legal Defense Fund had been used instead for a new combination coffee, soup and soda machine from Mr. Giovanni's brother-in-law's vending company, delivered to the Third Floor Faculty Room.

Jesse punched out after the last attendance was taken again and at 4 p.m. he drove home in silence, forgetting to put on the car radio.

"So," his father asked, "how was it, Mr. Teacher?"

"Was it everything you expected it would be?" his mother asked.

"I'm tired. I need a nap." He went to his room and ignored his mother's calls to supper. He pretended to be sleeping when his father looked in on him. When he finally got up at 9:30, he said he wasn't hungry and tried to watch TV. At 10:00, the thought of going back to school in the morning sent him to the bathroom, where he spent the next twenty minutes vomiting after he'd chased his grandfather out. He went to bed weak and tired, but he couldn't sleep.

Twenty minutes before Homeroom Jesse finally found the Third Floor Faculty Room, which was actually located between the second floor of the New Wing and the regular third floor. The only students in the halls were uniformed AV/ CM Squad members pushing in formation carts loaded with equipment. From the perspiration on their shirts they had been working a long time.

Even though he arrived early, the faculty room was already smoky. Four women were playing bridge at one end of the table, smoking between bids. Jesse recognized Red Farley and the man with the straw shoes from the General Meeting yelling at each other and playing hearts with a third man he didn't know. No one looked up when he walked in. His chairman Dick Janus was standing with a lit cigarette drooping from the corner of his lips, studying the selections on the new "Tom Keller Vending Machine." Jesse managed a faint smile and nodded, but Janus took his steaming cup out of the tray and left the Faculty Room without acknowledging him.

Jesse accidentally bumped the table with his new leather attaché case, a special gift from his father. "From one of my customers who sells luggage," he'd told him proudly when he gave it to him. "To make you look professional." The impact shook the coffee cups, spilling some on the table and drawing glares from the women.

"Cripes!" Red Farley yelled grabbing too late for his cup that emptied over the tabletop.

"Sorry." He sat in an uncomfortable vinyl chair in the corner where he watched teachers he didn't know enter the room. With every passing minute he felt the terror in his chest building like a fire. He was almost happy to see Sue Wellen and Terry Scapelli arrive together.

"Greetings, comrades," Terry called to the room. "Don't bother getting up, Red." No one even looked up. "And so begins another wonderful school year with my colleagues.

How's the new Keller coffee machine working, Red?" he asked when he saw him mopping up the table.

"Better than that flake Keller ever worked." He grumbled and played a card so hard he spilled more coffee. "Cripes!"

Sue sat down at the table in one of the metal folding chairs near Jesse. "Good morning."

"I'm resigning!" he blurted.

She laughed. "Good one." She opened her pocketbook and set out her makeup on the table in front of her.

"No, really," he said. "I typed the letter last night." He took the envelope from his pocket.

She looked up and saw that he was serious. "Resigning? Classes haven't started yet." Terry returned with two cups and handed one to Sue. "He says he's resigning," she told him, checking her makeup in her compact mirror. "He wrote the letter last night. Show him."

"What a great idea. I think we should all resign." Terry raised his cup to Jesse. "Until October at least." Jesse showed him the letter.

"You can't resign," Sue said. "You haven't taught a single class yet!"

"And you can't retire until you're fifty-five, somewhere around 2005. And you won't be eligible for Social Security until ten years after that in 2015," Terry said.

Jesse was fighting to hold in his emotions. "I'm not prepared. I'm so out of place. I don't know what I'm doing and nobody tells me anything." It came out in an uncontrolled stream. His voice cracked a little. The bridge players looked up briefly and went back to their game.

"It's a wise man who knows his limitations," Terry said casually. "I read that in a Chinese fortune cookie."

"You're serious," Sue said. The look on Jesse's face bordered on tears. "You're really not kidding. He's serious," she said to Terry.

"The fact that you don't know what you're doing shouldn't stop you. It hasn't stopped anybody here. Right, Red? Tell the kid how little you know."

"Up yours, Scapelli!" He looked up from the game. "I told him what to do yesterday. Remember, kid, don't let them smell fear or they'll eat you alive. What was the name of the guy that they hung out the window two, three years ago?"

The image of being suspended from the third-floor window gave Jesse something else to worry about.

"Don't listen to either of them," Sue said. "You can't just walk away. You signed an agreement, so you have to give the district thirty days' notice. You can't even *think* about quitting until you've tried it for at least a month."

"Or at least one full day," Terry said.

"My first year was a disaster," she said, touching up her lipstick. "Please, put that letter away."

"And have a cup of coffee." Terry offered his cup to Jesse.

Reluctantly he tucked the letter back into the inside pocket of his suit jacket. "Coffee gives me–"

"Gin!" the man with the straw shoes called over the noise in the room.

"What do you mean gin, Stanley?" Red said. "We're playing hearts!"

"Then hearts!" he said and laid his cards on the table.

"See what I mean. *Nobody* knows what's going on around here. You have to take it a day at a time. An hour at a time. Pretty much everything they told you in all those Ed courses–worthless. You can't worry about the unimportant things. And all those memos and papers and things they handed out yesterday. Meaningless. Don't sweat any of that crap."

"Those things always get done. Just do your lesson plans and prepare for class. Everything will work out," Sue added.

"And after a while you won't even have to prepare for class," Terry said. "School is like the government with a life of its own that grinds on no matter who's in charge. Christ," he mused, "to be so tender and virginal again. Were you ever so idealistic, Wellen? So young and innocent? I don't remember."

The bell rang and Jesse stiffened involuntarily in his chair.

"Just remember the three Bs of teaching. Breathe. Be yourself. Be sure your fly is zipped."

Reluctantly, the room emptied into the hall crowded with equally reluctant kids.

Jesse stayed close to them as long as he could. "What happened to him?" he asked.

"Who?"

"The teacher they hung out the window."

"Oh," Terry said. "They dropped him. But he wasn't much of a teacher anyway. And now he's an assistant principal, but I won't tell you which one." He led the way down a flight of stairs to the second floor. "Good morning, Mr. Giovanni," Terry said when he saw the assistant principal coming out of the Faculty Men's Room. He turned to Jesse and winked.

Mr. Giovanni cracked his neck and nodded. He made a mental note that the three of them were together again.

Jesse sighed and hurried off to find his classroom.

"Do you really think he'll be all right?" Sue asked.

"Of course, he can't miss. Didn't I give you the same advice?"

"I never checked my zipper."

"And that's the main reason you got tenure!" The Homeroom warning bell rang.

* * *

Red Farley was outside across the hall from Jesse's Homeroom. "Hey, kid," he called over the noisy students clogging the hall looking for their classrooms, "don't pay any attention to Scapelli. He's bad news. Divide and conquer! Survival of the fittest and all that crap! Just don't shoot your wad in Homeroom. You have five classes. If you want to see how it's done, stop by my door and listen to a pro." He winked. "Come on, move! Get to class!" he barked at a student who stopped to ask him a question. He just shooed the kid along and nodded at Jesse.

Homeroom was extended. After the Pledge of Allegiance, a moment of silent prayer or meditation, two verses of the National Anthem, countless student announcements and one by Mr. Lewis, Jesse barely had time for taking attendance, marking the absentees down on the official attendance cards and giving out the student programs. He was deluged with student questions he wasn't able to answer about program conflicts, room locations and working papers. And he certainly didn't have time to seat them in alphabetical order like the First Day Procedure Book required. When the bell rang his first Homeroom became history and the classroom emptied into the noisy halls. Alone, he heard his heart pounding in his chest, felt it under his letter of resignation inside his jacket pocket. He was alive, but didn't have time to dwell on it. There were only three minutes before the late bell and he had to get to Room 235 on the other side of the building.

He waited in the hall to compose himself until the room filled with students. He mopped his face, but the nervous flop-sweat had soaked his underwear and was running down his legs to his tight, uncomfortable leather shoes. All the nightmares of the past month had brought him to this. He inhaled and walked into the room. Squelching his impulse to smile, he didn't sneer either. He felt a slight trembling inside.

They quieted and watched him set his case on the desk before he turned and wrote his name on the board. "Good morning," he mumbled from behind the safety of his desk too low to be heard except by those seated directly in front of him. "My name–" He overcompensated and yelled. He had no control. "–is Jesse Tietjen." He knew he shouldn't have used his first name as soon as he said it. "Mr. Tietjen," he corrected. "And this is English 11 Regents–"

"Excuse me," a girl in the first row waved her hand. "My program says Business 10."

Jesse took his life in his hands and walked around his desk and into the middle of the row toward her though it might be a trap. "You must be in the wrong place." He reached for her card.

"Excuse me, new teacher. Mine says Business too."

"And mine."

"Me too."

They all called out at once waving their program cards.

"Business 10 and you're Mr. Milnow."

He looked at their cards. "Isn't this Room 235?"

"Room 335."

"Oh shit!" They laughed. "Oh, sorry." His face turned crimson. "*I'm* in the wrong place!" He grabbed his things from the desk and when he reached the door the man with the straw shoes strolled in, finishing a doughnut. "Mr. Milnow, where's 235?"

He pointed down the hall. "Other side of the building and up half a flight."

Jesse sprinted down the hall. He looked at his watch. It was already eight minutes into the first period. He was late for his first class. When he skidded around the corner he wasn't aware of a shadow in his path. His momentum caused him to collide with a crouching figure looking through the little window in the door into the classroom. His attaché case clattered against the lockers and the impact propelled the man through the opened door and into the room.

Jesse didn't stop. He grabbed his case and continued down the corridor. "Sorry!" he called back. "Late for class!" He zipped around the other corner without looking back.

"Ladies and gentlemen, it seems we have a surprise guest this first morning of school," Terry Scapelli said without changing the expression on his face when his classroom door burst open and Willy Zwill sprawled across the classroom floor. "You all know Mr. Zwill, one of our most illustrious assistant principals. Good morning, Willy. Starting administrative observations already?"

The AP twitched and rose to his knees. "Just checking, Mr. Scapelli." He looked around the room, removed a small memo pad from his pocket and a red felt marker. "Windows." He counted them and wrote the number on his paper. "Blackboards. Everything seems to be fine, Mr. Scapelli." He crawled to the doorway. "Carry on."

Jesse was out of breath when he reached Room 235. His students were inside and seated. He composed himself, took a breath and stepped inside. Every head turned and they went silent.

"Room 235, right?" He was still out of breath. "English 11 Regents?" He rested briefly on the end of the desk until he was able to write his name on the board. "I'm sorry for being late. I'm new here and there was this mix-up and–" He knew he was telling them too much, and he was about to tell them more, but a tall, gangly boy with wire rim glasses came in behind him.

"Sorry," he said. "Schedule conflict." His tightly curled hair made him resemble a dandelion puff or a liquid shoe polish applicator. "I was just transferred into your class." He handed Jesse a pink transfer slip. "You just go on with whatever you were doing, Mr."–he looked at the board–"Teegent?"

"Tietjen," Jesse corrected. "The second 't' is silent. And you are?"

"Virgil Loomis, Mr. Teeg, and all of my letters are noisy." The class laughed and Jesse actually smiled. Virgil loped to the empty seat in the back row and sat. His knees stuck out from both sides of the writing board.

"I was a kindergarten dropout," Jesse started, though he had no idea why. "I was five and I hated kindergarten." He paused. "Well, today, and the day is only an hour old, and my first day of kindergarten seventeen years ago have a lot in common." Several of the girls counted his age on their fingers. "I had two teachers. Old Mrs. Singer and the beautiful Miss DiMaio. I didn't like Mrs. Singer, but I *loved* Miss DiMaio the minute I saw her." He actually hadn't thought about her in years, but now when he pictured her face it all flooded back to him. They listened intently. "I was what you'd call a 'momma's boy,' so when my mother dropped me off that first day I cried. I made an absolute fool of myself in front of everybody, even Dorothy Marinzano, my very first girlfriend, who was also five, lived on my block and was in my class. I cried so much I threw up." He acknowledged their eews. "Back then I could make myself throw up whenever I wanted to, so they sent me home. But I managed to get through the next day only because the beautiful Miss DiMaio sat me on her lap during story time. On the third day when I didn't want to play clay, I hid under my wooden table and I got a splinter, which didn't do much to enhance my opinion of school." He stopped. "I just realized it. Yesterday in my Homeroom classroom I also got a splinter from my desk! An omen?" They laughed.

"Every morning during my short time in kindergarten we had a musical parade and marched around the room. Old Mrs. Singer played the piano and the beautiful Miss DiMaio the guitar. All the kid instruments were in the closet, so before the parade we stampeded to be first and grab the best instrument. To a five-year-old, best means the noisiest and that was the bass drum. Besides being loud, the drum led the parade, worn proudly around the neck of the lucky kid who grabbed it. The least instruments, the last to go and in the parade, the saddest of all the instruments were the lowly little triangles. There were two. One so small it wasn't worth hitting." He paused. "I *always* got that triangle." There were sympathetic moans. "Three days in a row! And I cried every day on the verge of throwing up. Oh, the indignity and the injustice of it all. On Friday, I cried so much the beautiful Miss DiMaio led me by the hand to the front of the parade where she removed the drum from the girl who beat out everyone in the class almost every day, and Miss DiMaio–"

"The beautiful Miss DiMaio," someone called.

"– the *beautiful* Miss DiMaio," he added, "fastened that drum around my neck. And she gave that bully of a girl my little triangle. I was the leader of the parade!" Everyone cheered. "And for one brief moment, for the first and only time in kindergarten, I thought, if they let me bang the drum, I could get to like it a little. If I could lead the parade every day, I might even love kindergarten. So there I stood, so proud with that big drum hanging around my neck! Old Mrs. Singer started the march on her piano and the beautiful Miss DiMaio strummed her guitar. My face beamed. Everyone was lined up behind me with their kazoos and tambourines, their pathetic wood blocks. And way in the back of the line where I would have been was that girl with the small triangle. I turned the drumstick in my hand to use the fat end, took a step and I banged. I hit it as hard as I could"–" He paused. He had them on the edge of their seats. "–and I broke a hole in the drum!" There was a collective gasp. "I was mortified. I couldn't even look at the beautiful Miss DiMaio's disappointed face." He took a deep breath, reliving the experience. "After I threw up they called my mother and I went home for the last time. I quit kindergarten and I never went back. And that's the truth." Jesse felt better than he had all week. "And don't you know, that terrible experience was nothing compared to the way it's been today."

There were cheers and applause and Jesse felt a smile form on his face.

The rest of the period he spent taking care of business and when the bell rang some of the kids stopped at the desk to wish him a better day.

Virgil Loomis was the last one out. "Great story, Mr. Teeg."

"Thank you, Mr. Loomis."

"Virgil, Mr. Teeg. Mr. Loomis is my father. Actually Dr. Loomis. My mother too. Dr. and Dr. Loomis. A pair a docs. That's an English joke. Paradox."

"I got it." Jesse laughed.

"What are your feelings about Jello, Mr. Teeg?"

"Jello? Can't say I feel one way or another. Why?"

"It fascinates me. Since last year I've been trying to convince Miss Orlando, my Art teacher and Senior Class Advisor to accept an idea I have, a performance art piece, for my end of the year Senior Project. It involves Jello. Filling a room six by six by six with virgin green Jello, that's been jelled in the room in one big solid cube and not shoveled in."

"Okay. But why?"

"I'd build an opening in the top of the clear plexiglass container I'm almost finished building, strip down to a Speedo and jump into it."

"Wait… wait… you're a senior? My class is 11th grade."

"I'm doubling," he said. "Obviously high IQ is no guarantee of performance. Last year I had some motivational problems. Mr. Keller and I didn't see eye to eye. He thought I was a wiseass and I thought he was just an ass. Did you know he's in jail now? His girlfriend's husband came home early, found them together and shot him. Maybe you read about it. It was in the papers." The late bell sounded. "Well, Mr. Teeg, I'm looking forward to your class this year. I'm on my way to the cafeteria for some breakfast. Anything I can get for you?" Jesse shook his head. Virgil waved and moved off down the hall. "Hey, Mr. Farley," he called when he passed him. "Looks like you and I have a date sixth period."

"Not if I can get you switched out first, Loomis." He saw Jesse. "I had the little bastards scared shitless. They didn't take their eyes off me the entire period. How'd it go with you? Hope you did what I told you."

"Okay." Jesse raised a two-fingers peace sign.

Red automatically returned Jesse's two finger salute with a single finger of his own. "Sorry," he said, "reflex action."

Jesse looked and saw that Red's fly gaped open. "No problem. I hope you get the same response from this class," he called. He slipped a finger under his jacket to check that his zipper was up.

"How's it going?" Terry asked, sipping at a cup from the vending machine. "Better than this tepid chicken-tasting coffee I hope!"

"It started off terrible, but it got better," Jesse said. "I was late for class and knocked some guy into one of the classrooms while I was running to mine."

"First period second floor?" Jesse nodded. "My room. And it was Willy Zwill."

Jesse's face turned ashen. "Is he okay?"

"As okay as he'll ever be. That makes two down in two days. Keep up the good work."

The afternoon classes weren't terrible either and neither was the drive home. That night he sat down at the supper table and ate something. He actually held a conversation with his parents about his first teaching day, careful not to get into too many details. He even shared some ice cream with his grandfather. Later, when he thought about going back in the morning there was a cold feeling in his stomach, like riding the Cyclone at Coney Island, but it passed and he didn't throw up. Before he went to bed he took his letter of resignation from his suit jacket pocket and put it in a compartment in his attaché case where he could still get to it easily.

"Mr. Tietjen?"

Jesse was marking the rest of the compositions he assigned his classes to write for their introductory themes. He thought the topic "My Fantasy Life" would be more interesting than "How I Spent My Summer Vacation," but it proved to be almost as tedious. Most of his first teacher weekend was spent trying to decipher bad handwriting, correcting bad grammar and approximated spelling. They were all pretty boring, except for Virgil Loomis's account of "Virgil in Green Jello," complete with illustrations of the chamber he was constructing.

"Mr. Tietjen," the voice came again from the doorway.

He looked up to see the woman with thick ankles who had kicked his class list under the table the first day. Instinctively he protected his papers.

"I'm Mrs. Butrum–" She didn't wait to be invited in and walked up to his desk. He looked at her blankly. "–Chairlady of the Sunshine Committee. I've been hunting you down for days. I put my notice about the building Sunshine Fund in your box personally the first day and I still haven't heard from you."

"Oh?" He didn't remember that particular ditto in among the rest. He hadn't actually gotten through all the papers yet. "I guess with all the excitement... I hope it wasn't something that required my immediate attention."

She smiled. "I thought you might be a little nervous about your first teaching job, so I gave you some time to adjust." Jesse nodded. "I imagine that long commute every day must be murder, with the roads what they are. A lot of added stress. So many thousands of people killed in their cars every year."

Jesse nodded automatically again and then looked up at her. "How do you know I commute from the city?"

"I read your personnel file. As Chairlady of the Sunshine Committee, it's part of my duties to know a little about *all* the teachers for special occasions like birthdays, funerals, next of kin, weddings and such. Last year the

Sunshine Committee covered three funerals and one wedding. I noticed you aren't married." She smiled. He shook his head. "Engaged? Seeing someone?" He was flustered. "Of course if you don't have the two dollars now for the Sunshine Fund–"

"I'm sorry," Jesse reached for his wallet and pulled out his last two dollars. Payday wasn't until the end of the week. He mentally calculated the change in his pocket and the amount of gas in the tank of his old Mercury. Maybe he could get a couple of bucks from his grandfather to tide him over. The old man wouldn't mind. He handed Mrs. Butrum the money.

"You know you never really do get over it. The nervousness, I mean. No matter what they say. In thirty years I still get the flux every September."

"The flux?"

She shook her head and lowered her voice. "The loose bowels. Of course the severe menstrual cramps that I used to get when I was a younger woman are a thing of the past since the hysterectomy. Can't say I miss what they took out and Lord knows I'm glad to be done with that monthly business. But since they removed a section of my lower intestine some seven years ago my digestion isn't quite the same."

"I see," Jesse said. He could feel himself tensing and the perspiration forming. He wiggled in his seat and his pants were stuck to the wood.

"I'll never forget my first year teaching." She was smiling again. "It was a disaster." Her eyes misted. "Had two deaths in the family not six months into the semester. Lost my mother first. And my father a month later. Did you have a good summer?"

"Y–yes, I suppose. And yours?" he added and regretted it immediately.

"Well, my husband passed early in July. Cancer," she whispered. "Just before the holiday weekend. He'd been sick for some time so it was expected and a blessing in a way."

"I'm terribly sorry."

"Thank the good Lord, Charles, that was my husband's name, put aside quite a bit so my daughter and I are pretty well off. She's unmarried as well, my daughter I mean, and not seeing anyone at the moment." She touched his arm. "My but August certainly was a scorcher wasn't it?" He shook his head and then wanted to kick himself. "That's nice." She smiled and waited.

"I *did* give you the money, didn't I, Mrs. Butrum?" He fished through his pockets for more.

She nodded and continued looking at him. "I was just thinking that it might be nice for you to meet her sometime. The two of you–"

He felt himself getting sick. "Excuse me, Mrs. Butrum," he interrupted, gathering his papers together, "but do you know if there is a men's room close by? It's kind of an emergency."

"I'm not sure about this floor. There' s one on the third floor and one by the cafeteria."

"Thank you." He got up. "It certainly has been interesting talking to you."

"Yes, it certainly has." She watched him fumble with his case and the papers. "If your stomach is upset I wouldn't suggest eating there."

"The men's room?"

"The faculty cafeteria. They're serving chili today and three years ago one of the teachers, poor man, was taken deathly ill. He spent a week in Intensive Care. The Sunshine Committee sent him a basket of fruit, but he wasn't able to eat it. So if your stomach has butterflies you should eat something light. I *never* eat in the cafeteria anyway. I can't afford to be too careful. With part of my intestines gone and all–"

Jesse bolted for the door.

"Do you live with your parents?" she called after him, but he didn't hear her. She circled his name on her paper and checked to see who was next on her list.

* * *

Mortimer Seymour Baltz became principal in 1964, after little Bernie Prahl, the first principal of R&G, retired for health reasons and then died two weeks later. Harry Dexter became the AV/CM Coordinator in October of the following year after Don Cooley, who occupied the seat, was electrocuted while sitting at his desk. Dexter received the telephone call from his uncle on Columbus Day. "You got the job," he said curtly. "Don't make me regret this."

His intention from his first day on the job was to make himself indispensable in the building, on a par with the custodians. Immediately he set out to consolidate his position, dismantling Cooley's slipshod operation and replacing it with his own. By the end of his first year he'd managed to erase all traces of his predecessor, except for a small framed picture of Don Cooley that he kept hanging on the wall of his office as a reminder that one could never be too careful where electricity was concerned. He inventoried every piece of equipment under his control, from the latest reel–to–reel Ampex Video Tape Recorders to the precise number of extension cords and created a complex cataloging system and index that he alone understood. He set up high, often arbitrary, standards to be followed by anyone who wanted to use *his* equipment, as he had come to think of everything in AV/CM as his. His signature controlled everything, and nothing moved without his personal approval. No one who failed to meet those standards and only a few who did ever got what they requested. Over the following years he compiled a meticulous history of teachers who offended him in word, deed or thought and he began keeping a file of personal information about each member of the faculty that might become useful.

"If this was Washington, DC," he told his wife, "I'd be J. Edgar Hoover."

The halls of R&G resounded with stories of projectors purposely sent to the wrong rooms, microphones dying midsyllable and record players perpetually revolving at the wrong speed. Dexter didn't try to prevent these stories from circulating; instead, he encouraged them. To add to the mystique, every month or so, he and his highly trained staff drew up new rules and new conditions for the requisition and the use of AV/CM equipment. The rules and forms weren't always placed in teacher mailboxes for ready reference, but failure to follow them resulted in long delays. More than two failures made the possibility of showing a film or listening to a record remote, and making it onto his Enemies List guaranteed never getting anything.

Harry Dexter wasn't a particularly smart man, but he was wise enough to know his limitations and he was shrewd enough to hold on to what he had. He took extreme precautions not to get fried on the job as Don Cooley had, so he made it a practice never to handle personally any piece of electrical equipment. And never did he even plug in or unplug a machine. Unlike many others, Dexter was content with his limited pool of power amid the other power pools within the school and the district, for the present at least.

The storage room behind his office was crammed with equipment on ceiling-to-floor shelves that lined the walls. Six members of the AV/CM Squad, or Dexter's Marauders as they were known, stood around a new Bell and Howell super eight projector listening intently as a boy with new captain's insignia and hash marks signifying three years of service, pointed to the partly dismantled machine. He indicated another part on the table. "Again, what is this?"

On the wall in his office behind Harry Dexter hung a large floor map of the building, speckled with different colored pins, indicating the exact locations of each piece of equipment presently out on loan. He was seated at his large wooden desk, thumbing through a tray of file cards he had removed from the steel file cabinet in the far corner. The index card taped to the face of the cabinet was neatly lettered in red marker: "CONFIDENTIAL–RESTRICTED ACCESS!" He always kept the cabinet locked, even when he was in the office, and he was the only one with the key. It was in these drawers that he kept accounts of his running feuds with the building staff.

One of the telephones on the desk rang. There were three of them. The black phone connected the main switchboard and all of the classrooms in the building. The white one was a direct outside line. And the red phone went to the principal's office. It was the black phone so Dexter let it ring seven times before he picked it up. "I'm a very busy man," he said automatically into the receiver.

"Dexter?" the voice at the other end was frantic. "This is Carl Hubby in Woodshop."

"Okay?" he asked in his usual bored nasal tone.

"I was supposed to get a film and projector for my classes–"

"Name of the film?"

"*Industrial Shelving*. It's not here and I need it! I don't have a lesson and these guys–"

"Super eight or sixteen millimeter?"

"Sixteen. Listen, I'm stuck for a lesson–"

"Did you preview it?"

"Last year." Mr. Hubby's voice intensified. "Dexter, I *need* that film!"

"Did you put in a proper requisition for it?" He located Hubby's requisition form in the wire basket on his desk.

"On the first day of school, for chrisakes! I put it in your mailbox personally." There was some noise at the other end of the line. "Sit down! Shut up! Don't touch that!" He was breathing heavily. "Hurry, Harry, please!"

"That's the problem, Hubby." Dexter turned around in his swivel chair and tapped the edge of his desk with a pencil. "The new AV/CM Bulletin stated that this year *all* requisitions for equipment must be filed in the box *outside* the AV/CM office and no longer put in my mailbox in the Main Office. You have to read those notices, Hubby."

"But, Harry, you don't understand! I'm desperate. This is a Track III class. Can't you do something? Send me anything! If I don't show them a film they'll tear the place apart. They'll tear *me* apart, Harry!"

"I'll see what I can do. But I can't make you any promises. I'm a busy man. The next time you want a piece of my equipment, Hubby, you'd better follow the rules. You have no idea the volume of work we handle every day. We don't have time to pamper any prima donnas who try to buck the system."

"But–" The phone went dead.

Dexter put the receiver back in its cradle.

"Ralph," he called to the squad's new captain. "That was Hubby in Woodshop. He said something about a film."

"Yes, sir." The boy came to attention. "I delivered it to the Biology Lab, just like you told me."

"Good. Good." He toyed with the pencil. "See to it that Hubby gets a record player right now. And maybe a filmstrip. Just pick one. It doesn't matter." He went back to his index cards. "But Ralph," he called, "no records and no filmstrip projector. Mr. Hubby still hasn't learned his lesson."

Jesse rushed into the Third Floor Faculty Room. He had only a few minutes to pee before the start of the next period. He was so looking forward to the three-day Rosh Hashanah weekend. God bless the Jews. He stood at the urinal, but nothing happened.

"Come on," he said. "You can do it. Atta boy. Come on. Come on. That's got it. Oh, yes, yes." The stall door behind him crashed open and Jesse wheeled around still holding on to himself. "Mr. Giovanni!" he said when he saw the assistant principal step out of the first stall. "I didn't know anybody was in here."

"Obviously." He shot him a look and cracked his neck. "What the hell are you're doing, playing with yourself?"

"No. I, er–"

The bell rang.

"Do you have a class now?"

"Yes, sir. I do. I, er–"

"Well, just be sure to put that thing away before you go. And wash your hands."

Jesse zipped up and went to the sink. He wet his hands and face before he remembered that there were no paper towels. He pulled his damp handkerchief from his pants and dried himself as best he could. Then he rushed out into the hall.

Mr. Giovanni went into the center stall and then into the third. He smirked, paused to check his hair in the mirror before he headed back to the Main Office.

Phyllis Lind was bending over the lowest drawer of the file cabinet when he came into the office. By her own admission she was one of a small group of women in the world who still didn't wear panty hose, but preferred garter belts and stockings with seams.

"Always looking good, Phyl," he said. He stopped and lingered and thought about that.

"Why thank you, Mario. Looking good is my life's ambition."

Her sarcasm wasn't lost on him. He cracked his neck and went into the Principal's Office. "Phantom's back in the toilet!" he announced. "Third floor faculty men's room. I wanted you to see it before I erase it."

"Fuck!" Mr. Baltz came around the desk and into the Main Office past Phyllis Lind. "I'll be out for a while, Miss Lind."

"Ms," she corrected.

Mr. Giovanni followed him down the hall to the elevator. It would have been easier and faster to walk up the stairs, but having an elevator key was one of the administrator perks and they made it a practice to ride whenever they could. When the elevator door opened, he pushed into the car before the student in a hip cast with a medical elevator pass could get off and she had to ride back up to the third floor.

Mr. Giovanni held the door to the faculty bathroom open and Mr. Baltz walked in. "First stall."

He pushed the green door aside and looked, but he didn't see anything.

"Behind the door. Eye level."

Mr. Baltz shut the door, squatted without sitting on the bowl and saw the message written in red felt marker. "Office of M. Seymour Baltz, Principal. Hours–irregular, like the man himself! Welcome to another school year–The Phantom."

"Son of a bitch!" He yanked the door open, but the return spring sent it flying back and it hit him in the head. "Fuck!" He opened the door slowly and walked out holding the bridge of his nose. "Get rid of it, Mario."

He reached the elevator in time to take a boy with leg braces back down to the first floor. He was trying to explain the whole ride down that he was late for class, but Mr. Baltz wasn't aware that the boy was even there.

Later, when they were both back in his office, he lit a cigarette and threw the match into the shrunken head ashtray. It was a stupid souvenir his mother-in-law had brought back from her cruise through the Panama Canal to Machu Picchu in Peru. The beady little dark eyes winked and reflected the overhead light like brown marbles. "What do you think, Mario?" he said.

"We know one thing." He picked a piece of long red hair that was wrapped in his carnation. "It wasn't anybody we suspected last year who left the building. Like Keller, or that other guy who got fired for exposing himself." He stretched and cracked his neck.

"Brilliant deduction, Mario. So what's your point?"

"It's a simple process of narrowing down the field. Cross everyone off the list who left. Then we eliminate anybody who called in sick today. And so on."

He punched the intercom button. "Miss Lind, bring me the list of all the teachers who called in sick or are out of the building today."

"*Ms.*" Her sleepy voice sounded over the intercom speaker. "The automated sick call in number isn't up yet."

"Then just get me a handwritten list of the teachers who are out today."

"There is no list. All of the teachers are in."

He let go of the button. "Shit! Any more ideas, Mario?" But he wasn't listening. He was picturing the seams on Phyllis Lind's stockings running up the back of her legs. Mr. Baltz crushed the cigarette out in the ashtray. "Earth to Mario. Come in Mario! I think you've been spending too much time with Noah Lewis!" He snapped his fingers.

Mr. Giovanni came back to reality. "We know that the Phantom is a man because all of the notes last year and this morning were in the men's toilet."

"You have a knack, Mario, for stating the obvious."

"So we can eliminate all of the females on staff. Unless, of course, it's a woman who's sneaking into the men's room to throw off suspicion. And we know that the Phantom always uses a red felt marker, right?" He paused. "So all we have to do is find who uses red felt markers. Then we collect the markers. End of problem."

Mr. Baltz sat back in his chair. "I am surrounded by incompetents!"

Mr. Giovanni stiffened and wondered how different things would be if he were taller.

New teachers came into the district every year. Some were filled with hope and enthusiasm and thought they'd make a difference, many weren't. Some were looking for an easy job, a placeholder until something better came along. And some just wanted to stay out of Vietnam. All were naïve and the majority quit in a year and moved on. The hard-core faculty of R&G remained virtually unchanged for decades, except for the teachers who died. The lucky ones lasted long enough to retire and returned occasionally to discover that pretty much everything was the same. Period to period, day to day, year in and year out the routine became set in stone–where people sat, their politics, the daily conversations and how to push each other's buttons.

Twenty minutes into fourth period, when Terry Scapelli sauntered into the Third Floor Faculty Room, he pretty much knew before he opened the door who would be there and where they would be. The only difference in the faculty room was the smell since the arrival of the new Tom Keller Vending Machine in September, a chickeny-coffee aroma. "Greetings, *comrades,*" he called, knowing how much that annoyed Red Farley. "No need to get up."

"Up yours," Red said without looking up from his cards. Instead of hearts, the game he played during the morning prep period, the afternoon game of choice with Stanley Milnow and Buddy Ritchie, the wrestling coach, was three-handed blackjack. Chuck LaFemina, the second librarian, never played, but always sat next to Buddy Ritchie and kept score of who owed what.

Terry thought about a cup of soup, but instead he pressed the button for black coffee and settled for tea with milk and sugar that tasted like all three. Then he drifted to the card game and looked over Red's shoulder because he knew he hated that too.

"Hit me!" Red said and Buddy Ritchie turned over a card. "Shit! Over again." He shrugged his shoulder. "Can you go stand someplace else, Scapelli? You're a jinx! And I can feel you behind me." He threw in his cards.

"I'm looking forward to the summer Olympics," Buddy Ritchie said, continuing with his college wrestling lament. "If I'd a tried out in my last year in college I probably woulda made the team. Been All-American. Won Olympic gold and made a lot of money doing endorsements. Did I ever tell you–"

"Yes," Stanley Milnow said, "many times. Hit me." He counted his points on his fingers. "And I should have listened to my mother who always wanted me to be a doctor. My brother's a lawyer and he's making a bundle." He waved his hand. "I stay."

"Once when I was in great shape I could bench-press the front end of a Volkswagen." He flexed the top of his body.

"Too bad about those hemorrhoids though, Buddy," Terry said. "How sad that piles cut short your hopes and your dreams to be on a box of Wheaties," he continued to tweak. "Maybe if you used Preparation H instead you coulda been a contenda!"

"Fuck you, Scapelli!"

"Only if you buy me dinner and drinks first."

Chuck LaFemina laughed.

"Thirteen, fourteen, fifteen," Red Farley counted. "Stop talking and hit me, for chrisakes. The period will be over before I win even once."

"Who won the pool last week?" Stanley Milnow asked, picking his teeth with the edge of his cards.

"For chrisakes, Stanley. You're getting blood all over the goddamn cards!"

He took the card out of his mouth and looked at it, and then he wiped the edge off with his fingers.

Terry circled around the table and came back to Red's chair.

"Marta the cleaning lady won high again. And Eddie the tattooed night custodian won low." He leaned forward. "Hit me, Stanley, for five card Charlie!" He got a seven.

"You're over, Red. That's twenty-two."

"I can count for chrisakes, Scapelli!" He threw in his cards.

"Anybody seen Milly Sadowski this year? She eats lunch in my cafeteria. Her knockers get served a minute before she does!"

Buddy Ritchie grinned. Chuck LaFemina blushed.

"Somebody should do something about the way they let them parade around here," Red complained. "We were better off when there was a dress code for students"–he looked at Terry–"*and* for teachers, Scapelli. This school went downhill when they stopped enforcing the dress code. It's indecent!"

"Indecent?" Stanley Milnow said. "If it's long enough and hard enough and in deep enough, it's in decent! I liked it when they wore miniskirts and hot pants. It made coming to work here almost tolerable. Now it's all that tie-dyed crap, and jeans." He lowered his voice. "Thank God for the shoe store or I'd never get to see a beaver."

"Shut up and deal, Milnow!"

"That Sadowski girl's really something. *Playboy* material. *Penthouse.* I keep giving her candy whenever I see her. An investment for when she graduates and comes back to visit her favorite teacher."

"And that would be you?" Terry scratched his beard. "Remember, her father's a cop."

"For chrisakes, Scapelli. You got goddamn beard hairs all over the table. No wonder I keep losing." He wiped the table with his sleeve after he lost another hand. "Speaking of losers, I got your friend Loomis in my class again., Scapelli. He looks like a bottle washer this year with that Jewfro."

Buddy Ritchie nodded. "A real freak. What's with him anyway?"

"Beside needing a bath and a haircut? The kid's a weirdo. A subversive. A goddamn radical. He's already questioning my authority and trying to organize the class! For chrisakes! Stop picking your teeth, you're marking the cards, Stanley!" he yelled. "You got your goddamn blood all over the picture cards!" He threw in his cards.

"Can I help it if I have bad gums? With the shitty dental plan we have in this shitty district, I can't afford to see a dentist."

"Your pal Loomis graduates in June. One less freak to deal with. And then the U.S. Army will take care of him. Make a man out of him."

"Like they did for you, Red? You ever been in the Army? Served your country?"

"I would've enlisted to teach those Asian bastards a lesson, but I have a heart murmur and my doctor wrote a note."

"I'm surprised to hear you have a heart," Terry taunted and Chuck LaFemina snorted. "My mother wrote a note for me to keep me out of everything. I have it here." He reached into his pocket and pulled out a folded scrap of paper. "'Dear Fill in Name Here,'" he read, "'Please excuse my son from Fill in Event Here, as he has a cold.' When the Selective Service Board read it they told me to go home." He took a sip of his tea.

"Bullshit, Scapelli. You're so full of bullshit. And you fill up your kids' heads with your bullshit too. No wonder there's no respect for authority anymore."

"Come on, Red. I'm very big on authority and interested in everything that will restore law and order to this country. I just read about some west coast doctor in the *Times* working on a solution for antisocial behavior."

"I don't believe anything you say, Scapelli, or anything in that lefty rag. Besides, psychologists don't solve problems, they create them. Coddling criminals. Psychiatrists are worse. All that touchy-feely shit. If they fired all the psychologists and psychiatrists in this district, and some of the guidance counselors, no offense intended, Rory," he called to the acting Guidance Chair down the end of the table, "nobody would notice and the place would run better." He waited for Terry to continue, but when he didn't, Red couldn't resist. "So what was his solution?"

"First of all the man's not a psychologist or a psychiatrist. He worked with criminals, chronic offenders, serial killers."

Red lost another hand while he was talking. He scowled at Stanley Milnow, who hadn't lost the deal all period. "What's the difference? Give the little bastards a boot in the ass instead of a pat on the back and watch how quick they straighten out. Like Loomis. The first thing I'd do if they put me in charge is give the freak a haircut. And *then* I'd give him a boot in the ass. Right, Buddy?"

Buddy Ritchie nodded. "I don't allow long hair on the wrestling team. And I make them wear jackets and ties whenever we have a wrestling match…whenever we aren't on austerity."

"You're a trendsetter, Buddy. But this guy is a medical doctor. An osteopath."

"What the hell kind of doctor is that?" Stanley Milnow asked.

"A bone doctor," Buddy said.

"How the hell do you know?"

"I had to take science classes, anatomy, pre-med health classes. You think Phys Ed is just playing dodgeball?"

"This doctor worked with the criminally insane and mental patients with a history of violent behavior."

"So," he asked again, "are you going to tell us? What was his solution?" Red was so predictable.

"He discovered that when he applied electroshock to an area of the brain he was able to neutralize certain muscles on his patients and all traces of violent behavior disappeared. You should know all about that stuff, Buddy, with your vast Phys Ed knowledge."

"Yeah, sure." He flexed his biceps and pectorals to show everybody.

"How'd he do it?" Stanley Milnow asked.

"A simple procedure, and cheap."

"Bullshit!" Red Farley said. "They can't do that. It's against the Bill of Rights."

"These are criminals, Red. They have no rights. Nobody cares about them. But that isn't all. Instead of neutralizing just *some* of the muscles, they neutralized all of them for the hard-core cases. Totally immobilized them. And then they didn't even need prison guards. It saved millions."

Farley thought about it. "Scapelli, you are so full of shit."

"You think so? Well, then you're never going to believe the next step. It's even better. After the subjects were incapacitated the staff decided to actually remove their bones!"

"Get the hell out of here!" Stanley Milnow said. "The bodies wouldn't have any support without bones. They couldn't stand up, or sit even."

"That's the whole idea."

"More bullshit!"

"The problem then becomes finding a suitable place to put the de-boned bodies."

"Tubs!" Stanley Milnow said.

"Exactly. Of course today they are only doing this to hardened criminals, but tomorrow the technology could be applied to kids like Virgil Loomis! Imagine that, Red. The ideal class! You wouldn't even have to bore them to death to keep them quiet! A class filled with tubs of de-boned kids. Like teaching Jello or a plastic bag full of chicken livers."

"You're an asshole, Scapelli."

Scapelli kissed Red Farley on the top of his sweaty head while everybody at the table watched. He picked up his cup and ran out of the faculty room toward the bathroom.

"I love that man," Chuck LaFemina said.

"Scapelli, you bastard!" Red yelled after him.

"He wasn't serious?" Buddy Ritchie asked. "They really can't do that, can they? And it would be illegal, right?"

Red wiped the top of his head with a napkin. He turned to Stanley Milnow. "For chrisakes, Stanley, would you stop playing with your teeth and go see a goddamn dentist."

"We don't have dental insurance."

* * *

At the end of eighth period Jesse stopped into the Main Office to check his mailbox before he punched out. Most of the other teachers were already gone and the door to Mr. Baltz's office was closed. Phyllis Lind was busy at her desk doing isometrics. Her eyes were closed. She was rolling her neck in circles and arching her back upright. Jesse felt a little like a Peeping Tom, but watched her anyway. And when he turned he was surprised to see Virgil Loomis sitting in the detention chair watching him watching Phyllis Lind. His face reddened.

"I, er... um, hello, Virgil. I thought everyone was gone." Jesse stammered.

"Isn't she something, Mr. Teeg?" He was holding a brown paper bag under his arm.

"Who? I hadn't noticed. I just didn't want to miss anything important." He walked over to his mailbox and pulled out some papers.

"She hasn't gotten to the best part yet–kegels. She told me she does a hundred a day to tone up."

"Why are you still here, Virgil?" he said to change the subject. "Isn't the building supposed to be empty?"

"Mr. G gave me detention. He got me on a three-twenty-seven, putting contraband toilet paper in the student bathrooms." He showed him the contents of the bag. "He's in there now with Mr. Baltz." He pointed to the closed door. "A big strategy meeting. He told me to wait here until gets out and decides what to do with me."

"Oh," Jesse said. "You wouldn't have an extra roll to spare?"

Virgil reached in and tossed Jesse a roll. "No frills is better than nothing at all."

"Thanks." Jesse put it into his mailbox with the rest of the papers he hadn't read.

"Ever noticed, Mr. Teeg, that Mr. G has issues with people taller than he is?" Virgil asked.

"No, I haven't."

"Did you ever see *The Caine Mutiny*? Humphrey Bogart is Captain Queeg. He's short and has an incredible inferiority complex. Mr. G even acts like Bogart with that thing he does with his neck and his teeth." Jesse looked at him. "Queeg is obsessive compulsive and focuses on little details like Mr. G. I've noticed that he spends a lot of his time in the bathrooms," Virgil said casually. "Not in a pervey way. But I think he was probably a bed wetter. Bed-wetters are often fixated on toilets later in life. Did you know Napoleon was a bed wetter? And he was short too."

Jesse shook his head. "Where do you come up with this stuff, Virgil?"

"Both my parents are psychiatrists and we talk." He pulled some papers from his pocket. "I've been taking notes. In the last two weeks I've done a study on the way Mr. G fills up the day." He looked at his index card. "Since the first day of school he's only spent two hours at most in his office. An hour for lunch every day. And four full hours every day in and out of the bathrooms. Four hours, that's two thirds of his day. Think of it, Mr. Teeg, two-thirds of his salary is earned in the toilet."

"How do you have time for all this?"

"Time management." He turned the card over. "On the other hand, Mr. Lewis spends most of his time eating. Mr. Zwill sneaks around. Did you know he was in a Japanese prisoner of war camp? And I haven't been able to find much about Helen O'Dell. She's a mystery. I can't be positive, but I don't think she has fingerprints!" He shrugged. "You ever been in therapy, Mr. Teeg?"

"Of course not. Why, have you?"

"All of my life. If my parents charged me just for the dinnertime conversation it would be a fortune," he said. "You've come up at the dinner table a couple of times."

"Me?" Jesse got defensive.

"I told them your kindergarten story and the consensus is separation anxiety and school phobia. Though it might be serious, it's not necessarily debilitating. I mean, you became a teacher."

"Well, that's a relief," Jesse said sarcastically.

"Of course my parents suggested you might be a masochist. And my mother thought the part about breaking the drum skin with the fat end of the stick was a disguised Freudian account about losing your virginity. You have lost your virginity?"

"Well, uh..."

"She asked me to tell you to give her a call if you're ready to confront your demons. She'll work with you and give you a special rate."

The door to Mr. Baltz's office opened and Mr. Giovanni walked through the office toward them. He saw Jesse standing with Virgil and did a Bogart.

"See what I mean, Mr. Teeg," Virgil whispered. "Hey Mr. G, I was just talking about you."

Mr. Giovanni motioned with his head for Virgil to follow him and he disappeared through the archway and down the two steps to the Administrative Alcove, where the assistant principals had their offices.

Virgil looked at Jesse and shrugged.

"Get in here, Loomis!" Giovanni's voice boomed through the alcove.

Phyllis Lind opened her eyes and smiled. "Kegels," she announced.

"I thought so," Virgil said.

"Loomis!"

He tucked his paper bag under his arm. "Coming, Mr. G." He walked through the archway. "Hang in there, Mr. Teeg. And give my mother a call." He grinned and waved.

In the News
October 1971

October 3

Pres. Nguyen Van Thieu of South Vietnam is reelected. He is the only candidate on the ballot.

October 6

The LA *Times* reports federal agents caught thirty-six illegal immigrants in a raid on a food processing plant owned by Romana Banuelos, named U.S. Treasurer by Pres. Nixon three weeks earlier. Nixon says on tape, "I want Otis Chandler's income tax." Chandler is the publisher of the LA *Times*.

October 7

Nixon announces Phase II of his economic plan that calls for wage and price controls.

October 16

H. Rap Brown "Minister of Justice" of the Black Panthers is captured following a shootout with police in NYC. He is charged with inciting a riot and carrying a gun across state lines.

October 21

Nixon nominates William H. Rehnquist to the U.S. Supreme Court.

Willy Zwill was a cautious man. He didn't like to stand out and call attention to himself. It was a lesson he learned quickly as a prisoner of war where being outstanding, tall, red-haired, different, could get you beaten by the Jap guards, or worse, cause you to lose your fair-haired head. So he learned to slouch, walk with his head down, stay in the shadows and blend into the background. It was something he carried with him twenty years later when he became an assistant principal. Returning now from his rounds he walked close to the walls to make himself inconspicuous. Before he moved he studied both ends of the corridor to be sure that no one was coming. He twitched involuntarily like a mouse about to come out of hiding into the open, made a quick dash to the opposite wall and slid into the recess of the door well. The corridor was still empty so he moved in increments until he was safely inside the Administrative Alcove. Still he stayed low. He nosed down at his office door and peered into the keyhole to be sure it was empty. Everything was dark inside. Then he remembered that his raincoat was hanging on the other end of the knob. He eased the door open a crack and slipped into the room, locking it behind him. Carefully he checked under the desk and looked into the closet. Only then did he switch on the light and sit in the creaking wooden desk chair. The sound still made him edgy whenever he moved.

Within seconds the telephone on his desk rang and that set off a paroxysm of uncontrolled motion. The phone rang four or five times before he managed to pick it up.

"Zwill," he said hoarsely into the black mouthpiece and listened for a response. The phone clicked. He twitched and replaced the receiver. Immediately it rang again and he grabbed it in the middle of the first ring.

"Who is this and what do you want from me? Leave me alone!" he shouted.

There was a brief silence and then, "Willy?" It was Helen O'Dell. "For a minute there I thought I dialed Harry

Dexter's number by mistake. He's always telling people to leave him alone. More day terrors?" Her voice softened. "Well, just hang in there. It's the weekend and we have Columbus Day coming up to look forward to."

"I know I've told you this before, Helen, but I have this strong feeling I am being watched. And I keep getting hang-ups on my phone."

"Mario was trying to reach you. Could've been him. He told me to tell you there's a special meeting in Baltz's office in fifteen minutes. On a Friday! It better be worth being late for Happy Hour at the Alibi." She was annoyed. "You're going, right?"

"Have you noticed anything strange going on around here?"

"Here? Always. You mean stranger than usual."

He pulled the receiver close to his mouth. "Someone is following me, O'Dell," he whispered into the phone.

"Are you having hallucinations again, Willy? Is your malaria acting up? Have you stopped taking your medication again?"

"This time I'm sure, Helen. I *know* I'm being followed–"

"Like you knew your neighbor across the street was a Russian spy. Have you actually *seen* anybody, Willy?"

He hesitated, "I... no... That's how good he is. But I can *feel* him, O'Dell. I hear voices and there's no one there. I hear footsteps and when I turn around the halls are empty."

"You're not sick, Willy. You're just in love." Her joke was lost on him.

"I'm positive it's the same person who attacked me from behind in the hall. And now he started calling my office to see if I'm here. He just called before you did and he hung up. I get hang-ups all the time, so I stopped answering."

"Um-hum," she said. She was eating something.

"It may even be more than one person."

"Mummmh?"

"I've had experience with this kind of stuff, Helen. My instinct tells me there's trouble lurking. And I learned to trust that prickle in the back of my neck."

"Maybe it's just your laundry detergent, Willy. Don't forget the meeting. Fifteen minutes. And don't ask any questions when Baltz asks if there are any questions. I want to get out of there while I'm still relatively young. It's Friday. And I don't want to miss Happy Hour."

"Helen?" He stopped her before she hung up. "Trust me and my instincts. I survived the Japs. So you just be extra careful until we know who they are and what they're up to. "

"Right, Willy. War is hell." she said. "Remember, no questions."

"Tell them I might be a little late for the meeting. I'll be taking the long way around the building."

* * *

From the stuffed chair Mario Giovanni was watching the principal line up a putt with the shrunken head ashtray set on the opposite edge of the rug across the office. He never liked golf. It was a game played by snobs, people who wore funny clothes and ugly shoes.

"Fuck," Baltz said when he missed the putt and the ball rolled under the table. He banged the putter on the rug. The smoke from his cigarette hanging from his lip curled into his eyes so he had to squint. He stroked through another putt and the ball veered to the right. "Shit!" He slammed the club down and the shaft bent.

"I never could understand the point of knocking a little ball into a hole. Hitting it as far as you can, that's a different ball game. And I can understand hitting a ball *at* somebody, but golf is stupid if you ask me."

"I didn't, Mario. It's for relaxation. That bastard Nessmith told me I had to relax if I didn't want to have a stroke. 'The game will help you to relax,' he said. Do I look relaxed? The only strokes he cares about are his and how much money I owe him whenever we play. Balls, Mario!"

He got out of the chair to retrieve the balls that had rolled under the table and set the balls in line on the fringe of the carpet. When Ollie Nessmith, the district doctor and Mr. Baltz's personal physician, ordered him to take up golf, the assistant principal had no choice but to go along and caddy.

"Since last spring I've lost enough money to him to pay for a fucking heart transplant. That bastard!" He thought about lining up another putt, wiggled his mustache and the live ash from his cigarette dropped down the front of his shirt. "Shit!" He patted it out, but not before it burned a small hole. "We've had enough of a workout for today, Mario."

The AP took the bent putter and balls and put them in the closet. Then he set the ashtray back on the desk.

The telephone rang and Mr. Baltz picked it up. "I told you I wasn't to be disturbed, Miss Lind–"

"*Ms* Lind. And it's your lovely wife. I told her you were in conference and you weren't accepting calls, but she insisted."

"All right, Phyllis. Put her on."

When he heard the click over the earpiece he didn't have a chance to say a word before she started, "Mort"– she insisted on calling him that no matter how many times he had told her he hated the name–"I think it's time for you to have another little talk with that secretary of yours. What does she mean, 'Sorry, he's in conference'? And her voice doesn't sound like a school. It sounds like a brothel. Talk to her. Or get rid of her."

"Yes, dear. I'll tell her to try and sound more like you. Miss Lind–"

"Ms," Mr. Giovanni corrected.

He glared down at Mr. Giovanni. "–is a Civil Service employee who took and passed tests for her position. And she's a member of CSEA."

"I don't care if she belongs to the Teamsters! But I don't have time now to argue. I have a nail salon appointment. Mother's coming for a few weeks. She called this morning. She arrives at JFK this afternoon."

Mr. Baltz turned away. "But, Edie–"

"There *is* no discussion, Mort. She's coming and that's all there is to it. These are tragic times for her. And we have to understand."

He twitched his mustache. "But it was just a goddamn dog and a poodle at that–"

"Mr. Miniver was more than just a poodle. He was Mother's companion. How can you be so callous?"

He exhaled a stream of smoke.

"Are you smoking?"

He stubbed out the cigarette in the ashtray. "No, dear. I was just breathing. Can't I breathe?"

"After I have my nails done, I have a fund-raising committee meeting at the club. Write it down. Her flight lands at four. Pan Am." She gave the details. "Don't be late. You know how she panics when no one is there."

"But I have a meeting–"

She barreled on. "I won't have time to cook much, so stop at Sonny Fong's Take Out Kitchen and pick up some Chinese for the four of us. I'm inviting Mr. Franks for dinner."

"But, Edie–" he whined.

"Be gentle with her and don't mention Mr. Miniver. That will make her more upset." The phone clicked.

"Women," Mario Giovanni said. "You can't live with 'em, and you can't bury 'em in your basement. Right, Boss?"

"Fuck you, Mario." He lit another Lucky.

* * *

Helen O'Dell stepped into the alcove. Willy's door was closed. She looked at her watch. Even if the meeting was short she would miss the best part of Happy Hour. The food went as soon as it was put out. Especially the wings... and the ribs. She started toward the Main Office but she wheeled around when she heard footsteps behind her.

"Hey, Ms O'Dell. Going to the meeting?" Virgil Loomis was holding a bunch of index cards. "I don't think Mr. Lewis is going. I saw him leaving the building about fifteen minutes ago."

"Why are you here, Loomis? The building's supposed to be empty at dismissal. Did Mr. Giovanni assign you detention again?"

"No," he shrugged. "I had an appointment with Mr. Aaron in Guidance that went late. Mr. Farley said he's suffered enough and objects to me being in his class again this year."

"Just go home. It's Friday, we're on austerity and I have better things to do than talk to you." She walked up the two steps through the archway into the Main Office and when she turned around Virgil was behind her. "Go! Now, Loomis!" She waited for him to leave and went into the principal's office. "Willy said he'll be late," she said slipping into an empty seat. "He thinks he's being followed by the person who attacked him in the hall last month. He's off his meds again and said something about a conspiracy. And Virgil Loomis just told me that Noah Lewis went home. I hope this isn't going to take long." she asked and looked at her wristwatch.

Mr. Baltz smoothed his mustache considering the possibility. "Conspiracy?" He lit a cigarette.

There was a quick knock, the door opened and Willy Zwill slid through. He twitched. "Sorry. I walked all around the building to get here from the opposite direction and then I backtracked to see if I was being followed."

"And?"

"I didn't see anybody, but I felt that I was being watched."

"Go back on your medication, Willy." He lit another cigarette and saw that the first one was burning in the ashtray. "Your report, Helen?"

"I stepped up surveillance on the classrooms and teacher desks, like you said, but there's nothing specific to report at this time." She looked at her watch again.

"Mario will bring you up to date on Operation Flush."

He stood up and removed the sheet covering the chalkboard. "Besides the attack on the first day of class here"– he pointed to the chalked building map–"there have been several occurrences of graffiti here." He indicated the Third Floor Faculty Men's Room. "Until recently they have been limited to the men's toilet, so all the evidence so far points to a male member of the staff, though there are a few females I have my eye on. He employs the same *modus operandi* in perpetrating his offenses, namely a red felt marker pen of this variety." He removed a marker from his inside pocket. "For that reason and for some things written on sign-in sheets and other documents, we have decided to call this individual–"

"Or individuals," Willy Zwill corrected.

"–or *individuals,*" Mr. Giovanni said, "the Red Felt Phantom."

They nodded in assent.

"The plan is to separate the Phantom from the red felt marker."

"But what if he switches to another color marker, Mario? Or a pencil?" Helen O'Dell asked, despite wanting to be out of there.

"Then we'll change his name."

"A list," Willy Zwill said quietly, and twitched. "We need to make a master list. That's what we did in the camp when the Japs knew we had a radio. and we knew there was an informant tipping off the Japs. We made a list of everyone we suspected and one by one eliminated names until we were left with one. Later we found out that the informant was a spy planted by the Japs and whenever he tied a knot in the lamp cord it was a signal he had information to pass. Needless to say we dealt with him severely–"

"That wasn't the Japs, Willy. It was the Germans. And it wasn't in your POW camp. It was in the movie *Stalag 17*."

Willy Zwill twitched. "Maybe. But a list would still be a good idea. First we find out who owns a red felt marker pen. Then anyone who has access to one. And then look for anyone with an opportunity, a motive or a grievance."

"The motive grievance thing isn't a bad idea," Mr. Baltz said. "In the next few days I want each of you to come up with individual lists. Everyone you've had trouble with last year, whoever got a bad observation or a formal reprimand or written up–"

"With a red felt marker, don't forget."

He nodded to the twitching Zwill. "And once you accumulate this data and we match it with a list of those who have red felt markers, I'll have Phyllis type up a master list. Then you will narrow it down until we find the individual–"

"Or individuals," Mr. Zwill said and twitched.

He sighed. "–and when we find out who it is I plan to charge him and fire him. I don't care how much a 30-20A tenure hearing costs the district to get rid of the bastard." He stood up. "Use every resource at your disposal and get on it immediately." He walked to the door and opened it. "Now I have to get to the airport."

Willy Zwill saluted. Helen O'Dell looked at her watch. And the three APs left.

"Gorilla theater? You mean like the Nairobi Trio on the old *Ernie Kovacs Show*? I loved that show."

"How do you know about the Nairobi Trio or Ernie Kovacs, Virgil? He died in 1962. That was ancient history." Terry Scapelli was sitting cross-legged on the desk of his Theater Arts class, an elective filled with drama kids and students like Virgil who needed another English half credit to graduate.

"I remember some things about the sixties, Mr. S. Black and white TV. The Beatles," Virgil said and waved his arms in the air. "And Woodstock. I was there with my parents, but I only vaguely remember it."

The class laughed.

"You remember Ernie Kovacs, but you don't remember Woodstock from two years ago?" He shook his head. "The word is *guerrilla*," he went on, "from the Spanish *guerra* which means *war* and not *go-rilla* as in big monkey! It's not a bunch of people dressed up in monkey costumes like Ernie Kovacs's Nairobi Trio and it isn't an event you buy a ticket to watch. It's improvisational street theater where the audience becomes part of the performance."

"Like 'Smile, you're on *Candid Camera*'?" somebody called out.

"But 'realer,'" he said with air quotes. "The term way back in the sixties was probably a 'Happening' or a 'Be In.' The TV show *Laugh-In* comes close.

"Virgil, you probably don't remember the 1968 Democrat Convention in Chicago either. It was Woodstock for the older generation, but with the Chicago police instead of rain. Abbie Hoffman, Jerry Rubin. Poet Allen Ginsberg. The Youth International Party, better known as YIPPIES. They brought guerrilla street theater to national TV." He stopped. "It gets me all excited just thinking about it, all that energy set loose."

"Tell us about it, Mr. S."

"I know you're trying to distract me," he said. "I'm too smart for that trick, but it will be helpful with your assignment." And he was off. "Before the Democratic convention began, the YIPPIES said they were going to put LSD in Chicago's water supply. And then they announced they planned to kill a pig on the streets to protest the war. Neither of which they did. But the pig thing was to prove a point. People were more upset at them killing a pig than they were about seeing the flag-draped coffins of human beings killed in Vietnam every night on the news. Abbie Hoffman touched a nerve. Chicago's Mayor Daley went crazy and ordered the police to crack down on the kids in the streets and there was a riot and violence the whole world watched live on TV while the Democrats inside the convention hall were nominating Hubert Humphrey, who would lose to Richard Nixon. Take a look at the black-and-white film footage. The Chicago Seven, Abbie Hoffman, Jerry Rubin and five other Yippies were tried for conspiracy and inciting a riot. In March 1970, Hoffman announced that he was going to defy the law against flag desecration and wear a shirt made from an American flag on the *Merv Griffin Show*. He created chaos and when he appeared the network blacked out his half of the screen so viewers wouldn't be offended or see the shirt, which, by the way, wasn't even made from a cut-up flag like he said it would be. That's Guerrilla Theater."

The classroom door swung open and Willy Zwill looked in. "Red felt marker pen, Mr. Scapelli?"

"Green tambourine and a yellow submarine, Mr. Zwill," he answered without hesitation.

Mr. Zwill nodded his head and closed the door, trying to decipher the code.

"A man walks into a room, says something, does something and it begins. As more people become involved the event takes on a life of its own. The participants aren't even aware they are part of a performance. The catalyst who started it all has no idea where it will go, because the event is happening live. It's spontaneous, improvised, although some parts of it may be planned. It's a very dangerous concept, subversive. And the results can be amazing, thrilling... or not. So–" He paused and waited for the buzz to quiet down. "That takes us to your assignment. Over the next few days I want you to consider some ideas for your own improvisational guerrilla theater. Then comes the hard part, staging it." The bell ending the period rang and they groaned. "We'll talk more tomorrow." Virgil hung back. "Ernie Kovacs, Virgil... I am impressed. What do you think about the assignment?"

"My head is exploding with ideas, Mr. S." He waved his hands vaguely.

Terry nodded. "I wouldn't expect anything less from you. Were you really at Woodstock, Virgil?"

"I was."

"I don't remember seeing you there. Come to think of it, I don't remember much about 1969."

Camelot

Official Publication of the Partnership of Parents and Teachers
in Association for better Farmington Public Schools
Harriet Stegle, President P-PTA

Vol. 1   Issue 1   September/October 1971

Sorry this first issue of *Camelot* is late, but two weeks in the hospital and one kidney less will do that! It sure was so good to see all your smiling faces on Orientation Day and it sure feels good to be "Back in the saddle!" even if it is with one kidney!

NEW EDITIONS: The elementary school libraries were not able to get all the titles they ordered last June as a result of austerity. But all is not lost. Some parents are making hand copies of selected books for use in the classroom. That's the spirit!

NEW ADDITIONS: Welcome aboard to the newcomers who have joined our Farmington Family. At West Street Elementary–Clint Garbus and Beverly Burke, daughter of itinerant reading teacher Larry Burke; at the Junior High – Helen Merry; and at the High School–Mike Hunt, Layla Bimenyenz and Jerry Tejent.

CONGRATULATIONS: Olivia Kunzintookis, West Street Elementary - it's a girl three times! Triplets delivered by C-section. And over the summer it was wedding bells for Phaedra Schwartz from the High School's Business Department. Now officially hyphenated, Fay Schwartz-Fine, she honeymooned in Europe with her new hubby Paul.

OLD FACES: Back from leave - Irene Pookey, Apple Hill Elementary; Don Norlick and Grace Sparks, Junior High.

CONDOLENCES: Sorry to hear George Fortis, High School, won't be back. George went out on a health leave last April, but without much success. Services were held in July.

NEWS AND VIEWS: Budget vote fails again... Contract negotiations break down... October is candy sale month!

See you next month with more news from the trenches!

FT Ass.
"Moderation + Mediation = Settlement"

FROM: Joel Maxwell, President FT Ass.
TO: ALL Farmington Teachers
Re: An Open Invitation

October is membership month. The Farmington Teachers' Ass. is opening wide in friendship and brotherhood. Join with your colleagues and let us be your voice of reason. Study our record. Read our posters. Compare our benefits and you'll "run to become a part of the FT Ass."—the only bargaining agent you will ever need. Professionals serving professionals.

See your building representative for details, and watch you mailboxes for special offers.

FU - 2
Farmington Union, Local # 2
"All we need is a few good men..."

Don't be fooled by the claims of a scab company organization that would have you believe they are a union. There is only one union in Farmington and that's us! FU-2! Not afraid to call a spade a spade, to take a stand, to draw a line in the sand! Let us stand together and fight everyone for your right to a contract! Don't be a professional SCAB! Join US not THEM! In unity there is strength! FU-2 all the way!

Dwayne Purvey, FU-2 President

The red telephone on Harry Dexter's desk rang, the direct line from Baltz's office. He squelched the impulse to pick it up and continued turning pages of the *National Geographic* where beautiful dark-skinned topless Polynesian woman beckoned him to retire to "Tahiti: Retirement Haven, Heaven on Earth." He let the phone ring three times before he picked it up. "I'm a very busy man," he voiced mechanically into the receiver.

"Cut the bullshit, Dexter. I know just how busy you are. I want you to check something out for me, so drop whatever it is you're reading and don't play your bullshit teacher games with me."

He dropped the magazine. "The squad is conducting a full inventory. Tuning up the equipment, changing all the projector bulbs, phonograph needles–"

"It's October, Harry, and another anniversary is coming up. Poor Don Cooley was such a mess they had a closed coffin at his wake."

There was a pause. "What can I do for you?"

"Red felt marker pens."

"AV 15-503R-73s?"

"Cut the crap. Red felt fucking markers!"

"That's the official designation for the red ones. The greens are 503Gs and the black ones 503Bs. If you want I can send you some of each. I got three cases."

"Keep your markers. I just want to know about the red ones and I want a complete list of all male teachers and staff who got a red felt marker pen through your office. How many people in the building have them?"

"Everybody. AV 15-503R-73s are SDI number 12."

"'SDI number 12'? Stop fucking with me."

"Standard Dexter Issue. Every teacher in the building got one on the first day of school in the AV/CM Survival Kit envelopes. We billed the district five bucks apiece for the kits. You approved it."

There was silence on the other end.

"A red felt marker pen was only one of the things included. There was a plug and socket, an AV/CM Official Handbook, a map of the building with–"

The receiver clicked.

He replaced the phone in the cradle and looked back at the humorous poster of Thomas Edison who more resembled Albert Einstein with his hair straight out and his finger in an electric socket. It was a gift from last year's graduating squad members. It brought back memories of Don Cooley's face. He shivered. "Hans! Miss Wellen gets a 16 mm projector in Room 312," he snapped, coming out of the trance. "Pick up the one in Woodshop and move it to her room now. Don't let Hubby tell you he needs it. Just take it even if he cries. It's just an act. He cries all the time. If he has a problem tell him to call me!." The boy clicked his heels, turned and double-timed out of the office. "Axle!" He removed a sealed envelope from his desk drawer. "Deliver this film to the Custodian's private cafeteria. And make sure it's still sealed when it arrives." The boy saluted. "The rest of you get on the projector bulbs and the phonograph needles. We have work to do."

He took his *National Geographic* and disappeared through the beaded curtain and into the Recreation Area in the back.

Jesse lived for the weekends, though Sundays were always hard for him. Even the veterans referred to the "Sunday blues." Coming back had been especially tough after the three-day Columbus Day weekend, but he had made it through another school day, through the first month and a half and with the exception of some car problems, with no major calamities. School wasn't actually fun, but things were settling down into a routine. His life wasn't easier, but at least it wasn't more difficult. He still had trouble sleeping nights, but he only threw up on Sunday evenings. Even Sue Wellen noticed and announced in the faculty room, "You aren't crying as much!"

He hurried out of the building and cut across the cinder track behind the school, the shortest distance between the time clock in the Main Office and Nelson's Auto Repair. In the morning Nelson said he'd have the rebuilt starter installed in time for his afternoon commute home. His attaché case was heavy, filled with quiz papers and ungraded essays, and he walked with a definite list to the side, which he corrected every so often by changing hands. At least the rain had stopped and the ride home shouldn't be so bad, if Nelson hadn't been overoptimistic and the car was ready.

As he approached the football field he saw a solitary figure in sneakers and athletic pants working out on the wet grass. The USMA sweatshirt was only partially covered by the Rosencrantz and Guildenstern Memorial High School team jacket and the chrome whistle bounced up and down on the end of a plastic lanyard with each jumping jack.

"Coach Boid?" he said when he recognized the Acting Director of Phys Ed.

Coach Boid dropped into a squat thrust position and counted off five quick ones before he stood up. His face was wet with sweat and rain in the afternoon chill. "Can I help you, son?"

"Jesse Tietjen." He extended his hand.

Coach Boid shook it. "Not much of a grip there, Jerry. You don't look like football's your sport. Maybe wrestling? Why don't you go see Coach Ritchie when the budget passes and he schedules tryouts?" He blew his whistle and Jesse flinched. "Let's go ladies!" he called over Jesse's shoulder to the empty field. "Pick 'em up! Lay 'em down! One, two! One, two! You caught me at a pretty bad time, Jerry. Afternoon workout," he said and looked him over. "You ever consider running track? Hurdles maybe? You have the body of a hurdler."

"No," Jesse said. "I'm not a student, Coach. I teach here. I was just on my way to get my car when I recognized you from your first day speech and thought I would say hello."

"Too bad. We could use a good hurdler when we get back on track. Come on, ladies," he called. "This ain't no social tea! Jumping jacks!" Coach Boid jumped and flailed his arms and legs. Jesse watched until he finished the set. "Yeah, Jerry, coaching ain't the fun it used to be. Especially in an austerity year. There's a lot of sweat and hard work. Come on, Slowotski! Move your keester!" He blew his whistle. "Everybody take a lap!" He circled his hand over his head. "What do you teach, Jerry?"

"It's Jesse, actually. And I teach English, Coach."

"Well, Jeffrey, think of coaching like reading a book," he said. "You gotta keep at it if you wanna finish. Come on, Slowotski! Stop dogging it! You can move faster than that!"

"Excuse me, Coach, but you do know," he hesitated, "there isn't anybody out there?" Jesse pointed to the field.

He looked at Jesse. "Certainly I know it. Do you think I'm crazy? Austerity, Jeff. There's no team sports program without a budget. And no sports means no practice. But that doesn't mean *I* can't practice. This is a *practice* practice. Just keeping my edge until *regular* practice resumes."

"Oh," Jesse said, pretending to understand.

"A good coach is a good coach with or without a team. I had a great team in sixty-six. Coulda been County champs. Lost in the playoffs by one point. Had three All-County players on the squad. Lost by one point." He shook his head.

"That's too bad."

"The kid fumbled the ball five yards from the goal line, the other team recovered and ran out the clock. One miserable point." He shook his head again. "Michael Slowotski. Five yards from the championship. I'll never forget him and I'll never *forgive* him." He dropped into a sit-up position. "But there's no sense crying over fumbled milk. Gotta think positive, right?"

"I guess so."

"I mean, what's that crap they say? It's not whether you win or lose, it's how you play the game. Right?"

"Right, Coach."

"Bullshit! Do you really believe that bullshit, Jeff? Show me a good loser and I'll show you a *loser*. You know what they call the guy who comes in second? First loser." He stepped toward Jesse and looked him in the eye. "You know who the real spark plug of any team is?"

Jesse hesitated. He didn't want to say the wrong thing. "The coach?"

"Damn right the coach! Kids come and go, but the coach stays year after year. Come on, you candy asses!" he called out. "Hendricks, give Slowotski more practice catching passes and holding on to the ball! Let's go, Slowotski! See if you can hang on to a football the way you hang on to your own balls!" He turned to Jesse and winked. "A good coach has to keep just as fit as his team. Keep his edge. Keep his old spark plug clean!" He did some knee bends and body twists. "You said English, right? You ever take a philosophy course in school?" Jesse nodded. "You ever read the one about a Greek who was walking around looking for truth, for the ideal, with a candle in his hands and marbles in his mouth or some crap like that?"

"I think you're mixing up Diogenes, who carried a lantern on his search for an honest man, and Plato, who was looking for the truth. Do you mean Plato's *Republic*?"

"I don't know what political party he belonged to, but what he said about perfection is true. It exists in the mind and not in reality. So if the *perfect* team doesn't exist in reality, than a team that *doesn't actually exist* must be perfect. You follow me there, Jeffrey?"

"Jesse," he corrected. "I'm not really sure–"

"Put another way, a *real* team can be a real hardship, a real handicap to the best coach. An ideal team that exists in the mind can't drop the ball five yards away from the championship. No losses. A perfect season. And any coach will tell you that's what it's all about."

Jesse nodded at the simple logic, but he just wanted to get his car and go home.

"You keep pitching, Jerry. And maybe some day you'll fill out. Baseball tryouts are in March and we should be off austerity by then." He blew his whistle twice. "Take another lap, ladies, and then hit the showers! Not so fast, Slowotski! You still have some catching practice." He started to jog. "By one point!" he said. "Move it! Pick 'em up! Let's go! Gotta run," he said to Jesse and he jogged off.

Jesse watched him disappear around the corner of the school. He really hoped Nelson had his car ready.

156

Three days of rain and wind knocked the rest of the leaves off the trees, and although summer had been over for a long while it was finally fall for real. The weekend had been a washout and Jesse felt cheated. He spent most of his time grading papers and when his alarm clock went off at six on Monday morning it was hard for him to get out of bed.

The bathroom door was shut and locked. The old man was getting worse, spending less time with the family in Brooklyn and more time in the trenches of France. He had started wearing his medals and he replaced his VFW cap with his old helmet he found in the basement. Armed with the old sword he carried back from Paris in 1918 buckled over his bathrobe, he was a danger to the house furnishings until Jesse's mother put an end to it. "No more broken lamps," she said and she hid it in the basement shanty.

Jesse heard the old man sloshing around in the sink or maybe the tub. "Come on, Pop," he called through the door. "Open up. I'll be late for work." He knocked again harder and when there was no response he tried a new approach. "Sergeant York? Open up, Sergeant! It's Private Tietjen reporting as ordered for the predawn patrol."

The water stopped running and the toilet flushed. The bathroom door opened and Jesse's grandfather was standing in his morning uniform–medals displayed on his pajama top and open bathrobe. "Patrol?" he asked. "I wasn't informed about a patrol."

Jesse pulled the bottom of the old man's bathrobe closed. "A special predawn patrol ordered by General Pershing himself."

The old man bowed his head. "God bless old Black Jack and the breasts that nursed him."

"I'll need to get into the Briefing Room before I set out."

"Of course. Carry on, Private. The briefing room is yours." He stepped aside and they exchanged salutes.

When Jesse was finished dressing he picked up his attaché case from the place on the dining room table where he wouldn't forget it. His grandfather was waiting at the door. "It's hell out there, son. We've already lost too many good men. You can't go alone. I'm going with you, Private. Where's my trench coat?"

Jesse shook his hand. "My direct orders from General Pershing are to go alone, Sergeant. He specifically said you are much too valuable to risk on such a dangerous mission." He held up his case. "I have to deliver these secret papers and I have to leave before dawn, Sergeant."

The old man stood aside and saluted. "Keep low and away from the wire." Jesse saluted back and left.

Forty minutes later he was moving with the traffic along the Southern State Parkway when the old Mercury lurched and made a noise that he didn't recognize. In the three years he'd owned the twenty-year-old antique he had learned to listen for new and different sounds and not to panic over every minor crisis. When he didn't hear the noise again he went back to tuning the radio. But two miles later it happened again, only louder and longer. Instantly he went to Standard Procedure One and turned up the volume so he couldn't hear the noise. Procedure Two involved singing over the sound of the radio. There was no Standard Procedure Three. The car began to vibrate and shake violently.

"Damn!" He used his hand to signal he was slowing and pulled onto the grass on the right. He looked under the hood and didn't find anything obvious. He kicked the tires and bent to check under the car. "Damn!" he said when he saw the drive shaft hanging at an oblique angle. He checked his watch. By the time he found a telephone and got a tow truck, class would be started. The prospect of being late for school was more upsetting than the car.

"Shitbastardhelldamnit!"

* * *

The bell for Homeroom rang. Students slammed lockers shut and ran through the halls to get to class. Others were in no hurry. It was only Homeroom.

Inside the quiet AV/CM Center the wall was draped with black crepe paper and the entire ten-member AV/CM Squad stood at attention. At a nod from Harry Dexter, three of them stepped forward with the wreath of plastic flowers, handed it to the coordinator and stepped back in line. At another nod the captain pressed PLAY on the tape recorder up on a mobile cart. Harry Dexter placed the wreath on the nail holding coupled male and female three-prong plugs attached to a length of visibly frayed electrical wire. Above that a framed yearbook photo of Don Cooley in happier days smiled down at them.

The mournful sound of "Taps" filled the office as the squad, lost in thought, stood silently and watched their leader with his head bowed, contemplating his own mortality.

It was another mid-October Don Cooley Memorial Ceremony.

* * *

Jesse reached a telephone well after eight o'clock. "Shit!" he said when he realized his attaché case with the school telephone number was a mile back in the car. Information gave him a nonworking number at Central. He tried it three more times to be sure. He was out of options when he remembered his Aunt Dimmy, who lived just a few miles from the school. Though her real name was Dimitra everyone in the family called her Dimmy, partly for short and partly because Aunt Dimmy wasn't known for her intellect. Growing up he had heard his mother's stories about her baby sister. He especially liked the one she told about Dimitra's first day in grammar school, a classic always recalled at family gatherings and holidays, mostly when Aunt Dimmy wasn't within hearing. He had heard it so many times he could recite it with his mother by heart. "How was your first day, Dimitra?" her mother, Jesse's grandmother asked. "Did you learn anything?" "The teacher likes me, Mommy," she reported. "Yes? How do you know?" "She said I'm a little bit smart and a little bit stupid." And that was when she became Dimmy.

He put the only change he had, a quarter, into the slot and dialed the number from memory and hoped that his memory was correct. He waited while it rang and rang. "Be home," he said to himself. "Please be home."

"Hello?"

"Hello, Aunt Dimmy. It's Jesse."

"Jesse?" she asked. "Jesse who?"

"Jesse. Your nephew Jesse." Talking to his aunt was a bit like talking to the Old Man. He waited, wondering how many other Jesses she knew. "Your sister Trudy's son." He waited again.

"Oh, *that* Jesse. How are you? How's your mother and father? How's Pop?"

"Fine, Aunt Dimmy. Everybody's fine. Listen, I'm in kind of a hurry. I'm calling–"

"I've been meaning to call them, but things have a way of getting by. How's college?"

"I graduated, Aunt Dimmy. Don't you remember? You came to the party. But–"

"So what are you doing now?"

"I'm teaching in Farmington. You sent me that newspaper clipping and I applied for the job–" He didn't want to get sidetracked and run out of time. "I'll tell you when I see you, but now I'm calling–"

"In town here and you haven't come to visit?"

"Listen, Aunt Dimmy–"

"You know your cousin Doris moved before Labor Day? To Washington, but I don't know if she's AC or DC. She called me yesterday. Her husband Buddy got a job with 'the Government.' That's what she told me, but I forget what he does. It's all a big secret–"

"Aunt Dimmy!" he shouted. "Aunt Dimmy, please." He lowered his voice. "I promise I'll come over and visit you to chat as soon as I can. But now I have a problem–"

"Procurement!" she said. "He's a procurer for the Government. Is there such a word? I'm not sure what it means, but it sounds important doesn't it–"

"Aunt Dimmy," he cut her off again, "please–I'm calling from a pay phone and I don't have any more money. Will you please listen to me, I'm in a jam, I have a problem!" he said all in one breath.

"You need money, Jesse?" She hesitated. "I could help you maybe a little, but–"

"It's not money, Aunt Dimmy. I'm stuck. My car broke down on the parkway on my way to school. I'm already late for class and I can't get through to the school. I have to walk a mile back to my car. It's dead on the parkway." He spoke quickly and didn't give her a chance to interrupt. "I need *you* to call the school for me." He considered his next words carefully. "Tell them that I had a *slight* accident." He thought it would sound so much better than just saying that the car broke down. "Tell them I'll be late and I will be in as soon as I can. Would you do that for me, Aunt Dimmy?"

"Tell them you had an accident?"

"A *slight* accident," he stressed. "Tell them I had a *slight* accident. A *slight* accident," he repeated. "With the accent, Aunt Dimmy, on the word *slight*. And tell them that I'll be in as soon as possible. You have a pencil? Write down the central switchboard number. Please call them as soon as we hang up. It's really important, a matter of life and death, Aunt Dimmy."

"I'll call," she said, "before I go out. I was heading out the door when the phone rang and it was you. Today is shopping day and then a movie with some of my friends so I won't be home until later–"

"Thank you, Aunt Dimmy," he interrupted. He asked her to repeat the number. "Just don't forget to call as soon as you hang up. I'm going to try and fix what's wrong with the car. You just be sure to call the school." He looked at his watch. "Class already started and they're probably wondering what happened to me, so please hurry. And thanks again, Aunt Dimmy." After he hung up he realized he hadn't told her to call the high school, but there wasn't anything he could do about it. He didn't have any more change and they would figure it out. Still it bothered him, but only until he got back to the car. "Fuck!" he yelled. His car was up on cinder blocks and the two front tires were gone.

* * *

"You have reached the central automated switch board of Farmington Union Free School District Seventy-One–"

"I'm calling to report an accident. My nephew–"

"Please listen to the following menu options. If you know the extension of your party you can dial it at any time–"

"–not a party. He's a teacher and he asked me to call. He had an accident–"

"At the sound of the beep slowly and clearly state the name of the party you are calling and you will be transferred. You have five seconds–" There was a beep.

"My nephew Jesse, Trudy's son. He had an accident. He told me it's a matter of life and death. This is terrible. Please I want to talk to someone, anyone–"

"Thank you. Your call is being transferred. It was a pleasure to serve–" The phone clicked and there was static in the receiver.

"Farmington Junior High School. How can I help you?" the voice said mechanically.

"Are you a person or a recording?"

"This is the Main Office. May I help you?

"My nephew needs help. He had an accident. He called and asked me to tell you. His car is on the side of the road dead, and I don't know who else might be dead, or if he's going to make it. I told him I'm going out for the day. He needs help–"

"His name? May I have his name please?"

"Tietjen. My sister Trudy's son, Jesse. When he called I thought he was still in college. He's my daughter's age and they played together when they were babies. But now she's in Washington AC or DC, I don't remember which. Her husband is a procurer. And now the poor boy's had an accident. It's terrible."

"I see. His name again?" She took it down and turned to the woman at the desk next her and shook her head. "An accident, yes, I got that." She wrote his name on a piece of paper. "I'll see to it that someone gets the message. Thank you." She hung up.

"Who was that?"

"Some nut." She twirled her finger in small circles at the side of her head. "Sarah, we don't have anybody named Tietjen working here, do we?"

"Not that I know."

"That's what I thought. Check the calendar. There must be a full moon." She dropped the paper on the corner of her desk.

* * *

The intercom buzzer that connected to the classrooms sounded on Phyllis Lind's desk. She pressed the button and the speaker crackled.

"Main Office," she said.

"You think you might send somebody up here to take care of the noise!" Red Farley held the phone so she could hear it. "There's nobody in 235. The new kid. And all that weird noise is driving me crazy. I think they're killing cats in there!"

"Mr. Tietjen isn't in his room?" She checked the absentee list and the call-in sheet. "He's not absent. Are you sure he's not in his room?"

He held the phone out again for her to listen. "If he *is* in there, they're killing him and you better send for the police instead!"

"Thank you, Mr. Farley. I'll take care of it."

"Make it fast!'

She hung up and checked. Mr. Tietjen's card wasn't punched in either. She checked the schedules to see which AP was available. Then she rang Mr. Baltz's extension.

"What is it now, Miss Lind?" he asked curtly.

"Ms, and there's no need for you to make whatever's bothering you my problem. I'm just looking for some direction here. I just got a report of a disturbance on the second floor."

He sighed. "So send one of the APs up there." He was about to hang up.

"Mario's wherever Mario goes. Helen is at Central. Willy Zwill had a doctor appointment and comes in later. So that leaves Noah Lewis. And do you really want me to send him all the way up to the second floor? Last time he went above ground level he got lost for the rest of the day."

There was a pause. "Can't you go up there, Phyllis, and check it out?"

"That's above my pay grade," she said.

There was an audible sigh. "Then send Noah."

"Your call." She hung up and dialed the assistant principal's extension.

* * *

Noah Lewis took the scenic route up to the second floor, stopping at the cafeteria to see what was on the menu. While he was there he put his lunch order in with Peggy McFeeley to save time. He hadn't been up above the first floor the entire second half of last year, and he was in no hurry now. He was surprised to see that it had a new paint job. But since he was color-blind he wasn't exactly sure of the color scheme, though he thought that particular shade of gray was pleasing enough. He turned the corner and he heard a strange sound filling the corridor. He followed it to its source and stopped outside Room 235. He pressed his ear against the door and tried to peer through the glass into the room but everything was dark. Slowly he turned the knob and opened the door.

"Ohmmmm!" filled the room in a single continuous tone, like the hum of an engine, the low vibration of an electric motor. It increased in pitch and intensity. "Ohmmmm!"

He felt along the wall for the light switch and flipped it with his thumb. A ghostly figure was sitting cross-legged on the desk wrapped in a white sheet with his eyes closed, surrounded by the rest of the class. The sound was coming from all of them. Their different voices picking up the tone, changing it, extending it in a single uninterrupted note, "Ohmmmm!" The smell of incense permeated the room as well.

The sheeted figure opened one eye and looked at the puzzled assistant principal. "Hey, Mr. Lewis," Virgil said.

"Sorry for the, auh, interruption," he whispered.

Virgil put his finger to his lips and the AP nodded. "Don't worry, I got this covered." He pointed to the light. "Do you mind turning that off when you go."

He switched off the light and backed slowly out of the room. "Ohmmmmmmmmmmmmmmmmm." The sound followed him down the corridor.

"Aren't you going to do something about that?" Red Farley called to him when he saw the assistant principal in the hall.

Noah Lewis didn't turn around. He just reached into his jacket and pulled a sandwich from his pocket. He waved it for Red Farley to see. "Lunch," he said.

"But it's only first period!"

"Early, auh, lunch." He hurried around the corner and was gone toward the security of the first floor and his office.

"Ohmmmmmmmmmmmmmmmm!"

* * *

Mario Giovanni quietly opened the door to the Third Floor Faculty Men's Room and stopped.

"Scab!"

"Asshole!"

"Ass-licker!"

"Moron!"

"Bastard!"

"Scumbag!"

Even if he hadn't recognized their shoes, he was a shoe expert, he knew exactly who it was behind the two closed stall doors. FT Ass. president Joel Maxwell always sat in the right stall, and FU-2 rival president Dwayne Purvey preferred the one on the left, always leaving the vacant center stall as sort of buffer zone between them.

"Spineless scab company jellyfish turd!"

"I'm rubber, you're glue!"

"Shit for brains!"

"Sticks and stones may break my bones, but names will never hurt me. When you die I won't cry because you're a fucking asshole!"

The rubber-soled shoes that Mr. Baltz ordered his staff to buy didn't make a sound on the tile floor. He entered empty stall and climbed on the edge of the toilet bowl, careful not to slip. He pulled himself up so he could look over the partition without being detected.

"Turd!" Joel Maxwell was paging through a copy of the New York *Times* that he had folded into a manageable size.

He turned and peeked over the top of the other stall where Dwayne Purvey was thumbing through a *Playboy*.

"Dildo!" He held up the centerfold and the AP recognized from the picture that it was an old issue.

For a long time the Farmington Teachers' Association was the uncontested bargaining agent for the teachers. FT Ass. worked hand in hand with the School Board and Central Administration to keep problems at a minimum and issues under control. They had a reputation as a "company union," not totally undeserved because officers of the FT Ass. invariably moved up and out of the classroom into administrative positions whenever they became available. When Dwayne Purvey and twelve vocal high school teachers started FU-2 the rivalry began and the faculty split. The eight elementary schools remained steadfastly loyal to the FT Ass., while the more militant high school joined the Union, and the junior high school staff was evenly divided. Unfortunately for the teachers with split loyalties, the two organizations provided them with about half the representation. Any potential cooperation between them was further prevented by the personal animosity between Maxwell and Purvey.

The rivalry didn't go unnoticed by Mr. Baltz. "Familiarity," he said at a meeting of district administrators, "breeds contempt. If they are fighting one another they won't be fighting us." He laid out his plan to keep the factions off balance and the two feuding presidents at each other's throat. He had Mario Giovanni, who was in charge of scheduling, arrange it so Maxwell and Purvey shared a classroom every year. They had the same prep and duty periods and the same lunch. The two of them spent more time together than they did with their families and all that shared time cultivated such personal hatred that neither missed an opportunity to express his contempt for the other in public or in private. They expended so much energy fighting one another, that neither the FT Ass. nor FU-2 could unite a splintered faculty and so the teachers found themselves working for years without proper representation or a new contract.

"Puke!"

"Ass wipe!"

He silently stepped down from the toilet, gave the stall a quick once-over for any new graffiti and then he tiptoed out of the bathroom.

"Jerk-off!"

Joel Maxwell didn't respond.

"I said, jerk-off!"

Nothing.

"Jerk-off!"

"Hey, Purvey, there's an article in the *Times* that must be about your family. They just found traces of an early civilization in central Europe that mated with animals. Your family's from that area, right? And didn't you say whenever your mother took you to the Bronx Zoo the monkeys threw their jizz at her?"

"Fuck you, Maxwell!" He pulled some sheets of toilet paper from the packet he was carrying, dipped them in the water and tossed the wadded paper over the top of the stall "Incoming!" he called.

"Purvey, you bastard. That's not funny."

"Scumbag!"

* * *

It wasn't quite ten o'clock when the phone rang. The old man was finishing a bowl of All Bran and the sound so startled him that he dropped his mess kit and had to dive under the table to retrieve it. "Command Post," he managed when he picked up the phone.

"Good morning," the voice at the other end said. "I'm trying to locate Jesse Tietjen."

The effect of a woman's soft voice was like a surge of electricity passing through him. He wiped the milk from his chin with the edge of his bathrobe. "Is that you, Suzette, *mon petit chou-chou?*"

"No, no. This is Ms Lind from the Rosencrantz and Guildenstern High School. Is Jesse Tietjen there. He hasn't reported for work today. This is his home isn't it? He's on our staff and–"

"Staff? General Pershing's staff?"

"Is there something wrong there?" she asked.

"I'd be the last one to complain, General. But since you ask I'll tell you. What we need here is more fire-power. Machine guns and those new tanks. And replacements for the men we've lost."

"Who am I speaking to?"

"York. Sergeant Horatio York. Fifteenth Cavalry Division, but most of the horses are dead, Sir, and we ate the ones that weren't killed. We were recently converted to Field Artillery."

"Listen, Sergeant York," she said very slowly, "is there anyone else there that I can talk to?"

"Not a soul. We've taken some heavy casualties from a raid in the middle of the night. And we were gassed."

"I thought you might be."

"This morning we sent a man out on a pre-dawn patrol. I'm the only one left, but I can hold out until the reinforcements arrive. You can count on me, General."

"I'm sure I can, Sergeant. But what about Tietjen? Is he sick today?"

"Out on patrol, sir. He left before the sun was up. A brave young man. Reminds me of my grandson."

"Well, I'm afraid I have some bad news then, Sergeant. He didn't get through."

He shook his head. "That's the second one in as many days." He paused. "I'd like to volunteer for the next patrol, Sir."

"Negative, Sergeant. You just stay put. We can't afford to turn your strategic position over to them. Sgt. York, you just carry on with what you were doing before I called."

"I will, General."

"Keep your head low and your gas mask close by at all times." She paused. "And, York, you'll be happy to know that you've been given a field promotion. You are now a captain."

"Thank you." He saluted. "And God bless you."

"Thank you, *Captain* York."

"About those machine guns and tanks?"

"I'll see what I can do," she said.

Terry Scapelli strolled into the Main Office just as she hung up the phone. He checked his box and stopped at the counter to sort out the mail. "Bill. Bill. Junk mail," he recited. "Memo from the principal. That one I can throw away."

Mr. Baltz walked through the Administrative Alcove on his way to his office. "No calls for the next hour, Miss Lind–"

"Ms."

"–unless it's my wife. And don't give her a hard time." He turned and stared at Terry's smiling face. "Don't you have something better to do, Mr. Scapelli, then just stand there bothering the busy secretaries?" He turned and went through the door into his office.

Terry's smile broadened. "Works every time," he said.

"What'?" she asked.

"I just smile whenever I see him. It bugs the crap out of him to see me so happy." He dumped all papers in the waste basket. "And speaking of happiness, good morning, Mrs. Butrum," he said as she came into the office.

"More like afternoon," she said, "and not that good if you ask me."

"You're right. It's so much later than we think." He looked at his watch. "And wasn't the weekend terrible. So much rain. It's just a matter of time before we'll have all that cold and nasty snow to deal with."

"I was just saying that very thing." She stuck some fliers in the boxes while she spoke. "Winter gets more and more dreadful every year. Especially out there in that drafty wooden T-Wing."

He took some of the papers from her and helped stuff the boxes. "You poor souls in the T-Wing." He pursed his lips. "I think Dr. Flackett and Mr. Baltz regard you 'T-wingers' out there as expendable. That's what they call you, you know, second class citizens. On the bright side we only have a hundred and fifty-six school days left until June. How's the Sunshine Committee? No casualties so far?"

"Not yet, but it's still early in the year. There are a few prospects, but it would be unprofessional of me to tell you who."

"How's your health? Your stomach? Your feet?"

She shook her head. "You know I hate to complain. And what's the use anyway? My stomach, my feet, my back, my veins? Everything is the same."

"That's wonderful, Mrs. Butrum. No better means no worse."

"I'm the lucky one," she said. "My niece's husband, he's about your age, the poor boy, went to the doctor with severe stomach cramps. He hadn't had a bowel movement in weeks. On his way to see the doctor he got hit by a car."

"It must have knocked the stuffings out of him."

"It sure did! Lord knows how he wasn't killed, thrown through a plate glass window like that. He required who knows how many stitches. Not to mention a transfusion. So what do I have to complain about? Even with less than a complete stomach, at least my bowels are regular and not rock hard like my niece's husband."

"That's good to know, Mrs. Butrum." He finished stuffing the last flier. "But all this potty talk has made me have to make a stop before my next class. It's always a pleasure, Mrs. Butrum."

She watched him go. "He's such a nice boy," she said. "If only he'd cut his hair a little, shave that beard and dress up. I remember how nice he looked when he started here." She took the seat next to Phyllis, opened the file cabinet and leafed through the teacher personnel files.

The phone rang. "Good afternoon," she said, "Rosencrantz and Guildenstern Memorial High School, Ms Lind."

"Phyl, this is Arlene Trent at the Junior High. By any chance do you have a Mr. Tietjen working there?"

"We sure do. But he isn't in and we've been trying to track him down all morning."

"Well maybe I can help. I got a call this morning from some raving woman. I thought it was a prank call. She was going on that her nephew Jesse Tietjen had a car accident."

"A *car accident* involving Mr. Tietjen?"

Mrs. Butrum perked up. She leaned back to pick up the conversation while she looked through the files for Tietjen.

"I didn't think much of it because the name wasn't familiar. And then I thought he might be in one of the other schools so I called all the elementary schools without much luck and junior high didn't know him either. I'm sorry for the delay in getting you the news."

"I called his house earlier. Any word on his situation?"

"Nothing other than the part about the car accident." she said. "Maybe he went home. You might try calling there again."

"Nothing too serious, I hope," Mrs. Butrum said when Phyllis hung up. She was wondering if flowers or a fruit basket would be in order.

"Apparently our new English teacher, Jesse Tietjen, was in a car accident."

"Oh? Is he okay? He seems like such a nice boy. I'd hate to think something terrible happened to him." Mrs. Butrum found his personnel file.

* * *

Trudy Tietjen walked into the kitchen with two bags of groceries in her arms. She set them on the table and went toward the hallway. She could hear the water running in the bathroom.

"Papa," she called, "I'm back!"

The water stopped and the old man came into the kitchen. He was dressed.

"What have you been up to?" She was afraid to ask.

"Nothing much. While you were out a woman from Jesse's school called," he said coherently.

"That's nice," she answered automatically, accustomed to not listening to the things he said.

"Said he didn't make it to work today." He went to the drawer and pulled out the box of aluminum foil.

"Who said? Who didn't?" She looked at the old man.

"The woman from Jesse's school. I just told you. Jesse didn't show up this morning." He tore a piece of foil and folded it into bars. "She also promoted me. Skipped right over lieutenant and made me captain," he added.

She wasn't listening and went to the telephone book where Jesse had written the number for the direct line to his school.

The telephone rang in the Main Office. "Rosencrantz and Guildenstern Memorial High School, Mrs. Butrum. How can I help you?" she asked mechanically.

"Good afternoon. I was wondering if you could help clear up a little misunderstanding. My name is Trudy Tietjen. My son Jesse Tietjen teaches English there and–"

"Oh, the poor boy," Mrs. Butrum said sympathetically. She was still looking through his folder. "I'm so glad you called. I'm the Chairwoman of the Sunshine Committee. The Committee has already started collecting money for flowers for the poor boy. And I have some questions–"

"Flowers?"

"I presume flowers are appropriate? Of course we could always substitute a basket of fruit instead, if the accident wasn't that serious."

"Accident?" His mother's voice reached a high note.

"We got the phone call a while ago. A delegation will visit him at the hospital, *if* he's in the hospital. It's part of my duties as the Chairwoman of the Sunshine Committee. Do you have the name of the hospital? But if his condition is worse, the funeral parlor. My, aren't the roads just murder these days? And with winter coming, you the number of head-on collisions will only increase. Why just last year we lost one teacher–"

"Funeral? Head-on collision?" Jesse's mother cradled the phone.

"I was telling Ms Lind, the secretary here that your son was such a nice boy. Of course I only saw him once or twice since school started. And so young. You have my deepest sympathy, Mrs. Tietjen." She waited for a reply. "Hello? Hello?" She looked at the receiver. "I was just speaking to Mr. Tietjen's mother," she said when Phyllis Lind returned to her desk, "but I think the poor woman hung up."

* * *

Fifteen minutes before the end of the day the AV/CM office shut down. The AV/CM Equipment Requisition Forms drop box outside the office was emptied. All the forms that were not completely filled out, contained misspelled words or sloppy penmanship were separated and stamped REJECT. It was Harry Dexter's belief that anyone using his equipment had to demonstrate their worthiness with correct grammar and good penmanship. The forms that passed this initial inspection were placed in the PENDING FURTHER ACTION tray, replacing those that were moved into the IN box for the next morning. It was also his philosophy that as with anything good, AV/CM equipment was worth waiting for. The rejects he dropped into the trash pail.

Before the dismissal bell rang the crepe paper was rolled up and the plastic wreath with Don Coolie's photo was put back in the cabinet, where they would remain until next year's ceremony. All that remained was the frayed wire and plug to serve as a reminder.

* * *

When the orange and blue Nassau County Police car pulled up in front of the high school, Virgil was sitting at the curb with his skateboard. He went over to the car and assumed the familiar position stretching his hands over the hood with his legs back and his feet apart.

The car siren chirped. "Move away from the car, Loomis!" the voice crackled from the loud speaker. "Step back from the car!"

"Just thought I'd save you some time, Sergeant Sadowski." He stood and dusted off his hands. He looked in the car. "Hey, Officer Guitano. How you been? I haven't seen you since you took Mr. Keller away last year." Sergeant Sadowski remained in the car while Officer Guitano slid out and opened the locked back door. "Mr. Teeg?" Virgil was stunned to see Jesse sitting sheepishly in the back seat. "What did they get you for? If you didn't already sign a confession or make a statement, don't say another word. I have some friends in the American Civil Liberties Union."

"Loomis," Officer Guitano said as, "just go home. It's late."

"Thank you." Jesse pulled his attaché case from the seat. His hands were dirty.

"Well at least you're not wearing handcuffs. That's a good sign. But you look terrible. Did they give you the rubber hose treatment? What happened to you?"

"Loomis," Sgt. Sadowski said rolling down the window. "I'm watching you."

"That makes me feel safe." Virgil went up to the car. "I'll probably see you this weekend. Millie and I are working on a project, and she invited me for dinner. I heard you got a new TV. Can I bring dessert?"

Officer Guitano laughed, adjusted his holster that got caught under him when he got back into the car and sat down. And the car pulled away from the curb with a lurch, kicking up pebbles.

Virgil waved and then turned and walked with Jesse toward the school. "Don't worry about anything, Mr. Teeg. I covered for you today. They didn't even know you were out until fourth period."

"That's not very encouraging and doesn't say much for my teaching, does it?"

He looked at Jesse's hands. "Bad day, Mr. Teeg?"

"That, Virgil, is an understatement."

The front door was locked. Jesse looked at his watch. He tapped on the window with his ring.

A large woman in a smock peered around the corner at the far end of the corridor and saw him with his face pressed against the glass. He banged again. She waved him away. "Is closed," she said in a heavy accent. "Go home. Is closed."

"Can I *please* use the telephone," Jesse asked. "It's an emergency. I'm a teacher. I work here."

She shook her head. "Is school. Not telephone place. School closed. Go home."

Virgil stuck his face up to the window. "It's all right, Marta. He's with me."

She dropped the mop into the bucket, wiped her hands on her smock and walked down the steps toward the door. "Is crazy here. When school is open kids is running out. When school is closed kids is coming in." She studied them through the dirty glass and shook her head before she opened the door.

"Thank you," Jesse said. "Is there a phone I can use?"

"Other side." She pointed down the corridor. "Is pay phone." She shook her head.

"Do you have change I can borrow?" he asked Virgil when he found the phone.

Virgil fished into his pocket and pulled out a handful of coins. "Be my guest, Mr. Teeg."

Jesse listened to the coins drop and register before he dialed his number. "Hello, Mom," he said when she picked up on the first ring. There was a moan and a thump at the other end. "Mom? Mom?" He turned to Virgil standing outside the phone booth. "I think she fainted."

"Does she do that every time you call?"

For the next half hour Jesse fed coins into the slot as he attempted to sort out the day's events while Virgil listened.

After he hung up he turned to Virgil. "I was just resurrected. My family thought that I was dead. They spent the afternoon calling hospitals. Trying to locate my body."

"More trouble!" Helen O'Dell said when she burst into the principal's office waving a crumpled piece of paper.

"Jesus, O'Dell, I haven't even had a chance to hang up my coat and hat." He skirted the covered portable chalkboard, opened the closet and hung them on the inside door peg. "What now?"

"Something about a dress code thing. Lots of chatter and notes and– What's that smell?" She sniffed the air and grimaced. "Like Pine-Sol and toilet!"

"It's nothing," he said quickly and shut the closet door. "I think the Science Department upstairs is doing sulfur experiments." His face looked worn and tired. "Mario worked on a student dress code last year memo. I'll tell Phyllis to get it out to everybody again."

"The problem is it isn't the students. I fished this memo out of a wastepaper basket in the third floor Women's Faculty Bathroom. They're planning some kind of a demonstration to wear pants suits." She handed him the paper.

He read the note. "'To all female staff members! Some of us have shown an interest in wearing pants suits instead of skirts and dresses. Your input is necessary to decide our possible future action. If enough of us get together we can make a change. Can we count on you to join us? More information to follow.'" He swiveled around in his chair. "Jesus Christ! I have enough problems without the goddamn women revolting." He smoothed his mustache with his thumb and index finger. "When do they plan this demonstration?"

"There's no specific date. It depends on the response they get. If enough women decide to challenge the district policy they'll stage a show of force and make a fashion statement. The bunch of them, that way you can't single out any individual."

"Another conspiracy. I don't have time to play with the girls. Tell Phyllis to get my 'Professionalism and Attire' memo from the files, run off copies and stick one in all the mailboxes.

That should head off anything they might have in mind." She nodded. "How is the red marker collection going?"

"Slow. Willy went from room to room and only collected eight." She pulled a paper from the front of her jacket. "This is the list of names and departments."

"That leaves a hundred and thirty-eight still in circulation if Dexter's numbers are correct. You're going to have to step it up, Helen. Mario said there's a mushrooming graffiti epidemic upstairs in the men's room spreading like a plague. He has his hands full just trying to erase it all! You have no idea what this is doing to me, Helen. I can't even go to the bathroom in my own school. I haven't been to the faculty toilet upstairs for a week. I feel like a prisoner in my own office. Besides being an embarrassment, a loss of face, it's putting a stress on my... system, if you know what I mean." She nodded. "I spoke to Flackett, that bastard, about diverting some of the district's Emergency School Fund for a private bathroom in my closet. Flackett hates me especially when it comes to allocating me funds. 'How's it going to look,' he told me, funding new construction of a private bathroom while the district is on austerity and there's no toilet paper in the toilets we have?' Of course the bastard has his own private toilet." He fished a cigarette from the pack on his desk. "Desperate times call for desperate measures, Helen, and I am getting desperate." He took a deep inhale of smoke. "You take care of that pants suits thing today. Double your efforts. Spread a little disinformation. Keep them off balance while you are keeping an eye on them. Don't let up on your early morning patrols of the desks and wastebaskets. Don't let this get away from you." He looked uncomfortable. "Now if you'll excuse me I have some business to attend to."

When she was gone he locked the office door and folded the newspaper under his arm. He opened the closet and the pine small got stronger when he went inside.

* * *

There was a knock on Willy Zwill's door. "Who is it?" he asked after a slight pause.

"Helen."

He opened the door a crack to make sure it really was her. Then he slipped off the chain and let her enter the dark office. "Hurry up!" he said. He twitched and looked over her shoulder into the corridor. "Did anybody follow you?"

She sighed. "Willy, I just came through the Min Office from a meeting with Baltz and I stopped at my office not ten feet away." She elbowed her way past him and sat in his creaking desk chair. She leaned back with her hands behind her head and put her feet up on his desk. "Boy, does his office smell foul. Open the window and air it out. But it's not nearly as bad as Baltz's. His office smells like shit. You have anything good to munch on?" She tilted forward, reached into a side drawer and found a bag of ruffled potato chips before he could answer. She squeezed the cellophane and he flinched when the bag popped. "You're slipping, Willy, and you better do something or you'll end up in the hospital again." She crunched some chips noisily in her mouth. "The chain lock's new and the blackout curtains–" She indicated the heavy drapes that were across the windows.

"Just taking precautions and tightening up security. But that's not all." He opened his closet door.

"A roll of chicken wire?"

"I picked it up at the hardware store."

"For when you retire and raise chickens?"

He felt comfortable with her, more so than with any of the administrators. He leaned in to her and whispered, "For inside my windows. It's a strong, tight mesh. And once I nail it in place it will stop any number of good-sized projectiles."

"You really are worrying me, Willy." She finished the chips and rummaged through his drawers for more. "You don't think that's a bit extreme?"

"Maybe you do, but I learned from past experience. I'd rather be over-prepared than be under. Having a secure base of operations is critical. A sanctuary."

She found an open pack of chocolate cookies and took a bite. They were stale, but she finished all of them including the last half one that was loose in the drawer. She looked at him.

This wasn't the first time she had witnessed his paranoia, but it was definitely getting worse. "Listen to me, Willy," she said with sincerity. "Despite all your peculiarities, I really like you and I hate to see you in such a state. But besides all that, if you had to take another leave of absence and go back to South Oaks for a tune-up, I don't want all the extra administrative work Baltz will dump in my lap." He was somewhere else. "Listen to me, Willy. We don't have a developing *situation* here. No conspiracy. No grand scheme to overthrow Baltz. Somebody is just writing on the bathroom walls, for chrisakes, and he isn't even writing about *us*. It could be anybody on the staff, Willy. I've been tempted myself. Nobody in the building likes Baltz, including Mario, who thinks he should be the boss. Baltz is treating graffiti like it's a threat to national security because he's an insecure asshole. All this 'Operation Flush' bullshit is bullshit. Baltz is a control freak who needs to be in charge of everything from the handwriting on the walls down to what people wear, like pantsuits. He thinks the fate of this building, the entire educational system as we know it and Western civilization depends on him. I like Mario, but I know he's a kiss-ass because he's an ambitious bastard who will do anything Baltz wants him to do so he can get ahead. Noah Lewis couldn't care less who's writing on the walls in the third-floor faculty toilet. He doesn't even know there *is* a third floor. If I had to bet, my money's on Scapelli. But like I said, it could be anybody. Baltz brings out the worst in people. Even Harry Dexter hates him and he's his nephew." She looked at him. "Willy, we don't have ambitions, so we just have to play the game until it's time to say *adios*. If Baltz wants me to root through garbage cans to 'collect intelligence,' I can do it. Hopefully he'll retire if and when we get a contract, but even if he doesn't, I'm only five years away from freedom. If he wants you to collect red felt markers, just do it. But don't for a minute take it seriously, Willy. And don't think any of this will make a bit of difference. Look around, Willy, and see the reality."

He did and studied the little office. "I think I'm going to ask Carl Hubby in Wood Shop to measure the walls. I just might line the whole office with sheet metal. And after I lay in a few provisions and get a little refrigerator for the perishables, I'll be self-sufficient and able to spend days without leaving the office." He thought for a second. "I seem to remember they have one they aren't using in one of the Home Ec rooms."

"You might consider a toilet too. You and Baltz." She shook her head. "He just told me he wants a private toilet in his closet; that way he never has to use the faculty facilities. Frankly, his office already smells like an old age home."

There was a knock on the door and he turned his head so fast his neck cracked. "Who is it?" he asked.

"Sunshine Committee. I'm taking up a special collection for Mr. Tietjen. He's a first-year teacher–" Mrs. Butrum said through the closed door.

"I already gave at the office," he replied.

"This *is* the office," she countered.

He twitched, reached into his pocket and felt some loose change. He opened the door as far as the chain allowed.

"The poor boy had a head-on collision yesterday on his way to school. I spoke with his mother and the woman is beside herself with grief. We are planning as a group to see him. I'll let you know if it'll be to the hospital or the wake as I get the details."

He handed Mrs. Butrum the money, a quarter, a dime and two pennies. She shook her head and dropped it into the brown envelope. He closed the door.

Helen was holding a stale Fig Newton covered with grit and dust she had discovered at the back of the drawer and was considering it. "I'm still hungry." She got out of the chair. "But I hate to walk all the way down to the cafeteria. I wonder what Noah Lewis brought for lunch today." She walked around him and opened the door. "You think about what I just said, Willy. I care for you too much to see you like this."

"And I care for you, so you be careful, Helen."

When she was gone he locked the office door and reset the chain. He removed the roll of chicken wire from the closet. He found the hammer and U nails he had taken from the Shop rooms.

* * *

Terry took a sip of his coffee and stuck his head into the classroom. He looked surprised when he saw Jesse sitting at his desk. "I see the rumors of your death and your arrest have been greatly exaggerated. That's really going to ruin Mrs. Butrum's plans."

"How did you know?"

"There are no secrets here. Virgil told me you were busted and Mrs. Butrum just hit me up for some money for the funeral wreath."

He sighed. "It was a mess," he said. "And what do I do with all of these compositions whoever had my classes had them write?" He indicated the piles of papers on his desk.

Terry brushed off the desk top into the pail with the back of his hand. "Busy work," he said. "They didn't get a sub so teachers had to cover your classes. I was in here 8th period. The kids know it's just to keep them quiet, but if they ever ask you about the essays they wrote the day you were arrested and died, tell them you misplaced them, but they got B's. That will keep them happy. And in a week they won't remember a thing. How's your car?"

Jesse looked at him. "I have a rental through my insurance. My old Merc wasn't worth fixing. So now in addition to everything else I have to buy another car before the rental runs out or I have to take the LIRR to work." He was glum. "One more thing to worry about."

"Let me know if you need a ride until you get a car. I can drive you to and from the station if it comes to that." He headed back into the hall. "Good morning again, Mrs. Butrum," Jesse heard him say before the Chairwoman of the Sunshine Committee came through the door like a charging bull. She wasn't happy.

"You have some nerve," she started. "Do you have any idea the trouble your practical joke has caused me and the Sunshine Committee? And your poor mother. The pain you put her through." Terry's head poked around the open door. "Being in charge of the Sunshine Committee is hard work enough, running around collecting money, making arrangements. I'm not a well woman myself and I don't have the patients or the stomach to put up with your shenanigans, mister. I have a good mind to–"

"Mrs. Butrum," Terry interrupted from the doorway, "did Mr. Tietjen tell you about his harrowing experience escaping death? He was very lucky. The car was totaled, but he escaped with barely a scratch. Not so lucky were the others though, the driver and his pregnant wife in the station wagon. Broken bones, multiple abrasions, contusions and a fire. The woman went into labor and they were on their way to the hospital when the husband got distracted and their car crossed the divider. This young man's a hero. They would have ended up in the morgue if Mr. Tietjen hadn't pulled them out of the burning wreckage before the explosion. Not only did he save the parents, but he also delivered the woman's baby, a healthy boy they named Jesse." Jesse looked at him with disbelief.

"No," she said, looking at Jesse with new admiration, "I didn't know. I had no idea. I thought you were playing a practical joke." She thought. "Maybe I could send the flowers to them even though they don't work here. I *am* the Chairwoman of the Sunshine Committee and *could* make an executive decision. You wouldn't know which hospital they were taken to?" she asked.

Jesse shook his head sheepishly. "I, er… um."

"No, it doesn't matter. I'll look it up in the newspaper. It would be a shame if the flowers went to waste." She turned to go and stopped. "Well, I suppose you might as well have this." She handed the manila envelope to Jesse. "It's what I collected from the faculty." She left the room talking to herself.

Jesse turned over the envelope. "Two dollars and thirty-seven cents?"

"A start toward that down payment for your new car." Terry examined the change. "This one's a Canadian dime."

Rosencrantz and Guildenstern
Memorial High School
UFSD 71
Farmington, New York

TO: All Teachers and Staff
FROM: M. Seymour Baltz, Principal
SUBJECT: Professionalism and Suitable Attire

Last year Mr. Giovanni and the Dress Code Committee consisting of Mr. Farley, Mr. Ritchie and Mr. Milnow, faculty members elected by you, spent months and a great deal of energy drafting a Dress Code for our students. If we expect our students to adhere to a higher standard of dress, can we expect any less from our teachers and staff? Teachers are professionals and as such expected to set an example for the impressionable youngsters that have been entrusted to our care. Dignity and character are represented by the clothes you wear. As the saying goes, "Clothes make the man!" *And the woman.* Teachers are expected to dress professionally at all times. Suitable professional attire for male teachers includes suit jackets and ties and collared white shirts. Like a smiling face, a pair of polished dress shoes is an indication of caring. For female teachers professional attire consists of dresses or skirts of appropriate length, suitable blouses and sweaters in cooler weather. Slovenly attire on men or woman wearing pants sends the wrong message to our students. Let us all set the highest standards possible. Look professional, be professional and be treated like a professional.

Rosencrantz and Guildenstern
Memorial High School
UFSD 71
Farmington, New York

TO: All Teachers and Staff
FROM: Mario Giovanni, Assistant Principal
SUBJECT: Red Felt Marker Pens

According to a recent bulletin issued by the manufacturer, the red felt marker pens that were issued in your First Day Procedure and AV/CM Survival Kit Envelope on the first day of school have been found to be defective. The manufacturer has recalled *all* red felt marker pens for inspection and replacement.

A box for the collection of red felt marker pens has been set up in my office. Teachers are to return their red felt marker pens before punching out this afternoon. Be sure your name is checked off the list when you return them. Our first concern is for your safety and well-being.

Be advised that paychecks will be issued at dismissal this afternoon to teachers who have complied with the red felt marker pen recall.

The Tom Keller vending machine was a natural boundary that divided the Third Floor Faculty Room into two separate but not necessarily equal halves. The women always sat at the end of the table furthest from the door and out of the draft, closer to the refrigerator. The men dominated the other section. Chuck LaFemina, the Second Librarian and Rory Aaron, the acting Guidance Chair, sat in the middle; Andi Roberts and Bobbi Andrews, Girl's Phys Ed teachers, occupied the center. The faces changed from period to period, but the seating arrangements never varied from day to day, a self-imposed monotony carried over from school year to school year. There was security in the predictable sameness, and teachers were by nature creatures of habit. Every June many requested and got the same lunch periods with the same friends who would take the same seats in the teacher's cafeteria and the faculty rooms the following September. Most new teachers and substitutes who violated the divine order of things usually got the message through subtle clues, teacher glances and whispered comments. Those who didn't were confronted by lifetime seat holders reclaiming their territory from some novice barely out of college. "It's like a dog pissing in the corners to mark his territory," Terry told Jesse when he sat in the wrong seat the first week of school. He never did after that.

Mrs. Butrum was a semi-regular in the Third Floor Faculty Room. She dropped in between Sunshine Committee duties, when she was after information, or if she had some new tragedy to share. Her position as Chairwoman of the Sunshine Committee entitled her to sit anywhere, but she generally settled down with the women bridge players–Claire Hutton, Rita Reed, Elsie Bergin and Helen O'Dell, who had recently joined the group to fill in until Vera Turk recovered from surgery–the "Four Horsewomen" as Terry Scapelli christened the group.

History teacher Claire Hutton always sat with her legs open. Had anyone cared to look they might have thought she was wearing fashionable textured nylons, but no one cared and they were varicose veins. She played a card, simultaneously spooning into her mouth the homemade cottage cheese and fruit mixture from the glass jar she brought to school each day without removing the Pall Mall dangling from the corner of her lips. Rita Reed from the Reading Department always sat to the left of Mrs. Hutton because the cigarette smoke was less and she could sneeze down toward the other end of the table where the men congregated. She wiped her nose between deals on a seemingly endless supply of tissues. Elsie Bergin, who wasn't exactly a teacher and not a secretary, sat across the table next to newcomer Helen O'Dell.

"A real tragedy," Mrs. Butrum said. "I went to his wake last night."

Claire Hutton played a card and rattled the bottom of the jar with her spoon to scoop the last of her cottage cheese. Her lips barely opened, but the cigarette wiggled when she chewed and talked. "Everybody you hear about these days is dead, dying or has cancer." Rita Reed fanned the smoke, blew her nose and nodded.

"He was always a practical joker. And he paid a high price for all of his foolishness this time. His wife, the poor woman, was grief-stricken and blames herself for the tragedy." Helen O'Dell was the dummy, content to watch and listen. "One minute he was sitting on the living room recliner enjoying an apple and watching TV, his wife told me, and the next thing he was jumping around the room making strange faces and noises. Like he had done at a party, she said, when he had everyone in stitches. Such a practical joker." The ash on Mrs. Hutton's cigarette dropped unnoticed into the cottage cheese jar. "His wife said she even left the dirty dishes in the sink to watch him jumping around. She said she didn't have time for his foolishness and had to clean up the kitchen. But he just threw himself down on the floor, where he wiggled around on the rug and held his breath. Of course his antics made her laugh. And both of them turned purple, from lack of oxygen and from laughing. So she stepped over him and went back to the mess in the sink. Twenty minutes later when she brought him a dish of ice cream she couldn't get him off the floor. And by then it was too late."

"Oh, the horror," Elsie Bergin said. The others nodded.

"The coroner said he choked to death on a little piece of apple. Luckily the children were asleep and missed it. He left the poor widow with three young ones."

Terry had walked into the room and caught the end of her story. "I guess he learned his lesson about playing practical jokes." He acknowledged the ladies with a nod. He went to the coffee machine and studied the menu before he dropped his money into the slot.

"Talk about death, dying and practical jokers and Scapelli appears as if by magic!" Red Farley said.

Terry waited for the cup to fall and fill with something brownish before he sidled up to Red and stood behind him looking at his cards. "You have a great hand there, Red. All you need is another jack for gin!"

Stanley Milnow pulled back the card he was about to drop on the pile.

"For chrisakes, Scapelli!" He threw in his cards and turned to face him. "I guess you didn't read the latest memo."

"What do you mean? I just turned in my red felt marker pen. Think I want to carry a potential killer around in my pocket? I'm not taking any chances with my health and safety!" He sipped from the cup and grimaced. "In fact I've turned in *all* of my writing implements, pens, two pencils and several suspicious pieces of chalk just to be sure." Helen O'Dell strained to listen.

"No, smart-ass, I mean the one about proper professional attire." He picked up the paper on the table and read from it. "'Teachers are expected to dress professionally at all times.'"

"I resent your implication, Red. I *am* a professional." He did a little model's walk and turn.

"A professional agitator! You're a disgrace, Scapelli."

"There are advantages to dressing the way I do, Red. For one, it keeps me out of graduation every year. Baltz would *never* let the parents see me looking like this. Right, Helen?" She nodded and turned away. "So in June, when the weather's hot and sticky and all you well-dressed professionally-attired teachers are sweating your asses off in the gym, I'll be here in the air-conditioned comfort of the good old Third Floor Faculty Room doing Helicopter Duty to keep the Grumman planes from landing on the roof."

"You're a goddamn slob, Scapelli. And you're why the kids have no respect for teachers anymore. When I went to school, teachers didn't dress like garbagemen."

"I take umbrage at that offensive remark, Red. You're just saying that because most garbagemen are Italians, from Naples, and I'm not even Italian."

"Bullshit, you aren't, Scapelli."

"I'm Sicilian. You and I have a lot in common, Red, once you get beyond our surface differences. My people are island people like yours are, Red. You're Irish, right? Ireland is an island and Sicily is an island last time I looked."

"Kiss my Irish Catholic ass, Scapelli! We have zip in common. Politics, philosophy, lifestyle. I voted for Nixon and will gladly vote for him again. You voted for Ho Chi Minh. I support the war in Viet Nam. You're a Vietcong. I stand up for America one hundred percent and you want to tear down everything that's good. I'm a Conservative. You are a Communist! We have *nothing* in common, Scapelli."

"Conservative and Communist," Stanley Milnow said with some satisfaction, "They both start with the letter 'C.' You got that in common." He picked up the apple that was on the table and wiped it on his pants. He took a big bite that left pink stains on the fruit.

"Shut the hell up, Stanley. Nobody asked you."

"There are other things the Irish and the Sicilians have in common. A passion for people, politics and poetry. And they all start with the letter 'P,' Stanley. And the Irish and Sicilians both share a keen interest in death."

Mrs. Butrum perked up at the mention of the word.

"You mean like in eat shit and die, Scapelli?"

"The Irish love wakes. And Sicilians are undertakers."

"Undertaking is a good business." Stanley Milnow took another bite of the apple and the juice spurted.

"Stanley, your goddamn apple's bleeding, for chrisakes! And what the hell do you know about undertaking anyway?

Jews don't become undertakers. It's the Catholics who have the market cornered because we believe in heaven and hell. Jews don't. Catholics go places after they're dead. Jews just stay dead."

He was offended at Red's comment. "I just meant that undertaking is a good business. No complaints from the customers and big bucks."

"You read *The Godfather*? Scapelli's I-talian Mafia *goombas* became undertakers so they could bury their murder victims in the same coffins with the stiffs."

"Sicilian," he corrected. "We Sicilians think of ourselves as separate entities."

Buddy Ritchie looked up from the football pool coupon in the back of the *Daily News*. "So how come you became a teacher and not an undertaker, Scapelli? Or a garbageman?"

"I could have had a great job as a garbageman, Buddy. I took the New York City Department of Sanitation test. And my Uncle Vito said he would pull some strings to get me on his truck. That's what we do. Jews take family members into the business, my people get the same garbage route. Undertaking is another story all together. My cousin Antney in California is very rich and famous. He used to work for Muzak until he got a million-dollar idea to combining Muzak and undertaking and now he's making a fortune."

"I suppose you're going to bullshit that he plays music for the stiffs."

"Much more than that, Red. He's in California so he does a complete profile of each client when he was alive. Job, hobbies, interests. Then he generates an individual musical program that begins at the wake. But music is just scratching the surface. He has state-of-the-art electronic equipment, video cameras and tape recorders, so the client actually greets the mourners when they approach the coffin. 'Hello. Nice of you to come. My, you look wonderful. How do I look?'"

"You're full of shit, Scapelli!"

"And it doesn't stop there. If the client is buried in an aboveground vault, there's a follow-up audio program piped right in, day and night. Radio DED. 'Good morning, Mr.

Stevens. It's a good day to be dead. The weather outside is frightful with temperatures expected in the twenties. And the stock market closed lower.' My cousin told me he's even working on a video program in the not-too-distant future."

"What if the guy's buried in the ground?" Stanley Milnow asked. He laid his cards on the table. "Gin."

"Right now video would be too expensive. But they do pipe in the audio."

"Unbelievable," Buddy Ritchie said, adding the score of the last hand. "California is really wacko!"

"He's bullshitting, Buddy. You really expect us to believe your bullshit, Scapelli? You must think we're morons, for chrisakes!"

He nodded. "It's true," Terry said.

* * *

Mario Giovanni grabbed the drop box and the list of names. He passed through the Administrative Alcove picking up speed, but Phyllis Lind's ass stopped him in his tracks and his rubber soles chirped on the tiles. She was changing to her after school shoes and she looked back at him without straightening up. "You're much too easy, Mario," she said.

He flashed a broad smile and lowered his voice. "We still on for later?"

She fluttered her eyelashes. "Door's open. He's waiting for you." She adjusted her stockings. "Don't be late. I'll get the movies. You bring the food, Pizza Man."

He bumped the door with his backside and went into the principal's office. "Here they are, Boss." He dropped the carton on the desk. "The Red Felt Phantom marker pen clean-up was a big success." He read from the list. "One hundred eighteen collected. Eight were previously destroyed. Three lost. And six are in the hands of administrative personnel, the four APs and Harry Dexter. He said he didn't have to give his up. And yours of course." He cracked his neck and did a Bogart with his teeth. "Everything is right here, wrapped up neat and pretty." The principal smoothed the ends of his mustache. "In the last few days there haven't been any new incidents." He sat in his usual place on the right. "So we have definitely turned the corner of this one. O'Dell thinks the women's pants suit thing is squashed. Said she hasn't heard anything new. Your memo let the wind out of their sails."

Mr. Baltz swiveled in his chair. "Good work, Mario." He leaned back and was the most relaxed he had been in weeks. "I'm working on another angle, Mario. I put it to Flackett after this morning's Principals' Meeting at Central about a project I'm planning. Of course I didn't give him all of the details, but the first phase is to convert the closet here in my office into a permanent executive washroom."

Mr. Giovanni looked in the direction of the closet. "O'Dell mentioned something about that."

"In the past weeks I've gotten accustomed to an executive toilet of sorts. It'll be nice to have a warm, clean place of my own. And if the war continues there's phase two, still in the planning stage, Mario. And it's very secret. I can't spell out the details to you right now, but as my right hand you'll know everything you need to know when the time comes for you to know it. And of course you'll have the use of my closet. I convinced Flackett it had something to do with a computer lab he could put his name on and he passed my construction plans over to Building and Grounds and they'll be around to take some measurements. With any luck construction starts after Parent's Night. If anyone wants information from you– The fewer people to know the better."

"Omerta." He pressed his finger to his lips. "My lips are sealed."

The principal swiveled around in his chair. "Meanwhile phase one of Operation Flush goes on as usual. What's Zwill up to?"

"O'Dell's concerned that he's not taking his meds. She said he's working on something big in his office. In the last few days I've heard a lot of noise coming from in there, but he hasn't opened the door or answered his phone."

"Stay on top of that too, Mario. We can't afford to have Zwill go off again."

FT Ass.

"Wherever professional people negotiate."

FROM: Joel Maxwell, President FT Ass.
TO: ALL Farmington Teachers
Re: October Membership Appeal

For a person with foresight, for a person with integrity, for a person who sees teaching as more than just a job, for the professional that you are... there's only one place to be and that's in the FT Ass.

FU - 2

Farmington Union, Local # 2
"Unions made America great. Join a great union. FU-2"

RU fed up? RU mad? F U Kn Rd this U Kn Gt a Gd Jb w/ Hi R Pay N bet R Ben E fits. FU-2 or FU!

Dwayne Purvey, President FU-2

Rosencrantz and Guildenstern
Memorial High School
AV/CM Department

To: All Teachers
From: Harry Dexter, Coordinator AV/CM Department

Effective immediately no new requisitions for AV/CM equipment will be accepted and *no* requisitions will be processed through the first week of November. This is due to the recent red felt marker pen recall and plans to issue replacement marker pens combined with the extensive preparations required for an AV/CM Department display to be exhibited on Parent's Night, Thursday, October 25th.

Teachers who have submitted equipment requests previous to this memo and have received confirmations for use of requested equipment, be advised that those confirmations are null and void during the above mentioned blackout period.

This retroactive policy is one small step toward holding the line on the backlog of old paperwork that must be cleared before any new paperwork will be accepted and *any* equipment released. It is one giant leap forward toward November normalcy when a new policy for submitting AV/CM equipment requisition slips will be announced to take effect when the AV/CM Department office is reopened for business.

The AV/CM Department and the Library were the two most guarded, secret, semiautonomous sub-organizations in R&G Memorial High School. The AV/CM Department was more visible with its high-profile uniforms and memos, and it exerted a far more reaching influence on the daily lives and routines of the teachers. The Library preferred anonymity and maintained a low-profile to remain undiscovered, inaccessible and impenetrable to infiltration. Even the elite Custodial Corps under the leadership of Stash Polakas, Head Custodian, the most powerful individual in the building and perhaps the district, had difficulty.

With the exception of the day before the student body arrived when the doors to the Library were flung open for first-day Department Meetings and on Parent's Night, when the eighteen hundred brand new volumes were put on display for the taxpayers of Farmington, the Library went unnoticed by blending into the woodwork of the second floor and was made practically invisible by the camouflaged, splotch-painted walls to all but the most trained eyes. Inside, the First and Second Librarians, along with their staff, passed their days from September to June in relative solitude and peace.

Ovita Haupt, a tenacious woman with a clubfoot and a severe dowager's hump she developed in her later years, became the original school librarian in 1945, when Rosencrantz and Guildenstern Memorial High School opened its doors. For more than twenty years her stooped-over world consisted of cataloging the cartons of hard-covered volumes, cases of old paperbacks, some without covers, yellowed newspapers and magazines, many of which were destroyed in the book burnings of the mid-1950s. "Limping Iron Lady," as Miss Haupt was called by supporters and detractors alike, also spent a great deal of her working day picking up change thrown on the floor by students to see her bend. "And I saved every penny," she admitted in her June 1965 forced retirement speech, "to buy a brand-new Chevrolet and drive it to my new house in Florida. So who's laughing now?"

In August, School Board president, Donald Blight, appointed his only daughter, Marjory Maureen, the part-time picture-taking person for district events as First Librarian. Quickly nicknamed "Moron Blight," she was totally unqualified for either job. Her controversial promotion triggered much dissension, especially among the supporters of elfish Chuck LaFemina, Ovita Haupt's faithful assistant, the assumed shoe-in for the job. But in the end President Blight's decision stood and Chuck remained Second Librarian.

But the battle wasn't over. The two librarians clashed over everything, beginning on day one. Their internal conflicts became public when Blight locked LaFemina in a storage closet and threatened to leave him there until he was "a rotting, maggot-festering corpse." Slow Charley, the assistant custodian, finally released the Second Librarian before he had a bigger mess to clean up. Several mediation sessions produced a fragile though uneasy peace and a dividing line drawn through the center of the Library that partitioned it like North and South Vietnam. Donald Blight lost the next School Board election, but "Major Mo," his pet name for his mannish daughter, stayed on.

Jesse didn't find the Library until the middle of October, when he happened to stop directly in front of two doors painted to look exactly like the walls. He had never noticed them before on his PB rounds of the second floor. He pushed and went into a small, dark alcove. There was a printed sign on the closed, more formidable doors: "STOP! YOU MUST HAVE AN OFFICIAL LIBRARY PASS SIGNED BY YOUR OFFICIAL CLASSROOM TEACHER AND COUNTERSIGNED BY YOUR OFFICIAL STUDY HALL TEACHER DATED WITH TODAY'S DATE, YOUR OFFICIAL HOMEROOM NUMBER AND SECTION LEGIBLY DISPLAYED IN THE UPPER LEFT-HAND CORNER!"

A bronze letter drop with a hinged cover leered at him. Below it was another sign: "DEPOSIT SIGNED AND DATED LIBRARY PASSES ONLY!"

Jesse knocked. There was no response. He looked for the doorknob, but there was none. He knocked again, harder. A metal peephole cover swung aside and an eye appeared at the opening above the letter drop. "Deposit your library pass!" the eye said in an annoyed voice.

"I don't have a library pass,. I was just–"

"Then you can't come in. Can't you read, stupid?" the eye asked with no attempt to hide the contempt it felt at being disturbed from whatever it was doing before he knocked. "And if you can't read why are you here?"

"I'm a teacher–"

The eye blinked. "Do you have some identification to prove you are what you say?" the eye demanded.

Jesse patted his pockets and came up empty-handed. He took out his wallet from his back pocket. "Is a license good? Or a Draft Card?"

"I'm not interested in your Selective Service classification or how old you are. You're not trying to buy beer here. Do you have anything that proves you're a *teacher*?" The eye squinted with a growing annoyance.

"I'm new. This is my first year. My first teaching job–" He looked through his wallet again. "I don't know what you want. They didn't give me anything to prove–"

The eye sighed. "All right. I'll make an exception this one time. But the next time you try to come in here make sure you have something better than a license. Now hold it up where I can see it!   Hold it closer!" Jesse nodded and complied immediately. The eye looked over the license and paused. "Any convictions?"

He turned it around to show that it was clean. "Do you want to see the registration? It's a rental until I get a new car." He was trying to be helpful.

The eye glared. "What are you, a wise guy? I'm doing you the favor." The eye checked over the license again. "Tejent?"

"Tiet*jen*," he corrected.

"Whatever. You can come in, but just this once."

"Thank you." Jesse smiled. He heard the sound of a dead bolt sliding on the other side and a key turning in the lock. The door opened on large hinges that creaked and Jesse stepped into the Library.

The eye belonged to a chubby girl with a bad case of acne who couldn't have been more than a junior. She scowled at him.

"Thank you," he said again and walked into the room. There was a large sign with one word printed a foot high —"NO!"—and a freestanding life-size cardboard figure of a policeman reaching for his gun guarded the way into the center of the room. "DON'T YOU DARE!" the sign next to him cautioned.

"STOP! TIME-STAMP YOUR LIBRARY PASS BEFORE PASSING BEYOND THIS POINT! INSERT PASS HERE AND HOLD!" The time clock with a red tag attached was a newer model than the one in the Main Office. "SDI 446. Not to be removed. Service by anyone other than a certified AV/CM technician is forbidden. Read and refer to the instruction sheet concerning the proper use of this equipment. Your failure to do so, abuse or misuse of this equipment will result in its immediate recall to AV/CM!"

The machine belched when Jesse passed by.

Everything in the Library was in even, straight rows— the wooden chairs, the tan formica-covered tables. The windows were uniformly opened and the shades were level. Jesse saw a half dozen or so students seated in the center, boys at tables on the left, girls on the right. No one looked up when he approached. Except for the sound of his shoes on the brown tile floor it was absolutely silent–and motionless. No one talked, no one moved. There were no books on the tables. No one was reading. He approached one of the students and he saw it wasn't a real person. It was a dressed, life-sized soft sculpture propped up in the seat. He checked some of the others and discovered that they were too. He considered asking the eye, but he didn't want to tax their already strained relationship with questions. Instead he went to the book shelves.

"FICTION: DO NOT REMOVE BOOKS!"

He reached up and took down the first one he touched, *Dead Souls* by Nikolai Gogol, and he looked back over the top of the cover at the silent crowd. When he heard the approaching footsteps he thought it was the eye and quickly replaced the book in its slot.

"Oh, it's all right," the voice behind him said. "You're a teacher. You can remove the books. That silly sign is only for the students."

Jesse turned and looked into the clear moist eyes of Chuck LaFemina he recognized from the faculty room.

"Deirdre, the security girl, pointed you out." He offered his manicured hand. "Official introduction, Chuck LaFemina the *Second* Librarian, but you can call me Chuck or Chucky."

"Jesse Tietjen. English Department." The handshake lasted longer than was comfortable. "Can I ask you something? Those things over there are nylon statues?"

"Only some," he said shifting his weight on his tiny feet. "A couple are real. But it's hard to tell them apart isn't it? They are very lifelike. Soft sculptures the Art Department made for the Library. Stuffed like a pillow and dressed. They're amazingly detailed." He leaned closer to Jesse and whispered, "Anatomically correct, if you care to look." He touched Jesse's arm.

"Uh, no... no thanks. I'll take your word for it. But why?" Jesse asked.

"Having the Library full of students looks good if anyone from the Board of Ed or Central Administration or the State ever drops in. But these are so much easier to handle than the real ones. Quieter and cleaner." He looked at the book that was still in Jesse's hand. "You like the Russians?" He took the book. "I have a fondness for the French."

"I read André Gide," Jesse said, "in college. And Sartre. In English. My ability in French leaves a lot to be desired."

"I'll bet you're a Gemini, aren't you?"

"I am," Jesse said. "Does it show?"

"I *adore* Geminis. I'm a Taurus. Gemini and Taurus are very compatible signs." He touched Jesse's arm again. "Excuse me a minute." He called over Jesse's shoulder to one of the live ones who had moved from his chair and was about to take a dictionary from the Reference shelf. "Sonny, that's a no-no. You can use it there, but don't remove it from the stand." Jesse saw the boy still reaching for the book. "Tenth-graders just haven't learned the rules yet. The older kids *never* cause trouble. They never come to the Library."

Before the boy's hand made contact with the dictionary a blur moved across from the left, a dark, hulking figure that intercepted the boy in mid-reach, grabbing him by the scruff of the neck and replacing the book in one fluid motion. "What's the matter with you, boy? You deaf?"

"Who's that?" Jesse whispered.

"That dyke," he replied with unmistakable sarcasm, "is the *First* Librarian, *Moron Blight*."

She shook the surprised boy and his feet brushed the floor. "The sign says do not remove! That means you. Now pick up your crap and get out of here! You're banned! I don't want to see your acne-covered face in here until May!"

"Overkill and emasculation. But I can't do anything. The Reference Section is on *her,* and I use the word loosely, side," he said a little too loudly.

She stormed over and closed in on the two of them, ignoring the line of demarcation. "What's that, you prissy little pansy ass?"

Chuck LaFemina ducked behind Jesse. "You're on my side of the line," he said, keeping Jesse between the two of them.

She laughed. "Pussy!"

"Don't you wish."

Jesse forced an embarrassed smile. "I, er, um..." he said in an attempt to disarm the situation.

"Nobody asked you, pretty boy!" She got in Jesse's face and came up to him eye to eye. She turned and crossed to the other side of the line.

"Bitch," Chuck LaFemina called, but he made sure it wasn't loud enough for her to hear. He composed himself and smiled. "Oh, don't let her scare you. She's just showing off. She does that whenever any of my friends come up to visit. Always trying to assert her masculinity."

Jesse wanted to flee to the safety of the halls. "Yeah, well, I have to go," he said and moved toward the door.

"Now that you know we are here," Chuck said as he took Jesse's arm, "I do hope you'll be back. And if you're ever interested in brushing up on your French, I have an extensive collection of French books at home with some interesting and rare engravings."

"Actually," Jesse stammered, "I'm really very busy... with lesson plans... this being my first year and all... but thanks anyway."

"Maybe some weekend, when things settle down. I'll put you on my To-Do list."

"Is that the right time?" Jesse pointed to the clock above the desk. "I'm on duty now and I have to run. Really." He broke for the door. The time machine clicked at him as he passed.

"Don't be a stranger."

Deirdre, the security girl, looked annoyed. She put down her copy of *Tiger Beat Magazine* and pointed to the time clock. "You didn't punch out," she said as the large doors closed behind him. He heard the lock click and the bolt slide back into place. The bell rang, ending the school day and Jesse was caught in the crowd of screaming, frantic students hurrying to get out of the building.

Terry stepped out of the Third Floor Faculty Bathroom and recognized Willy Zwill tiptoeing along the corridor. For all of his attempts at stealth, the flap-flap-flapping wheel of the AV/CM cart he was pushing would have been enough to disrupt the entire third floor. But it was too early for anyone to be in class.

Terry watched the AP disappear around the corner of the hall and hurried to catch up with him. "Good morning, Willy," he said.

The AP didn't hear him approach and jumped. He wheeled around flinching and fumbling inside his jacket as the rolling cart careened into the lockers with a loud bang. "Scapelli!" he said. "Don't ever sneak up on a man like that. Never. It's the first rule. You don't know how close you came–" He felt his chest. His heart was pounding. His face twitched violently.

"Sorry, Willy. I didn't mean to startle you. You're in early. Somebody kick you out of bed this morning?" He looked at the cart. "Did you join the AV Squad or are you working for Stash Polakas to pick up some extra cash?" The large box on the cart that was now only half covered with a sheet. "Is that one of the little refrigerators from Home Ec, Willy? You planning a party? I heard about those wild administrator parties every month."

"What parties? I was never invited to a party." He stepped between Terry and the cart and centered the little refrigerator on the cart before he pulled the sheet back in place. "No parties. Just a project that I'm not at liberty to disclose right now. So do me a favor and keep a lid on it." He used his fingers to lock his lips. "You didn't see me and we never had this meeting." He winked or twitched and Terry winked back.

"Like Sergeant Schultz says, 'I see nothing. I know nothing.'"

He looked puzzled. "Sergeant Schultz? Do I know him?"

"No worries, Willy. My lips are sealed."

The AP checked the corridor before he resumed his journey down the hall. The sound of the flap-flap-flapping wheel picked up intensity as he picked up speed. Terry fell in beside him. "You might call this an insurance policy." He just couldn't resist. "I always liked you, Terry. Like me you're an individual, one of the few holdouts around here who hasn't bought a Jap car."

"I never forgave them for Pearl Harbor, Willy," he said. "The bastards. That's why I drive a Volkswagen."

"Exactly! I'm a good judge of character and I know you *are* a person who can be trusted." He looked around. "If I told you, you'd be surprised at some of the things that have been going on around here. So what I'm going to say might seem a little strange–"

"Nothing you say ever seems strange, Willy."

"Thank you. That means a lot to me." He leaned in closer. "Have you been followed? Around the school, I mean. Seen faces in your windows? People skulking in doorways, hiding in the shadows? Heard mysterious footsteps? Strange voices? And turned around to find nobody?"

He nodded. "Now that you mention it, there was somebody looking through the keyhole of my classroom awhile back. And I do have the distinct feeling that I'm being watched."

Mr. Zwill looked relieved. "I knew I wasn't paranoid."

"You know, just because we're paranoid doesn't mean they aren't out to get us."

"Exactly!" He shook his head "Helen O'Dell said I'm imagining things. This all started with Baltz and is now trickling down. He's been spending a lot of his time and energy trying to catch whoever it is that's writing stuff about him on the bathroom walls. He's consumed with it."

"Is he now?"

"We have meetings about it. He's developed elaborate plans to stop it. Like that whole red marker recall. A ploy. I can't go into the details. But despite his efforts it seems to be spreading faster than we can contain it."

"No! Really?"

"I don't know if you know this, but I was assaulted in the halls the first week of school! I've kept it quiet not to cause a panic. Since then, I've been followed around the building. And in these last few days I'm convinced that someone is watching my house!"

"You're kidding."

"This is too serious to kid about, Terry. I've been taking longer and longer routes around the building to get from place to place when I'm here and more and more complicated routes between home and school. Sometimes it takes me an hour to go the six miles."

"Any idea who it is?"

"I haven't figured that out yet, but I'm a patient man and I'm working on it. I have a few suspects in mind. Not to name names, but that Toby Wong in the Math Department got my attention. Those years I spent in that Jap POW camp have taught me follow my instincts. You know I was head of camp intelligence and morale officer," he boasted, "responsible for security *and* keeping up spirits in that hellhole. My experiences there have helped me here to handle tricky situations."

"I'm sure they were the very qualifications that got you the job here, Willy."

"I shouldn't be telling you this. 'Loose lips' and all. But I'm in the middle of preparations to set up a home base of operations in my office. That's what the refrigerator is really for." He patted the covered box. "This little beauty, along with some other innovations, will make my office self-sustaining and the best fortified position in the whole building. Like a little fallout shelter away from home."

"You have a fallout shelter at home?"

"Of course. State-of-the-art! First thing I did when I moved into Levittown was dig a basement and stock it." He looked at Terry. "It would be too difficult and too expensive to do that here, so I'll settle for a safe room."

"How are you doing this, Willy? And does anybody else know?"

"It's on a need-to-know basis, and not too many people need to know. Most of the money is coming out of my emergency slush fund. All the APs keep back a few bucks from school trips, book sales and stuff just in case. I've kept the expenses to a minimum by scavenging what I could here and at home. I was also on the salvage committee in the camp," he said with pride. "Once everything is in place I won't have to leave my office for days. You might want to keep that in mind if things get bad."

"Oh, I will," Terry said.

"Of course administrators have priority."

"Without a question. Where would this place be without our administrators?"

"I know I don't have to tell you again, but keep a tight seal on what I just shared. There's no way of knowing exactly who is listening."

"I understand," Terry assured him.

"I'm not giving up without a fight. The next thing is to convince the other administrators to fortify themselves for when push comes to shove."

"It's a comfort, Willy. Many of us in the lower echelons will be able to sleep easier to know that."

During their entire exchange Willy hadn't flinched once. "Don't get too complacent," he warned. "You watch my back and I'll watch yours. If you see anything strange, report directly to me."

"Right. Maybe when you're finished with the refrigerator job you'll bring the cart to my room. I have a few things that I need moved. A filing cabinet and some stage props."

He gave Terry a thumbs-up. "I'll drop by before the end of the day." He checked over his shoulder, twitched and started the cart in the direction of the elevator. He took a few steps and turned. "Drop by my office sometime and check out what I've done." He turned and continued down the hall until the flap-flap-flapping of the wheel disappeared.

Terry watched him before he headed back to the Third Floor Faculty Men's Room.

In the News
November 1971

November 5

Indian Prime Minister Indira Gandhi meets with Pres. Nixon to assure him India has no desire for war with Pakistan. Nixon later tells National Security Adviser Henry Kissinger, "We really slobbered over the old witch."

November 12

Nixon announces he will withdraw 45,000 more troops from Vietnam by February 1972.

November 14

Nixon signs the Revenue Act of 1971, an amendment to the Economic Stabilization Act that had already controlled wages and prices. Phase II provides "tax cuts of some $15 billion over the next 3 years to stimulate the economy and provide hundreds of thousands of new jobs."

November 22

Guerrilla fighting escalates on the border of East Pakistan. India masses 12 divisions near the border.

Rosencrantz and Guildenstern
Memorial High School
UFSD 71
Farmington, New York

TO: All Teachers and Staff
FROM: M. Seymour Baltz, Principal
SUBJECT: Parent's Night
November 4, 1971

C O N F I D E N T I A L

I would like to take this opportunity to remind you that the annual Parent's Night festivities are scheduled for this evening. In preparation for the event, to insure a smooth operation and facilitate an even flow of the expected masses, teachers must legibly print their names and subject areas on an index card and fasten it to the door of your room or rooms before the end of the regular school day.

Although posters and displays in each of your classrooms are technically not mandatory, you should remember that a tastefully attractive display makes a good impression, creates an attractive atmosphere and lends to the appearance of education. Atmosphere and learning go hand in hand. Therefore, the Art Department Office will be open all day today for you to pick up your decorative supply kits. Since the District is on austerity a nominal cost will be collected from each teacher. If you do not have the money, it will be deducted from your next check.

In addition, a complete list of the names and Homeroom sections of the children of School Board members will be in the mailboxes of the teachers who have these children in their classes. Be sure to read the list if you don't already know who they are. Wash all chalkboards and scrub graffiti from all desks. Be certain that all classroom equipment is in operating order.

Duty teachers will remain on their posts throughout the evening.

A display by Mr. Dexter and the AV/CM Department will be ongoing during all lunch periods in the Student Cafeteria. In the event that a parent plans to visit the Library, teachers should consult their building maps for its exact location. The Library will be open.

The parents pay your salaries, so keep them happy. Avoid unpleasantness at all costs! There is to be no discussion of individual students with parents, no mention of the austerity budget and no reference to the lack of a teacher contract. Together we can make this the best Parent's Night ever.

As a wise educator once said, "The flower of learning flourishes in the garden of warm smiles and is nourished with the fertilizer of pleasantness." So it wouldn't hurt to put your best face forward and spread a little fertilizer.

The afternoon of Parent's Night, the building emptied faster than usual. Teachers who lived close by rushed home to eat and rest before their return performance in the evening. Others hurried off to the Alibi or the Stikitt Inn to consume as much alcohol as necessary in the between hours to fortify themselves and carry them through the long evening. A cold, steady downpour was the ultimate finger in the eye. But on a positive note, the rain would keep down the numbers for the ordeal that was Parent's Night.

The Custodial Corps was mopping and sweeping the floors when Virgil walked down the deserted hall past the Student Cafeteria. He stopped to watch the AV/CM Squad setting up their Parent's Night video display. The long lunch tables were against the far walls, the chairs stacked to the sides, leaving a wide clear expanse of the floor for their equipment. Squad members had set up movie and slide projectors around the perimeter with phonographs and audio tape recorders. Three squad members huddled around a large Ampex videotape recorder and several TV monitors were set up at strategic points in the cafeteria. Virgil carefully stepped over the cables duct-taped to the floor **and** passed in front of one of the three big box studio video cameras on wheeled tripods and he waved when he saw himself on the monitors. "I didn't know we had all this stuff, Axle," he said to the captain overseeing the preparations. He leaned closer to the camera for a better look. "Can the students use these?"

"Don't touch anything, Loomis! I don't have time. I'm a very busy man." He looked through the viewer and fine-tuned settings zooming in for a close-up on the "Audio Visual Curriculum Material Multi-Media Presentation" message on a music stand. "There's a glare on the sign. I can't read the words. Somebody tilt it so I'm not seeing a glare," he barked impatiently. "And camera two focus is out again. Who touched it?" Virgil looked through the camera two viewer. "Do you mind, Loomis? This is very sophisticated equipment, to be handled only by trained AV/CM personnel." He fiddled with the lens ,but the picture got worse.

"Zoom in all the way and then adjust the focus. Then zoom all the way out. The image will always stay in focus," Virgil said.

Axel did it and it worked. "Yeah, well, you just keep your hands off the equipment, Loomis." He was annoyed.

Virgil watched with great interest when one of the others selected one of the large one-inch videotape reels from the box and placed it over the spindle. He carefully threaded the end of the tape around the wheel, through the gate, past the recording head and onto the empty reel on the other spindle. He pressed the play button.

"Stand by for picture," Axel called. The monitors went dark and then flickered and test numbers counted down on each of the large screens. "Stand by for sound." There was a series of beeps. "We have picture. We have sound. We have program!" The prerecorded program began and the cafeteria erupted in loud cheers. The first five notes from *2001: A Space Odyssey,* quiet at first, grew in volume through the speakers around the room. "Cue lights." The cafeteria went dark and a black light strobe exploded in flashes that could trigger an epileptic seizure. As the music faded, a spectral voice rose. "There is nothing wrong with your eyes. There is nothing wrong with the TV. During the next ten minutes you will be transported on the ultimate trip. The spectacle of sight and sound you are about to experience is only one example of how the AV/CM Department under the able direction of Harold Dexter is working to bring better learning through modern technology to your children. Special thanks to Principal M. Seymour Baltz for his support. So now sit back and enjoy the program."

Virgil was totally engrossed as the black light strobes continued and then stopped and a side shot of the front of the high school materialized on each of the dark TV screens. The camera panned across the lawn. "This is our home." The camera zoomed in along the cement walk for a medium shot of the center entrance. Then the picture dissolved and rematerialized in front of the closed door of the AV/CM Office. A disembodied hand appeared in the frame and opened the door as the camera dollied in on Mr. Dexter working behind his desk. He didn't look up, but continued signing and moving papers from one pile to another. When the camera finally came to rest he looked up and made eye contact with the visitor. "Oh," he said. "You surprised me. I wasn't expecting you so soon and I didn't hear you come in. I was busy with the duties of the Coordinator of the Audio Visual and Curriculum Materials Department." He smiled. "I'm Harold Dexter, one of the busiest people in the school." He got up, walked around and sat on the edge of his desk. "Every day this office processes volumes of papers for the distribution and collection of the most modern, up-to-date electronic equipment your children use during the course of their school day. The AV/CM center is an indispensable part in our school today, and the classroom of the future will rely more and more on audio and visual equipment, from videotape to the coming computers. Yes, that's right. Computers are coming to the classroom and when they do, this office will work even harder to keep your children on the cutting edge of education."

The picture of Harry Dexter's smiling face faded into a shot of the first floor hall. "A typical day in your child's school day begins and ends at the locker. Here are some typical students starting another typical day at R and G." Three Squad members in civilian clothes came smiling down the halls, opened their lockers, removed their books and filed off smiling toward class. The scene faded. "Here we see the lovely Phaedra Schwartz-Fine from the Business Department teaching her class the finer points of touch-typing, a skill that will come in handy until computers replace typewriters." Her smiling face faded in. "Keep your fingers on the Home Keys." The large diamond on her left hand sparkled into the lens. The picture cut to the cheerful faces of the secretaries in the Main Office. "Our able secretaries perform their duties helping to keep the school humming and running on track." The camera zoomed in for an extreme close-up of Phyllis Lind bending over the bottom drawer of a file cabinet.

A montage of clips showed an assembly in the auditorium, silent students passing through the halls and the

Guidance Suite, where counselors were too busy guiding Squad member students to notice the camera. "Guidance counselors are ready to help solve the problems today that may crop up from time to time and to chart a career course for students in the future. And no day would be complete without a hot and nutritious lunch served every lunch period by our friendly cafeteria personnel." In the Student Cafeteria the cheerful cafeteria staff in hairnets scooped generous heaps of roast beef onto the plates of Squad members waiting eagerly in a quiet, smiling line.

The screen went dark until a tight close-up of Mr. Baltz's face appeared. Slowly the camera zoomed out to reveal him seated behind his desk in his office looking very official, almost presidential with an American flag over one shoulder and the school flag over the other. He handled a stack of papers, compacting it like a deck of playing cards. "Welcome to another Parent's Night. I am Seymour Baltz, principal. This special program you have been watching is an example of how your school tax dollars are being used to benefit your children." His tone was warm and sincere, his eyes shone with integrity and there was a slight shine of perspiration on his forehead that glistened in the light when he tilted his head. "To insure the highest standards and the greatest achievement for your children, we need your support and your money." He managed a smile. "Please pass the budget."

The camera cut to a brief final shot of Harry Dexter still signing papers in his office. He looked into the camera. "Even without a budget, we at AV keep doing our job. But passing the budget would make it easier for us to give your kids what they deserve."

The picture faded, the program ended and the lights came up to the cheers of the AV/CM Squad. They rewound the audio and video tapes and set the counters to zero for the evening presentation one final time.

"I'm sold. They'll love it tonight," Virgil said. He reached into the box of tapes and picked up a reel. "What's this?"

The captain took the tape and replaced it in the box. "Just mind your business, Loomis, and keep your hands off the equipment. This doesn't concern you. Now, if you'll just go away—"

"I was just wondering. I'd really like to use it sometime."

"Well, you can't." He moved him toward the door. "Attention everybody," he called and they formed a line in front of the equipment. "It's a wrap. Parent's Night starts at seven thirty. You will report to the AV Office at seven sharp in clean, full dress uniforms. The first presentation begins at eight during the first lunch period. Squad dismissed!"

Virgil watched them as they filed out.

* * *

"Jesus, Jesse," Sue Wellen said when she saw him in the Third Floor Faculty Room, "you really look shitty."

"I feel shitty," he said. He could smell the alcohol coming from her. "I've been sick to the stomach all day. And dinner at my aunt's didn't help. I've been sitting here since six-thirty trying to decide if I want to throw up." He was sweating even though the room was cool. And he was puffing on a cigarette.

"You're sounding more and more like Mrs. Butrum." She laid out her compact and makeup on the table and inspected her face. She looked at the full ashtray that was in front of him. "Since when do you smoke?"

"Since I bought a pack of cigarettes this afternoon because I'm so nervous."

"It's only Parent's Night." She applied makeup on her cheeks and cleaned the corners of her mouth with her fingers. "You should have come out with Terry and me and had a couple of martinis for supper. Then you wouldn't be worried about anything." She watched him puff without inhaling. "You really look stupid smoking." He put the cigarette out in the ashtray. "Relax. You know how to do this. You've been teaching for two months. The parents are just older and not much better than their kids." She took a small can out of her pocketbook, sprayed the air and sniffed it. Then she checked the label. "Have to be sure it's breath spray." She aimed a blast into her mouth. "Last year I used a feminine hygiene spray by mistake. It tasted terrible, but I had some of the fathers following me around all night!" He didn't smile. "That was a joke. Lighten up." She saw the growing panic in his eyes. "This is easy and can even be fun."

"What am I going to say to them? What do you do?"

"It's only ten-minute class periods. Easy to fill when you're programmed to do forty-five minutes. Even with ten minutes between each class a lot of the parents will get lost and pop in late if they don't give up and go home early. Just keep talking up to the bell and don't give them a chance to ask any questions. Stop worrying. And as a last resort you can always give them a test. Red Farley does that. Or don't say anything. Tom Keller did that last year, but he was stoned. He sat in a student desk with the parents and didn't say a word. They just thought the teacher didn't show up and they left." She teased her hair. "Just be yourself. They'll love the new young teacher their kids told them about."

More teachers came into the faculty room.

"There you are, Sue Ellen. We've been looking for you. I thought we agreed that we were all going to meet for dinner. We waited for you."

"Sorry, Phay," she said. "I forgot. I went for drinks with Terry. I hope you didn't wait long."

"We didn't. You remember my husband Paul." He looked bored already with his hands in his pockets. "Paul, you remember Sue Ellen Wellen from the bridal shower. She gave us one of the four fondu sets." She turned to Jesse, who looked up for the introduction. "I don't know who you are."

"Jesse Tietjen," Sue said. "He replaced Tom Keller. Jesse, Phay Fine and her new husband Paul."

"Phaedra *Schwartz*-Fine," she corrected. "I've decided to go with the women's lib hyphenated thing to keep my identity. Too bad you didn't meet us, you missed a good meal. We found the most delicious French restaurant, *Chez* something or other that opened recently in town. It's so *kicky,* and *so* expensive. It's a good thing Daddy gave me his American Express Card. I'm sure he'll deduct it as a business expense. Paul hates French food, but he indulged me." She patted him.

"Nice dress," Sue said.

She modeled the dress. "Isn't it stunning? A two-month anniversary gift from Paul." She touched the front and the diamond engagement and matching wedding band glittered. "Actually Paul picked out something else in a different style and color, but I exchanged it for this one."

"Red is my favorite color. A perfect choice for tonight. You certainly have fine taste, Paul," Sue said sarcastically.

"Well, come on, Paul." She pulled his hand out of his pocket. "There are some other people I want to show you off to. Don't forget to stop by the cafeteria, Sue Ellen, and catch me on Harry Dexter's tape. I'm featured."

"Absolutely," Sue said without looking up from her mirror. "Nice talking to you, Paul." When they left she looked at Jesse. "See, it could always be worse. You could be Paul."

Terry came bounding through the door. "I just saw Phay and Mr. Phay."

"In that stunning dress Paul picked out in another color and a different style." She looked him over. "And you look stunning too! New sneakers?"

"New laces. I couldn't afford new sneakers. We're on austerity and working without a contract."

Jesse checked his watch. "Maybe nobody will show up," he said nervously.

The door opened. Noah Lewis was wearing his plaid Parent's Night vest under his regular school suit. He looked around uncertainly.

"Greetings, Mr. Lewis," Terry said jovially. "What brings you all the way up here on the third floor?"

"Someone, auh, said there's an icebox where I can, auh, keep my sandwich?"

"Refrigerator, Noah. Gee, you really haven't been up here in a while. We got rid of the icebox a few years ago when we got electricity. And now we even have the new Tom Keller Vending Machine."

"There hasn't been much call for me to, auh, get beyond the first floor,. But, auh, somebody took the icebox from the Home Ec room where I, auh, used to keep my sandwiches. This one is tuna fish, and I, auh, didn't want to take a chance of it going bad before tomorrow."

Willy Zwill poked his head inside just as the bell sounded in the hall. "Battle stations everybody! Zero Hour!" And another Parent's Night was officially under way.

* * *

"Parent's Night is a time for fun," Terry explained as the three of them walked toward their assignments through the hall crowded with already confused parents.

Jesse said gripped his attaché case so tightly his hand hurt. "Look at them all."

"Don't worry. The numbers go down with each passing period. By the end of the night the ones that are still here will be zombies wondering the halls."

"They won't be able to figure out the schedules their kids made out in Homeroom because of the bad handwriting and the mistakes they made by accident or on purpose," Sue added.

When Terry spotted a couple that looked like Iowa tourists lost in Manhattan for the first time he stopped. "Can I help you?"

"The Bernard H. Prahl Auditorium?" The man showed him the schedule.

"We don't have an auditorium. Do we?" he asked Jesse and Sue. "I think you're in the wrong building." A look of panic crossed their faces. "Just kidding. It's on the first floor, and you're on the third floor."

"What's the easiest way to get there?"

"Actually, there isn't an easy way from here. But go around the corner and up half a flight of steps. You really have to go up before you can go down." He pointed. "One of the kids dressed like Mormons or Jehovah's Witnesses will escort you. Have a great Parent's Night."

"Thank you." They hurried off holding on to one another.

"Check her out," Sue said indicating a woman with a leather mini-skirt and white go-go boots.

"She's a mother?" Jesse asked.

"You're a teacher?" the woman asked Jesse. "A lost woman. Where's Room 220? I can't read a damn word my kid wrote on this." She held out her schedule and touched his arm.

He smelled her perfume. "Room 220?" he stammered.

"You must be new here." She spelled it. "T-w-o-t-w-e-n-t-y."

"I like this woman," Sue said with admiration and took charge. "You might assume that 220 is on the second floor, but you'd be wrong. It's in the main building through that door," she pointed, "down around the corner and then up a short flight of steps. It's actually on the third floor."

"Maybe I'll just go across the street and get a drink."

"Now I really like you," Sue said. "You'll find it. Down, around and up."

"See *you* around," the woman said and patted Jesse before she continued down the hall.

"I think she likes you, Jesse," they said in unison.

A cluster of greasers with slicked-back hair, cut-off shirt sleeves and leather vests watched Sue approach. One of them whistled. "Track III parents," she said and opened the door. "Let's go, boys. And don't ask me for the bathroom pass!"

Homeroom was a mini version of the regular day with the Pledge and the National Anthem followed by announcements. Mr. Baltz appealed to them to pass the school budget at the next vote. A breathless Mr. Lewis tried to explain the abbreviated schedule. The bell ending Homeroom rang in the middle of Mr. Giovanni's attempt at clarifying Mr. Lewis's announcement and the parents filed like cattle into the halls to face the remaining eight periods.

* * *

Jesse stood in the hall before his first-period class trying not to sweat or look nervous. He gave directions to lost parents and realized he had become familiar with the school. It gave him a modicum of confidence.

"Found it," the blonde in the miniskirt said when she passed him. "What are you doing later?"

"I, er, um...." he stammered, all his confidence gone.

She winked and continued to the end of the hall, waved and blew him a kiss before she disappeared.

The seats were almost full inside his classroom. He scanned the faces, trying to match parents to their kids. In the back, Jesse was positive, a Loomis occupied Virgil's seat. He had the same hair, wire frame glasses with dark tinted lenses, but he looked too young to be Virgil Loomis's father. Jesse stared and realized it *was* Virgil who looked over the top of his dark glasses and nodded. Jesse didn't understand why Virgil was there, but felt somehow relieved that he was. Except for the scowling man who never blinked, next to Virgil, the other parents paid close attention. He gave them an overview of the class, his homework policy and testing. When he heard himself he sounded like he knew what he was saying. And his timing was perfect. He asked, "Are there any questions?" as the bell rang ending first period.

Most of the parents hurried out the door to get to their next class on time, a few hung back to thank him. The scowler came directly at him and for a second Jesse thought about running.

"Frank Reardon," he said. "Gruber's parole officer." He never took his eyes from Jesse, measuring him. "Problems?"

Jesse didn't recall a Gruber in his classes, but he didn't want to get the man angry. "No," he said quickly. "No problems."

"Call me if he gives you any," he handed Jesse his card, "and I'll beat his heart in!"

Virgil came up to the front. "You did okay, Mr. Teeg, for your first time. The verdict was favorable. Three women thought you were cute. One thought you were too young to be a teacher. The lady in the front said you looked just like her nephew. But the guy who just left didn't like your tie. He said that only fairies wear flower ties."

Jesse looked at his tie he had worn special. "What are you doing here tonight, Virgil?"

"It's Thursday night and my parents have their group therapy session. So I thought I'd drop by." He sat on Jesse's desk. "If you don't mind a critique? You talked a little fast and your eye contact was weak in the beginning. But you got better as you relaxed. And you stopped sweating too."

"Well, thank you for calling it to my attention, Virgil."

"Just trying to help. Do you know what TM is, Mr. Teeg?"

"When you clench your teeth so tight at night that your jaw hurts. Jesus, am I doing that too?" He opened and closed his mouth and felt his jaw muscles.

"That's TMJ," he said. "I mean Transcendental Meditation. It's a way to find your center and relax. You should consider trying it. Meditation could make you a different person, even just ten or fifteen minutes. I meditate an hour a day every day."

"You did say *meditate,* just to be clear?"

He grinned. "Some incense, my headphones and Ravi Shankar playing the sitar. I'll make you a tape."

"What could anyone possibly meditate about for an hour?"

"I just focus on my breathing until it becomes automatic. Then I start seeing things. Making connections. Time and space. Past, present and future. Einstein said time is relative and it *is*. Everything is connected and everything is the same. Like the end of the movie *2001* when the astronaut is a fetus and an old man at the same time. Life and death. A return to the womb. While I was in a deep meditative state and saw everything so clearly I got the idea for the room filled with green Jello." He looked at Jesse. "One time I even saw God."

"You saw God?"

"Only once and only after I had forgotten the names of everything I knew and all words were erased from my memory and my body started to vibrate."

"Maybe the music was too loud."

"Seriously, Mr. Teeg, my body pulsated with a three-beat rhythm and my body *became* that three-beat sound. It filled me completely. Three beats. Life and energy and everything became clear and I knew what it was, the meaning of life, but I didn't know what to call it. I saw all of mankind in a line from the beginning through now to me and into eternity. And all of it was moved by the same three beats that formed into a word. One single word. But that word was something I couldn't say because it was something sacred. Something unsayable, you know?" Jesse looked at him. "And then I realized that the sacred Word *was* God, just like the Bible says, 'In the beginning was the Word, and the Word was with God, and *the Word was God*.' But still I didn't dare say it. Not then, anyway." He took a deep breath. "Did you know, Mr. Teeg, that Jews aren't supposed to say the name of God? They aren't even supposed to write g-o-d? So they put a dash in the middle." He took a deep breath. "Anyway, in that one instant I understood it all. Creation. Life. Death. The Buddhists say they can send their mind out of their body. Astral travel. The idea is that if they time it right they can switch bodies just before their soul recycles and they can live somebody else's life. Live forever. I'm still working on it."

"But what about the word you didn't say."

"Frumily?"

"Frumily? What's frumily? *Frumily* is God's name?"

"Not God's name. Frumily *is* God."

"Frumily is God?"

"Well, not any more. Frumily *was* God. But the instant I said it the word lost its power. Frumily was my God. But you'll have to do your homework to find your own God. Everybody does." He stopped "Don't you have another class, Mr. Teeg?"

Jesse closed his mouth and looked at his watch. "Oh, shit."

"I'm heading down to the cafeteria. AV is doing a multimedia presentation during the lunch periods and I want to get there early to see it." He turned when he reached the door. "For the record, Mr. Teeg, I *like* your tie."

* * *

Mr. Baltz was in his office across from Dr. Flackett and Mr. Adornau. When the School Board president took a small cigar from his pocket, the principal was on his feet and around the desk fumbling with his Zippo to light it.

"Thank you, Seymour." He blew a perfect ring that passed over the principal's head like a halo. "What's this that Don tells me about some money for a toilet and some computer thing?"

"A few thousand."

"Eight thousand," Dr. Flackett said.

"We're on austerity. And didn't we just put in your new cesspools, Don? Aren't there enough toilets in this place already. And who's ever going to use a computer?"

"We can always scale back the computers to save some money. And those are student and faculty facilities, Lalo. This is for an *executive* toilet." He nodded to his AP sitting in the corner, quietly following the dynamics of the meeting. "The plans, Mario. I took the liberty of having the plans drawn up by Trey Brinker to expedite matters when it's approved." He laid out the completed blueprints on the desk.

"That was rather presumptuous," Mr. Adornau said, flexing his political muscle. "You mean *if* it's approved. Eight large is a lot of money for one toilet. I just had my bathroom at home done for five and it has Italian marble and a sunken Jacuzzi!"

He was prepared. "Then we can cut some more expenses," he opened the door, "and put it in here and save on new construction." They sniffed the heavy smell of pine that filled the office. "Moths. I'm fumigating," he explained. "The closet *is* small but a half bath would fit–a sink, toilet, a small stall shower. I don't need a sunken Jacuzzi," he joked. "Mario's brother-in-law works for a licensed plumber. He's willing to rough out the pipes on his own time for practically nothing and he knows somebody who knows somebody who can get the fixtures way under cost. And Stash's crew will do the finish work and be happy to make some extra cash. So the whole thing will come in around three thousand." He gestured vaguely "If you ask for seven and get six you can return two when the job is done under budget and look good. That leaves a thousand for, er, computers or anything else you think may be needed." Mr. Adornau sat back and puffed his little cigar. "For a fee, Ollie Nessmith will even say I have a medical condition that makes the installation a necessary expense. You know how it is, at my age it's a long run up to the third floor. And you can write the whole thing off as a medical expenditure and save the District more money. It will look great in the year-end budget report."

"How will it look if you get money for your toilet while we don't have toilet paper for their kids?" Dr. Flackett broke his silence, pleased by the annoyance on the principal's face. "The taxpayers will be outraged when they hear and vote the Board out of office."

"The taxpayers won't find out, Don," Mr. Adornau said. "We'll divert the funds from Emergency Educational Expenses in a closed session. Let's keep the figure at the original eight thousand, just to be sure there's enough. In the end *everybody* walks away happy with a few bucks in their pocket." He stubbed out his cigar in the mouth of the shrunken head ashtray.

"Thank you, Lalo. Mario will call his brother-in-law to get the ball rolling as soon as you release the money. And I'll tell Polakas to get his boys ready. I'd like to get everything done before the New Year." He came around his desk without looking at the superintendent and put his arm around the Board president. "Now let's have some fun watching the parents try to get from class to class."

Mr. Giovanni held the door open for them and they stepped into the Main Office with Dr. Flackett tagging behind.

"From everything I've seen here, Seymour, you run a tight ship."

175

"It's all a matter of control. This year we have fewer kids in the halls because we cut the time between classes to three and a half minutes."

"I do indeed like what I see. Miss Lind." He winked at her when he passed her desk.

"Ms."

When the elevator door opened on the third floor, Terry was coming out of the faculty bathroom. "Good evening, gentlemen." He flashed a peace sign.

"You know Mr. Scapelli," Mr. Baltz said with a forced smile. "He's a senior member of our English Department."

Mr. Adornau narrowed his eyes. "You always dress like that?"

"Of course not. Working without a contract and with the salaries in this district, I can't afford to dress up like this every day. These are my special for Parent's Night clothes."

Mr. Baltz looked at his watch. "Isn't it almost time for the bell, Mr. Scapelli? Don't you have a class next period? You don't want to keep the parents waiting."

"Oh, that's all right, Mr. Baltz. I'm wearing sneakers." He showed them his feet. "With brand new laces, soI can make it to any part of the building in under three minutes."

Mr. Baltz smoothed his mustache nervously and took the Board president by the arm as the bell rang. "Let me show you the Library."

"Peace." Terry held up two fingers.

"The new media section in the Library is very popular with the students. There's always a full house." Baltz moved them down the hall.

"You let him teach looking like that?" Mr. Adornau said.

"He has tenure. When they get tenure, it's almost impossible to get rid of them, though God knows we've tried."

* * *

Jesse was exhausted by the time the last bell rang and the last parent finally left his classroom. He had arranged with his Aunt Dimmy to sleep over so he didn't have to make the long drive home and back again in the early morning.

"Hey, Mr. Teeg, did you get down to the cafeteria for that presentation?" Virgil called

"I didn't have the time, Virgil."

"Too bad. You missed a great show, even better than the one they had planned. I'm sure you'll hear about it. See you in a few hours. I have to run. My ride is waiting."

While the others were fleeing the building into the drizzle, Jesse packed his attaché case and dragged himself to the third floor for a long overdue pee and maybe a soda. Sue Wellen was sitting by the window and looked up when he came into the Faculty Room.

"I see you survived," she said, checking her hair and her makeup in the reflection. "See, I told you it wouldn't be so bad."

"Barely." He took a deep breath. All the sodas were gone. He got a coffee instead. He watched a cup drop into the tray and fill halfway with something brown and half with something yellow. He poured it out in the sink and dropped onto the couch.

"So?"

"It's over," he said simply.

"Come out for a drink with Terry and me. I'm too wired to go straight home."

"My aunt is expecting me. But thanks for asking. How was your night?"

"As expected. Those greasers turned out to be in the wrong class. But one guy stayed and kept asking me for my phone number. When he followed me to the bathroom I told him to fuck off. But the rest of the night went okay." She looked at her face in her compact mirror, applied some lipstick and shut the case.

There were still a number of parents looking for the exits, but most of the teachers were gone.

"I left plans on my desk," Terry said when he met them in the office. "The day after Parent's Night is always a 'mental health' day to make up for the anguish and the extra hours I put in without getting overtime." He punched out. "You heard about the screwup in the cafeteria? Somebody put in the wrong tape and AV showed a porn video instead of the planned presentation!"

"No!" Sue said.

"Virgil told me. He was there. Said it took a minute before anyone realized what they were watching. Nobody knew how to turn the thing off so Dexter literally pulled the plug. Baltz had a shit fit when he got to the cafeteria, but everything was taken down by then."

When they got outside, Virgil was talking to the blond woman in the miniskirt. He ran over to them. "I can't talk now. I'm getting a lift home."

"Really?" Sue said. "She's old enough to be your mother, Virgil."

"My older sister, anyway. I met her in the cafeteria. Her daughter Nancy is in the junior high and she's having trouble with algebra. She asked me if I would tutor her. She thinks I'm a student teacher. And she said I could drive her Karmann Ghia. It's a four-speed stick!"

"You can't do that Virgil. You don't know how to drive. You don't have a license. And you're too young!" she persisted.

"I have my learner's permit." He waved to the woman when she honked the horn.

"Come on, Virgil," she called. "We have miles to go before we sleep."

"I'll be right there, Mrs. Robinson."

"Mrs. *Robinson*? You gotta be kidding me! And she's literary too, paraphrasing Frost. I'm impressed," Terry said.

"I gotta run. I may be a little late for first period, Mr. Teeg, if I come in." He trotted to the car and slipped into the driver's seat.

"Poor Virgil. I sure hope he knows what he's getting himself into," Sue said.

"Poor Virgil? I'm thinking more poor Harry Dexter!" He looked at Jesse, watching wistfully as the the car lurched and bucked out of the parking lot. "And poor Jesse. In the words of poet John Greenleaf Whittier, 'For all sad words of tongue and pen, the saddest are these, *It might have been.*'"

By ten fifteen the building was completely empty, except for Eddie, the tattooed night custodian, who materialized from somewhere in the sub-basement. He only had a few hours to get the floors swept, the desks realigned and the building ready for the morning's onslaught. The sound of Iron Butterfly cranked out from the boom box on his cart and filled the halls. "In-a-gadda-da-vida honey, Don't cha know that I love you? In-a-gadda-da-vida baby, Don't cha know that I'll always be true?" sounded the end of Parent's Night.

143

Harry Dexter didn't sleep the entire night in anticipation of the preschool confrontation he had to face.

"What's the worst thing he can do to you? You're related. He can't kill you," his wife said.

"Obviously you don't know what my uncle is capable of. Let's just say I've seen him at his worst. Even if I have to grovel–" His voice trailed off.

"You have tenure. Even if you lose the AV job, you can still go back into the classroom, can't you? And in ten years you're eligible to retire."

He shuddered. "I could never do that again, Shirley. Spend even a year with those kids. They hung me out the window! It would kill me! It almost did!"

And so the night went until a dreary Friday morning dawned.

Baltz's Buick was in the reserved space in the courtyard so he knew it was useless to hope his uncle was lying dead somewhere on the side of the road. Still he played with the fantasy while he stood in front of the closed door of the Principal's Office. His hands were sweating, so he wiped them on his pants and he knocked softly. There was no response. He gathered all the courage he had and knocked again, harder.

"Come in!"

He touched the brass doorknob with one finger, half expecting to get electrocuted. Don Cooley's face flashed before his eyes and he shivered. When nothing happened he palmed the knob and turned it slowly. He pushed the heavy door open, but didn't step in immediately, waiting for something heavy to fall on his head, a booby trap, an ax to swing like a pendulum from an overhead wire into his face, the floor to open beneath him and drop his body past the secret fortress of the Custodial Corps and into the bottomless pit below. But nothing happened.

"I said come in, Harry." He sounded calm, standing with his back to the door, hunched over his putter.

Dexter paused when he heard his first name. It was something his uncle only did around the dinner table during the High Holidays or when he needed a favor. This confused him. He stepped inside and even peeked behind the door in case Mario Giovanni was hiding there with a garrote. Nothing.

"Please shut the door, Harry." His voice was almost a whisper. He took several short practice putts over the golf balls that were lined up on the rug at his feet.

"Mr. Baltz–" he started, apologetically "Uncle Seymour," he began again. "you are my godfather. The patriarch of the family. My mother's only brother. You know that I would never willfully do something to compromise you–"

"Sit down Harry," he interrupted without turning around. The words were even and calm.

Dexter strained for any signs of tension. Perhaps all of the therapy, the stress and anger management programs had finally helped his uncle. And maybe, as unlikely as it was, he had even come to see some humor in the previous night's event. And then it happened. The principal tightened his grip on the putter and swung hard. The three balls exploded off the club, bounding to different parts of the office, One ricocheted off the wall and caught Dexter over his eye. Baltz turned, holding the putter upright like a weapon. The tension on his face stretched his mustache like a caterpillar above his teeth. He swung the club over his head in lethal circles like a Scottish claymore. The air whistled.

Dexter stopped rubbing what he knew would become a welt later in the day and froze like a mouse caught out in the open. "Really, Uncle Seymour," he said in a rush of words, "I don't know how–"

"A fuck film with a special message that it was being presented with my cooperation and support. To parents! On Parent's Night!" His hands tightened around the grip of the club until his knuckles turned white. He brought it up above his shoulder and managed only with great effort not to bring it crashing down on Dexter's skull. He could never explain it to the police. The muscles in his right cheek began to twitch,

181

giving his mustache a life of its own. "You bastard, you can be easily replaced. For two hundred and fifty dollars, Mario assures me, two broken legs can have you gone on disability. For two hundred fifty more you can disappear."

"But I–"

"The Superintendent of Schools, that incompetent asshole, was standing there. The president of the School Board. For two months I've been kissing his fascist anti-Semite ass!"

He lowered the putter and Dexter looked up through his hands protecting his head thinking that the worst danger had passed. But suddenly, in an about-face, Baltz lunged at him from the side. He grabbed him around his throat, knocking the chair off its legs, and held Dexter suspended in the air, his face turning from red to purple as the fingers tightened around the Adam's apple.

"I owe my sister nothing, you fuck! My obligation is done. Do you have any idea what your fiasco will cost me?"

"You're... choking me... Uncle Seymour..." he stammered with great difficulty, trying to break the hold with his hands. But his words had no effect and he felt himself blacking out.

The office door burst open and Willy Zwill stuck his head into the room, freezing them in a grotesque tableau. "Oh," the assistant principal said. "I didn't know you were here. I was on my early morning rounds and I heard some noise. But I see you're busy. Sorry to interrupt." He twitched, backed out and closed the door.

Mr. Baltz exhaled and loosened his grip. His breathing returned to normal. The crisis had passed. "I'll be all right," he said to Dexter who was feeling the indentations on his throat. "I'm okay now." He composed himself and straightened his tie and his jacket.

"You... almost... strangled me to death," he said in a high Mickey Mouse voice.

"Pick up the chair, Harry." He was back behind his desk and pulled a cigarette from the pack and lit it.

Dexter cleared his throat and sat. "I swear to you it wasn't me or anyone from the Squad. I questioned every one of them. Somebody deliberately sabotaged the program. Someone out to humiliate you, me, AV. It was well coordinated so it may involve several students." His voice was returning close to the normal range.

"A student conspiracy?"

"I've kept pretty extensive dossiers. People here now. Graduates with grudges. It'll take time, but I will review *all* the student records. And then disgruntled teachers who didn't get equipment. That may take even longer."

Mr. Baltz sat back in his chair. "You do that while I try to mend fences with Adornau and Flackett. That just leaves your expense in the matter." He did some mental calculations. "Five hundred should help put things right again."

Dexter swallowed hard. "Dollars?" It was a lot of money, but worth it not to have his legs broken or getting disappeared. "I don't have that kind of money lying around and I don't want to involve Shirley in any of this. Can I do it in installments?"

"I'm a reasonable man. You can spread out the payments. Fifty cash the beginning of the month until the end of the school year. That comes to"–he did some more calculating–"four hundred and a balloon payment for the balance the end of June." He smoothed his mustache with his thumb and index finger. "Starting with today's paycheck."

"You'll have to wait until I go out and cash my check at lunch. But I can give you twenty now." He reached into his wallet. He handed over the bill. "Do you think you could give me a receipt?"

"Get out of my office," he ordered. "Consider yourself lucky you're still able to walk. And make sure you're back after lunch with the rest."

When Dexter was gone he pocketed the money and pondered a new conspiracy theory. He hadn't considered the possibility that it might involve students and teachers. He pulled a large accordion folder from his desk drawer. It was a suspect list containing the names of teachers who had filed an official grievance in the past five years, those who were vocal opponents at faculty meetings, teachers with complaints about schedules, class assignments, duties, and anyone with a personal ax to grind. Terry Scapelli's name appeared in every category. His dress, irreverent attitude, the smart-ass way he always stuck his face into the Main Office with that shit-eating grin infuriated the principal and made him first among the usual suspects. He thumbed through the files on Dexter, Flackett, Adornau and twenty-two other people. The one marked "Scapelli" was the thickest. It was full of anonymous faded, typed and hand-printed dittos he had collected over the years that had been posted on bulletin boards, subversive messages that were in teacher mailboxes. Some had even come addressed to his office via inter-school mail, always in a new brown manila envelope without a trail of names that could be traced. The satirical messages, bogus memos and off-color cartoons lacked any means of identification, but he had compiled them all, along with anything else he hoped might one day implicate Scapelli in "conduct unbecoming a teacher" to be used against him in any future 30-20A tenure hearing.

When he was finished with that, he opened his desk drawer and turned off the voice-activated audio tape recorder. He had bought it in his local Radio Shack to record secretly everything that went on in his office, another way of keeping an ongoing and accurate history of things. Not even Mario Giovanni had a clue that everything he'd said since the beginning of the school year was on the record. He rewound the tape and played the Dexter episode until he came to the part about money. Then he carefully erased that portion of the tape.

Camelot

Official Publication of the Partnership of Parents and Teachers
in Association for better Farmington Public Schools
Harriet Stegle, President P-PTA
Vol. 2 Issue 2   November 1971

It's hard to believe that October is gone so soon and Fall is in the air. The leaves have turned, so can the holiday season be far behind?

Out of the Mouth of Babes: Cliff Beiner is the franchise owner and manager of the new Dunkin' Donuts that recently opened to rave reviews at 215 Jerusalem Avenue in good old Farmington directly across from Wicks Mortuary and Dick's Sporting Goods. Well, Dunkin' Donuts sponsored a poetry contest for all the Farmington grammar school students. The topic? Appropriately "The Changing Seasons"! And the winner is (drum roll please) West Street Elementary School's 4th Grader Alicia Gretes, who said it best in this cute little ditty she composed and recited at her school's assembly.

> When the weather's hot and sticky
> That's not the time for Dunkin' Dickie.
> But when the frost is on the pumpkin,
> That's the time for Dickie Dunkin'.

For her efforts, owner manager Beiner presented the lucky Alecia with a $25 in-store only gift certificate that will buy a lot of donuts for her to dunk! Way to go, Alicia!

NEWS AND VIEWS: Since the last budget vote was the *last* budget vote and it went down in defeat, it looks like another full year on austerity! But be of good cheer. Not reaching a contract settlement with the teachers means money that would have been spent on their salary raises and fringe benefits has been diverted by President Adornau and the School Board to the Emergency Educational Expenses Fund to pay for emergency expenses that crop up in this austerity year! Way to go, Lalo, always looking to save Farmington's taxpayers money.

Remember November! That's the slogan of the month. Be sure to place your P-PTA Florida orange and grapefruit orders. They'll make the perfect Christmas/Chanukah gift! Mark it on your calendar.

Coming Soon! You can look forward to the Annual Cookie and Cake Sale, the House Plant Extravaganza and the Magazine Subscription Drive all coming in the New Year.

See you next time with more news from the trenches!

FT Ass.
"The bargaining agent with foreign appeal."

FROM: Joel Maxwell, President FT Ass.
TO: ALL Farmington Teachers
Re: The Numbers Don't Lie

Fifty-four percent of all the teachers in the Foreign Language Department prefer the Farmington Teachers' Ass. Ooo La La! Wouldn't you? We must be doing something right! See your building representative and join today!

FU - 2
Farmington Union, Local # 2
"When we all stand together no one stands alone."

Fed up? Tired of empty words? Inaction? Angry you're still working without a contract? Ready and willing to do what MUST be done to get a contract? Then say in one loud voice in good old plain English that can not be ignored–FU-2!

Dwayne Purvey, FU-2 President

Joseph E. Scalia

Rosencrantz and Guildenstern
Memorial High School
UFSD 71
Farmington, New York

TO: All Teachers and Staff
FROM: M. Seymour Baltz, Principal
SUBJECT: Parent's Night

To paraphrase Erasmus *(Bartlett's Familiar Quotations)*, "Give knowledge and the darkness will disappear of itself."

That is what some of you did capably and professionally at last week's Parent's Night. As I passed through the building I couldn't help overhearing all the parent comments and compliments when they had their eyes opened to what we are doing here at R&G.

Congratulations on another successful Parent's Night. Good job well done.

Rosencrantz and Guildenstern
Memorial High School
AV/CM Department

To: All Teachers
From: Harry Dexter, Coordinator AV/CM Department

Please read carefully this "New Policy Procedure Addenda and Clarification" and attach it to last week's "New Policy Procedure Regarding the Use of AV/CM Equipment" for easy future reference. It represents a further modification to the recently modified and soon to be implemented policy regarding the use of AV/CM equipment that will take effect next week when the AV/CM Center reopens for business. It will remain in effect until further notice, or until the end of the school year.

Effective immediately there is a one-dollar nonrefundable expediting surcharge payable in advance on *all* AV/CM equipment. Separate fees apply to each requisition form and will expedite equipment requested. No bulk requisitions will be accepted.

Teachers who use AV/CM equipment for a number of days will be charged an overnight storage fee of twenty-five cents for each night the equipment is held over.

MESSAGE FROM THE UNDERGROUND!
STILL NO CONTRACT!
AND THE FUTURE LOOKS GRIMMER...
HERE ARE SOME PRACTICAL THINGS THAT <u>YOU</u> CAN DO TO HELP SPEED UP THE PROCESS OF NEGOTIATIONS!

Since teachers don't deal with garbage collection, the production of useful goods and products or anything practical, there is no way to measure what we do. We deal in the realm of the intellect, the odyssey of the mind. Our brains are our only stock in trade. So...

1. DON'T THINK AS MUCH. MAINTAIN AN IDLE MIND FOR LONGER AND LONGER PERIODS OF TIME IN THE CLASSROOM THROUGHOUT THE DAY, THEREBY WITHHOLDING VALUABLE INTELLECTUAL RESOURCES.

2. FILL YOUR LESSONS WITH MORE AND MORE "**UMs**," "**ERs**"AND "**AHs**." DEVELOP A **STUTTER**. THESE SIMPLE STEPS WILL EFFECTIVELY FURTHER REDUCE THE AMOUNT OF ACTUAL INSTRUCTION TIME IN A 43-MINUTE PERIOD BY AS MUCH AS 18 MINUTES. THIS WILL ADD UP OVER THE COURSE OF THE YEAR.

3. IT'S A SCIENTIFIC FACT THAT **ALCOHOL DESTROYS BRAIN CELLS**. BY SIMPLY CONSUMING JUST **TWO DRINKS** OF SCOTCH, VODKA OR BEER EACH AFTERNOON AFTER SCHOOL WE CAN **REDUCE THE COLLECTIVE INTELLIGENCE OF THE STAFF BY 15 TO 20 I.Q. POINTS**, THEREBY MAKING THE FACULTY DUMBER. THREATENING TO DRINK OURSELVES INTO TOTAL IGNORANCE CAN BE A MOST EFFECTIVE TACTIC IN CONTRACT NEGOTIATIONS WITH THE SCHOOL BOARD.

LOWERING TEACHER EFFECTIVENESS WILL LESSEN STUDENT PERFORMANCE ON STANDARDIZED AND REGENTS EXAMS, DRASTICALLY REDUCE THE NUMBER OF GRADUATING SENIORS ACCEPTED BY GOOD COLLEGES AND THE NUMBER OF THOSE WHO WILL RECEIVE COLLEGE SCHOLARSHIPS.

4.   TEACH **WRONG INFORMATION**. START SLOWLY AT FIRST BY MAKING LITTLE MISTAKES, THEN GRADUALLY INCREASE THE VOLUME OF ERRONEOUS MATERIAL INTRODUCED INTO YOUR LESSONS. MATH TEACHERS MIGHT BEGIN BY STATING THAT **X ALWAYS EQUALS 7**. ENGLISH TEACHERS SHOULD MISSPELL WORDS (E.G., **FARM IS SPELLED E-I-E-I-O**). SOCIAL STUDIES TEACHERS TEACH ABOUT THE **WAR OF 1813**. SCIENCE TEACHERS CONSIDER TELLING STUDENTS THAT IT IS PERFECTLY SAFE TO **MIX AMMONIA AND CHLORINE BLEACH** WHEN CLEANING THE TOILET. OTHER DISCIPLINE AREAS SHOULD BE CREATIVE IN THEIR APPROACH **(BUT DON'T BE TOO CREATIVE, REMEMBER WE ARE WORKING WITHOUT A CONTRACT)**.

5.   GIVE MORE **WRONG ANSWERS** TO STUDENT QUESTIONS. WHAT WAS GEORGE WASHINGTON'S LAST NAME? **DC.** WHO WAS ANONYMOUS? **A FAMOUS GREEK WRITER AND THE AUTHOR OF COUNTLESS POEMS AND OTHER LITERARY WORKS**. WHO WAS GRANDMA MOSES? SHE WAS **MOSES' GRANDMA**.

Joseph E. Scalia

IF WE <u>ALL</u> WORK TOGETHER AND NOT WORK AS MUCH, WE CAN ACHIEVE OUR COMMON GOAL–A CONTRACT IN THIS LIFETIME!

"Why doesn't Shakespeare just speak English?" one boy called out from his seat. "Or why doesn't somebody translate it into English?"

The class was barely into *Romeo and Juliet*. After a week of cajoling, Jesse had finally convinced them that they *would* understand the play and maybe actually *like* it. "Shakespeare *did* speak the English of his time, but he wrote poetry. And translating it into regular English, as you say, would destroy the poetry. Nobody walked around the streets of Elizabethan England talking like Shakespeare wrote. Of course they used the words of their time like *'thou'* and *'thine,'* which were singular pronouns"–he held up one finger–"for *'you'* and *'yours.'* We use *'you'* for one or more than one person. But nobody walked around speaking in iambic pentameter."

"Huh?"

"That's a poetic rhythm. Ten syllables. Five unaccented alternating with five accented syllables." He picked a line from the play. "Listen and you'll hear it. You can count them on your fingers. 'But *soft* what *light* through *yon*der *win*dow *breaks*?'" He repeated as they counted. "But Shakespeare wasn't perfect and not every line has ten syllables. The next line has eleven. 'It *is* the *east,* and *Ju*liet is the *sun*.' Unless you pronounce her name Jul*yet*." He repeated the line. "The rhythm is a bit off too, but you get the idea. Whenever he needed an extra syllable he added an accent mark on the e and made *'blessed'* into 'bless*éd*.' If he needed fewer syllables he contracted words and it becomes *'blest.' 'Over'* becomes *'o'er.'*"

"Neat. That's why his spelling is so messed up."

"Yes. It's no mystery. So I'll tell you what we are going to do. Before we read each scene I'll outline it so you know what it's about. I'll translate the hard words while we're reading it. And after we've read it we'll discuss what we read. And after all that if you're still confused just ask me to stop and explain and I will. And one other thing, when you read it, don't stop at the end of a line unless there's a comma or a period. You'll be tempted, but read it right through. It will sound better and make more sense. When we finish reading the play," he had promised, "I'll show you the Zeffirelli *Romeo and Juliet* that came out a few years ago."

The first day he assigned them parts, little ones to the reluctant and shy kids, a line or two, bigger parts for anyone who wanted one. And he moved the desks and set up the front of the classroom like a stage so they could see what was going on. It was slow going at first, but he had brought them successfully through the first act and they were asking for parts.

Now he had them poised around the balcony in Act II, scene 2, and he had them in the palm of his hand. "This is the most famous scene in the play. So if you don't mind I'd like to be Romeo."

"How come you always get the good parts, Mr, Teeg?" Virgil asked.

"Well, Virgil, partly because I'm a ham and partly because you wouldn't know they were good parts if I didn't read them!" They laughed. "But if you would like the part be my guest."

Virgil looked over the the lines that ran on for pages. "On second thought, you can have it, Mr. Teeg."

"Who would would like to be my Juliet?"

Audrey the red-haired girl in the second row, whose face turned the color of her hair whenever he called on her, who sighed every time Jesse looked at her, who hardly said anything in class and always waited in the hall after class to watch him pass, raised her hand tentatively.

"Audrey, you will be my Juliet." He smiled. "So let's recap. Romeo is moping around because Rosaline doesn't love him. When he learns she was invited to the big masquerade party at the Capulets, his family's sworn enemy, he crashes it with some friends and falls in love at first sight with Juliet, the young daughter of Capulet. At the end of the evening he ditches his friends, doubles back to Juliet's garden and sees her on the balcony. She's not aware he's below her window when she begins talking about her feelings for him. Got it?" They nodded. He cleared his throat and began the scene. "'She speaks, yet she says nothing. What of that? Her eye discourses. I will answer it.' Ten syllables," he pointed out and moved closer to Juliet, seated on top of his desk for height. "'I am too bold. 'Tis not to me she speaks,'" he whispered.

"'O Romeo, Romeo, wherefore art thou Romeo?'" she read on cue, delivering the words like a young teenage girl in love. Her face was flushed and her voice trembled.

Jesse was impressed. "She's not asking *where* is Romeo, as you might think," he explained. "'Wherefore' means *why*. She's wants to know why is this person she loves a Montague, her family's sworn enemy. Her words surprise him. His next lines are a soliloquy and you know that means?"

"Spoken out loud to himself so the audience hears it," they recited.

Jesse nodded. "'Two of the fairest stars in all the heavens, having some business, do entreat her eyes to twinkle in *their* spheres till they return. What if her eyes were there.'" He raised his arm toward the clock on the back wall. He had seen the Zeffirelli film at least half a dozen times, had copied every detail of delivery, gestures, and he had fallen in love with Olivia Hussey's innocent Juliet. "'They in her head? The brightness of her cheek would shame those stars, as daylight doth a lamp; her eyes in heaven would through the airy region stream so bright that birds would sing and think it were not night. See how she leans her cheek upon her hand! O, that I were a glove upon that hand, that I might touch that cheek!'" He was standing so close to her and his voice lowered to a whisper. Juliet was breathing heavy.

"BUZZZZZZZZZZZZZZZZZZZZZ!" The sound from the PA, between sheet metal running through a power saw and the warning buzzer at a nuclear power plant meltdown, shattered the mood. Everyone jumped. Juliet looked terrified and Jesse dropped his book. "Buzzzzz! Buzzzzz! Buzzzzz!"

"What is that?"

"Bat Phone, Mr. Teeg! Commissioner Gordon."

"Where is it? How can I stop it?" He looked around. He didn't want to lose them. "Where?"

"In the little metal cabinet in the corner."

Jesse couldn't pull the door open.

"It's locked. Use your key."

"I don't have a key!" he said over the buzzer that refused to give up. He tried to pull it open.

Virgil trotted up the aisle fishing a small key from his pocket and unlocked the metal cabinet. Jesse pulled and the rusted hinges complained. Inside the metal door "Break Baltz!" was printed in red marker.

"What?" he said into the receiver, but the buzzing continued.

"Press the white button."

Jesse did. "Who *is* this?" the voice at the other end demanded.

"Who is *this*?" he asked. "You called me and interrupted–"

"I, auh, asked you first!" the voice countered. "Now, you, auh, tell me who this is!"

"Jesse, um, Mr. Tietjen."

"Well, Mr. Tietjen, there, auh, is a student hanging outside from your, auh, window!"

"No there isn't."

"Auh, Yes, there is. A student is hanging from your, auh, window!" he repeated.

"I think you are mistaken, Mr. Lewis," Jesse said. "I just looked and nobody's hanging from my window."

"Mr. Tietjen," he said again emphatically, "He's not just hanging, he's, auh, swinging from your window. I, auh, can see him in the courtyard from my, auh, office. I am watching him now."

"My classroom isn't on the courtyard, Mr. Lewis. You must be looking at the wrong room."

"I see him," he insisted. "He's swinging back and forth with one, auh, hand now."

"My room is not on the courtyard side." He opened the door to check the number. "Room 234 is on the street side of the building. And there is no one swinging outside any of my windows. I am looking now."

"You're, auh, positive?"

"Definitely. Room 234."

"Then what room is he, auh, hanging from?"

"I don't know. I'm on the *opposite side* of the building trying to get through the balcony scene of *Romeo and Juliet–*"

"You have a balcony? What's the, auh, number of the room across the hall from you?"

"I'm not sure. Either 235 or 303." He still hadn't figured out building layout, except for his own classrooms.

There was a pause.

"Well, auh, it doesn't matter now. He just fell." He paused. "Be sure you stop by the Nurse's Office today. You have to fill out an accident report and I have to, auh, call an ambulance." Click.

Jesse replaced the phone and closed the cabinet. The class waited. "I can't begin to explain." He picked up the book from the desk and opened to the page where they'd left off.

"'O Romeo, Romeo! Wherefore art thou, Romeo?'" the red-haired Juliet continued, her voice filled with emotion. "'Deny thy father and refuse thy name. Or if thou wilt not, be but sworn my love,'" her voice caught at the word, "'and I'll no longer be a Capulet.'"

The buzzer sounded in a classroom somewhere across the hall.

Friday was a perfect mid-November morning. The summer heat was a distant memory replaced by the invigorating crisp and clear autumn air. Christmas was on the horizon and Thanksgiving was only a week away. But Willy Zwill didn't notice any of that. He was focused on one thing, fortifying his office. He had spent the previous week gathering everything together and he slept in his office Wednesday night to be in place Veteran's Day morning when the building was closed. That way he could work without raising suspicions and without interruption. It had taken him most of the early hours to unroll the sheet metal and attach it to the walls. Even with the new heavy-duty hinges, the reinforced door opened and closed with some difficulty. He tightened the chicken wire across the window and covered it with new blackout curtains. The rest of the Veteran's Day, he painted the entire office so his modifications wouldn't be easily detected. The little refrigerator liberated from Home Ec was stocked and now his office was an almost impregnable fortress.

There were some unforeseen problems. The extra layer of insulation made the room unbearably hot, and because of the modifications to the window he wasn't able to open it. His requisition for an air conditioner was rejected by Buildings and Grounds because of austerity. So whenever he was in his office he changed into a pair of shorts and a camouflage shirt reminiscent of POW camp days. Whenever he left the sanctuary he changed back into his civilian clothes and stowed his warm weather gear in the closet with the yellow Civil Defense helmet and bullhorn with a strap he attached to his wrist during state-mandated air raid drills and emergency evacuation exercises. Baltz had made him the building CD warden.

He opened his office door as far as it went and peeked through the crack into the Administrative Alcove. It was empty. He undid the chain. The other AP doors were shut and there was no sound except for the secretaries pounding away on their typewriters. He shut the door and it locked. When he had time he would replace the school lock with a new one that had a dead bolt. He patted his jacket pocket for the pliers and screwdriver he would need on this foray. The first rule of survival was be prepared to take advantage of unexpected opportunities. On a recent building patrol he had discovered exactly what he wanted and he planned to liberate it now with extreme prejudice.

He took the long way around the building to the student cafeteria and smelled the boiled franks and burned beans up on the third floor. Only the spaghetti and vomit cheese that was always on the Thursday menu smelled worse. From outside the cafeteria he watched the noisy students lining up to be served. Their sterilized metal trays were still hot from the boiling water and their ice cream melted over the edge of the dessert compartment into the main course. He stepped over the debris, the paper and food stuff that always littered the cafeteria floor. He moved undetected through the kitchen food preparation and storage area until he reached the door marked "Private."

He waited, watching the backs of the serving women too busy scooping franks and beans and yelling at the kids to notice him. He picked up an industrial size can opener from the counter and stuck it in his pocket, a bonus. Emilio, the dishwasher with the gold tooth, was enveloped in a cloud of steam, obliviously scrubbing and scraping the large pots with burned-on beans. His music was so loud Zwill heard it from his earphones. Emilio had been demoted to washing because of the obscene kissing noises he made at all the girls whenever they passed him on the serving line.

Zwill slipped into the corner of the food manager's empty office and headed toward the electric motor sound of the large exhaust fan turning in the window. He opened a metal folding chair and set in front of the window, careful not to step on the back of the seat and collapse the chair when he climbed up. He pulled the screwdriver from his pocket to unscrew the four brackets holding the fan at each corner. He was stretching to reach the one that was furthest away.

"Hey, Mr. Z."

Joseph E. Scalia

"Christ, Loomis! You almost gave me a heart attack!" The AP's foot kicked back and the folding chair collapsed under him. The screwdriver clanged in the spinning fan, shot through the air and sank blade first into the wall. He grabbed for the fan cover and his clawing fingers caught in the grating for a moment until his added weight pulled away the two brackets still holding it in place. The spinning fan hung from the window and continued running, swinging erratically from side to side inches from his face.

Virgil put his lunch down on the table covered with a red checkered cloth and a burgundy rose bud in a vase. "Seriously, Mr. Z, shouldn't one of the custodians be doing that? And you really should unplug electric appliances before you poke them with a screwdriver while standing on a metal chair. You could electrocute yourself. Didn't one of the teachers electrocute himself a few years ago?" He wiped his mouth with a cloth napkin, got up and pulled the plug from the wall outlet. He helped Mr. Zwill to his feet.

"Thank you." He wiped his greasy hands on Virgil's napkin. "What are you doing here? Why aren't you out there eating with the rest of them?" He retrieved his screwdriver from the wall and went back to unscrewing the other brackets.

"I have an arrangement with the serving ladies. You expecting a heat wave? It's too late for Indian summer."

"A private administrative matter, Loomis. On a need-to-know basis. I need it and you don't need to know why." The second bracket was off and the fan came away from the window. He put the handle of the screwdriver in his mouth. "A little help here," he mumbled.

Virgil took one end and they rested the fan against the counter. Mr. Zwill looked around the kitchen very carefully. "This fan makes me completely independent now," he said cryptically

Virgil nodded his head. "You don't mind if I finish. The period will be over in a few minutes. Can I offer you something? Mr. Lewis loves the baked potatoes and sour cream. He hardly ever misses when he knows I'll be having them."

200

He shook his head. "I have stuff back in the office. Unless there are some canned goods you can spare?"

Virgil looked on the shelf and handed him a can of colossal black olives. "Take these. They don't serve olives anymore, or peas since last year's food fight."

Zwill checked the expiration date and dropped it into his jacket pocket. Then he swung around suddenly and looked behind him. Nobody was there. "Ever have that feeling of eyes boring into your back? Like somebody is watching you? Following you?" He wheeled around again.

"These *are* worrying times."

"Do you know something, Loomis? What have you seen? What have you heard? Strange things have been going on since the first day of school. And it's getting worse." He leaned in. "You're a student so you don't know the half of what goes on here. Undercurrents. Politics. Intrigue. You'd be surprised by some of the things going on in this building."

"Things?"

"Exactly. Things." He touched his finger on the side of his nose. "There are things I could tell you that would curl your hair." He looked at Virgil's curly hair. "There are things seething, fermenting under the calm surface. These are troubled times." Virgil took a forkful of twice-baked potato. "As someone very wise recently said, just because I'm paranoid doesn't mean they really aren't out to get me." He struggled to pick up the fan. "Did you know I spent three years in a Jap POW camp?"

"I might have heard. I'm sure it was a defining traumatic experience that's had a lasting effect on your grasp of reality."

He put the fan down again. "I don't know about that, but I *know* when I'm being followed. If you don't believe me, just tag along behind me and see for yourself."

"I have a class, Mr. Z, and an appointment with Mr. Aaron—" he hesitated. "And won't they miss that fan?"

"I'm an assistant principal. Rory Aaron is just a Guidance Counselor. If you watch my back I'll watch yours and write you a pass. As for the fan—I'm an assistant principal."

He gripped the fan in a bear hug and started for the door. "You just stay far enough behind me and you'll see. We'll take the long way back to my office."

"I'll be right behind you, Mr. Z," he called to the assistant principal. Virgil finished his tea, wiped his hands and his mouth and cleared his table. "Thank you, Mrs. Papadopoulos," he said to woman behind the counter. "I hope Diana feels better. I'll call Diana later with the work she missed. See you tomorrow."

* * *

Helen O'Dell walked around the counter in the Main Office toward Mr. Baltz's office. Her face was flushed with the exertion of hurrying down from the Third Floor Faculty Room. Phyllis Lind was repairing a broken nail with an emery board. "Is he in?"

"He said to hold his calls and not let anybody in for a quarter of an hour." She glanced at her wristwatch. "That was a half hour ago."

"New watch?"

"A Lady Bulova," she said, "from Mario to express his appreciation."

"The two of you went away for Veteran's Day? How'd it go?"

"Well enough." She wiggled her wrist. "Gold-filled and twenty-three jewels." She put down the emery board. "He should be finished by now with whatever he was doing. But I should warn you he's been more awful than usual this last week." She pressed the intercom button with her repaired nail. No response. She pressed it again and shrugged. "Looks like he's not answering. Unless he's dead." She pressed the button a third time and held it down.

"What!" he demanded a little out of breath. "I told you not to bother me. Have you no regard for my privacy?" Privacy was a major concern and when his office was remodeled he specifically had Stash Polakas remove the window with an unobstructed view of the secretaries in the Main Office. "Get rid of it. I don't like being on display like goddamn fish in a

Chinese restaurant." Following that he also had him install a door buzzer under his desk.

"That was thirty-five minutes ago! Helen's here and says she *has* to see you. So don't shoot the messenger!"

There was a pause. "Give me another minute." He was seated behind his desk with a folded copy of *Newsday* under his arm when he buzzed her in.

"It looks like the women have united! I just found this posted in a corner of the bulletin board upstairs." She unfolded the sheet of paper and placed it on his desk.

"'An open invitation to all fashion conscious women, faculty and staff. You are cordially invited to attend a tea this afternoon at dismissal in Home Ec Room 11B in the T-Wing. This social gathering of women only is to discuss today's trends in current fashion. Tea and cookies baked by the Home Ec classes will be served along with the lively conversation.'" He dropped the paper on his desk. "You interrupted me for this? A social tea? What do I care about an afternoon blab fest of women?"

"The meeting was yesterday! And it was about the pants suit thing again!"

"I thought you took care of that last month."

"Apparently not. I have it on good authority at yesterday's meeting they planned a show of strength next week."

"Next week? Next week is Thanksgiving."

"They took a head count of everyone who said they'll come in wearing pants. Teachers, secretaries, hall mothers. I found similar memos in different classroom waste baskets this morning and that one in the Faculty Room."

He lit a cigarette. "This was your project, Helen." He swiveled around in his chair. "We do have a dress code on the books–"

"They researched it. A dress code won't hold up legally. They have the case law. According to recent court decisions, it isn't legal."

"What about another more strongly worded memo? That should head them off. You know what a bunch of cows the women are."

"They agreed to ignore any memos. Strength in numbers. They figure you can't do anything if most of the women come in wearing pants."

He crushed out his cigarette and lit another one. "You really let this get away from you, Helen. So, what do you plan to do now?"

She shrugged. "Give in?"

"And lose face? It will look like I've been pressured, outwitted. And I will not have my authority as principal compromised by a bunch of PMSing women in pants. I wear the pants here!" He drummed his fingers on the desk. "I have an idea. Assuming you're right and the women won't scatter like a bunch of old hens and assuming they show up on Monday morning wearing pants, it's going to be *my* fucking idea!"

"I don't follow you, Chief."

He took the gold Cross pen from the desk set his wife bought him to celebrate Bernie Prahl's announcement that he had cancer and was retiring. He thought for a minute and scribbled a short paragraph on his memo pad and handed it to her. "Have one of the secretaries type it up. No, wait! You said there were secretaries at yesterday's meeting? So you type it up in your office and keep it to yourself. Then personally run off enough copies for the entire building and sit on them."

She looked at him. "Sit on them?"

He sighed. "Keep them under wraps until right after the dismissal bell. It's Friday, so the place will be a ghost town before the second bell. Then I want you to put a copy in everybody's mailbox. I'll compose another memo about building use and have Phyllis put that one out to prevent private meetings in the future–" The intercom cut him off. "What *now,* Miss Lind?" he demanded.

"*Ms,*" she corrected. "The police are here."

"The police? For what?"

"I don't really know, but two police cars, a paddy wagon and an ambulance are in the courtyard. And there are more cop cars on the front lawn."

He tilted the blinds and looked through the window. The police vehicles were parked carelessly in the courtyard with their lights flashing. "What do they want?"

"Something about a riot. You'd better get out here."

"Fuck!" He skirted the edge of the desk, pulling Helen O'Dell from her seat. "Get that done!"

Eight Nassau County cops in riot gear carried truncheons and shotguns and were pacing around nervously in the Main Office. "Jesus Christ!" he said. Sgt. Sadowski was standing over Phyllis Lind's desk looking down her blouse. "What's going on here, Boris?"

"You put in a call about a riot in progress on the campus."

"I didn't make any calls! What riot? I don't see a riot. I don't hear a riot. Do you see a riot in progress?" His face was red and his mustache wriggled.

"*Alleged* riot," Officer Guitano corrected.

"Riot's what the 9-1-1 dispatcher said. Some antiwar protest that went bad. Or a nut in the clock tower with a rifle like that guy at Texas University who killed a dozen people."

"Fourteen," Officer Guitano corrected, filling in the details. "Whitman, Charlie Whitman in 1966. A U.S. Marine. Stabbed his mother to death before he went on a rampage. Wounded thirty-two. An incredible shot."

"Aren't you a walking encyclopedia, Louis," Sgt. Sadowski said. He looked at the dispatch he was holding. "Mr. Zwill called–"

"Zwill?" Mr. Baltz roared.

Terry entered the Main Office attracted by the commotion of sirens and flashing lights. "What's up, Phyl?"

She shrugged and pointed at the pileup near the alcove. "Something about Willy Zwill and a riot."

Terry joined the crowd. Mr. Baltz elbowed his way through the police in their riot gear with their guns drawn who clogged the passage. Helen O'Dell trailed behind holding the paper she had to type. "Loomis!" he shouted when he saw Virgil seated in one of the chairs. The door to Mr. Zwill's office was closed. "What did you do?"

"Where's the riot?" Sgt. Sadowski asked.

"Alleged–" Officer Guitano started and thought better of it when he saw the expression on his sergeant's face.

Virgil raised his hands. "I don't know anything about a riot. Mr. Zwill just asked me to watch his back because he was being followed."

"Being followed? Jesus Christ!" Mr. Baltz took a deep breath.

"Was he?" Sgt. Sadowski asked.

"He was," Virgil said. "Look out in the hall."

They opened the door to the main corridor. "What the hell is this?" Mr. Baltz shouted when he saw the single file line of students stretching from the office door back along the corridor until they disappeared around a corner.

"I counted more than three hundred on my way here," Terry offered. "It goes up to the third floor, down the hall to the other side of the building, back into the cafeteria in single file. I just came from there. I asked them what was going on, but nobody on the line knew."

"Why are there three hundred students lined up in single file?"

Virgil waved his hands vaguely. "I was in the cafeteria eating my lunch and Mr. Z said something about being followed. He asked me to watch his back and find out who it was. I told him I had class and a guidance appointment, but he insisted, so I did what he asked, trailing him at a distance. One kid after another lined up behind us as we passed, very quiet, very orderly. Mr. Zwill noticed when he turned on the second floor and saw the line behind him. It was like he was the Pied Piper, you know, leading all the kids out of Hamlin. When he started running I ran to keep up with him. Then everybody started running. For a man his age, he's pretty fast. When he made it into his office he slammed his door and told me he was going to call the police. He hasn't come out since."

The muscles on Mr. Baltz's face began to twitch. "Get back to class, Loomis! Everybody," he called to the line, "get back to class now!" Sgt. Sadowski gave a sign to his men and they moved out rapidly to disperse the crowd. Mr. Baltz banged on the AP's door. "Are you in there, Willy? Open up!"

"They've got the place surrounded, Willy," Terry called, forming his hands into a megaphone. "Come on out with your hands up!"

"Do you mind, Mr. Scapelli!" Mr. Baltz turned the doorknob, but it was locked.

"You could break it down or shoot off the lock," Terry said. Officer Guitano had his hand on his gun. "It would be a real waste not to take advantage of all that firepower."

"Mr. Scapelli, this is a serious matter and no time for one of your tasteless comments." He took his master key, put it into the lock and pushed the door slowly. A rush of hot air hit him in the face.

Inside the dark office Willy Zwill was squatting behind his desk, his eyes just visible above the top of the desk and below his yellow Civil Defense helmet. "Thank God it's you," he said to them.

Virgil hadn't dispersed with the others. "Hey, Mr. Z, you were right. You *were* being followed."

"I knew it. I told you. I told everybody!" He looked relieved, vindicated.

"Jesus Christ!" Mr. Baltz said. "Jesus H. fucking Christ!"

**Rosencrantz and Guildenstern
Memorial High School
UFSD 71
Farmington, New York**

TO: All Teachers and Staff
FROM: M. Seymour Baltz, Principal
SUBJECT: New Building Use Procedures

November 22, 1971

It has come to my attention that the building and its facilities are being used to conduct personal business, hold meetings and carry on unofficial school activities without the prior knowledge and consent of the building principal. That is in violation of the district's "Buildings and Grounds Use" policy as outlined on page sixteen of the Teacher's Handbook. "The principal of each building is directly responsible for the facilities (rooms, desks, chairs, erasers, chalk, etc.) in his building; as such the principal is accountable to the Superintendent of Schools and the School Board concerning the use of said materials."

Though use of the building has been tolerated in the past, it will no longer be permitted with the district on austerity budget. Outlined below are the *new* procedures that have become necessary to safeguard the building, the children, the staff and faculty.

1. CLASSROOM VISITATION: Classrooms are for learning, therefore teachers are no longer permitted to interrupt ongoing instruction by "dropping in" or visiting another teacher without first securing the permission of a Department Chairman, Assistant Principal or the Principal. This restriction does not pertain to PA announcements and Guidance Counselors may continue to interrupt instruction at any time in

the course of the day. No "outside visitors," students or adults, are permitted in classrooms during school hours. All visitors must sign the Guest Register in the Main Office where an Official Visitor's Pass will be issued. If a guest lecturer or speaker is scheduled in a classroom during the course of the school year or at a teacher-sponsored after-school meeting, the sponsoring teacher must submit for official consideration the name of the guest lecturer, a topic outline of the subject matter, as well as a detailed copy of the text. This must be done at the time a room reservation request is filed with Mr. Lewis (See Procedure # 4).

2. TEACHER MAILBOXES: Teacher mailboxes are expressly for *official* school business, including, but not limited to, *official* memos, *official* notices and *official* announcements. Teachers wishing to use mailboxes for individual and personal contact may no longer do so. The distribution of *unofficial* fliers, *unofficial* leaflets, personal letters, notes and/or memos will require *official* sanction, which may be obtained be submitting all *unofficial* communications to building administration for inspection and *official* approval, thereby making them *official* and eligible for distribution in teacher mailboxes.

3. USE OF DITTO MACHINES: Ditto machines in the Faculty Room, stencils, duplicating fluid and copy paper (whenever these become available if a budget is passed and austerity ends) are the property of the District and to be used solely within the educational structure of the school day. They are *not* for personal use. Teachers who supply their own stencils, duplicating fluid and paper are not permitted to use the District-owned ditto machines to run off material, be it educational, noneducational, personal correspondence or otherwise. And these materials may not be distributed in teacher mailboxes (See Procedure # 2).

4. CLASSROOM USAGE BEYOND THE REGULAR SCHOOL DAY: During austerity the building is to be evacuated at dismissal. Teachers wishing to secure use of a classroom for meeting purposes beyond regular school hours will no longer be permitted to do so. Effective immediately

teachers must submit in writing a formal room request on an official Room Request Form (which will soon be available) one week in advance of the date desired,. Completed forms with the teacher's name, date requested and specific purpose of the meeting will be submitted to Mr. Lewis for review.

Observing these simple procedures will insure the best possible use of this, your building, and the best possible education of the youngsters in your charge. Strict adherence to the rules will assure a secure workplace and the safety of your students, as well as your own. It will enable Administration to keep track of your comings and goings within the building, avoid any future misunderstandings and prevent further difficulties or embarrassment.

These policies are effective immediately!

Rosencrantz and Guildenstern
Memorial High School
UFSD 71
Farmington, New York

TO: All Teachers and Staff
FROM: M. Seymour Baltz, Principal
SUBJECT: Pants Suit Ensembles

Friday, November 19, 1971

C O N F I D E N T I A L

In response to a recent question posed by a distaff member of the faculty earlier last week, the wearing of *suitable* pants suit ensembles by female members of our staff is completely appropriate. Therefore, official permission has been extended today, Friday, November 19, to those who may wish to wear such suitable pants suit ensembles in the future.

As agreed Sue Wellen pulled her car into the Faculty Parking Lot at 7:15. Other cars were already there, clustered in a corner close to the back entrance of the school. It reminded her of the westward-ho-ing pioneers that circled their wagons every night for security. She recognized Phyllis Lind's new Plymouth Barracuda. "I decided to go with the green to match my eyes instead of the red that goes with my hair," she announced to the Faculty Room card game. "I might want to change my hair color. Besides the car looks so much hotter in racing green." Phaedra Schwartz-Fine's Caddy was next. Helen O'Dell opted not to park in her reserved AP spot in the courtyard and was sitting alone in her new Pinto. She waved as Sue drove past and parked, while she watched the other cars arrive for the next several minutes. Some of the women who normally drove alone had carpooled for moral support. They all sat waiting for the bell to start the historic day–reflecting, talking, worrying and wondering if they would regret their decision. Gradually, almost grudgingly, the rest of the parking lot filled and teachers dragged themselves back from the weekend with no awareness of the gathering storm in the parking lot.

The first bell rang. Sue finished applying her makeup, pressed her lips together and put her case back into her pocketbook. As if triggered by a Pavlovian signal, the women opened their car doors in unison. They fashioned themselves into two lines, roughly in size order, and they marched into the building quietly and in an orderly fashion, like a reverse fire drill. The procession wended past the Gym and the Cafeteria, toward the Main Office. They were invisible to the crowd of students opening and slamming lockers in the corridor. They stopped at the entrance to the Main Office and clasped hands. "All for one and one for all, ladies!" Elsie Bergin who was not exactly a secretary or a teacher said. And they filed through the door.

Carolyn Butrum was already at her station behind the counter where she waited every morning for the late bell so she could keep track of the teachers who arrived late. It wasn't an official duty, but she liked the quasi-administrative power she felt when she issued her warnings, "That's the second time this week you're late, dear. Don't make this a habit. Looks like you'll have to set your alarm to wake you up a little earlier." She watched the women enter and her mouth hung open. "My," she said with as much sweetness as she could muster, "don't all of you look very... lovely... in pants." She watched as they emptied their mailboxes and she sighed. "Oh good Lord," she said to no one, "what is this world coming to? In my day teachers were revered. Women teachers, and they were mostly women, never used makeup, were unmarried and always dressed modestly and wore white gloves." She tutted. "Nowadays is it any wonder the disrespect the kids have for authority? They already dress like hooligans and now that women are wearing pants to school it won't be long before they start coming to school naked, teachers and students! There are no standards."

Frank Lovejoy, the director of shows, was standing by his mailbox. "I just hope I'm still working here when that day comes," he said. "I look forward to it."

Mrs. Butrum sighed and shook her head. "I rest my case."

All morning the women in their suitable pants suits ensembles smiled and waved and nodded whenever they passed in the halls. By midday pants were old news. The door to the principal's office remained closed all day. He didn't once respond to the many knocks on his door or pick up the telephone when it rang and in the afternoon when the building was empty he took his things and went home.

Tuesday morning the building buzzed with excitement, partly because of the "Revolt of the Women," as Terry Scapelli had proclaimed the event during his previous day's lunch period in the Third Floor Faculty Room, partly because Thanksgiving was only a day away and partly because of the flier in all of the mailboxes despite Mr. Baltz's memo the previous Friday restricting their use. Someone had also posted them at various locations around the building.

UNITED 0=> MALES <= 0 UNTIED
ATTENTION ALL OPPRESSED MALES!

Inspired as we were by our sisters in arms, those valiant women of R & G who pulled up their skirts to show the Fashion Police just who wears the pants, a contingent of male members of the faculty met Monday afternoon to create UNITED MALES UNTIED, draw up a Constitution and unanimously ratify the following platform for UMU:

1. We are in agreement that clothing is an expression of one's personality.

2. Every man has the right and the duty to be an individual and express his originality in a time when Society would make him conform in an IBM world.

3. In these changing times the archaic conventions and outmoded attitudes toward sex, drugs, Rock and Roll and dress must be reevaluated.

4. A man is not measured by the size of his jib, his tools or his suit jacket and tie.

5. Just as the horse and buggy gave way to the horseless buggy and the skirts came off for the pants, the jacket and tie must be our final frontier.

6. The time for talking is passed.

7. In accordance with these conclusions the entire membership of UMU has decided on a course of action now.

NO LONGER CAN WE TURN OUR HEADS IN COLLARS THAT ARE TOO TIGHT! NO LONGER WILL WE LIVE UNDER THE YOKE OF OPPRESSION, SO APTLY SYMBOLIZED BY THE TIES WE HAVE BEEN FORCED TO WEAR AROUND OUR STIFF NECKS!

LET EVERY MAN, THEREFORE, BE FOREVER FREE TO DECIDE HIS OWN ATTIRE! AND SO DECEMBER 7TH HAS BEEN DESIGNATED AS "BURN A TIE FOR FREEDOM DAY"!

IF YOU REMEMBER PEARL HARBOR AND REMEMBER PEARL BAILEY, REMEMBER TO BRING YOUR TIE AND BURN ONE SMALL TIE FOR MAN, ONE GIANT BARN FIRE FOR MANKIND! MATCHES FOR THE OCCASION WILL BE PROVIDED BY UMU!

Respectfully Submitted, Recording Secretary, United Males Untied

* * *

By his prep period Terry was bored and restless so he left the teacher's cafeteria, stopped at the Main Office to check his mailbox and then took a walking tour of the building. That always was a great way to see the educational process at work that went on behind closed doors. The Home Ec hall was always quiet. Sylvia Berkowsky was standing over her girls working their sewing machines like a foreman in a garment center sweatshop. The stuttering sounds of typing ricocheted down the Business corridor where Faye Schwartz, now Fine, warned, "Fingers on the home keys, people. Fingers on the home keys." Several students were nodding in Stanley Milnow's class and so was Stanley at his desk. Then he swung through the fire doors on the second floor where the AV/CM Squad was maneuvering equipment carts like parking lot attendants. He heard Red Farley yelling at someone down the end of the hall. And he stopped outside of Sue Wellen's room on the third floor where everyone was writing.

"Anybody home?"

"Test," she said from her seat behind the desk where the New York *Times* crossword puzzle was opened in front of her.

She put down the pen she always used to fill in the boxes. "What are you doing up here during your prep?."

"They're cooking farts in sauerkraut for lunch, another high-sodium austerity special, and I had to get away. If you take a deep breath you can just about detect it just above that rotten egg sulfur smell from the Chemistry Lab."

She inhaled. "No cheating," she said to the class. They were writing feverishly. "I'll be watching you from the hall." Several boys watched her cross the room.

"You have fans," Terry said. She turned and the boys' heads dropped back to their test papers. "And I have to tell you, Wellen, as much as I support a woman's right to choose her wardrobe, there is something to be said about the woman's movement especially from behind in a miniskirt!"

"You mean like Mrs. Butrum, Pig?" she countered. "What's new with the suit jacket and tie thing?"

"They're lining up taking sides in the 'Great War of the Suit Jackets and the Ties.' History will remember it that way. When you're a bitter old spinster teacher you'll be teaching it with other great battles as Bunker Hill, Gallipoli, Midway and the Bulge, my dear *Ms* Wellen."

"And you're long gone making folded origami birds in the Mary Muldoon Home for Retired Teachers?"

"The Union put out a position paper that's in all the mailboxes pledging unanimous support for UMU at the tie-burning ceremony. The Association is standing firmly behind its 'no position' position. Half its members plan to boycott any tie-burning event; the other half plan to attend." He pulled out the ditto from his pocket and handed it to her. "I just found that in my mailbox. Seems there's another group, CREWP, the Coalition of Righteous Educators for Wardrobe Parity pushing for the rights of cross-dressers who want to wear suitable pants suits ensembles without ties."

"Here comes *El Exigenté*!" She pulled in from the doorway.

Mr. Baltz glided silently down the hall in a crash course aimed directly at them. "*Miss* Wellen," he said with an artificial smile that made him look like "The Demanding One" from the Savarin Coffee commercials. "You have a class going on in there? And Mr. Scapelli," his tone was unctuous, "have you chosen to become a new class member?" He rocked on his crepe soles while he waited for a response. "Didn't you get the memo that was distributed yesterday about unauthorized visitations between teachers?"

"I'm not visiting, Mr. Baltz. This is official business. I'm coordinating with *Ms* Wellen about the revolution."

The principal raised his eyebrows. "The revolution?"

"I teach a unit on the American Revolution," she offered. "And the History and English Departments plan to work together so our students make connections."

"Team teaching," Terry said. "We'll read selected historical literature and co-ordinate activities in both our classes."

"Activities? Oh? Just what activities do you have in mind, Miss Wellen?" His smile stretched his mustache so tight it looked like it would snap.

"Staged demonstrations," Terry said before she could answer. "Historical vignettes. Impromptu great moments in history like the old TV series *You Are There*. I'm sure you remember that. Figures from the Revolutionary era in improvised scenes and settings." He leaned forward on his right leg, placed his left arm behind his back and struck a familiar pose. "You know the painting of Washington in the front of the boat crossing the Delaware. That's where the improvisation comes in. How different might history be if he had a head cold?" He did an exaggerated sneeze. "'Hey, quiet down. The British'll hear us. And sit down before you capsize the boat!'" He paused. "If the English/History thing goes well, the Music Department plans a ballet version of the Battle of Trenton. The Drama Department has a Bob Newhart routine featuring a really annoyed Paul Revere telephoning the news about the British coming! You see where we're going with this, Mr. Baltz?"

"I know *exactly* where you're going. Mr. Scapelli." His smile faded. "It all seems very creative. Both of you will write up a detailed account for me to include in my monthly report to

Dr. Flackett. He's very interested in what teachers do with their free time and can include it in his district newsletter for everyone to see."

"Absolutely, Mr. Baltz," he said without hesitation. "But I want to do a good job with this, so I hope you're not in a rush."

"Take your time, Mr. Scapelli. Say next week after Thanksgiving?"

"I'll be away for the holiday. Can you give me another week? By the end of the first full week in December?"

"Of course, Mr. Scapelli." He forced another smile. He removed a small calendar from his jacket pocket and wrote it down. "I'll be expecting it on my desk by the tenth."

"Hey, Mr. S, Ms Wellen. And a special hey to you, Mr. B," Virgil said when he turned the corner, arms dangling and head bobbing, and almost ran into them.

"Loomis, why are you out roaming the halls?" the principal demanded with redirected anger. He tucked his chin into his neck. "Where do you belong now?"

"Here, in Ms Wellen's." He handed her his pass. "Back from my guidance appointment with Mr. Aaron."

Mr. Baltz took it out of her hand and examined the time. "Does it take twenty minutes to get here from Guidance?"

"I was talking to Mr. Farley and Coach Ritchie. Did you know we have a secret wrestling team during austerity? They were discussing it. They practice in the gym locker room every day after school. Mr. Farley's Coach Ritchie's assistant. I told them I wanted to go out for the team. That's what took me so long."

"Just get in there, Loomis." He handed back the pass and turned with a little rubber squeak. "Now if you'd be on your way, Mr. Scapelli, Miss Wellen can resume her class."

"You going to your office, Mr.Baltz? I'll walk with you and give you more details about that team teaching unit." He fell into step and they headed down the hall.

"You just have it on my desk, Mr. Scapelli, and I'll read it then."

Sue turned to Virgil who was watching them go. "Virgil," she said, "you are a breath of fresh air in a building that smells of sauerkraut and rotten eggs!"

"Thank you, Ms Wellen. And I've been in the Boys' Room reading some very complimentary things people are saying about you too." He smiled. "Do I still have to take that test?"

The level of excitement ramped up day by day during the shortened week leading up to the Thanksgiving recess as the temperature outside dropped. Only the day before Christmas break was more exciting. Student attendance dipped daily and by Wednesday it was down to a third. Teachers who could afford to wait until the following Monday for their paycheck called in sick Tuesday night to get a head start on the most traveled day of the year. Those who showed vibrated with anticipation of the coming four-day weekend. There were fewer fights in the halls–student as well as teacher. Conversations replaced arguments in the faculty room, for the most part, and teachers who never smiled walked around grinning like idiots.

Throughout the day the paycheck line moved by Phyllis Lind's desk. Her flying manicured fingers flew, dipped into the shoebox and retrieved each check from the batch of alphabetized envelopes automatically while she carried on a running conversation with each teacher in front of her. Dip, pull, present, open, replace the empty envelope.

"Nice pants. But I still like to see a woman's thigh," Stanley Milnow said.

She finger-walked over the remaining envelopes and located his at a glance by the red spots at the corners. "Here you go, Stan." She passed it to him holding it by the edge with her long nails. "Thank you for sharing."

He pulled out the check and looked at the amount, absently picking his teeth with the corner of the envelope before he dropped it on her desk. "Taxes and Social Security. That's the reason I'm teaching."

"What did the queer say when he brushed his teeth and his gums started bleeding?" Red Farley asked when he saw the blood-stained envelope.

"I really have no idea, Mr. Farley." She handed him his check.

He leaned in closer. "Whew, that's a relief. Safe for another month!"

"What's that supposed to mean?" Stanley Milnow said. "You think I'm queer?"

"It's a joke, Stanley. A homosexual with bleeding gums. Safe for another month. You know. Like a woman when she gets her you know. But for homos."

"I know what a woman's you know is, but I don't like what you're inferring. I'm a married man."

"Implying," Terry said. "Red was implying you're queer and you were inferring that you are from what he said about your bleeding gums."

"Mind your own business, Scapelli."

"Just trying to educate you." He stopped in front of Phyllis. "Baltz," he announced. "M as in 'My, didn't I used to run this place?'" He stuck his hand out to be paid.

"You're too late. As you might expect, he always gets his first."

Terry slid the green check out of the envelope and winced. "It's a sad state of affairs, Phyl. I think I'm worth at least twice as much as they pay me, yet every payday the message I get is I'm only half the man I think I am."

"Not in my book, Mr. Scapelli." She winked.

"You always know just the right thing to say to sooth a man's bruised ego. That's one reason I love you, Phyl."

"And the other reasons?"

"You always smell great."

"Shalimar. Any others?"

"You're a great dresser. And speaking of that, any blowback from the flagrant and blatant act of civil disobedience by you and the distaff members of the faculty?"

"Hardly a word all week. He isn't talking to me except for barking occasional orders. He's been holed up in his office like Nixon in the Rose Garden. Helen said he hasn't talked to her either since Monday. Speak of the devil and he appears."

The aroma of Pine-Sol wafted into the main Office when Baltz opened the door and Terry took a deep breath. "I smell pine forest, Phyl. Are you growing Christmas trees in there, Mr. Baltz?"

He ignored the comment. "Miss Lind–"

"*Ms.*"

"–are you finished with those checks yet?"

"A few more after Mr. Scapelli."

"Don't you have a class? A duty period, Mr. Scapelli? Someplace else to be other than on top of Miss Lind?"

"*Ms.*"

"Actually there's no place I'd rather be, and it's my prep period."

"Then go prep and let the secretaries do their work."

"I was just telling Phyllis how great she smells and how much I like that outfit she's wearing. Like it was tailored just for her. That's one of the best suitable pants suit ensembles I've seen all week."

She smiled. "Why, thank you, Mr. Scapelli."

Sue came into the office talking to Helen O'Dell, both wearing pants suits. Baltz glared at his assistant principal, who turned away. "Don't take all day, Phyllis. And bring your steno pad when you're finished." He made a dismissing gesture with both hands. "You've been paid, Mr. Scapelli, so you can be on your way. This isn't a singles bar." He went back into his office with another puff of pine.

"He's still not happy." Sue took her check, looked at the amount and put it into her pocketbook.

"And I don't blame him," Terry agitated. "It's disgraceful women wearing pants. How am I expected to tell the men from the girls?"

"Women." Sue sucked in a deep breath and stuck out her chest. "Twelve of us on Monday, twenty-two today. I'd say the women won this one."

"I don't think so, Wellen. Baltz's memo was in all the mailboxes with last Friday's date before the first 'suitable pants suit ensemble' stepped over the threshold on Monday. So technically he gave all of you permission to wear them. So in a split decision the judges have to award it to him."

The buzzer on her desk sounded angry. "Phyllis, are you still socializing out there? Come in here, if it isn't too much trouble, so I can dictate a memo."

Terry spoke loudly into the intercom. "Thank you, *Ms* Lind for all that very interesting information. You can trust me to keep it in the strictest confidence."

She let go of the button. "That's going to give him a case of heartburn the rest of the day and make the rest of my week a *picnic,* thank you very much, Terry." She took her steno pad from the drawer, opened the buzzing door and disappeared into the pine forest beyond.

* * *

Jesse looked at the clock on the back wall. "Everybody listen up. Your assignment over the Thanksgiving weekend–"

There was a collective moan. "It's a holiday. We're going away. That's not fair. Nobody else is giving assignments."

The classroom door burst open with a bang that made them jump. A dark and hairy hulk of a kid filled the doorway with one long arm hanging by his knee and the other hand tucked inside his belt.

"Fumbles Kavernicki!" someone called from the back.

"Eat me!" he sneered. He turned to Jesse. "You in charge here?"

"Apparently not. How can I help you?"

"Mr. Fink in Shop sent me out for a Lesson Stretcher."

"We don't have Shop equipment here. This is an English class."

He wiped his nose with the back of his hand and left.

"You're welcome," Jesse called. "Just feel free to interrupt me anytime–"

Kavernicki stuck his head back through the open door. "You talking to me?"

Jesse cleared his throat. "Happy Thanksgiving."

He frowned, ducked out and disappeared.

Jesse closed the door. "Where was I? Oh, right. The assignment for the weekend I want you to–" They grumbled louder. The door crashed open again and Jesse flinched.

"Mr. Fink said stop screwing around," Kavernicki said, "and gimme the Lesson Stretcher!"

Jesse approached the boy cautiously with both his hands visible to show him that he was unarmed. "Mr. Kavernicki... is that your name?" he said calmly and quietly. "I don't know what a Lesson Stretcher is. But take your time. Look around. If you see what Mr. Fink is looking for, you are welcome to take it."

He looked. "I don't know. You're the teacher. I never seen one."

Jesse lowered his voice even more. "Mr. Kavernicki, please go back and tell Mr. Fink that the teacher in Room 234 searched and swears he doesn't have *any* Shop stuff in his English class. Tell him I don't know what a Lesson Stretcher is, but if I ever come across a Lesson Stretcher in the future I'll to send it to him. Can you remember to tell him all that?" Jesse walked him back to the open door. "And, Mr. Kavernicki, in the future if you knock, things would go so much easier on me, the class and the wall. Again, happy Thanksgiving to you and your family." Jesse watched him disappear down the hall. He tried to get back on track. "Now, for the third time, I want you to be sure–"

Several minutes later there were two light knocks, a pause and then the door flew open. The knob crashed into the wall, chalk toppled from the ledge of the blackboard and a window shade snapped up. "Mr. Fink is really pissed at you. More than he's pissed at me!" He was a winded from running back and forth. "He says for *you* to cut the shit. His words. And if you send me back to him one more time he's coming up here personally!"

There was a collective ooh. "Don't worry, Mr. Tietjen," someone called out, "you can take him. Mr. Fink's about a hundred!"

"He says call the office if you don't know what you're supposed to do."

Jesse went to the phone and picked it up.

"Main Office," Phyllis Lind answered. "How can I help you, Mr. Tietjen?"

"I'm having a little problem," he mumbled into the mouthpiece. "Mr. Fink keeps sending a kid up from Shop for some kind of equipment. A Lesson Stretcher? Three times I told the kid I don't have one, but he's back and Mr. Fink is making threats."

"I see you didn't do all *your* homework, Mr. Tietjen. The official 'Lesson Stretcher Memo' was in all the mailboxes in September. The revised list was out last week. Just a minute and I'll check the list for you." He waited. "You're supposed to send him on to Ms Bimenyenz in Room 110. She's next on the list."

"I don't understand."

"The Lesson Stretcher list. Mr. Fink sends his kids to you. You send them on to Layla Bimenyenz on the first floor and she sends them up to"–he heard her turning the page–"Mr. Humphrey on the third. He sends them to the Library. And so it goes, on and on until the end of the period."

"But why?" he whispered with his mouth close to the receiver.

"Did you ever hear about the truck driver who was delivering canaries, Mr. Tietjen?"

"I don't think so."

"Well, every few blocks the driver stopped, ran around the truck and hit the sides with a big club. When somebody saw it and asked why, the driver explained he was carrying a ton of canaries in his half-ton truck, so he had to keep half of them flying at all times. The Lesson Stretcher is how we do that here. It was Helen O'Dell's idea for keeping problem kids out of the AP offices. Holidays are always the worst. I suggest you read that memo as soon as you get the opportunity. For now, just sign his pass and send him on to Room 110. If there isn't anything else? Happy Thanksgiving." She hung up.

He replaced the receiver and looked at Kavernicki doing chin-ups on the door jamb to impress the girls. "Mr. Kavernicki, Ms Bimenyenz in Room 110 has your Lesson

Stretcher." He signed the pass and Kavernicki grunted and left. "Good luck with your quest," he called after him.

Jesse turned to the class and the bell ending the period rang. There was a mad scramble for the door. "Wait! The assignment!" he said to the empty desks and gave up. "Aw, what the hell. Happy Thanksgiving," he called.

"Mr. Tietjen?" Audrey from his morning class was in the hall and handed him a card. "Happy Thanksgiving." She hesitated. "My mother said if you didn't have any place to go for Thanksgiving dinner tomorrow, you're welcome to come to our house."

He smiled. "Thank you, Audrey. And please thank your mother." He was genuinely touched. "But I'll be with my family."

"I thought you would. Happy Thanksgiving." She joined the crowd in the hall.

The card was signed "Love always." He smiled again. And then he pictured poor Kavernicki and how many other lost souls strung out around the building on a wild goose chase for something as elusive as the Holy Grail. He wondered if they would be trapped in the building over the long weekend and miss their turkey dinners.

* * *

Pieces of orange and black crepe paper left over from Halloween were taped to the painted cinder block wall in the Third Floor Faculty Room with cardboard Pilgrims, turkeys and cornucopias. Over the ditto machine a sign announced "The P-PTA, Harriet Stegle, President, wishes the faculty and staff the happiest and healthiest Thanksgiving ever!" Under it was a tray of homemade doughnuts donated by the Home Economics Service Club, where the reams of ditto paper and duplicating fluid during non-austerity years would have been. The center of the table was covered with a special paper Thanksgiving tablecloth and a 3D crepe paper turkey centerpiece. Harriet Stegle herself and a number of P-PTA mothers mingled with the noisy teachers, filled coffee cups and served doughnuts while they buttonholed teachers to join the organization.

It was standing room only. Even the Guidance counselors who rarely left the safety of their offices were there in force. Most of the year, spotting a counselor was rarer than seeing a UFO. They were also out during Guidance Testing Week in September, appearing at the beginning of the test periods with their #2 pencils and booklets and collected everything at the end, to be redistributed the next morning. The time between, they waited in the faculty lounge drinking coffee. And they returned for the June promotion meetings, where they pressured teachers to pass their failing students.

"We are advocates for the students," Betty Gabel, a second-year twenty-something counselor announced breathlessly at the faculty meeting before the September Guidance Testing Week extravaganza.

"What does that make us, their adversaries?" Terry had called out from his place in the auditorium to applause from the teachers.

John Hiller, the oldest counselor on staff, hovered by the doughnuts stuffing an assortment into a plastic bag. "For Thanksgiving tomorrow," he explained. "The double plastic bag will keep them fresh. I'm going to a friend's for turkey dinner and I want to bring a nice dessert." His reputation for being the cheapest person in the building stemmed from his personal accounts of riding the LIRR for free by hiding in the bathroom whenever a conductor came around to punch the tickets. "Not every day, of course, maybe three out of five. I still buy a ticket just in case I get caught. But it's saving me a fortune."

The bridge players resisted all attempts to infringe on their space at the end of the table and held their ground against all comers, making it clear intruders had no right interfering with the normal daily routine even during the holidays.

"Really!" Claire Hutton yelled at Armando Bello, the Foreign Language Chair who wore capes when the weather turned cold. He banged her in the back of the head and knocked her Pall Mall from between her lips. It fell into the glass jar she refilled each night with cottage cheese and fruit for her lunch every day. "Go backo where you belongo," she said and fished the cigarette from the bottom, picked the ash off her lunch and spooned out another helping.

Mrs. Butrum watched them play. "So many people here I haven't seen in years. It's like the Catholics who only go to church on Palm Sunday and Ash Wednesday when they can get something for nothing." She stopped her knitting. "Lordy, is that John Hiller over there? I thought he was dead. I think the Sunshine Committee sent flowers to his wife." She declined a parent offer of more coffee. "It kills my stomach, dear, what's left of it. But I'll have another powdered doughnut. They aren't as greasy this year."

"I bet his wife thought he was dead too," Rita Reed said and blew her nose into the balled lace handkerchief she held with her cards and everyone laughed. "Carolyn, you're getting sugar on your pot holder," she warned.

"It's a baby sweater." She dusted off the knitting.

"A black baby sweater?"

"The family's in mourning. You remember that dreadful wedding I went to last month?"

"And she's having a baby already?" Elise Bergin asked.

"She *was* having the baby before the wedding. That's why they got married."

"Well, you know what they say," Claire Hutton announced with a snicker, "the first one takes only about seven months. All the others take nine."

"That's the least of their problems," Mrs. Butrum said, resuming her knitting. "The bride's brother disappeared from home when he was seventeen and no one heard from him in years. Somehow he found out about his sister's wedding and said he would show up at the reception and they decided to surprise their father. But that turned out to be a terrible mistake. The plan was to turn off all the lights while his long lost son came into the hall, turn them on again and yell surprise. Well, the poor man had a massive coronary and died right there in the middle of the dance floor."

"That's terrible!" Helen O'Dell said.

"Only sixty-two. Can you imagine. Nobody could leave until the police, the coroner and an ambulance arrived."

"So what did they do?"

"Well, the groom's family paid the band to stay overtime, but hardly anybody danced. It was so strange to hear the 'Hokey Pokey' while they all just sat there." She held up the sweater. "I just want to get this sweater finished before the poor girl has a miscarriage. With all the excitement, she's been staining." She put down the knitting and took a bite of her doughnut.

Mrs. Hutton played a card. "It would really be a shame," she said, "if she loses the baby after they went to the trouble and the expense of getting married."

Rita Reed wasn't fast enough to retrieve her handkerchief and sneezed on her cards

"*A votre santé,* Rita," Terry toasted her with his coffee cup.

"My, but aren't you the happy one," Mrs. Butrum said.

"Just a very valiant false front, Mrs. Butrum. I always find the holidays to be so depressing."

"Exactly what I was telling the girls." She nodded to Helen O'Dell, who was trying to sneak a peek at Rita Reed's cards. "Lost both my parents within a month of each other between Thanksgiving and Christmas my second year teaching. The ground was so frozen we had to wait until the spring to bury them. This year it will be exactly thirty-two years."

"Well, I hope you have a happy Thanksgiving this year." He made his way through the crowd and stopped by Red Farley and Stanley Milnow.

"This is you, Scapelli," Red called over the noise, holding a blue ditto in his hand. "This United Males crap. It's you."

Terry took the paper and read it over. "I already dress to express my personality, Red. For years." He dropped the ditto on the table. "This was obviously written by someone who's repressed, some suppressed individual with issues, not unlike yourself, Red. In fact, I wouldn't be surprised to find that you're behind this tie-burning thing."

"Don't bullshit me, Scapelli! This was written by someone with no regard for law and order and decorum in an attempt to undermine the structure of our society. By somebody who is out to destroy suit jackets and ties irregardless of the impact it will have on the future of the educational system in America!"

"Just between you and *I,* Red, it was written by somebody with good grammar. I suspect by someone who is beyond suspicion." He looked over at Buddy Ritchie talking to Coach Boid. "Maybe the Phys Ed Department. They wear sweats. " He pointed his finger. "Buddy Ritchie, *j'accuse!*"

Buddy Ritchie stared over at his accuser and raised his middle finger. "Accuse this, Scapelli."

"The Phys Ed Department has the perfect opportunity to meet and plan God knows what in the Athletic Office," he continued, appealing to everyone around him. "Answer me this if you can, Buddy Ritchie, just what do you Phys Ed people do all day in that little office near the gym away from prying eyes."

Buddy gave him the finger with two hands.

"Considering your rationale, Dr. Nessmith has to be a suspect," Stanley Milnow said. "He wears a white coat and hangs out in that little medical area." He sat back and watched the flies looping lazily in the air by the unused Tom Keller Vending Machine until one landed near the opening where the cup dropped. He pulled a rubber band from the collection around his wrist, looped one end on the tip of his index finger and pulled the other end back to his eye like a bow and arrow. He squinted, took careful aim snd let the rubber band loose. It covered the distance in a flash and caught the surprised fly dead center, mashing it on the front of the machine.

"Nice shot, Stan," Terry said with great admiration and applauded.

"Practice," he said, "whenever I have free time in the shoe store." He pulled two more rubber bands from his wrist and got off two quick shots, completely obliterating one fly and shooting a wing off the other. The wounded fly circled down like a World War I biplane in a dogfight, crashing and writhing around with one crumpled wing beating ineffectively against the floor. He stood, picked up two of the flies and placed them in his napkin.

"Milnow, you are disgusting!" Red dumped his doughnut in the garbage can.

"What?" He put the folded napkin in his pocket. "For my son's frogs."

"Ollie Nessmith," Terry mused. "You might have hit the nail on the head there, Stan. Between examining the cheerleader squad for breast cancer and giving scoliosis tests to the girls' track team, he'd have plenty of time to run off volumes of dittos. I never did trust that man." He saw Dave Bowden sitting by the window. "And then there's the Science Department and their lab coats." He waved and Dave lifted his coffee cup in salute.

"Smoke and mirrors, Scapelli. All this shit"—Red held up the ditto—"points back to you. It has your fingerprints all over it."

"You're the one holding it, Red."

"He's right," Stanley said. "Your fingerprints are all over it now."

"Answer me this, Red. Are you grown man enough to dress yourself, or do you need Big Brother to zip you up in the morning? Shouldn't a man's wardrobe be a matter of personal choice?"

"Like birth control," Stanley Milnow offered. "But that's really a woman's problem."

The others were listening. Even the four horsewomen looked up from their game.

"This whole suit jacket tie thing," Terry continued and walked over to Joel Maxwell, "might be a ploy to draw our attention from the real issue, our bargaining agent still hasn't been able to negotiate a contract." He picked up a cruller and held it in front of him like a microphone. "As president of the Farmington Teachers' Association, Mr. Maxwell, what do you have to say about that?" He looked at the crowd waiting for an answer.

"We're working on it."

"And your position on suit jackets and ties? Is the Association supporting UMU's position on jackets and ties?"

"The Farmington Teachers' Association is taking a position of 'no position' on that position!"

"Chickenshit!" Dwayne Purvey yelled from across the room.

Terry carried his cruller down to him. "Then I take it that the Union is on opposite sides from the Association."

"Three hundred and sixty degrees," Dwayne Purvey said looking contemptuously at the rival president.

"I'm no math teacher, Dwayne, but that would actually put you exactly where the Association is. I think you mean hundred and eighty degrees." Terry waved his cruller. "So then can we assume that you and the Farmington Union are planning to support United Males Untied?"

"FU-2 supports them one hundred and eighty percent!"

"And are you going to participate in any tie-burning?"

"Including–" He stopped and looked at the ditto Terry showed him. "I wasn't aware of any tie-burning."

"Chickenshit!" Joel Maxwell taunted.

He grabbed Terry's hand holding the cruller and shouted into it. "Not only will FU-2 support the tie-burning on December seventh, Maxwell, but the Union will be there to strike the first match! So F you, too! And what do you think of that?"

"I think you have bad breath, Purvey. I can smell you from here."

"Oh, yeah?" He rushed over and caught Joel Maxwell's tie with his fingers and flipped it into his face.

"Yeah!" He pulled Purvey's shirt out of his pants.

The two men grappled as the crowd surged around them, some trying to break them up, others goading them on. Maxwell had his hands around Purvey's neck. "You son of a bitch!"

Purvey grabbed the tails of Maxwell's suit jacket and ripped it up the seam all the way to the back of the collar. Maxwell threw a punch that was deflected by Chuck

LaFemina's head when he came in for a closer look and landed on Purvey's shoulder.

"Jesus Christ! Jesus Christ!" His nose started bleeding.

The commotion ended when teachers broke up the two main combatants and escorted them separately from the room.

"See what you started, Red," Terry said shaking his head. "I just hope you're satisfied. You and your United Males Untied!"

In the general confusion Helen O'Dell placed her cards on the table and slipped out unnoticed. If she reported everything to Mr. Baltz, maybe she would get back into his good graces and he would talk to her again.

Thanksgiving was in the rearview mirror. Over the long weekend the temperature dipped and the official countdown to Christmas began. Monday morning the building was especially cold because the District had turned the heat off. It would take a week before the building became tolerable, and longer after New Year. Every extended holiday, boilers broke, water pipes froze and the custodians worked overtime. Twice a year when the clocks were turned back or ahead for Daylight Saving Time nobody knew the right time and bells went off throughout the day so the PA had to announce the end of each period.

Slow Charley the assistant custodian was Florence Sooter's greatest success story in all her years teaching the special CRMD kids. Sometimes referred to as "Sooter's Retards" or the "Criminally Retarded and Mentally Deranged" by those less sensitive, CRMD actually stood for Children with Retarded Mental Development. The class consisted of those identified by Guidance early on in elementary school. They were then segregated from the general population and remained in a self-contained classroom through high school graduation. CRMD kids spent their days learning basic survival math, counting to a hundred frontward and backward, by ones, twos, fives and tens, doing simple addition and subtraction, making change and going on field trips. Charley was the shining beacon Florence Sooter pointed to in the hallways whenever anyone questioned the necessity of special education. "He graduated CRMD Class Valedictorian in June 1965," she crowed, "and in September he became the assistant custodian!" The job had been created especially for Charley by Stash Polakas, who had developed a fondness for the boy when he was a student.

In 1968, Charley became famous, an overnight celebrity, after the movie *Charly* was released. The film, based on a Daniel Keyes short story, "Flowers for Algernon," was read in all the tenth-grade English classes. It is told through the journal entries of the lovably retarded Charly Gordon, who undergoes experimental surgery to make him smarter. The success of the surgery becomes obvious in the daily journal entries as Charly's language, grammar and thinking improve and develop to the point that he outstrips the doctors who operated on him and becomes a genius. But it only lasts for a brief time before Charly sadly reverts to his former retarded self. Cliff Robertson won "Best Actor" for his Charly. Every year when the tenth-graders read the story, Slow Charley's fame resurfaced anew with tales circulated around the school that the assistant custodian was the real Charly Gordon. And for weeks every year he couldn't go down the hall without signing autographs. He was a celebrity.

Mario Giovanni leaned back in his desk chair and the sound made him cringe. Last June, he had asked Charley to hit it with some oil, or better, grease the spring. Now whenever he saw Charley around the building he reminded him, but Charley was "Charly" and if he wanted it fixed he'd have to do it himself. He rocked back and forth until he couldn't stand it any longer. Through his open office door he watched Phyllis across the Administrative Alcove behind her desk at the far end of the Main Office. He liked watching her, especially when she was unaware he was watching. From his drawer he took the pair of opera glasses he had confiscated from one of the boys trying to spy on the girls in their locker room and put them up to his eyes.

"Great ass!" He studied her swiveling around in her chair, a sit-down modern dance routine. She was always doing something to stay in shape. He stretched his neck and fingered the flower in his lapel, pinched it and smelled his fingers. He watched her get up and gyrate her way between the other secretaries toward him through the archway and disappear into the walk-in vault between the Main Office and the Administrative Alcove. That was where they kept the exams, whatever petty cash or other valuables that came in and out of the building. He inhaled. Even from this distance a faint trace of her Shalimar reached him.

He held his chair steady and got up without a sound. Willy Zwill's door was closed because he was still out sick.

Even though he said he was perfectly fine, Baltz insisted he take a week of mental health days just to be safe. He wouldn't be back until Monday. He saw Helen O'Dell's silhouette through the frosted glass of her office window, reclining behind her desk with her legs up. He looked at his watch. She was like clockwork. After lunch and a snack it was nap time. The sign with the OUT and IN clocks suction-cupped inside Noah Lewis's door indicated that he would return in forty-five minutes, but that was its perpetual promise whenever the door was shut.

He walked quietly through the empty alcove, setting his feet down so the rubber soles on his shoes wouldn't chirp on the tile. He paused in the doorway of the vault where he saw her bending over an open drawer and felt a shudder of excitement. He pulled his lip back across his teeth and reached out. His hands passed below her arms and he felt side boobs. He cupped and pressed them gently like ripe melons. "Surprise!" he whispered and his front end contacted her rounded bottom.

She didn't jump. She didn't make a sound, but relaxed and backed against him slightly. "Not now, Seymour!" she said without turning around. "I told you I'm much too busy to fool around now."

"Seymour?" He pulled his hands away.

"Oh!" She clasped her hand over her mouth in an exaggerated gesture like a silent film star. "It's you, Mario."

"*Seymour?*" he said again, with genuine hurt in his voice.

"Stop being such a little boy." She laughed, but he wasn't amused. "I knew it was you because it was an underhand grip and Baltz is strictly overhand."

"Now you're making fun of my height!" He stretched his neck.

"I smelled your Aqua Velva before you were halfway here." She tousled his hair. He stretched and stood taller. "Besides, how many times have I told you that size doesn't matter. At least when it comes to height. But if this makes you feel better–" She stepped out of her heels, but was still an inch taller.

"I only have a minute. I have a meeting with *Seymour*," he mocked. He put his arms around her ass and pulled her closer.

"Don't wrinkle my new pants," she said. "I just bought them. What do you think?"

His disappointment showed. "I hate pants. Skirts are so much more *user friendly*." He reached behind him and pulled the vault door closed.

"And don't mess my hair," she said. "I just had it done."

* * *

Virgil was sitting in the detention chair, elbows on knees and his bobbing head in his hands watching the secretaries work, choreographing their movements to some inner music. He watched Phyllis Lind step from the vault and walk through into the Main Office, scoot around the desks and sit. He waved when Mr. Giovanni followed shortly after. "Hey, Mr. G."

"What are you grinning at, Loomis?" he asked, straightening his jacket. "What did you do this time?"

Virgil got out of the chair. "Mr. Farley," he said, "sent me out in a fit of rage and a burst of passion at the beginning of the period." He removed a red hair that was caught in the flower on the AP's lapel. "Are you wearing Shalimar, Mr. G?" he said.

"Never mind me." He cleared his throat and stretched his neck. "Tell me what happened now?"

"A debate."

"In math class? Didn't I tell you to leave Mr. Farley alone and not talk politics with him?"

"It wasn't about politics, Mr. G. It was about math."

"What could you possibly debate about in math?"

"Mr. Farley said Euclid was the only real important name in modern geometry, and I brought up Nikolai Ivanovich Lobachevsky, a Russian mathematician in the field of non-

Euclidean geometry who disproved Euclid's fifth postulate about lines and points and parallels."

"Is there a *point* to this, Loomis?"

"I told him that Lobachevsky's new geometry replaced Euclid's."

"And he threw you out for that?"

"Not right then. Mr. Farley said Nikolai Ivanovich Lobachevsky was a commie. But I knew he meant Nikolai Ivanovich *Lenin,* which is what I told him. And he said *all* Russians are commies. So I said calling Lobachevsky a communist because he was Russian would be like saying Euclid was homosexual because he was Greek."

"Then?"

"Nope." He waved his hands in the air. "He said because Euclid was the *father* of geometry he couldn't be homosexual, and that I had better take back what I said. I told him it was an analogy and that I hadn't actually said Euclid *was* homosexual, although I thought he *probably* was. Then things got personal. Mr. Farley said I was a blight on the earth and a general nuisance, a pain in the ass in his class, and that people like me should be cut out of society like a cancer. He said he hated me, but that he was going to pass me this time so I could graduate and get drafted. That way the army would make a man out of me and send me off to the jungles of Vietnam to be killed." Virgil took a breath. "I asked him if he was ever in the army and if they had made a *man* out of *him*. He said his teaching job got him a deferment, so I said that the army probably wouldn't have made a man out of him anyway."

"I'm sure he loved that." Mr. Giovanni was getting impatient. "So he threw you out."

"No. The conversation turned to music and according to Mr. Farley, rock and roll and groups like the Beatles and the Rolling Stones are responsible for the downfall of Western Civilization. He said that John Lennon, whose name is the same as Nikolai Lenin, is a commie, and that the Beatles would never last as long as Frank Sinatra, who is twice the singer as all of the Beatles and the Stones combined. And he said that Mick Jagger is an immoral prancing little faggot, his words, with a drug problem, who'll be dead from an overdose before he's thirty. I reminded him that Frank Sinatra is in all likelihood an alcoholic womanizer, who associates with known Mafia members and has ties to organized crime." He paused.

"And?"

"That's when he threw me out." Virgil handed him the student referral.

Mr. Giovanni looked at the first word of the long account "Insubordination" and didn't bother to read the rest. He folded the referral and stuck it into his pocket.

"So," Virgil asked "how we going to handle this one?"

"You just sit here in the detention chair for the rest of the day and then go home. And stop bothering Mr. Farley." He shook his head and started for Mr. Baltz's office.

"Works for me, but hey, Mr. G–"

"What now, Loomis?"

"I really don't think I should yell it." He lowered his voice. "There's some lipstick–" He handed him a tissue. "Before you go in there you probably want to wipe your face and your chin."

His face flushed almost deeper red than the lipstick. He wiped it, looked at the smudge and put the tissue into his pocket. He walked around the counter past Phyllis Lind who was touching up her lipstick. She pressed the intercom on her desk and he could hear it inside the office.

It took a moment before Baltz replied. "What is it, Miss Lind?"

"Ms. And Mr. Giovanni is here for the meeting."

The door buzzer sounded and the AP stepped inside the principal's office. "Sorry I'm late."

Baltz looked tired. "It hasn't been an easy couple of weeks, Mario. Besides the bullshit here with Zwill and the cops and some lingering fallout from Parent's Night, Edie's mother is staying at the house again, in my bed, and I am sleeping on the pull-out couch."

The damp circle on the desk blotter made Mario think Helen O'Dell wasn't the only one who napped on her desk after lunch. He touched his face and absently sniffed Shalimar on his fingers. The office smelled too, of air freshener and something else he couldn't quite identify.

"I'm getting too old for this shit, Mario. It just may be time for a change."

"You're not talking about quitting, or retirement, are you?"

"Maybe sooner than you think." The overhead fluorescent light accented the deep circles under his eyes. "Everything that should be down is up. My cholesterol, blood pressure. And everything that should be up is down. Nessmith told me I need to take a little vacation, or I may get a permanent vacation. When I do go, Mario, I'll need a successor. O'Dell dropped the ball with the pants suit thing and joined them. I can't trust or depend on her. Noah Lewis–" He shook his head. "And Zwill's heading for a straight jacket and a semiprivate room in South Oaks. So that leaves you." He looked around the office. "Someday, Mario, all this could be yours."

"I'm honored that you hold me in such high regard." His legs kicked back and forth excitedly. He smiled and smelled his fingers again. He couldn't wait to tell Phyllis.

"Meanwhile, the jacket and tie thing is getting out of hand and I'll need you to be on top of it." He lit a cigarette, took a deep puff and handed over a ditto sheet. "Read this."

"'Our sisters have asserted their freedom and now it is our turn to stand up to oppression! Come to an important UMU strategy meeting to finalize plans for the upcoming tie-burning.'" He turned it over and looked on the back. "There's no date, time or room number."

"Your perception is astounding, Mario. Maybe it's a phony. Maybe the whole UMU thing is intended to get a rise out of me. But I sure as hell don't want to lose another battle after the pants thing. That's why I want you to track this down to its source. If it *is* real, I want you to head it off!" He crumpled the ditto and threw it toward the wastebasket, but it hit the rim and bounced along the floor. "Handle it." He nodded. "My money's on Scapelli."

"Scapelli hasn't worn a tie or a suit jacket in years. So why would he be involved?"

"To 'Break Baltz'! It just smells like the kind of shit he pulls. Like writing on the bathroom wall."

"Speaking of that, I removed the screws from all the toilet seats in the men's room like you suggested, but it hasn't helped. There's more writing than ever–in different handwriting and colors now. So much for the marker pen recall." He got up to retrieve the paper. "The comments are nastier, very personal."

"Show me!" he said, stubbed out his cigarette and bolted out of the office.

"Hey, Mr. B," Virgil called after the two of them rushing past, but the principal didn't respond.

* * *

"Elevator's temporarily out of service," Slow Charley said, pointing down the shaft where the Head Custodian was standing on top of the car banging the cable with a wrench. "Stash says it'll be fixed in a few–"

"Shit!"

They climbed the four flights of steps up to the third floor and had to catch their breath before busting through the door of the faculty toilet. The doorknob crashed into the tile wall and echoed off the tiles in the confined area. Stanley Milnow was standing at the urinal next to Red Farley and he turned involuntarily in the direction of the noise. The redirected stream of urine splashed on Red Farley's pants leg.

"Jesus fuck! You're pissing on my pants, Stanley!" he yelled and turned his own apparatus on the shoe salesman. "What the hell kind of homo bullshit is that?" he raged, red-faced, and slapped at the offending organ.

"What are *you* doing, Farley? Now you're pissing on me!" He slapped Red's hand away from his crotch and grabbed Red's.

Oblivious to the drama unfolding in front of him, Mr. Baltz flung aside the green door and ran into the first stall. "BALTZ HAS NO BALLZ!" was written in red. Under that someone else had scribbled in blue ink, "His wife duz!" He unsuccessfully tried to rub off the words with the palm of his hand, gave up and went into the second stall. "BREAK BALTZ!" was in red. "Eat shit MSB!" was in blue. "...and die, tyrant!" was added in thick green crayon. In the third stall the red message was an invitation to anarchy. "TODAY PANTS SUITS, TOMORROW NO SUITS JACKETS OR TIES!" The other messages were "HELTER SKELTER" and "KILL THE PIGS!"

He dipped the end of his handkerchief into the bowl. "You get the other two stalls, Mario."

He watched his boss on his knees wetting and wiping, attacking the handwriting. A part of him felt pity for what the man, his idol, his role model had become. The rest was filled with disgust and elation at the prospect of taking over after his breakdown. The other two remained speechless, watching him with great curiosity.

"I'm the principal of this school, entitled to respect!" He came out of the stall short of breath, his face dark. "When I catch the bastards responsible–" He saw them for the first time still holding on to one another. "What the fuck are you two morons doing? Zip up your pants, you deviates, and get to class before I call the police and have you both arrested!"

He disappeared as suddenly as he had entered and when the four students inside the elevator saw him coming, they frantically pressed the button and the door shut when he was less than a foot away. He banged on the door, jammed his elevator key into the slot and turned it, but the only thing it produced was the emergency alarm when the car got stuck between floors. That was mistaken for the dismissal bell and the third floor filled with students. In seconds the two administrators were overrun by the stampeding crowd rushing for the lockers.

"Jesus Christ!" Baltz yelled. The stream moved him like a twig caught in rushing water running along the curb toward the sewer. He got sucked through the doorway and flushed down to the second floor. When the actual dismissal bell rang, a larger crowd flooded the second floor and carried him upward like an erupting volcano back to the third floor.

"Hey, Mr. Baltz." Virgil's smiling face greeted him when he finally reached the Main Office, bruised and wrinkled. "Mr. G just went into your office. You really look–"

"Fuck you, Loomis," he said between clenched teeth and continued without stopping. Virgil shrugged and went back to the detention chair.

"Up!" he exploded when he saw Giovanni in his desk chair. "Go see Polakas now and tell him to get somebody up there to the third floor to scrub all that shit off the walls! And I don't care if he has to do it himself! Now!"

He pulled the damp handkerchief from his pocket and wiped his face, but remembered why it was wet and dropped it on the desk blotter. He grabbed the phone and dialed the three-digit in-house number on the black phone.

"Dr. Flackett's office," the receptionist answered, after five rings.

"You took long enough," he barked. "Seymour Baltz. Put Flackett on and hurry up!"

"The Superintendent is in conference–"

"Interrupt him!"

"I'm sorry, Mr. Baltz. He left orders not to be disturbed–"

"Do it! This is an emergency."

There was the muffled sound of voices and the phone clicked. "Hello, Seymour. What's your emergency now? Another conspiracy?"

"I need that bathroom expedited. We agreed. Adornau promised the funds."

"That was before Parent's Night?" Silence. "You're lucky he let the incident die and kept it out of the papers. I convinced him not to demand your resignation."

"I'll settle for less. Four thousand. The two of you can do whatever with the difference."

"No can do, Seymour."

He played his trump card. "How's your wife, Don? Still getting chemo? I am so sorry. And your secretary? The young one, really attractive, though not my type. She answered the phone, right?" Silence. "I'd be the last one to talk, but some people are saying you bypassed all the Civil Service red tape shit to hire her. But people will always talk and they love to gossip. Some people don't understand leaving a sick wife to go on a superintendent junket with a young and very attractive secretary. The Bahamas, wasn't it?"

"Are you trying to blackmail me?"

"Blackmail, Donald, is against the law. What I'm doing here is negotiating." He had regained the initiative. "I don't give a flying fuck who you're *schtupping* now. All I want is five thousand dollars–"

"You said four."

"The project just got more expensive. But you'll still have enough to take your secretary to the next conference over Christmas. The word is you booked it, right?"

There was silence. When the superintendent spoke his voice was lower. "I'll talk to Lalo and maybe I can sell it to him, but not as your toilet. I'll need something good to call the expense."

"Call it Project X for all I fucking care! Tell him it's for an experimental learning program… with computers. Make something up. You're a bullshit artist. It goes with the job. Just get the money, Don." He hung up the receiver. "That is how to handle an asshole," he said aloud to himself.

He lit a cigarette from the pack of Luckies. He checked that his office door was locked, picked up the folded copy of *Newsday* on his desk and went into the pine-smelling closet. Once he got the funds he was considering some ideas that would take "Project X" well beyond his executive toilet.

In the News
December 1971

December 3

The 3rd Indi-Pakistani war begins when India intervenes in the Pakistani civil war. Pakistan attacks Indian airfields and India mobilizes its army after nearly 10 million Pakistani refugees pour into India.

December 9

Pres. Nixon vetoes legislation calling for the establishment of a national day care system.

December 16

Pakistani forces in East Pakistan surrender to the allied forces of India and the new country of Bangladesh, which accuses Pakistan of war atrocities and the deaths of some 3 million people during the 9-month civil war.

December 18

Pres. Nixon devalues the dollar.

Despite the secret CIA-directed force of 30,000 indigenous Laotian tribesmen and hundreds of millions of U.S. dollars to strengthen anticommunist strongholds, North Vietnamese troops capture the Plain of Jars in Laos.

December 22

Pres. Nixon signs an extension of the Economic Stabilization Act, allowing him another year in which to right the economy.

December 23

Pres. Nixon signs the National Cancer Act and declares war on cancer.

December slid in on Wednesday. The building was finally warm enough that Red Farley could no longer see his breath as he walked through the halls, but the chill still made his nose run. He looked puffy from the Irish knit pullover sweater under his jacket that he kept in his classroom closet for such occasions, or maybe some of that was from too much Thanksgiving. Since the sweater rarely saw the light of day and had never been cleaned over the years, the white wool had grayed. He was humming Wagner's "Ride of the Valkyries" in time with his steps. Unlike most teachers who hated PB Duty, he loved making his rounds.

"Silence and speed are the keys to my success for catching them in the act," he boasted in the faculty room when a discussion of PB Duty came up. "Peeing or pooping?" Terry quipped.

Red quietly opened the door to the boy's room on the second floor and slipped in. It was empty. The radiator was warm so he leaned against it to absorb the heat. "There's nothing like the smell of methane and Pine-Sol in the morning," he said and delivered a long, almost musical two-note fart into the silence that reverberated off the tiles.

Immediately a voice answered from the far stall. "Hey, Mr. Farley."

He jumped. "Loomis, what are you doing sneaking around in there?"

Virgil came out holding a copy of Tolstoy's *War and Peace*. "Just catching up on my reading." He went to the sink, put the book down on a dry place and washed his hands. "Still no toilet paper." Virgil pulled a black bandanna with a white peace symbol from his back pocket and dried his hands.

"Pass, Loomis?" His voice boomed in the enclosed space.

"You feeling okay, Mr. Farley? I heard you clearing your throat. You really don't sound well. It might be a good idea to stop at the nurse's office, it being flu season and all. How was your Thanksgiving?"

"Don't worry about me, Loomis. And my Thanksgiving is none of your business." He picked up the book and dropped it like it was hot. "More Communist propaganda. Don't they read American books in English class anymore? Nice stories like that Tom Sawyer thing or Huckleberry Hound. Pass." He held out his hand.

"I'm reading Tolstoy on my own." He unfolded the damp pass and handed it over for closer scrutiny.

"It's wet!"

"Water mostly. And those brown stains–"

He dropped the pass, turned the faucet and ran water over his hands. He looked at the empty paper towel dispenser and dried his hand on the front of his sweater.

"I bought a Twix in the cafeteria. Nothing to have a stroke about." He patted Red Farley's arm.

"That's assault, Loomis! Don't you touch me! Don't you *ever* touch me again!" His complexion went almost purple.

"Technically unconsented physical contact with another person, even where the contact is not violent but merely menacing or offensive is battery, Mr. Farley. You're much too defensive. You have to relax. You look like you're going to explode! Hypertension is a leading cause of death in teachers–"

"Are you threatening me now, Loomis?"

"No, I read that in an article in *Psychology Today*. Did you know the second most common ailment teachers suffer is varicose veins."

"Don't you worry about my veins, Loomis."

"Do you eat a lot of red meat? Fast food? It's no good for your heart. Studies show that red meat makes people more aggressive. Eating more vegetables along with regular exercise would bring down your stress level, lower your aggression, cut your chance of having a heart attack in half and bring down your weight too."

"Thank you, *Doctor* Loomis. I weigh exactly what I did when I wrestled in St. Patrick High School for Boys." He sucked in his stomach and pumped out his chest.

"Heavyweight division?"

He ignored the comment. "For your information, not that it's any of your business, I *do* exercise. I work out with Mr. Ritchie's wrestling team. I'm assistant coach, smart ass."

"There aren't supposed to be extracurricular activities during austerity, Mr. Farley."

"That's what you know, smart-ass. Austerity won't last forever. There's a secret Wrestling Team preparing for when austerity ends. A select group training in the locker room every afternoon, keeping sharp for when competition starts up. Not that you'd even know where the locker room is, Loomis. Your mommy probably had the doctor to write a note excusing you from gym."

"My mommy *is* a doctor. And so is my daddy. Where do I sign up if I wanted to join?"

"You're not fit, Loomis. Coach Ritchie has a 'No Long-Haired Weirdo' policy. Thank God he still has high standards. His wrestlers are always well groomed and wear suit jackets and ties whenever they go to wrestling meets. Maybe you should join the Students for a Democratic Society instead."

"Oh, I already belong to the SDS, Mr. Farley." He took out his membership card. "Would you know if there are other secret clubs and teams that meet? The Debate Club? Cheerleading? Or is it just wrestling?"

"Get the hell out, Loomis. Pick up your pass, your Communist Manifesto and your SDS card and get out of my sight!"

He was out of breath when he resumed his PB Duty duties armed with his new Standard Dexter Issue black marker. In the first stall he attacked the latest graffiti, changing it to GO BOOK YOURSELF and MILLY SADOWSKI SOCKS BIG COOK. That was easy. In the second stall he moved rapidly sketching a bathing suit on a rather interesting drawing of a nude female with exaggerated genitalia, and he left I WANT YOU TO SOAK MY CLOCK on the back of the stall door. In the third stall he deftly handled an EAT SHIP, but he stopped short when he encountered MISS WELLEN HAS GREAT MELONS! His marker was poised, but his mind was blank. He pulled out the official PB Duty alphabetized correction ditto for help. "M" was MELONS-less. He reread the message and pondered the possibilities. "Damn kids!" he said returning the list and the marker to his pocket. He pushed open the stall door and started for the Main Office.

* * *

The secretaries were busy on the phones and pounding their typewriters. Everything was in motion, especially Phyllis Lind, who was sharpening a handful of #2 pencils to stockpile them for Guidance Testing.

"You know, Phyllis–" Elsie Bergin called to her from her folding chair at her temporary workplace by the window. She was folding Guidance notification letters and stuffing them into envelopes to be mailed to every parent about the upcoming test schedule, "–we have an electric sharpener in the vault that would make the job easier and faster."

"Thank you, Elsie. I'm a traditionalist and prefer doing it by hand. And it gives me a little exercise too." She turned the little handle in tight circles and with each quick rotation her behind circled as well. She looked over at the three boys from Auto Shop admiring her technique and she gave the #2 a few more cranks. "Nothing like the pump and grind of the old universal gear box to keep that motor purring, hey boys?" she said and winked. They blushed. "You boys better get back to shop class," she added, "before your pants explode."

Mrs. Butrum was seated at the personnel file cabinet with some teacher folders opened in her lap, situated perfectly to listen to the conversations around her. She nodded when Red Farley hurriedly rounded the counter, turned left without acknowledging her and disappeared through the archway down the steps into the Administrative Alcove.

"Well," she tutted at his rudeness, "some people. I wonder what has him in such a snit that he can't even manage a civil hello." She fingered through the folders and pulled out Frederick Farley's folder.

Mario Giovanni's office was empty and Zwill was still out sick. Helen O'Dell's door was closed and a "Meeting Do

Not Disturb" sign in her window. Only Noah Lewis was in. "Good afternoon, Mr. Lewis–"

He was seated behind his desk staring blankly out the window into the courtyard. He turned when he heard his name again. He had a vague smile on his face as if coming out of a pleasant dream. "Mr. Farley, I, auh, was just thinking to myself, it won't be long until Christmas, and, auh, then June can't be far behind."

"I have a problem, Noah. I was just on bathroom patrol–" It was the wrong thing to say.

The smile on the AP's face disappeared. "Bathrooms are, auh, Mr. Giovanni's area of, auh, responsibility and expertise."

"I know. But he's not in his office. Zwill is still out cuckoo and O'Dell's door is closed. I need help now–"

"Well, Mr. Farley, I, auh, am right in the middle of something and I, auh–" His hands were in motion as he fumbled with the desk drawer. "I, auh, was just going on my, auh, lunch break." He pulled open the center drawer and felt around inside without looking.

"Lunch? It's almost dismissal."

"Auh, late lunch." He pulled out a partially wrapped sandwich and looked at it with great interest. "Cheese!" he said excitedly. "Imported, auh, Swiss cheese, with spicy brown mustard on white bread! My favorite. I forgot that I, auh, made an imported Swiss cheese sandwich–" He showed him.

"That's great, but I just need some direction. This won't take long. It's about something that was written in one of the stalls–"

"As I, auh, said that falls under Mr. Giovanni's, auh, sphere of administrative responsibility. Especially the writing on the walls part, and I, auh, wouldn't want to infringe on his domain." He opened the wax paper and prepared to take a bite. A piece was already missing from the corner of the sandwich. He reached into the side drawer and removed a container of orange juice with a straw stuck into the top. "Now if you'll excuse me, it's, auh, lunchtime."

Red backed out and shook his head. "Never an AP around when you need one."

"Looking for me, Red?" Mr. Giovanni called out from Helen O'Dell's office. Her door was open and they were sharing a bag of Cheez Doodles.

"PB Duty problem," he said, "and Lewis is out to lunch."

Helen O'Dell sat back in her chair with her hands behind her head. She leaned forward and dipped her yellow fingers into the bag for more Doodles.

"What's the problem?"

"Second-floor boy's room. Somebody wrote 'Miss Wellen has great melons.'"

"Great melons, huh? Well, they're right about that." He stretched his neck and nodded at Helen O'Dell, who nodded back, cramming a handful into her mouth and wiping the yellow cheese powder on the jacket of her pants suit. "So what's your problem?"

"I don't know what to do. The ditto list you gave out is no help."

"That's because 'melons' isn't an obscenity."

"I think that in this case it is," Red said and he looked to Helen O'Dell for consensus. "What do you think, Helen?"

She reached for the bag. "The implication is there. 'Melons' obviously refers to her boobs. At least that's what I get from it."

"But technically melons are a fruit and therefore they are not obscene."

"What about banana? Banana is a fruit too," Red Farley countered. "But if someone wrote, 'I want to stick my banana up Miss Wellen's—'"

"That's different. Your example is clearly describing an obscene *action* with a banana. An unnatural act, sodomy with a piece of fruit. And the word 'ass' is on the list I gave you. But the 'melons' comment as written simply says that Miss Wellen *has* melons—"

"*Great* melons," he corrected.

"That doesn't matter. It's a statement that indicates ownership of a piece of fruit… big or small… or great."

"Although," Helen O'Dell offered, "it is obvious that the comment about Wellen's great melons is a suggestive reference to her body parts. It would be more obvious if it said, 'I want to suck on or lick Miss Wellen's melons.'"

"Great melons," he corrected. "Then it *would* be obscene because it is describing a physical action again."

"Wait," Red said, "are you saying it's obscene because of the word 'suck'? Then you are saying that sucking anything is obscene. I suck Lifesavers. Babies suck bottles. That's not obscene, is it?"

"That's a tricky one all right." The AP thought about it. "But babies also suck tits, and 'tits' definitely is obscene."

"What about 'breasts,' I mean in the case of babies?"

"Hmmmm, Yes, that's another good one."

"So what do I do? I can't just leave it up there on the wall."

"I know," Helen O'Dell replied. "Why not cross out 'melons' and write in 'tits' and eliminate any ambiguity. Then you can simply change 'tits' to anything that fits!" She smiled. "That rhymes."

"Problem solved, Red," he said stretching his neck and reaching for the last Cheez Doodle. "Now go take care of it."

Red Farley pulled out his marker and rushed from the office.

"O'Dell," he said to her when they were alone, "now I know why you're an administrator. You are a genius in your own right."

"Anybody in the hall?" she asked.

He stuck his head out. "Free and clear."

"Want to shoot some hoops?"

"Here? Now?"

She opened her desk drawer and pulled out a ball the size of a softball. "Nerf Ball," she said, "Brand new. I bought it at Stern's. Made of foam for indoors." She threw it to him and he ducked. "I put the hoop on the back of my door."

He swung around in the chair and pushed the door shut with his foot in one fluid motion. "You're on."

"What do you make of all this tie-burning stuff?" The ditto was on her desk.

"Probably just a lot of bullshit. But Baltz thinks there's something to it and gave me *carte blanche* to shut it down. Told me he felt pressured, under siege. Said he couldn't take it and mentioned he might even take some time off, a leave, maybe even retire." He shook his head. "He was actually crying the other day. It was pathetic."

"Just because of some writing on the walls? If I knew that was all it took to get rid of him!"

"He wants me to stick around late to keep an eye out for any meetings. And he wants me there if they have a tie-burning on the seventh like they said. He doesn't want another pants suits incident."

"But you'll miss happy hour."

"A man's gotta do what a man's gotta do, Helen, and I'm a man. Maybe next year at this time I'll even be *the* man." He took a shot at the basket and missed. "Twenty-one game, but you have to win by two. And you have to spot me something."

She considered it. "Okay. Seven points."

"I was only going to ask for five."

"Take six then."

"Okay, six, but if I win you buy the next snacks. Winner's choice. I call Ring Dings!"

"Sucker!" She let go with a righthand hook shot that dropped right through the hoop. She grinned. "Nothing but net! Six to one. Oh, and if you get it in you go again... and the other guy has to get the ball."

He complained and went to retrieve the ball.

Camelot

Official Publication of the Partnership of Parents and Teachers
in Association for better Farmington Public Schools
Harriet Stegle, President P-PTA

Vol. 3   Issue 3   December 1971

Where does the time go? It's getting so I can't seem count to 28 anymore. And when I told my husband I was late this month, he passed out! Of course I was referring to this issue of Camelot! Wasn't November here and gone in a blink? And now that Thanksgiving is behind us, we have the Christmas/Chanukah vacation to look forward to.

AROUND THE DISTRICT:
Elvis the Pelvis meets Nelda the Pearl... Last week Nelda Pearl, fifth-grade teacher at Willis Elementary, broke her pelvis in a "freak accident" when she tripped over several of her students during story time. No children were hurt in the incident! You can send get well cards to Nelda c/o Happyvale Rehabilitation Center in Amityville, where she will undergo months of intensive physical therapy after she completes detox for substance abuse. Lucky her! She will be out for the rest of the school year.

Too much of a good thing? I have it on good authority that Elisa Hyman at West Street Elementary School will take advantage of the Christmas/Chanukah/New Year break to finally schedule that breast reduction surgery she has been talking about for years! That should be my problem, my husband said, but I guess half a loaf is better than none.

On the brighter side of life... War hero and former World War II POW Willy Zwill, Assistant Principal at R&G Memorial HS, is back behind his desk after a brief R&R. Willy was captured by the Japanese somewhere in the Pacific and held as a POW for 4 years. Last month he suffered a temporary relapse of stress fatigue that triggered an attack of malaria. But he has recovered nicely. Welcome back, Willy, just in time to see a revolution, on the fashion front.

Aren't they lovely...? It's no more up-skirt drafts on those cold winter days and no more chafed thighs for the courageous women at R&G. The gentler sex took a stand for comfort and practicality and made a fashion statement in the process. They are now parading around that drafty Klaus Brinker, Jr. Temporary Wing in pants suits!

Also from the High School... A memo received from R&G's United Males Untied reminds everyone to, "Remember Pearl Harbor! Remember the ceremonial tie-burning to be held in the faculty parking lot after school. Come one, come all, come make it happen!" I'm not exactly sure what the plan is, but Camelot wishes UMU great success with their school event.

NEWS AND VIEWS:

Here's the latest on the P-PTA Florida orange and grapefruit orders. It seems the company that took the orders has filed for bankruptcy, so there won't be any citrus this year in your Christmas stockings or hanging from your Chanukah bushes and there will be no reimbursements either. So far all attempts to recover any of the money that was collected have been, well... fruitless!

See you next time with more news from the trenches!

"It's been two weeks, Mario, and you still have nothing concrete." Mr. Baltz paced around behind his desk. His concern was obvious from the two cigarettes he was smoking, one in his hand and the other curling a string of blue smoke into the air from the shrunken head ashtray. He picked up the dittos that covered his desk blotter. "You haven't been to a single meeting. None of you can even say for certain if there have been meetings. Well, today's the day. Even Stegle's bullshit newsletter says there's going to be a tie-burning and we're no further along on this.." He lit a third cigarette.

The three assistant principals looked vaguely like a tableau of the three monkeys. Helen O'Dell had an index finger in her ear. Mario Giovanni stifled a yawn. And the recently returned Willy Zwill in the center rubbed his twitching eyes until he saw kaleidoscoping stars. Noah Lewis wasn't present. He rarely attended regular cabinet meetings, so they never told him when an emergency session came up.

"In exactly three hours," he said looking at the wall clock, "and sixteen minutes–"

"Eighteen minutes," Willy Zwill corrected. "The school clocks are two minutes fast. Mine's synchronized with the official Naval Observatory in Washington, D.C., so it beeps right on the hour, right to the second," His reddened eyes sent out a spasm of separate blinks like Morse code. Since his return to school his twitching had increased, although everyone pretended not to notice.

"Willy, now is not the time to tell me if the big hand is on the three or the four," he said brusquely. "We're talking about more important matters–"

"Actually, this is a digital. A Timex. There is no big hand. Only numbers that are much easier to read. And in the night if I press this button a light–" He showed them his watch.

"In a little more than three hours," Baltz ignored him, "that goddamn ceremonial tie-burning will take place unless *we* can come up with something to prevent it."

"Or will it?" Mario Giovanni said. "They're predicting rain."

"That's great. One of you knows the time and the other the weather." He paced toward the window, held the venetian blinds away from the dirty glass and stared out into the courtyard. The ground was dry. "The sky is blue, Mario."

"But it's definitely clouding up." There was barely a trace of optimism in his voice. "What's the latest, O'Dell?"

She removed the earpiece to a little portable radio in her jacket pocket. "Barometer is falling. Dew point is up. There's a cold front coming down from Canada. They are reporting a sixty percent chance of late afternoon showers on this station. The other station has it at seventy percent starting as snow flurries and then changing to rain, possible thunderstorms, heavy at times, with high winds."

Zwill twitched and raised his hand tentatively. "What are the chances–" he started weakly

"Speak up, Willy, if you have something to say."

He sat up straighter in his chair. "When I was a POW back in the camp the Japs rationed our drinking water so we went for a long time without a shower. And we had to depend on rain. I remember we had a guy in the camp, a Navajo, who brought on the monsoons every year with a rain dance. Maybe we could–" He stopped and sat back in his seat.

"Dance?" Mr. Baltz stubbed out all three cigarettes in disgust.

"Not dancing." Zwill recovered. "I saw it on TV and it was done by seeding the clouds with potash and dry ice." His whole body shook with excitement. "We could check with the custodian to see if he has any lying around. Then maybe we could get the Science Department to mix up a batch, go up on the roof with a helium balloon or a rocket and seed the clouds. It's worth a try–"

"Or you can call an emergency faculty meeting for this afternoon," Mario Giovanni said, "and keep them late, until it gets dark."

"At best that would only delay the event for an hour or so."

"And *then* we can make it rain."

"Enough, Willy, about making rain and that POW crap. We know you were in a camp thirty years ago and ate rice with maggots and drank pee. But this is now and we need to come up with a plan of action for a real problem in the real world."

The office door opened slightly and Noah Lewis stuck his head through the crack. "Oh, here you are." He was holding a brown bag with LUNCH lettered across it. "Sorry I'm, auh, late. I was having my lunch. But I, auh, didn't get the notice about the meeting. I thought meetings were always Monday. If I did, I, auh, forgot, or maybe I, auh, heard from somebody that it, auh, was called off." He shut the door behind him and sat in a chair in the far corner

"What did you just say?" Mr. Baltz asked.

"I, auh, said I, auh, thought it was called off–"

"That's it, Noah!" Baltz yelled. "It's brilliant and it's so simple!" He smiled. "All we have to do is put out a ditto before the end of the day announcing that the tie-burning thing was canceled. Early enough for everyone to read it, but late enough so nobody can refute it." He thought. "Nothing official looking. It can't be an actual memo. Something hand-printed, simple and to the point. Mario, take this down in caps! 'Attention all members of United Males Untied! This afternoon's ceremonial tie-burning has been canceled due to the weather.' And maybe add a drawing."

"I have an idea," Helen O'Dell sketched a frowning smiley face with a tear rolling down, an open umbrella and several lines to indicate the rain. She held it up for them to see.

"That's it! Mario, you run them off, enough to go around, but don't let anybody see you." He looked at the wall clock. "Then wait until a half hour before dismissal to get them out. Drop a few on the floor in the halls, a bunch on the front counter near the time clock, on the bulletin board and the table in the faculty room. And don't forget the faculty men's bathrooms. But whatever you do, don't get caught. We want this to look like it came from them and not from us. Get on this right away." He walked over and opened the door for them. "Willy," he said when he saw that he was still upset, "I'm sorry I spoke the way I did. I've been under a lot of strain. No hard feelings? And thank you for your service."

Zwill flinched when he felt the principal's hand on his back.

Mr. Baltz shut the door behind them. Noah Lewis was still seated in his chair near the wall eating a cookie. "Meeting's over, Noah. You can go back to whatever it is you were doing."

"Auh?" He looked around and saw that the others were gone. "So soon? Hardly worth coming." He picked himself out of the chair and left.

Mr. Baltz rubbed his palms together. It just might work. There was a knock on his door and he pressed the buzzer. "What did you forget, Noah?" he said, expecting the assistant principal. Terry Scapelli walked in and his face dropped. "What do *you* want, Mr. Scapelli?"

"That thing you asked me to do before Thanksgiving. The piece for Dr. Flackett's monthly report–"

"Oh, yes. I thought you had forgotten"–he had forgotten–"and I was just going to have Miss Lind call you and ask for it."

Terry pulled out a sealed white envelope. "I did it as a press release to save you the trouble of having to write one yourself." He opened the envelope. "If I may," he began. "A multi-faceted and many-talented individual, whose artistic abilities range from published poet and fiction writer to graphic artist and actor, Terry J. Scapelli must be considered a true *Renaissance Man* in every sense that phrase conjures up. Besides the enormous amount of time he spends preparing his lessons for his students, Mr. Scapelli is quite often called upon by his colleagues to showcase his talents in and out of their classrooms. These additional demands on his time have taken the form of numerous requests for Mr. Scapelli to appear as a guest lecturer, to read his poetry and to demonstrate his skills in the area of improvisational theater technique. In order to do so, quite often Mr. Scapelli has to sacrifice his own free time, going without lunch or the benefit of an unassigned period just to keep up with all the requests for his many talents. Mr. Scapelli is currently working on a grand improvisational theater piece with Ms Sue Ellen Wellen and the Social Studies Department he admits will not be completed until the end of the school year in June. He takes great satisfaction in assisting his colleagues in any way he can. Requests for his services are often and ongoing. Teachers wishing to work with Mr. Scapelli can contact him directly in writing and place their requests in his mailbox at R&G Memorial HS." He paused. "I hope it's what you wanted, Mr. Baltz." He refolded the paper, replaced it carefully into the envelope and handed it to the principal.

Mr. Baltz dropped it on his desk and looked at his watch. "Now, Mr. Scapelli, is there anything else? I will see that Dr. Flackett gets this. Now if you'll excuse me, I have to use some of my talents as principal." He walked him out and waited for the door to close. He pulled the envelope from his desk, crumpled it into a tight ball and threw it into the wastepaper basket.

EXTRA EXTRA

THE WAR IS OVER!

**Administration Assumes A New Position On Suit Jackets
And Ties!
Ceremonial Tie-Burning Is The Deciding Factor!**

(Dateline: Farmington, New York—December 8, 1971)

For a time it was questionable whether yesterday's scheduled tie-burning would take place, due in part to the rain and a last-ditch attempt by radical right-wing tie-ists to confuse the members of UNITED MALES UNTIED. The eleventh-hour circulation of bogus handbills falsely announced the cancellation of the event. But 30 years to the day after the bombing of Pearl Harbor, a day that will forever live in infamy, on December 7, 1971, the forces of good once again triumphed over the Evil Empire. 15 male faculty members and 7 female diehards in suitable pants suit ensembles assembled in the faculty parking lot after school and managed a successful tie-burning.

These stout and steadfast individuals braved the steady downpour in the name of truth, justice and freedom. After one UMU member tore off the offensive tie from his neck and jumped on the roof of a Volkswagen bus, another managed to strike the waterproof match that eventually sent the damp symbol of male oppression to a smoldering end. Immediately a chain reaction like an atomic fireball over Hiroshima had all of the males in attendance immolating their ties. In the heat and the passion of the moment, one unidentified pants-suited woman stripped off her brassiere and threw it into the burning pile. "It is the least I can do to show my support... by burning my support!" she shouted to the cheering crowd, prompting several of the other women to do the same.

The weather may have dampened the ground, but not the spirits of the demonstrators who spontaneously broke into song, singing an unprecedented three choruses of the movement's revolutionary anthem, "Suit Jackets and Ties Bah Bah Bah... Cha Cha Cha!" Immediately after the fire died to embers and the smoldering embers turned to ash, the crowd marched in a human chain to The Alibi Bar and Grill where they toasted their success! Ah, the sweet taste of victory!

A dramatic announcement concerning the Administration's new position on attire is forthcoming at this afternoon's faculty meeting.

Willy Zwill dropped the account of the tie-burning on his desk. Even with the fan his office was still extremely warm and he was wearing a pair of brown tropical shorts and a T-shirt. He jumped when the telephone rang and considered not picking it up. But when he heard the muffled bang on his wall he knew it was Helen O'Dell. She did that whenever she knew he was in and wasn't picking up and she needed to talk to him.

"Did you see it, O'Dell?"

"The ditto? Of course I've seen it. Everybody's seen it."

"No, the event. I was just reading the account and I don't know when all that happened. I didn't see any of it. I was there in my car across from the parking lot right after dismissal and I waited for hours. Nothing. I drove around to the athletic field to see if maybe they were there. And then I checked the parking lot at the Administration Building. I even got out of my car and walked all around the school in the pouring rain in case they were hiding. I was drenched and I went back to my car again and I fell asleep." He sneezed. "Now I have a cold from sitting there in my wet clothes." He sneezed again. "These are some very insidious people we're up against. But I think they saw me and waited until I left."

"Bless you," she said and heard him blow his nose. "It never happened, Willy. The whole thing is a sham. A charade."

"What do you mean? I was there."

"So you said and you didn't see anything. Mario was in his car yesterday across the street and says he saw you and he stayed until after you left. So you were there and Mario was there and nobody else was there, Willy!"

"Score! Two points!" he heard the voice in the background.

"Sneaky bastards. The whole thing smells a little fishy to me, O'Dell. I'm working on a few angles and I have a few suspects. I think Wong in the Math Department might be involved."

"You're not hearing me, Willy. You got anything to eat? Me and Mario are starving."

"Wong's a little sneak. Inscrutable," he went on. "I've been watching him closely. Ever notice that he never looks you in the eye when he talks to you? And he drives a yellow Datsun 240Z. A yellow Datsun, O'Dell! What could be more obvious? Those people may smile a lot, and nod their heads, but you can't trust them. They're still holding a grudge for those two A-bombs. It was no coincidence that the tie-burning and Pearl Harbor were on the same day. I have a keen nose and this smells like Wong. I lived with them, O'Dell."

"That was Japan, Willy. Toby Wong's Chinese."

"Japs, Chinks. They're hard to tell apart," he said.

There was a rustle of cellophane into the receiver and the sounds of chewing. "I could go for some Chinese." She muffled the phone a moment.. "Mario says he could too. Want to go out to Sonny Fong's, Willy?"

"I'm too busy. My gut is telling me it's Wong. But I have to figure out who all the others are."

"Willy, there are no others. It didn't happen."

He picked up the ditto and read it. "The account describes it in detail."

"It was all a hoax. But Baltz is pissed because whoever is behind that ditto called *Newsday* with an account of the phantom tie-burning–"

"The same Phantom that's writing on the bathroom walls. It's all coming together now, O'Dell."

She sighed. "*Newsday* sent a reporter to Flackett for a statement about the District's position on a dress code. Flackett got on Baltz and Baltz wants to head the whole thing off before it becomes another *situation,* so he scheduled a special meeting of the entire faculty this afternoon. That's the other reason I called you."

"They're even more diabolical than I imagined. Masters of deceit, O'Dell."

There was more chewing. "What about that Chinese?"

"I plan to drop in on Wong to see what I can pick up from him."

"Maybe you should forget about Wong and remember the meeting. Baltz wants us to line up for the march in, a show of solidarity." There was a muffled sound as she covered the mouthpiece. "Mario says he wants some of those great chocolate chip cookies you baked." More chewing. "And don't forget to wear your jacket and tie to the meeting. If you show up without one that would *really* piss Baltz off." She covered the receiver again. "Mario wants to know if you have any Fritos? We're both starving."

He hung up the receiver and opened the center drawer of his desk. He reached deep inside and felt around until he found what he wanted. The old wooden handled Nambu Type 14 8mm pistol he had smuggled back from the camp. He had cleaned the rust and oiled it and it worked, mostly, though the magazine would only feed three bullets before it jammed. It felt good in his hand. "I'll be ready for whatever happens." He laid the pistol down carefully on the desk blotter and changed his clothes.

He liked the weight he felt when he inserted the pistol into his pocket. It couldn't be seen but the handle was in easy reach. He twitched, dropped one shoulder and shook his hands to loosen up his fingers like an old Western gun fighter. He turned and tried a fast draw, but the Nambu caught in the opening of his pocket and fell to the floor. "Concentrate and practice," he told himself and went through the routine several times before he put the gun away.

He removed the tin where he kept his home-baked cookies. He picked out four of the smaller cookies from the foil, reconsidered and put one back. He found the open bag of Fritos, remembered to stick the clip-on tie into his collar and left the office.

* * *

The faculty room buzzed with the usual talk about the kids who were already checked out for the holidays. "They are gone already," Claire Hutton said, "so there's no sense trying to teach anything new."

"It seems to happen earlier and earlier every school year," Rita Reed offered. "How many more school days do we have until Christmas?"

"Too many."

"Paul and I are flying out Friday night right after the Christmas party. Originally he wanted to take a ski vacation in Colorado, but Daddy was able to get us a great package in a warm climate. So we'll be in Kauai," Fay Schwartz-Fine told a disinterested Sue Wellen, "that's in Hawaii, its least-known island."

"I know where Kauai is, Phay, I teach social studies."

"So now the problem is I'll have to go shopping for a whole new wardrobe–"

There was grumbling about the weather, the special faculty meeting scheduled for the end of the day.

"It's not right, Maxwell, that they call a meeting without any notice," Stanley Milnow complained to the association president. "I have to get to work and isn't there something in the contract about that?"

Joel Maxwell shrugged. "We don't have a contract."

"And whose fault is that?" Dwayne Purvey called from his seat by the vending machine.

Marta had just lost her money and hit the front of the machine several times with her palms. "Is no vork!" she complained. "Is taking money and no vorking!"

"Besides, what's the meeting going to be about anyway? Austerity? Guidance testing? Is that so important it can't be covered with a ditto or wait for the regular faculty meeting? I'm not going."

"Word to the department heads," Dick Janus said, lighting a cigarette from the end of his other cigarette, "is it's about the tie-burning. All the building administrators were told to be there early and be properly attired."

"What tie-burning? There was a tie-burning?"

"Where you been, Milnow?"

"At the shoe store."

"There was no tie-burning," Red Farley said. "That was all bullshit. And I'm sure Scapelli was behind the whole thing."

Jesse listened and watched while he corrected quiz papers. And so it went from period to period throughout the day.

Five minutes after the dismissal bell sounded, a crowd formed in front of the Bernard H. Prahl Memorial Auditorium reminiscent, Jesse thought, of his first day three and a half months ago. Was it *really* three and a half months? Was it *only* three and a half months? He joined the throng of reluctant teachers and squeezed through the doors to the area in front of the stage where teachers jostled to pen their initials on the Official Faculty Meeting Sign-In Sheet, the final checkpoint after punching out to prevent any early escapees. After signing they rushed for the remaining choice seats by the exits.

The Science Department always arrived first and in a group in their white lab coats. They occupied the section by the parking lot exit. The other teachers filled in the empty places close to them and toward the back. The volume of sound increased steadily with the growing crowd and several brown-shirted AV/CM Squad members with folded arms stood off to the side watching with amusement.

At exactly three o'clock the back door of the auditorium opened and the procession of administrators, including Dr. Flackett, and department chairs walked in solemnly quiet from the corridor. All the men and Helen O'Dell wore suit jackets and ties. The APs found their chairs and remained standing, waiting for Mr. Baltz to take his position at the podium. He looked serious next to the superintendent, who was nodding and talking to several people wearing press credentials. One held a camera and snapped pictures while the other took notes on a small pad. Mr. Baltz shook his head and forced a smile. He indicated the empty seats in the front row, where they sat with Dr. Flackett.

"You don't think we're going to have a group picture?" Sue asked Terry. They were seated together a row in front of Jesse. "I'll have to put on a better face." She patted her hair and looked in her pocketbook for her makeup case.

"It looks like everyone is putting on a better face," he said. He had picked his wardrobe specifically for the day, worn elephant bells that were embroidered where car battery acid had made little holes on the legs and a Joe Cocker Woodstock tie-dyed shirt. He watched as Mr. Baltz went to the podium. He looked drawn and somber. His chin made deep furrows in his neck. Terry began to clap and the sound of his solitary applause rose over the drone of the crowd. Others were inspired and began clapping.

Mr. Baltz looked back at Terry, who nodded acknowledgment and continued clapping. When the auditorium quieted, he cleared his throat. "'Tis the season," he began. "Between the holidays, the disruption upcoming Guidance testing will be causing and the weather, you veterans know what that means in the next weeks. So to head off any problems before they happen, we have new measures to tighten control of the building." He adjusted the microphone and fiddled with the dittos someone had left on the podium. He turned them over and read, "THE WAR IS OVER! Administration Assumes A New Position On Suit Jackets And Ties! Ceremonial Tie-Burning Is The Deciding Factor!" When he processed the message his mustache twitched several times and and he tucked his chin farther into his neck. "Mr. Giovanni will outline them for you." He crumpled the ditto and stuffed it in his pocket.

"This week the emergency telephone chain calling list should finally be in your boxes. When you get it, keep it where you will remember you put it and use it if you have to! We don't want a repeat of last year when people on the top of the chain didn't call the people under them and half of you showed up in a blizzard when the school was closed." He checked the list. "In addition, there is a new plan to cut down on student cutting. The custodians have started to remove all the inside door handles from entrances and exits except for those at the main entrance."

"You can't do that," Dwayne Purvey yelled. "What if there's a fire?"

"We have that covered. Helen O'Dell is drawing up new escape routes through the building to the main entrance. They should be in your mailboxes after the snow chain list is finished."

"Unacceptable–"

"Shut up, Purvey," someone called from the back of the auditorium. "We want to get out of here before Christmas." That was followed by the sound of jingling keys.

"But–"

"Now if there aren't any other questions?" Mr. Baltz cut him off.

"What about the suit jackets and ties?" someone called, but he chose not to hear it.

"You are dismissed," he announced and turned off the microphone.

"That's twenty-two minutes I'll never get back in my life," Sue said as the administrative procession reversed course followed by the press, passed up the aisle and into the corridor. "We needed a special meeting for that?" She stood at her seat and put on her coat, waiting for the crush to clear at the doors that still had inside handles. "What a waste. Not even a group picture."

"Are you kidding? It was a stunning meeting," Terry proclaimed from his seat. "Weren't you watching? The Science Department knocked a full eight seconds off their exit record. Stanley Milnow fell asleep and slid out of his seat. Granted that isn't anything new, but it was certainly entertaining. And the new door handle policy is almost as groundbreaking as when the nurse demonstrated the proper procedure for detecting head lice and half the faculty got head lice. Though it wasn't as good as when Harry Dexter's demonstration of the overhead projector started a fire and set off the alarm. But in my opinion, this meeting was a stunning victory for United Males Untied."

"How do you figure?" Sue asked. "He didn't say a word about suit jackets and ties."

"Precisely. What could he say? That's why the War of the Suit Jackets and Ties, as it will henceforth and forever be remembered, will live on in glory. When the faculty realizes what has happened, and they will in a few days, they will start showing up at school looking like me."

"God. I hope not," Sue said.

"It's official! The war is over!"

"Vietnam?" Jesse asked from where he had been sitting. "Did I miss something?"

"Even better. Starting tomorrow, faculty members can wear anything they want to school. Well, maybe not you until you get tenure."

And the war *was* over.

Terry was right. The day after the faculty meeting, three teachers came in wearing jackets but no ties. On Friday the jackets were gone and on Monday even Red Farley gave up his suit jacket for the sweater he kept in his closet.

That alone would have been enough to make Mr. Baltz furious, if it hadn't been for the Sunday edition of *Newsday.* Education Writer Mike McQuinn's piece, "Breaking Ties With Tradition—No More Pencils, No More Books, No More Suits and Ties" in his column was the first thing Baltz read. In part McQuinn said, "It's certainly not the high school I remember as a student when my teachers may have been boring, but they looked like teachers. The men in their cheap, ill-fitting suits and ties and tight collars, the women in dresses frumpy though they may have been. But today it's a different picture and Farmington's Rosencrantz and Guildenstern Memorial High School looks like it will be the first to let a teacher dress code fall by the wayside. In November the women of R&G flouted what was long-standing policy and began wearing pants suits. On December 7th an *ad hoc* group calling itself 'United Males Untied,' administered a *coup de grâce* with a ceremonial tie-burning that put an end to dignity, decorum and suit jackets and ties. Which leads one to ask, 'If a teacher burns his tie in a demonstration and nobody prevents it, does anybody really care?' Building principal, M. Seymour Baltz, and Superintendent, Dr. Donald Flackett, would not comment. And no one from United Males Untied could be reached."

In addition to McQuinn's column, the Editorial Page pushed the matter further with "How Can We Expect Johnny to Read When His Teachers Don't Know How to Dress?" The *Newsday* editors, no fans of "overpaid and under-worked Long Island teachers," stoked the fire. "They're showing up to class more relaxed in T-shirts and bell bottoms, tie-dyes and rags. Not the kids! We're talking about today's high school teachers! And no one seems able or willing to stand up and say 'Enough is enough!' Is it any wonder that taxpayers vote down school budgets year after year?"

Even the picture they used with the article made Baltz look bad. "You know," his mother-in-law said when she saw it. She was staying with them again. "I never noticed just how much Morton looks like President Nixon!"

* * *

He tried to reach Stash Polakas all morning, anxious to get construction started on his executive toilet. And he had another project he was considering. He picked up the phone again. It was still busy. Redial. Still busy. Redial. He pressed the intercom button.

"Yes, Mr. Baltz?" Phyllis Lind asked. "How can I help you this time?"

"Why is the phone to custodian's office still busy? I've been trying to reach Polakas for the past hour," he said brusquely.

"I don't know how the phones work. I'm just a secretary and that's above my pay grade," she said sarcastically. "I've been here at my desk all morning taking phone calls and answering questions about the newspaper article. I haven't had a break. I haven't been to the lady's room and I haven't gotten to the midterm test schedule you said you wanted immediately." She took a quick breath. "And someone must have called the Fire Department because the Fire Chief just showed up to check that all the door handles removed from all the exit doors have been replaced. So maybe the custodians are busy putting them back on. Or maybe the phone is busy because they took it off the hook. They do that sometimes. Now if there isn't anything else you want, I have to answer *my* phone because *I* didn't take *it* off the hook."

He huffed. "Miss Lind–"

"Ms!" She clicked off the intercom.

"–I'm the principal–" he reminded her too late.

A second later she was back. "And if I didn't have enough to deal with, now your wife is on the phone!"

"Shit!" He exhaled. "Tell her I'm busy. Tell her I'm doing observations, tell her–"

"Too late. I'm an executive secretary and I made an executive decision. I told her you were in. Please hold."

The phone on his desk rang. "Morty," she said in a rush, "Mother has an appointment with the dermatologist to remove some things and since we will be in the city we decided to have an early dinner and catch a show. There's nothing in the refrigerator, so make your own arrangements for tonight."

He sighed. "I'll just have the leftover eggplant from Don Vito's on Tuesday night–"

"We're taking that over to Mr. Franks before we go into the city, so he shouldn't go without. You pick up something on your way home from school."

"But, Edie–"

She muffled the phone with her hand. "Mother says don't dawdle after school because you have to walk the new puppy. And when you do, don't forget to put paper down when you walk her. She's paper trained and won't make her business outside unless you put paper."

"But I–"

"If you pick up Chinese for yourself, get some extra steamed dumplings, the pork ones, not the vegetable, and an egg roll and maybe an order of spare ribs for after we get back if we're still hungry. Are you writing all this down? Don't leave it in the container or everything will taste like cardboard. Put it in the new Tupperware I bought at the Tupperware party." She added as an afterthought, "If you decide you don't want Chinese for yourself, pick it up for us on the way back from getting whatever it is you get for yourself."

"But I–"

"Can't talk or we'll be late for the doctor. Smooch." The phone clicked.

"Smooch my ass!" he said.

"Excuse me!" Phyllis Lind's asked over the intercom. "Are you talking to me?"

"Oh, Jesus, Phyllis, have you been listening?"

"Please. I have better things to do with the little time I have. If there aren't any other special requests, I'm going to the cafeteria. It's *Fiesta Mexicana* Wednesday."

"Shit!" He turned off the intercom button and hung up the phone. Then he picked it up again and dialed the custodian's office. It was busy.

By midafternoon he decided to take more direct action. He wheeled around on his chair and was on his feet in one motion. "I'll be out, Phyllis," he said to his secretary. "If anybody needs me–" She was on the telephone and didn't acknowledge him. He scowled and continued around the counter.

"Hey, Mr. Baltz." Virgil called from the detention chair.

He furrowed his neck. "Loomis! Why are you always here? What is it this time?"

"Jello, Mr. B." He reached under the chair and pulled up a doubled brown shopping bag. "I was collecting it in the cafeteria." He tilted the top open so that the principal could see the contents. "It isn't exactly what I had in mind. I would have preferred one solid block of green Jello and this is kind of a color mixture. But sometimes you have to compromise, you know? Sometimes you just have to settle–"

"What are you talking about, Loomis?"

"You must have fantasies, Mr. B. Something you always wanted to do?"

His face relaxed for just a second and his eyes lost their intensity. An almost-smile briefly replaced the deep scowl as visions of Tahiti drifted into his head. He snapped back to reality. "I don't have time for fantasies, I'm the principal. And I don't have time for you, Loomis or for Jello no matter what color it is." He pointed to the bag that had darkened in places where the moisture seeped through. "Get rid of it!"

"I have a two more bags in my locker–"

"Get rid of it all!" He turned to go.

"Oh, there's just one other thing. Remember the secret wrestling team I told you about?" He shifted the Jello from one arm to the other. "I'm being discriminated against by Coach Ritchie and his assistant, Mr. Farley. It has something to do with my hair. So I thought you might be able to speak to them?"

He stopped and turned to face Virgil. "Loomis, just what do you think a high school principal does all day? If you have a problem, observe the proper protocol. Make an appointment with your guidance counselor and when that doesn't help, go see the assistant principals."

Virgil nodded his head. "But I just thought you could take care of it and save everybody grief. Especially with all that bad press in *Newsday*. I really didn't want to get into a legal battle with attorneys or involve the American Civil Liberties Union when a word from you–"

"The Jello, Loomis. Take care of the Jello." He left the office.

Virgil jiggled the bag and watched the multicolored contents pulsate almost like it was alive. He shrugged and started out the door for his locker. "Hey, Mr. Teeg," he said when he passed Jesse at his mailbox. "Are you interested in some Jello?" He pulled out a handful and stuck it in his mouth.

Jesse looked into the bag.

"About twelve pounds in this bag." He shifted it in his arms. "I collected it in the cafeteria from all the lunch trays and I have about twice as much in my locker."

"So you're really going to do it then?"

"I thought so, but there's been a minor little setback. Mr. Baltz just ordered me to get rid of it."

"How are you going to do that?"

He fell into step beside Jesse. "Flush it probably, after I get the rest of it out of my locker."

* * *

The Custodian's Office and its adjoining work area were located in the Klaus Brinker Jr. Temporary Wing at the farthest end of the building complex, out of the way of prying eyes and foot traffic. Semi-independent and nearly autonomous, it functioned as a feudal principality might have under the neglectful eye of a disinterested lord, because no one in the District actually knew who was responsible for its operation. Building and Grounds had a *laissez-faire* attitude as long as things got done eventually, and if the theft of materials for little side jobs like house painting, decks and dormers the custodians did on their free time wasn't blatant, could be ignored or covered up. There was never a shortage of side jobs for the Head Custodian and his Custodial Corps. Even a number of teachers worked with the crew on construction projects and picked up extra cash over summer break to supplement their income. There were no classrooms in the remote Custodial Zone, or anything remotely educational, so Mr. Baltz rarely visited there in person. He conducted business with the Head Custodian by telephone or through diplomatic courrier, usually Mario Giovanni.

Now he moved silently, ghostlike in his rubber-soled shoes down the hall, staying close to the lockers along the wall. He had learned the importance of surprise in his teacher days and employed it with great success as an administrator. He startled a group of students standing by their lockers, who scattered when he materialized from the shadows into the middle of them. He caught two teachers laughing and chatting and they retreated into their classrooms and shut their doors as he approached. He derived great satisfaction from the fear he stirred in the minds and hearts of his teachers. Given a choice between being loved or being feared, he chose fear. They called him *El Exigenté*, "The Demanding One," and that was one of the names he liked and encouraged.

The custodian's office door was decorated with a big Christmas wreath and blinking lights. He turned the knob and walked in without knocking. It was empty. A greasy sign, probably from a gas station, was nailed to the back wall of the office. "Due to insurance regulations, customers are not permitted beyond this point." He paused, then pushed through the beaded curtain into the work area and looked around in amazement at the clutter of half-repaired pieces of his school. Desks, several portable chalkboards, mimeograph machines and things he couldn't identify were strewn across the floor or suspended by chains from the ceiling at various stages of disrepair. Floor-to-ceiling shelves were crammed with smaller parts of bigger parts. The long workbench was pristine and tools hung from the peg-board in their outlined places. In the corner, a faded American flag bumpersticker proclaimed "THESE COLORS DON'T RUN" next to a peace symbol poster with the slogan "THE FOOTPRINT OF THE AMERICAN CHICKEN." The workroom was empty too.

"Fuck!"

He turned to go when he heard a sound like an alarm siren from behind the maze of venetian blinds hanging up for restringing. He pushed through the tangle of bent tin slats and saw the blue back of one of the custodians. He was seated at a worktable cranking the handle of a pencil sharpener. The siren sound came from his throat. When he turned faster the sound grew in intensity. When he slowed, the siren gradually tapered down. When he stopped, he opened his eyes and was surprised to see the principal standing next to him. He stood and the keys on the large ring attached to his belt jingled like spurs. "You can't be in here," he said.

"I can be anywhere and everywhere, I'm the principal. Remember, Charley, when you were in school here and I came to a Christmas party in Mrs. Sooter's class? And we were all wearing party hats."

Charley smiled. "The Christmas party. I remember. You gave me a flashlight that never worked."

"Where's Mr. Polakas?" he asked.

"Not here."

"I can see that. Where is he? I've been trying to reach him for hours."

"Lunch."

"In the cafeteria?"

He shook his head. "Downstairs."

"Would you get him?"

He shook his head and jingled.. "Stash says, 'Charley, lunch. Nobody bothers me.'"

He was losing patience, but he forced a smile and spoke slowly and very deliberately. "Listen, Charley, it's very important. Can you call him?"

"An emergency? Stash says, 'Charley, only for an emergency can you bother me.'"

"Yes, an emergency. Call him. Tell him that Mr. Baltz has an emergency and needs to see him!"

He nodded, picked a large wrench hanging from the peg-board and banged three times on the pipe that ran down through the floor into the sub-basement. He waited and then banged three more times. After a short delay came a response, two echoing clangs through the pipe from somewhere below. Charley unscrewed the end cap and spoke into the opening.

"Mr. Baltz says it's an emergency. I told him lunch–" There were some garbled words and the custodian turned to Mr. Baltz. "Did Hell freeze over?"

"Tell him it's an opportunity for him to make some extra money."

Charley relayed the message. "Stash says he'll see you downstairs." He replaced the end of the pipe and pointed to the heavy steel door marked "Danger–High Voltage!" He pulled it open and the hinges creaked.

Mr. Baltz hesitated and recoiled. "Who's that?" He pointed to the tattooed man sleeping on a cot

"Eddie the night custodian. He sleeps here during the day. Stash says he'll meet you at the bottom."

He stepped around the night custodian and peered into the dimly lit hole. He grimaced and stepped into the darkness. Charley jingled and the door shut behind him. He hugged the wall to maintain his balance and carefully went down the uneven steps one at a time. Behind him he heard the siren crank up again. When his eyes grew accustomed to the darkness he saw that the long, steep stairway curved toward the bottom and disappeared to the right into the bowels of the earth. The air was heavy with dampness and the odd smell of sulfur. He took an audible breath and when a shadow moved across his feet he almost lost his balance. He steadied himself against the rough wall that was damp from the water runoff from aboveground. White patches of thick niter covered some of the surface. The momentary remembrance of an Edgar Allan Poe short story, "The Cask of Amontillado," flashed through

278

his mind and he half expected to bump into a skeleton chained to the wall. Or maybe the Clay People from the old Flash Gordon movie serial he had watched at Saturday matinees as a kid would separate themselves from the walls. Instead he bumped into another steel door at the bottom of the steps. He hesitated and pushed against it. The spring-mounted door gave way easily and he had to cover his eyes until they became readjusted to the bright light.

He emerged into a different world. The concrete walls, the niter, the dampness were behind him. Before him the sub-basement room was well-lit, fully climatized and carpeted. The area was huge, sprawling–a fantasyland. The central hall had passages that branched in different directions. The emerald-painted boiler pipes glittered in the overhead lighting and twisted like towers and spires. They ran the length of the hall and disappeared into the ceiling.

It was the first time he had been to Oz. "Holy shit!" he exclaimed.

Stash Polakas, a tough-looking man shaped like a fire plug with hairy arms stood in front of him holding a beer. He took a drink and wiped his mouth with his napkin. "Money?" he asked.

"This is incredible, Stash! I had no idea."

There were several other custodians, people he had never seen around the building, seated at a table eating, drinking and smoking. The jingle of keys, muffled by the thick rug, the acoustical ceiling tile and the background music, punctuated their movements. The delicate sweetness of incense or perfume floated through the air.

"We manage, Seymour." The head custodian settled back in his place at the head of the table. Smoke from a thick, hand-rolled cigarette curled up from the ashtray. He took a deep drag and offered it to Mr. Baltz.

"I'm trying to quit," he declined.

"Now what was that about money?" He exhaled.

"A little side job."

"An extension on that deck we put in for you two years ago? How's it holding up?"

"No, something here in the building. You've seen the plans for my office?"

"A toilet. Yeah. A very little job. Hardly an emergency." He shook his head. "A simple installation. There's no money in it for me."

"But there's something else. A little secret private job that I'll pay for directly in cash. No work orders. No invoices."

He poured some coffee from his thermos. "Yeah?"

"I'm calling it 'Project X.' It involves a little renovation of the utility closet in the area of the faculty bathroom on the third floor."

"Another toilet job?" He shook his head.

"Not exactly." He removed an envelope from his jacket pocket. "I have the plans and a list of materials right here."

He looked over the paper. "Electrical wire, switches, lumber, soundproofing. Mirror?"

"The mirror is a special order. You have to keep it under wraps. This is top secret."

He took another drag from the cigarette and passed it around. "It looks like an interesting job. But I'll need the money up front. And I'll need a helper."

"One helper. Your most reliable man."

"There's an old Polish saying. 'A noisy cow gives little milk.'"

"I don't know about that, but I want you to do the work yourself and when nobody is around. And I want it done by the day school reopens after New Year."

"So you're asking me to work over the vacation?" He did some mental calculations. "There's a new Polish expression. 'Twenty-two hundred dollars will buy a lot of silence.'"

"I was thinking more along the lines of five hundred cash, after all your expenses, of course."

"I wouldn't consider it for less than–" He picked a number out of the air. "Say sixteen hundred."

Mr. Baltz did some calculations of his own. "Say an even thousand and we have a deal. But I need your personal guarantee that it will be operational the first day in January when we come back. Deal?"

He hesitated. "Okay, deal."

"I just happen to have that exact amount." He handed him another envelope with the cash. They both laughed and shook hands. "You'll get the balance when you let me know the cost of the materials."

The pipe clanged and the custodian unscrewed the cap. "What is it now, Charley?" He put his ear close to the opening and listened. "What kind of emergency?" He paused. "In the student toilet? Can you describe what it looks like?" He thumbed through the bills and slipped the envelope into his bib pocket. "Thick and lumpy? That could be anything. Today is *Fiesta Mexicana* Wednesday." He nodded. "Not like anything you've seen before? Well, get the plunger, Charley. It's in the drawer in my office. I'll be up in a minute with the snake." He screwed the cover back on the pipe.

"What's the problem?"

"A real emergency. The second floor is flooded from an overflow coming out of the boy's bathroom. The toilet's clogged. Charley says it's a gooey jelly stuff, all different colors." He stood up. "You'd be surprised at some of the things we find in the toilets."

Mr. Baltz nodded. "Not at all, Stash. I've been having some of the same problem myself. But now, with your help, all that is about to change."

**Rosencrantz and Guildenstern
Memorial High School
UFSD 71
Farmington, New York**

TO: All Teachers and Staff
FROM: M. Seymour Baltz, Principal
SUBJECT: Christmas/Chanukah Holiday Time
December 20, 1971

C O N F I D E N T I A L

Once again the Christmas/Chanukah holiday season is upon us, a sacred time for many, a time for all those holiday parties and the time for my yearly reminder.

The U.S. Constitution, re-enforced by recent Supreme Court decisions, provides for the separation of church and state. It is against federal law as well as district policy to display seasonal religious symbols of any kind in any classroom in any school, including, but not limited to, nativity scenes and/or menorahs. To avoid parental complaints and possible litigation this sacred Christmas/Chanukah holiday season, I have expanded the definition of "religious symbols" to include Christmas trees, colored lights, spinning tops, pictures of Santa Claus, Father Christmas, St. Nicholas and/or any of his other aliases.

In the past the Music Department went through the building during the last period on the last day of school before the break singing Christmas carols and Chanukah songs, but not this year. In a further effort to avoid a legal backlash and to keep a "lid on the pot," the Chorus will not be caroling in the halls during the last period Thursday afternoon before the Christmas/Chanukah/New Year holiday.

All teachers are reminded that holiday parties Christmas/Chanukah or other, with the exception of Mrs. Sooter's CRMD class, are never permitted in any of the classrooms.

Like the rest of you, I am looking forward to this long awaited break in the school year. On behalf of my staff, Mrs. Baltz and myself I would like to extend our sincere wishes for a happy, non-sectarian, non-denominational holiday season and a healthy New Year 1972 to all of you.

Joseph E. Scalia

Rosencrantz and Guildenstern
Memorial High School
AV/CM Department

To: All Teachers
From: Harry Dexter, Co-ordinator AV/CM Department
December 20, 1971

Due to the added burden created by increased teacher demand for AV equipment, the AV/CM Department has been forced to reduce its hours of operation during the last week of school before the break. The office will be closed to the public and AV equipment will be unavailable during odd periods on odd days, even periods on even days and Homeroom periods each day this week. If these equipment "brown outs" are not successful in allowing the AV/CM staff to catch up with the volume of paperwork, the office will be closed all day Wednesday, December 22nd and the AV/CM office will suspend operations completely on December 23rd for the purpose of collecting equipment currently on loan.

Teachers are strongly cautioned not to attempt to hoard AV/CM equipment in their classrooms in the misguided hope of using it until the end of the week. WE KNOW WHERE EVERYTHING IS AND WHO HAS IT!

Equipment requisitions for the next calendar year must be submitted to AV/CM during the first week of January upon our return, *if* the AV/CM office is open. Requisitions that are not accompanied by the customary Equipment Usage Deposit fee will not be processed and will be disregarded. Information regarding the requisition of AV/CM equipment for the next school year beginning in September 1972 will be in your mailboxes in the spring.

From myself and all the members of the AV/CM Squad, a heartfelt Merry Christmas/Happy Chanukah and a very Happy New Year!

Union Free School District 71
Office of the Superintendent
Central Administration Building
Farmington, New York

From: Donald F. Flackett, Superintendent
To: All Faculty and Staff
Subject: Account for Your Blessings
December 20, 1971

During this year fraught with so many problems such as war, political uncertainty, an austerity budget and unresolved teacher contract issues, a story comes to mind of the man who complained because he had no shoes until he saw a man who had no legs. In that legless spirit I ask all of you to step back for a moment and take stock, not of the things you lack, but of all the things you have. It is time to account for and count your blessings–a job, the roof over your head, a full stomach, as well as a full tank of gas even if it means having to pay more and maybe even wait on long lines!

In the coming year it is my sincere hope that we can all join hands and sing in perfect harmony, just like the Coca Cola commercial says. I'd like to buy you all some Coke to make each and every one of you happy!

And there is no better time than now, as you prepare your two-week escape from school, to announce a coming change. Upon your return in January and in the spirit of cooperation, Farmington Schools will introduce higher educational standards and greater levels of responsibility for teachers to help the children of Farmington become everything they can be in the New Year. Just as you will demand more from your students, the district will demand more from you, and hold each and every one of you accountable for the success and the failures of your students. When you return in the New Year rested and tan, be ready to work harder than you have ever worked!

Details and an explanation of the upcoming changes in the New Year will be available in each school in each teacher's mailbox as soon as they are completed.

"Peace on earth and good will toward man," is the message of the season, and in that spirit, I wish you and yours a happy, healthy and peaceful holiday and a prosperous New Year.

Camelot

Official Publication of the Partnership of Parents and Teachers
in Association for better Farmington Public Schools
Harriet Stegle, President P-PTA
Vol. 4 Issue 4   Special Early Holiday Edition   December 1971

Well, the holidays have arrived and not a second too soon, thank G-D! I wouldn't want to be the one who has to stop and tie my shoes when the last bell rings on Friday and all those bodies bolt out the doors to hit the beaches, kind of like John Wayne in *The Sands of Iwo Jima,* one of my all-time favorite movies made by the Duke.

And just where is everyone heading this year to work on those tan lines?

The district is sending School Board President, Elliot Adornau, to a meeting of the Association of School Board Presidents in sunny Las Vegas. Originally Lalo was going with his wife, but she's too ill. Get well soon, Ruth. So his able-bodied new secretary, Anne Costigan, will take her place and pick up the slack. While in Lost Wages Lalo will participate in a series of workshops to learn how to drive a hard bargain in negotiating teacher contracts. There just may be a teacher contract in the not-too-distant future, if the slot machines and blackjack tables don't reclaim some of the money the district plans to save by the hardball tactics Lalo picks up. Anybody wanna bet?

I have it on good authority–Paula Flackett herself, wife of our beloved Superintendent–that they will leave for the Superintendents' Convention in Buenos Aires, Argentina, a day early to avoid the Christmas/Chanukah travel crush. *Olé,* you lucky ducks, and don't forget the sunblock. I understand it's summer down there!

Ted Mitchell, principal of Old Dutch Mill Elementary, and wife Alice will once again escort a P-PTA sponsored tour to Europe for P-PTA parents. Last year it was the Bahamas, this time the destination is the island of Ibiza in the Mediterranean, somewhere off the coast of Spain. My bags are packed and I'm ready to go. We all leave at midnight! My *sombrero* is off to those of you who can't get away, for whatever reason, and will have to put up with the little monsters running around the house for the next two weeks! I'll bring you back a souvenir!

AROUND THE DISTRICT:

Congratulations are in order for Roger Underwood at the Junior High. He's the only male Home Ec teacher in the District. And lucky Roger won a contest sponsored by Fleishman's Dry Yeast. His winning slogan ("America, be leaven it or be leavin' it!") was good enough to win the $500 first prize and a case of dry yeast. Now Roger (he's not married, ladies!), all you have to do to make your life complete is find a woman with a lot of dough!

NEWS AND VIEWS:

You teachers may think you have it tough today. But here's a list of things that women teachers, circa 1915, would have had written into their contracts.

1. Not to get married.
2. Not to keep company with men.
3. To be home between the hours of 8 PM and 6 AM, unless in attendance at a school function.
4. Not to loiter downtown at the ice cream stores.
5. Not to leave town at any time without the permission of the chairman of the school board.
6. Not to smoke cigarettes.
7. Not to get into a carriage or a car with any man except a father or brother.
8. Not to dress in bright colors.
9. Not to dye your hair.
10. To wear at least two petticoats at all times.
11. Not to wear dresses more than two inches above the ankle.
12. To keep the school neat and clean, and to light the fire in the boiler by 7 AM each morning.

My, you've come a long way, baby! Let's hope School Board President Adornau doesn't find out about it on his trip to Vegas!

Season's Greetings and a happy 1972! I always seem to do better in the even years. See you next year with more news from the trenches!

FT Ass.

"Never rough. Never harsh. Never an unpleasant aftertaste if we negotiate."

FROM: Joel Maxwell, President FT Ass.
TO: ALL Farmington Teachers
Re: Special New Year's Membership Benefit

Does the state of the economy have you considering other options? Is the specter of Death staring you in your face? Are you wondering how your family will manage when you're gone? Don't worry, be happy! Because now you can rest in peace!

FT Ass., in conjunction with Khalil Hormuz, President of American Limited Life and Home, is happy to announce an offer too good to resist, a term life insurance policy for *every* member of FT Ass.! According to the terms of the policy, ALLAH agrees to pay a $1,000 death benefit to any member in good standing who dies and $2,000 if that member dies in the classroom!

So if you stand a chance of dying on the job, and recent Government statistics show that teaching is a high-stress occupation, you need this protection that will take effect on January 1, 1972. If you are presently not a member of FT Ass., join today. You owe it to yourself! You owe it to your family!

FU - 2

Farmington Union, Local # 2
"The Union With an Attitude!"

In an effort to offset the economic pinch of working without a contract for so long, FU-2 is making you an offer you can't refuse! It's a reduction in membership dues for the next 50 people who join. So now, the cost of becoming part of the "in-crowd," of presenting a united front in negotiations, of standing shoulder to shoulder with your comrades in fraternity and solidarity has just gone down! You get twice as much for only half the regular dues!

Interested? See your FU 2 building representative as soon as possible. This offer won't last!

Season's Greetings from Dwayne Purvey, President FU-2

Jesse was up to his elbow, trying to dislodge the ball of papers that had accumulated at the back of his mailbox. In the middle of the memos, the impersonal, pre-printed Christmas card from the School Board that was sent to each member of the faculty and staff, there was something marked IMPORTANT SECOND NOTICE dated October. He considered taking it over to Phyllis Lind, but she was talking to Mr. Giovanni, and he didn't think it wise to let the assistant principal know he had neglected something important. He folded it and put it back in the pile.

"If they'd put the money they spend on all this crap in the mailboxes toward our salaries," Terry said and held up the generic School Board Christmas card before he tossed it unopened into the pail, "they might have enough money for a contract and a decent raise!" He leafed quickly, one by one, through all the memos and tossed them all, except for Dr. Flackett's. "'A new spirit of cooperation,' 'higher educational standards' and 'greater levels of accountability,'" he quoted. "You know what *that* means," he said to Jesse, "more work for less pay, and make sure nobody fails! Interested in taking a little field trip?" he asked. "I have to run an errand before the end of the period."

"I can't. I, um, er–" Jesse stammered. "There's only fifteen minutes and I–"

"Plenty of time." He shrugged. "I was just going to pick up your Christmas present. And remember when you get mine don't spend more than ten dollars. It's the rule."

"You're kidding, right?" He was never sure when Terry was serious. "I didn't know anything about Christmas presents."

"Take a ride with me," Terry said as Mr. Baltz entered the Main Office. "I promise to have you back in time. Besides," he raised his voice, "it's the week before Christmas and everybody's a little bit more forgiving in the spirit of cooperation. Right, Mr. Baltz? I was just telling young Mr. Tietjen that if we're a little late getting back before the end of the period nobody will notice in all the growing confusion."

"I'm sure Mr. Tietjen has enough to worry about, being a first-year teacher, without you leading him down the road to ruination before he even has a *chance* of getting tenure." He smoothed his mustache with two fingers and looked directly at Jesse, who turned away and began leafing busily through his papers again. "I'm sure you read my memo about maintaining control in the building, Mr. Scapelli. The time to tighten the reins is before things get out of hand. As teachers and administrators, we all have jobs to do."

"Read it? I practically can quote it from memory. We can all quote it. It's the same one you put out every year."

The principal walked past him and around the counter. Terry followed and stopped at Phyllis Lind's desk where she and Mario Giovanni were deep in conversation.

"Hello, Ms Lind, Mr. Giovanni. Making vacation plans?" The assistant principal's face flushed. "Oh, should I not have said that? Was it a secret?"

"Not everybody will have free time during *your* free time, Mr. Scapelli."

"Administrators are always on duty," Mr. Baltz added.

"Speaking of which, I heard a funny story this morning on the radio on my way in," Terry said. "Did you hear it, about the man in a hot air balloon who realizes he's lost?"

"No, Mr. Scapelli, I can't say that I have. And I don't have the time to listen to it now–"

"Well," Terry started anyway, "this guy in the hot air balloon drops down and sees a woman on the ground. 'Can you help me?' he calls down to her. 'I promised a friend that I would meet him in an hour, but I'm lost and I don't have any idea where I am.' The woman says, 'In a hot air balloon about thirty feet above the ground somewhere on the east coast of the United States.' The guy in the balloon says, 'You must be a teacher.' The woman is surprised. 'I am,' she says. 'How'd you know?' 'Because everything you just told me is technically correct, but your information is useless. I'm still lost because you haven't been any help at all.'"

"Is there a point to this, Mr. Scapelli?"

"I'm getting to it, Mr. Baltz. The woman says, 'You must be an administrator.' So now it's the man who's surprised. 'I am, but how did you know?' 'Because you don't have a clue where you are or where you're going. You got where you are because of a large quantity of hot air. You made a promise to someone you can't keep, and now you expect *me* to solve your problem. The fact is you are in exactly the same position you were in before we met, but now it's somehow my fault that you are!'"

Phyllis laughed out loud and Mr. Baltz stared at her. "Are you sure she isn't a secretary?" she asked.

"I don't get it," Mario Giovanni said.

"I'll explain it to you, Mario," she said. "Going to the holiday party on Thursday, Mr. Scapelli?"

"Wouldn't miss it."

"I am saving you a dance."

"If I don't see you later in the week," he said to Mr. Baltz, "I'd like to wish you a hap–"

Mr. Baltz turned and went through the door to his office and closed it hard.

"–py New Year!" he called and went back to his mailbox. "Somehow," he said to Jesse, who had been listening, "I don't think I'll be getting a present from Baltz either."

The excitement in R&G increased daily as December dropped away, like an Advent calendar counting down to Christmas. On Thursday, the eve of Christmas Eve, it reached a fever pitch. And it continued building with each passing class–unmistakeable, electric, palpable! Freedom and a ten-day vacation loomed. And the students were excited too. Each morning a deluge of control dittos and official memos flooded the mailboxes and PA announcements incessantly interrupted classes, reminding everyone that the holiday started on Thursday afternoon at dismissal and not before.

During Thursday's extended homeroom the overhead PA box clicked on again followed by finger tapping and blowing sounds. "This is Mr. Baltz, the principal. Stop all work. Stop all work." That was his standard protocol whenever he took to the airwaves.

"Why does he have to announce who he is?" a boy in Sue's Homeroom said. "I knew it was him as soon as he started blowing. And we don't do any work in Homeroom."

"Thank you for that vote of confidence, Angelo. Now be quiet and listen to our leader or he will cancel Christmas."

"He can't do that. Can he?"

"In the spirit of this holy season," he went on, "I want to wish each of you a peaceful and joyous nonsectarian holiday whether you celebrate Christmas, Chanukah or that new one, Kwanzaa." He paused. "I want to remind everyone that vacation doesn't start until the dismissal bell today." There were loud cheers throughout the building. "You are expected to attend all your classes after the assembly program, maintain proper order and follow the school rules until the end of the day." There were boos. "Attendance will be taken in each class, the names of absentees sent directly to my office and checked against the official absentee list. Cutting will not be tolerated. Cutters will be identified immediately and the Attendance Office will follow up with phone calls home throughout the day." More boos. "So happy holidays and enjoy your vacation.

I look forward to seeing all of you next year." The PA clicked off.

An hourlong assembly conducted by the Music Department playing nondenominational seasonal songs followed Homeroom, followed by shortened regular classes. Despite all the warnings, attendance dropped off each period, except for the kids who never missed a day. The halls were full of roving revelers smart enough to celebrate inside where it was warm instead of joining those who ran out of the building and were dancing outside in the freezing cold. Jesse gave up early any thought of actually teaching the lesson he had prepared and he was sitting behind his desk alone in his classroom. The last bell rang and a muffled roar arose from the teachers. He was exhausted, but the realization that he made it to Christmas and the prospect of an almost two-week vacation made him giddy.

"Hey, Mr. Teeg." Virgil Loomis called from the doorway. He was dressed in a Santa Claus suit. "I'm sorry I didn't get around to play for you today." He tooted the first few bars of "Oh Tannenbaum" on his kazoo. "The halls were lovely, dark and deep, and I had promises to keep, and miles to heft before I left."

"Almost Robert Frost. I'm impressed, Virgil. But then again you always impress me. I thought you weren't allowed to go around caroling," Jesse said.

"That confidential memo only mentioned the Chorus singing during the last period, Mr. Teeg. It didn't say anything about students kazooing! And I started after the assembly and nobody stopped me all day." He broke into a verse of "Jingle Bells." "Anyway," he said when he finished, "have a good time at the school party. I'm on my way to play a few tunes for the people in the Main Office. Nonsectarian seasonal greetings, and Merry Christmas too!"

"And to you and your family, Virgil."

A few minutes later Sue stopped by and Jesse was still behind his desk. "Who's ready for a par-*tay*?" she said. "Get many presents?" She was carrying a shopping bag overflowing with Christmas gifts.

Jesse smiled and showed her a bottle of English Leather. "This from Audrey."

"Ah, the red-haired girl who follows you around all day. Love is grand." She dropped the bag on his desk and pulled things out. "Well, I got an umbrella. A box of hand-embroidered hankies. Perfume. Dusting powder. Two 'Best Teacher' mugs. And from the boys in my Track III class," she reached inside, "a can of natural scent Vespré Feminine Hygiene Spray. I don't know if it's a hint or wishful thinking on their part. Though I am curious about that natural scent thing, an adolescent boy's fantasy. How do you suppose they came up with the natural scent?" She sprayed a bit in the air and looked disappointed when she sniffed it. "There's nothing natural about that smell." Jesse laughed and she swept everything back into the large gift bag. "Terry's warming up his VW. I told him we'd meet him. We can all go together in one car and stop at the bank first before the party."

Jesse grabbed his attaché case and a brown shopping bag from inside the footwell of the desk.

"What's all that junk?" she asked.

"Book reports. Five sets. One from each class."

"Rookie mistake. You're such a first-year teacher," she taunted. "Didn't anyone tell you never make an assignment due *before* a vacation?" He handed her a present and looked embarrassed. "What's this?" She opened it. "Oh, that's very sweet. a 'World's Best Teacher' mug. You can never have too many." She gave him a kiss on the cheek and his face flushed.

On their way out of the building they saw the custodians already pushing their wide brooms down the halls in an attempt to clear the debris. They were in a hurry to get to their own Christmas party in the sub-basement.

Terry was in his car, where the VW's defroster was desperately trying to melt the ice his scraper left behind. Jesse opened the door for Sue and she looked in. The back of the car was piled with old newspapers, a spare tire and some other things. "You live in here?

"Don't mind the mess. It's the indication of a creative mind. Throw your stuff on top." He dusted off the seat with a rag. "You both have to squeeze in the front."

Jesse got in first and Sue climbed onto his lap. When they were settled Jesse handed Terry a present. "I got this for you.".

"I bet it's a coffee mug," Sue said digging in to her pocketbook for her makeup case.

"Thanks," Terry said. "You can throw it in the back with the others." He turned on the windshield wipers that smeared a small opening in the ice and he stepped on the gas.

The weighted down VW sputtered and shuddered as he aimed it through the slush pools and the ice patches that punctuated the parking lot. The car bumped over the curb and Sue bounced in Jesse's lap. He didn't react, but he was painfully aware of her movement and the smell of her perfume. Even in the cold car he felt warm and he began to perspire. "Is that a pistol in your pocket, or are you just glad to see me?" she asked trying to draw on some lipstick. Jesse's face flushed deep red.

At a traffic light Terry reached behind him and felt around. "Here," he said, handing a cardboard box to Jesse, who took it and looked at it. "It's a tape recorder for your first faculty Christmas party. It's an event you'll want to keep for posterity."

Jesse pulled it out and read the tag hanging from it. "Standard Dexter Issue 2117?"

"I borrowed it from AV two years ago." He turned to look at him. "Tonight you're going to see and hear things you never imagined."

"And you won't recognize these people," added Sue.

"Probably. I don't know most of them."

"No, I mean the people you think you've seen during the daytime become something else at the Christmas party. Last year Red Farley passed out in the women's toilet. And Tom Keller stole the bartender's tip jar," Sue said, dropping her makeup back into her bag. "There's a lot of hugging and crying and kissing. By the second round of drinks it turns into a regular orgy." She swiveled around and pursed her lips at Terry. "How do I look?"

"Fantastic," he said. "I can hardly see the scars, or the road." He wiped the foggy inside of the windshield with his hand, which only made the visibility worse. "If we time it right, when we get there a lot of them should be pretty well oiled."

"It's funny," Jesse said. "But I never pictured teachers having a good time."

"Oh, nobody has a good time," Sue said. "They'll complain the whole time about everything. The cost. The time it started. The time it ends. The room. The decorations. The drinks. The food."

"Tonight you'll see teachers in a new light," Terry said. "The Christmas party shines a spotlight on a bunch of stressed-out and repressed people with their guard down."

"Is there always so much stress? It must get easier."

"The material, yes. But teaching is war, if you're any good at it. You have to keep fighting. Keep pushing the envelope."

"If you stop trying, you start dying," Sue said. "That's what you told me my first year. And when you start counting the years to retirement, you're already dead."

"Stress is part of the job. Along with high blood pressure and all the chalk you can steal. Good teachers have to be stressed and afraid so they will keep growing. They have to stand up and tell the truth, expose the lies and reinvent the system so it can be renewed. Good teachers are dangerous. Great teachers are revolutionaries. That's why teachers are the first ones they put up against the wall."

"My," Sue said, "Aren't we being seriously philosophical today?"

Terry was wound up. "Good teaching isn't keeping the floors clean, the shades even and the desks in straight rows. It isn't keeping kids in their seats, but getting them on their feet. It's cutting through the bullshit and blowing the doors off. It's not teaching them *what* to think, but *how* to think and question *everything*."

She looked at Jesse. "He does this sometimes, but if you wait long enough it will pass."

"When it comes to education, everyone has an ax to grind. Taxpayers who hated school vote the budget down every year to get even. They now sit on school boards and want to cut teacher salaries because 'it's a part-time job with summers off and home by three.' And everyone from the parents to the school board, the unions, the secretaries up to the custodians, and all the special interest groups trying to protect their special interests knows best when it comes to teaching, except the teachers."

"Are you almost done?"

"Almost. Kids come and go. Some love you, some hate you and a few make you want to quit. All you have to do is give them something they will remember and take away with them. And I don't mean the present perfect tense of irregular verbs! You know what the really sad part is about being a teacher?"

"The crappy lunches?"

"It's that you may never know if you've made any impact at all."

"Then why do it? Quit." Jesse said. It was Christmas break and he was getting depressed. "Why spend your life being miserable and doing something so unrewarding."

"It's easy to burn out, and even easier to settle."

"So why do *you* do it?" Jesse asked again.

"To get rich, of course. And for all the vacation time," Sue added.

"For Virgil Loomis and kids like him who may come along. They are our best hope."

"God bless Virgil!" Sue said.

"Amen! I'll smoke to that!" He poked his finger into the ashtray and picked out the longest brown butt he found. "Anybody want to party before we get to the party?" He lit the stub with the cigarette lighter and offered it to Jesse.

Jesse pulled back and shook his head with a look of panic on his face. "No, thanks, I– er, What if the cops–"

"Hey, it's the seventies," Terry said and passed it to Sue.

"I'm so glad you got all of that out of your system. He usually does it *at* the party." She looked out the window. "It's snowing again!"

Big flakes, heavy and wet, pressed against the windshield and stuck momentarily before they were smeared away by the streaking wiper blades. In a matter of seconds the grass and the sidewalks were covered. They used the drive-thru window at the bank to cash their checks.

"Battle stations," Terry said, steering the straining VW up the long, steep driveway of the Hand Maid Inn. It was a colonial building, large and historical, where, it was said, Gen. George Washington once slept. The parking lot was almost filled with snow-covered cars. "Get ready to lose your virginity!"

* * *

The building was empty and the halls had been reclaimed. The eerie silence was broken by a periodic metallic ping that resonated down from the third floor and filled the corridors.

"What's the matter, Charley?" Stash Polakas stood in the faculty toilet yelling at the wall. The tiles had been removed over the two sinks, and a bare section of cinder blocks lay exposed where the old mirror had been mounted.

The banging on the other side stopped. "I can't find the hole," came the muffled response.

"If I put some hair around it I bet you'd find it soon enough!" He heard Charley laugh and he shined his flashlight through the tiny opening. "Are we through? Do you see the light, Charley?"

There were some other sounds. "I think so."

"Well, get your eye away. I'm gonna shove a bar through. Tell me when you see it. The quicker we get this done, the quicker we get to the Christmas party."

"Here it comes... I can see it... I can feel it... Owwww!" he screamed.

The custodian pulled the bar back."You idiot! I told you to get your eye out of there. Are you okay?"

"April fool!" Charley laughed again.

"You got me there good, Charley. You nearly scared the crap out of me. I was wondering what I was going to tell your mother when I showed up at the door with her half-blind son. When we go downstairs I'll buy you a drink, okay?"

"But aren't the drinks free, Stash? I thought the drinks were free."

"Everything is free at the party. So let's get this demo done and get down there, okay?" He slowly repositioned the bar. "Just keep your eye out of holes where they don't belong because I am pushing my rod into this one." He heard Charley really laugh. "And when it comes all the way through take that sledge hammer and tap it gently–"

There was a loud bang. The cinder block wall erupted and crumbled in a choking cloud of dust. When it settled, Charley was standing on the other side of the large hole with his mouth open. His sweaty face covered with gray powder made him look like a statue. "You said hit it and I did it!"

"You sure did!" He stuck his pipe between his teeth. "I hope you didn't break that goddamn special mirror or it's coming out of the money I'm paying you."

"I think it's okay." He held the glass in his dusty hands and turned it around "But I can only see myself on one side."

"That's because like you, it's special. Now put it down before you drop it, Charley." He helped him through the opening in the wall. "We've done enough for today. Let's go downstairs, hit the showers and maybe get loosened up in the hot tub. Then I'll buy you that drink. We both earned a couple a drinks."

"But I thought the drinks were for free at the party, Stash?"

"They are, Charley, but I'll buy you one anyway, because I like you." He slapped him on the back and raised a cloud of dust from the uniform. "But don't drink too much tonight. We have to come back up here early tomorrow to clean up this mess. I want to finish the job before Christmas Eve." He led the way out of the bathroom. They stepped into the open elevator and took it all the way down to the sub-basement.

A solitary figure moved through the shadows, attracted by the noise and the light on the third floor. It paused in front of the door to the faculty toilet and looked in at the rubble on the tile floor, the large hole in the cinder blocks. Then it went around and opened the door to the Utility closet. The image of a dusty Santa Claus reflected in the mirror on the floor. He stepped inside and saw everything and before he left he took his red marker pen and added the letter "F" to "Utility."

* * *

"Rosencrantz and Guildenstern Memorial High School Educators Holiday Party," the sign in the lobby said and an arrow pointed to the right. "Ye Olde Out-House Room."

"Educators sure sounds impressive," Sue said when she read it.

"That's because there are administrators here. Otherwise we'd still be just teachers," Terry said.

They elected Jesse to take the coats to the checkroom. A hard-looking woman behind the counter was smoking a cigarette and reading a romance novel, *Cheap Date*. She was dressed in what the Hand Maid Inn had decided a colonial serving wench might wear, a low-cut top that revealed the age spots on her breasts and a white apron too short to hide the tight black Capri pants that outlined the contours of her crotch. Jesse handed over the three coats and felt guilty for staring at her lips. "Do I tip you now or when I get them?"

"You can put your tip in my jar anytime, hon," she said.

Jesse's face flushed. He didn't have any change, so he dropped a dollar into the tip jar.

"For that I'll give you a real kiss." She puckered her lips and Jesse backed away. "Thank you, sweetie." She blew him a kiss instead.

The "Ye Olde Out-House Room" was on the first floor of the Hand Maid Inn. Once it had been outdoors, where the outhouses of the original inn stood, but the area was enclosed with large windows and had become a patio in recent years. The windows were slid open in spring and summer, but now they were closed and covered with heavy drapes for privacy and to keep down the draft. There were pots of flowering artificial plants and trees to add a sense of the outdoors. A low brick knee wall surrounded the rectangular cement fountain in the center of the room and created a shallow two-foot pool of water with assorted coins that dotted the blue painted bottom. Tables were arranged around the perimeter of the room with a small dance area between them and the buffet carts. A tired-looking combo played behind the sign announcing them as "The Decrescendos." The trio consisted of three music teachers, Vinny Dimitris on the accordion, Herb Gateway playing the sax and Bob Powell behind the drums, brushing a snare and tapping the cymbals. The Decrescendos seemed disinterested playing for Mr. Baltz, who was on the dance floor with his wife. And beside them Mario Giovanni was doing his best to hold up a silver-blue-haired woman who looked remarkably like an older Mrs. Baltz, paying more attention to the shivering little dog she was holding than to the dapper assistant principal.

"We'll have to leave earlier than I said, Morty. Mother can't eat anything from the buffet, so we'll have to get something on the way home. And this room is terrible. It's so drafty, And the band—"

Mr. Baltz sighed and nodded and eyed his AP who dutifully tapped him on the shoulder to change partners.

The cash bar was at the far end of the room where a long double line of teachers stood in front of the two frantic bartenders trying to fill orders and mix drinks. This year, to keep down the cost of the party, non-drinking teachers outvoted the drinkers, who had to pay for their own drinks.

"It was the most terrible thing I ever heard," Mrs. Butrum said to the Four Horsewomen sitting at a table away from the cold draft. "They'd put off their camping trip for years until the children were old enough. So when my nephew got laid off he decided to turn lemons into lemonade, a camping vacation for the whole family, even his mother-in-law. The poor woman was living with them ever since she lost everything in the fire." She picked over the tray of hors d'oeuvres offered by a waiter and grabbed a handful she put on the already full plate of the very bored chubby girl sitting next to her. "They took the kids out of school early, packed up everything and set out before the sun was up. Drove all day into the mountains to a private campground somewhere up in Canada. But right after they pitched both the tents, unpacked everything, the sleeping bags the cots, all the food, they realized the poor woman apparently had a massive coronary and died hours before!"

"Oh, the poor thing," Rita Reed sympathized. She sneezed into her holiday handkerchief.

"How awful," Elsie Bergin said.

"Of course the kids were upset after driving all that way. And by then it was dark and getting cold, so they had to break camp and repack everything again by flashlight. When they were finished the woman was as stiff as a board so there was no way to put her *inside* the station wagon, so they rolled her in one of the canvas tarps and tied her to the roof."

"Oh, goodness."

"And then, of course, they had to drive all the way back home across the border to the States with a dead body on the roof! All the questions, all that red tape would tie them up for days. So they decided not to say anything to the border guard and luckily nobody checked. You can imagine it was a terrible trip back with all the crying. They were all so exhausted driving all day and then into the night so they decided to stop at one of those dreadful places on the Thruway to eat and get a little rest. And wouldn't you know, when they came out of the restaurant the station wagon was gone! Car, camping equipment, mother-in-law! Everything! Disappeared into thin air."

"How terrible."

"They reported the stolen car, but didn't say anything about the woman in the luggage rack. And three days later the State Police called to say they'd recovered the car, but all the equipment was gone. They haven't found the poor woman to this day, it's over three months!"

"How awful," Claire Hutton said, dangling the lit Pall Mall from her lips. "Your poor niece lost her mother *twice* in one day."

* * *

"What a shit party!" Red Farley grumbled from his seat close to the bar. He had two shots and two beers in front of him. "I've been to a lot of shit parties over the years, but this one is the worst."

"It was worse last year," Buddy Ritchie said.

"Last year? Are you kidding?" Stanley Milnow shook his head. "Last year's party was the best. Drinks were included." He lowered his voice. "And you remember that little French teacher with the fat ass who worked on the other side of the building. What was her name?"

"Fat Ass," Buddy Ritchie said matter-of-factly.

"Well, after the party we got a room in the Asian Palace Motel. I didn't get home until the next morning. Was my wife pissed." The expression on his face changed as he remembered. "Boy, could that little Frenchie move her fat ass!"

"What a shit party," Red said again, draining a shot and a beer.

"Glad to see you are all having such a great time," Terry called from the bar. "From way over here your resemblance to the Three Wise Men is uncanny."

"Up yours, Scapelli." He finished his second shot.

"And a merry Christmas to you too, Red. Sweet vermouth on the rocks with a slice of lemon," he said to the bartender. "And the guy over there who raises his hand said he'll pay for it." He raised his drink and toasted the table. "Thanks for the drink, Red." Red stuck his arm in the air and gave him the finger. "That's the true Christmas spirit."

"Don't give me 'Christmas spirit,' Scapelli. Christmas is a religious holiday and you're a goddamn pagan heathen."

"I spent twelve years in Catholic schools and I have the scars to prove it." He carried his drink to their table. "I have a cousin who asked me to invest in his business enterprise that's going to make millions. For a while I was thinking about letting you boys in on the ground floor, but now that you said what you said and hurt my feelings–"

Buddy Ritchie was checking out the women, trying not to listen and get sucked in. Stanley Milnow's ears perked up. "What?" he asked. "I didn't say anything."

Terry sipped his drink and thought for a long time. "All right, Stan, in the spirit of the season. Bible Bubble Gum cards. He's ready to pull the trigger and take his company public."

"Old Testament or New?"

"Both."

"Smart. Opens the market to Jews and gentiles."

"That's blasphemy. Is nothing sacred to you, Scapelli?" Red reached for his beer and knocked over Stanley Milnow's glass.

"Fuck! You spilled my drink!" He scooped the glass upright and salvaged some of the contents with his cupped hand. "You owe me another drink, Red."

"Not blasphemy at all, Red. It teaches kids religion and cashes in on their desire to collect trading cards. And these are top quality artistic photographs right from the Bible. I've seen them. Noah's Ark, Moses and the Burning Bush, Jesus Teaches the Rabbis in the Temple. That's his rookie card. And on the back, instead of batting averages the card lists the Bible quotations, book, chapter, verse and lines for easy reference. Five different cards to the pack and a piece of bubble gum. Now how could that be blasphemous? Jesus, Hebrews and a chew."

"I think it could work," Stanley Milnow was nodding his head.

"My cousin's done the market research. But wait, there's more. After the cards he plans to expand into the religious toy market. Mattel is interested. A whole line like Barbie and Ken. Think of it. Holy Family dolls with different action sets. A wetting Nativity scene, Jesus gets circumcised, walks on water, throws the moneylenders out of the Temple. The big money is in the clothes. Lots of outfits like the 'Mary Goes to Temple Dress.' And even more in the accessories. Kids will line up for 'David's Super Whamo Slingshot,' the 'Saint

Joseph Workbench' with a complete line of tools. There's even a series of carpentry projects from the 'Jesus Builds a Birdhouse' kit for beginners all the way up to 'Jesus Adds a Dormer to the Manger.'"

"Fuck you, Scapelli."

"No, no. I can see it," Stanley Milnow said.

"What a crock of shit," Buddy Ritchie said. "And what a shit party."

* * *

"All these people, Helen." Willy Zwill was hunched in a corner of the room with his back to the wall. "They make me nervous."

"Uh-huh." She held her plate close to her face while she forked some Chinese into her mouth. "Relax, Willy. It's Christmas. Peace on earth to men of good will and all that crap."

He took another long look around the room and his face twitched. "I have that sinking feeling in the pit of my stomach again."

"Maybe you're hungry. Have something to eat." She offered him her almost empty plate.

He recoiled and covered his mouth. "You know that rice makes me gag."

"Then try the ziti."

"Can't you sense it, Helen? The air is charged with electricity."

"Those are the Christmas lights, Willy."

"Something just doesn't feel right to me."

She looked down. "That's because you spilled your drink, Willy. There's a Bloody Mary all over your pants." She attacked the stain with her napkin. "I'll have it off in a second." She bumped into something hard. "Willy, I'm really impressed with what you're packing under there."

"Don't you worry what's what in my pants, Helen." He jumped to his feet and pulled his jacket down. "I have to move, Helen. I can't just sit still. A moving target–"

"I know, 'is harder to hit.' And while you're up, Willy, get me another helping of the ribs."

He walked slowly around the edge of the dance floor and disappeared into the potted plants along the wall.

* * *

Jesse inched along toward the buffet carts. He smiled at Phyllis Lind who was dancing with Mr. Giovanni, a tango to the laid-back tempo of the Decrescendos. He watched them glide around the floor. They danced well together, like they'd done it before, like they'd practiced. When he turned back. Noah Lewis had cut the line in front of him.

Jesse smiled. "Merry Christmas, Mr. Lewis. From the looks of this line I hope there's enough food for us. We'll be on line a long time."

"Auh?" The assistant principal looked at his watch. "Time? My watch seems to have stopped." He wound the stem and put it to his ear.

"I meant that we have quite a wait–"

"Two years and, auh," he counted on his fingers, "six months until retirement. I, auh, have been reading and studying the matter very carefully. Did you know that a person can retire very comfortably in Poland?" He beamed.

"I hadn't really thought about it, Mr. Lewis. This is my first year."

He nodded. "Well, it's never too early to start planning your getaway. When you do retire, you, auh, should consider Poland. With a pension and Social Security, I, auh, can live like the King of Poland. All my life I dreamed about living in Krakow."

Jesse nodded and they inched closer to the food.

* * *

"Check out the ass on that one." Stanley Milnow moved away from the bar, his hands filled with drinks. "Look at that ass!"

"No tits," Buddy Ritchie said.

"What's her name?"

"Layla Bimenyenz. Thirty, divorced, a kid, but no tits."

"With an ass like that she doesn't need tits."

* * *

"You're a kiss ass, Maxwell!" Dwayne Purvey stood in the center of a small crowd with a drink in one hand and Joel Maxwell's tie in the other.

"And you're a whole ass, or is that an ass *hole*? And you can kiss my ass!"

"No brains!"

"No balls!"

They were face-to-face.

"Kiss my ass!"

"Eat me!"

Chuck LaFemina laughed and covered his mouth. He was standing close to Rory Aaron.

"Fuck you!"

"You wish."

"Such wasted energy," Rory Aaron said. "Come on, let's go, Chucky. This *macho* shit is tiresome."

* * *

"I don't understand," Buddy Ritchie complained to no one and everyone around the bar. He held his drink and watched Terry and Sue on the dance floor. When Jesse passed he pulled him over. "You're English, right? What is it about you fucking English teachers that all the women are attracted to? What's your secret?" He watched them dancing closer. "I mean, I'm better looking than Scapelli. And I could kick his ass any day, any time. I bought her drinks but I won't go home with her. So what's the secret? Do all you English queers read poetry while you eat pussy? Tell me. I really want to know."

"I'm new here so I really can't say."

"I hate him. I hate all you English fags."

"Mr. Tietjen," Mrs. Butrum called across the dance floor.

"Oh, oh! Better run kid, before it's too late. Here comes big butt Butrum, that old bag with her fat ass daughter." He turned in a circle and fled. "Merry Christmas."

Her daughter, in a pink chiffon party dress, looked annoyed as her mother dragged her reluctantly toward him. Jesse wanted to escape, but they were on him.

"This young lady is my daughter Lucretia I told you about. Mr. Tietjen is a first-year English teacher, dear." She offered her daughter to him. "I thought it would be nice if you two young people met. I bet you'll have a lot to talk about." Jesse nodded. He put down his drink and extended his hand, which Lucretia looked at but didn't accept. "Lucretia can be a little shy. And she's probably tired because she just drove down from college in Buffalo."

"Oh?" he said. "SUNY Buffalo?"

Lucretia didn't respond.

"No," her mother answered, "a private finishing school up there. Lucretia just loves to dance. She studied dance when she was little. Maybe you two might–"

He smiled politely though he felt a sense of panic. "I'm afraid I don't dance. A sports injury in college–"

But Mrs. Butrum was relentless. "The both of you have so much in common. Lucretia wants to be a teacher too."

"That's very nice. Very commendable."

"Lucretia, tell Jesse all about yourself," She pushed her toward him. "I think I need some more ginger ale. My stomach seems to be acting up a bit. Remember to be nice, Lucretia," she said and walked toward the bar.

Jesse watched her go and his frozen smile faded. Lucretia stood silently shifting her weight from one foot to the other, the only sign of life she gave. "So, you want to be a teacher, Lucretia?" He tried to make polite conversation at the same time scanning the room for Sue and Terry.

"Call me Lucy."

"What subject area, Lucy?" He took a big mouthful from his drink that made him choke.

She stepped up closer to him and whispered, "Do you want to come back to the house and fuck around?"

Jesse choked again. "Oh, thank you, but, um–" He looked around the room. "I'm not alone. I came here with someone. Over there." He pointed to where Sue was now doing shots with Dick Janus. Buddy Ritchie was standing in the fountain with his pants rolled up, watching her and shaking his head.

"If you're worried about my mother, I can come back to your place."

"Again, thank you so very much for the offer. As tempting as it may be, I, er, um–" He sidestepped away from her. "Would you excuse me for a minute?"

"I'll give you my number. Or if you give me yours, I'll call you."

"Really," he said, "I have to go. But good luck. With college and dancing and teaching and whatever–"

"If you change your mind I'll be here until after New Year. I'll suck your dick!"

The passing line of bunny hoppers led by Layla Bimenyenz with Stanley Milnow tucked up right behind her wound its way around the floor. "Having a good time?" Terry called. He and Sue had attached themselves to the tail end.

"A ball," Jesse said and pointed to his watch.

"Yeah, in a bit."

Jesse turned, excused himself to the sad-faced Lucy and he hurried out to the lobby where Red Farley was slouched in a chair. His face was red and his shirt bagged out of his pants as if he had come apart at the seams. His head bobbed unsteadily and he watched the room in motion. Then the Decrescendos broke into "The Hokey Pokey" and the crowd responded, putting things in and taking them out.

"Merry Christmas, Red," Jesse said.

"Si' down. Si' down, kid." He made room next to him. "Life," he waxed philosophically, "is very short."

Jesse looked behind him, glad that he hadn't been followed, and then he looked at his watch again. Some of the teachers were already leaving. "Sometimes," he said, "it seems to go on forever."

"'Zackly right," he slurred. "Christmas sucks. And what a shit party this is. Are you having a good time?" His eyes were watery and unfocused. "I know I am." He signaled for another drink. "But you ever won'er if there isn't something better? I mean betteren this shit party–"

"Only every day."

"–I mean way down in your soul, in the bottom of your stomach?" He tried to focus on Jesse. "I can feel something's trying to burst out–"

Jesse put a little distance between them.

"'Scuse me." Red got to his feet with some difficulty. "I think I have to puke."

Jesse watched him totter away.

"Are you ready to go?" Sue asked. "I was looking all over for you."

Jesse jumped off his stool. "I'll get the coats!"

The counter at the checkroom was empty. Jesse waited for help and when no one came he decided to take advantage of the opportunity and stop in the toilet. He opened the door marked MENS, resisting the temptation to correct it, and stepped into the small, dark alcove. When he pushed the inner door it banged against something hard, so he pushed harder. It turned out to be Red Farley's head. He was sprawled across the tiles on his stomach.

"Are you all right, Red?" Jesse bent to help him.

"Don' tush me," he said. "If you tush me I'll throw up."

"But your head? It's bleeding. Your foot is in the urinal."

"It's nice an' cool in here. An' I'm comforbull. Don' tush me. Don' tush my foot or I'll throw up."

Jesse reluctantly stepped over him and went to the farthest urinal. "Baltz is the anti-Christ," was written in red marker on the wall above it. He finished quickly and zipped up. "I'll send help," he called to Red on his way out.

"Don' yell," Red mumbled. "If you yell I'll throw up."

The checkroom was still vacant. He looked around for help and decided to take matters into his own hands. He raised the hinged countertop and slipped inside with the coat checks

313

and searched through the rack for his numbers. Whimpering moans from the back stopped him dead.

"Oh, God! Oh, my God!"

Slowly he separated the hangers and saw Stanley Milnow and the serving wench naked on a pile of coats.

"Yes, yes, yes!"

"Oh, God! Oh, yes! Oh, Stanley!"

Jesse quickly and quietly found the three coats. He dropped the check stubs onto the counter, started away and then took back fifty cents from the dollar he'd left earlier.

Sue and Terry were waiting for him in the lobby. She was holding the floral centerpiece and he was carrying a pot of plastic plants. "Wasn't it everything we told you it would be?" he asked.

"And more," he said honestly. He shook his head.

Outside everything was covered in white, lending an air of wonder and unreality to the scene. It was still snowing lightly.

END OF PART ONE

Part II

In the News
January 1972

January 7
Pres. Nixon announces that he will seek another term in office.
January 9
Reclusive billionaire Howard Hughes, speaking by telephone from the Bahamas to reporters in Hollywood, says his purported biography by Clifford Irving is a fake.
January 20
Nixon gives his State of the Union message and calls for bipartisan support to create jobs, increase income and attain full employment through increasing industrial competitiveness.
January 24
Democrat Sen. Edmund Muskie of Maine wins the Iowa caucus for the presidential nomination.
In Guam, Shoichi Yokoi, a WWII Japanese soldier, is found by hunters near the Talofofo River. He had survived since 1944 in adherence to his army code of never surrendering. Upon his return to Japan as a national hero, Yokoi says, "It is with much embarrassment that I return."
January 25
Pres. Nixon makes public the secret peace talks from May 31, 1971, that included a cease-fire-in-place, US withdrawal and the return of prisoners from North Vietnam. His eight-point peace plan for Vietnam calls for POW release in return for withdrawal.
January 30
In Londonderry, Northern Ireland, British troops fire on a civil rights march. 13-14 people are killed on "Bloody Sunday" by soldiers of the First Parachute Regiment, six of whom are only 17. The British embassy in Dublin is burned down. One man who is photographed being arrested and taken into British army custody was later found shot dead. According to British government authorities, the march to protest internment was "illegal."

On Monday, January 3, 1972, the faculty, students and staff of Rosencrantz and Guildenstern Memorial High School trudged back from the long Christmas/Chanukah vacation through slushy snow. It had been a cold week with temperatures in the teens, but a New Year's Eve thaw turned the streets runny and gray. Although it was barely into winter and there were six very long months left to the school year, for the faculty and staff at R&G, and for teachers across Long Island, turning the page at the beginning of the new calendar year was the psychological point that marked the beginning of spring and the downhill slide to summer.

Mr. Baltz arrived at the building unusually early on this first day. He didn't bother to stop at his office to hang up his coat or take off his new galoshes, a Chanukah gift from his mother-in-law and Arnold Franks, her boyfriend, though he hadn't been a boy for more than sixty years. She was back in West Palm Beach finally. He had convinced her to fly on Christmas Day. "Everyone knows it's the best time to go into the City to see a show, or to travel. All the *goyim* are home opening presents." The plane touched down just after noon at the West Palm Airport with the three of them aboard, and he spent the week after Christmas avoiding the Florida sun and his mother-in-law.

The telephone call he expected from Stash Polakas came on New Year's Day. "Yeah," the Head Custodian assured him, "we finally finished your project. What a pain in the ass. A much bigger job than you said. I needed to hire another man to get everything done in time. I paid him out of my own pocket and threw in a little bonus to keep his lips sealed. And the toilet in your closet is done too. You owe me another–five hundred." He knew that Polakas was lying, but he wasn't about to quibble.

They arrived at JFK Airport on Sunday with the rest of the holiday travelers and he was too keyed up to sleep much Sunday night. In his haste to get upstairs he hadn't bothered to check his private facilities. He'd have plenty of time later to give the new executive john a good workout. He was focused on finally unmasking the Red Felt Phantom. He clumped through the halls directly to the third floor.

"Hey, Mr. Baltz." Virgil Loomis greeted him from out of the darkness. "Happy New Year."

The principal jumped and grabbed his chest. "Loomis, you scared the shit– What the hell are you doing in the building at this hour?"

"Mr. Farley sent me out on a Lesson Stretcher back in the old year, so I thought I'd get an early start and take up where I left off. Punctuality is one of my New Year's resolutions."

"What are you talking about, Loomis? What do you mean 'Lesson Stretcher'?" He was annoyed that his plans had been disrupted and that Loomis knew about the Lesson Stretcher, a concept so super secret, even the name wasn't to be spoken. It was Helen O'Dell's brainchild from her WAC days when veterans sent new recruits all around the base in a wild goose chase for some nonexistent thing. She adapted the concept of the Lesson Stretcher to get disruptive kids out of the classroom and move them through the halls on a phantom quest. Like the phone chain call list for emergencies, snow days and school closings, the Lesson Stretcher list, updated every September, kept a steady flow of troublemakers moving from room to room, teacher to teacher. And most important, it kept them out of the AP offices where they used to collect like flies and became an administrative problem.

"Loomis, this is the first day back. It's the New Year. It's not even seven o'clock. It's dark out. We are still on austerity and nobody is supposed to *be* in the building for another hour."

"I know that, Mr. B. But last year *before* the vacation I wasn't being all that I could be, so I made several resolutions–"

"I really don't care, Loomis, and I don't have time for the new you or the old you. Do you have a pass?"

Virgil patted his pocket and pulled out a clump of pink paper, the official red Lesson Stretcher pass, the universal signal alerting teachers on the receiving end of approaching trouble and for them to send whoever was holding it along the prearranged route ad infinitum, or at least the end of the day. "I'm sorry. I left it in my pocket when my pants went through the wash."

He didn't touch the wadded pass. "Go sit in the Cafeteria and don't move until the bell rings, and then go to your classes."

He waited for Virgil to turn the corner before he continued. He stopped in front of the (F)Utility closet and carefully felt over the top of the doorjamb for the new yellow key where Polakas said it would be. He made sure the corridor was completely empty, unlocked the door and stepped inside. The door shut behind him and he was in complete darkness. He felt for the two switches, flipped one and the closet filled with light. He turned it off, hit the other one and a red glow turned the closet into an observation center, as he imagined the inside of the Pentagon War Room might look. It was perfect. He edged forward and slowly lifted the blackout shade. His smiling face reflected back at him as in a dark mirror. He did resemble Richard Nixon, he thought, blood-red in the light. He touched the switch again, the light faded, his reflection disappeared and he was looking through the one-way glass at the three stall doors and the urinals in the faculty men's room. It was a beautiful sight, well worth anything he had to pay that crook Polakas. He wrung his hands in glee. He was ready now and knew it would be just a matter of time before he caught the Phantom in the act. Maybe even on the very first day of operations.

For the next half hour he watched returning teachers stream in and out before classes began, and he was amazed at how many of them didn't bother to flush or wash their hands. After the Homeroom bell he locked the closet, slipped the yellow key into his pocket and went back to his office to take care of his pressing matters. He clumped into the Main Office humming.

"Somebody sounds like he had a good vacation." Phyllis looked at the clock on the wall. "A little tardy on our first day back?" she said. "Did we over-sleep?"

"Happy New Year, *Ms* Lind." He was unfazed by her taunt.

"FYI, the three APs were just here looking for you, like the Magi out of the East. And they were bearing gifts. Should I let them know you're in? Are you accepting callers?"

"Give me about ten minutes," he said and let himself into his office.

She pressed the intercom button. "He's here, Mario. But I don't think it's the real Baltz. It's like that body-snatcher movie and he's been replaced. However, I like this one better. He said to give him a few minutes to settle in."

* * *

He was smiling broadly behind his desk when the three APs came in with matching smiles.

"I really love that buzzer security feature," Willy Zwill said. He examined the doorframe and tested the electric lock with his fingers before he pushed the door closed with an authoritative click.

"Happy New Year! We were wondering if everything came out all right?" Mario Giovanni nodded in the direction of the new executive toilet.

"Beyond my expectations."

"We bought you a little something to *christen* your new potty." Helen O'Dell produced the gift-wrapped package she had been hiding easily behind her back. She laid the package on his desk.

"I already did that, Helen," he joked and they all laughed.

"All of the assistant principals chipped in."

"Except Noah Lewis," Willy Zwill added.

"Well, thank you. But you shouldn't have." He pulled off the wrappings. "Washcloths and towels." He held them up. "Both marked 'His.' That's very thoughtful."

"The lady in the store had to break up a set and charged us extra," Zwill said. His eye blinked in an uncontrolled twitch.

"Can we see it?" she asked, indicating the closed door.

"Of course." He walked them over and the four of them packed themselves into the tiny room, inspecting the little sink, the mirrored cabinet and bowl, the walls and floor. Everything was tile and finished in serene shades of blue.

"Beautiful," Helen O'Dell said.

"And it smells good too. Pine."

"If it was a little bigger I could've had a stall shower." He flipped off the overhead light and switched on the vanity light over the mirror. The third switch started a little exhaust fan in the ceiling.

"Where does the exhaust go?"

He shrugged. "Upstairs somewhere. I'm not exactly sure. But I think it's tied into the vents in the Science Lab."

*　*　*

He pulled the Moroccan leather-bound register he had bought in Florida, a gift to himself. Stenciled in eighteen-karat-gold letters on the cover was the title he'd decided on, *Memoirs of a Secondary Schoolmaster by M. Seymour Baltz*. He opened to the first page. He thought long about an opening sentence. He wanted something quotable, something memorable for future generations of secondary schoolmasters. He had considered borrowing from Dickens: "It was the best of times; it was the worst of times," but rejected it, partly because he wasn't sure what it meant. He twisted the cap off his Waterman fountain pen with the extra fine nib, another gift to himself and wrote, "Project X–First Entry–January 3, 1972: A secondary schoolmaster is like a wartime commander-in-chief who is besieged by enemies, undermined by traitors and surrounded by incompetents, whose every decision has life-and-death ramifications that impact those under his charge. The tide of battle is changing at last. It is regrettable that half a school year has been wasted. But I may be getting ahead of myself." Those four sentences took a lot out of him. "The first day back turned out to be a surprisingly easy one. I am elated at the new facilities and spent most of the morning running up and back to The Observatory. It tired me out, but I was able to take a short nap after lunch. My 'Fortress of Solitude,' as I have chosen to name the new toilet, is very convenient, I can come and go as I please."

That was enough for one day. He closed the book and replaced it in the side drawer. He picked up the magazine on his desk and carried it to his Fortress of Solitude. He admired the towels he had arranged with great care on the rack over the sink. His and His. He dropped his pants and sat before he reached his free hand and switched on the exhaust. Somewhere on the second floor in the Science Lab the breeze coming from the air exchanger increased slightly and carried with it the new aroma of Pine-Sol into the room. It mingled with the lingering scent of rotten eggs and sulfur, the ghosts of science experiments past, and no one seemed to notice.

Union Free School District 71
Office of the Superintendent
Central Administration Building
Farmington, New York

From: Donald F. Flackett, Superintendent
To: All Faculty and Staff
Subject: From Kindergarten to Beyond! "No Child Left
              in the Lurch"
January 6, 1972

Welcome back to a New Year. Now get ready, because 1972 is the year Farmington UFSD 71 raises standards for our students and for our teachers across the board–"From Kindergarten to Beyond!" Beginning this semester, academic tracking for ALL students will be eliminated! Basic Level Track III, non-Regents students will be "Leveled Up" into mainstream Regents classes! Ready or not here they come–and that will mean new challenges, especially to you teachers.

As Superintendent my goal is to make sure my plan is a success. That means teachers will be called on to develop new curricula in all subject areas to provide for varied and individual learning needs and insure "No child will be left in the lurch," the new slogan for the new year and beyond. To that end, compulsory weekly professional training and development workshops will begin this month for every teacher in the district, insuring that the new curricula is implemented at all levels and without exception. It will be an even greater challenge because the District remains on austerity through June.

There are no funds in the budget to buy new textbooks for "Leveled Up" students or to compensate teachers for training and curriculum development, or for attending the compulsory workshops. So you will have to "do more with less," the other slogan for the new year.

I am confident you will all rise to the occasion. Your end-of-the-year performance evaluations depend on it! In addition to the coming academic changes, new teacher performance evaluations are in development at Central to measure teacher success and failure, and they *are* coming soon!

Joseph E. Scalia

Camelot

Official Publication of the Partnership of Parents and Teachers
in Association for better Farmington Public Schools
Harriet Stegle, President P-PTA
Vol. 4 Issue 4   January 1972

Well, here we all are back again where we started, but in a new year with new tans and new plans! All I know is if you are like me, most of those New Year's resolutions have already gone by the boards.

RESOLUTIONS AROUND THE DISTRICT:

Lois Barone, Kindergarten teacher at Old Dutch Mill Elementary–"My resolution is to stop beating my kids. My biological kids, I mean. I will continue to beat the kids in my class."

John Hiller, Guidance Counselor at R&G–"My resolution is to sock away some extra money for retirement. I'm eligible to go, but I won't put my papers in until we get a new contract–and a raise."

Sylvia Berkowsky, Home Ec Chair at R&G–"My resolution is to bring style and good fashion, skirts and dresses back to the classroom. I want teachers to become good role models for their students like they used to be." When I asked her as a follow-up just how she plans to do it Sylvia who is no fan of pants suits and a relaxed dress code, didn't answer. She smiled mysteriously and winked. "It's a spring surprise, but don't be surprised when you see lots of homemade skirts and dresses among the budding flowers."

NEWS AND VIEWS:

Knock three times if you're OCD!

District School Psychologist Les Manley is finally back from an Association of School Psychologists (ASP) conference held over the break. The topic, "Coping with Obsessive Compulsive Disorder in Our Schools." In Les's official report submitted to Central he said, "Originally scheduled for a single afternoon, it took two full days to cover the conference agenda. So many people were eager to share their personal experiences with OCD, but setting up the tables and deciding on the order of speakers took the entire afternoon. And finally getting a motion to adjourn the conference turned into a two-day marathon."

See you next time with more news from the trenches!

Joseph E. Scalia

FT Ass.
"We value You."

FROM: Joel Maxwell, President FT Ass.
TO: ALL Farmington Teachers
Re: Free Insurance

The Farmington Teachers' Ass. is happy to announce a new perk. Effective January 1, 1972, ALL members of FT Ass. were covered by a $1,000 limited term life insurance policy! This benefit is free of charge and provided by the Limited Term Life Insurance Company. Non-members, now is the time to join and take advantage of this added benefit.

FU - 2
Farmington Union, Local # 2

"Unions - From Cradle to Grave!" (And now beyond!)

FREE FREE FREE FREE FREE FREE FREE FREE FREE
FREE FREE FREE

You're worth more to *us* alive than dead! That's right! Of course, there is no substitute for a warm body in the classroom. But here's the better news. Now, if you should die, FU-2 will insure you for $2,000! That's 100% more than the competition. And if you die while you are "still in the harness," so to speak, in your classroom, your survivors will have a cool $4,000 double indemnity because you had the good sense to say "FU-2!" Heart attacks are the leading cause of classroom deaths! Cancer and high blood pressure are things to look forward to for the career teacher, and death by any of these conditions is covered by this policy. Of course nobody wants to go, but now you can go with 100% more peace of mind knowing that as a member of FU-2, there's up to $4,000 in cold cash sitting in the pot at the end of the rainbow.

Dwayne Purvey, President FU-2

The Teacher's Cafeteria was filled with the usual crowd in their usual places. Jesse learned early the seating protocol in the faculty room, at meetings in the auditorium and the teachers' cafeteria. Seniority ruled. When he set his tray on the wrong table in the wrong place at the wrong time, his mistake was promptly corrected. "That's where we sit," Sylvia Berkowsky, Home Ec Department Chair, told him and stood over him until he had found another place.

So now he inched his tray along the serving line and waited to place his order with Peggy McFeeley, the Teacher's Cafeteria lunch lady. But that wasn't really necessary because he always ordered the same thing, turkey and Swiss on a Kaiser roll with mustard and some pickles on the side. She had it ready and handed it to him with a smile. "Happy New Year and enjoy."

John Hiller was the only person who didn't have an assigned seat and sat wherever he wanted. That was not so much a perk for being the most senior guidance counselor on staff, but because he was in and out of the Teacher Cafeteria all day and jumped from one open place to another. This period he was at a table by the radiator where he always stashed his frozen rolls every morning behind the curtain so they would thaw. All day he helped himself to the butter and jelly on the service cart and enjoyed his "free lunch," as he called it. Coffee wasn't free. Each cup was fifty cents, but refills were, if you used the same cup. So John used his styrofoam cup from period to period and refilled it. Before the end of the last period, he rinsed it in the drinking fountain and stored it overnight in the teacher refrigerator for the next morning. He kept backup cups in the freezer and he bragged he could go for weeks before he had to pay fifty cents for another cup.

Jesse carried his tray to the table and sat next to Terry, who didn't look up. He was deeply engrossed in discussion. "The question is what does the Union plan to do about this." He waved the superintendent's memo in the air. "This is a clear violation of the terms of our contract."

"We don't have a contract," John Hiller said, dunking a roll into his coffee cup.

"And that's why the terms of the old contract remain in effect by state law. They can't change anything," Dwayne Purvey said.

"But they *are*. Teacher-developed curriculum with no compensation. Compulsory afterschool workshops mean an increase in the workday. No tracking means bigger class sizes. And new teacher evaluation forms!" Terry was on a roll.

"I'm too old for this crap," John Hiller said and buttered another roll. "I can retire whenever I want. I could just put down my roll and coffee and walk out that door today if I wanted to. But I won't give them the satisfaction until we sign a new contract and I get my raise and my retroactive pay. That will go toward increasing my final average salary. Then I'll retire."

"You've been retired for the past ten years, John," somebody said.

He laughed and pulled another roll from his bag.

"The Union Executive Committee will meet to consider our options–"

"The Association isn't sitting still for this either," Joel Maxwell called over from another table. "While you consider your options, Purvey, the Association is already acting."

"How's that, Maxwell? Volunteering to conduct the workshops?"

"Up yours. This morning we ordered 'Teacher Working Without a Contract' buttons for all our members to wear on assigned days."

"That should do it," Terry said sarcastically.

Jesse ate his sandwich and watched the exchange like a tennis match, his head pivoting back and forth.

"Without any push back from the Union and the Association, Flackett will get his plan through, write up a paper about how innovative it is and use that as a stepping-stone to a higher-paying job in a richer and better school district. And the teachers will be left holding the bag and doing the grunt work. How'd Flackett say it–doing more with less. Isn't that right, Les?" Terry turned to Les Manley, the school psychologist at another table trying to be invisible.

Jesse looked over. He had seen him walking the halls, touching the walls, but didn't know his name. "That's the school psychologist," Sue told him when he asked her about him. "I'm surprised you saw him outside his office, a little closet across from the Main Office near Attendance. Les is a *little* agoraphobic and only leaves it when he has to. And he's *a lot* OCD, so when he's out in the open he has to keep one hand on a wall. Crazy, huh?"

The school psychologist heard his name and looked up. "What?" he asked and then looked for an escape route.

"More with less. That's what Flackett said," Terry quipped. "So what more does Flackett want, Les?"

"I don't really know, Mr. Scapelli." He managed a weak smile. "But if I hear anything I'll get back to you." He looked at his watch. "Oh," he said touching his tray three times before he dumped it into the trash. "Late for an appointment." He got up, placed his right hand on the wall and felt his way out of the cafeteria.

"So when are you getting those buttons?" Terry asked.

"I'll need a bunch of them," John Hiller said.

"They're free for all our members, John," Joel Maxwell said. "So you can't make money selling them."

A SPECIAL MESSAGE
FROM THE OFFICE OF
THE SUPERINTENDENT OF SCHOOLS
DR. DONALD F. FLACKETT, SUPT.

Leveling Up! Details and Clarification. Is This Plan on the Level?

January 10, 1972

In my final memo of 1971, I tossed down the gauntlet when I asked teachers to join hands with administration in an effort to heal old wounds and begin the New Year with a new spirit of cooperation. In last Thursday's memo I announced an end to academic tracking and plans to impose higher educational demands and greater levels of accountability on the teachers.

Many have asked exactly how this can be done in a climate of distrust, austerity and the absence of a teacher contract? Let me respond by saying that I am prepared to expend all of the District's resources, including the revenues and the accrued interest realized from still not reaching a contract agreement with the teachers, to insure the success of my plan to raise standards, extract more from the teachers and leave no Farmington child in the lurch. This is how it will work.

Eliminate *all* **Basic Level** classes. Students, previously identified as **Non-Academic, Slow Learners, Reluctant Learners, Track IIIs, Special Ed** and **General,** often referred to euphemistically in closed sessions at Board of Education meetings as **Gee-Whiz Kids, Losers, DERs, DUHs or Duds,** will be moved up into academic **Regents Level** courses. This process, called "Leveling Up," beginning first at the high school level in English, and then to all levels and each academic area of every school, will immediately raise the educational standards and the class sizes. To assist teachers who will be held accountable for the success of my plan, I have prepared a primer of new administrator-speak to familiarize you with the specialized terminology. All teachers will memorize the following terms in preparation for their upcoming "Teacher Competency Test" in the spring.

1. **Oxymoron:** Comes from the prefix *Oxy* (as in Oxford University) meaning "intelligent"; and *moron* meaning "stupid" or "absurd." An **oxymoron** is a contradiction in terms, such as "plastic-glass," "deafening silence," and "light-heavyweight," "**Leveling Up**" (see #2 below) and "**Forced-Cooperation**" (see # 3 below).

2. **Leveling Up:** Comes from the word *level* meaning "even" or "at the same place" (e.g., "Is this new plan on the level?"); and the word *up* meaning "not down" and/or "at a higher level." When the two words are combined the **oxymoron** (see #1 above) "leveling up" results. In my plan, everyone will be **Leveled Up,** except those students already on the **Regents Level** at the proposed level. Similarly, students on the **Honors Level,** whose parents exercise considerable political clout in the school district, will not be affected by the changes, since these students are already up a level above the **Regents Level.** Moving **Honors Level** students down to the **Regents Level** and mixing them with **Regents Level** students and previously **Basic Level students** newly **Leveled Up,** would actually be **Leveling Down**, which is not desirable. (Note: The phrases **Leveling Up** and/or **Leveled Up** are preferred to the phrases **Up Leveling** and/or **Up Leveled,** although **Up Leveling** and/or **Up Leveled** may sometimes be used in place of the preferred phrases.)

3. **Forced Cooperation**: In the interest of making the new **Leveling Up Plan** or **LUP** work smoothly, students previously in different academic levels other than **Honors** will be *required* to cooperate and assist one another. **Regents Level** students already familiar with course requirements and procedures will be paired with newly **Leveled Up** previously **Basic Level** students in what is called **Peer-Pairing**. **Peer-Paired Partners** or **PPP** will become the mainstay of the plan. In addition to the **PPPs**, **Peer-Paired Teachers** or **PPT** from different scholastic disciplines, many of whom have been harboring grudges for

years and haven't spoken to one another in decades, will be *forced* by my new plan to cooperate and work together, hence the term **Forced Cooperation.**

4. **Lu-Lu:** The newly combined **Leveled Up** classes will no longer be designated as either **Basics** or **Regents**. Instead they will be referred to as **Lu-Lus**, from the combination of **Leveled Up** and **Losers** (another euphemism often used at Board meetings). Depending on the number of **Lu-Lus** (formerly **Basic Level** students) in each of these newly combined classes, the newly formed **Leveled Up** classes may indeed be real **Lu-Lus**.

5. **Adapted Downward Aquatic Modification** or **ADAM:** Since the new plan is intended to *raise* standards, the curriculum will not be *watered down* to accommodate those who have been **Leveled Up**. *Watering down* the curriculum would only work against the new plan by lowering the newly raised, higher standards. However, some **Leveled Up** students may initially require additional assistance beyond that available from **PPPs** and/or **PPTs**, as provided under **Forced Cooperation** (see #3 above). This may necessitate a slight readjustment in the new *higher* standards. The term for such a readjustment is **Adapted Downward Aquatic Modification**. In the simplest sense this entails slightly diluting the curriculum by adding just enough water to the mix in the hope that what is stuck to the bottom will float to the top.

To further meet the needs of the newly **Leveled Up** students, a list of required reading for next September's English classes has already been compiled. The new titles are a result of careful **Adapted Downward Aquatic Modification**. They will replace the actual books that students have read for years in the good old days before **Leveling Up**. For those who are unable to read, the district also plans to expand its collection of movies, tapes and/or cartoon versions of the classics so former **Basic Level** students will be able to comprehend.

The list of new required books includes:

A Tale Of One City　　　　　*Catch 11*
Romeo Or Juliet　　　　　　*The Hardy Boy*

Little Woman
The House of the 3.5 Gables
Mediocre Expectations
I Almost Remember Mama

The Sound Or the Fury
Crime Or Punishment
The Old Man Or The Sea
The Halfback Of Notre Dame

As Farmington's success spreads across the state and the country, my educational plan will become the model for the nation, propelling America's education forward. Today Farmington, tomorrow the world!

**Union Free School District 71
Office of the Superintendent
Central Administration Building
Farmington, New York**

From: Donald F. Flackett, Superintendent
To: All Faculty and Staff
Subject: Official Memo of Clarification of Leveling Up
               Misinformation
January 14, 1972

Monday's memo circulated under the heading A SPECIAL MESSAGE FROM THE OFFICE OF THE SUPERINTENDENT OF SCHOOLS DR. DONALD F. FLACKETT, SUPT. purporting to contain "Leveling Up–Details and Clarification–Is This Plan on theLevel?" was *not* on the level and was *not* an official memo from this office as alleged.

The purpose of this *official* official memo is to set the record straight.

As Superintendent of Schools, I am on the "ground floor," so to speak, in all matters regarding the education of students in Farmington School District UFSD 71. That being said, student grade level tracking for Basic Level classes as it existed WILL be eliminated in the Spring Semester. Honors Level classes WILL NOT be affected and will not change.

However, district administrators, including myself and all of the assistant superintendents, have *never* referred to Farmington students functioning on a lower academic level, or those in Special Education classes, as "Losers," "Gee-Whiz Kids," "DERs," "DUHS" or "DUDS" euphemistically or otherwise, at School Board meetings or anyplace else, per the bogus memo.

In addition, to the best of my knowledge, there is no intention on the part of the Board of Education to change the reading curriculum. Parents and taxpayers alike can rest assured that *no* additional money will be wasted on new books to replace the worn and dog-eared volumes, the classics that have become a mainstay and been used in the district for decades.

Finally, the "Leveling Up Plan," as well as the "administrator speak" and "terminology" contained in the counterfeit memo is a complete fabrication with no basis in reality. Its sole purpose was obviously to disseminate false information in an attempt to spread confusion and create panic throughout the district. To prevent this from happening again, teachers and staff are directed to disregard all unofficial memos that may appear in their mailboxes. To assist you, in the future all official memos from Central Administration will contain the words "Official Memo" posted prominently on the page.

It should be noted that the concept of a Teacher Competency Test referred to in the false memo is not completely without merit, and such a test is currently under consideration for construction in the future.

"Is he in, Phyl?"

She shook her head. "I haven't seen him since this morning, Mario. He was here for a little while and then he was gone. Said something about being out of the building for most of the day."

"He didn't mention anything to me about it. Did he say where he was going? Were the other APs with him?" He looked worried.

"No." She picked at her nail polish. "But he had a new folding chair with him."

"What for?"

"He wouldn't say. And told me to mind my own business when I asked. So now I'm minding my own business." The phone on her desk rang and she ignored it, continuing to apply polish to her nail. "Then he told me to handle anything important that comes up. I'm considering pulling a surprise Fire Drill. Or maybe just sending everybody home early. What do you think?"

"Did he seem mad at me?"

"He's always mad at somebody, Mario. Yesterday he came back after being out of the office all morning furious about something. He told me to call Stash Polakas and have him remove all the stall doors in the faculty men's toilet."

"The bathrooms are *my* responsibility, Phyl, and he never even mentioned anything to me about it. Did he say why he wanted to remove the doors?"

"Something about 'sanitary issues.' I told him if he was concerned with sanitary issues maybe he could finally put in the vending machine in the women's room we've asked for forever."

He wasn't listening. "Did he mention anything about his mother-in-law at the Christmas party?" He looked worried. "I was drinking and I might have gotten a little carried away. Did I say or do anything to embarrass myself?"

"You mean *at* the party or *after*? I know I'm still waiting for that 'special delivery' you couldn't deliver."

"I told you that never happened to me before. And I promised to make it up to you. I mean, did I say or do anything offensive to make him mad at me? He's been avoiding me."

"He's avoiding everybody. Everybody but me!" She fanned her nails with the papers on her desk. "Here's the schedule for midterm week he had me type up. And this is the schedule for the spring teacher observations I had to rush because he needed it now. And worse news for you, Mario, he said he can't do any observations and he wants you to split them with the other APs, including the follow-ups before the June countdown."

He looked at the schedule. "Now I'm sure he's mad at me. What the hell do I know about observing English classes?" He stretched and cracked his neck and went back to his office.

She started painting her other hand when Coach Boid came into the Main Office looking agitated. "I gotta see Seymour, Phyllis," he said, barely stopping in front her desk. "It's important."

"He's not in, Birdie, but he told me to take care of anything important."

"Well," he slid the baseball cap to the back of his head, "last week I got this call in my office from some guy who said something about wrestling. Said he represents the ACLU. I thought it was that new All Conference League thing in Connecticut and didn't follow up. But the guy left another message yesterday. Said it was serious, but when I looked them up I couldn't find any ACLU listed."

"Can't help you, Birdie. But you can go tell Mario. He's in his office and doesn't have anything else to do."

He marched into the alcove.

"I got my hands full with the midterm schedule and observations," the AP said and showed him the papers. "Did you check with Buddy? He's the wrestling coach."

"I did. The guy from the ACLU called Buddy too, a couple a times. Turns out he's a lawyer representing a kid named Loomis—"

"Virgil Loomis?"

"According to Buddy. He said the ACLU guy claims the kid's being deprived of his rights. He wants to join the secret wrestling team, but was told he can't because his hair is too long."

"Do we have a secret wrestling team?"

Coach Boid pulled off his cap and scratched his bald spot. "Fuck if I know. The guy said if Loomis doesn't get on the team they'll send somebody to the school. I didn't know anything about any secret wrestling team, Mario. Do you think Seymour knows anything about it?"

"I'll ask Phyllis," he said. "She knows everything." He picked up the phone and dialed her number, but she didn't pick it up. "Shit!"

He was happy with the new director's chair. After sitting so long on the metal seat of the folding chair, he needed one that was softer and taller. It hadn't been cheap, but it was worth the price. Now he was able to look out directly into the faculty toilet from behind the mirror and sit more comfortably for longer periods of time and enjoy his lunch, half a cream cheese sandwich on date nut bread and a container of apple juice. With the stall doors removed he had an unobstructed view of Stanley Milnow sitting in the middle stall reading the newspaper. He lost count of the number of times the business teacher was in the bathroom between periods during the course of the day. Milnow spent as much time in the toilet as he did in the classroom. "Stanley Milnow–possible enlarged prostate and/or irritable bowel syndrome," he made a note in the log he was keeping. That might come in handy in the future.

Baltz watched him less than a foot away lay the newspaper aside at the sink and turn on the water. The spring-loaded faucet snapped back immediately. The teacher turned it on again and held the faucet with one hand while he rinsed the other. Then he reversed the process. He flicked both hands to shake off the cold water and when droplets splattered over the mirror Mr. Baltz flinched. Then he ran his damp hands across his hair and leaned forward to study his reflection close up in the speckled mirror. He ran a wet index finger into and around both nostrils, paused and stared. "What are you looking at? Are you looking at me?" he asked into the mirror. "Are you looking at *me*?" In the darkness Mr. Baltz pulled back from the glass. In the bathroom, Milnow peered into the mirror. "You must be, and I can't blame you. Handsome devil." He winked and fired a finger-pistol shot at his reflection in the mirror. Then he pulled out a length of dental floss from his jacket pocket and stuck it between his teeth.

Inside, the principal stepped closer to the mirror so that six inches separated the two of them. "Yeah," he whispered, "I am looking at you!" And he watched with disgust as Milnow rooted around until his gums bled into the sink.

"No wonder the women can't keep their hands off you, Stan." He dropped the bloody string into the pail, cocked his finger again, winked and took another shot at the mirror.

Baltz was nauseated, but there was something exciting about being a voyeur, able to watch the secret lives of others unfold before his eyes. Like Scrooge in *A Christmas Carol* when he goes back in time undetected. Like Jimmy Stewart in *It's A Wonderful Life*. Like the Invisible Man who comes and goes as he pleases. "I'm the Invisible Man," he whispered. "And I see everything!"

He was about to leave when the door banged into the tiles and Mario Giovanni barged into bathroom. "Scattering your message on the bathroom walls again, Stanley?" he asked.

"Only on the mirror this time, Mario. I leave it to the poets and the malcontents to do the writing. Besides, they took the doors off the stalls. Now I can't even crap in peace."

The AP turned to look. "When did that happen?" He stepped into each stall to check for new writing, but there wasn't any.

"This morning while I was taking a dump. Polakas and Slow Charley came in and yanked them off. When I complained, Stash said if I had a problem to take it up with Baltz. Midterm proctoring assignments ready yet? I hope you don't screw me over again this year, Mario."

"Phyllis gave them to me to review, Stan. With all the other things I have to do around this place now that our fearless leader is nowhere to be found most of the time, I'll get to them when I do. Besides, what do you care? Everybody downstairs knows you'll call in sick during test week and miss your proctoring assignments."

"I won't miss them at all, Mario. Midterms are the best time for a trip to Atlantic City. Noah Lewis already made reservations. A bunch of us are going. Why don't you come along?"

"Good for Noah Lewis," he said sarcastically. "While you guys are playing I'll be here on shit detail doing Baltz's dirty work and all the other shit details he comes up with." He stopped at the mirror and looked at himself and stretched his neck. "Jesus, Stan, you got blood all over! Good thing Baltz isn't here to see it or he'd have you polishing the glass. And me cleaning the toilets! The bastard."

"Fuck him and the midterms. You really oughta come to AC. We got comps for dinner and a show."

"I promised Phyllis–"

"Pussy-whipped." He snapped his hand and made a whip-cracking sound. "And you're not married. If Baltz didn't have you to handle things he might even appreciate you more. Think about it, Mario."

"I will."

When they were gone he jotted down their conversation into his log. It was an eye-opening insight into his number one AP. He also realized he couldn't be out of his office all day, day after day, without raising suspicions. Mario was complaining and Phyllis was asking him questions. To avoid a mutiny he needed a plan for more efficient use of his time. He switched off the light, opened the door, checked the corridor and left the Observatory. Observatory, he thought, sounded so much better than coming out of the closet.

The days leading up to midterm week were especially hectic. The deluge of memos from Central, official and otherwise, teacher concerns about new curricula and larger classes packed with non-Regents kids added another layer to the stress. And rumors of new teacher evaluations based on student performance and test scores circulated daily, compounding the strain of five months of austerity and the absence of a teacher contract. The removal of the stall doors in the Third Floor Faculty Men's Room was the final factor in creating the perfect storm inside R&G. Tempers flared, old grudges were intensified and new grudges were begun.

"Things are really bad," Sue told Jesse, "when Dwayne Purvey and Joel Maxwell are talking to one another unarmed and agree to a joint Union and Association faculty meeting."

"I really don't understand what it's all about," Jesse said.

"But you're going, right? You have to go as a show of support and solidarity."

"Well," he hesitated, "I have a lot of papers to grade and averages to do before the midterms. And I was hoping–"

"No excuses. You're going. Everybody has to go. This is beyond important, it's about the future of teaching here in the District. Bring your papers and grade them at the meeting. Just show up after school today right after dismissal in the auditorium!"

So he did.

After the dismissal stampede to vacate the building, Jesse reluctantly made his way to the Bernard H. Prahl Memorial Auditorium through the littered halls and that made him sad. He remembered his elementary school was always clean, even at the end of the day. Anything on the floors was "educational litter"–broken crayons, pencils. or on occasion, a lost hat or a mitten. That was because, he thought, elementary kids love their school. And they especially love their teachers and put them on an altar higher than their parents. The halls of R&G were filled with paper airplanes, gum wrappers, actual trash and even spit. Today they were clogged with disgruntled teachers deciding whether to go to the meeting or go home.

There was a sense of *déjà vu* as he approached the small crowd that triggered the pangs in the pit of his stomach he'd felt on that long-ago first day. At least he didn't cry or throw up as much, but he still wasn't able to relax and most of his home time and weekends he spent marking papers and planning lessons. He felt the inside pocket for his resignation letter and panicked when it wasn't there. Then he remembered it was in his attaché case. Yes, he had definitely made progress. He took a deep breath.

"Step up! Step up! Come in! Come in!" Dwayne Purvey called to passing teachers like a carnival barker. He had a large "FU-2" button pinned to his lapel "This is an important meeting. You can't afford to miss it."

"Come in! Come in!" Joel Maxwell said, handing "FT Ass." and "Teacher Working Without a Contract" buttons to everyone who passed into the auditorium. "Come to the meeting if you want a contract. If you want dignity and privacy, if you want the doors back in the faculty bathroom."

"This isn't going to take long I hope," Phaedra Schwartz-Fine commented. "I have important things to do."

Justine Bell, a teacher Jesse vaguely recognized, pressed a flier into his hand when he passed. She was a Jehovah's Witness and had spent her hall duty periods trying to convert him since September whenever she saw him, until he found another route around the building. He read the Witness pamphlet, *Awake!,* with its simplistic pastoral scene line-drawing of people and wild animals side by side in harmony. "Wouldn't you like to live in a world like this? Keep right with God. No left turn. John 27." Jesse slipped it into his pocket and went through the doors.

The auditorium wasn't very crowded, but the noise level far exceeded the actual number in the seats divided along affiliation lines with the FU-2 on the left, FT Ass. on the right and small clusters, like dandelion clumps, between the two. Chuck LaFemina and Rory Aaron sat together in the middle. Phaedra Schwartz-Fine slipped into the vacant seat next to Sue who was paging through the opened New York *Times* draped across the back of the seat in front of her.

"I really can't stay. I hope it isn't long. I'm meeting Daddy and we have an appointment with the divorce attorney at four. Paul and I are done!"

"That's nice, Phay," she said absently.

Terry was in a heated conversation with Red Farley and Stanley Milnow on the other side of Sue. Carolyn Butrum, Rita Reed and Claire Hutton were ranged across a row in front of them at various stages of knitting, crocheting and knotting yarn.

"Attention," Joel Maxwell banged on the microphone. He was at the podium. "Will the teachers at the back please take seats and shut the doors so we can begin."

Jesse climbed into a row behind the three women and his attaché case bumped the back of the seat. Mrs. Butrum turned and tutted at him. "Sorry," he said. He dropped into his seat and jumped up too late to avoid the wad of chewing gum. He hit the back of Claire Hutton's head and knocked the Pall Mall she was smoking from between her lips.

"Do you mind?" She brushed the ashes from the crewel she was knotting, a forest scene stretched out in a large wooden hoop that lay across her lap. She readjusted her hair and Jesse realized it was a wig.

"Sorry. Excuse me. Gum on my seat."

"It sure isn't a very good turnout," Mrs. Butrum said. Her head moved up and down as she counted the stitches she had just knitted. "Darn. I missed count." She pulled out the entire line and started again. "At this rate I'll never get it finished in time."

"Yes, a sad turnout," Rita Reed echoed, blowing her nose and fanning the air to dissipate the smoke from Mrs. Hutton's cigarette before she made several more stitches in the handkerchief she was crocheting.

"People love to complain," Mrs. Butrum said, "but no one bothers to show up."

"Such a shame."

Jesse pulled at the gum stuck to his pants. He felt like he was in the scene with Madam Defarge from *A Tale of Two Cities.* "Off with their heads!" he said under his breath and Mrs. Hutton turned to look at him.

"Can we get started?" Joel Maxwell began.

Dwayne Purvey made a noisy entrance through the rear door and went directly to the podium. "Just a minute, Maxwell, I thought this was going to be a joint meeting. A show of solidarity." He twisted the stand microphone in his direction. "I don't recall anyone delegating you chairman."

Joel Maxwell twisted it back. "As the elected president of the only officially recognized bargaining agent in this school district it stands to reason that the Association–"

Dwayne Purvey turned and bent over. "Kiss my officially recognized ass, Maxwell!" They wrestled briefly for the microphone.

"I'm in charge here."

"Over my dead body, Maxwell." He grabbed the microphone.

"That can be arranged."

"This meeting is now in sess–"

Joel Maxwell flicked the button and turned off the microphone. "Up yours, Purvey." He grabbed it from Dwayne Purvey's hand. and switched it back on. "I call this meeting to order!"

"It appears that this is two meetings and my half of the meeting," Dwayne Purvey announced, "will not respond to your call to order." He leaned into the microphone. "All Union members are directed to disregard the Association portion of the meeting."

During the scuffle for control of the podium, David Bowden and two other science teachers got up and escaped through the side door.

"Point of order," Richard Everett, the senior teacher in the History Department and oldest teacher in the district, called from the back of the auditorium. Everett prided himself on his knowledge of history and was a self-proclaimed expert in Parliamentary Procedure. A lifelong Farmington resident and the unofficial town historian, he attended all the School Board meetings where as a taxpayer he vocally opposed raising teacher salaries and voted against the school budget if it meant increasing town taxes. "I'm old-school," he announced. "I started teaching when teachers didn't care about salaries. I would teach for free." Everyone knew he was a company man and a direct line to the building administration. He often dropped in on Mr. Baltz "to chat" and fill the principal in on the things he observed and overheard around the building. That was one of the reasons teachers called him "Dick."

He pushed his walker forward down the center aisle with some difficulty. "As a member of neither organization"– he claimed every September he wouldn't join either as a matter of principle and to maintain his impartiality, but it saved him having to pay dues, a considerable amount over the years–"I don't support either side. So I volunteer to act as Parliamentarian that we might act civilly as a unified body. I propose a compromise and designate both Presidents Purvey and Maxwell as co-chairmen and split the microphone time. It is now exactly three twenty-two."

The Phys Ed Department stood up en masse and hurried out noisily.

"A point well taken, Mr. Everett. I would like to go on record as far as the Farmington Teachers' Association is concerned that you would be more than acceptable to act as Parliamentarian. It's not my intention, nor has it ever been my intention to block the progress of this meeting or prevent the free exchange of information. But if the other side–"

"The 'other side,' you bastard, finds Mr. Everett even more acceptable than your side does."

"Point of Personal Privilege," Mr. Everett said. "Now can we have that in the form of a motion to make it official."

The Driver Education people packed up their things and left.

"Wouldn't that be a Point of Order and not a Point of Personal Privilege?" Red Farley asked.

"I stand corrected, Mr. Farley. It would be a Point of Order."

"Is there a motion to the effect–" Joel Maxwell asked

"I so move," Mr. Everett said. "But we need a second."

"I second the emotion," Stanley Milnow called from the back.

"Discussion on the motion?"

"What exactly are we voting on," Mrs. Butrum said, without looking up from her knitting.

"I'm not sure." Something Dick Everett said, but I wasn't listening."

"Since there is no discussion," Mr. Everett announced, "I call the question."

"I call and I raise," Stanley Milnow called.

"Now we need a vote on the motion to call the question by a show of hands. All in favor."

Hands went up.

"Opposed?"

Some of the same hands went up again.

"Motion to end discussion carried," Mr. Everett announced. "Now on the motion itself. All in favor? Opposed?"

It was carried by the same mixed number.

"In order to insure that everyone in the hall gets an opportunity to be heard," Mr. Everett proposed, pulling a sheet of paper from his class notes, "I propose we keep a speaker's list. Anyone wishing to speak for or against a proposal will raise his or her hand and I will record the names on this pad. Mr. Purvey, I have your name first."

"Finally–"

"Another Point of Order," Mr. Everett interrupted. "According to *Robert's Rules of Order,*" he pulled out a copy from his book bag, "under Parliamentary procedure, old business is always first. And then we go to new business."

"There is no old business, *Dick*! This is a new meeting with only new business. Dr. Flackett's unilateral changes to the working conditions. Teachers working without a contract, the new teacher evaluation forms and the stall doors in the faculty toilets."

"Point of Information then," Mr. Everett said. "That would be in the Faculty Men's toilet as the doors in the Faculty Women's toilet are still in place. Is that correct?"

"The Faculty *Men's* toilet," Dwayne Purvey corrected.

"Point of Order." Mr. Everett read from *Robert's*. "If there is no old business we will still need a motion to dispense with it to move on."

Six more people left.

"Is there such a motion?" Joel Maxwell asked.

"So moved," Mr. Everett offered.

"Second that emotion a second time," came from the back.

"All in favor," Mr. Maxwell said in the interest of speeding things along.

"Point of Order," Mr. Everett interrupted. "According to–" He held up the book, "We need discussion before any vote. All motions have to be discussed. I have this speakers list." He held up the sheet of paper.

"Is there any discussion?" Joel Maxwell asked. There was none. He looked at Mr. Everett. "Now what?"

"We have to call the question again."

"Anyone? Call the question?"

"So moved," Mr. Everett volunteered.

"Called and raised!"

"Is there any discussion on the motion to call the question?" Maxwell asked, determined to get it right.

"Point of Information," Mr. Everett offered. "According to *Robert's*, a motion to call the question is non-debatable."

Mrs. Hutton stood and packed her things. Her cigarette dangled from her lips. "I have to get home before the dog poops on the new rug. Let me know what they decide tomorrow, *if* they decide anything." She started up the side aisle and collected three more people as she went.

"All in favor? Opposed?"

Only half the people present voted. The union side was confused about whether or not they were still boycotting, so they abstained.

"Jesus Christ," Dwayne Purvey said, "we've been here for forty-five minutes and haven't gotten to the point! There are no damn doors on the stalls in the men's toilet."

"Is that what this is all about? The men's toilet? I thought it was about a new contract. Or the budget." Mrs. Butrum picked up her things.

Purvey went on. "Two years ago they took the metal eating utensils from the Teachers' Cafeteria and replaced them with plastic ones that break. They said it was because the dishwasher was broken and they couldn't keep the silverware clean. That was two years ago! Even before austerity they reduced the number of mimeograph machines to cut down on the amount of paper we use. Then they removed the paper. Now they took the doors off the stalls in the Third Floor Faculty Room in direct violation of the laws of privacy and decency."

Rory Aaron raised his hand and got on Mr. Everett's speaker's list.

"Mr. Aaron?"

"It's barbaric. The plastic utensils are useless. Bring back the silverware!"

Chuck LaFemina nodded in agreement. "I second that!"

"We're talking about the stall doors. The doors are just the tip of the iceberg!" Dwayne Purvey said when he once again had the floor.

"I have to run," Phaedra Schwartz-Fine said to Sue, who was working on the crossword puzzle. "Let me know what happens with the iceberg."

"Nothing is being done because the administration has ignored all the informal requests to correct the problem and the lame-ass Farmington Teachers' Association, the *official bargaining agent,* is too chickenshit to file a formal grievance!"

"Just a minute, Purvey–" Joel Maxwell grabbed for the microphone.

"All we ever get from you is excuses, delays and stalls!"

"And now the stalls don't have doors!" Chuck LaFemina called from his seat and everyone remaining laughed.

"Exactly!"

"Purvey, you bastard–"

"It's time to stand up for ourselves. To show Baltz we have balls. "

Sue looked up from the puzzle. "Is that the direction we're going? Who has the biggest balls?"

"Don't think standing with big balls isn't a problem, Wellen," Terry said.

"It's time to stand up to Flackett and Central Administration! To let them know we won't tolerate any unilateral changes in working conditions. We demand a contract! We demand input! It's time for a change!"

"And no more plastic forks! We want real silverware back in the cafeteria again!"

"If we don't take action to stop this growing cancer today, tomorrow we will all be working longer hours for less pay–"

"Exactly," Terry called. "That's what Flackett's plan is all about!"

"And we'll be eating off paper plates!"

Purvey fought off Maxwell's attempt to grab the microphone. "I make a motion–"

"Second!" came from Stanley Milnow at the back of the auditorium.

"Point of Order," Mr. Everett interrupted, "according to *Robert's Rules of Order*"–he pointed to the book–"if either of the co-chairmen wants to make a motion, he has to vacate the chair first."

Joel Maxwell grabbed the microphone. "I demand an opportunity to answer the personal attack on me!"

"That would be a Point of Personal Privilege, right, Mr. Everett?" Red Farley asked.

"It would, Mr. Farley."

Some of the women from the Home Ec Department hurried for the doors.

"The Farmington Teachers' Association has always been the voice of reason and worked hard in an attempt to accommodate–"

"Accommodate my ass, Maxwell!"

"You are out of order, Mr. Co-chairman," Mr. Everett said, "but I will put your name first on the new speaker's list."

"You can shove your list, you dick!"

Rory Aaron and Chuck LaFemina left.

"Point of Order," Mr. Everett said. "I'm afraid we can't take a vote today." He looked around the auditorium. "There don't seem to be enough people present. We'll have to call for a quorum."

"Bullshit!"

"A call for a quorum," Mr. Everett ignored the comment, "is a motion according to *Robert's Rules*–"

"Roll up Robert's and shove him up your ass with your list, Dick!"

"I'm afraid you are out of order again!" He did a quick head count. "And by my unofficial count there is definitely not a quorum present. There are only sixteen people present. Thirteen," he corrected when three more teachers left. "Since there is not a sufficient number present to represent the faculty, as Parliamentarian I would respectfully recommend a vote to take no vote and thereby table the vote until another meeting of the faculty can be convened–"

Purvey made a grab for the microphone and missed. "This *was* a meeting of the entire faculty, you asshole!" Mr. Purvey shouted without a microphone. His face was almost purple.

"Come now, Mr. Purvey. Thirteen people can hardly represent the entire faculty. Twelve," Mr. Everett corrected.

"All in favor of taking no action signify by saying 'aye.'"

Four hands went up.

"Opposed?"

Dwayne Purvey was the only one left from the union to oppose the motion.

"The vote to take no action passes," Mr. Everett said.

"Now the Chair–"

"Co-chair," Mr. Everett corrected.

"The Co-chair," Joel Maxwell amended, "will entertain a motion to adjourn."

"So moved," Mr. Everett said.

"Second," Stanley Milnow called as he left through the back door.

"Meeting adjourned."

Jesse left the auditorium exhausted.

January dragged and it was snowy. By the second week it had already snowed twice, not enough to close the school, but just the right amount to make Jesse's commute a nightmare and add two hours to his drive. He hadn't seen the sun in weeks. He got up earlier and earlier and left for school long before sunrise, and he drove home in the gloom of night. He was ready for another vacation, but that wouldn't be until the middle of February. And there was more snow in the forecast for Midterm Test Week.

"If it snows tonight and school is closed tomorrow, Mario–if Baltz reschedules midterms and thinks I'm doing all that work over again–" Phyllis told him Sunday night. "You better pray it doesn't snow."

"I'm praying, Phyl, but it has nothing to do with snow. So now could you turn down the light and turn over?"

The snow held off, but it was bitter cold. The best thing about test week was the change in routine; the *worst* was the change in routine. Each day two two-hour testing blocks followed an extended Homeroom with early dismissal after the second test. Teachers with less seniority proctored the exams while veterans were assigned relief duty so proctors could use the bathroom and eat lunch. After Homeroom, Jesse went to his proctoring assignment, distributed test materials and watched for cheaters.

His relief, Stanley Milnow, showed up ten minutes late and Jesse only had thirty minutes, not enough time to get to the teacher's cafeteria, eat and return. "Don't look for me tomorrow, kid. Or the rest of the week." He sat at the desk and opened his *New York Post*.

Jesse trudged to the Third Floor Faculty Room. With his thumbnail he scraped a small circle in the ice that had formed on the inside of the window clouding the glass and he squinted through the opening. Despite ABC weatherman Tex Antoine's reassurance the that there would be no snow, it was snowing. The wind was blowing it almost horizontally. Jesse let out an audible breath, anticipating the nightmare ride home and then back in the morning when English exams were scheduled. A depressing thought, as was the realization that he still had ninety-four school days to get through, no Saturdays, Sundays or holidays. But the school year was down to double digits. Ninety-four was long-range; he just had to focus on the more immediate problem, getting through the week.

It wasn't just snow that was in the wind. To save money, Dr. Flackett had directed Buildings and Grounds to pull the plug on all nonessential electric equipment in the district during the two-week Christmas/Chanukah vacation. Apparently that included the Tom Keller Vending Machine and the refrigerator where forgotten teacher lunches spent two weeks moldering and decomposing in the balmy temperature within. Jesse sniffed. Three weeks after the juice had been turned back on, the sickly sweet smell emanated from the refrigerator and the vending machine, a trifecta of tuna fish, chicken soup and death. The aroma was strong enough to support a small squadron of flies tirelessly weaving knots in lazy loops in the air by the vending machine. And it kept down the number of teachers spending time in the faculty room.

Joel Maxwell was seated near the window marking papers. The math test had been the first one on Monday. "Done!" he announced to nobody in particular. "Gotta love short answers and these Scantron answer sheets!"

Jesse quietly hated him. The English test, which should be first because it involved so much reading, was next to last. He'd have to work all weekend correcting essays to get grades in on time Monday morning.

Marta the cleaning lady was spread out on one side of the long table, clogging the aisle with her cleaning supplies eating her lunch–something onion, something sardine, something garlic on black bread. On the other side, Marjory Maureen Blight, the first librarian, was asleep. After his first and only visit to the Library Jesse hadn't seen her much. Her mouth hung open and she was snoring, quiet little sounds punctuated by great throaty gusts. She occupied the most comfortable chair in the room, a command position she assumed whenever she was in the faculty room. Her feet were up on another chair blocking Jesse's way. He was in the horns of a dilemma. He didn't want to approach Marta and get pulled into a conversation he wouldn't understand, and he certainly didn't want to wake "Moron Blight," as Chuck LaFemina named her, and face her wrath. Jesse slowly lifted his left leg over the sleeping First Librarian, keeping his attaché case well up and away when her eyes snapped open and her hand shot up.

She took held Jesse's genitals in a death grip. "What are you doing, maggot?"

Jesse winced, inhaled deeply. "Just... passing... through!" he said in pain. "Changing to a warmer seat."

The cleaning lady looked up, took in the tableau and shook her head. "Teachers is crazy," she said.

"How'd you like me to snap these off and feed them to you with eggs!" She tightened her grip.

"I... wouldn't. You were... snoring so comfortably... and I didn't want to bother you–" She let him go and shut her eyes. "Thank you." He passed over her quickly and sat. "It's rough getting back into the swing of things after a vacation–" But her mouth dropped open and she was snoring again. He turned and looked out beyond the icy window at the wet large flakes accumulating on the car tops and the street. Then he watched Marta eat.

She leaned her chair back from the table and without rising dropped money into the coin slot on the machine. It fell hollowly and she pressed a button, but nothing happened. She got to her feet and began fiddling with the row of buttons, pressing them one at a time and then all at once. Still nothing. Jesse watched her growing anger. She pounded the side with a heavy fist, jiggled the coin return, alternated that with pressing and banging. Nothing. "Farking machine is money stealer!" she announced in her heavy central European accent and gave the front of the machine a forearm smash. "Phetew. I spit in face of farking money stealer machine!" She kneed it approximately in the groin.

Joel Maxwell watched. Moron Blight opened one eye.

"Somnabitch! Is farking money stealer machine!" It gurgled once and a small brown mouse tumbled onto the cup tray. "Oh yiii!" she yelled and jumped back. "Is farking mouse in coffee machine! Is mouse!"

The terrified mouse turned its tiny body to escape back up the cup chute. Marta lunged, but the mouse was gone. She hit the front of the machine again and a cup fell into place, followed by a steamy, brownish fluid that filled the cup halfway. Marta picked it up, sniffed and sipped. "Is farking mouse shit in coffee cup! Is mouse shit!" She gagged and poured the contents of the cup into the sink. "Mouse shit! Even in old country is no farking mouse shit in coffee!" She put the rest of her sandwich into the pocket of her apron and wiped her hands. "Marta is putting sign on machine. Nobody is drinking coffee with mouse shit!" She stomped out of the room grumbling and passing Dwayne Purvey in the doorway.

Joel Maxwell smiled. "Purvey," he called. "Just the man I was looking for. Can we talk for a minute?"

"I only have a few minutes, Maxwell, and I don't want to waste it on you."

Maxwell threw up his hands in surrender and looked at Jesse. "I give up. You saw I tried." He turned to Jesse and back to Purvey who sat on the other side of the table. "All this meaningless antagonism. It has to end. Come on, Purvey, it's a new year and we're both grown men. We can't continue doing this. It isn't fair to our membership. Can't we all just get along in the best interest of the teacher?"

Purvey didn't respond. The scars of mistrust were deeply cut. He hummed suspiciously.

"Okay, so last week's meeting didn't go well," Maxwell continued. "Let's put that behind us and work together now, starting today. If we do there's no telling what we can accomplish. In unity there is strength and you can catch more flies with honey than with vinegar."

Purvey swatted at the air and scattered the ones flying above his head.

"Come on, Dwayne." Purvey raised his eyebrow when he heard his first name. "With all the shit that's going on here, we need to start getting along. I'm not saying we have to become friends, but we have to end this petty rivalry. Look around. Next week is February. Another year on austerity and still working without a contract. Baltz is ecstatic. He has us at one another's throat. Divide and conquer. And now Flackett thinks he can do whatever he wants." He paused. "So what do you say we stop the infighting and merge our efforts for the good of everyone concerned?" He reached into his pocket and pulled out some change. "To show you that my heart is in the right place, let me buy you a cup of coffee. Come on, Dwayne, what do you say? A cup of coffee. And then who knows?" He dropped in the coins before Purvey could refuse. The machine hummed. "How do you take it?"

"Light and sweet, like me," Purvey said.

Maxwell looked at the panel, pressed the right buttons and the cup dropped with authority onto the tray. It filled and he placed it on the table in front of Purvey. "Enjoy it," he said.

Purvey eyed the cup with some doubts. "And what do you want in return"–he tried to use his first name but couldn't–"Maxwell?"

"Nothing. Absolutely nothing. No strings attached. This is a new year and I've made a few resolutions. Sharing a cup of coffee is much better than screaming and yelling. Don't you agree? Let's bury the past. Drink up. *L' chiam!*" He raised his empty hand in a toast. "To life! And a contract!"

Purvey took a cautious sip. "Yuk," he said and grimaced. "Not enough sugar!" Then he tipped his cup to Maxwell and took a long swallow.

"You should only be healthy. As Dr. Spock says, 'Live long and prosper.'" Maxwell's smile broadened. He flashed a Spock split-finger salute and he left the room.

A minute later the door flew open and Marta returned with a piece of cardboard and tape. She was still muttering to herself when she saw Dwayne Purvey with the cup in his mouth. "Stop!" she yelled. "Nobody is drinking coffee! Coffee is poison!" She held up the sign she had printed, "No Vorking! Poizin! Is farking mouse shit in coffee cup! IS POIZIN!"

Purvey looked down his nose into the cup at the residue at the bottom and he retched. He dropped the cup on the table and retched again.

"Teachers is crazy. Is always talking never listening. Is worse than farking kids. I tell other teacher is mouse in machine. Why then you drink coffee with mouse shit? You like mouse shit? You crazy teacher."

"Maxwell!" he screamed. "You fucking bastard! You miserable, lying, fucking bastard!" he managed between heaves.

Marta shook her head as he darted past her. "Even in old country in worst times is eating dogs, cats... but nobody is drinking mouse shit." She posted the sign on the machine. "Teachers is crazy." She made little circles with her finger by her head at Jesse sitting with his mouth open next to the snoring librarian.

Willy Zwill had been contemplating the piece of smoked salmon on the plastic fork over his plate. He sniffed it, put it back, then changed his mind and brought it to his nose again.

"Jesus Christ, Willy," Mario Giovanni said. "Are you going to eat it or make love to it? Take it or put it back, but don't breathe all over it, for chrisakes!" His tone was harsher than he intended and his annoyance misplaced. His stress level increased dramatically in the new year and he was really upset with the boss.

"I know I did something to piss off Baltz, but I don't know what," he had told Phyllis earlier. "I'm out of the loop and I don't like being treated like the other APs."

"Is that what this failure to launch is all about, Mario?" Phyllis had asked him after another disappointing letdown. "You're out of the loop and it's causing performance anxiety?" But he hadn't responded.

Zwill twitched. "I don't eat sushi!" he said. "Sushi is *raw* fish. Japanese fish." He picked up a piece in his fingers and smelled it.

"This is lox, Willy. It's not raw, it's *smoked* salmon. It's Jewish fish!" Mario pulled his lip back and cracked his neck.

"Jewish fish?" Noah Lewis asked. He stopped forking slices into his sandwich from home. "I, auh, thought salmon was Canadian fish, like Canadian bacon."

"It's Canadian bacon?" Zwill said. He picked it up and sniffed it again. "Smells like something I vaguely recognize–"

"Fish, Willy. It smells like fish!" Helen O'Dell crammed the last of the garlic bagel into her mouth. She looked for the napkin that had dropped from her lap. When she didn't find it she licked the cream cheese off her fingers and wiped them on the front of her jacket. "Great spread, Chief," she said with her mouth full. "What's the occasion?"

They were at a cabinet meeting in the principal's office, standing around the card table covered with a tablecloth, plates, bagels and an assortment of stuff to put on them.

"Administrator Appreciation Day, and why the hell not? They hold an appreciation day every year for teachers. This is my way to tell you that I know I haven't been available much recently. But even in my absence the machinery grinds on and that's due, in part, because of you," he said with an exaggerated smile. "The good news is, barring a disaster today, that midterm week went smoothly and the February break is coming up. Graffiti in the men's room is down considerably since the stall doors were removed." He looked serious. "But not without complaints. Dick Everett was in yesterday and told me he heard talk of letters to the newspaper and the Department of Health." He fixed himself a sesame seed bagel with cream cheese and lox. "I want all of you to do what you can to increase the rift between Maxwell and Purvey. Drive the wedge deeper between the Union and the Association. Whatever it takes. Teacher observations start next week before the February break. You're all going to be busy, especially with Flackett's new forms. But I don't want observations to distract you from your other duties. Helen, step up your early morning patrols so we don't get blindsided by another incident." She nodded. "Mario, you have a lot to do, including the third-floor bathroom. I want to see more of you in and out up there to keep up the pressure." He paused. "Willy, Noah–" Noah Lewis was looking out the window into the courtyard. "You two just continue whatever it is you do." He looked at his watch. "I don't want to rush you, but I have to get back to Central. So take your bagel and finish eating in your office–"

Noah Lewis got up and picked over the tray. "For lunch later," he said and he filled his lunch bag with crackers and the plastic container of chopped liver.

The principal made a show of looking at his watch again. "Now get out there and get busy." He moved them toward the door.

Mario Giovanni hung after the others left. "I was wondering... we haven't spent much quality time together lately and... Are you mad at me? Did I do something? Say something—"

"Don't be silly, Mario." His tone was unctuous. He smoothed his mustache. "What could you have possibly said or done I might have seen or overheard, even in your most private moments when you thought you were alone? Besides, you above all should know, if you did do something, I wouldn't get mad. I'd get even."

"That's a relief." He took a deep breath. "I wanted you to know that I'm working on something with Sylvia Berkowsky and the Home Ec Department that just might turn this pants suit thing around. 'Skirt Day,'" he said. "She's planning for all the girls in Home Ec to design and make their own skirts. And on a specific day to get everybody in the school, students, faculty and staff to wear a skirt on 'Skirt Day.'" He looked pleased. "And the best part is my idea, a follow-up 'Dress-Up Day' to bring back suit jackets and ties. We'll do it every year."

"Great idea, Mario. It does have great possibilities. Put it in a memo when you've worked out the details. But now I have to go. You get back into the bathrooms and next week get a head start on those observations. Unfortunately, my schedule at Central will keep me busy, so you will have to do some of my observations as well as your own" He opened the door wider.

* * *

Friday afternoon the end of Midterm Test Week, the building emptied in record time. Only the secret cross-country team had the run of the place, quite literally. Track coach Gary Schultz, inspired by Buddy Ritchie's secret wrestling team's secret workouts, quietly reactivated his secret track team. He began a program of intensive training in the event the budget passed before the end of the school year. Phil Rizzoli, the varsity baseball coach, said he was planning a secret spring training. Temperatures hadn't been above freezing all week and Wednesday's layer of snow was still on the ground, so secret track practice moved indoors. When the building was vacant the secret track team members began doing laps up and down the stairways and through the corridors with rags wrapped around their sneakers to keep down the noise. Folding chairs became hurdles and in minutes the runners were strung out along the darkened corridors.

Dwayne Purvey stalked cautiously down the third floor corridor staying in the shadows. He pulled back when the door of the (F)Utility closet opened in front of him and he hugged the wall. He was surprised when Mr. Baltz materialized like a phantom. He stuck his head out, checked the empty corridor and hurried quickly and quietly down the hall in the other direction. Purvey was curious and wanted a closer look, but the closet door was locked. Maybe another time, he thought. Now he had other things to do. He hung back in an alcove and waited until the running sounds faded before he continued on. Shifting the brown paper bag he was holding he proceeded to the Third Floor Faculty Room. Two more runners turned onto the floor down at the end of the corridor and ran toward him. Fortunately he saw them before he heard their rag-covered sneakers clumping on the tiles and he ducked into the recess by the water fountain just in time to let them pass.

The faculty room was empty. He closed the door behind him and locked it. The only sound in the room was the electric whir of the vending machine motor and the occasional click of the refrigerator. Quickly and carefully he set down the paper bag and removed the contents he had gone out to buy during his prep period–an aluminum pie pan, a small spool of string and a box of plastic Cling Wrap. He laid them out and reached deep inside the bag for a smaller package wrapped in stained brown paper that he set beside the other items.

"Shit!" he said when the torn Cling Wrap tangled and clung to itself. "Fuck!" He peeled it apart with difficulty and held the sheet by the edges so he could lay it on the floor in front of the vending machine. Then he took the new number two pencil from his pocket and tied a length of string to the eraser end with a double knot. He laid the pie pan on the center of the sheet of Cling Wrap and propped it up ons side with the pencil, eraser side down. Then he delicately played out the string along the floor to the couch opposite the machine, careful not to pull the pencil out of place. When he was satisfied with the arrangements, he went back to the table and tore open the small paper wrapped bag. Immediately the smell of sharp cheese filled the room. "I want the sharpest, smelliest cheese you have," he had told the man behind the counter who broke off a piece for him to taste. It was so strong it had made Purvey's eyes water. "Perfect!" Now he lifted the chunk of imported French Camembert and laid it carefully on the plastic wrap directly under the tin. He rechecked everything and tightened the slack on the string. Then he settled cross-legged on the couch with a copy of *Soldier of Fortune* magazine and he waited.

Two hours later he was engrossed in the middle of the article "Why the Vietcong Will Never Win the War" when from the corner of his eye he noticed a tiny movement in the shadows. Slowly and quietly he set down the magazine and watched the mouse give up the security of the coffee machine and venture into the dark room. Purvey held his breath. The mouse moved farther into the room to sniff around the edges of the Cling Wrap and the cheese. Its little whiskers vibrated nervously. Purvey's years of experience as a bow hunter taught him patience, still it was difficult to squelch the impulse to move too hastily. He waited until the mouse was directly under the pan and lost in the deliciousness of cheese. He tugged, the pencil flew and the pan fell silently over the unsuspecting rodent.

"Gotcha!" he said with the catch of excitement in his throat. But when he tried to get off the couch his folded legs were unconscious beyond asleep. He couldn't feel the floor under him and stumbled like a man on stilts. He massaged his knees and calves until some of his circulation was slowly restored and the needle pain he felt became a tickling sensation. He limped forward awkwardly toward the pan across the floor on stiff limbs, like some grotesque creature in a monster movie.

Without raising the pan, he pulled the Cling Wrap edges taut around it forming a perfect seal. Then he turned it over slowly and looked at his prize. The mouse gaped into Purvey's grinning face and panicked. It ran around the slippery inside of the pan in vain for a hiding place. Its little chest heaved up and down, its feet unable to get traction. Suddenly the mouse stopped, took a last deep breath, urinated and rolled over on its side, dead.

Purvey packed everything back into the bag, unlocked the door and left the building unnoticed.

Monday morning Helen O'Dell wanted to get in earlier than usual, so she showered Sunday night to save time and in the morning just threw on the blue jumper she had laid out. She stopped for coffee and a buttered roll in the 7-Eleven, ate most of it before she pulled her Pinto into the reserved number four AP space in the empty courtyard. It was still dark.

The courtyard was parking just for administrators, department heads, guidance and the secretaries. But because there never were enough spaces in the teacher lot, they often tried to sneak into the courtyard unnoticed and park there. Austerity made it even worse because most teachers arrived at the same time just before the morning bell and battled for parking spots. In January, the union and association came up separately with a plan to pressure the district into signing a contract. Teachers lined up every morning to march in as a group and punch in *en masse* at the bell. Association members were in the courtyard and the union people in the parking lot. In the afternoon they reversed direction after the dismissal bell, which created a morning pileup in the Main Office and an afternoon stampede out. However, no one in the district, the school board or the community got the message, cared or even noticed.

O'Dell fished the last piece of the roll from between her teeth with her finger, drained the coffee. She brushed the crumbs from the front of her jumper, licked her fingers one more time and wiped them on the old army jacket from her WAC days. She still fit into it, *if* she left it unbuttoned and didn't breathe. This was her favorite time of the day and she enjoyed being there early. The building was empty and quiet. She passed Eddie the tattooed night custodian in the dark hall and he grunted. She punched in her time card, strolled to her office where she hung her jacket and she started her rounds. She was still hungry. The buttered roll was more of an appetizer than breakfast. She found a very stale Fig Newton in the back of her desk drawer, picked off the dust and lint and gobbled it.

When Baltz had commissioned her with the intelligence gathering job he told her that no one was above suspicion or beyond scrutiny. "Be discreet, be thorough and be creative. But don't get caught!" he warned her. "You have *carte blanche* to poke your nose and your fingers anywhere." So she added the APs to her daily rounds.

Mario's was her first stop. She unlocked his door and rummaged through his drawers. She read a letter from his cousin Vito, who was in Florida doing time for insurance fraud. "I have no problem taking the fall and doing the time as long as I know the family is taking care of my family while I'm away in the country and they make good when I am back." There were love notes from Phyllis Lind, matchbooks from The Galaxy, a by-the-hour motel. She knew he also dallied there with other women on staff, mostly just hit-and-runs. She peeked through his 403B stock portfolio and poked into the wastepaper basket. There was nothing to eat.

Next came Noah Lewis's office. The desk was completely empty except for a copy of *How to Retire in Poland and Live Like a King* with the bookmark still in page two hundred and sixteen. The novelty partially-eaten rubber sandwich wrapped in wax paper was within easy grasp in the center drawer. He dragged it out whenever there was an emergency he wanted to avoid. "I'm, auh, having lunch. Come back later," he said showing them the sandwich. The old-timers knew it was fake, but it worked with new teachers.

Zwill's was the only door she couldn't open with her passkey. It hadn't worked in months, but she tried again. It fit into the lock, but didn't turn. She tested the door and threw her weight against it, but it didn't budge. She pressed her ear against it and listened. Sometimes Willy arrived earlier than she did, and he often stayed later than everyone. She suspected that there were times he even slept in his office overnight. She heard the low hum of a fan's electric motor that he kept running day and night. She could feel the vibration through the door. It started a sympathetic rumbling in her stomach.

Generally she headed next for the Guidance Office, where there was never much of any value. Then it was the Home Ec classrooms on the first floor. After a weekend there wouldn't be anything worth eating until Wednesday at best. So she cut short her usual rounds and took the elevator to the third floor. The light in 301 was on. She tiptoed to the door, careful that her rubber soles didn't squeak on the tiles. Joel Maxwell was behind the desk leafing through *Newsday*. Every year he and Dwayne Purvey were assigned the same lunch, duty and prep periods and they shared classrooms. That was Baltz's idea to keep them preoccupied and unfocused. Divide and conquer.

She looked at her watch and knew Maxwell would stay there until it was time to go outside to marshal the FT Ass. crew for their mass sign-in. She also knew his lunch was in the faculty room refrigerator. He always had interesting treats and enough of them that he wouldn't miss one or two. She hurried quietly down the hall to the empty faculty room. She'd check the room for useful information after she ate something. After all, Baltz told her, "A good administrator must never be afraid to open up all the locked doors, hunt out and pursue intelligence at the source. Show fearless initiative. Rely on your instinct and fall back on your military training." So she had also incorporated the faculty room refrigerator in her hunger for information, though she suspected Baltz would be annoyed if he found out she was getting more than information from the teacher lunch bags.

She pulled the handle and opened the little refrigerator. A gust of air chilled her ankles. The effort of crouching pushed out a little fart and she laughed. Farts were always funny to kids and teachers. She reached her hand deep inside, past the two smaller bags, and grabbed Joel Maxwell's. His was always the biggest. She opened the bag. Monday was usually Sunday leftovers and that could be a real treat. She passed over a piece of homemade holiday fruitcake, an apple and an orange and scouted a small bag of Fritos, a juice pack, a Snickers, three Laughing Cow cheese wedges and some chocolate chip cookies. She ate a cookie and took a cheese wedge for later. Wrapped in plastic were three sandwiches. Three? Maxwell usually had two at most. She was curious about the third. She picked the biggest one, weighed it in her hand and unwrapped it–a sesame seed roll, thick and full and dark. A piece of roast beef would be nice, she thought. Carefully she opened the roll and peeked in.

* * *

The scream reverberated through the halls and was clearly audible all the way to the first floor where teachers who had marched in after the bell were trying to get to the time clock and their mailboxes. It stopped everything. Even the late-comers still in the courtyard and the parking lot heard it.

"And so begins another day," Terry said.

Mrs. Butrum, who never punched in, was already in her classroom when she heard the scream. As slow as she was, she was the first to reach the scene. Breathless from the exertion she opened the door to the faculty room. "Oh, my Lord! Oh my goodness! Oh, how terrible!"

Helen O'Dell was lying in the middle of the floor in front of the open refrigerator. Next to her was the open lunch bag and the seeded roll. A tiny brown mouse partially wrapped in a piece of leafy lettuce stared up at Mrs. Butrum. She grimaced and reached down to feel for Helen O'Dell's pulse. Her body was warm, but she was just as dead as the frozen mouse, its sad brown eyes clouded gray.

"She's dead. The poor woman's dead!" she told Harry Dexter who was the second to arrive. "I'm no expert, but from the looks of that surprised expression on the face she had a massive coronary."

Dexter looked at Helen O'Dell's body. Her blue jumper skirt was hitched up, exposing her heavy white thighs. He sighed. His wife had suggested he consider taking a different position other than the AV job, one with less responsibility, and now, he knew, there would be an opening for assistant principal.

* * *

Mr. Baltz pulled the tan Buick Regal into the courtyard and into the number one parking slot. Mario Giovanni's car with his "ITSMARIO" vanity plate was in number three, between the empty space where Noah Lewis parked and next to Helen O'Dell's Pinto. He locked the door and chirped the alarm that echoed in the courtyard. He stopped and chipped some dried bird droppings from the hood with his thumbnail before he walked into the building.

The AP looked like the comic stereotype of an expectant father with his hands behind his back pacing nervously in front of the entrance to the Main Office. When he saw the principal he rushed down the hall to meet him. "Trouble, Boss." The worried look on his face intensified. "We got big trouble up on the third floor. *Big* trouble!"

Baltz panicked. His color paled as visions of discovery drained the blood from his head. He felt faint. "What did they find? I can explain–"

"It's O'Dell. She's dead!"

"Oh, thank God. For a minute–" He stopped himself as the meaning of the words registered. "What do you mean O'Dell is dead? Our O'Dell? Are you sure? She can't be dead, her car is parked outside."

"Dead, Boss. Really dead. Third Floor Faculty Room dead. Harry Dexter's up there now with the body, and Mrs. Butrum. She found her. I roped off the area with duct tape to keep everybody out and waited for you."

He tried to remove his overcoat and his galoshes. "Let me just put these–"

"No time. You better hurry, Boss. Something's fishy."

He clumped up to the third floor. A crowd had gathered around the faculty room door trying to get a peek.

"Stand aside please. Out of the way." The two of them elbowed through. Helen O'Dell's body was lying where it fell.

"Oh, it's terrible," Mrs. Butrum lamented. She was seated on a chair fanning herself with her attendance envelope.

Mr. Baltz reached down to adjust the dead woman's skirt. "What happened here, Mrs. Butrum?"

"She's still warm, the poor woman. She must have been eating. There are cookie crumbs in her mouth."

"And that?" he pointed to the sesame seed roll on the floor next to her body.

"A frozen mouse, would you believe?" She was back on her feet pointing to the little creature that was thawing into a small growing puddle of wetness on the floor. "Lord knows what she was doing with that."

"Mario," he whispered, "call the police and tell them to send an ambulance. Then lock this door, for God's sake. And keep it quiet. I don't want the whole building disrupted." He smoothed his mustache and forced his face into a smile. "Helen is fine," he said to the growing crowd. "Just a little woozy. The rest of you, get ready for class. Helen will be okay. She just fainted."

"But–" Mrs. Butrum tried to interrupt.

He moved in front of her. "She just told me it's probably from something she ate that didn't agree with her."

"But–"

"She's very embarrassed by all the fuss. She said she'll be fine after she rests a bit and for you to go about your business. And she asked to please not say anything to get the students all upset," he added and dispersed them.

"But... she's dead," Mrs. Butrum said. "She didn't faint. She didn't say a word because she's d-e-a-d!"

"Yes, yes, Mrs.Butrum, I know that. I know she's dead. You know that. I just don't want everybody else to know and start a panic. So please don't say anything to anyone until the police arrive."

"But what about the mouse?"

"You don't know anything about a mouse, Carolyn. Now you get back to your class. Mario and I will handle everything. Homeroom's about to start. And thank you for your help." He opened the door and nudged her through it.

Harry Dexter stepped up. "Shirley and I were talking about me giving up AV for something less stressful. When do you suppose the district will post the AP job vacancy–"

He pushed Dexter out of the room and shut the door in his face.

"Boss," Mr. Giovanni said when they were alone, "if you give me a hand we still have enough time to move her into a classroom before the police arrive."

"Why the hell would we do that, Mario?"

"To collect the insurance. O'Dell's entitled to death benefits. And according to the terms of the new policy if she dies in the classroom she collects double indemnity. That's at least a couple a grand, Boss. But to collect she has to die *in* the classroom. I read all the small print." He did a Bogart and stretched. "A couple a grand. Better in O'Dell's pocket, if you know what I mean."

The Homeroom bell sounded.

"Just make the goddamn call to the police, Mario. Then clean up this mess and get rid of that fucking mouse before they arrive. I don't want any more trouble than we already have."

* * *

Twenty minutes later the blue and orange county police ambulance screeched into the courtyard followed closely by two squad cars. The blinking lights and screaming sirens punctuated the "Star-Spangled Banner" and Homeroom was extended while everyone on the courtyard side pressed against the windows to see what was going on.

"Who is that?" Terry asked from his classroom. He watched the EMTs wheel the stretcher into the courtyard, the front wheel of the crash cart flap-flap-flappping in rhythm to the pulsating red and yellow lights.

"Looks like Helen O'Dell," Virgil Loomis said. "And she doesn't look very good. In fact, she looks very dead."

The EMTs loaded her into the back of the ambulance and carried her away, horns blaring, sirens wailing and lights blinking.

Inside the principal's office, Sgt. Sadowski was waiting to wrap up the loose ends while more police milled about in the Main Office. "There are just a few questions, Seymour," he

371

said with his pad and pencil in his hand. "It shouldn't take very long." He opened the notebook and thumbed through it. "It's just that there seem to be a few minor discrepancies I'd like to resolve."

"Discrepancies?" Mr. Baltz faltered lighting a cigarette. "Well, I wasn't here when they found her. Mario Giovanni–" A knock at the door stopped him. "That's him now." The AP came in leading Dr. Nessmith, the school physician, and the two of them sat down.

"She was out on morning rounds, I understand?" Sgt. Sadowski continued consulting his notes. "So who actually discovered the body?"

Mr. Giovanni raised his hand tentatively. "I did. And she was in a classroom when I found her. I want to make that clear and a part of the official police report."

"According to this," he looked at his pad, "she was in the faculty room. And Carolyn Butrum said she was the first to arrive."

Mr. Giovanni thought quickly. "That's right," he said. "Mrs. Butrum *was* the first one to arrive in the faculty room where Helen was still breathing when I got there. So when you said 'body' I was confused. We moved her from there to a classroom so she'd be more comfortable... and have more privacy," he added. "And that's where she died. In the classroom. And I was there when she died. In the classroom and *not* in the faculty room. Dr. Nessmith here, the school doctor, will verify that poor O'Dell wasn't dead until after we got her into the classroom. Right, Ollie?"

"That's correct, Sergeant." He rubbed his nose with his thumb and index finger and looked away.

"Mrs. Butrum said something about a frozen mouse?"

"Mouse? What mouse? Did you see any mouse, Mario?"

"Mouse? I didn't see any mouse." Mr. Giovanni lowered his voice. "You have to understand, Sergeant, Mrs. Butrum has a tendency to become a little overwrought sometimes. A little hysterical." He winked and moved his finger in little circles by his head. "She's not always all there at all times, if you catch my drift." He looked around for corroboration.

Mr. Baltz shuffled through some papers and puffed his cigarette.

"Maybe she meant frozen mousse? Last week I observed the Home Economics classes and they made a frozen mousse. Chocolate. Delicious. And there was so much of it left over I think that it was put in the refrigerator in the faculty room."

"Of course," Mr. Baltz said. "It has to be frozen mousse."

The sergeant nodded. He crossed out something and wrote something else. "Next of kin?"

"None that I know of," Mr. Baltz answered. "We're checking. O'Dell had no family. She said she was raised in an orphanage in the midwest, I think. After that she joined the Women's Army Corps. And later she got her degree and administrative certification through the GI Bill. O'Dell tended to stay to herself. Lived alone."

"*We* were O'Dell's family," Mr. Giovanni added with a catch in his voice. His lip quivered. "And this school was her home. She was a good *man* and I was proud to serve with her. We're all going to miss her."

Sgt. Sadowski nodded again and wrote something else in the pad. Then he closed it and put it back into his pocket. "Thank you for your cooperation, gentlemen," he said. "Just routine, you understand." He turned to Doctor Nessmith. "Doc, if you come with me you can give me the Death Certificate you signed. That way I don't have to wait for the coroner."

"Take care of that, Ollie," Mr. Baltz said.

"We'll touch base later, Ollie," Mr. Giovanni added.

"Happy to help, Sergeant." Dr. Nessmith followed him out of the office and in another few minutes the two squad cars screamed out of the courtyard.

"Mario, what the fuck are you trying to do?" Mr. Baltz demanded when they were alone in his office.

"It was just a little lie, Boss. Ollie did examine her and he said she could have been alive when he did. And it'd be a shame not to collect that money. Maybe as much as four grand, Boss. She had a policy with the association *and* the union. An insurance bonanza. And being an orphan and all with no heirs. She said she was going to put me down as her beneficiary." He shrugged. "Nessmith doesn't have a problem as long as he gets a little something for his troubles. I'm willing to pay him from my share. And we can split the rest."

The principal lit another Lucky and took a deep drag, "I just don't want this to come back and bite me on the ass."

"No problem guaranteed, Boss."

"Now, what were you saying the other day about this Skirt Day thing?"

Mario Giovanni smiled. He was happy to be back in the man's good graces.

In the News
February 1972

February 12
Sen. Ted Kennedy advocates amnesty for Vietnam draft resisters.
February 13
U.S. intensifies bombing against North Vietnam.
February 17
Pres. and Mrs. Nixon depart on his historic 10-day trip to China. He is the 1st U.S. president to visit a country not diplomatically recognized by the U.S.
February 22
Pres. Nixon meets with Mao Tse-tung and Chinese Premier Chou En-Lai in Beijing. In a joint communique, later known as the Shanghai Communique, both countries agree to increase their contacts and for the U.S. to withdraw gradually from Taiwan.
February 24-25
Less than two weeks before the New Hampshire presidential primary, the Manchester *Union-Leader* publishes a letter to the editor alleging that leading Democratic candidate and Maine senator, Edmund Muskie, approved a racial slur of Americans of French-Canadian descent (an important voting bloc in New Hampshire), and notes: "We have always known that Senator Muskie was a hypocrite. But we never expected to have it so clearly revealed as in this letter sent to us from Florida." The crudely written letter becomes widely known as the "Canuck Letter." The next day, the paper's publisher, William Loeb, publishes an attack on Muskie's wife. An angry Muskie denounces the letter and the editorial, calling Loeb a "gutless coward," and in the process apparently bursts into tears. The media focuses on Muskie's tears and the "weakness" it implies. As a result, Muskie's standing in the polls begins to slip, and when votes are cast in New Hampshire, Muskie receives only 48% of the vote, far less than predicted. The letter is later found to have been a "dirty trick" of the Nixon campaign committee.

February 24

Hanoi negotiators walk out of the peace talks in Paris to protest U.S. air raids on North Vietnam.

February 25

Paul McCartney and Wings release "Give Ireland Back to the Irish." Written by Paul and his wife Linda, the song is in response to the events of Bloody Sunday in Northern Ireland on January 30, 1972. It is soon banned by the BBC.

February 27

At his farewell banquet with Chairman Mao, Pres. Nixon remarks in his toast, "This was the week that changed the world."

February 28

Pres. Nixon addresses the nation via television to discuss his trip to China.

The news of Helen O'Dell's passing spread within the building in minutes, like a California brushfire in August. And it was around the district before the end of the school day. That night at its regular monthly Monday meeting, the School Board observed a moment of silent prayer to honor Helen O'Dell's memory and to commemorate her loss. Then it voted down a motion to allow teachers and staff members time off from class to attend her funeral, though no funeral arrangements had yet been made. Board President Adornau made a motion allowing teachers to take time during the school day, provided that it was charged to their personal leave or it was deducted from the pay of those who didn't have the time to use. The motion was passed unanimously.

On Wednesday morning the flag by the War Memorial on the front lawn of Rosencrantz and Guildenstern Memorial High School was lowered to half-mast. It was frigid outside, but the climate inside the building was warmer and friendlier, often the case when the reminder of mortality hits close to home. Based on the conflicting stories that circulated, everyone had a theory about how poor Helen O'Dell met her end.

"What happened?" Dwayne Purvey asked. "What's going on? The flag is at half-staff and everyone looks so glum." He was waiting in the Main Office with the rest of the crowd to punch in.

"Where the hell have you been, for chrisakes, under a rock?" Red Farley asked.

"I was absent. Out sick. Monday and Tuesday. This is my first day back, so how would I know?" he answered defensively.

"Somebody snuffed O'Dell for chrisakes!"

"Helen O'Dell?"

"With a frozen mouse," Stanley Milnow added.

Dwayne Purvey paled. "A frozen mouse–"

"Or a poisoned frozen mousse. There are conflicting versions and the jury's still out."

"You look like shit, Purvey. Maybe you shoulda stayed out another day."

* * *

In the faculty room teachers carefully walked around the smudged chalk outline of Helen O'Dell still in the center of the floor. Someone had drawn in a smiley face and printed the message, "Have a nicer day than mine!"

Some laughed, some were appalled, most didn't notice and the ghost of Helen O'Dell didn't prevent anyone from using the refrigerator. It also didn't stop the growing number of rumors, innuendoes and conspiracy theories that were advanced freely by everyone but Dwayne Purvey, who remained silent except to announce when anyone asked that he was not in the building and had been out sick for two days. The general consensus regarding the cause of death, based on the eyewitness testimony of Mrs. Butrum, was heart attack.

"The expression on that woman's face was unmistakable. Oh the horror. I'll never forget it or that frozen mouse in the seeded roll defrosting on the floor next to her."

"I heard it was frozen mousse."

"It was definitely a mouse. And if you ask me, I think she was purposely scared to death by someone with a grudge. And that would make it murder by heart attack."

"O'Dell ate herself to death!" chemistry teacher Herb Lupus said with authority, looking like a doctor in his white lab coat. "Clogged arteries from all that crap she put into her body over the years. I used to eat with her." He was soaking a stale cruller in the pale tea that looked like a urine sample in the beaker he used as a drinking glass.

"Then what about the mouse Mrs. Butrum saw? A frozen mouse."

"It wouldn't be the first time she imagined seeing things. She's delusional."

"There wasn't any mouse," Mario Giovanni offered. "It was a mousse. It was a frozen mousse the Home Ec Department made in class!"

"A poisoned frozen mousse?"

"We didn't make any mousse, but that would be a good project to do after the girls finish making their skirts for Skirt Day," Sylvia Berkowsky said.

"Maybe it was two, two, two things in one. A mouse *and* a mousse!" Terry Scapelli quipped stepping over the smiling outline. He pulled out a roll of Certs and offered it. "Tastes like a candy, works like a breath mint."

"For chrisakes, Scapelli, you're standing on Helen O'Dell!" Red Farley exploded. "Don't you have any respect for the dead?"

* * *

"And the official cause of death?" Elliot Adornau asked. He was seated across from Mr. Baltz in the principal's office.

"Heart attack. It's all here in the police report." He passed over the paper.

"And all that talk about rat bites? What's with that? I got calls from parents threatening to keep their kids out of school and three exterminators who want to fumigate the building."

"Misinformation, Lalo. No rats. No mice. Just mousse. So, that should be the end of it."

"Except, of course, we'll have to hire a replacement." He pulled a small cigar from the tin box in his pocket and offered one. Mr. Baltz declined and lit one of his Luckies. "I have a niece who wants the job. We'll have to go through the motions of posting the position and doing bullshit interviews."

"Of course. But it might be a good idea to wait at least until we dispose of Helen."

"How's that Project X thing going? The programmed learning, individual instruction thing, wasn't it? And Flackett said something about computers?"

"Right." He inhaled deeply. "Right," he said again. "A real innovation. A company in Palo Alto is willing to supply us with a computer terminal here that connects with the one they have in California. They'll provide all the lesson modules and punch cards and Westinghouse will underwrite the cost for three years. I'm sure this whole computer stuff won't catch on, but we'll look good and it's practically for free. Mario Giovanni has all the details."

"And if the computer thing works out, who knows, we can get rid of a few teachers." He blew a smoke ring. "And you got your toilet too?"

"A real beauty," he said with genuine pride.

"Mind if I see how we're spending the teachers' contract money?" he laughed. "I'd like to send a little something down the line to Flackett's cesspools."

"Of course." He gave him a tour of the facilities.

* * *

Harry Dexter looked around his office at the things he had acquired over the years. He leafed through the invoices and the requisitions. He derived a great satisfaction from all that power he had at his fingertips, a pride in knowing that not a movie could be shown, not a record played, not a single frame of boring filmstrip advanced without his official sanction. Since he'd taken over AV from dead Don Cooley's cold electrocuted hands, the job defined him and gave his life meaning, so it would be difficult to give it all up. But he knew being an administrator would be much less work and pay more. He opened the file folder on his desk and stared at his yellowed résumé. He was eminently qualified, at least on paper, for Helen O'Dell's position whenever it would be posted. He wavered. Did he really want to give up his little principality for a closer reserved parking place in the courtyard?

He found a clean sheet of paper and rolled it into the carriage of his brand new, just out of the carton IBM Selectric II electric typewriter. He paused and searched for the right words. It wouldn't hurt to be ready if he decided yes.

* * *

Willie Zwill was late man on Monday morning and when he arrived in the building Helen O'Dell was already gone, so he never got to see her. The news about her death made him sad, but it was not a complete surprise. He had warned her, but she dismissed his concerns for their well-being. Right after he heard he went directly to his office and locked himself in and remained *incommunicado* for two days, growing more morose.

Now he sat motionless behind his desk, hunched over, unshaven and depressed. He reached for the telephone on his desk and for the thousandth time he dialed Helen O'Dell's three-digit extension. He listened to the hollow ringing in the receiver and through the muffled walls. "I told you, O'Dell," he said to the ringing in his ear. He'd heard that it was a heart attack, but of course he had his suspicions. "I warned you to be careful, to watch your back on the first day of school, but you laughed. I told you to trust my intuition. But you had to learn your lesson the hard way. I can't believe you are gone." His eyes filled with tears and he replaced the receiver in the cradle. A knock at the door made him twitch. His body tensed, but he remained silent and motionless hoping whoever it was would go away.

"I know you're in there, Mr. Zwill." It was Mrs. Butrum. "I can see the light from under the door."

Damn, he thought. He'd have to remember to do something about that. "I'm busy. Go away. Leave me alone."

"Collection, Mr. Zwill. The Sunshine Committee is collecting for Helen O'Dell. Surely you wouldn't want to say no to Helen?" Reluctantly he went to the door and opened it a crack. "I know the two of you were close." She pressed her weight against the door, but his foot was wedged solidly behind it. "Such a shock. Such a tragedy." She inserted her shoulder and extended the envelope she was holding. "I know you didn't see her, but I'll never forget the look on poor Helen's face." She shook the envelope and lowered her voice. "There's something not right going on here. A cover-up."

"I told her... I told Helen, but she wouldn't listen."

"And I told the police, but did they listen? Did they believe me? No. I know what I saw, and I definitely saw a frozen mouse on a roll. A seeded roll. A mouse sandwich. Not a mousse. Who would ever eat a mouse?"

"I ate my share," he said. "The Japs fed us rice, but if you were lucky there were mice. Rice and mice," he said.

"It's criminal. A conspiracy. And now this campaign to discredit me. A slap in my face and a slap in the face of the Sunshine Committee. But I won't let it go." She shook the envelope again. "Donation?"

He reached into his pocket and pulled out a wrinkled dollar that he dropped into the envelope. "Neither will I. Not until poor Helen is avenged."

"Thank–"

He shut the door and bolted it and then went back to his desk. Of course there was a conspiracy and it was so obvious now that even Mrs. Butrum could see it. It was time for someone with balls to step up and switch on the light, expose the cockroaches for everyone to see. That reminded him and he rummaged around for something to seal the crack at the bottom of his door.

Again he dialed Helen O'Dell's line. "I never thought I'd be spending a dollar on you like that, Helen." With his other hand he opened the desk drawer and found the 8mm Nambu. It smelled of oil. He had disassembled it, cleaned and fine-tuned it and now the action moved like it did the day he stole it from a camp guard on the day the Japs surrendered. "It's not over yet, Helen. It's just beginning. I give you my word on that, Helen."

It was late Thursday afternoon when a flustered Mrs. Butrum stopped at Phyllis Lind's desk in the Main Office. "Isn't he in there *yet*?" she asked, indicating the closed door.

"Sorry, Mrs. Butrum." She shook her head. "I haven't seen him since this morning when he said he was going out to do some observing. He didn't even come back for his lunch today."

"I've been to every classroom throughout the day, would you believe, and I haven't seen him." She was more agitated than usual. "Nobody's seen him!" She looked at her watch pinned to the top of her dress. "I still have so many things to do. I can't spend my whole day trying to track down a phantom."

At her word Mr. Baltz rushed into the office, skirted the front counter and barreled down on the two women. "Speak of the Devil. Here he comes now and it looks like he's on a mission, headed for the executive john. Best get out of his way, Mrs. Butrum!"

But she stood her ground directly in his path, blocking access to his office. "I've been looking for you all day!" she said as though she were talking to an errant student. "I need a few minutes of your time right now!"

"Carolyn, I'm not going to toss that mouse-mousse thing around with you again. You saw the police report. I'm out of patience and I don't have any more time for your theories. In the heat of the moment you were mistaken. It's understandable. Even Dexter who arrived right after you says there wasn't any mouse. Now if you'll excuse me–"

He tried to make his way around her, but she wouldn't back off. "It's official Sunshine Committee business," she said, "for poor Helen O'Dell and–"

"I gave yesterday, Mrs. Butrum. Five dollars." He moved to get around on her other side. "I really have to *go* and you are in my way. Let's just let poor Helen O'Dell rest in peace and get on with the school year." He feinted left and when she committed, her weight carried her too far and he passed her on the right. He opened the door.

"That's exactly what I'm trying to do." She was right on him in his slipstream and in the office behind him before he could shut the door. "This *is* about Helen resting in peace. It's about her funeral. No one's claimed her body yet, so the Sunshine Committee had an emergency meeting. The poor woman is just lying there waiting in the County Morgue for deliverance. So the Committee voted to claim her. Lord knows, it's the least we could do for one of our own. The way she went and all, like a horse in the harness."

"A very noble gesture, Mrs. Butrum," he said eager to get her out of his office. "I'm sure she would be proud of the efforts of the Sunshine Committee."

She was on a mission. "We collected enough money for flowers, but apparently there won't be a wake or any place to hold a service. Which means there's no place to send the flowers. So," she brushed a piece of lint from the front of his jacket, "this morning the Committee voted to have a short wake, a memorial service and a burial. Something simple but fitting, and with dignity."

"Fine." He went to his wallet. "How much more do you want me to chip in?"

She held his arm. "The Committee just needs your approval for the removal of the tables and chairs in the student cafeteria. Lord knows I tried, but Mr. Polakas and the custodians won't do it without a work order. And you have to sign a work order. The florist will have everything set up tomorrow after school, but the tables and chairs have to be moved out of the way right after the last lunch period." She waited for his reply.

"Tomorrow? For what? What are you talking about?"

"The service, Mr. Baltz. I just told you. The Committee has arranged everything. The County hearse will deliver Helen sometime tomorrow after the last lunch period, but before the end of the classes so there is time to get her ready. The wake will begin right after school. It being Friday and all, the cafeteria won't be used until Monday. And the County agreed to transport her for the burial on Saturday morning."

"Where, Mrs. Butrum… where is this all happening?"

She was annoyed and looked at her watch again. "In the cafeteria, Mr. Baltz. Haven't you been paying attention?"

"You're going to bury Helen O'Dell in our cafeteria?"

She let out an exasperated tut. "Don't be stupid," she said in her teacher tone as though she were talking to one of her Track IIIs. It froze him. "Now try and follow what I'm saying. The wake will be in the cafeteria tomorrow afternoon after school." She looked at him sardonically for understanding. "The burial will take place on Saturday morning after a memorial service. Not in the cafeteria. In the war memorial on the side lawn. Of course you will want to say a few words. Originally the Committee considered cremation, but we decided burial would be better and–"

"Mrs. Butrum, you went ahead and planned all this for our cafeteria and the war memorial?" He tucked his chin into his neck and became very officious. "I'm afraid I can't allow you to do that. It's out of the question. It's not possible. I don't have the authority and besides it's unsanitary and I'm sure it's against the law."

"The Committee has taken care of everything. Building and Grounds has already given us the use of the cafeteria for free. We have clearance from the Department of Health. The Committee spoke to Mr. Adornau and all of the other School Board members on the phone. And I contacted Dr. Flackett's office earlier about the details. Lord knows all the planning that's gone into everything and you don't have to do a thing except sign that work order."

"But the war memorial? She can't be buried there."

"She can and she will. Our research discovered that the war memorial on the side lawn is erected directly over the town's very first cemetery. The Committee applied for a variance with the clerk at Town Hall and they were only too happy to approve it." She showed him the paper with the official seal. "We even picked out a little headstone. But that won't arrive until after it's been engraved. Are you following all of this?"

Mr. Baltz was silent. "And just who is paying for all of this, Mrs. Butrum?" he asked

"Oh," she said, "that's the best part. Helen O'Dell is. Actually her insurance policies are. The Committee checked it all out. She's entitled to collect on the district insurance, and she gets the new member benefit from the Association and the Union. Since poor Helen had nobody, no family, no heirs, the money is just sitting there. Thanks to Mr. Giovanni's moving her into the classroom, that comes out to a little more than five thousand dollars, enough to cover everything!"

"Mario said she designated him as her beneficiary."

"The Committee checked with Central, the Association and the Union and apparently Helen left the beneficiary space blank."

"But her estate–"

"There isn't any estate. She was an orphan and had no family."

"Her will–"

"No will." She paused. "And here's the best part. Because the insurance papers hadn't been filed, it was a simple matter to fill in the Sunshine Committee as her sole beneficiary. The Committee voted on the spot to do it. The papers were notarized and backdated." She lowered her voice. "Technically it may not be quite on the up-and-up, but it's Helen's money after all and what better way to spend it than on Helen as a final bash, a kind of going away party for her? The Committee hand-delivered the applications to the insurance companies today, along with copies of the Death Certificate signed by Dr. Nessmith and they issued checks for the full amount–five thousand one hundred and fifty-seven dollars!" She produced the three checks made out to the Sunshine Committee. "Now the only thing that's holding everything up"– she produced another folded sheet of paper from her pocketbook–"is your signature on this work order."

"But Mrs. Butrum, I can't take the responsibility for all this."

"Not your problem, Mr. Baltz. You don't have to. The Committee is on top of everything and everything is working smoothly. We'll start setting up tomorrow at the end of school and close up at night."

"But–"

"We'll be able to wheel her into the cafeteria refrigerator overnight. She should keep very nicely in there. Besides it's only for one night and the refrigerator will be practically empty for the weekend. Lord knows that's a break. The itinerant speech therapist, the one with the lisp," she looked at her list, "Warren Pace, says he'll be happy to officiate at any ceremony. He's an ordained Cardinal in the Life of the Universe Church. It's nonsectarian, so there won't be any religious conflict, and nobody can be offended. And the price is right, he'll do it for free."

"But–"

"I put you on the program to say a few words, along with Dr. Flackett and Mr. Adornau. Then we thought we'd open it up to anybody else who wants to remember poor Helen. Saturday morning the hearse will pick her up at the back door of the cafeteria and deliver her around to the memorial for interment. The Committee has taken care of everything."

He signed grudgingly.

She smiled. "I'll just trot this down to Stash Polakas and we can get the funeral rolling. It's going to be a party!"

All day Friday the school was alive with the arrangements for Helen O'Dell's wake and well before the final bell the student cafeteria was in transition. Mrs. Butrum stood in the center of the activity, directing the movements of the separate groups like a choreographer. Some were hanging black crepe paper left over from the Halloween dance around the inside of the windows and over the doors. Custodians were pushing wide brooms back and forth as in a well-rehearsed ballet to clear the accumulated garbage from the student lunch periods. People were stacking chairs, folding and moving tables to the perimeter. Already more than half of the floor area was empty.

"Now, Charley dear," Mrs. Butrum said patiently to the custodian, "I like what you're doing with the folding chairs. It shows real creativity and independent thinking, but I think having the chairs in rows and all facing in one direction would be nicer." He nodded and began rearranging them. "And maybe you could have them facing that window," she pointed, "where the coffin will be instead of the back wall. We'll put poor Helen approximately here." She positioned a chair for him. "Now that I got you started, do you think you can manage it, dear, about ten rows"—she held up both of her hands—"of twelve across. That's all of your toes and two of mine." She lifted her foot. "And that should be enough. If we need more you can always add them later." Charley nodded. "We'll leave the first row for the Sunshine Committee, Mr. Baltz and the administrators." She checked the list of names she was holding. "Dr. Flackett, Mr. Adornau and the rest of the School Board, and the remaining *living* assistant principals, of course."

"Hey, Mrs. Butrum," Virgil said when she bustled past him. He had been watching everything from the doorway. "How are the preparations going?"

"Splendidly, Virgil dear," she answered without taking her eyes off her checklist. "Everything is going splendidly, thank goodness. Those flowers," she called to the florist, "should be separated. One wreath on each side of where the casket will go. Put the red bleeding heart on the left and the good luck horseshoe on the right."

"You look busy."

"I am, dear. Very busy." She took inventory of what still had to be done. "And always more to do." She walked through the cafeteria to the kitchen and Virgil followed. "Wouldn't you know, the County was a little earlier than expected with their delivery. Luckily the refrigerator was ready." She opened the large aluminum door and they went into the walk-in refrigerator. "She arrived with the lid closed, but that made me feel so claustrophobic. Besides an open-casket wake is so much more satisfying for everyone, don't you think? It gives everyone a chance to see poor Helen one last time. How do you like the coffin? The Sunshine Committee was torn between bronze or wood. We went wood. It's so much more elegant and warmer."

Helen O'Dell reposed in a dark mahogany coffin with the bottom half closed, her head exposed on a satin pillow. Her hair was styled and she was wearing her army jacket that was buttoned. She lay facing a row of hanging bolognas and cheeses.

"She looks very peaceful, very natural."

"Yes, dear. They did a wonderful job. They got that surprised look off her face. But I just don't like her hands." They were folded emptily under her round and ample chest. They stepped around the casket for a closer inspection. "She looks as though she's holding herself up. And I don't think it would be right for people to walk away with that image as their last impression of the woman. She should be holding something other than herself, don't you think?" She reached into her pocketbook. "Maybe a pair of rosary beads?" She put them into Helen's cold hands.

Virgil shook his head. "It's better, but still not right."

"What about a flag?" She removed a small American flag wrapped around a stick and put that into Helen's hand.

He walked around the coffin to take in the full effect from every angle. "She looks like she's leading a parade."

"A lace hankie?"

"Somehow I don't think that she was the lace hankie type." He searched around the refrigerator and found a bunch of celery stalks. He selected the smallest ones and offered them to Mrs. Butrum.

"Celery?" She wrapped the empty hands around the stalks. "That *does* look much better. And considering she was eating when she went, it's appropriate, poetic. You are such a gem, Virgil dear. Thank you."

* * *

When the bell rang at the end of the day, there wasn't a stampede to the cafeteria to pay their respects to a fallen comrade, as Mrs Butrum had anticipated. And ten minutes later the cafeteria was still practically empty. She fretted and fussed and nervously rearranged things at the buffet table that the caterer had prepared and the cafeteria staff set up.

"I'm so upset," she said to Helen O'Dell, who was now out of the refrigerator and reposing peacefully in front of the large window backlit by the setting February sun. The bleeding heart and horseshoe floral arrangements were at each end of the open casket, the bottom half of which was draped with an American flag, a tribute for her military service. Inside Helen O'Dell clutched her slightly wilting celery. Mrs. Butrum knelt on the velvet covered kneeler borrowed from Saints Cecil and Cecelia Church and prayed. "Dear Lord, You know I don't ask for much. Well, not very much. It is Friday and happy hour starts at three, but please, if You would, open people's hearts and send a large crowd to make this event a success. Amen." When she turned some of the chairs were filled, and more people were drifting in. She turned back. "Thank you," she whispered.

Stanley Milnow followed Red Farley directly to the buffet table for a closer look at the fare. "This is better than the Christmas party," he said, loading his plate with cheese cubes and olives.

"That *was* a shit party," Red complained. "And this one is free besides."

"Free? I chipped in a buck."

"Looks like I got supper for tonight," John Hiller said as he forked cold cuts, rolls and potato salad into plastic bags. "Maybe even lunch on Monday."

"Lunch?" Noah Lewis said joining the growing line up around the table.

"Great news," Phaedra Schwartz announced to Sue Wellen, "I'm Phay Schwartz again. I signed the divorce papers and now I'm ready to par-tay! In fact I'm planning a little "Good Riddance Paul" get-together in the faculty room next week with a few of the girls."

"Ann Landers said you have a year to send out thank-you cards for your wedding gifts, but what's the protocol for returning them and for the ones from the bridal shower we threw you last spring before the wedding?" Sue asked.

"Most of the wedding gifts are still under warranty," Terry added. "If you hurry and return mine I might be able to get a refund on that fondu set I bought you."

"This is bullshit, Phyl," Mario Giovanni muttered under his breath.

"What is?"

"It's not fair," he sulked. "All that money they wasted on flowers and this spread. Not to mention that coffin. It could have gone to better use."

"Let it go, Mario. Just be happy for the send-off Helen's getting. If she were alive today and here to see this turnout, she'd be so happy."

Willy Zwill sat silently in the corner with his back to the wall, watching the crowd. His twitching was much worse. His face was gaunt and there were deep circles under his eyes.

The R&G Madrigals, accompanied by Mr. Dimitris and his piano, performed a medley of three songs, "How Merrily We Live," "Rise Up My Love" and "Ha Ha This World Doth Pass." Virgil Loomis in whiteface, striped shirt and beret mimed his way among the mourners. He walked against the wind, got trapped in a box and had a tug of war with himself before he reached the coffin miming tears to the applause of everyone but Dr. Flackett and the School Board. B Orchestra arrived and played an extended version of "God Bless America" under the direction of Herbert Gateway.

"Thank you all for coming," Mr. Baltz said to the thinning crowd. "I am sure Helen is looking down on us now from wherever she may be, happy and proud at being remembered this way. Tomorrow is the burial service and before the rest of you run out the door for happy hour, Mrs. Butrum wants me to remind you that the county van will be here tomorrow morning–" He looked at Mrs. Butrum who was basking in the glory of a perfect wake.

"At nine thirty sharp," she said.

"Those of you who plan to attend the internment, please arrive before they do so we can get Helen into the ground and get on with things of the living, as I am sure Helen would have wanted. Now get home safe and see you in the morning."

When the cafeteria was empty Mrs. Butrum closed the coffin lid. She directed Charley to wheel Helen back into the refrigerator where she would spend the night in repose with the buffet leftovers.

87 Saturday

The drive home took Jesse forever. It rained Friday evening, a steady, cold, hard rain that fell all night. And when the temperature dropped overnight everything froze. The added weight of the ice knocked down tree branches and power lines and early Saturday morning, sometime well before daylight, the freezing rain turned to snow, a silent downfall that covered the ice, brightened the slush and gave everything a dreamlike quality.

"You can't go," his mother said when Jesse announced he had to drive back to school. "It's Saturday. There's no school on Saturday. And it snowed."

"I really have to go," he said, "to show my respect."

"WINS news says the streets are ice. They haven't even cleared the accidents from last night. Stay home. It's the weekend. Please."

He knew his drive back would be a long nightmare and in all likelihood by the time he arrived the funeral would be over and he'd just have to turn around for home. But he went anyway.

The weather kept Mrs. Butrum from getting any sleep. All night she was at the window watching and fretting. Before the pale sun was up she drove her Jeep, her winter car, to the school and used her passkey to let herself into the dark and empty building, where she went directly to the cafeteria. She got Eddie the night custodian to roll Helen out of the refrigerator and the two women waited for the daylight and the day to begin, hoping for the sun.

When Jesse finally pulled into a spot in the teacher's parking lot he thought everything would be over, so he was surprised to see cars scattered randomly and at odd angles close to the building. He shuffled carefully along the narrow shoveled path the custodians had cleared that was icing over again. Inside Helen O'Dell still reposed between the two wreaths where he'd last seen her. She was alone and virtually ignored by the smaller gathering of mourners who milled about impatiently near the windows. He joined Terry and Sue.

"Never thought we'd see you this morning," she said.

"I know. I probably should have stayed last night at my aunt's house," Jesse said. "It took me forever and I thought I was going to be too late."

"You didn't miss a thing," Terry said. "O'Dell's still dead."

"Everything's on hold until the County van arrives to transport her around to the war memorial," Sue added with a tut.

Terry emptied his coffee cup. "After they plant her she will become a forever part of R&G's lore. I know I'm looking forward to spring and what will come up!"

"That's awful!"

"This is terrible," Mrs. Butrum worried. She was by the open coffin. The celery in Helen O'Dell's hand had long gone limp in the heat of the cafeteria. "And everything was going *so* nicely."

Willy Zwill clumped across the floor in his unbuckled galoshes. All morning he walked back and forth from chair to coffin to view the body. His eyes were red-rimmed.

Mr. Baltz sighed audibly and shifted his trench coat to check his wristwatch again. Mr. Adornau and Dr. Flackett joked and laughed off to the side. Chuck LaFemina and Rory Aaron watched Special Ed teacher Warren Pace with a much higher regard in his scarlet cardinal robes. He was well into his Life of the Universe Church pitch to Red Farley.

"No, really. It's *not* a pyramid scheme like AMWAY. I ordain you for a one-time fee of fifty-five dollars, a small investment. Once you become an ordained bishop you can collect fifty-five bucks for each minister you ordain. Cash. And when you become a cardinal like me, you collect a little fee each time one of your bishops ordains a new minister. And the best part is as clergy you are tax-exempt and your house is also exempt of property taxes because it's your church. You have to love America."

"I *do* love America, but–"

"When you're a minister you'll love it even more. I haven't paid any taxes, sales or income, in two years." He handed Red a business card.

The level of the conversations in the room grew steadily louder.

"Mrs. Butrum," Mr. Baltz called with annoyance, "it is after eleven thirty. Don't you think this has gone on long enough? We've been waiting for"–he looked at his watch again–"two hours. Some of us who are alive may have other plans for the rest of the day."

Mrs. Butrum's face dropped. "Maybe we could carry her out? Or perhaps we could load her into a station wagon–"

"Frankly, Mrs. Butrum, I don't give a damn. Just hurry up and do something!"

"Does anyone here have a truck or a station wagon?" she called over the din of conversations.

Willy Zwill raised his hand. "A Chevy Nova station wagon."

"Good." She approached the assistant principal. "Instead of waiting any longer for the County van, we'll move the event along and move Helen ourselves. So if you would be so kind as to back your station wagon close to the door, Mr. Zwill, the men will load her in and we can be on our way." He nodded and clumped out to get his car. "I'll need a few able-bodied men," Mrs. Butrum announced, "to help carry Helen out the door when Mr. Zwill arrives with his car. In the coffin, of course." She smiled and patted Helen before she closed the lid with a sigh. "And after we get her loaded, he'll drive her around to the memorial."

It took some maneuvering to get the 1964 Chevy Nova over the ice. The rear wheels turned and skidded and the station wagon slid sideways, until it was finally close enough to the building.

"Now if we might have those volunteers."

Red Farley stepped forward, joined by shop teacher Murray Fink, Terry and Jesse and the impromptu pallbearers strained to lift the heavy coffin with some effort. After the heat of the cafeteria, the cold outside air and wind felt especially brutal, and it was difficult for them to hold the brass handles and move Helen over the ice. Fitting her into Mr. Zwill's car wasn't easy either, with Mrs. Butrum supervising and everyone calling out suggestions.

"She's sticking out over the back bumper," Mrs. Butrum observed. "Do you think you might get some rope around her end so we don't lose the poor woman again?"

Willy Zwill found a piece of old clothesline and tied Helen O'Dell securely in place. Just as he was finishing the last of an intricate series of knots, the blue and orange County van swung into the parking lot, siren wailing and red light turning. It slid to a stop while the crowd inside the cafeteria broke into a collective cheer.

"Well," Mr. Baltz said to Mrs. Butrum talking to the van driver and attendant, "you might as well leave her where she is. It will only waste more time moving her out of Zwill's trunk and into the van." He tapped his watch. "Can we just get this show on the road?" He turned and walked back into the warmth of the cafeteria.

Mrs. Butrum rolled her eyes at the two men who were waiting for direction. "If you dears just take the flowers, we'll keep things the way they are. Lord knows poor Helen's been shuffled around enough."

They collected the wreaths and stuffed them into the back of the van.

"Now," Mrs. Butrum said to the crowd waiting inside, "the Committee had originally planned to have a cortege of cars drive around the school behind the van to the memorial, but the weather hasn't made that easy. Should we still try to take the cars or do we walk? It's up to you to decide."

The mourners huddled to discuss their options, and after debating the matter thoroughly, they voted by a show of hands that it would probably be easier and faster to walk. The distance from the back of the cafeteria to the war memorial on the side by the tennis courts was less than a hundred yards in a straight line along the front lawn.

When everyone was ready, Mrs. Butrum gave the signal for the two-car funeral procession to begin. Mr. Zwill's Nova wagon with Helen O'Dell hanging over in the back spun out of the parking lot dead slow, spitting snow and ice. The County van, red bubble light turning, crawled along behind with the flowers. The band of mourners, bunched together as they were for warmth and security, started out across the snow-covered lawn, advancing awkwardly in tight formation, holding arms to keep from falling, rocking side to side like a flock of penguins over an ice floe. It took them almost fifteen minutes to make the hundred yards.

As the Sunshine Committee's research revealed, the memorial on the right side of the lawn in front of R&G, honoring those who served in four wars, was indeed erected on the site of the town's first cemetery. When the high school was expanded years later, a portion of the original burial ground was reclaimed for the construction. The bodies, including town founder, Ephram Hickler, were exhumed and relocated to the new cemetery and the portion not used for the expansion was paved over and converted into three composition tennis courts. The land adjacent to the new tennis courts became a war memorial by default when the two granite boulders proved to be too heavy to be removed. Bronze plaques greened with age were inscribed with the names of Farmington's war veterans and attached permanently to the boulders. There they remained, shaded by a stand of scrub pines and ornamental shrubs, virtually forgotten, except on Memorial and Veteran's Days, when plastic commemorative flowers were laid there by a diminishing number of aging, uniformed VFW members. On warm spring days the area around the Memorial was a favorite hiding place for the class cutters who smoked and made out there in the bushes, and for the vandals who tagged the boulders with spray-painted graffiti.

The two cars skidded up Second Street, around the front of the school and down Fourth Street toward the yawning, open grave in the middle of the Memorial, where they came to an angled halt. Mr. Zwill and the men in the van waited for the others to arrive and together with the unofficial pallbearers they carried Helen O'Dell toward her final resting place.

"Can we get started?" Mr. Baltz asked and didn't wait for an answer. He nodded at Dr. Flackett and Mr. Adornau, who were scheduled to speak first.

"In the interest of saving time," the superintendent said, bundling himself against the wind, "I think I will forgo my prepared statement and say simply that Helen O'Dell will be sorely missed by all and she will be hard to replace."

Mr. Adornau puffed on his small cigar. "Ditto," he added and turned to Mr. Baltz. "Take it, Seymour, if you have anything you want to add."

The principal pulled a sheet of folded paper from his coat and cleared his throat. "Helen O'Dell was a colleague," he began, "and a team player. She was committed to her job and she was a dedicated assistant principal. In the four years she worked for me she always did whatever I asked her to do. But now she's dead. And in a way, it is fitting that we bury her here on school grounds, because it will enable Helen O'Dell to continue doing her job and keep an eye on things, something she so ably did when she was alive. May she rest in peace."

"Rest in peace," the collective voices echoed his sentiments as he folded the paper and put it back into his pocket.

"Life, as silly as it may seem at times, is just a short trip. Out of one hole and into another," Cardinal Warren Pace said, beginning his benediction. "Helen O'Dell's ticket was punched prematurely and her journey has come to an untimely end. Although I didn't really know her well, or personally, she did observe my classes on at least one occasion and gave me a relatively good write-up. So I am saddened by her premature burial. Now, as we send her body into the earth to nourish the flowers and the trees, let us remember her not as she is in death, but as she was in life–a little overweight perhaps, and often out of breath. Ashes to ashes, dust to dust."

The cold and ice had turned the newly dug ground too solid, so instead of dirt the mourners tossed handfuls of snow into the grave and the two County workers and two custodians held the ropes that lowered Helen O'Dell into her frozen hole.

Virgil Loomis took a kazoo from his jacket pocket and played a mournful rendition of "Taps," no less touching than trumpeter Army Sgt. Keith Clark's, whose broken note that November 1963 afternoon brought tears at the JFK funeral almost a decade before. Willy Zwill and Mrs. Butrum cried.

"I'm so happy," she said on their walk back, "that everything went so well. In the long run, I mean. It was a glorious funeral."

"Well, there's another good thing," Terry commented when he was standing back inside the cafeteria with the others. They had remained for the post-burial buffet arranged by the Sunshine Committee and paid for by Helen O'Dell, her final thank-you to the mourners.

"And what the hell would that be, Scapelli?" Red Farley said reaching for a roast beef sandwich while balancing a full plate of potato salad and a cup of hot coffee.

"O'Dell being out there on the side lawn should keep the number of cutters, smokers and the fornicators out of the bushes at least for a little while."

Willy Zwill remained behind. He was the last to leave the grave site. He waited until the District plow pushed the final clods of frozen earth back into place. "You'll not be forgotten, O'Dell," he said and placed a flower on top of the mound.

And so Helen O'Dell was laid to rest and belonged to the ages for all eternity, or until the District needed more tennis courts.

Camelot

Official Publication of the Partnership of Parents and Teachers
in Association for better Farmington Public Schools
Harriet Stegle, President P-PTA

Vol. 5 Issue 5   February 1972

AROUND THE DISTRICT:

Flags were lowered to half-staff last week as tragedy struck and the District mourned the passing of one of its own. It is with great sadness that I report the passing of Helen O'Dell, the 4th AP at R&G. Helen, a former WAC, was hired in 1966 and served until January 31st, when she died doing the thing she loved best, servicing the taxpayers of Farmington. Her wake on Friday afternoon in the High School cafeteria was followed by a brief nondenominational service on Saturday morning, attended by colleagues and district dignitaries, who braved the snow and ice to say a final farewell to Helen. Her remains were laid to rest with dignity and decorum in the bushes of the War Memorial on the side lawn of R&G, where she will be memorialized with a small, but tasteful, rose-colored headstone as soon as it arrives from the stonecutter. When you get the chance, drop by for a look-see.

CONGRATULATIONS:

Kudos are in order for Chairwoman Carolyn Butrum and the R&G Sunshine Committee, who conceptualized, planned, choreographed and executed the best funeral since the JFK assassination. The event was a great success and, except for the weather, went almost flawlessly. There is consolation in our grief to know that if Helen O'Dell were alive today, she'd be proud to be buried where she is, with all the dignity she deserved.

It's no longer FINE for Phaedra Schwartz-Fine, whose divorce was FINE-ally FINE-alized. Phay, who was married just last

June at a lovely wedding I attended, is back to being unhyphenated again. "And that's just FINE with me," she said. But actually it's now just Schwartz again!

NEWS AND VIEWS:

Here are some of the comments that I overheard at Helen O'Dell's funeral.

M. Seymour Baltz, Principal: "I hope this is over soon. Helen will be hard to replace."

Donald F. Flackett, Superintendent of Schools: "Helen O'Dell was a big woman who left a big hole. And I don't just mean the one on the side lawn of the High School. Life goes on, so we will soon have to fill Helen's hole. Again not the one on the lawn... or any other you might be thinking."

Noah Lewis, First Assistant Principal: "Great spread. The sandwiches were fresh and the potato salad had little pieces of bacon in it and something else I couldn't identify, like dill. Yes, it was dill. And I didn't know I even liked dill."

Mario Giovanni, Second Assistant Principal: "Helen had a voracious appetite and wicked hook shot."

Willy Zwill, Third Assistant Principal: "I heard the stories about a mouse or a mousse and I smell a rat! This isn't over yet!"

Dwayne Purvey, President Farmington Union Local # 2: "I don't have anything to say. I don't know anything about any mouse or mousse. For that matter, I was out sick on Monday and Tuesday the week she died and that's on the record."

Warren Pace, Bishop of the Life of the Universe Church: "Besides funerals I do weddings and ordinations if you are interested in becoming a minister with all the benefits that go along with it. Call me for details. Here's my card."

AROUND THE DISTRICT:

FLASH—Central Administration is now accepting applications for the recently vacated AP position at the High School. Interested qualified individuals can submit résumés to the Superintendent before the February break next week. All applications will be reviewed and interviews will begin in the early spring.

That's all for now. See you next time with more news from the trenches!

"Miss Lind–"

"Ms."

"–Phyllis, I'll be out observing again," the principal said. But it had been a slow afternoon because there was not much to observe in the Observatory. Stash Polakas had to put the stall doors back after the Health Inspector showed up.

"A serious health code violation," the inspector had told Baltz, casually rubbing his thumb and fingers together, but got no response. "There are numerous complaints and very little wiggle room." He waited again. Nothing. He became very officious. He filled out a citation. "As principal it's your obligation to see that the doors go back on immediately. Failure to do so and the school district will face legal action." He handed over the paper. "Call your custodian. I'll wait and make sure the job's done."

Even though there wasn't much to see, time in the Observatory was still better than real teacher observations. He was getting restless. He drummed on the writing table he had moved into the closet and he looked at his watch. There was still another hour until the dismissal bell. He was about to leave when he heard voices.

"My crotch is a semiprivate affair, not something to be held up to public scrutiny, or judged by some advertising industry sniffing standard!" Red Farley said, deep in the middle of conversation. "Haven't you heard of using regular deodorant or a splash of cologne?"

"Regular deodorant is for the underarms and cologne burns my balls!" Stanley Milnow said. "They already *make* crotch sprays for woman. Why not men?"

"If you want your balls to smell like a flower just use one of them."

"Those are feminine products."

"You know, Stanley, for a teacher you really are stupid! Just like all those other people out there being manipulated, a slave to Madison Avenue, for chrisakes! There's no difference."

"Then let me ask you this, Red. Do you order Tab instead of Diet Coke? Ever smoke Virginia Slims?"

"Of course not. Those things are for women."

He smiled. "I rest my case."

"What case? What fucking case are you resting, Stan? What's your point? It's stupid. Crotch spray for men is unnecessary, and it's… fruity."

"Not according to the latest research." He shook the newspaper he was holding. "It's right here in *The Post*. The company is sponsoring a contest to name their new product. Something strong and masculine." He found the place on the page. "The winner gets a cash prize and two weeks at the Playboy Mansion. I wouldn't mind winning, that's all I'm saying. Scapelli had some good ideas for names."

"Scapelli is an asshole."

"*Penisimo*. He came up with that one. That's a great name! I wish I thought of it."

"He's still an asshole. I see the doors are back." Red pulled the newspaper out of his hand and disappeared into one of the stalls.

Stanley Milnow went behind the other door and they continued their conversation. "Something really manly. How does *Hard On* sound to you? Something outdoorsy. Or *Tackle and Rod* 'for the sportsman in you'? Maybe *Bum Wrap* for men with a broader problem area? What do you think, Red?"

"I think you're a bigger asshole than Scapelli."

Both toilets flushed at the same time and they came out of the stalls together. Stanley went up to the mirror, opened his mouth and poked around his gums with his finger. "'It's *Cock-Sure* to be secure!'" he said. "I like that one. Or maybe 'Dickery Dew' spelled d-e-w. It has a nice, gentle sound to it."

"How about *Foul Balls,* for chrisakes!" Red Farley sniffed the air. "Don't you wipe your ass after you take a dump? No wonder you're looking for a deodorant spray."

"*Foul Balls*. Good one. And what the hell are *you* talking about? You're the one always complaining about the hemorrhoids."

They left the bathroom still arguing.

Baltz logged in their names, date and time into the pad. Then he wrote a brief outline of the conversation and numbered it. He left the Observatory and entered the toilet for a closer inspection of the stalls. He opened the first one and it was clean. He checked the second and it was clean too. He peeked into the third stall. Clean. He came out with the folded newspaper. He realized he really had to pee and probably wouldn't make it back to his office. What the hell? He was alone and there wasn't really any need to be uncomfortable. He tucked the newspaper under his arm and stepped up to a urinal. "BREAK BALTZ!" was printed in red marker at eye level.

"Fuck!" he said. He licked his finger and started rubbing out the words when the bathroom door opened.

Terry stopped whistling his version of the Beatles' "Hello, Goodbye" but he when he saw the peeing principal. "Looks like I caught you with your pants down, Mr. Baltz. Well, open anyway." He deftly slipped into the space next to him, ignoring the unspoken every-other-urinal protocol when permitted.

"All the places to pee and all the bathrooms in all the world and I picked this one this time," he said unbuttoning his jeans deftly. "You know, it's amazing. All my years here at R&G I've peed next to department chairs, assistant principals, school board members, but this," he paused dramatically, "this is unprecedented. This is the first time I've ever peed next to you, Mr. Baltz. Which makes this a special occasion, an historic moment for me."

"That's very interesting, Mr. Scapelli." His face was as red as the red smear on the wall.

"To take it a step further, Mr. Baltz, I don't recall anyone in the faculty room *ever* mention peeing next to the principal. In fact, there are people who have a theory for that. Would you like to know what it is?"

"Not really, Mr. Scapelli. I'm just interested in taking care of business and getting on with business. Which you might do as well. But I'm sure you're going to tell me anyway."

"The theory is that principals don't pee because their, er, apparatus"–he pointed down into the urinal–"is removed when they get the job."

Mr. Baltz twitched his mustache.

"I hope that's not true for assistant principals. Is it? Because I was giving some serious thought to applying for Helen O'Dell's spot. But not if I have to give all of this up." He looked down at himself. "Consider the possibilities with me as your new AP. It could be the beginning of a beautiful friendship. The two of us working together. What do you think, Mr. Baltz?"

He snorted involuntarily, considered some retort, but gave it up.

"It's just something else for you to ponder," Terry said. He turned toward him and looked down. "Jeez, me peeing next to the principal. What a coup. And now I can hardly wait to tell everybody that it's really no big thing." He buttoned up and shook his head.

Mr. Baltz flushed and left without saying another word and without washing his hands.

"X-Y-Z. Don't forget to examine your zipper, Mr. Baltz."

The week after Helen O'Dell's wake and funeral the building settled back into a routine and business as usual. The stall doors were back up, six months on austerity had become a way of life, a minor speed bump everyone worked around. There was still no contract or any prospect of one and teachers worked around that as well. Joel Maxwell and the FT Ass. encouraged teachers to wear their buttons. He assured everyone their efforts were having an effect and that there were other activities in the works. The following week teachers were told to wear black every Friday as a symbol of their mourning, not for Helen O'Dell, but the lack of meaningful negotiations. Some did, most didn't. Of course the only ones who saw the buttons and black were the students.

Dwayne Purvey was unusually sullen and more quiet, trying to remain below the radar. He sat alone and left whenever discussions turned to Helen O'Dell and the theories surrounding her end. And there was no lack of theories, many involving frozen mice. Willy Zwill was daily more morose, but nobody noticed because he was also less visible, spending most of his time in his fortress office. And Noah Lewis called in sick Thursday and Friday to get a head start on his trip to Poland during the February break. So all the weight of administrative responsibility fell on Mario Giovanni.

"I'm all alone, Phyl," he complained. "Zwill's fading fast and keeps himself locked away in his office. Noah Lewis is eating pierogis in Warsaw or Krakow and looking for retirement villas. And Baltz... Where the hell is he?"

"Every morning he tells me he's going out to observe."

"Well, I haven't seen him anywhere. He's not here and he's not at Central. I've called them, but they haven't seen him either. He's a ghost. I've been abandoned! I'm doing everything. I'm running the factory alone."

"You can add to your to do list answering my phone if it rings. I have to go to the lady's room." She grabbed her pocketbook. "But there just might be some changes in the works, from what I've been hearing." She raised her eyebrows.

"What did you hear? What do you know?" He followed after her. "Tell me."

"I don't know anything for sure, but I've heard his complaints on the phone to his wife about stress, lack of sleep and all the bad press." She leaned in and whispered, "The power behind the throne is pushing him to take time off. A leave. Or put in his papers before things get any worse."

"Worse, huh? Did she say how much worse they have to get? Did *he* say?" He trailed her through the Administrative Alcove. "You know, Phyl, we both could use a little break. And I've been working on that 'little problem' I've been having. So why don't you come into my office and we'll see if anything comes up—" He patted her butt.

She tutted him and rolled her eyes. "How original. I don't have time now, Mario. I want to stop by upstairs for Phay Schwartz's *bon voyage* party. Her divorce is final and she's celebrating. She leaves tomorrow for the Bahamas with her new fiancé. You're coming up? There's food. The vultures will be out in force. John Hiller said he was going up and camping out after Homeroom. So if you want to eat something you better do it quick."

He cracked his neck. "I was hoping it was an offer you wouldn't refuse, Phyl, but obviously you don't have time for me—"

"We'll have time for that all next week when we're off. Cheer up. We'll be on vacation. Life is beautiful and it's payday." She reached into her blouse and produced an envelope with his check. "Special delivery."

He pressed it to his face. It was warm and smelled of her Shalimar.

* * *

The day before any vacation passed more slowly than usual. Attendance in Homeroom was down drastically and it got less class to class as the day wore on. Only students afraid of getting cut slips or those whose parents didn't want them home showed up and stayed around all day. Not enough kids to teach anything, not that teachers planned lessons, but too many to turn off the lights, lock the classroom door and hang out in the faculty room all day. Friday before the February break was at best a holding action.

Willy Zwill opened his door tentatively and peered into the alcove before he stepped out of his office. "Good afternoon, Willy." Terry's voice caught him by surprise and he scurried back inside like a cockroach caught in the middle of a room when the light goes on. Behind the relative safety of his office door he leaned against it. "Is everything all right, Willy?" Terry tapped on the door.

"What do you want? I don't have anything for you."

"It's Terry Scapelli, Willy. Sorry if I scared you. I don't want anything from you. Just my check."

"I don't have it."

"I know. I was on my way to get it from Phyllis."

"You're alone?" He opened the door a crack and his blinking eyeball appeared. He was perspiring.

"From the little I can see, Willy, you don't look too well. I guess with Helen gone… and being understaffed you're looking forward to the break to regroup."

"We're not understaffed!" he protested. "Maybe stretched a bit thinner, but we're ready for anything. Always ready. *Semper paratus*!"

"I saw that Central is running an ad in the paper this weekend for the open AP position and will start interviewing next week. It won't be too long before you're at full strength."

"We don't need another assistant principal. The four of us are just fine."

"Four?" He looked into the eyeball. "Only three, Willy. Helen's dead. Don't you remember? We buried her out on the lawn by the monuments last week. You transported her in the back of your station wagon."

He lowered his voice to a whisper. "Don't you believe every rumor you hear. O'Dell's not dead. It's misinformation, a trick. A false flag. That's what we want everyone to believe. She's gone underground. Undercover to infiltrate the conspiracy. Learn their plans. I was just talking to her on the phone. I talk to her every day when she checks in to report."

"Oh?" he said.

"O'Dell will be back in that office soon and you'll see. But don't you say a word to anyone. Loose lips sink ships. It's a secret. But he who laughs last laughs the loudest." He laughed, shut the door and slid the chain back in place.

Terry was still shaking his head when he passed through the archway into the Main Office and Phyllis saw him. She picked his check out of the box and handed it to him.

"Have you seen Zwill? I was just talking to him. He worries me." He handed her back the empty envelope and slipped the check into his pocket.

"Is he still talking to Helen?"

"That's what he told me. On the phone."

"I'll call Doc Nessmith and tell him Zwill's meds need to be readjusted again."

"I'm not sure what's worse for Willy, being depressed or having Ollie Nessmith taking care of him. Although I've heard Ollie's an expert when it comes to giving the scoliosis exam to the girls every year."

"What's going on out here?" the principal said when he stepped from his office and heard them laughing. He was annoyed. "What's so funny?"

"Mr. Scapelli just made me laugh," she said.

"Always the funny man, Mr. Scapelli. Always at the center of things.."

"I am the guilty party."

"Of what exactly *are* you guilty, Mr. Scapelli? Are you hiding something you'd like to confess?"

"I suspect deep down we're all hiding something, Mr. Baltz. Me, you, even the president of the United States is guilty of something."

"I can't answer for Richard Nixon, but have a clear conscience and I have no problem sleeping at night. But while I have your attention, Mr. Scapelli. You've been storing some things in the closet in the Administrative Alcove… stage props, costumes? Well, it all has to be removed. The custodians are cleaning out Helen O'Dell's office and need the storage space. So if you want it, move it or lose it." He smoothed his mustache with his fingers and was prepared for an argument.

"Absolutely. I'll get on it immediately."

The response surprised him. "I don't mean that you have to do it now... today, Mr. Scapelli. After the February break and before Easter. Before the new AP comes onboard." He forced a smile.

"I'm one of the candidates and I am looking forward to my interview. Meanwhile, is there anything else you need me to do?"

"Just cleaning up your mess will be quite enough." He turned abruptly and went back into his office.

"You're applying for Helen's job?" she asked.

"Of course not. I'm not that crazy. It's just part of my new strategy, Phyl. Systematic unpredictability to keep him wondering."

"And how is that working?"

He leaned in to her. "Sometimes when we pass in the halls I pretend he isn't there and I walk right by. Other times when he's down one end and I'm on the other, I go out of my way to call to him, wave and say hello. He doesn't know what to expect. I'm telling you, he's a nervous wreck, Phyl. Have you noticed he's flinching like Willy Zwill whenever he sees me? The other day I was on the third floor headed to the bathroom and I called to him down the hall. When he saw me headed his way, he turned and ducked into the utility closet so we didn't have to interact."

"I'm surprised you've seen him at all. Mario hasn't seen much of him at all. Says Baltz is becoming a phantom."

"Maybe *The Phantom.* All I know is he sweats whenever he sees me coming."

"Men. All that wasted energy that could be used for good." She shook her head.

* * *

Zwill was seated behind his desk in the growing gloom. It had been a long, lonely week. He hated that Helen O'Dell was away. She seemed to be gone longer than usual. Sick? Jury duty? He knew it was something, but he didn't remember what. When he heard sounds in the alcove he went to listen. After he installed the peephole he'd picked up at the hardware he wouldn't have to open the door to see what was going on. He turned peered through the crack in time to see Phyllis coming out of Mario's office with him and pass through the alcove. Noah Lewis's office was dark and the door closed, the light in Helen O'Dell's office was on.

"She's back," he said, when he saw a silhouette moving around behind the curtain. He stepped into the alcove, pressed his ear against Helen's door and listened to the music coming from inside. "Welcome back, O'Dell!" He pushed the door open.

Someone was hunched under the desk tuning his radio. The unexpected intrusion made him jump and bang his head. "Owww!" he yelled.

"You're not O'Dell! What are you doing with all her stuff? And what have you done with O'Dell?" He was on the man in an instant and had him by the throat in a choke hold.

Slow Charley couldn't speak. He couldn't breathe either. They toppled over the desk locked together, scattering papers, knocking over O'Dell's lava lamp that shattered on the floor. The assistant custodian struggled to loosen the death grip around his neck, feeling desperately over the desktop for something that might save him before he passed out. His hand closed around what felt like a gun, and it was, the cork gun Helen O'Dell used for target practice during her downtime. He lifted it and fired point blank. The cork exploded with a pop and hit Zwill in the eye. Stars blazed around him and he momentarily loosened his grip enough to enable Charley to suck in a revitalizing gasp of air before felt his broom and brought the handle up swiftly into the assistant principal's stomach. That knocked the wind out of Zwill who crumpled to the floor. All the yelling brought secretaries and teachers running in from the Main Office.

"You're crazy! Cra-zy!" Charley gasped when he could talk. He felt the finger indentations on his throat.

"What... did... you... do... with... O'Dell?" Zwill managed between breaths.

"What's going on here?" Mr. Giovanni demanded pushing through the crowd clogging the doorway.

Charley held the broom handle with one hand like a long sword, keeping the fallen Zwill at bay; the other felt the damage to his throat. "I was just cleaning the office like Stash told me. He tried to kill me. He's a crazy man."

"Okay. Nothing to see here. Go back to what you were doing," Mr. Giovanni said. "Just a minor misunderstanding. Go back to what you were doing. Nothing to see." When the knot of curious onlookers slowly dissipated. he turned to the custodian. "Sorry, Charley. Mr. Zwill has been under a lot of stress recently. You go see the nurse and then finish what you were doing. I'll take care of Mr. Zwill. You okay, Willy?" He helped him to his feet.

"Shot. I was shot in the eye. And one of them tried to gut me with a sword. They were all here in her office, but I stopped them. How's O'Dell? Where's O'Dell? Is O'Dell okay?"

"She's fine, Willy, but I better get you to Doc Nessmith."

Immediately word of what happened, or what people said happened, spread throughout the building and by the end of the day there were detailed conflicting accounts. One had Willy Zwill attacked by a former disgruntled student he'd suspended back in 1967. Others told of the "Vandals," a local gang, who were thwarted by the AP in the process of looting dead Helen O'Dell's office. Zwill lost an eye in one account and was gut-stabbed in another. One of the more bizarre stories said nothing of gangs or stabbings, but had the assistant principal surprising a derelict who had wandered off the street and was about to treat vacant AP office as his private toilet. By the time the bell rang at the end of that very long day, everyone agreed on one thing; the February break that was a true harbinger of spring couldn't come soon enough.

79

As long as it had taken to arrive, February break flew by and school was back in session before Jesse realized he had been off. Blue Sunday was a blur. Monday the attendance was still down for students and teachers who were slowly drifting back from vacations in warmer climates or skiing the Colorado Rockies or the Alps.

In the faculty room Phay Schwartz showed off her sunburn and her new engagement ring to Sue, Terry and everyone close enough to hear. "Daddy's having the old ring made into a necklace for me. This diamond is much bigger." She flashed it in the light and rainbows bounced off the walls and reflected on the ceiling. "I got the worst case of sun poison and I spent the last two days flat on my back in bed with Maurice. Did I mention that he's a wealthy Wall Street financier?"

"Several times," Sue said.

"Maurice and I are planning a June wedding."

"You mean *another* June wedding," Terry clarified.

"Will you be wearing off-white for this one?" Mrs. Butrum asked.

"I trust we won't be expected to give you *another* gift," Terry said. "You can just keep the fondu set I gave you for the last one."

* * *

A beaming Noah Lewis arrived back from Poland late on Tuesday filled with stories of cheap real estate opportunities, his clothes smelling of sausages and cabbage.

"Poland? Really?" Red Farley asked. "That's a commie country, Noah."

"Exactly," he said between bites of kielbasa. "That's why, auh, everything is so cheap if you, auh, have money. All those abandoned buildings. Blocks of them. Entire, auh, neighborhoods. Mimi and I, auh, made a downpayment on a place in Krakow that we, auh, will pay off in five years. If you want my advice, Red, buy a place in Poland and live like a king when you retire."

"Do the commies allow kings in Poland?" Stanley Milnow asked.

* * *

"What'd you do on your vacation, Jesse?" Terry asked. He was standing in front of the mirror in the faculty bathroom.

"Marked papers," he said from the urinal. "That's what I always do. Mark tests, essays, creative writing assignments."

"That goes with being an English teacher." He leaned in for a closer look at his reflection. "In my next life I plan to come back as a Phys Ed teacher and just throw out balls–basketballs, volleyballs, dodge balls. Then sit back, relax and watch them kill one another. Or maybe I'll be an administrator and do nothing at all."

"Seriously, how do you manage? You never seem stressed. Nothing bothers you."

He laughed. "Well, the first thing I learned was to stop having things due before a vacation. That helped the most. And I hardly bleed on all those compositions."

"Bleed?"

"Red ink. Nobody ever reads all those pithy comments anyway. They just want to see the grade. They'll keep writing 'a lot' as one word no matter how many times you circle and correct it. And most will never understand the difference between 'their,' 'there' and 'they're.'"

"But you read them?"

"Their papers? Of course. Always. Mostly. But I'm no longer a fanatic. You have to make time for yourself or you'll burn out before you get tenure."

"*If* I get tenure."

"Did you see this?" Terry pointed to the tile next to the mirror.

Jesse flushed, zipped and went to the sink. He washed his hands and dried them on his handkerchief. He had learned to carry more than one. "'Break Baltz'?" he read. "Yeah, I've see it before, among other things, all over. On walls, in stalls, inside the fire alarm boxes."

"Yeah," Terry said, "but somebody has just taken it to another level. This one is rubber stamped."

* * *

Mr. Baltz was on a mission. He put his key in the elevator and when the door opened there were people he didn't know inside. "Who are you? And why are you in my elevator?"

"We're looking for the Library on the second floor–"

"Well, this is the express to the first floor." He shooed them out. "Take the stairway it's healthier. Library's one flight down. Good luck finding it." He inserted his key in the panel and shut the door. When it opened again on the first floor there were more people waiting. "Jesus Christ!" He pushed himself through them and dashed down the hall into the Main Office without slowing and turned into the Administrative Alcove. "Wake up, Mario!" he yelled and barged into the AP's office, slamming the door against the wall.

He was slouched in his seat behind his desk, his face hidden by the book *Love Story* propped up in front of him. He jumped awake, the hardcover dropped to the floor and he looked into the irate scowl of the principal. "I wasn't sleeping. I was reading."

"She dies at the end! Now you don't have to read it." He stuck the end of a Lucky Strike into his mouth and lit it. "While you're dreaming your life away, Mario, I was just upstairs on the third floor, in the toilet. The writing is everywhere. In the stalls, on the walls. Even inside the fire alarm boxes! And now that bastards aren't just writing it, they're using a rubber stamp. 'Break Baltz' was stamped everywhere in green ink! I even found it on memos posted on the bulletin board outside the Main Office for everyone to see! It's growing like a cancer. So there will be no sleeping, and certainly no time for reading either."

"With O'Dell gone and Zwill crazier than bat shit, I've been early *and* late man for a month. I'm exhausted. I can't do much more."

"The building is getting out of control. Where is my help? Where did my devoted staff go, Mario??"

"You do know O'Dell's dead, right?" he said. "Zwill may not think so, but he's just a few steps short of a straitjacket. Noah Lewis got back from Poland yesterday, but he called in to say he starts jury duty for a week." He hesitated.

"With all due respect, you haven't been around much to help. So that leaves just me."

"Just because you don't see me doesn't mean I'm not here, Mario." he said cryptically. "Strangers are wandering the halls and hijacking the elevator."

"It's the people interviewing for O'Dell's spot. Flackett's been parading them around the building. I don't know anything about the elevator."

Baltz looked through the window. "I saw Zwill wandering around outside before by the monuments. What the hell is that idiot doing there?"

"He's out there all the time he isn't hiding in his office. He told me he goes out every day to visit O'Dell. Said she's the only one he can talk to, the only one who understands him and that she calms him down. There's something seriously wrong with him, Boss."

"You think? There's something seriously wrong with everybody, Mario. That's why they're all here."

"Nessmith has him on medication, but it hasn't helped. He's really depressed. He showed me a bunch of death poems he's carrying around, by Edgar Allen and Emily Dinkins. He almost killed Slow Charley. Said he had a flashback and thought he was back in the camp. When we got back on Monday he was snooping around the backstage area looking through a box of props and handcuffed himself to a doorknob. Stash had to cut him loose because Slow Charley wouldn't go near him after the fight. And then when Willy was free, he didn't say a word about what he'd done. Just locked himself inside his office. I'm worried he's going to blow and maybe take one of us with him."

"*I'm* stressed! We're *all* stressed! It's a stressful job." He inhaled deeply on his cigarette. "When does Noah Lewis get back from jury duty?"

"Not until next week at least, if then. Phyllis said he called again during lunch and told her he was selected as the foreman on a murder case–the one in *Newsday* where the guy wanted his wood chipper back from his next door neighbor who borrowed it. They got into a fight and the owner of the chipper ended up in the chipper and all over the neighborhood. Noah gave her all the details. He said the guy's as guilty as sin, but that they still have to go through the motions of a trial before they convict him." He looked at his boss, who was slumped in the chair. "Does it really matter if Noah's here or not? So until O'Dell is replaced it's just me."

"Everybody knows the job is going to Adornau's daughter or niece or girlfriend. But that bastard Flackett is dragging his feet as long as he can to make me sweat." He couldn't find an ashtray so he put out his cigarette in the silver bowl, the AP's award for twenty-five years of service in the District. "Leadership, Mario, is a heavy load to bear, and it takes a heavy toll. Do what I tell you and it just may pay off in the not-too-distant future. I'm not planning to be here forever, Mario, and I am grooming you for greater things. Maybe you'd have more time if you cut back on lunch. A little less pasta wouldn't hurt." He patted his stomach. "And if you gave up your DJ job on the weekends–maybe you wouldn't be so tired. Just until we get back to full strength." He picked a hair from his AP's shoulder and examined it. "Perhaps if you spent a little more time sleeping at home on your own bed, Phyllis would get more work done too."

"Fuck!" he said when Baltz was gone. He dumped the dead Lucky from his bowl into the wastebasket and polished the dark spot with his handkerchief before placing it back on the desk. He pulled the toothpick he had been carrying since lunch from his pocket and stuck it between his teeth and let it settle at the corner of his mouth. He felt his stomach, looked at his reflection in the window. He sucked in his gut, reached over and tried to touch his toes a couple of times. "Too much pasta, my ass," he said. "I can still touch my toes–almost."

"Oh, I'd recognize that face anywhere," Phyllis quipped from the alcove when she saw him bent over and he jumped up quickly. "I just saw Baltz leave."

"Do I look fatter to you, Phyl?"

"Let me feel." She put her arms around him and saw the book on the floor. "You finished *Love Story?*"

"I don't have to now. Baltz told me she dies at the end." He retrieved it, moved some things around to make room in his desk drawer and dropped it in.

"What's all that stuff?" she asked before he slid the drawer closed.

"Nothing. Something I found. A rubber stamp pad." He changed the subject. "I think I just got another *promotion,*" he said sarcastically. "Something new has popped up, and Baltz wants me on top of it."

She moved her hand down from his belt. "No question about it, Mario. You do feel a little chubby. But now's not the time to see what it is. Polakas called. The toilets in the girls' locker room are overflowing again."

"The overflowing toilets in the girls' lockers are more regular than the girls!" He looked at her. "I'm afraid I have some bad news, Phyl. Baltz wants me to put in more time, so we may have less time together on the weekends–just until things here settle down a bit–"

"Not a problem," she interrupted. "I made plans this weekend."

"–but the good news is–" He stopped. "You made plans? What plans? I thought we had plans."

"Phay Schwartz's bachelorette party with the girls. So it works out for everybody." She turned to leave. "Oh, before I forget. Somebody from the ACLU keeps calling and asking for Virgil Loomis. He says it has something to do with the wrestling team. I told Baltz, but he told me to tell you to handle it."

"Shit," he said. "I thought *we* had plans–"

The first week back after the February break ended on a positive note. There weren't any emergencies worse than the plumbing problem in the girls' locker, nothing that involved the superintendent or the newspapers, the police, or dead bodies. The days were noticeably getting longer, which was another good thing. Even better, the number of remaining school days was shorter. Mr. Baltz looked at his desk calendar where seventy-seven was written in red. He counted. Only four and a half weeks until Easter and West Palm Beach. Interviews for O'Dell's slot, though meaningless, were ongoing, and as much as he hated the idea of having one of Lalo Adornau's women– daughter, niece, girlfriend, whatever–on his staff, he needed somebody there. Lewis and Zwill were useless when it came to teacher observations, and if Mario didn't get help fast, he'd have to do some. The principal of a high school had more important ways to spend his time than sitting in boring classes doodling on a legal pad seemingly writing comments, pretending to pay attention to lessons he didn't understand or care about.

Absently he flipped open the Zippo lighter with a snap of his fingers. It had belonged to a shop student he caught sneaking a smoke in the courtyard. He ambushed the surprised boy in the breezeway. "Smoking is a filthy habit and bad for your health. Put out that cigarette immediately and give me that lighter. And get back to your class before I suspend you!"

He pulled a Lucky from the open pack on his desk, put the flame from the Zippo to the end of it and inhaled deeply, drawing in lighter fluid fumes with the smoke. He sat back savoring the moment, snapping the lighter open and closed between his fingers and thumb several times with a satisfying click. It was a skill he had acquired through years of repetition. "Muscle memory," he said and stared down at the closed leather-bound *Memoirs of a Secondary Schoolmaster* on his desk blotter. The content wasn't exactly what he'd had in mind when he considered writing about his career as a high school principal, but still he had managed to fill about a third of the pages since the new year. He launched a series of smoke rings before he opened the cover and leafed through the contents. Tracing his finger down each page, he paused now and then to reread an entry.

The intercom on his desk buzzed. "Willy Zwill's pacing around out here," Phyllis said. "He's been waiting to see you for about a week." She muffled the mouthpiece with her hand and whispered into the phone. "And he looks very *fragile,* so be kind. I think he's been sleeping in his clothes."

"Okay, Phyllis," he sighed and he pressed the buzzer on his desk.

The door opened and the Zwill tentatively stepped inside. He saw the backlit figure behind the open book, with bright light radiating shafts through the halo of smoke around his head and actually thought for a brief moment that he had stumbled into Judgment Day. He shielded his surprised eyes and hung back blinking and twitching.

Baltz hadn't seen much of his assistant principal since Helen O'Dell's funeral and he was genuinely shocked at how terrible he looked. There were deep circles under his eyes and his twitching was worse than ever. "Come in, Willy," he said forcing a smile. He stubbed out the cigarette and closed the book. "Miss Lind said you wanted to see me? You're looking–" He searched for a good word, but gave it up. "You look like you've lost a few pounds. Have you been eating, Willy?"

"No appetite."

"Have you been sleeping?"

"Not much at home. Insomnia." His eyes were ratty. "But I try to catch a few winks in my office whenever I can."

"Something bothering you, Willy?"

"It's O'Dell. I just can't wrap my head around it."

"Of course. I understand. It's only been a couple of weeks, Willy. We all miss her and we're all still shocked by her sudden loss. But like they say in that song, 'Something something something something… life goes on.' And you have to get on with your life. You have to man up, Willy."

There were tears in the AP's eyes and his lower lip quivered. "I'm trying. Really I am." He twitched. "I know I've been through a lot worse. But this has me thrown. There are so many unanswered questions, conflicting stories and I'm trying to make sense of it all."

"Let it go, Willy, and let O'Dell rest in peace."

"I'd like to, but the voices won't let me. I stop by to see her every day."

"Voices? What voices?"

"The ones I sometimes hear," he said.

"You're hearing voices now?"

"No, not now. I don't always hear them, and I don't know what they are saying, but it's voices all right, trying to tell me something."

"Those voices… they aren't telling you to save France, are they, Willy?" The AP didn't catch his Joan of Arc reference. "Mario tells me Ollie Nessmith changed your meds and prescribed some new antidepressants. Are you taking your medication?"

He looked the principal directly in the eye. "It has nothing to do with taking medication or not taking it. It's not a delusion. I hear voices. And I'm sure it's O'Dell. She's been trying to communicate, trying to tell me that something's very rotten here in Rosencrantz and Guildenstern."

Baltz lit another cigarette. "You need to get some sleep, Willy. You're exhausted, on the verge of a relapse, and neither of us wants that to happen. Take a few days off and then come back refreshed. It'll be Easter soon and we'll be off for a week."

"I can't," he said. "I *need* to be here, close to O'Dell. She will never be able to rest in peace until"–he twitched–"I solve her murder. I gave her my solemn pledge to find the truth and free her soul."

"Don't be crazy, Willy," said Baltz and regretted his choice of words. "You're letting your imagination get the best of you. There are no voices and definitely no murder. Helen O'Dell was overweight and out of shape. She died from a heart attack." He stood up and walked across the office. When he raised his arm to put it around Mr. Zwill's shoulder, the AP cowered involuntarily. "Willy, talk to Ollie. Go see him. Do it for me. Have him adjust your medication, before they carry you out of here too, in a straitjacket. I don't want to lose you, Willy. I can't afford to lose another one of my APs." He led him gently to the door. "If you won't take time off, use this weekend to clear your head. Ask Ollie for some sleeping pills and after a few good nights of sleep things will look better, I promise. But please, no more talk about hearing voices or murder. Losing O'Dell the way we did is unsettling enough for everybody, the students and the staff. Crazy talk will only make matters worse." He opened the door and walked him into the Main Office. "Go see the doc and then go home early and get a head start on the weekend." He watched him leave and turned to his secretary. "Make sure Willy goes home after he sees Nessmith, Phyllis. I'll be out doing some observations until after lunch."

"Before or after I finish this other work you want done today? And would you like me to drive him home or just follow him there?"

"That won't be necessary. But you can tell Mario to look in on him tonight on *his* way home."

* * *

After leaving his Observatory he returned to his office through the Administrative Alcove. All of the AP doors were closed. "Hold all my calls, Phyllis," he said when he passed her. "I'll be busy writing up my observations."

Inside he pressed flat a blank page in his book with one arm, and from his jacket pocket he removed the slips of paper containing his notes. He sorted and arranged them in order in a neat pile.

"Project X—February 25, 1972," he wrote. "Phase One was a qualified success. I have learned things about people in this building I never anticipated. However, there are also several unexpected issues I didn't expect. Time is the first. The Observatory demands more time than I am able to devote and it already occupies most of my working hours and that has taken a toll. The unexpected and sudden loss of Helen O'Dell is another. The suspicious circumstances of her death have Willy Zwill babbling about murder. He has always been marginal and on the ledge, so to speak, but now he is hearing voices and talking to the dead. If nothing else his behavior is fueling unrest in an already restless faculty. From the beginning the police had questions about the circumstances. Damn Mario Giovanni and his harebrained insurance scam. Too many people are involved and one careless remark could easily reopen an investigation into the matter. It would be a short leap from mousse to frozen mouse to insurance fraud. They always follow the money and that would lead them right to Mario, and for all his talk of loyalty, he'd roll over in a second and escort them right up to my office. It is imperative that I make it to the end of the school year without another incident.

"With the stall doors back up it is impractical for me to continue running into the toilet from the Observatory to inspect the walls. Besides the risk of detection, I am not as young as I used to be and all that running back and forth is hard on my legs. The writing, since the stall doors were replaced, has actually increased and it appears that it is no longer the work of just one individual. The red marker recall was another failure. Now the comments are in different colors and different handwritings. And most recently someone started using a rubber stamp. Most of the offenses seem to take place when I am not in the Observatory, which suggests that the culprits may be aware of my schedule. I have formulated plans that will allow me constant surveillance–I call it Phase II. I just need to get the stall doors removed again."

He picked up the cigarette that was burning down in the ashtray, took two more puffs and crushed it out in the shrunken head.

"On a positive note, the dossiers I am compiling are filled with valuable information about many male members of the faculty and it occurs to me that my job would be considerably easier if similar observation posts were installed throughout the building, including the women's faculty toilet– not for any prurient interest, but for the intelligence it would reveal. It is unfortunate that Helen O'Dell is dead, because she would have been the natural choice to man such a station. At any rate, depending on who replaces her as AP, it is something to consider for Phase III."

He blotted the last part of the entry so it wouldn't smudge and closed the book. He twisted the cap back on his pen, replaced everything in the desk drawer and locked it. He picked up the phone and pressed the two digits that connected him to the Custodian's Office. "Stash," he said, "I have a job for you, setting up electronic equipment upstairs in that closet."

"It's easy enough."

"Let me talk to Dexter and if you pick up everything before the end of the day, do you think you could get it done over the weekend? It's a rush job, I know, and it's going to involve some overtime. I'll come by your office later and we can discuss details." He waited for the dial tone and called AV.

"I'm a very busy man–"

"I know just how busy you are," he cut him off midsentence.

"–and that's why I am unable to take your phone call at this time." It was a recording.

"Fuck!"

* * *

"Mr. Dexter?" a quiet voice called from the door.

"I'm a very busy man," he responded automatically from somewhere inside. "And the office is closed for inventory."

There was a brief silence. "Mr. Dexter?"

Something in the voice lifted him from his chair and led him to the half-opened Dutch door. A pretty young girl with blond hair stood there smiling. Her Paul Newman blue eyes shot through him like the fusillade of bullets that stopped Butch Cassidy and Sundance in the freeze frame. He almost gasped at her blinding beauty. "Yes? How can I help you?" He pushed his thinning hair back with his hand.

"Ms Lind in the Main Office said I should see you about the AV Squad." She tilted her head and her hair moved in waves back behind her shoulders and shimmered in the overhead light. "I'm new here. From Middle Valley High School in Ohio." She extended her hand and he took it automatically. "Patti-Ann Wood. We moved because my father is an engineer at Grumman. He's building the F-14 Tomcats. That's a fighter jet," she said.

He was still holding her hand when he released the catch on the door and opened the lower section. He led her into his office. "Come in. Please sit down." He offered her a place on the couch next to his desk.

"I seem to be following in his footsteps because I'm a nut when it comes to electronics and motors. I'm planning to go to college and become an engineer too. I have a passion for mechanical things. Small battery-powered motors. I've always been good with my hands. That's why I want to be on the AV Squad."

"Believe it or not, Patti-Ann, that's how I got my job here, because of electricity. And the AV Department is one of the most important parts of this school. The AV Squad is efficient, sharp and well disciplined. Each member is handpicked and willing to follow orders. How do you think you would do when it comes to taking direction?"

Her blue eyes opened wide and sincere. "Back in Middle Valley I received the 'Eager to Please Award' for my work in the Service Club. And the Junior class voted me 'Girl Most Likely to Go All the Way.'"

He opened the desk drawer and revealed an assortment of snacks. "Cookie? Something to drink? Coke? The cooler is full."

"Oh, no thank you. I have lunch next period."

He removed a red thermos and two glasses. "Some hand-squeezed orange juice? I squeeze it myself." He shook it, poured two frothy drinks and added a cherry to each from a jar of maraschinos. He handed her one before she could refuse. "Have you had much experience–I mean working with electricity?" He put down his drink and removed the coupled plugs and wire hanging on the wall. "You're familiar with these?" He slipped them apart and then slid them back together, in and out rhythmically. He handed them to her.

"Sure. It's a two-pole three-wire 125 volt 20 amp male and female plug in a black and white nylon case, double-wall construction, a transparent terminal cover with clear window and teardrop wiring pockets." She looked closely at the separated parts. "And both sides are pretty much fried." And she examined the wire attached to each end. "That insulation looks like it was cut and removed to expose the wire. Anyone plugging or unplugging it would get a big surprise–125 volts and 20 amps. Which could be fatal flowing across their heart."

He looked over her shoulder and the expression on his face changed.

"Mr. Dexter," Mr. Baltz said. He had slipped quietly into the office. His chin was tucked into his neck.

Dexter jumped up from his seat, grabbed the plug from her hands and crammed it into his desk drawer. "I didn't hear you come in."

"Obviously. Your phone message said you were busy with inventory. I hope I'm not interrupting your busy work."

"Were you standing there long?" He pointed to the couch. "Patti-Ann Wood," he said formally, "this is Principal Baltz. Patti-Ann is a new transfer student to R and G, very interested in joining the AV Squad," he fumbled. "Phyllis sent her up. Her father is a Grumman engineer." She smiled. "Well, then," Mr. Dexter said recovering slightly, "I'd like to see you later, Patti-Ann. If you get a pass you can come back during lunch or Study Hall and we can go over the schedule of your periods. And you can meet some of the other squad members. Let me validate your pass so you don't get in trouble." He slid the yellow slip into the time clock and it registered the day, date and time with a hostile snap–along with the AV/CM insignia.

"Thank you so much, Mr. Dexter." She took the pass and she tossed her head back. Her hair tumbled over face and covered one eye in a Veronica Lake effect. She smiled, brushed it aside with her other hand and left.

"Lovely girl. Very, very lovely," he said. "And an incredible knowledge of electronics. She wants to be an engineer like her father. Patti-Ann Wood." He prattled on. "It's just a shame there aren't more opportunities for girls in the field. In fact, it would be a great idea to start a program here–"

"Cut the shit, Harry. At the moment I don't care if Patti-Ann would or wouldn't." He looked around the equipment room. "I need some things." He walked to the shelves. "A tape recorder with a microphone, one that turns on whenever someone speaks, and some blank tapes."

"I have a reel-to-reel that records in stereo with two microphones. Great quality. Or one of the new cassette recorders. The quality isn't as good and it only records monaural, but it's smaller and much more convenient and you don't have to worry about threading a tape through the recording heads. The tape comes in a little plastic case you just pop into the machine. I prefer the reel-to-reel for the sound quality, but it all depends on what you are planning to record–"

"Just give me a tape recorder, Harry. I'm not interested in the lesson. Now get me that stuff."

Dexter handed Baltz a requisition form. "If you could fill out the paperwork for my records–how long you'll need it, where it will be stored and approximately when it will be returned–"

The expression on Mr. Baltz's face cut him short. "I want that stuff now and I don't want any bullshit. So put it on a cart and put it aside for Stash Polakas to pick up this afternoon." He turned to leave and saw a bunch of items covered in blue plastic. "What's all that?"

"Black and white Ampex CC-452 studio video cameras on wheeled tripods." He pulled the plastic off and rolled one over. "They're a little dusty because we haven't used them since we made the Parent's Night video."

He did some quick calculating. "Is it hard to work?"

"The AV Squad is fully trained in the proper care and the use of such a complex–"

"Show me!" he demanded.

"Now? The course takes two weeks–"

"What's this for?"

"The on/off switch." He switched it and nothing happened. "It has to be plugged in to a power supply and there are cables that connect the camera to the video recorder." He pointed. "That's the Ampex-7000 one-inch reel-to-reel recorder on the cart. But if you want to see what you're recording, you need a TV monitor."

"Show me!"

"It's highly technical. Very sophisticated. It requires an expert–"

"Dexter, if you don't shut up I'm going to wrap that electric cable around your neck and strangle you. Now plug the fucking thing in and show me! Fire up what has to be fired up, connect whatever needs to be connected and show me how to use it!"

He bit his fingernail. "I don't usually handle the electricity part. Usually one of the Squad... Could you do it? Plug it into the wall over there?"

Reluctantly the principal took the plug and stuck it into the socket and the viewfinder in the camera came to life. "And what's this?" He pointed to a wired box.

"A remote switch, I think–"

"Remote control? I need this too. Now show me everything... how to set up and how to film."

"Tape," he corrected. "It's not film, it's tape, like audio tape only it's video."

In minutes the recorder was threaded and humming. The TV monitor came to life and the picture in the camera view finder popped up on the TV the screen. Twenty minutes after that, by the time the bell rang to end the period, Baltz knew as much about video recording as Dexter.

"You can add this to the cassette recorder. I'm taking it all," he said. "Have everything here ready for Polakas when he comes to pick it up. And anything else you think I might need."

* * *

Stash Polakas came down the darkened hall toward the Administrative Alcove pushing a loaded AV cart. The keys on his belt jingled like spurs and he did a little twist step that changed the tempo. "Come on, Charley. Hurry up. Get that electric drill you left in the storage closet," he called into the darkness behind him, "and let's get this done so we can go home."

Charley, slightly less decorated with free-hanging objects, followed at a slightly different pitch, pushing a second cart with a TV monitor and carrying his toolbox. With every step they played a syncopated metallic composition, consciously changing their rhythm to improvise the tune. Charley did a little skip step and Stash wiggled his hips. They entered the alcove. The head custodian picked through the keys from his heavy key ring. "Damn it!" he said. "I can't find my number three. Drop all that shit and check your ring. If you don't have a number three, I'll have to go all the way back downstairs to get one."

Charley dropped the tools and fingered the keys until he found the right one on the ring. "Here it is. Number three." He smiled with satisfaction and held up the key.

The custodian took it, opened the door and handed back the key ring. When he hit the light switch on the wall, nothing happened. He jiggled it a couple of times, but there was still nothing. "You replaced the bulb, right?" Charley nodded. "Then the circuit breaker must be off. With all the shit they have in here I can't find anything." He felt around in the dark for the drill and walked into a painted scenery flat. "Damn it!" he complained. "I'll go trip the breaker." He looked at Charley's cart. "Where's the BX cable? Did you take the BX cable?"

"I thought you did."

"How we going to run electric cable without cable, Charley?" He lit his pipe. "I'll get the cable. What else did you forget for me to pick up while I'm there?" He looked at Charley, who was still playing with his keys. "You listening to me, Charley? You understand what I just said?"

"I know. I know." He nodded, looking into the dark closet. "You get the cable and I'll find the drill."

"I don't want you to hurt yourself or I'll have to do *all* the work upstairs. So just wait until the lights go on and I'll be back as soon as I can."

When Stash was gone, Charley stepped inside the dark closet. "I don't need light." He felt around for the drill. When he moved one of the cartons on the overhead shelf it started an avalanche. He lunged to stop it, but his weight detached the shelf. It set into motion a chain reaction of cartons, shelves and stage flats that knocked him into the door slamming it shut. When the dust settled he was under everything sealed inside the closet in total darkness.

In his office Willy Zwill snorted and opened his eyes. He had been dreaming when a noise outside wrenched him from sleep. In his dream, Helen O'Dell was very much alive, clawing frantically at the inside of her coffin. "Willy, help me!" she pleaded, "Somebody... somebody please help me!" He came fully awake, dazed and confused, sweating, his heart was racing. At first he didn't know where he was, until gradually he recognized his office. It was dark and the light coming from the window was wintry dim. He couldn't tell if that was because of the time, the dreary weather or the mesh covering the glass. He looked blearily at his watch and saw that it was nearly five p.m. Despite what Baltz told him about leaving early to get a head start on the weekend, he had stayed and fallen asleep at his desk and he had slept through the dismissal bell again. His body was stiff. He considered changing out of his shorts into street clothes before heading home, but he knew he'd end up sitting in rush hour traffic. He rocked in his chair

"Hem me–"

He heard the muffled sound coming from somewhere behind him and stopped rocking. At first he thought it was the hum of the exhaust fan, but it wasn't turning. "What?"

"Hemmm meeee!"

Maybe the voice was coming from the CB radio that he kept in the closet for emergency communications when the grid went down. Inside the closet the radio indicator light was off.

"Who is it?" he called. He walked the perimeter of the room, trying to isolate the sound. Slowly he opened the office door. "Somebody there?" he asked,. The alcove was empty and dark. He shut the door and began to twitch.

"Hemmmmm meeeeee!" It was the sound of distress, of someone in pain.

"What are you saying?" he asked. "I can't understand you. What do you want?" He felt along the wall with his hands and pressed his ear against the sheet metal. "O'Dell?"

"Help me, please!" the voice said distinctly through the wall.

He jumped back and then he cupped his hands and yelled, "Is that you? Are you there?"

"Yes. Yes, it's me. I'm in here."

"What do you want from me? What can I do?"

"Help me! Please! I'm trapped under all of this weight–"

"Then you're alive?"

"Yes, alive. But I'm stuck. I've fallen and I can't get out!"

"I knew you weren't dead," he said with excitement. "I told them you weren't dead." He yelled to the walls and the sound echoed back metallically. "I'm coming to get you, O'Dell. But I have to find a shovel. Don't worry, I'll get you out of there."

"I can't breathe. I'm suffocating."

"Hold on. I'm coming. I'll dig you out of there." He threw open his door and ran out of the office and down the dark hall. In minutes he was by the monument at the side of the building on his hands and knees frantically scraping at the frozen ground with the broken snow shovel he found outside the empty Custodian's Office.

He was so intent on his mission to save Helen O'Dell that he didn't notice when the two police cars arrived, although their sirens were blaring and their lights blinking. The old woman who lived across from the school had called them. She called the police regularly to report trespassing students. And she was the same woman who called in false alarms to watch the students parade out of the building. This time she reported a dark figure crouched in the shadows of the monument. "He's armed and possibly naked, in the bushes engaging in some lewd behavior."

"Drop the weapon," Sgt. Sadowski repeated over the speaker from the warmth of his car, "and step away from the hole."

Two other officers approached with their guns drawn.

"I'm coming, O'Dell. I'll get you out of there."

"Give it up. We've got you surrounded! Drop the shovel or we'll shoot!"

U.S. Army Cpl. Willy Zwill turned and watched as the two Japanese soldiers closed in on him. "Not this time, you little yellow bastards!" he yelled. "You're not going to get me this time!" He rose to his feet and charged forward with his snow shovel raised to strike.

"Stop resisting! Stop resisting! Drop the weapon! Stop or we'll shoot!"

But in the end they didn't shoot, though it took all three of them, including Sgt. Sadowski who had to leave his car, several minutes to subdue the ranting lunatic. Together they rolled on the frozen ground. Willy Zwill, determined to avoid capture, gave as well as he got. The police, were just as determined to bring to justice the would-be grave robber, or child molester dressed in nothing but a Hawaiian shirt and tropical shorts lurking in the freezing February darkness. Huffing, puffing and bruised, they eventually snapped on the handcuffs and dropped the pervert into the back of the squad car.

"Let me go, you yellow bastards! She's alive, I tell you. She's alive! They thought they murdered her, but she's alive. I have to dig her up! Get her out before she suffocates!" He shouted until both cars drove off into the gathering gloom and the curious onlookers, attracted by the lights and the commotion, went back inside their houses.

Mr. Baltz got two phone calls late Friday night, from Stash Polakas informing him that the job was done, and an hour later from the police. After the second he immediately called Mario Giovanni, who reluctantly dragged himself out of bed, judging by the muffled exchanges Baltz heard in the background, and went to the Second Police Precinct where he spent the rest of the night waiting. Saturday morning Willy Zwill was moved to the Nassau County Jail pending a Monday appearance before a judge, who remanded him to South Oaks Mental Hospital that afternoon for evaluation.

Monday before Homeroom the faculty room buzzed with stories that grew throughout the day like a snowball rolling downhill, contradicting details about what had happened in the bushes by the War Memorial Friday night.

"The man had a total breakdown and I saw it coming," Mrs. Butrum clucked. "I doubt if he's ever coming back."

"I heard he was naked in the freezing cold, exposing himself to the neighborhood," Betty Gabel, the first-year guidance counselor said to John Hiller, who was dunking his frozen roll in coffee and peeking down the front of her blouse.

"Creepy," he said. "But with that temperature Friday night, I'm sure wasn't a big thing."

"He was digging up poor Helen O'Dell for God knows what perversity he had in mind, I just don't know."

"I never liked the way he looked at me," Phay Schwartz said. "Always flirting. He made me feel very uncomfortable the way he ogled me. Always winking."

"I never liked the way he looked at me," Toby Wong said, looking up from his *Times*. "And he didn't like me very much either. I can't prove it, but I always suspected he was the one keying my Datsun Z."

"One of the neighbors saw it all and she said he attacked the police with a bayonet screaming 'Banzai!'"

"He's lucky they didn't shoot him."

"They're falling fast by the wayside," Terry announced in the Third Floor Faculty Room Tuesday afternoon. "Two down and just two more to go. Three if you count Baltz."

"I suppose that means they'll be interviewing for two APs now," Red Farley said.

"Hey, Stan, you're always looking for ways to make extra money," Terry said. "I think I might have an idea you might want to consider investing in."

"Yeah? What?"

"T-shirts. I threw this one together last night as a prototype." He opened his jacket. "I SURVIVED THE ROSENCRANTZ AND GUILDENSTERN MEMORIAL HIGH SCHOOL 1971-72 SCHOOL YEAR!" was printed in red. "The only expense would be the shirts in assorted sizes. For two hundred bucks you can become a silent partner and double your investment at least. Of course the actual shirts would be semiprofessionally silk-screened by Mary Jane Orlando in the Art Department. She already did sketches of Baltz and the four APs on the front like Mount Rushmore, with O'Dell and Zwill crossed out. What do you think, Stan?"

"That's pretty cold, Terry. But I like it. I'm in for a hundred."

"There's a sucker born every minute," Red said. "You're an insensitive asshole, Scapelli! And if you believe him you're an even bigger asshole, Stan. He's trying to suck you in again. I can understand O'Dell on the shirt. She's dead. But Zwill's not dead, he's just crazy."

"I'm positive he's not coming back," Mrs. Butrum reiterated.

"If you don't invest you're going to kick yourself when everybody on the faculty is wearing them, Stan," Terry said. "This one is a moneymaker."

* * *

"Mr, Giovanni doesn't look very happy now he has to do all the observations," Sue said when they saw him down the hall with his clipboard. "I predict a bunch of 'Needs improvements' on the evaluations."

"Thanks a lot for that. Like I don't have enough to worry about already," Jesse said.

"Here's something that might help you with observations, but you have to get your classes to work together," Terry said. "In September I tell them that whenever an adult walks into the room to jump to their feet without hesitation and sing the 'Good Morning Song.'"

"I don't know that one."

"No matter who comes through the door, Baltz, Flackett, anybody, they are to jump up together no matter what lesson is going on and sing loudly and in unison: 'Good morning. Good morning. A new day is dawning. Up Father! Up Mother! Up Sister! Up Brother! Good morning. Good morning. Good morning to you.'"

"But why?"

"Besides surprising whoever walks in, it unifies the class against the intruder. It creates a community and gives them power. They aren't sure at first, but after a few times they love it. And after the first week they jump up and sing every time my door opens and an adult comes in." He sipped from the cup he was carrying. "The next thing involves observations. I tell them not to worry if someone comes in to observe us and go on as usual. And this is the best part. When I ask a question the kids who *know* the answer are to raise their right hand. The ones who *don't know* their left hand."

"I don't understand."

"Every question every hand in the room goes up. They all have their hands raised. Total class participation. Of course, I tell them, I'll only call on those right-handed kids."

"He gave me the same advice my first year," Sue said, "and it does work. Unless you get observed in a Track III class where they don't know their left from their right."

The bell rang. "Let the observations begin, Mario," Terry called to the glum assistant principal as they passed him.

* * *

Monday morning the beleaguered assistant principal knew how things would play out. Baltz wouldn't expect him to do *more with less*, he'd expect him to do it *all* with *less than nothing*. He got him through Monday by cutting back on his other duties and pacing the teacher observations. He cut the time he spent in each classroom by half, skipped lunch and by the end of the day he completed ten observations, a one-day personal best. Tuesday he was beyond tired and already running behind by the end of third period and he knew the number would be lower. Baltz was nowhere to be found. Neither was Noah Lewis, who was in the final stages of preretirement and at best managed only two or three observations in several years. And he handpicked those–Home Ec, where he could sample the cooking, and Shop, where he brought personal items he needed repaired.

He had just spent half fourth period in a French class where he briefly nodded out during irregular verbs and now he was headed to watch Herb Lupus blow things up in chemistry. At least he wouldn't fall asleep there, and maybe with a little luck Herb might blow out the windows again and set the lab on fire. A fire drill would break up the day. There were some positive things about doing observations–intimidation. The teachers called him him Mini Mussolini behind his back, intending it as an insult, but he reveled in it. He liked the power he exerted, especially over the new teachers, just walking down the corridor with his clipboard visible. He got a great deal of satisfaction seeing their panicked expressions when he slipped into a classroom unannounced and went unnoticed until the teacher looked up and saw him seated in the back of the classroom and panicked. He loved it when saw fear in veterans, including the grizzled and burned-out old-timers who became unnerved when he spent most of the observation feverishly jotting things down on his clipboard. It didn't matter that he was making a shopping list or trying to remember the names of the fifty states or the U.S. presidents. As long as he was writing, it gave them something to think about, to worry about. The most difficult aspect of teacher observations was trying to remember a lesson to reference and find fault with when he wrote it up later. The creative part was writing a critical evaluation without saying anything for which he might be held accountable.

In the Third Floor Faculty Men's Room after a pee and a superficial inspection of the stalls he checked his fly, stopped at the mirror and flashed a Bogart. He turned to leave when he heard something that stopped him. He pressed his ear to the wall. A whirring–like running water or leaking pipes? An electric motor? Electricity and water didn't work well together. He didn't have time now, but he'd tell Stash and have him check it out.

For his afternoon observations he decided to paralyze a few first-year teachers. It would be less demanding and it was always fun to watch new teachers freeze like deer caught in the headlights. He narrowed his victims to English or Spanish, between Jesse Tietjen he knew would turn red and sweat the entire period, or Layla Bimenyenz, who had a nice ass and was better looking than Tietjen. He opted for the latter and rechecked his Master Room Schedule.

He trotted down the steps to the second floor and passed the storage room someone had turned into a STO(P)RAGE ROOM with a red marker. That was actually fitting because the airless and windowless room had been an In-School Suspension holding cell for hardcore, antisocial students when the Lesson Stretcher didn't work. Solitary confinement. But after numerous complaints by parents whose kids developed sallow complexions from the lack of sunlight, ISS was moved to a small room on the first floor. Now the STO(P)RAGE ROOM was a place where the custodians kept their cleaning supplies, hid *Playboy* centerfolds and napped. He stopped when he saw the flickering light leaking from under the door and illuminating the dark hallway. Muffled sounds came from inside. He sniffed and smelled smoke. Something was burning. He pulled the door open.

"Shut the door! Shut the door!"

"Fweep! Fweep! Fweep!" The sound was liquid drops of fire like tiny tracer bullets dripping into a water bucket in the slop sink. Each molten droplet lit up the room for an instant until the water below extinguished the fire. "Fweep! Fweep!"

"What the hell is going on here?" He felt along the wall for the light switch.

"Oh, hey, Mr. G."

"Loomis? What are you doing in here!"

Virgil's eye was pressed to the viewfinder of a Kodak Super 8 camera on a tripod aimed at a flaming plastic dry cleaner bag. It had been wound up and knotted in several places along the plastic. The "rope" hung from a wire hanger attached to one of the overhead light fixtures directly above the metal bucket of water in the sink. A small flame slowly climbed up the plastic from knot to knot and burning droplets dripped with an eerie fweeping sound into the water below, collecting into an island of smoldering dark plastic.

"What the hell, Loomis! Do you want to burn down the school!"

"I got this new Super 8 for my birthday and I'm making a movie, Mr. G. For Mr. Scapelli's class. An independent study project. I'm trying to simulate the air war in Vietnam with burning plastic bombs raining fire from the sky. Of course the effect isn't quite the same with the lights on." He adjusted the camera. "I'll add an audio track with sound effects, splice in some action scenes and war photos. And voice-over narration. Would you consider doing it? I have a script. What do you think?"

"Are you crazy, Loomis? You're not allowed in here! And you started a fire on school property! That's arson." He was outraged, but he couldn't stop watching the plastic as it burned and continued to drip, speeding up while the flame crawled up the plastic rope between knots, slowing as each knot unraveled and disappeared in flaming droplets. "Put that out before it sets off the alarm!"

"It's dripping into water." Virgil blew out the tiny flame and smoke rose like a small dark string.

"You have detention." He pulled out a detention card from his pocket and began filling it out. "You're lucky I don't suspend you. Or worse, expel you for violating the County fire code," he stammered. "For smoking on school grounds... for being a smart-ass! Pick one!"

"I have a fire extinguisher." He pointed to the red torpedo on the floor. "I wasn't smoking and nothing caught fire."

"For the unauthorized misuse of official school property!"

"It's not misuse, it's schoolwork. And Mr. Polakas gave me permission to use the storage room. As long as I didn't set myself or anything else on fire. He gave me the fire extinguisher."

"It's time, Loomis, that you realized this is a school and no place for fun." He handed him the card. "Detention this afternoon... and for the rest of the week."

Virgil hesitated. "This afternoon, Mr. G? Afraid I won't be able to make it. I have a previous appointment." He pulled a notepad from his pocket.

"A previous appointment? This isn't a country club, Loomis, that caters to you and operates according to your schedule." He stretched and stared. "Detention. This afternoon and the rest of the week. No excuses."

"My schedule will be free–"

* * *

Mr. Baltz was ecstatic with the video setup that worked perfectly, even better than he'd hoped. It would be even better once he was able to turn it on and off without being there. Maybe something voice-activated like he had for the tape recorder in his office, or a motion sensor. Polakas could install it over the door in the bathroom and wire it to the video recorder. There must be something. It might cost him, but it would be worth it not to spend his time in the closet. He slipped through the door and headed in the direction of AV. Maybe Dexter had what he needed in all that crap and he wouldn't have to buy it. He sniffed the air. Something was wrong. It wasn't the usual school smell–gym socks, chalk dust and an undercurrent of vomity cheese. Something was burning.

He followed his nose around the corner where Mario Giovanni was engaged in a dispute with–he sighed–Virgil Loomis.

"What's going on here, Mr. Giovanni?" He stood silently in the open doorway and startled the both of them. "And what is that awful smell?"

"A minor misunderstanding, Mr. Baltz," Virgil explained. "It's nothing serious, really."

"Do you mind, Loomis?" The AP grimaced. "He asked me." He turned. "Burning plastic, but it's out now. Loomis started a fire in the sink–"

"Not a fire exactly," Virgil interrupted. "More like a controlled burn. Just dripping, burning plastic."

"Are you out of your mind lighting a fire in *my* school!" He looked at the sink. "What's that?"

"A Zilch," Virgil offered. "Like a laser light show with sound. I'm making a movie for independent study. Mr. Scapelli." He lit the plastic bag with a lighter and started it dripping again.

"Mr. Scapelli, I should have known."

Mr. Giovanni blew it out. "I told him that was grounds for automatic suspension. Expulsion. I assigned him a week's detention, but he says he won't go."

"He won't go?" He turned to Virgil. "You *will* go to detention today, Loomis, and for *two* weeks!" Mr. Baltz said with finality. "Case closed."

"No disrespect, Mr. Baltz," Virgil said, "but I didn't say I *won't* go. I told Mr. G I *can't* go today because I have a previous appointment about the secret wrestling team. You remember? We talked about it."

"What secret wrestling team?"

"I told you about it a while ago. Mr. Ritchie turned me down when I tried to join because he doesn't allow 'long-haired faggots,' his words, on his team. I tried going through channels like you suggested, but it didn't work. So this afternoon I have an appointment with my attorney, who agreed to take the case. IF I miss the appointment who knows when it will be rescheduled. Do you have any idea how busy the American Civil Liberties Union is these days?"

"You have an appointment with an ACLU attorney about a wrestling team? Why wasn't I told about this?"

"My lawyer tried. He called everybody involved and sent letters, but he got no response." He took out the attorney's card and handed it to Mr. Baltz.

"'Arthur Rubens, Esq., Attorney at Law, The American Civil Liberties Union.' Do you know anything about this, Mario?"

"I'll check with Phyllis. She may have mentioned something–"

He frowned. "Then you'll start serving your detention tomorrow, Loomis. Mr. Giovanni change the date on the card and make it ending in two weeks," he said emphatically. "Detention tomorrow, Loomis. No excuses. Be there."

"I'm afraid I can't make tomorrow either, Mr. Baltz." He handed back the detention card for correction. "We're meeting with Students for a Democratic Society. They've pledged support and depending on how my meeting with Dr. Flackett goes, they plan to stage a student demonstration. *Newsday* agreed to cover it."

He smoothed his mustache with his fingers and exhaled. "Will you handle this, Mario? With all the teacher observations, I don't have the time." He turned and left as quietly as he had arrived.

Virgil looked at his calendar and ran his finger down the page.. "I'm filled up into March, Mr. G. It would be better after Easter. I should be free when we get back from the vacation–"

Mr. Giovanni stretched his neck, "March then. Two weeks, Loomis. Report to detention on Monday–" He looked at his calendar. "–March twentieth. And not another word."

"Tuesday the twenty-first is clear," Virgil said, rechecking his own calendar.

"On March twenty-first! And that is an order!"

"Fine, Mr. G. I'm writing it down now." He filled in the square. "See how easy that was? Now if there isn't anything else?" He picked up the camera and tripod. "I have an outdoor shoot that I want to get in the can before the light is wrong. I'll just go with what I got here now." He picked up the equipment and left.

When he was alone, the AP stepped inside the STO(P)RAGE ROOM and closed the door. He switched off the lights, pulled out a pack of matches and relit the end of the Zilch. The room pulsated with light and the fweep fweep fweep of dripping plastic. It was mesmerizing. He'd have to show this to Phyllis at home. After a couple of drinks it would be better than TV. The hard look on his face relaxed as he watched. He was smiling, until the sound of the fire alarm brought him back to reality.

March 1

Attorney General John Mitchell resigns and immediately assumes the position of chairman of CREEP, the Committee to Re-elect the President.

March 10-12: National Black Political Convention in Gary, Indiana, draws 8,000. The National Black Assembly or National Black Political Assembly/NBPA is formed and the convention approves a National Black Political Agenda to be taken to the Democratic convention in Miami Beach in July.

March 16, 1972: Pres. Nixon dismisses busing as a means of achieving racial integration and seeks legislation that would deny court-ordered busing. Nixon asks Congress to halt busing in order to achieve desegregation.

March 20-30

Pres. Nixon confirms plan to bug Democrats. John Mitchell, director of CREEP, and his aide Jeb Stuart Magruder discuss the proposal made by G. Gordon Liddy to plant electronic surveillance devices on the phone of the chairman of the Democratic Party, Lawrence O'Brien. Pres. Nixon's chief of staff, H. R. Haldeman, confirms that Nixon wants the operation carried out. On March 30, in a meeting held in Key Biscayne, Florida, John Mitchell approves the plan and its budget of approximately $250,000.

Congress approves the Equal Rights Amendment (ERA) and it is sent to the 50 states, where it will eventually die.

Vietnamese students in the U.S. take over the Vietnamese Consulate in New York for an afternoon to protest the war and the South Vietnamese government; the occupiers are arrested, but all charges are dropped to avoid further bad publicity for the Thieu government.

**Rosencrantz and Guildenstern
Memorial High School
AV/CM Department**

To: All Teachers
From: Harry Dexter, Coordinator AV/CM Department
Subject: March Equipment Inventory
March 3, 1972

Attention! The period after the February break and before Easter is one of the busiest times for the AV/CM Department, second only to the even busier end of the year rush on equipment that occurs during the run-up to final exams in June. To avoid equipment shortages during the periods of peak demand, the AV/CM Department will conduct an inventory during the remainder of March, perform routine maintenance and assess which equipment is in need of repair and overhaul. This March inventory will include all machinery currently out on loan. Teachers are directed to check desks, cabinets and closets for "lost" or "misplaced" AV/CM materials including film and slide projectors, record players and tape recorders and return them immediately to the AV/CM center.

Your cooperation is expected. Failure to cooperate with this directive could result in drastic future equipment shortages. Hoarding will not be tolerated! In the next several days, key-equipped AV/CM Squad members will make surprise classroom visits and remove equipment they find. Any teachers attempting to hide items will be denied access to any AV/CM equipment for the duration of the school year.

In addition, the AV/CM Department will be closed for the three days during Holy Week before the Easter/Passover recess. Teachers wishing to use equipment during the brief period between the conclusion of the two-week March inventory and before Holy Week when the office will be closed, must file the appropriate forms no later than tomorrow.

Requisitions for equipment received after tomorrow will be returned to your mailboxes unread.

UFSD 71

Camelot

Official Publication of the Partnership of Parents and Teachers
in Association for better Farmington Public Schools
Harriet Stegle, President P-PTA

Vol. 6   Issue 6   March 1972

AROUND THE DISTRICT:

Congratulations to the recently divorced Phaedra Schwartz, formerly Fine, now not so much, also once burned is not at all shy. She came back from February break in the Bahamas with sun poisoning, a rock Elizabeth Taylor would wear and a new fiancé, Wall Street financier Maurice Snediker. They plan to tie the knot at the end of the school year. Another June wedding?

THE ELEMENTARY SCHOOLS HIT THE TRIFECTA:

When Principal Ted Mitchell, Old Dutch Mill Elementary, sent his students home last week with a note to their parents, he also sent them with a little something extra–lice! The good news is Old Dutch is finally out of dutch now that the outbreak of those creepy crawlers are on the run. The bad news is some of them have hopped on over to Willis Elementary and West Street Schools! Well, they do say three's the charm!

SKIRT DAY:

Sylvia Berkowsky, Home Ec Department Chair has just two words, Skirt Day! Coming soon to the high school near you. "It's going to be the fashion statement of the year!" according to Sylvia, who has high hopes of bringing style and good taste back into the schools.

AROUND THE BEND BUT ON THE MEND:

R&G's Assistant Principal Willy Zwill is coming along, according to reports out of South Oaks Mental Hospital, where a weeping Willy was taken on February 27 for observation and evaluation. He is undergoing treatment for depression and nervous exhaustion. That is no doubt due to the recent loss of AP Helen O'Dell, who died in R&G in January under what some people are calling "suspicious circumstances"! The

School Board has yet to fill her AP position, and it just may have a second slot to fill with Willy Zwill's future still in doubt.

IN THE NEWS:

Interviews have been endless with candidates parading into and out of Central for weeks. Among the finalists vying to be the new AP spot is my own son Seth. Teachers may remember Seth from his student days. He's a product of the Farmington School System. Unfortunately in his junior year at R&G, on a dare Seth touched the LIRR third rail and tragically lost an arm. Last year he was turned down for a Phys Ed substitute teacher position in the district because he couldn't meet the push-up requirement. Good luck this time, Seth! And luck to the other interviewees whose faces in the crowd I recognized–School Board President Elliot Adornau's "niece" who wouldn't tell me her name, School Board member Walt Walters' nephew Ross Walters, even though he is still working on his administrator's license at C. W. Post, and Reading Teacher Rita Reed. May the best one-armed man win.

That's all for now. See you next time with more news from the trenches!

"Believe me, Seymour, I'm doing the best I can with what I got to work with, no matter what you may think," Flackett said into the phone. "The ad in the *Times* brought out a troop of characters last week all trying to escape from the City, like rats deserting a sinking ship. What a crew. 'I want to work in the country,' one guy said in his application. I sent a bunch of them over to the High School just to get them out of here and make some room. I'm sure you saw them parading like a bunch of ducklings through the halls."

"I'm getting desperate, Don. I need an AP yesterday!"

"I saw your nephew Dexter's name in the pile. Why the hell would he want to give up his little plum to be an AP?"

"He was never the brightest bulb on the tree. What about Adornau's, er, niece. How long before she's approved?"

"I'm not getting in the middle of that shit. Lalo called me and told me to pull her application. Said his wife found out about the two of them and threatened to file for divorce and take the kids and the house after she made a public scene. So Lalo handed over his cock and balls and now he's staying close to home, at least until it blows over."

"Just hire somebody… anybody… other than Dexter. A warm body to fill the gap! Noah Lewis has been retired since he started the job. Zwill is still in the looney bin and Mario Giovanni is ready to kill me."

"You know the protocol. The process takes time, Seymour. We have to go through the motions and see them all to keep everybody happy."

"It's teacher observation time and I need all hands on deck now. Speaking of hands, what about Stegle's kid? She's been on the phone every day pushing him."

He laughed. "The one-armed bandit? At best he'd only be able to lend a hand. Besides, you know the unofficial district policy involving job replacements to maintain the balance of power and preserve the *status quo*. An Mick replaces a Mick, a Wop a Wop, a Jew a Jew, and always man replaces a man, a woman replaces a woman. I'm assuming O'Dell was a woman, even if she was a WAC. So her job goes to another woman. We're just lucky she wasn't a minority, or we'd be looking for one of them."

"Pick somebody in-house. Temporarily. Even if it's a man. I know Chet Montrose, the Math chair applied. He applies for anything that will get him out of the classroom."

He looked at his list and sighed. "No can do, Seymour. Now I have to go. There's a lineup outside my office waiting to be interviewed. So many of them, my secretary gave them numbers like in a bakery. You just have to be patient and do the best you can... do more with less." He hung up the phone and smiled. "Up yours, you bastard," he said.

"Fuck you very much," Mr. Baltz said into the receiver.

* * *

It was well after four o'clock and Virgil was still sitting quietly on the vinyl chair in Reception at Central Administration. He had been in the waiting area long enough to watch the long procession of nervous interviewees pass through Dr. Flackett's office. He encouraged each of them as they went in and consoled them when they came out. He recognized Rita Reed from the High School, but none of the others. And he had spent the time leafing through most of the magazines that were scattered over the top of the wooden table. He read the articles "Nixon's Secret Plan to End the War in Vietnam" and "Front Runner Ed Muskie, the Dems' Only Hope to Win White House!"

Under the pile he found a scratched hand-made fluted metal candy dish that was used as an ashtray. The inscription under the crusted ash read: "Presented by the Metal Shop students of the Graduating Class of 1967 to Dr. Donald Flackett, Farmington Superintendent of Schools for all you have done to further education."

"Dr. Flackett certainly has a wide and varied reading interest," Virgil said to the secretary to make conversation. "*Popular Mechanics, Life, Look, Redbook, Reader's Digest, Modern Bride* and *Farmers' Weekly*. Does he read all of them?"

450

"Only the ones with pictures, but don't tell anybody." The intercom on her desk buzzed and she pressed the switch.

"Are we done for the day, Miss Costigan? Are they all gone? Can I finally get out of here?"

"There is still someone here to see you, Dr. Flackett," she said formally and winked at Virgil. "A student from the high school, Virgil Loomis. He's been waiting patiently for hours."

"About?"

She looked at Virgil. "The high school wrestling team," he said.

"Give me a minute and then send him in... Shit!" the superintendent said before his finger was off the intercom completely.

She shook her head. "It's nothing personal. He feels that way about everybody."

She walked Virgil to the door and knocked as a formality before she opened it and let him in. The room was large and airy. The imposing mahogany desk was centered between two floor-to-ceiling windows with an unobstructed view of the new Administrative Parking lot.

Dr. Flackett was backlit in his chair. "Come in," he said brusquely to Virgil, who was already in. "Sit." His eyes were slits, a trick he used in negotiations and card games.

Virgil sat in the straight back chair across the desk.

"What's your problem and why does it involve me?"

Virgil slid the chair in closer. "I hope you don't mind, Dr. Flackett." He pulled a cassette recorder from his pocket and placed it in front of him on the desk. "My attorney suggested that I record our meeting for him and so there aren't any misunderstandings later on just in case there's a lawsuit."

The superintendent was rattled. "Lawsuit? Attorney?"

"He said it's better to get everything on the record. And if you object he instructed me to end the meeting and call him immediately. He's standing by and will have the papers served and make it more formal." He looked into the superintendent's eyes that had widened a bit. When there was no objection he switched on the machine and positioned the microphone across the desk. "Don't be nervous, Dr. Flackett. Just talk naturally. The mic is very sensitive for its size."

"You have an attorney?"

Virgil removed a card from his pocket and handed it to him. "Arthur Rubens. He's really very cool."

"You have an ACLU attorney?" He fingered the card. "So what is all this about?"

"The high school wrestling team."

"We're on austerity. There is no wrestling team. There aren't any teams on austerity."

"It's a *secret* wrestling team. And there are other secret teams as well."

"Oh? What do you want from me? And why would it involve attorneys?"

"I want to join the team," he explained. "It would look good on my college application. Varsity Wrestling. I've been trying to join since December, when I learned about the team, but Mr. Ritchie, the coach, refused. I've been up the chain of command. Coach Boid didn't help. Mr. Baltz said principals have more important matters to deal with. The assistant principals weren't any help. I tried all of them. Mr. Lewis said he was going out to lunch every time I asked him. Mr. Zwill is just out to lunch. And Mr. Giovanni said he didn't have time for me, that he didn't have time to pee." He leaned in and lowered his voice. "I thought he meant prostate problems, but he really is overworked, Dr. Flackett. He's always done a lot, and now with Helen O'Dell on the front lawn, he's doing practically everything over there." He leaned back. "But that's another matter. Today I'm here to speak to you personally before we take the school district to court. I told my attorney I thought you would be reasonable and that we could get the problem cleared up before wrestling season is over and that I could get my Varsity letter."

"What exactly is your problem with Coach Ritchie?"

"It's more *his* problem with *me*. And besides the fact that he doesn't like me, it's hair," Virgil said. "My hair is too long. And he won't let me on the secret wrestling team because he requires crew cuts. He said my hair is girlie and a safety hazard. But even if I get a crew cut I can't be on the team because I 'look like a faggot and he doesn't allow long-haired faggots' on his team. I told him discrimination against long hair or faggots is illegal. And when nobody I talked to at the high school helped, I contacted the ACLU."

"Virgil." His tone took on a more fatherly level. He was silhouetted in the fading light. "Is it really necessary to involve the court system in our little family problem here? With draft dodgers burning draft cards and flags and running off to Canada and people like Cassius Clay refusing to serve their country. Don't you think getting up on your white horse and tilting at every windmill that comes along is a waste of your time and energy?" He opened the file that was on his desk. "Looking through your school record here, I see that you have a bit of a reputation for being a trouble–" He eyed the tape recorder. "Let's say for being a bit of a nonconformist. Not that there's anything necessarily wrong with a little nonconformism now and then." He puffed himself up and smiled. "You might not know it to look at me, but I had a reputation for being a rebel myself back in the Korean War days. I was the only recruit in the entire company to grow a mustache. Of course they made me shave it off, but I had planned to shave it for my wedding pictures anyway before I got home. My wife-to-be said she didn't like it. Said it irritated her face." He rubbed his thumb and index finger over his bare lip absently. "I loved that mustache almost as much as I loved my wife. And I still miss that mustache." He sighed. "What I am trying to say, Loomis, is that even a nonconformist has to conform sometimes. Hair is not important."

"My sentiments exactly, Dr. F. And that's what I told Mr. Ritchie. Hair is *not* the issue."

"I am glad you agree. Now let me tell you another little story about when I was a high school principal in a really tough school in Hell's Kitchen in the City. They didn't call it that for no reason. Every kid there was bad. There wasn't a good one in the batch. But there was this one really rotten apple, mean and vicious with long sideburns and greased-back hair in a ducktail. They called it a DA because it looked like the back end of a duck. That was the style back then, like Elvis Presley before he went to Las Vegas and put on all those silly jumpsuits. Well, this boy, I'll call him Butch, got expelled and everyone gave up on him. Everyone but me, that is. A month after I expelled Butch, he got into trouble with the law and the judge gave him a choice, 'Go back to school or go to jail!' So Butch came crawling back to me with his ducktail between his legs and he asked, no, he begged me to be readmitted. And do you know what I did?"

"You had him thrown out of your office?"

He forced a smile. "No, I told him if he wanted to get back into school and my good graces he had to do two things. He had say 'please' and he had to make a gesture to show me that he was sincere, prove to me that he had really changed. He had to do something everyone could see before I would even consider signing the papers that would get him back into school and keep him out of jail. He had to shave his head! And do you know what he did?"

"He decided to go to jail?"

"No!" He scowled. "Because he *was* sincere, because hair wasn't really important, he made the gesture. So I had the local barber come into the auditorium and right there at an assembly in front of the entire student body he shaved Butch's head right down to the freckles!" Dr. Flackett sat back contentedly in his chair to let his words hit home and sink in.

"And?" Virgil asked.

"And what? Weren't you paying attention? Sometimes to prove a point, to prove yourself to others, you have to make a gesture, a sacrifice. You have to give up something you value."

"Yes, yes, I understand. And you're applying that to our situation… to me and the secret wrestling team?"

"Now you have it. Hair wasn't important then and it isn't important now. It was the sacrifice Butch made that was important. The gesture of giving something up."

"Yes, yes. I see, Dr. F."

"Then you'll do it? You'll agree?"

"To make a sacrifice? Certainly I will."

Dr. Flackett clapped his hands and rubbed them together. "Bravo. And *you* wanted to involve a lawyer." He smiled. "See how easy that was without a lawyer. And you don't even have to shave your head, you just have to cut that bush of yours and I'll see that you get on the secret wrestling team, and that you get a Varsity letter for your sweater.

"Cut my hair?" Virgil looked puzzled.

"Yes. You just agreed that you would."

"I agreed to make a gesture, not to cut my hair. You said the hair wasn't important–"

Dr. Flackett's face darkened. "Of course the hair was important! Weren't you just listening? I made that dirtbag shave off all his hair to prove a point to him. To teach him a lesson and let him know who was in charge. And he learned it!" His face was red. "So you *have* to cut your hair!"

"I'm sorry," Virgil said. "I don't mean to get you upset, Dr. F. I *will* make a gesture, a sacrifice to show that I am sincere, because, as you said, it is all about the sacrifice, isn't it? So," he thought, "my sacrifice will be to clip my fingernails." He held up his hands.

Dr. Flackett grabbed the end of his desk and launched himself out of his chair. "Get out of my office, Loomis," he exploded. "Out! And take your tape recorder and your wiseass attitude and your long frizzy hair with you!"

Virgil picked up his recorder. "You have my attorney's card. He'll call you to work out the details for a meeting before the hearing." Virgil passed through the door and into the waiting area.

"So, how did it go, Virgil?" Miss Costigan asked with a smile.

"Surprisingly well," he said. "And kind of the way I figured. He's a great storyteller. But if you're planning to go in there, you might want to wait a little while."

March was midway done and the only thing inhabiting Helen O'Dell's office was her ghost. The flood of applicants for the open AP position became a stream and then a trickle. The large pool of candidates had been reduced to lowest terms until there was only one left.

"Come in, Mrs. Reed." Dr. Flackett stood up behind his desk to greet her. "Please have a seat, Rita, and we will begin."

She stepped in timidly behind him and he ushered her to the straight back wooden chair strategically placed almost in the center of the room far away from the desk and walls. It was bathed in a circle of light from the overhead recessed fixture, not unlike an interrogation seat. Dr. Flackett crossed directly in front of her and leaned against the front of his desk.

"Thank you." She sat and immediately began twisting her lace handkerchief.

"Relax. We're all friends here," she heard from behind her and turned to see School Board President Adornau seated in a stuffed chair in the shadows puffing on a little cigar. She covered her nose with her handkerchief. "I hope you're not feeling sick," he said. "That's one of the things we'll be taking into consideration, Mrs. Reed. Sick days. We can't afford to hire another sick assistant principal." There was seriousness behind his attempt at humor.

"I do have allergies," she explained and daubed her nose to illustrate. "I'm very allergic to cigarette smoke." She coughed.

He took a deep puff and blew out a cloud into the room. "This is a cigar." She coughed again. "Is there anything else you're allergic to that might prevent you from doing the job? How many sick days have you taken in the time you've been teaching here?"

His directness flustered her. "I-I don't know… exactly, but I'm sure it's on my attendance record. I called in every time. But it was never more than the number of sick days we get every year. Even after my daughter was born and I took an extended leave. I've even managed to bank a number of days just in case of an emergency."

"You're not planning on having another child, are you?"

She flushed. "My youngest is in high school," she said. "I really don't think so."

"But you're not ruling it out entirely?" He puffed his cigar. "So I assume it still could be possible."

"You're... I... I suppose." She twisted in her chair to face Dr. Flackett.

"It's been almost two months since Helen O'Dell's passing and we are very eager to fill the position with the most qualified person," the superintendent redirected. "And that has been more complicated than you may imagine. Farmington is made up of different kinds of people. Different nationalities, religions, politics... hardworking, middle-class, blue-collar people for the most part. It's a microcosm of the outside world. One of my jobs here is to preserve a balance and keep everybody in the town happy. And how do we do that, you might ask. We go out of our way to preserve that status quo. Helen O'Dell was a woman, so it is only right to replace her with another woman." He smiled. "And we think *you* are *that* woman."

"Well, thank you," she said, recovering some of her composure.

"I'm sure you've noticed, Rita, that there aren't many female assistant principals in the schools. A few at the secondary level and none in the elementary schools. Some men tend to be threatened by women in positions of authority. They feel that a woman can't do as effective a job as a man because... well, because she is a woman. Because of certain... female bodily functions–"

She twisted in her seat again.

"Are you frigid, Mrs. Reed?" Mr. Adornau blurted.

"I'm comfortable," she said.

"Are you menopausal? Is the baby factory shut down?"

Dr. Flackett stared at him. "What Mr. Adornau means–" he said trying to wrest control back again.

"What I mean, Mrs. Reed," he continued, "in purely economic terms, what are the chances of giving you the position and then losing you?"

"I'm afraid I don't understand–" She wrung the handkerchief in her hands.

"If you got yourself knocked up. Or if there were 'female issues' that prevented you from doing your job every month." He stubbed out his cigar and looked for a place to put it. "We need to discuss some considerations, some concessions we expect before we officially offer you O'Dell's position, Rita."

"I still don't follow–"

"Men and women are different. And I for one say God bless that difference," Dr. Flackett interjected. "Mr. Adornau is being practical. He's asking, and not very well, if you are a *real* woman in the fullest sense of what that entails. Could you function in such a high-stress job without the monthly 'woman thing' getting in the way–"

"Are you still getting your 'friend'?" Mr. Adornau asked.

"Please–" Dr. Flackett tried to interrupt.

"You aren't a lesbian, are you, Mrs. Reed? If you were, that would eliminate the pregnancy thing and make you a safe gamble at least on one level. One of the boys. Though it would be a moral issue. Can't have lesbians working with our children."

"I'm a married woman–" she protested and on the verge of tears.

"Once you get the job–" Dr. Flackett said, trying to comfort her.

"*If* you get the job," Mr. Adornau interjected.

"Assuming you become an assistant principal, Rita, the district would rather you die in the position, like Helen O'Dell. Or retire, of course. But we don't want to lose you to any of that woman stuff."

"Hysterectomy," Mr. Adornau announced. At the word she clenched her knees together. "That's the District's position, Mrs. Reed. If you aren't planning on any more children, as you say, what's the problem? A hysterectomy is the only sure way to take the worry out of being close."

"And it's not such a bad operation, Rita. Many women younger than you go through it as a matter of routine." Dr. Flackett handed her a tissue to wipe her eyes.

"A rite of passage."

"And your hospitalization and major medical covers most of it and the District will kick in anything over and above what insurance doesn't. And here's a bonus, we won't charge your time out against your sick days, so you won't lose any of them. A sort of good faith offering and a way of saying welcome to administration. It's a win win."

"And because the 'procedure' is job related, you can declare it as a deduction on your income tax. The way I see it, another win-win. You're sitting pretty. Promotion. Bigger salary. Your own office. It's your call."

Dr. Flackett smiled. Mr. Adornau blew some smoke rings and Rita Reed blew her nose and knotted her handkerchief.

Superintendent of Schools
UFSD 71
Central Administration Building
Farmington, New York

From: Donald F. Flackett, Superintendent
To: All Faculty and Staff
Subject: Sensitivity
March 16, 1972

In their most recent bulletin, the Bureau of Home Economics Education of the University of the State of New York focuses on the matter of sensitivity in education. The questions they propose for Home Economics Educators may well be asked of all teachers of every subject at every grade level. So, I reproduce them here for your attention that you may be impelled to examine your own classroom behavior and be more sensitive to the needs of your students.

1. Have I tried to become familiar with the backgrounds and the abilities of my pupils?

2. Have I done the same with my colleagues in an effort to know them as individuals?

3. Have I developed a good rapport with everyone–students, parents, teachers and administrators?

4. Am I flexible and willing to adapt, to change and let go of old ideas, outdated methods and stubborn opinions?

5. How well am I able to adjust?

6. Do I provide for the special needs of my pupils?

7. Am I sensitive to the needs of others? To their feelings?

8. What am I doing to make better my classroom, my school, the world?

Teachers are asked to take stock, make changes, be more aware and become more sensitive. But if you can't do that, at least try to be relevant in your lessons!

"Is that really you, Loomis? I don't believe it!"

"Sweet."

"Way to go, Loomis."

"*You're* a wrestler?"

The comments came as Virgil headed down the corridor and he couldn't help smiling. He was wearing the maroon and brown Varsity sweater with a gold wrestling team letter. "Hey, Mr. S," he called into Terry's classroom through the open door and flashed him a thumbs-up, "I just got it! And now I'm on my way to the Main Office to show everyone."

"I am definitely impressed, Virgil." Terry shook his head and watched him saunter down the hall to the staircase and the Administrative Alcove.

He was happy to see Mr. Giovanni and Phyllis Lind. They were sharing a plate in the AP's office. "Hey, Mr. G, Ms Lind."

"What is it now, Loomis?" He shifted the toothpick from one side of his mouth to the other and picked up a french fry with his fingers.

"I just wanted to show you my sweater. But if you're busy I can come back another time. I just got it in my school mailbox this morning with a note from Dr. Flackett after he met with my attorney."

"Wonderful," he said sarcastically. "You have a mailbox here?" He turned to Phyllis. "He has a mailbox? Why does he have a mailbox? Students don't have mailboxes in school. I barely have a mailbox."

Virgil shrugged. "It's unofficial," he said. "I used my Label Maker and put my name on an open cubby. The secretaries use it for my detention slips and all the notifications I get. And now the occasional delivery. It's easier than trying to find me. Right, Ms Lind?"

"That's right, Virgil dear. And that sweater is stunning. It makes you look so virile," she said fingering the letter.

Mr. Giovanni cracked his neck and stretched. "Yeah, it's wonderful."

"I haven't shown Mr. Ritchie yet. I was planning to head to the gym after I showed you."

"I'm sure he'll be as thrilled as I am."

"I got the sweater the same day the secret wrestling team season ended, just in time for the yearbook picture! They're scheduled for this afternoon for the *Maroon and Brown*. The official team picture will hang in Mr. Ritchie's office in the Boys' Gym along with all those from past years forever." He nodded. "A reminder of what hard work and determination can achieve, Mr. G. I'm really looking forward to taking my place alongside the rest of my teammates."

"But you weren't *on* the team, Loomis. There wasn't even a team because we're on austerity."

"That doesn't matter, Mr. G. It's for posterity, you know. History. Years from now people will be looking at that yearbook. Generations of R and G alums will see that picture, a little faded maybe, long after I graduated, long after you're gone, Mr. G, and someone in the Library Xed out your face with a marker. They will see me and maybe I will serve as a role model and they will be motivated to succeed."

"That's beautiful, Virgil," Phyllis said and patted his arm. "You *are* a role model. A philosopher and a poet."

"Thank you, Ms Lind. You've always encouraged me during my years at R and G." He went into the alcove. "I'll keep you informed and let you know how the pictures turn out. If the photographer takes individual shots, I'll ask him to make some extra copies and give one to both of you."

"I can't wait. Now close the door and don't let it hit you in the ass when you go."

"He's so cute," she said. "So tall and so handsome. Isn't he wonderful?"

"Yeah, wonderful," he replied and stretched his neck. "And he's got his own mailbox."

"Hello, Virgil. That's a very nice sweater."

"Thank you, Mrs. Butrum. I was just showing Mr. Giovanni and Ms Lind."

"And I was just on my way to find them." She knocked on the door.

"What is it now, Loomis? Go away," he complained. "Jesus, it's like Grand Central Station in here."

"Sunshine Committee," Mrs. Butrum called through the closed door and opened it. "Collecting." She shook the brown manila envelope. "Hello, Phyllis. Glad that I got you too."

"What are you collecting for this time?" he grumbled. "Didn't the Sunshine Committee get all of Helen O'Dell's insurance? Why do you need more money?"

"For a get well basket for poor Rita Reed." Mrs. Butrum moved the envelope closer.

"What's wrong with her?"

"Female problems," she said and lowered her voice. "Total hysterectomy. It came on suddenly, the poor woman. She seemed well enough, but yesterday out of the blue she went into the hospital. Here yesterday, gone today. She'll be out until Monday. The good news is when she returns she'll be the interim AP and move into Helen's office, at least until the end of the year."

"I didn't know that," he said and stretched his neck. "How do you know that?"

"The Sunshine Committee has its sources. As for Helen's insurance money, the Committee spent every penny on her funeral arrangements and burial."

"I suppose the Sunshine Committee will present an accounting? For the faculty, I mean. To let them know just how their money is being spent." He reached reluctantly into his wallet when she shook the envelope in front of him and he pulled out a dollar.

"While you have that thing out, Mario, put something in for me too," Phyllis said.

* * *

"Wrestling team… Varsity sweater," Jesse said when Virgil stopped by to see him at the end of the day. He looked at the gold letter. "A varsity letter. Congratulations. I didn't know you were a jock, Virgil."

"Well, Mr. Teeg, the truth is I've barely been in the Boys' Gym since ninth grade, even during the years when we weren't on austerity. In seventh grade, I fell off the ropes and broke an arm. In eighth a dodgeball broke my nose. In ninth, it was an ankle not quite going over a hurdle. I have a note so I don't even have to show up in Gym ever." He opened his wallet and unfolded a well-worn yellowed paper. "'Dear To Whom It May Concern, Please excuse Virgil Loomis from Gym because he is allergic to physical education. Respectfully, Dr. Cynthia Bohl-Loomis PhD, MD.' My mother plans to write me another note for when I turn eighteen and have to register with Selective Service for my Draft Card. 'Please excuse my son from the war in Vietnam because he has a strong aversion to death.'"

"Let me know if that works for you." Jesse looked at him. "In high school I was on the Rifle Team, but I didn't letter. I missed making varsity by this much." He indicated an inch with his fingers. "The targets we aimed at had twelve bull's-eyes on each sheet and whenever we shot each of us had twelve bullets. After the varsity qualifying competition there were thirteen holes in my target and I got disqualified. Later I learned that a senior took another bullet and put an extra hole into my target. He made the team instead of me."

"That really sucks, Mr. Teeg."

Maybe it was for the best. In college I heard that he became a Marine sniper in Vietnam and got killed." He sighed. "So tell me, if you don't go to gym, how did you get your letter sweater?"

"Persistence, Mr. Teeg," he said. "I'm on my way *to* the gym now to show Coach Ritchie my sweater and for the secret Wrestling Team yearbook picture. He still doesn't know I made the team."

* * *

"Awright, awright, awright, ladies!" Buddy Ritchie's voice resounded through the locker room and echoed off the tile walls. "Playtime's over! Shower time's done! Cut the grab ass and suit up for pictures." They ran past him and he snapped the towel from behind his neck. It caught the slowest kid on the backside with a stinging slap that left a welt. "Still too slow and too fat, Jocko," he taunted. Jocko rubbed his rear and Buddy Ritchie who followed him into the dressing room.

"Kavernicki, are those hickeys all over you? Are you dating a girl or a vacuum cleaner?"

"A Hoover," somebody called over the laughs. "Kavernicki's girlfriend sucks like a Hoover."

"You mean a *who-uh*," Buddy Ritchie said. "Are you dating a who-uh, Kavernicki?" Everyone but Kavernicki laughed. Buddy Ritchie turned on one of the others. "What are you laughing at, Bonafido? You never had a date. Going out with your sister doesn't qualify. And stop pulling on that thing. It'll grow... eventually." He snapped the towel at him. "Everybody be suited up and ready by the time I get out of the shower. I want all of you lined up before the yearbook geek shows up to take our picture." His towel cracked again and they flinched. He sat on the bench in front of his locker and undressed.

"Hey, Coach," Virgil said. He had followed the sounds.

"What the hell are you doing in my locker room, Loomis? This is a place for men."

"I'm here for the team picture, Coach. I got a message from Dr. Flackett that they were today–"

"Team picture? You got a lot of damn gall coming in here." He stood and took a step toward him in his supporter and socks. "Get the hell out of here, Loomis, before I really get mad and let somebody hurt you."

"And I also wanted to show you this." He put on his sweater.

Buddy Ritchie's face burned beet-red. "Get that off, Loomis. You're not worthy to wear that sweater and that letter. And you sure as hell aren't going to be in the team picture."

"Not according to Dr. Flackett's memo. He made arrangements through my attorney." He produced a paper.

"I don't care what Flackett may have told you, but just so you and me are on the same page, I wouldn't be *seen on the same page* in the yearbook or any other place with you. You're not an athlete, Loomis. You're a radical, a smartass and a fraud. But I'll tell you what I'll do, Loomis. I'll ask you three questions and if you can answer even one of them I'll let you be in the team picture and I'll stand next to you in the yearbook naked!"

"How could anyone resist that offer, Coach?"

"What's the name of the man who holds the major league record for most home runs?" He waited. "Too tough for you? Then tell me the sport Steve Prefontaine will dominate in the summer Olympic games." Again he waited. "Okay, here's an easy one, a softball. Who's Duke Snyder?" He waited and then he chortled. "I knew you wouldn't know, Loomis. You're good for nothing, Loomis. Certainly not worthy to be standing here in my locker room and definitely not in any team picture. I don't ever want to see you here again." He picked up his soap and walked into the showers. "Sports builds character, Loomis, and character is what you lack," he called over his shoulder and the sound of the steaming water. "It's a coach's job to mold young boys into men, to build them up, Loomis. With you there's nothing to build. You're not a man, Loomis. Sportsmanship depends on honesty and fair play, and you didn't play fair getting that sweater. You're penalized fifteen yards for unsportsmanlike conduct." He peeled off his supporter and his socks and stepped under the water. "Honesty, Integrity, Fairness and another one I can't remember right now are the Four Horsemen of athletics... the Tinkers to Evers to Chance of Good Character, Loomis. Mr. Farley was right when he said you are a little puke, Loomis. You'll never be one of my boys." He ducked back under the water. "And you can forget about college, Loomis. With the bad recommendation I'm going to put in your file, you won't even get into Nassau Community College. So get ready to say hello to the U.S. Army and good ol' Vietnam. If you're lucky they might make half a man of you before you come back. *If* you come back. So have a good life. I hope you like rice because you're gonna be in those rice paddies sooner than you think."

"My mother wrote me a note, Coach," he said and he turned to leave.

Kavernicki, Bonafido and Jocko were crouched on the ledge above the showers so Coach Ritchie couldn't see them from below. Virgil watched them peeing together in three streams that arched down into the steaming shower water below.

"You're a loser, Loomis. L-o-s-e-r." He rinsed the shampoo from his hair, filled his mouth with water and spit it in Virgil's direction like a fountain.

"So what you're saying, Mr. Ritchie, is that I am definitely out of the team picture?"

"Haven't you been listening to me? That's your problem, Loomis, you never listen. Now get the fuck out of here. But know this, what goes around, comes around, and if there's any justice in this world, you'll get yours eventually. It's called Comma."

Virgil backed out. "I guess you're right, Coach. Comma is a bitch." He touched the letter on his sweater and left.

Monday was the first day of spring, at least according to the calendar, and spring always held out hope for a new beginning. Though winter was officially over, it didn't get the memo and it was still hanging on. The weekend temperature was only in the thirties and the forecast for the week ahead was the same. Major league baseball would begin in two weeks on April 1, if the players didn't go out on strike over pension and arbitration issues as they were threatening. And most important, there were only eight more school days until the Easter/Passover break.

Monday was also the day Willy Zwill, like Lazarus returning from the dead, returned to work after being away for three weeks. They had held him at South Oaks for the court-ordered observation and evaluation and then beyond. He was tested, diagnosed, treated and released.

"The rithium," the little Asian said to Zwill on his first day, "is for depression, but take two weeks to kick in. You no worry, Mr. Wirry. Soon you be new man. You be better than new man." The sight of the squinty-eyed doctor wielding a needle sent him into flashback-induced spasms. "New experimental psychotropic drug FDA approve any day now for general use I combine with electroshock make voices go way chop-chop. If not completely, will keep them from dominating all your conversations." He held up an electric cattle prod. "This make you spill your guts, Yankee pig dog. Now you tell when Mac Arthur come back to Philippines and where he land," he ordered, or so Willy heard.

The effects of the combined treatment were nothing short of miraculous. In three days, Zwill's twitch disappeared. He was able to sleep. He ate real food and his sallow complexion improved. In his second week, the screaming voices stopped yelling, a number of them stopped completely and the ones that remained used their inside voices inside his head. Helen O'Dell was the last to go. She stopped talking to him after another round of electroshocks. And he stopped answering her shortly after that at lunch one afternoon during his final week, when he returned to the table with two servings of fruit salad suspended in green Jello for himself and Helen. Suddenly and without saying a final good-bye, she disappeared.

It turned out that his Inquisitor wasn't Asian at all, but a third-year resident named Zed Dvorkas, a Columbia med school graduate with wire-rimmed glasses, a bad cigarette habit and perhaps more than a little Mongolian ancestry in his Russian-Israeli bloodline. As promised, Willy's depression lifted two weeks to the day, exactly fourteen days after his first dose of Lithium. And four days after that he was released with a handshake, a pocketful of prescriptions, an armload of plastic lanyards and half a dozen pre-punched woven leather wallets he had made in arts and crafts, and hope in his heart. As Dr. Dvorkas had promised, Willy Zwill was a new man.

He arrived home to his empty house and the silence was deafening. The level of water in the fish tank was down and all his tropical fish, unfed for three weeks, were dead and floating in two inches of murky green, foul smelling muck. Piles of *Newsday* littered the front of his house, bills, circulars and Chinese take-out menus clogged the mail slot. Yes, he was home, a new man, but without the voices to keep him company the house was cold and empty and Willy was alone. The Friday night he was released, he missed his first medication. Saturday he overslept, skipped breakfast and his morning dose of pills, and the rest of the day was a blur. By Sunday he forgot everything. The TV was full of Democrats–Edmund Muskie, George McGovern and George Wallace and news of the presidential election in November dominated the airwaves. A smiling President Nixon announced more troops were being withdrawn from Vietnam *and* a step-up of bombing attacks on Cambodia. At nine he tuned to *Bonanza* on NBC. The episode, "A Place to Hide," was slow-moving even for that Sunday night series. The plot involved Confederate Col. Cody Ransom who had fought for the South during the Civil War and escaped to Mexico with his men at the end of the war. Ransom's wife, played by an actress he recognized, but whose name he didn't know, and her little girl turned to the Cartwrights for help because her husband wanted to stop being an outlaw and surrender. He watched Ben Cartwright and his two remaining sons, Hoss and Little Joe, help Rose Ransom redeem her husband's good name. He never understood why Adam Cartwright left the show. The family said he had gone to sea or moved to Europe or the East Coast to run that end of the business. But Adam was the least of the Cartwrights, and by the time the story was wrapped up, Willy was tired.

After a tepid shower he noticed the light blinking on his answering machine, a PhoneMate 400 Helen O'Dell had given him for his last birthday. "So we can always keep in touch," she wrote on the card. when she gave it to him. He rewound the tape and listened to his outgoing greeting: "I am not here and I will not return your call." He fast-forwarded through all the old messages, mostly sales pitches and prank calls, the curse of having a listed number. Then the muffled voice message stopped him. "Willy... Willy..." He sat up straight and his body stiffened like it did with the electroshock treatments. "... come back... we need you... Willy, things... worse than ever... see you morning meeting tomorrow.... Click." Helen O'Dell was back! He replayed the message several times before he fell asleep to the sounds of all those familiar voices in his head. The new Willy was gone and he was back to his old self again.

* * *

He arrived especially early in the morning darkness and pulled into his parking spot. He watched his breath rise and disappear as he walked across the courtyard. He opened the locked door with his key and moved instinctively through the hall toward his office. The sounds, the smells, everything was familiar, everything the same. It was a comfort to know that nothing had changed in the weeks he had been gone, except for the large drooping sign that was curled and hanging partly off the wall in the Administrative Alcove. He pressed the tape that had come loose and refastened the top corner so he could read what it said. "WELCOME and Congratulations from the faculty and staff and the Sunshine Committee." He smiled. Leave it to O'Dell to think of everything.

His office, unopened for three weeks, was musty and dusty, so he spent the hour before anyone else arrived bringing it up to pass inspection. He waited in the dim light for the bell and the morning meeting with Baltz and the old crew.

* * *

After the Pledge, the National Anthem and a barrage of morning announcements, Homeroom ended and Willy was almost ready to begin to face the world on the other side of the door. He would have preferred to ease himself back slowly, unnoticed, without a fuss, but apparently the faculty, staff and Sunshine Committee had different plans for his return. As uncomfortable as he felt, he would graciously accept whatever surprise they were planning. He peered through the crack into the empty Administrative Alcove where his "WELCOME" sign had fallen off the wall completely. He pulled his shoulders back, steeled himself and took a deep breath. "Banzai!" he said under his breath. From somewhere distant he heard the strains of the theme from *The Bridge on the River Kwai* and realized he was whistling it. He marched into the Main Office prepared to act surprised, but nothing happened. None of the secretaries looked up. The teachers rummaging through their mailboxes didn't notice him. Was he even there? Maybe he was still home in bed dreaming. Maybe he was still in South Oaks and Monday was chicken and dumplings, his favorite. Maybe all the stuff they gave him in the hospital had made him invisible.

"Good morning, Mr. Zwill," Phyllis said softly and slowly. Baltz's memo had given very clear instructions: "Don't make a fuss. Don't make any sudden motions or loud noises and don't even acknowledge that Mr. Zwill has been away. It's business as usual."

"They're all waiting for you inside."

Her words popped his chicken and dumpling dreams like a balloon and the disappointment showed his face.

"Is everything all right, Mr. Zwill?" she called to him.

"Yes, yes. Why wouldn't everything be all right?"

"Hey," Red Farley's voice boomed. "Look who's here, Stan! Welcome back to the crazy house," he said and headed around the counter to shake hands.

"Don't you mean welcome back *from* the crazy house?" Stanley Milnow followed him.

"A little sensitivity there, Stan. Everybody knows the man was in the booby hatch. I was just trying to make light of it and not call attention to his breakdown." Mr. Zwill flinched when he saw them coming at him. Red clapped him on the back and the sound filled the office like a pistol shot. "Jeez, Willy," he said, "I thought you'd come back rested and tan after three weeks vacation. But you look like… crap. What the hell did they do to you in there?"

"I had a friend in South Oaks," Stanley said, "He went a little crazy and tried to kill his wife and his mother-in-law. They took him away in a straitjacket and gave him electric shocks in the head that cured him. But he was never the same. He never tried to kill either of them again when he got out. But his wife left him and he killed himself. So how *you* feeling, Willy?"

When Phyllis noticed the AP twitching, she walked over and escorted him away. "They're waiting for you inside, Mr. Zwill." She aimed him toward the door and turned to them. "I just heard the bell, boys. You don't want to be late for your classes. You can catch up with Mr. Zwill later."

Mr. Baltz was behind his desk when Phyllis led Willy into the office. The other three APs were in place. "Good, you're here," Mr. Baltz said matter-of-factly. "We can begin. Take a seat, Willy."

He slipped into the open chair and looked around at the nodding smiling faces–Noah Lewis, Mario Giovanni… the woman. He stopped and studied her. She wasn't Helen O'Dell.

"You know Rita Reed from the Reading Department, Willy. While you were away, Rita was appointed interim assistant principal to replace Helen, at least for the remainder of the school year. She starts officially today. On Friday, when you were… still out, she came in and we had a little welcome slash get-well party for her. Rita was just in the hospital. You must have seen the banner outside your office when you came in this morning."

He didn't reply.

"You look great, Willy," Mario Giovanni exaggerated. "It's good that the crew's back–"

"Cruise?" Noah Lewis opened his eyes with interest. "You were on a cruise? Where? How, auh, was the food? On a cruise the food is always, auh, good. And it's all you can eat."

Mr. Baltz lit a Lucky from his pack and Rita Reed covered her nose with her handkerchief. "So we are finally back to full staff." He turned to face her. "We all know that filling Helen O'Dell's shoes will take time, Rita. So be patient and don't expect to accomplish miracles. Use this week to get a feel for the job. Mr. Giovanni will help you through it and do some of the more demanding things while you get acclimated." He glanced at his number two, who sighed and sank a bit lower in his seat. "But you *can* start observations. Phyllis will give you a list of teachers who haven't been observed yet. Pick some. Start with people you like. Or with people you don't like. It's entirely up to you. You've been around long enough to know how it works. Drop in, stay a while, find something wrong and write it up. It's easy." He exhaled smoke that made her cough. "For the rest of you, now that Willy is here with us again, it'll be easier for everyone." He stood up. The meeting was over. "We only have eight days until the break. So get out there and keep a lid on things. It'll be April when we come back and before you know it, final exams, graduation and summer vacation."

Willy Zwill passed silently through the Main Office into the Administrative Alcove and followed Mario Giovanni into his office. When the AP sat in the desk chair he saw Willy standing inside the door. "Jeez, Willy, I didn't hear you behind me. You scared the shit out of me."

"Stealth training," he said simply.

"What can I do for you?"

"That woman in Baltz's office... She isn't O'Dell. Where's O'Dell? What happened to O'Dell?"

"You know she's gone, Willy." He shook his head. It was *déjà vu*! "You just spent three weeks in the hospital. Didn't they explain that to you? Didn't they help you to understand what happened to her when you were there? O'Dell's dead, Willy."

"Bullshit! O'Dell called me. Last night. I listened to her message on my answering machine. Said she wanted me to come back as soon as possible. That she needed me. That everything was worse and that she'd see me at the meeting."

He sighed. "That wasn't O'Dell, Willy. That was me. I left you the message. O'Dell's dead," he said again. "We buried her on the side lawn by the monuments. Don't you remember the funeral in the cafeteria? You took it hard. You and Helen were close. Everybody knows that." He let what he was saying sink in. "That was over a month ago, Willy. All that pressure, the loss. You snapped. You tried to dig her up. They called the police and you attacked them. That's why they took you away." Zwill's face was blank. "What the hell did they do to you in that place? Are you going to be okay, Willy? Are you taking your meds?"

"Of course *I'm* okay," he said. "It's that impostor pretending to be O'Dell that worries me!"

Camelot

Official Publication of the Partnership of Parents and Teachers
in Association for better Farmington Public Schools
Harriet Stegle, President P-PTA
Vol. 7 Issue 7 Special Easter/Passover Edition March 1972

AROUND THE DISTRICT:

Principal Ted Mitchell, Old Dutch Mill Elementary, has announced another outbreak of lice in his school. But the good news from Old Dutch is that the rat infestation is finally under control. Not so much in Willis Elementary and West Street Schools where "Rat Patrol Exterminators" has placed baits throughout the buildings to attract the rodents. A memo warns parents of both schools to instruct their children not to eat any of the brightly colored "candies" they may find lying around the buildings or bring home with them.

FROM THE "WIN SOME, LOSE SOME DEPARTMENT"—It was a relatively speedy recovery for former R&G Reading Teacher, Rita Reed. Rita's early onset total hysterectomy seemed to come out of the blue right in the middle of her interview for the late Helen O'Dell's AP position at R&G. After a brief post-op stay in Meadowbrook Hospital, she was released in time to assume the interim position in a year when Principal Seymour Baltz seems to have his share of problems with his building administrative staff. Rita was a complete woman one day and the next day an AP, interim though it may be. Way to go, Rita, and good luck. When a door closes, a window of opportunity opens. Although she lacks administrative experience, Rita edged out all the other more qualified candidates for the AP job that had been held by Helen O'Dell until her untimely and mysterious death. Those who were interviewed included my own (disappointed again) son Seth, who hasn't been quite the same since he was denied employment for the second time in the school district he once attended. Oh well, with the way things are going at R&G, maybe another AP opening is on the horizon.

WELCOME BACK

It's welcome back Willy Zwill to R&G from his three week R&R, or at least that is what they are calling it. For those of you who may not remember, Mr. Zwill suffered a nervous breakdown in late February. After attempting to dig up Helen O'Dell from the monuments on the side lawn of R&G where she was buried, Willy was carted off to jail by Farmington's Finest in handcuffs. Later he was remanded to South Oaks Mental Hospital for observation, evaluation and treatment. People held out little hope for his return, but return iron man Willy did on Monday with a "clean bill of health" and bright and cheery future ahead of him… or so they say.

In the spirit of the solemn holidays we will celebrate next week, I want to wish a very happy Easter to all you Christians. And to the few Jews who have not yet moved from Farmington to the more affluent Jericho, may the Angel of Death quietly pass over your house this Passover!

Rosencrantz and Guildenstern
Memorial High School
AV/CM Department

To: All Teachers
From: Harry Dexter, Coordinator AV/CM Department
Subject: Easter/Passover Hiatus
March 22, 1972

No AV/CM equipment will be available until the ongoing inventory is complete. So don't ask!

The AV/CM Department would like to wish all of you a very happy Easter and Passover.

Rosencrantz and Guildenstern
Memorial High School
UFSD 71
Farmington, New York

TO: All Teachers and Staff
FROM: M. Seymour Baltz, Principal
SUBJECT: Disturbing Incidents

It has come to my attention that in the past week a number of "disturbing incidents" have occurred in and around the building that have gone unaddressed until now. These incidents, in the form of "unwanted deposits" for want of a better term, have been uncovered in various isolated locations around the school. The first "deposit" was detected on the second floor landing of the back staircase by one of the assistant principals when he stepped in it on a routine building inspection. It didn't take long for him to realize the exact makeup of what he had stepped in. The incident caused him considerable consternation and resulted in damage to a pair of expensive leather shoes. A second "deposit" was discovered in the backstage area of the Bernard H. Prahl Memorial Auditorium. And the third particularly offensive deposit was left on the floor in the middle of the elevator.

Behavior of this sort will not be tolerated. If it continues the authorities will be informed. If you have any information about these "deposits" or the "depositor," please contact Mr. Giovanni in his office.

Jesse could hardly believe it, he had actually made it through the entire winter to spring. The weather forecast, according to Tex Antoine, called for warming temperatures and sunshine for the weekend. And then there were only three days of school until Easter vacation. He took a deep breath. He sure had come a long way since those September nights when he wanted to quit. And he hadn't thrown up in months. He hadn't thought about his letter of resignation for a while either, and he had actually moved it from his attaché case to his desk at home. Although he couldn't say that he was actually happy, for the first time he was able to make plans to get away for a few days when he was off instead of marking papers and planning lessons. He passed through the Administrative Alcove shortcut to the Main Office and heard himself whistling.

"Hey, Mr. Teeg," Virgil's muffled voice called from somewhere in the alcove.

Jesse stopped short. "Virgil? Where are you?"

"I'm in the closet."

He looked at the open door of the storage room he didn't know was even there. Jesse peered into the room filled with boxes and things. He stepped inside cautiously and looked around. "What is all this stuff? And what are you doing in here?"

"Theater props and stage flats from the looks of it. And costumes." He stepped forward and was wearing a Roman helmet and breastplate under his letter sweater. "I got detention. And Mr. Scapelli thought I could help move stuff out of here to the backstage area."

"Mr. Scapelli gave you detention? I'm surprised. What did you do?"

"No, Mr. Giovanni gave me the detention from when I was making a movie and he thought I was trying to burn down the school. When Mr. S saw me sitting in the detention chair he got me paroled. So here I am in the closet." He pulled the short sword out of the scabbard strapped around his waist and flailed it in the air. "*Et tu, Brute?* Then fall, Caesar.'" He held his side, staggered back against the stage flats and died. Dramatically. Then he jumped up and bowed. "How's that?"

"Not bad, Virgil." Jesse poked through some of the boxes. He found a pith helmet and a curved wooden saber painted silver. "You're not the only one who knows *Julius Caesar.* 'I draw a sword against conspirators. When think you that the sword goes up again? Never, till Caesar's three and twenty wounds be well avenged. Or 'til another Caesar have added slaughter to the sword of traitors.' On guard, vile cur!"

"I'm impressed, Mr. Teeg. On guard!" He launched his attack and the two swords clacked together in noisy battle.

Mr. Giovanni's voice boomed through the alcove. "What the hell? What's going on in there, Loomis? And who else is in there?"

Jesse lowered his sword, Virgil lunged and scored a hit. "*Touché,* Mr. Teeg. You really have to keep your guard up at all times."

"Mr. Tietjen?" Mr. Giovanni stared at Jesse and cracked his neck. "What are you doing in there?"

His face was red. He dropped his saber. "I, uh. We, uh—" he stammered.

"Well, Mr. G," Virgil said coming to his rescue, "we were just doing some Shakespeare. I'm sure you heard that all the world's a stage, and men and women playing many parts, so we were just playing."

"And I'm sure you both heard that this is a school and you're not supposed to be playing and having a good time. Loomis, I agreed to let you help Mr. Scapelli. You're supposed to be cleaning up the mess in there and not creating one." He turned to Jesse. "Mr. Tietjen, I remind you that you are a teacher, not one of the kids. I strongly suggest you act like a teacher, a *first-year* teacher at that. Now leave Loomis alone and go find someone your own age to play with." He turned and continued through the alcove into the Main Office.

"Sorry, Mr. Teeg. He's been more grouchy than usual lately."

"It's my fault, Virgil. Mr. Giovanni's right. I should know better. Boundaries."

"Do you think before you go you might give me a hand moving this stage flat out? It's the biggest thing and the heaviest. I can handle all the other stuff, but that brick wall is definitely a two-man job." He pointed to the brick veneer wall. "Mr. Scapelli went to get a cart from Mr. Polakas to roll everything backstage." He took one side of the flat. "If you grab the other side, we can lay it against that wall and I'll clear all the smaller stuff."

Together they tugged and pulled and dragged the flat out with some effort and propped it against the far wall in the alcove. Virgil laid some boxes and smaller flats against it. "That should keep that brick walls from tumbling down. Thanks, Mr. Teeg. I got the rest."

Jesse went into the Main Office, but returned a few minutes later. The alcove was filled with what Virgil had already emptied from the storage room.

"What's up, Mr. Teeg? You look upset."

"You wouldn't happen to have a movie projector in all that stuff by any chance? Seems I'm too late to get one from AV." He showed Virgil his rejected yellow AV requisition form. "I *was* planning to show that new *Romeo and Juliet* movie three days in class next week before vacation. Now it looks like I won't be until the end of May, if at all."

"The Franco Zeffirelli *Romeo and Juliet*? I saw it when it first came out in 1968. It was my first serious encounter with puberty." He sighed. "I was thirteen and I fell in love, Mr. Teeg, with Juliet. Or with Olivia Hussey, who played Juliet. She was an older woman. Fifteen then, and she stole my heart."

"Yeah, Virgil. I know. I fell in love with her too when I saw the movie." Jesse's face misted over until he realized how inappropriate he sounded.

"You do remember, Mr. Teeg, that there's a naked boob scene in the movie, right? It's quick, but it was a welcome sight for my thirteen-year-old eyes." They both sighed. "I'd sure like to see that movie again. If you give me that form I might be able to get you that projector, Mr. Teeg. Sometimes it's just a matter of knowing who to ask." He dusted his hands. "Sometimes it's knowing how to ask."

Jesse handed it over and followed him in to the Main Office.

* * *

Willy Zwill sat behind the security of his desk while the faint breeze from the exhaust fan in the window passed over him. Despite the moving air, the office was hot from the sheet metal insulation and he was perspiring. He had changed from his shorts and T-shirt into his regular clothes because he wanted to make a foray through the building. All the noise in the alcove outside his door had kept him in place, but he was a very patient man. Patience was something he learned during his POW days, and once again it paid off. It was finally quiet. He pressed his ear against the door, paced around the office and went back to the door.

"You think it's a trick?" he asked.

"Could be, Willy Boy," the voice answered. "So don't be too hasty to rush into anything. 'Patience is survival,'" the voice repeated the familiar mantra. "Maybe just a little peek."

Zwill switched off the lights and quietly slid the chain. He turned the key in the special pick-proof lock and slowly cracked the door. Everything was dark. Not dark like when the electricity is turned off, but dark like the inside of a cave, the bottom of a grave. He pulled the door open all the way. "Bricks!" he exploded. "We're bricked in!" He began to twitch uncontrollably. He was sealed inside behind a solid wall of bricks. He pressed and pushed, but it didn't budge. He put his shoulder to the bricks. They didn't yield an inch. "The yellow bastards buried us alive... like they did to Helen!" Just the mention of her name brought tears welling up in his eyes. "The bastards buried us alive!"

* * *

Jesse followed Virgil through the archway back into the alcove pushing a 16mm projector on an AV cart. "How can I thank you? I can't believe he actually gave you this projector when you vouched for me."

Virgil smiled. "Mr. Dexter wants to be appreciated and his work valued. That hard exterior is just a cover up. Underneath beats the heart of a frightened child who needs assurance, love and appreciation."

"You're very enlightened, Virgil. And you saved my life. What can I do for you?"

"Well, there's Mr. Scapelli's cart for the flats, but no Mr. Scapelli," he said. "Maybe, Mr. Teeg, you could help me load everything and move it into the auditorium before the bell rings?"

"Deal. Put the smaller things on here." Jesse pushed the projector cart forward. "And I'll help you with the flats on the big cart."

"Be careful, Mr. Teeg. You're not as young as you used to be. And you don't want to hurt yourself before the vacation."

* * *

Willy Zwill's back was against the closed door. He looked at his wristwatch. Apparently he'd been out for some time. As he slowly recovered his first thought was that he was inside the hot box in the Cabanatuan prison camp in the Philippines. "Yellow bastards," he mumbled. But then he remembered his actual predicament, which wasn't much better. That set off a spasm of uncontrolled twitching.

"Don't panic, Willy Boy–" the familiar voice said from somewhere in the darkness. "This is not the time. Clear your head. Think. We've been in worse spots and we survived. When the going gets tough and all that shit. The phone, Willy Boy, use the telephone to get help."

He went to his desk, picked up the receiver and automatically dialed Helen O'Dell's extension.

"Rita Reed," a strange voice answered at the other end.

"Where's Helen O'Dell?" he demanded. "I want Helen. What've you done with her?"

There was a pause. "Helen O'Dell's dead–"

"Bullshit, you lying bastard! You yellow lying bastard!"

She slammed down the receiver.

He dialed Mario Giovanni's extension, but there was no answer. And Noah Lewis didn't pick up either. "They knocked out central command. Everyone's gone." He redialed again with the same results. The office was getting hotter and perspiration rolled off his face and under his collar.

"Forget them, Willy Boy. You're all that's left. The only one. You're the last hope. So pull yourself together. Think. What did you do in the camp?"

"A tunnel! Of course, a tunnel. I headed the tunnel committee." He ran to the closet where he kept the things he had scavenged from his earlier forays around the camp. "I'll dig my way out." He pulled out two ladles and a bent fork. "We can put the dirt in bags in our pants and scatter it in the yard like we did. That way the bastards won't get suspicious. But this time we'll tunnel down deeper to get under the wire. And–"

"That's a scene from the movie *The Great Escape*, Willy Boy. Besides, it'll take too long. We don't have time. We need to get out now!"

"Right. We'll go right through the wall into Noah's office. And with his help we can dig out the others if it isn't already too late." He pushed aside the desk chair and attacked the far wall at the baseboard with the bent fork. It broke immediately and he tossed it across the floor. Then he tried the ladle, but it didn't last much longer.

"You can't tunnel through sheet metal, Willy Boy."

He tried unsuccessfully to pull it away with his fingers, but it wouldn't budge.

"The window, Willy Boy. Try the window."

He ran to the window and tried to pry loose the double layer of wire mesh. But the extra-long staples were set too deep and they didn't move. "Trapped!" The perspiration poured down his shirt and his pants. He began to hyperventilate. "Those bastards lured me into a trap and snapped it shut on me like a rat. Like a rat in a trap… Like the frozen mouse they used to kill poor O'Dell!" He rocked back and forth and heard the howl of a wild animal, a terrible sound he realized was coming from him.

"Easy, Willy Boy. We can't lose it now. We may be trapped, but they didn't count on one thing. Think."

Suddenly his face turned to a grin and he remembered. He stopped rocking and jumped to his feet. He pulled open the desk drawer and scattered everything that was in his way. He reached in and felt around until he found what he was after, the Nambu in the back of the drawer. His hand trembled when he touched it. The gun oil smelled sweet. "We'll shoot our way out!"

He dug deeper into the drawer and located the four loose 8mm bullets. He had cleaned and polished them until the brass casings gleamed. He pressed the release on the pistol, pulled the empty magazine from the handle and carefully slipped the bullets into the clip. Then he pushed it back in place until he heard it click and he took a deep breath.

"A drink first, Willy Boy. To steady the nerves before we rendezvous with Destiny."

From the cabinet above the little refrigerator he took out the half-empty bottle of cognac he had been saving and poured some into the glass tumbler. "One for you"–he continued pouring–"and one for me." Then he raised the glass and paused until he thought of an appropriate toast. "Remember Pearl Harbor," he said and downed the drink.

"Now, Willy Boy, it's time to show those bastards what we're made of!"

He pulled the large cocking knob at the back of the gun as he moved forward to the door. He heard a shell slide into the chamber. With his other hand he struggled unsuccessfully with the chain lock, tucked the pistol into his belt and went at the second lock. "Old Willy Boy isn't about to go down without a fight. No sir." He pulled and his hand slipped off the knob. He flew backward at the same time a deafening explosion reverberated inside the office. He wanted to run, to dive for cover, but he couldn't move. He hadn't quite grasped the meaning of the blast until he looked down and saw the blood pooling on the floor and the jagged hole in his shoe where some of his toes had been.

"Those bloody yellow bastards!" he yelled. And then he passed out.

* * *

Mr. Baltz was feeling pretty good when he left the Observatory. The video camera was a brilliant idea. He was gathering a trove of unexpected intelligence about his faculty and staff, even more valuable than what he had hoped for in his pursuit to unmask the Phantom. He added Dwayne Purvey's name to the growing list below Rory Aaron and Chuck LaFemina, John Hiller and Herb Lupus. He had them all on tape and enough on each of them to use the next time he had a problem. Who knew the secrets lurking in the hearts of men?

He moved swiftly and silently through the hall toward the elevator. He was still waiting when the sudden blast made him jump. "What the fuck!" he said. "The boiler!" He turned the key in the panel and pushed the elevator button a bunch of times without results. Then he turned and ran down the three flights to the Main Office. He was winded and his face dark when he turned to the main corridor. The halls were filled with curious teachers and students and the crowd clustered outside the door to the Administrative Alcove slowed him down.

"What happened?" he demanded, pushing his way to where Rita Reed was holding her balled handkerchief over her nose and crying hysterically. "What the hell happened?"

Mrs. Butrum was banging on Willy Zwill's closed door. "Mr. Zwill! Are you in there? Can you answer me?"

Rita Reed blew her nose. "I don't know," she managed. "An explosion in Mr. Zwill's office I think. First I got an obscene phone call and then there was this terrible bang. What did I get myself into? I don't want this job. I want to go back to being a teacher. What in God's name did I do to myself?"

"Oh, stop whining," Mr. Baltz snapped, "and make yourself useful! Call the police and an ambulance!" He leaned against Zwill's door and listened. "Willy, are you in there? Are you okay?" He tried the knob and it turned, but he couldn't open the door.

"It's jammed. Something is jammed against it," Mrs. Butrum said. "Do you think he's dead?"

He stared at her. "Willy? Talk to me. Willy!"

Mario Giovanni pushed his way into the crowded alcove. "What's going on? What happened?"

"Break it down, Mario." He pointed to Zwill's door.

The AP looked at him. "But I just got here."

"Break the door down now, Mario, it's an emergency!"

The AP straightened his jacket, cracked his neck and backed up into the crowd that was gathered behind him. He ran and hit the door with his shoulder, but it didn't open and he bounced back a little dazed.

"Again, Mario! Again!"

He hit the door harder and it gave slightly. And then together they all pushed and were able to force it open further.

"Oh, my God," Mrs. Butrum said when she saw the blood and Mr. Zwill lying in it. "I knew it. I knew it. He's dead!"

"Maybe we should move him into a classroom," the AP said feeling his bruised shoulder. His suggestion brought a murderous glare from the principal. "I mean so we're not slopping around and stepping in all that blood. I don't want to ruin another pair of shoes."

* * *

Seventeen minutes later, police cars again screamed into the courtyard with their lights flashing and the sirens growling and stopped next to the county ambulance. Their lights bounced around the walls as people filled the windows hoping to see something.

"He's not dead yet, but he's in shock," the Filipino EMT said. "He's lost a lot of blood, from what looks like a single non-life-threatening bullet wound in the foot. The more serious injury is the cracked skull he got from when you knocked in the door and hit him repeatedly on the head. I gave him a shot, but they'll take X-rays to see if there's any brain damage. The police will have questions about the bullet wound."

He pulled the strap tight on the gurney. Willy Zwill rolled back to semiconsciousness and looked into the slanty eyes of his captor as he was being wheeled from the office. "You shot me, you little Jap bastard," he snarled weakly but defiantly. "You should've killed me because if I get the chance you'll be the dead man!"

"You die soon enough, yankee pig dog. You be dead man velly soon! But first we make you talk, yankee dog," he taunted with a smile that revealed several gold caps.

Zwill closed his eyes. "Never. I'll die first. Remember... Pearl... Bailey! Remember... pearl... earrings!" he mumbled and closed his eyes.

"He may lose the rest of his toes. That wound looks pretty bad. And who's this Pearl Bailey he's ranting about?"

Sgt. Sadowski shook his head and looked at his notepad. "A single bullet wound from one gunshot concurs with what witnesses are saying. Nobody actually saw the event, but the shot was heard by numerous people." He held up the old Nambu with a pen through the trigger guard. "We recovered this relic with three more bullets in the clip." He showed them. "Fortunately he only shot himself. I don't know what else he was planning. We'll question him when he's out of surgery. You were lucky; you dodged a bullet... actually three of them." He smiled at his little levity. "But you sure are having a run of bad luck when it comes to assistant principals this year," he said to Mr. Baltz.

"Willy Zwill was always a little tense." Mr. Giovanni was talking to the two plainclothes detectives who had arrived on the scene in an unmarked car. "He just got out of South Oaks last Friday. He wasn't the most stable. Very nervous, a little flighty. He was a prisoner of war... in the Pacific... captured by the Japanese. I always thought he was a little off center, out of balance. And he definitely got crazier after we lost Helen O'Dell. She was another assistant principal who died the end of January. They were close."

One detective wrote something on his pad. "Would you say he was disgruntled? Do you think he planned to shoot anybody else?" the other detective asked.

"That's hard to say."

"What about this Helen O'Dell. Exactly how did she die?"

"Exactly? Helen died from natural causes," Mr. Giovanni said quickly, avoiding eye contact. "Well, if you consider a heart attack or heart failure natural. It was something heart related. In one of the classrooms," he added. "There was definitely no foul play."

They nodded.

A third man approached Mr. Giovanni when the other detectives moved to question other witnesses. "If you wouldn't mind," he said, "I have a few more questions for you." He looked at his pad. "Can you go back to Helen O'Dell? I understand there's been some talk about foul play by some people in the building. Do you think there might be a link? Did either of them have any enemies that you know of? Anybody who didn't like them? Who might be nursing a grudge and want either or both of them dead?"

"Look around," he said and cracked his neck. "This is a high school. School days, school days, good old golden rule days my ass. Remember what it was like when you were in high school? Well, it got worse. Years filled with anger and hatred. Students hate the teachers. Teachers hate administrators. And administrators hate everybody."

The unidentified man wrote it in his pad.

"Like most of our students, you graduated high school after four or maybe five years. We don't graduate. We're trapped here forever, until death or retirement. And as far as grudges go, everybody has at least one grudge. There are teachers in this place who haven't talked to one another since 1956! And you can bet that everybody here wants at least one somebody dead." He watched the man write in his pad. "Like I told the other detectives, Helen O'Dell died in a classroom of a heart thing. The school doctor was there and he filled out the death certificate. There were no suspicious circumstances and no foul play. She probably ate herself to death. Helen could pack it away. She was a big girl. And Zwill recently had a little breakdown and just got back to school on Monday after three weeks in South Oaks Hospital. The only connection is that they were both APs in this snake pit."

The police left the building after the ambulance pulled away with Willy Zwill secured inside.

"What did I, auh, miss?" Noah Lewis asked. "Someone in the lunchroom said the, auh, police were here again? I, auh, went home for lunch and came back as soon as I, auh, finished eating."

"It's Willy this time, Noah. And it looks like there's going to be another AP opening," Terry Scapelli said.

"Auh?"

After Mr. Baltz dispersed the crowd, Stash Polakas arrived with Slow Charley, a mop and a bucket and things went back to the new normal.

Rita Reed was shaking behind the desk in Helen O'Dell's office with Mrs. Butrum trying to comfort her. She was pale and her eyes were red. "And for *this* I had a hysterectomy?" she sobbed. "I don't need any of this. I just want to go back to my quiet classroom."

"I know, I know," Mrs. Butrum said. "But look at the bright side. At least you don't have to worry about your monthlies any more. Lord knows that's a blessing."

Are Our Schools Really Safe?
by Mike McQuinn, Education Writer

(Sunday March 26, 1972) Beginning at the age of five, children have been routinely packed up for school and shipped out by their parents. They place their babies on creaky, bouncy, yellow School Buses without a second thought, except, perhaps, for the absence of seat belts or that their kindergartener may come back after that first day of school with news that Mommy and Daddy are the Tooth Fairy and there is no Santa Claus!

But besides those expected dangers, exactly how safe are our schools?

Judging from the administrators and teachers at Rosencrantz and Guildenstern Memorial High School in Farmington, not very safe at all!

Assistant Principal Willy Zwill is a veteran of WW II and former POW who served in the Pacific Theater, survived the Bataan Death March and spent years in the Japanese prison camp of Cabanatuan until he was rescued. But his luck ran out on Friday when Zwill became the victim of gun violence resulting in the loss of four toes on his right foot and making him the latest casualty in a school plagued with casualties.

"He is the second AP in two months to bite the dust," according to AP Mario Giovanni who admitted that the injured Zwill was always a "bit unstable," possibly the result of having been a POW. Giovanni went on to expound on Zwill's history of mental illness and paranoid behavior. "He was always a loner who kept locked away in his office and he only got worse after [Assistant Principal] Helen O'Dell died and we buried her on the side lawn."

Helen O'Dell, herself a veteran who went into Education after serving with the Women's Army Corps, became the first casualty on January 31 when she died inside Rosencrantz and Guildenstern Memorial High School under mysterious circumstances. Though the cause of her death was originally listed as "heart failure" on the death certificate signed by school physician, Dr. Oliver Nessmith, it has now come under question. "I know what I saw," Carolyn Butrum, Chairlady of the Sunshine Committee exclaimed, "and I saw a frozen mouse in a roll on the floor next to poor Helen's body! Maybe we'll never know the truth about that mouse or what really happened to that poor woman. Is it a coverup? I can't say for sure, but it's a mystery–right up there with the Kennedy assassination, poor woman."

Zwill's shooting has raised questions about motives and possible links between both events among others on the staff. Joel Maxwell, President of the Farmington Teachers' Ass., minced no words. "The teachers are in their second year working without a contract with no raise in salary and no sign of a settlement on the horizon. Farmington shows its lack of concern for its teachers by repeatedly voting down the school budget year after year. Austerity has now become a way of life. Is it any wonder that teachers are resentful. And that resentment has a way of bubbling to the surface," he said.

Asked if it is possible someone nursing a grudge might take out their frustrations on those in authority or even on the children in the Farmington schools, Mr. Giovanni answered without hesitation. "Look around. School days, school days, good old golden rule days my a**. Remember what it was like when you were in high school? Well it got worse. Years filled with anger and hatred. Students hate the teachers. Teachers hate administrators. And administrators hate everybody." The beleaguered assistant principal continued, "We don't graduate. We're trapped here forever, until death or retirement. Everybody here has at least one grudge. Some teachers haven't talked to one another since 1956! And you can bet that everybody here wants at least one somebody dead."

The assistant principal went on to paint an unflattering picture of a high school where the principal spends a great deal of his time trying to catch the "Red Felt Phantom" who has been writing threatening insults and posting them throughout the building. "If that isn't enough, feces have recently started popping up around the building, everywhere except in the toilet! And I haven't even mentioned Parent's Night back last

November, when somebody tampered with the planned video presentation and replaced it with a pornographic tape. The guilty party was never found and the incident is pretty much forgotten."

Mysterious deaths… random shootings… pornographic tapes… What next? So again I ask you, how safe are our schools? For the parents of Farmington, and possibly in other schools on Long Island, in New York State and across America, they may have more to worry about than no seat belts on school buses, the Tooth Fairy and Santa Claus. No wonder Johnny can't read, he's much too busy dodging bullets and trying to avoid stepping in poop!

* * *

Monday morning copies of the Sunday *Newsday* story were on all the bulletin boards in the school. In the Third Floor Faculty Room there were ditto copies highlighted in yellow on the table as well.

"Somebody's in big trouble today," Sue said.

"And for once it isn't me," Terry quipped.

"I wouldn't want to be Mario Giovanni, that's for sure."

"But I sure would like to be a fly on Baltz's wall when Mario gets in. Dust off your résumés, boys and girls. We just may be in the market for yet *another* assistant principal!"

And so it went.

* * *

"He's waiting for you, Mario," Phyllis said when he stopped at her desk. "Be careful."

"Did he say anything?"

She shook her head. "Be very careful."

He stepped into the office and closed the door. Mr. Baltz was standing at the window looking into the courtyard. He didn't turn. At least, the AP noted, there was no plastic drop cloth under the chair in front of the Baltz's desk to catch the blood spatter. And he didn't see a baseball bat in reach. He moved into the room cautiously. "I… can explain… Really… I…"

"Sit, Mario." He turned and his face was dark. "No, Mario. Closer. Sit closer," he said tonelessly when the AP slid into Noah Lewis's seat in the corner farthest away.

"I had no idea–"

He raised his hand and cut off his attempt at an apology. "For years, Mario, from your first day as my assistant principal, I started grooming you. I told you then to prove yourself and your allegiance, don't do anything to embarrass yourself... or me. I said, and one day you would be sitting in my seat. But you let me down, Mario." He took a breath. "Is it possible I misjudged the level of your incompetence? You can't be that stupid, can you?" Again he put up a hand. "That leads me to wonder then if it's outright sabotage."

"I'm sorry... I didn't know–"

"*Newsday*, the Sunday edition, Part Two." He scanned down the page picking out words and phrases. "'Unstable... a history of mental illness and paranoid behavior... a loner... driven by paranoia and obsession... phantom writer... feces at various locations around the high school.' And then, if that wasn't enough, you idiot, you dragged up that Parent's Night fiasco again! What were you thinking? *Were* you thinking? Is it your wish to have me resign in disgrace? Or are you trying to kill me? See me dead??"

"I swear I didn't know the guy was a reporter. I thought he was one of the detectives. He had a pad–"

"Do you even have a clue what you've done? The police are asking questions about O'Dell again. An *Eyewitness News* report on TV is calling for the investigation to be reopend. Exhume O'Dell's body if necessary! That long-haired hippie loudmouth who reported all those abuses in Willowbrook State Hospital, Gerald fucking Riviera, is leading the charge and covering the story." He pulled a Lucky from the pack, lit it and started a coughing fit. "On top of all this shit, I'm going to be sick for vacation." He stubbed it out in the ashtray. "I don't want Gerald Riviera, or anybody else running around investigating my school!"

"Rivera. Geraldo with an 'H' Riv*era*," he corrected.

"Gerald Riviera, Geraldo Rivera, who gives a fuck! I don't want either of them airing our dirty laundry, poking into dark closets, finding something else to make me an even bigger laughingstock. Whenever I pick up my phone somebody's laughing. Flackett, that miserable bastard, and Adornau, that *dago* asshole. And Stegle called me over the weekend *at home*, the stuttering bitch. This morning I had a note from her in inter-school mail about hiring her fucking moron of a son to replace Zwill, that lunatic son of a bitch. Everybody in the building knows that Zwill's crazy, but it's you, Mario, that told everything to a *Newsday* reporter. It's you that is responsible for bringing down what I worked a lifetime to build!"

"I was tired... I haven't slept much... I'm doing everybody else's job around here–"

"Just remember, if the ship sinks, you're going down with it. It was you who got rid of the mouse."

"But you told me–"

"And you came up with the idea to put O'Dell in a classroom. That's insurance fraud. If you don't fix this, Mario, there may well be more than one body that needs explaining." He rolled up the newspaper and tucked it under his arm. "Now get the fuck out of here and think of something to make it right."

In his private toilet Baltz lit another cigarette and tried to relax. He watched the smoke curl up over his head until it was caught by the exhaust fan and sucked into the science classroom above him. He separated the newspaper sections and read his horoscope. "'There are changes on your horizon. Embrace them.'" He paged through the comics. He never understood "Doonesbury." In this one, some unemployed man sitting on a chair asks his wife for a beer. She says they got a package all the way from Vietnam. The note is from their son B.D., who says he bought his father a toffee-toned hand-drilled bowling ball in Hong Kong. In the next to last panel the man and his wife are ecstatic as he twirls the ball on his finger and shouts 'Whoopee!' In the last one he is thinking, 'A good bowling ball sure can take the sting out of being unemployed," whatever that was supposed to mean. It wasn't even funny.

He was restless. He knew if he went out he'd have to face all those smirks and snide comments, especially if he ran into Scapelli. He tried putting for a bit, but kept missing the ashtray, which only made him more tense. So he bit the bullet and left. "I'll be out for a while on official business, Miss Lind–"

"Ms."

"If that Stegle woman tries to reach me again, tell her to take it up with Flackett. And if that *Riviera* Rivera guy calls and says he wants to make an appointment to see me, I won't be available until June sometime."

"And what do I say if Walter Cronkite calls?"

He took the elevator to the third floor and went directly to the (F)Utility Closet… his Fortress of Solitude and source of solace.

"It's a disgrace!" Red Farley was livid when he stormed into the Third Floor Faculty Room. "It's beyond disgusting!"

Moron Blight, the First Librarian, opened one eye on the couch where she was napping. "What the hell is that foul smell?"

Rita Reed gagged and pressed her handkerchief to her face.

"Geez, Red, you stink," Stanley Milnow said. "You better check your diet and go see a gastro doctor."

"Funny, Stan. The Phantom Shitter struck again!" he roared. "That degenerate pinched a loaf right inside the door of my classroom! And I slipped in it. It's on my shoe, my pants–" He looked for paper to clean himself.

"You're tracking it all over the floor," Mrs. Butrum said and Rita Reed retched.

"What am I supposed to do? There's no paper towels."

"Austerity," Joel Maxwell quipped. "The district reaps what it sows."

Mrs. Butrum and Rita Reed both handed him tissues.

Terry entered the room followed by Jesse, who held the door for Sue Wellen. "What's that god-awful smell?" she asked.

"Red stepped in shit. At least that's what he says. Though he might be lying because he has it all over his pants,." Terry couldn't resist.

"In my opinion, the solution to all this shit is simple–a contract," Joel Maxwell continued, on his political soapbox. "If the District gave us a decent contract with a decent raise there wouldn't be any need for disgruntled employees to be shitting around the building or shooting assistant principals."

"In my opinion the solution is simpler," Red Farley said, wiping the sole of his shoe with the tissues. "We have the resources right here in this school. So how difficult would it be to collect a specimen from everyone in the building and have the Science Department do an analysis and compare the results to what the Phantom Shitter left behind?" He held up the tissue.

"That's disgusting."

"It could work."

"I love the smell of feces in the morning," Terry said. "It makes me homesick and reminds me of my tour in Nam where they fertilize their rice paddies with 'night soil.'" He turned to the ladies. "That's a polite way of saying doody." He pointed to Red. "That whole country smells just like that."

"What you smell, Scapelli, is all the bullshit you've been spreading around here for years," Red said. "You were never in Nam."

"The hell I wasn't and the hell you know. Right out of college ROTC before I started teaching."

"Bull... shit!"

"Think what you will, Red. Say what you want. Then how do you explain this?" He reached into his back pocket and pulled out a bandanna that turned out when he opened it to be a flag–a single orange star in the center, a dark blue patch below and alternating red and yellow stripes radiating above.

"What's that supposed to be?"

"It's the flag we captured the morning my platoon went into the village of Qwang B'dang, my friend. And by 'we' I mean me and the boys from Charlie Company, a unit of the America I Division's 11th Infantry Brigade. Always the first ones in the shit... slogging through the rice paddies. It took us all day to neutralize the village... capture all those woman and children and those old men. Oh, the things I've done, Red, and the things I've seen." He sighed. "And just as a point of information. Charlie Company was the same Charlie Company that went into My Lai in 1968 with Captain Ernie Medina and Lieutenant William Calley in command."

"Oh, *you lie* all right, Scapelli. You're the biggest goddamn liar I know."

"Like I said, think what you will, Red. But I know what I know and I know I have this flag to prove that I was there." He folded it carefully and tucked it into his back pocket.

The bell rang and there was a collective groan from the teachers who had to face another class. Only Moron Blight didn't move.

"So, let me get this straight," Sue said. "You went to Vietnam right out of college ROTC?" She counted on her fingers. "That would mean you were there in 1960, around the time Eisenhower sent in advisors and about two years before Kennedy sent some more." She continued counting. "That would be four years before the Gulf of Tonkin in 1964, when U.S. combat began." She shook her head. "I don't think so."

"Well, I may have exaggerated a little. Can't argue with a social studies teacher," he said to Jesse.

"And isn't that the Arizona state flag?" Jesse asked. "I seem to recall seeing it when I went to the Grand Canyon."

"The Arizona state flag?" Terry was shocked. "It can't be the Arizona state flag. When the LST landed and the ramp dropped, we went into Qwang B'dang guns blazing."

"LSTs were used in the D-day landing and they transported tanks. Higgins Boats landed the troops." Sue added.

"Oh, God. I'm totally embarrassed." Terry looked horrified. "If what you say is true that means those paddies I slogged through were... Arizona rice paddies? Then that must mean," he paused, "and I shiver to think that... all those people we neutralized were... Arizonians!" He took a deep breath and covered his face. "What have I done Wellen? I fear that I made a terrible mistake. And now I just may have to reevaluate my entire life."

A SPECIAL MESSAGE
FROM THE OFFICE OF
THE SUPERINTENDENT OF SCHOOLS
DR. DONALD F. FLACKETT, SUPT.

SPECIAL COLLECTIONS

March 29, 1972

In response to the number of disturbing incidents concerning unwanted "deposits" by a Phantom Depositor recently reported at the High School during the past weeks, I feel it is my "doody" to take definitive action to prevent Mr. Baltz's problem from escalating and becoming mine. Effective immediately, all teachers and staff at R&G are required to provide my office with a stool sample specimen. Specimens may be hand-delivered to Central Administration or sent via Inter-School Mail by the end of the day. Each specimen must be identified with the name of the specimen provider and the time of its collection. All specimens will be analyzed in-house by the Science Department under the direct supervision of Science Chairman Dr. Calvin Kulp. Specimens will be categorized and identified by name and compared to those that have been left behind at the high school.

Those who are unable to provide a specimen today because of the short notice, or for physical or psychological reasons, Fleets Enemas will be available in the Health Office throughout the day. Specimens not deposited today must be submitted properly labeled upon the reopening of school on April 10 after the Easter/Passover break. Under no circumstance should anyone attempt to provide a stool sample specimen of a pet or a person other than themselves.

A SPECIAL MESSAGE
FROM THE OFFICE OF
THE SUPERINTENDENT OF SCHOOLS
DR. DONALD F. FLACKETT, SUPT.

CORRECTION AND AMENDMENT

March 29, 1972

In the previous memo, all teachers and staff were instructed to submit their properly labeled stool sample specimens to Central Administration either in person or by way of Inter-School Mail. This was an error. Specimens are to be delivered to the Administrative Alcove in the High School where collection boxes will be provided outside Assistant Principal Mario Giovanni's office.

In addition, because the Phantom Depositor has been more active and has enlarged his (or her) "deposit" range in recent days, teachers and staff dropping off their specimens with Mr. Giovanni will be issued plastic bags for use to cover their shoes. The District will not be responsible to any teacher or staff member who declines the protective plastic bags and is not financially liable for any unprotected shoes that may become ruined.

Furthermore, because the assistant principals at the High School seem to be "dropping like flies," flak jackets will soon be available for any surviving administrator who wishes to wear one.

Note: Flak jackets will NOT be available for teachers.

Red Farley walked into the faculty bathroom. "It really galls me to see that Loomis kid strutting around with his smug, smart aleck attitude, flaunting his Jewfro in everybody's face and wearing a wrestling letter on a Varsity sweater. And now Buddy Ritchie says he's trying to pull the same ACLU lawyer crap with the other secret teams! That kid has no sense of decency and no consideration for others." He let go of the door and it closed on Stanley Milnow's hand.

"Owww! My hand!"

"There was a time when the teachers ran the school, but not anymore. It started back in the sixties in the colleges. NYU, Columbia and Berkley. No respect. And we let them get away with it. Now high school kids are calling the shots. I can only imagine what it will be like in ten years. And speaking of shots, if they'd killed a few more radicals at Kent State, things would be a lot different today. I have to take a dump."

"You know, Red, if you were the Phantom Shitter you wouldn't have to come in here." He held his hand under running water. "You could shit anywhere." He shook his wet hand and examined his face and teeth in the mirror. "If we ever get a contract I hope we get dental insurance so I can get these gums fixed." Red laughed. "What's so funny about gums?"

"Just reading the writing on the wall." He laughed again. "A lot of people really hate Baltz. You got a marker?"

"Black okay?" He walked over to the stall and handed it under the door. "Who do you think it is?"

"Writing on the walls? From the looks of it, everybody."

"No, I mean the Phantom Shitter."

"I guess we'll find out after they analyze all the samples. You know I had that idea first. Somebody in the faculty room must've heard me and told them at Central." He opened the stall door. "Here's my sample. Did you drop yours off yet?"

"When we get back from vacation." He took back his marker. "But if you had to guess, who do you think?"

"It's not you and it's not me. Unless you're hiding something. I figure it has to be somebody with the run of the building. A custodian… Polakas? He'd be crazy to pull shit like that. Maybe Slow Charley. More likely one of the night crew who has less chance of getting caught."

"It could be a woman. It's a lot easer for a woman to set, squat and drop."

"Not if she's wearing pants. Besides, women don't do shit like that."

"Maybe a dyke would. That librarian. She looks like she would drop a deuce without a second thought." He cocked his head and leaned closer to the wall. "Do you hear something, Red?" He pressed his ear against the mirror. "Sounds like humming. Like an electric motor."

Red pressed his ear to the wall. "Any humming you hear is in your head, Stan."

"Maybe it's termites swarming?"

"It's a cement wall! Come on, I want to drop this sample off at Giovanni's office so I can get out of this place fast at the end of the day. What are you doing for Easter?"

"I'm a Jew. I celebrate Passover."

"Okay, so what are you doing for Jewish Easter?"

As soon as they were gone, Mr. Baltz rushed into the bathroom and he didn't care if anyone saw him. He pushed open the stall door and the walls were covered in different handwriting and in different colors, printed and in script. "BREAK BALTZ BALLS," "2 APs DOWN 2 TO GO" with "DEATH TO ALL TYRANTS" "NO CONTRACT NO WORK" under it. Behind the door was the greatest number of messages printed in red and green that had been altered with black marker. He grew more enraged as he read each of them. "BOOK BALTZ!" "BALTZ SOCKS BIG HAIRY COOKS" "BALTZ IS A COOK SOCKER" "BALTZ EATS SHIP" and "I WANT TO BOOK SUE WELLEN AND SOCK HER PITS!" At least, he thought, Red Farley was still doing his job.

In the News
April 1972

April 1

The first Major League Baseball strike begins.

April 3

Pres. Nixon enacts legislation devaluing the dollar.

Actor Charlie Chaplin returns to the U.S. after twenty years' absence.

April 4

In further response to the North Vietnamese Easter Offensive, Pres. Nixon authorizes a massive bombing campaign targeting all NVA troops invading South Vietnam, along with B-52 air strikes against North Vietnam. "The bastards have never been bombed like they're going to be bombed this time," Nixon privately declares.

April 5

The Harrisburg 7 trial ended in mistrial after 11 weeks. Fr. Philip Berrigan and Sr. Elizabeth McAllister were declared guilty, but only of smuggling letters in and out of prison. Librarian Zoia Horn, who had refused to testify at the trial, becomes the first U.S. librarian to be jailed for refusing to testify. She is freed after 20 days when the jury is deadlocked on conspiracy charges.

April 7

Vietnam veteran and pilot Richard McCoy hijacks a United Airlines jet and extorts $500,000 in a copycat version of the DB Cooper crime. He parachutes into a Utah desert, but is later caught with the money in his house and is sentenced to 40 years in prison.

"Crazy" Joe Gallo, flamboyant mobster, is gunned down at his 43rd birthday party in Manhattan's Umberto's Clam House.

April 13

The first Major League Baseball strike ends.

April 16

Apollo 16 blasts off on a voyage to the moon.

April 17-30

Watergate burglar Eugenio Martinez and White House aide E. Howard Hunt, ratchet up the activities of the White House "Plumbers" operation. Martinez is not yet aware of the nature of the team's operations, but believes he is part of a black-ops, CIA-authorized organization working to foil Communist espionage activities. Hunt gives team member Bernard Barker $89,000 in checks from Mexican banks to cash for operational funds, and orders Barker to recruit new team members. Barker brings in Frank Sturgis, Virgilio Gonzalez and Reinaldo Pico, all veterans of the CIA's activities against Cuba's Fidel Castro. Plans are discussed to break into Democratic presidential candidate George McGovern's campaign headquarters. Hunt says they are going to find evidence proving that the Democrats are accepting money from Castro and other foreign governments.

**Union Free School District 71
Office of the Superintendent
Central Administration Building
Farmington, New York**

From: Donald F. Flackett, Superintendent
To: All Faculty and Staff
Subject: Official Memo of Clarification
April 10, 1972

Before the Easter/Passover break two memos purporting to be from this office appeared in teacher mailboxes at the High School. By way of summary, these memos referred to a plan to collect stool sample specimens from every teacher and staff member at the school for analysis in an attempt to identify the individual or individuals responsible for the unwanted deposits that have been left behind around the building. The memos also indicated that flak jackets would be distributed to administrators who want them.

Be advised that it was a hoax! The memos were bogus and definitely not official memos from my office. There is no intention to collect and analyze stool sample specimens from the faculty and staff at this time and those that were sent to Central Administration by Inter-School mail, along with those left with Mr. Giovanni at the High School have been discarded.

However, there may be some merit to the idea of flak jackets.

Welcome back.

Rosencrantz and Guildenstern
Memorial High School
UFSD 71
Farmington, New York

TO: All Teachers and Staff
FROM: M. Seymour Baltz, Principal
SUBJECT: Safety and Sanitary Concerns in Schools
April 10, 1972

Attention! Recent events have raised questions about the safety and well-being of our students, as well as sanitary conditions within our school. Both are of paramount concern. Therefore, in the coming weeks security patrols will be stepped up around the building. Mr. Giovanni's amended duty list for teachers will be in the mailboxes today. Beginning tomorrow and until further notice, all teacher preparation periods will be cut and teachers will be assigned areas of the building to patrol during those twenty-three minutes.

Efforts are now underway by the Custodial Corps to systematically sanitize the entire building in the coming days and weeks. To this end the stall doors in all the student bathrooms have already been removed. The stall doors in the Third Floor Faculty Men's Room will once again be removed tomorrow. Stall doors in each of the Faculty Women's Rooms will also be removed in the interest of gender equality and to acknowledge passage of the Equal Rights Amendment to the Constitution on March 22nd.

Once the removal is accomplished, the custodians will begin a systematic operation to steam the facilities and sanitize them. During the brief period that the doors will be down they will be inspected, repaired, repainted or, if necessary, replaced with new stall doors. Your patience and understanding is appreciated. All stall doors should be back in place before the new school year in September.

Joseph E. Scalia

Camelot

Official Publication of the Partnership of Parents and Teachers
in Association for better Farmington Public Schools
Harriet Stegle, President P-PTA

Vol. 8 Issue 8   Spring Edition   April 1972

How about that Geraldo Rivera? The *Eyewitness News* investigative reporter, fresh from his successful exposé earlier this year about the gruesome conditions and neglected mentally disabled children in the Willowbrook School on Staten Island, has been seen around the high school. And he's asking questions! No stranger to Long Island, he hails from just up the road in Suffolk County's West Babylon and his mother is a dear friend. When little Jerry Rivers, as I knew him, is "on the case" there's no place to hide. Give 'em hell, Geraldo! And I want to go on the record, he's much better looking than he appears on TV.

AROUND THE DISTRICT:

On March 24, R&G AP Willy Zwill, who had recently returned from a three-week stay in South Oaks, was once again chauffeured from the building courtesy of Nassau County. Mr. Zwill was wheeled out on a gurney with a smile on his face, though some said it was more like a grimace of pain, a song on his lips, "Remember Pearl Harbor," and a number of toes shy. But it's nothing but good news for Wee Limpin' Willy, who was moved from Meadowbrook Hospital back to South Oaks. And reports are that he is recovering nicely from a concussion after surgery to remove a blood clot and a portion of his right foot. Visitors who saw him last said that Willy was popping wheelies in his chair and practicing other tricks like picking up a handkerchief from the floor with his teeth.

Willy Zwill's bad luck means good luck for someone because it looks like there's another Assistant Principal position to be filled. And that gives the powers that be in Central another opportunity to finally "do the right thing" and give an able and deserving local boy another chance. But enough said.

CONGRATULATIONS:

The winter bowling league finally ended last week and trophies were presented to all the participants. Everyone gets a trophy! Congratulations to Ann Bernadette Flannery from the Junior High, who finished with the lowest score, and Head Custodian Stash Polakas for highest series and total pins. "It's in the blood," Stash said at the award dinner held at the Mid-Way Alleys. Atta boy, Stash. You showed them your skill and you're Polish (Ha! Ha!).

CONDOLENCES:

Sincerest condolences to Martina Freety, Kindergarten teacher at West Street Elementary, on the loss of her mother.

And prayers to the Burkes. Larry is the itinerant reading teacher servicing all the elementary schools. They are mourning the passing of their seventeen-year-old cocker spaniel, Trooper.

NEWS AND VIEWS:

Well, it's official. After all the hoopla, the buildup and the hard work, the date for Skirt Day at R&G has been finally set– Monday, April 17! According to Sylvia Berkowsky, Home Economics Department Chair, "Once upon a time teachers dressed like professionals and students came to school neat and clean. Boys wore slacks and girls wore dresses and skirts. My how standards have fallen. That gave me the idea for Skirt Day. It's a perfect opportunity to raise those standards back to where they once were. And it's a chance for our Home Ec girls to reveal their assets and show everyone what they are made of. Skirt Day will be a way to acknowledge their hard work and showcase the skirts they've designed and been sewing all year. In fact, it will be a perfect way for *everyone* to participate and dress up. Hooray for Skirt Day. Monday, April 17! Everybody wear a skirt!" You heard the woman, everybody wear a skirt!

That's all for now. See you next time with more news from the trenches!

Message from the Underground
"Hell yes, I'll go wherever I wanna to go!"

FROM: The Phantom Pooper
TO: ALL Farmington Teachers
RE: The Potty Manifesto

There is something rotten in Rosencrantz and Guildenstern and it's coming from the toilets!

Not only have we endured another school year without a contract, two years with no salary increase and yet another austerity budget, but now we are expected to just sit there and take it while further indignities are dumped on us! To wit, the April 10 memo "Safety and Sanitary Concerns in Schools"!

The removal of stall doors from the faculty toilets goes beyond the bounds of indecency! It is a blatant attempt to further demean us and strip a faculty, already stripped of dignity with our pants and underwear around our ankles, of whatever little dignity remains. But we're not just going to sit there and take it! There can be no rest, only unrest in restrooms without stall doors!

Teachers, now squatting in the glare of this public humiliation, jump to your feet in unison. Stand tall together shoulder to shoulder in a show of solidarity. Shout in one voice for all to hear, "Hell no, we won't go!" To paraphrase the immortal words of John Lennon, "All we are saying is keep on your pants!"

AND SO IT IS RESOLVED THAT APRIL 14, HAS BEEN DESIGNATED AS BUILDING-WIDE POOP OUT DAY!

Keep out of the faculty bathrooms tomorrow and join your colleagues, men and women, who will stand and remain standing until all the stall doors have been returned! What then, you may well ask, will you doo when you have to make a doo?

Doo what I, the Phantom Pooper already doos, any place in the rest of the building will doo!

Dwayne Purvey had tried to keep a low profile for more than two months, while he waited for Helen O'Dell's dust to settle and for her to rest in peace. But when Willy Zwill flipped out, shot himself and Mario Giovanni stirred up the whole mess again, the ghost of Helen O'Dell arose from the dead. He hoped all the interest generated by the *Newsday* article and the TV and radio coverage would die down during the Easter break when school was closed, but instead the story developed legs, was picked up on the wires and went national. Reporters from as far away as Washington state showed up in town and were nosing around. School Board meetings were packed and signed petitions circulated calling for a full investigation. In the wake of Helen O'Dell's wake and what followed, Purvey was conspicuously absent from the faculty room, the ongoing conversations and theories. Citing "personal issues," he stepped back from all of his union activities and handed over leadership to Frank Stagiano, the militant vice president of FU-2, and slipped further into the shadows. So much so that Mrs. Butrum was surprised to see him in the halls.

"When I asked Mr. Maxwell what happened to you he said you had testicular cancer! How are you feeling? I haven't seen you much and thought you were out sick. The Sunshine Committee was going to send you a basket of fruit." She lowered her voice and her eyes to the front of his chalk covered pants. "Have you started chemo?"

Dwayne Purvey was in the middle stall in the faculty bathroom when he heard the door open. He picked the papers he was correcting from the floor, pulled his feet up and hoped whoever it was would come and go and be on their way.

"Wham! Wham! Wham!" a hand pounded on the stall door.

He lurched forward and grabbed his pants. "What the fuck! Somebody's in here!"

"And somebody's out here to take the doors off the stalls."

"You just have to wait."

"The hell I do. You stay there and keep doing what you're doing and I'll have the door off in a minute."

He recognized the voice. "Maxwell, you're a fucking idiot."

"Oh, yeah? I'm out here scaring the piss out of you and you're stuck in there with your pants around your ankles." He pounded on the door again. "So who's the fucking idiot, Purvey?"

"You have a hell of a lot of nerve telling Butrum that I have testicular cancer. She's such a big blabbermouth she told everybody—"

"I didn't tell her you had testicular cancer. I told her you don't have any balls."

"Fuck you, Maxwell! When I get out of here I'm going to kill you!"

"Like you killed O'Dell?"

"Wh-what are you talking about? I wasn't even in school that day. I was absent when O'Dell died."

"Maybe yes, maybe no. I don't know how or what you did, Purvey, but all that talk about a mouse makes me think you had something to do with it." He went into the first stall and shut the door. "They're all sniffing around, Purvey, and it won't be long before somebody makes a connection and then you're the one that's fucked."

Silence.

"The handwriting is on the walls, Purvey." There were muffled sounds. "And while you're reading what's on the walls, look overhead. In coming!"

Purvey looked up as a barrage of flaming tissues sailed over the top of the stall and rained down on top of him. That was followed by a second wave and a third.

"What the fuck! Are you insane, Maxwell! I'm on fire!" He stomped out the flaming paper and pounded out the smoldering ashes on his shirt. "I'm going to kill you, Maxwell. This time, this time, Maxwell, it'll be your chalk outline on the floor."

Silence.

* * *

Baltz was in the Observatory reviewing the videotape. He fast-forwarded through the beginning and backed it up when he saw Purvey and Maxwell. He replayed it several times and laughed each time. "Assholes. Even bigger assholes than I thought." He turned up the volume and he listened until he heard Helen O'Dell's name. It stopped him and he played it back again and again.

When the bathroom door opened, Stash and Slow Charley came in wearing their makeshift hazmat suits—yellow rubber rain slickers, dishwashing gloves, galoshes and goggles. "You get the doors, Charley. I'll crank up the steamer. And we we'll be out of here in no time."

There was a rumble as the steam machine came to life. In minutes the mirror clouded over with mist and the bathroom filled with steam. Baltz heard them moving around on the other side of the one-way mirror, but the steam was too thick to see through. When the fog lifted they were both gone and so were the stall doors.

April 17 began with great promise. It promised to be a beautiful day and everything said spring. According to Tex Antoine, the warm weekend weather would hang around into the week at least through Wednesday. The crocuses were up, the forsythia popped and tree pollen covered everything like yellow snow. It made Jesse sneeze, but it was worth it. Life was almost good again. Even with Daylight Savings Time still two weeks away, it was noticeably lighter longer. The light at the end of the tunnel was actually the early morning sun, so his commute was not in total darkness. Better yet, as the days were growing longer, the number of days until June was getting shorter–faster, like toilet paper unwinding at the end of the roll.

After months of teasers, posters taped to the walls in every corridor of the building, promotional announcements on the PA every morning and afternoon and fliers crammed into every teacher's mailbox for weeks leading up to the big event, Monday, April 17 was finally here. It was Skirt Day, the brainchild Sylvia Berkowsky, the Home Economics Department Chair, hatched way back in November when the pants suits arrived and fashion standards and good taste came to a screeching halt. That cold November day in the faculty room she announced her yet-to-be formed idea.

"It is my hope," she said to people who weren't really listening, "that the Skirt Day 1972, the first many, will be like a finger in the dike–" That caught the attention of Andi Roberts and Bobbi Andrews, two Girls' Phys Ed teachers in the back corner of the Faculty Room. "–the first step in stopping the ever-sliding standards of dress among students and some teachers." All eyes turned to Terry Scapelli. "Skirt Day will become the vehicle to restore beauty and good taste to these school corridors."

Like Ladybird Johnson's vision of a more beautiful America without billboards, Sylvia Berkowsky painted her glorious picture of a Skirt Day so successful it would become an inspiration, an institution, serve as the model for all the Skirt Days to follow at Rosencrantz and Guildenstern, and that would create a fashion revolution across Long Island and America. Terry stood and applauded when she finished her speech.

For Sylvia, Skirt Day was practical as well as idealistic. It was a way for the new Home Ec Department Chair to justify her recent promotion that came with a substantial salary increase and a decrease in the number of classes she had to teach. Its success would guarantee her tenure by showcasing her administrative abilities as well as her creativity. So, in the months that followed her January proclamation, every Home Ec teacher was ordered to participate and every Home Ec class became, like a turn-of-the-century Lower East Side sweatshop, a hive of secret activity where girls, under the watchful eyes of their teachers and the scrutiny of Sylvia, conceived, designed and created their very own fashions to be unveiled and worn by them on the first Skirt Day.

A month before the big event, signs began to appear on official bulletin boards: "Skirt Day is coming!" In a well-coordinated advertising blitz, each day messages appeared taped over doorways and tacked to every flat surface around the building: "Monday, April 17, is Skirt Day!" Two weeks before Skirt Day, the first announcements were broadcast over the PA system after AM exercises and repeated just before the PM dismissal bell. "Skirt Day is next Monday. Don't forget to wear a skirt." A week before, teachers were directed to remind their classes every day leading up to Skirt Day. And on the Friday before, an official letter addressed to every parent of every student signed by Sylvia Berkowsky went home to each household in the district, explaining Monday's event and ending with the sentence: "*Everyone* wear a skirt on Skirt Day!"

Despite all that orchestrated enthusiasm, none of the teachers seated around the table in the Third Floor Faculty Room seemed in a great hurry to put out cigarettes, finish their coffee or rush to class when the Skirt Day morning bell sounded. Red Farley and Stanley Milnow continued playing Hearts without any indication they had even heard the bell.

"Excuse me," Terry said, "I believe that was the signal for the Skirt Day ceremonies to begin." He stood where he had been sitting, rolled up the legs of his jeans revealing a well-worn pair of construction boots and droopy white socks, reached into the stained, brown #10 shopping bag he had been holding and pulled out a bundle. He shook it open and it became a gray wrap-around midi-skirt that he tied in place around his waist. He adjusted the length of the purple shirt he had specifically selected for the occasion and smoothed the wrinkles. Then he pulled out the elastic holding his ponytail and shook his head so that his hair fell free and natural.

"Oh, shit!" somebody said. "Here we go!"

"What the hell is wrong with you, Scapelli?"

"It's Skirt Day, Red." He strode to the door and then he was out in the hall, swallowed by the throng rushing to get to their lockers before Homeroom.

* * *

A high school is like a living organism, an ant colony or a creature with a brain and a nervous system. Some things travel slowly, others faster than light. So before Terry had passed down the hall, the message "Mr. Scapelli is wearing a dress!" exploded around the building. It echoed to the furthest outposts of R&G. It reached the lunch ladies in the cafeteria, who shook their hair-netted heads. All of the guidance counselors drinking coffee in their offices heard it, except for John Hiller, who hadn't punched in yet. And it trickled down even to the custodians in the sub-basement. The news got around the building in a flash, helped along by Mario Giovanni, who was on his morning rounds when he saw Terry standing outside Room 215 directing traffic before the opening day ceremonies began.

"Good morning, Mr. Giovanni. Did you forget it's Skirt Day? Nice shoes," he called to the assistant principal who stopped just for a second to gawk before he sprinted down the hall in the direction of the Main Office.

Minutes later a very red-faced Mr. Baltz was barreling down at him from the far end of the corridor. "Come with me,

Mr. Scapelli. Now!" he ordered in a rush when he had the breath to speak.

"But, I have a class. Mr. Baltz."

"Someone will be here to cover. You come with me NOW!" He turned to the crowd of students who had bunched up around them. "The rest of you," he bellowed, "get to class immediately!"

Terry followed close behind, sucked along in the principal's jet stream, down the stairs from the second floor, then up again to the first, beyond the Music Room where some teachers and students applauded as they passed, around the corner and by the Bernard H. Prahl Memorial Auditorium into the main corridor. Mr. Baltz pushed open the door to the Main Office and Terry was a step behind him, his hair streaming over his purple shirt and his wraparound Skirt Day midi skirt catching air. The secretaries, late-arriving students, parents dropping off their kids or forgotten lunches went silent when the two men burst onto the scene. It was like an old cowboy movie where the bad guy comes through the swinging saloon doors and everything freezes. All eyes followed them around the front counter, past the secretaries' desks to Mr. Baltz's office.

"Nice ensemble–" Phyllis started when Terry walked by her desk, but Mr. Baltz cut her short with a killing look.

He slammed his office door and Terry slipped into the chair in front of the principal's desk, modestly crossed his legs at the knees and arranged the hem of his skirt so only his construction boots and droopy white sock showed.

"What's the meaning of this, Mr. Scapelli!" he raged. apoplectically.

Terry brushed back his hair with his fingers. "It's Skirt Day, Mr. Baltz."

"Scapelli... you know very well... that was intended for the girls and the women on staff."

"Mr. Baltz, I have to respectfully disagree. There have been signs posted all over the building for months. Everywhere. On all the walls in all the halls and even in the glass display case right outside the Main Office. And they all say, 'Everyone wear a skirt.'"

The principal's face twitched involuntarily and he suppressed the impulse to dive across his desk, scattering everything on top of it, to grab Terry by the throat and hold on until he stopped moving. "Scapelli, you are a smartass bastard. A thorn in my side for years. You have no regard for decorum. No respect for authority... for me... and you delight in breaking the rules just to 'break Baltz balls'! You are an instigator, a provocateur, a saboteur and responsible for many of the problems in this building. And when I can prove what I know in my heart, it is going to be my greatest pleasure to begin a 30-20A tenure hearing and see you gone, no matter how long it takes or how much it costs the District."

"Be all that as it may, Mr. Baltz, first and foremost I am an English teacher, and as part of my duties as such, I deal with the precise meaning and use of the English language," he said calmly. "If you actually check, I am sure that you will see there is not a single sign, flier or Skirt Day poster that mentions 'girls' or 'women.' So you can see how I, a well-intentioned male full of school spirit, in a show of solidarity with the Home Ec Department and in support of Sylvia Berkowsky, as well as the Equal Rights Amendment that will soon become the twenty-seventh Amendment to the Constitution, might have been misled by the wording on all those signs."

"Bullshit! That's the only thing you are full of, Scapelli!" He pulled a Lucky from the pack, lit it and exhaled a stream of smoke across the desk.

Terry uncrossed and recrossed his legs, careful to keep the hem of his skirt modestly over his knee. "If someone wanted to make the case in a court of law, not that I'm saying I would, the ACLU might be very eager to take up the cause. The exclusion of fifty percent of the school population from participating in Skirt Day, a sanctioned school event, could be seen as 'sexism' and that would make you a 'sexist.'"

"More bullshit!" He leaned forward, his tone became menacing. "Don't fuck with me, Scapelli!"

Terry sat up straighter in his seat. The expression on his face became serious and so did his tone. "I picked this specific day to teach my classes a lesson on sexism, sexual stereotyping, sexual discrimination, sexual oppression and gender stereotyping as it occurs in John Steinbeck's book *The Pearl,* required reading for the class. Everything that is wrong in the story can be seen in the modern world through events like Skirt Day. I've been planning my lesson for months, Mr. Baltz. It's detailed in my plan book and Dick Janus, my department chair, read them, approved them and signed my plan book last week as required by you, Mr. Baltz. My ass is covered and it is my intention to return to my classes and tell them everything that happens here." He leaned forward in his chair. "So don't fuck with *me!*"

He reached for another cigarette and was about to light it when he realized one was already lit. "Well, Scapelli," he said more calmly, "I'm sure your ACLU buddies eager to undermine America and further erode the American school system would be only too happy to take up your cause all the way to the Supreme Court."

"Seymour," he replied with smug familiarity that stung the principal, "I'm not looking for trouble. I was just using Skirt Day as motivation for my classes and present another brilliant lesson they will remember and talk about at my party when I retire. But I don't want to be insubordinate. So if you tell me exactly what you want me to do, we can both save face and get on with the more important matters of educating America's youth."

He fingered his mustache. "Don't think for a second that I bought any of that shit, *Mr.* Scapelli. But this isn't what's going to take you down. I reluctantly agree with you about getting on and since you asked, I would *prefer,*" he picked his words carefully, "if you didn't wear your skirt in the halls."

"Fair enough." Terry nodded. "But I *will* continue to wear it for the rest of Skirt Day in my classroom! With Helen O'Dell down and Willy Zwill out for the season at least, I still haven't been observed this year. So if you have the time today come up and watch today's lesson and write it up as a formal observation." He uncrossed his legs, rose from the seat and turned away modestly. He unrolled his jeans before he unwrapped, removed the skirt and draped it over his shoulder. He stopped at the door. "Kudos to Sylvia Berkowsky. Her vision for Skirt Day has inspired me and she's also given me an idea for my classes. Hat Day. It's coming soon. I'll let you know more about it."

The secretaries turned to watch Terry came through the door into the Main Office holding his skirt.

"So?" Phyllis asked. "It was pretty quiet in there. We expected to hear furniture hitting the wall. Did he have a massive coronary?"

"No. We came to an agreement when I explained how whatever he did in there could become a sexism lawsuit." He held up both hands and mugged in a parody of Richard Nixon's two-finger victory salute. "Not so bad for what started out as a joke."

The buzzer on her desk sounded. "Send the next one in, *Ms* Lind, and tell Scapelli he's late for class!"

"Ms? Your sexism discussion must have really made an impact," she said. "That might be one the first time he called me 'Ms'!" She turned to the detention chair. "Virgil, dear, Mr. Baltz said he will see you now."

Virgil came around the counter. He was wearing a white ballet top, matching tights and a stiff lace tutu that stood out around his waist. "Hey, Mr. S. Love your skirt. You don't think I overdid it with this, do you?"

"Not a bit, Virgil. It's very tasteful." He gave him a thumb's up. "A little advice, if you don't mind. You might want to keep 'sexism' and 'sexual oppression' handy when you talk to him."

"That *was* the approach I was planning, Mr. S."

Virgil disappeared into the principal's office and Terry rushed up to his classroom. He re-skirted in front of a most attentive class. Then he presented his prepared lesson to them and the young substitute teacher sent to cover his class who didn't want to leave.

And so Rosencrantz and Guildenstern Memorial High School's first and only Skirt Day came to an end.

"Hat Day?" Sue asked. "What the hell is Hat Day? And didn't you have enough trouble this week with Skirt Day?"

He shook his head. "I don't know. I just made it up in Baltz's office. But the more I thought about it, the better it sounded. I had to come up with an angle to make it educational and I did last night."

"Of course you did."

From his pocket he pulled a small, worn paper lunch bag, which he had formed into a vague hat and placed it on his head. The front of the bag was torn into a flap that formed a short brim. The rest of the bag was a folded band like ear flaps along three sides. Over the brim he had drawn a five-pointed red star. It resembled the cap Chairman Mao wore. He put it on. "Everybody in my Senior Honors English class will wear paper hats."

"Twelfth-graders? Kids who got their college acceptance letters and are almost old enough to vote? Never happen."

"Sure will. I'll make it part of the unit on Orwell's *Animal Farm* and tell them they're being graded. They're so worried about their final grade averages and class standing they'll do anything."

"You can't grade them for wearing paper hats."

"Can too. I can do anything. I'm the teacher."

"For how long?"

"A week."

"Definitely never happen."

"Bet? Winner gets dinner and drinks at the place of his choice."

"The place of *her* choice will definitely not be Sizzler."

"*His* choice could be something homemade. And maybe breakfast instead of dinner. Waffles."

"You wish," she said.

"Bet? We can work out the details after I win." He extended her his pinkie.

"Bet." They locked pinkies.

"Today I tell my class."

Red Farley and Sylvia Berkowsky came into the faculty room together. She turned away when she saw Terry. She hadn't spoken to him since Skirt Day.

Red saw the paper bag. "Nice commie hat, Scapelli."

"I'm going to have all my kids wear one. Next week is Hat Day Week, Sylvia. What do you think, from a professional Home Ec point of view?" She ignored him. "I was thinking if Hat Day is a success maybe next year we can combine it with Skirt Day?"

"I have nothing to say to you, Mr. Scapelli... ever."

* * *

"So let's be sure that you all understand the plan, boys and girls. On Monday everybody comes to class with a homemade paper hat. If you want you can go with my design, the classic Chairman Mao. Or perhaps a Che Beret. Or design your own. Something plain. Something fancy. Embellish it. Decorate it. Put on lights, feathers, whatever. Use your imagination to make your hat unique. And then you'll wear it next week. Are there any questions?"

There were many and they all came at once. "Is everybody in the school doing this? Do we have to wear them around the building? This isn't one of your pranks to make us look silly, right? And if we wear them you'll give each of us extra credit? How about a hundred? A hundred for every day we wear them for the entire week?"

"No... No..." He pointed. "Sure." Point. "Right, it's not a prank and besides, you people don't need my help to look silly." Point. "Absolutely." Point. "Let me think about that one. A hundred every day for the entire week?" He paused just briefly. "Okay."

"Point of information here, Mr. Scapelli," Paul Locatelli the schoolhouse lawyer said. He rose to his feet with his thumbs in his belt, a perfect imitation of Spencer Tracey in the movie *Inherit the Wind*. "Before we go any further, and so we understand that we are all on the same page."

"Yes, Mr. Locatelli, what is your point of information?"

"You're saying in front of all these witnesses that anyone who wears a paper hat in this class next week will get the grade of one hundred in your marking book... every day for five days... for a total of five hundreds, right? And you aren't tricking us."

"Yes, Counselor. You are one hundred percent correct, sir, five times. But I expect everyone in the class to do it."

"We get that no matter what kind of hat we make, even if it's just a paper bag or a folded newspaper." Terry nodded. "Would you please state your response for the record?"

"Correct. But even if it is just a paper bag or a folded newspaper, it still must be worn in class each day for the entire week. Just so you aren't trying to trick me."

"We just have to wear it *here*, not around the building, to other classes, or anything like that."

"Correct again." Some were still skeptical. "But wait, there's more. I'll tell you what I'm gonna do. You say you're not satisfied. You say you want more for your money. Today we're starting a new book"–they groaned–"George Orwell's *Animal Farm.* You're going to love this book. It's filled with lots of cute little talking animals. So this is what I'll do. If you wear your hats all next week, I won't give you a test on the book when we finish–"

"Or while we're reading it," Paul added.

"You drive a hard bargain, Counselor." He sighed. "Okay. Or while we're reading it. I won't give you *any* tests on the book. And here's something even more extra special. At the end of the week we'll have a contest and vote for the best hat. The winner will be exempt from the final exam in June."

"You can do that?"

"Of course I can do that. Just like I told Ms Wellen, I can do anything I want. I'm the teacher."

"So, one more time, just to be absolutely clear. *All* those extra hundreds will go toward everyone's class average. There will be *no tests* on the book at all. And the winner doesn't have to take the final?"

"Yes, Counselor. That is correct."

"Can we have it in writing?"

"Of course." He turned and listed the terms and conditions on the side board: "One. April 24 to 28 is Hat Day Week. Two. Everyone agrees to wear a paper hat. Three. Everyone who makes and wears a paper hat will receive one-hundred extra credit for each day for five days. Four. There will be no test on the book, 'AF,' for short," he said, "during or after we read it. Five. The winner of the best hat contest on April 28 will be exempt from the final exam in June." He signed his name with a flourish. "Satisfied? And I'll leave that right there on the board for everyone to see." In block letters he wrote "DO NOT ERASE!!!"

"I'm in," Paul said and they all nodded in agreement.

He pulled a box of well-worn paperbacks from the closet and passed them. "Before the bell takes you away and closer to the weekend, your homework assignment–" They groaned. "I didn't promise no homework." He pointed to the board. "Beside designing and making your paper hat, read the the first two chapters of George Orwell's wonderful book *Animal Farm*. Don't skip over the Introduction." He knew they wouldn't read it. "Let me leave you with this thought," he called when the bell rang, "'All animals are equal, but some animals are more equal than others.'"

* * *

"So?" Sue asked. She was leafing through all the papers in her mailbox. "Did they all laugh at you?"

"Are you kidding? I got them so worked up they can't wait until next week."

"How'd you manage that?"

"I bribed them with many, many promises."

"Not fair," she said. "But by Monday I bet only two of them at most will show up with paper hats. The rest will say they forgot."

"I'm way ahead of you, Wellen. I'll have a supply of newspapers and paper bags on hand."

"Definitely not fair!"

He pulled out the papers from his box and looked at them. "Anything in all this crap I should care about?"

"The letters of intent for next year aren't out yet."

He stuffed it all back. "If there's anything important they'll send a follow-up. Right, Phyl," he called across to her, "you'll buzz me in my room if it's anything critical?"

"Don't I always, Mr. Scapelli? But would you at least clear out some of the old junk so we have room for new junk?"

"Of course." He pulled it out again and dumped everything into the waste basket. "No need to bother with any of that, young Tietjen," he said to Jesse who was lost in reading through the contents of his mailbox. "Have a great weekend, everybody ,and don't forget your paper hat on Monday."

"What paper hat?" Jesse asked Sue.

"He's trying to get his seniors to wear paper hats in his class for a week."

"Why?"

"Because he wants to… and because he's having fun."

"I never have fun. I just make lesson plans and mark essays. When does the fun start?" He was annoyed. "I don't have time to play games in my classes. I guess once you get tenure you can slack off."

"Slack off? Play games? You think Terry's slacking off? He works harder than anyone in this building. He's a master teacher. He's so good he makes it look easy. His students are learning things without knowing they're being taught!"

"Wearing a skirt and a paper hat?"

"Yes. Skirt Day was brilliant! Years from now his students will still remember the day their crazy English teacher wore a skirt to school. And they'll remember the lesson he taught them about thinking for themselves. If you want to learn how to teach, timing and technique, go and observe him when you have a free period. I did for three years. I'm not sure where he's going with this paper hat thing, but you can bet there's more to it than just getting a bunch of seniors to put bags over their heads for his amusement–" Suddenly it occurred to her. "Damn Scapelli! I'm going to *lose* that bet! Damn him!" She laughed.

"I tell you, Phyl, I'm tired of being his whipping boy. He blames me for everything, even this Phantom Shitter shit! I'm still out there all alone. I can't remember the last time I saw Noah Lewis. He's been retired in his mind for years, but has he *actually* retired and nobody bothered to tell me?"

"I see him every other Friday when he collects his checks." They were sharing lunch in his office with the door closed.

"Forget Rita Reed. She hides in O'Dell's office all day cowering in the corner afraid to come out. If I didn't hear her sneezing and blowing her nose through the wall I'd think she was as dead as O'Dell. I know all the stress is affecting *our* relationship, Phyl. I can't take much more or *do* any more! Still he has the balls to tell me that O'Dell dead is more help to him than me alive. Every time I turn around he's on my ass. And I'm getting those stress-related boils on my ass again."

She let him vent, put down her sandwich and looked at him. It's been a while since somebody was on my ass." She waited for his reaction. He always reacted to her double entendres, but there was none. "You must really be sick."

The phone on his desk rang and he reached automatically and picked it up.

"Mario–" Mr. Baltz said into the phone.

He covered the receiver. "Fuck!"

"Thought you'd never ask," she said.

"Baltz," he mouthed silently, but she knew by the expression on his face.

"–I was just up on the third floor looking into the faculty bathroom–" He corrected himself. "–I was *in* the bathroom looking. The stall doors are back up again!"

"Board of Health contacted Phyllis. It's a code violation and they had lots of complaints. They're sending another inspector to make sure the doors were up and stay up, and they will fine for every day the doors were off. You weren't around, so I had Phyllis call Flackett. He ordered her to get Stash to put them up again. I was just looking out for you."

"Shit." There was silence. "What about the observations? Done yet? I want them done and written up before Phyllis puts out the teacher Letters of Intent."

"I can't guarantee it. I'm all alone out there–"

"Do what you have to do, Mario, to get it done. You're holding up the works." He hung up and the AP slammed the phone down, picked it up and slammed it down again.

"What now?"

"*We* have to get all the observations done before *you* can put out the Intent Letters. And *he* was pissed about the doors."

"He'd really be pissed if he knew who made the phone calls to the Department of Health."

"I have to do all of the remaining observations in a week."

"How many more? Give me your schedule."

He opened the desk drawer and handed it to her. She dialed the phone. He could hear it ringing through the wall.

"Rita," she said, "this is Phyllis. Mr. Baltz wants you to do some teacher observations today. Write these down." She gave her a list of names and room numbers. "I know... I know... I understand... but he was adamant that *you* get them done today, Rita. And there will be more tomorrow and Friday. Thank you." She hung up and dialed again.

"Who are you calling?"

"Noah Lewis. His unlisted number. Noah," she said when he answered, "this is Phyllis Lind... Yes, yes, I know you're out to lunch... I know you're at home now, that's why I called you there... Yes... yes... We have an emergency, Mr. Lewis," she said in her best secretary voice and cut him off. "No... no one else is dead, at least as far as I know... The emergency is teacher observations. Yes, Mr. Giovanni does them. But with Helen and Willy gone... They've been gone for a while, Noah... Mr. Baltz told me specifically that he wants you to do teacher observations today... Mr. Giovanni is already observing... Yes, that 'new woman' is observing as well. And she's not really new, you know. She's taught reading here for years. Rita. Rita Reed... Yes... yes... Just a second, Noah. Mr.

Baltz was just yelling something. Yes, Mr. Baltz. I'll relay your message. Sorry, Noah, he's very upset," she whispered. "He said to put down your lunch and get back here now. Of course I can't repeat everything he said. He gave me a list of teachers that *must* be observed by you today. He specifically said for you to drop everything and do it." She looked over the list. "Mr. Scapelli's English class is one. Yes... Mr. Baltz knows that your background isn't English, but Mr. Scapelli should be easy enough to understand. When you finish that one, there are four more classes to observe that may be a bit difficult... Okay then... You just do Mr. Scapelli and I'll see if I can convince him to cut the others down to two or three. I'll have the list for you when you come in. I'll give Rita Reed the more difficult observations... Oh, you're very welcome, Mr. Lewis. Stop at my desk as soon as you are back." She hung up the phone. He was awed by what he had just witnessed. "And that, my dear Mario, is why the secretaries run the school."

* * *

Noah Lewis found the third floor just where Phyllis Lind said it would be, but it seemed different–warmer since the last time he was up there. Of course that was back last December, when he pushed the wrong button on the elevator. He walked past the (F)Utility Closet. The Third Floor Faculty Men's Room would be his orientation point to Room 310, but before he made his way there he stopped inside. It looked pretty much the way he remembered. Except on closer inspection, there was more graffiti on the walls and inside the stalls. He read it. Some of it was very funny. One was about him. "Noah Lewis can't walk and chew gum at the same time." He laughed. Of course he could. He was chewing gum and had just walked into the toilet.

Still there was no toilet paper, so he wouldn't be able to take care of the business he hadn't finished at home. He went to the urinals and read while he peed. He didn't flush, didn't wash his hands at the sink. Instead he examined himself in the mirror making small circles on his stomach with his left hand while patting the top of his head with his right. "Who says I can't do two things at once?"

He checked the sheet Phyllis had given him with all the information he needed for the observation and made his way to Mr. Scapelli's class, which was well in session. He opened the door and before he could step inside the class jumped up and began to sing. "Good morning, good morning, a new day is dawning…" they sang more or less in unison.

He backed out and pulled the door shut. Confused, he checked the room number and the information on his sheet. He opened the door and again they sang, "…Up father, up mother, up sister, up brother…"

He retreated, cracked the door open and stuck his head in. They were on their feet. "…Good morning, good morning, good morning to you!"

"Mr. auh, Scapelli? I, auh, was just a little confused by the, auh, greeting. I thought it was a Music class." He looked at his watch. "It's lunchtime, auh, not morning."

"Well, you are welcome any time, Mr. Lewis." The class was still standing and Terry motioned for them to sit. "To what do we owe the honor of your visit here to the third floor?"

"I, auh, came to observe."

"Well then, come all the way in… please… and observe away."

He looked around the room. "Is this a party? I see all of your students are wearing, auh, paper hats."

"Almost all. Except for those two over there in isolation." He pointed to two girls sitting together in the corner. "Eileen and Alexis decided they weren't part of the team." The class booed. "Eileen decided she didn't want any part of this and didn't even make a hat. Isn't that right, Eileen?" She looked at him coldly. "And Alexis joined her after the first day. So we put the two of them in the corner because they aren't part of the group. Isn't that right, class?" They booed again. "If you want, you can wear Alexis's hat. Would that be okay with you, Alexis, if Mr. Lewis wore your hat?" She didn't look up or protest when he retrieved her paper hat from his desk and handed it to the AP. "We're reading *Animal Farm*, Mr. Lewis.

I'm sure you're familiar with Orwell's book. It's all about talking animals."

"Auh? Sure," he said uncertainly. He put on the paper hat and adjusted it as he walked to an empty seat in the back of the room to observe.

"Now would somebody bring Mr. Lewis up to date on where we are in the story?" Every hand in the class shot up, some right, some left. He looked around the room and called on a girl waving her right.

In the News
May 1972

May 1

South Vietnamese troops abandon Quang Tri City to the North Vietnamese Army.

May 2

Col. Pham Van Dinh officially surrenders Camp Carroll (Cam Lộ) to the North Vietnamese and Viet Cong, their first major victory during the Nguyen Hue Offensive.

J. Edgar Hoover, head of the FBI from 1924 to 1972, dies in Washington.

May 8

In response to the ongoing NVA Easter Offensive, Pres. Nixon announces Operation Linebacker I, the mining of North Vietnam's harbors along with intensified bombing of roads, bridges and oil facilities. The announcement brings international condemnation of the U.S. and ignites more antiwar protests in America.

May 15

Alabama's Gov. George Wallace is shot and critically wounded in an assassination attempt by Arthur Herman Bremer while campaigning for the Democratic presidential primary and shaking hands with well-wishers in the parking lot of the shopping center in Laurel, Maryland. Wallace is left paralyzed from waist down.

May 16-18

A voice-activated taping system attached to Pres. Nixon's telephone on his study desk in Aspen Lodge at Camp David becomes operational.

May 19

Kathy Boudin and Bernardine Dohrn, members of the Weathermen, set explosives in bathroom of the U.S. Pentagon.

May 22

Pres. Nixon arrives in the Soviet Union for a summit meeting. He is the first sitting president to visit the U.S.S.R.

May 28

Operatives working for the Committee to Re-elect the President (CREEP) burglarize the Democratic National Committee headquarters in the Washington, DC, Watergate office complex. Electronic bugging equipment is installed at Democratic National Committee headquarters in the Watergate building.

May 30

Three members of the Japanese Red Army recruited by the Palestinian Popular Front for the Liberation of Palestine-External Operations attack Lod Airport near Tel Aviv, killing 26 people and injuring 80 others. Two of the attackers are killed, a third, Kōzō Okamoto, is captured after being wounded.

Camelot

Official Publication of the Partnership of Parents and Teachers
in Association for better Farmington Public Schools
Harriet Stegle, President P-PTA

Vol. 9 Issue 9   May 1972

I don't know about you, but it's hard for me to believe that it's already May!

AROUND THE DISTRICT:

Overheard in one of the elementary schools: "If April showers bring May flowers, then what do Mayflowers bring? Pilgrims!"

Founder's Day Dinner will be held on Friday, May 5, at Chez Antoine's. The festivities begin at 7 PM. This year's Founder's Day honoree has not yet been named, so you'll have to buy a ticket ($40) to see who it will be. **The Founders Day Parade** will kick off on Saturday morning at 9 AM. The traditional open car caravan, weather permitting, filled with dignitaries including this year's honoree will begin at the Administration Building. The parade route will wind through all of Farmington and take the cars past each of the schools before it ends where it began at the new Administrative Parking Lot. So come early. Find a good spot and pick your seat. If you take neighbors and friends, you can pick their seats too.

Congratulations yet again to Phaedra Schwartz, typing teacher at R&G, formerly Fine, now Snediker, or is it Fine-Snediker? "Originally we were planning a June wedding right after school let out, but circumstances changed. Daddy thought it would be best not **to** wait to tie the knot, so he booked us a long weekend in Vegas. I called in sick and Maurice, my new hubby, and I eloped! We've been partying ever since. Of course we still plan to have that big official gala wedding party in June not to disappoint everybody who wants to give us gifts."

I couldn't help but notice and I have to wonder… is all that "partying" the reason Phay has traded in her high fashion wardrobe for looser fitting clothes? You know what they say, once on the lips, forever on the hips. But perhaps there are more congratulations due soon? Only Phay can say for sure!

ON THE MEND

Willy Zwill, the hard-luck AP at R&G, is almost fully recovered from surgery to remove the remaining toes from his right foot. Sharpshooter Willy "accidentally" shot off most of them while cleaning his pistol in his office back in March. That has left him with a bit of a hitch in his giddyup so that the inmates at South Oaks Mental Health Center, where he was transferred after the surgery, have started calling him "Hopalong Willy"! "Any day now" is the word from South Oaks psychiatrist Dr. Chu Phat regarding his release. "We are trying to regulate his medications again so he no longer hears the voices that returned soon after his first stay with us." According to Dr Chu (or is it Phat?), "There have been fewer violent outbursts during private sessions and Willy no longer needs to be restrained. He has become more socialized." Another sign that Willy is on the mend is that he has joined with the other patients in Arts and Crafts, where he quickly graduated from weaving lanyards and making vinyl wallets to sculpting with stone. Apparently his knack with a hammer and chisel has impressed everyone in South Oaks. Who knew he had such latent talent? He is doing so well there is talk of letting him out on a supervised weekend furlough. "He won't be back… at least for the rest of this year," said Carolyn Butrum, Chairlady of the Sunshine Committee at the High School. "No matter what they say, the poor man is a mess." So it looks like there's another opening that will need filling.

NEWS AND VIEWS:

There's no denying it, May is the beginning of the end, starting with the Founder's Day Dinner and Parade and culminating with the Memorial Day weekend! It is hard for me to believe that another school year is almost over. Looking back in retrospect, as we come around that last turn and head for the finish line, it really hasn't been such a bad school year after all. Granted we began by voting down the school budget several times, but we are learning how to live with austerity. And our teachers have grown accustomed to working without a contract. But even beyond our little school family, 1972 is looking bright and it can only get better! The war is finally winding down and there is light at the end of the tunnel. In the words of our beloved President Richard M. Nixon, who is well on his way to a second term, "Peace with honor is at hand." Yes, America, the sky's the limit. Two more Americans landed and drove their Rover on the Moon. And if that isn't enough good news, the Summer Olympics are on the horizon in Munich, Germany, and we have all those gold and silver medals to look forward to. It's a great time to be an American. Let us be joyful and rejoice as this great American Memorial Day holiday approaches! Let's make this a time of great celebration, the happiest Memorial Day ever!

See you next time with more news from the trenches!

"Hat Day Week turned out to be the best week of school ever, Wellen!" Terry announced before he was even inside the faculty room. He raised his two hands in a Richard Nixon victory salute and dropped his head between his hunched shoulders. The paper bag hat with the red star, more wrinkled and stained, was on his head.

"Better than Skirt Day?"

"Miles! And I do believe you lost a bet to serve me breakfast in bed," he said and everyone looked up.

"I'm not so sure about breakfast and certainly there was never any mention of bed. You're telling me they actually wore their hats for the entire week? All of them?"

"Except for Eileen Meehan and Alexis Gross. The others did. I gave them hundreds every day like I promised. A promise is a promise after all. And no unit test, We voted for the best hat and the winner gets exempted from the final exam. They were so ecstatic they plan to nominate me Farmington's High School Teacher of the Year! Now about our bet, Wellen, when can I expect to collect?"

"The whole school heard it, Scapelli," Red Farley called across the room from his card game. "Not only did you cause trouble, now you're *in* trouble for what you did. My Track III kids almost rioted when they saw that paper bag foolishness. Now they want extra credit. I told them only if they wear *plastic bags* over *their* heads."

"Be careful or they'll put one over *your* head, Red?" Stanley Milnow said and laughed.

"Shut up, Stan, and pay attention to your cards." Red was angry. "Your bullshit won't fly this time, Scapelli. Making a mockery of education again after that Skirt Day thing you pulled. I reported you to the Collegial Professionalism Committee and when they meet I'm making a motion to censure you for being unprofessional. You can't *buy* Teacher of the Year with extra credit. Maybe *Easiest* Teacher."

"Easiest teacher? Wasn't that your girlfriend, the substitute you chased around all last year. The one who reported you. What was her name again?"

"Up yours, Scapelli."

"This afternoon," Terry said to Sue when they were in the hall, "my class is going to be very interesting. "Today is when they learn the real lesson."

* * *

There was a low buzz in his classroom when Terry slipped in and closed the door. The dusty blackboards had been erased and washed clean. All traces of the paper hats were gone and the room was cleaner than it had ever been, except for his desk that was piled with papers and things. Every September he told his classes, "If I am ever absent it's your responsibility, your duty, to make sure the sub doesn't clean my desk. It looks pristine now, but over the course of the year it will develop a fine patina of dust and papers and become completely covered. A sub might be tempted to clear off the top and put things into drawers, but all of you have to stop anyone who tries to clean! If anything is moved, if anything *on* my desk is rearranged, I will know it. And I am holding all of you personally responsible." So his desk remained untouched.

He walked to it, opened the top drawer and pulled out composition paper. "Okay, boys and girls, clear your desks for a test on *Animal Farm*." They looked around uneasily and waited for him to say he was joking, but he didn't. He handed paper to the first person in each of the rows. "Take one and hand the others back. Name and date on the top."

"Wait! What? You said no test!" they erupted.

"What are you talking about? First question–"

"You said no test if we all wore paper hats. And we did... last week!"

"Don't be absurd. Paper hats? This isn't elementary school. You're high school seniors."

"You gave us extra credit–"

"A hundred points–"

"Every day for five days!"

"I don't recall any of that." He looked at Eileen Meehan and Alexis Gross who were back in their regular seats. "Did you girls wear paper hats last week?" They shook their head.

"You wrote it in your marking book."

He opened his marking book and showed them the empty spaces. "You must have dreamed it."

"You erased the numbers! I can see them."

"It's not fair."

"We had a contract," Paul Locatelli said officiously. "You wrote it on the board and signed it."

He looked over at the board. "I don't see anything."

"You lied to us, Mr. Scapelli!"

"You all lie all the time. 'The dog ate my homework.' 'I forgot it at home.' Everybody lies. *If* I lied, and I'm not admitting that I did, it wouldn't be the first time you've been lied to. Right, Paul?"

"But this is different. You're not supposed to lie. You're a teacher." He was furious. They were furious.

"What happens when people you trust, people who aren't supposed to lie, lie? 'I solemnly swear to tell the truth, the whole truth and nothing but the truth.' Perjury is a crime. Do you think witnesses in court lie? Do cops ever lie when they testify? On a police report? The people you elect? What happens if your own government lies to you? People you trust, people you depend on?" There was silence. He turned to the two girls. "How come you didn't participate, Eileen? And how come you joined her the first day, Alexis?"

"I read the Introduction like you said and, I knew what you were doing."

Alexis nodded. "It took me a little longer to realize you were the pigs in the book who lied to all the other animals to get power."

"So you just admitted it. We *did* wear hats!" Paul said.

"You ladies are the real winners here," Terry said. "You put up with a lot from your classmates and from me. I was pretty rude to you. But even with all that peer pressure and abuse you didn't give in. For that you both get hundreds! And like I promised, you are both exempt from my final exam!" He applauded them.

"You can't do that. It wouldn't be fair to the rest of us."

"Life's not fair, boys and girls. That's your lesson. Ever hear the quote 'Power corrupts and absolute power corrupts absolutely'? In here I have absolute power, so I make the rules and I decide what's fair."

"It's a breach of contract. If I took you to court–"

Terry smiled. "Not if I control the courts. Not if I rewrite history and change the rules, which I did. I took advantage of you. Your trust. I manipulated you. Orwell said it in this book, 'All animals are equal, but some animals are more equal than others.'"

"That's an oxymoron," Paul said. "You can't be 'more equal.' It's a contradiction!"

"Exactly Orwell's point. And that's not just the way the world worked during Orwell's time and the Communist Revolution. Look around today. Do you think President Richard M. Nixon is truthful all the time? That he is bound by the same rules as the rest of us?"

"He should be."

"Agreed. But is he? What happens if *you* break the law? Decide you don't want to pay your taxes, or get drafted into the army and refuse to go? As citizens we have a duty to defend our country, but what if the government isn't telling us the whole truth and nothing but the truth? What if, to paraphrase what Eileen said, the government is the pigs?"

They weren't happy, but there was growing understanding.

"Last week while we were reading somebody asked, 'How could the animals be so stupid?' And I had to smile because when I looked, all of you were sitting there wearing your hats. I duped you. I didn't play fair. And all of you fell for it, except for these two. So if you learn anything from this, I hope it's that you can't just go through life following blindly. You have to question. You have to think for yourself." He opened the book. "That being said, I suggest we revisit *Animal Farm* and maybe actually read the Introduction. There's a a lot more to this book than silly talking animals. And when we finish I want you to take a few minutes before the end of the period to use that paper and write down your reactions to the past week." He pulled his hat from his back pocket, unfurled it and put it on his head. He struck the pose of the pig Napoleon on the book cover.

"Good morning ladies and gentlemen, and you too, Mr. Farley, on this fine May day," Terry announced cheerfully, but nobody in the faculty room looked up.

"May Day is a commie holiday."

"It's May, it's Wednesday and it's 'Hump Day.'"

"How I hate that expression. It sounds so… obscene," Mrs. Butrum tutted to Rita Reed who blushed.

"Nonetheless, all's right with the world because early this morning I got mine! And I assume you got yours, Ms Wellen. Did you? Did you get yours?"

"That sounds even more obscene."

All the heads in the faculty room pivoted in unison toward Terry and back to Sue.

"You know what happens when you 'assume,' Mr. Scapelli," Sue said in a formal tone. "You make an ass of you and me. But since you asked, as a matter of fact I did get mine, probably before you got yours. Thank you very much!"

Heads swung again.

"The pleasure was all mine, Ms Wellen."

"Oh, Lordy," Mrs. Butrum said and Rita Reed covered her face with her handkerchief.

"For chrisakes, Scapelli, do we have to be subjected to your inappropriate comments? It's bad enough we have to listen to your appropriate comments. Nobody here has any interest in hearing your smutty, suggestive innuendos about your sexual exploits, real or imagined."

"Speak for yourself, Red. I am," Stanley Milnow said.

"Innuendos? Methinks that Mr. Farley didn't get his this morning. And now *you're* the one that's talking dirty, Red."

"What do you mean dirty? I didn't say anything dirty."

"Oh, don't be coy. Everyone knows *in you endo* is the Italian word for sodomy."

Mrs. Butrum and Rita Reed gathered up their things and got up to leave.

"I have no idea why you are taking offense at what I said, Red. In fact I am deeply offended at your offense. It's your dirty mind that's the problem. With your Italian sodomy talk. I was just saying in all innocence that this morning I got mine, referring to my Letter of Intent."

"And I got mine too," Sue added.

"Are the letters out?" Mrs. Butrum asked.

"Phyllis Lind was putting all of them in the mailboxes when I came in," Sue said.

"Apparently not *all* the boxes," Terry amended. "Only the people they want to come back next year. Maybe that's why you didn't get yours, Red. Maybe they are trying to tell you something."

"Up yours, Scapelli. I have tenure."

"Don't you mean in *my* endo? See, there you go again with your dirty mind in the gutter and your filthy mouth."

Red got up abruptly from his seat. "I'm going down there now to get mine, smartass! Come on, Stan."

When they were out the door Terry laughed. "He's going to be really surprised. I took his letter out and stuck it in Virgil's box."

"Virgil Loomis has a mailbox?"

Terry looked over at Jesse sitting silently by the window during the exchange. "Why so pale and wan, fond Tietjen? You look pretty glum."

"I didn't get mine either," he said.

"So that should be a good thing. Didn't you write a letter of resignation on your first day?" He got two coffees from the machine and handed one over to Sue.

"It's May and you're still here. Big accomplishment considering if we didn't stop you, you'd have been long gone," Sue said to help. "You've come a long way, baby, since September."

"It sure is an accomplishment." Terry said. "And nobody's hung you out the window. In fact, from what I hear, some of your kids may even like you. You definitely made it further than Helen O'Dell. Isn't that right, Dwayne?" he called over to Dwayne Purvey, who was listening while pretending to read the *Times*. "She only got to what, the end of January?"

"Why are you asking me? How would I know about Helen O'Dell? I was absent the day she died." He folded his paper and stormed out.

"What was that all about?" Sue asked.

"Beats the hell out of me."

The door opened again. "I got mine!" Stanley Milnow said and held up his letter.

"How about you, Red? Did you get yours?"

"*In you endo,* Scapelli!"

* * *

"I don't care that Polakas got some directive from Flackett and won't remove them. I want those stall doors in the faculty men's room down again, Mario, if you have to take them down yourself. You're always bragging about how handy you are. Take a damn screwdriver and a pliers or whatever you call them and take the doors down. I don't want anything to obstruct my view into those stalls." The assistant principal looked at him. "I mean, I don't want the bastards able to hide behind closed doors." He lit a cigarette.

"There's going to be a revolution."

"I really don't give a shit, Mario. If they don't like it let them go someplace else."

"Speaking of going someplace else, there was only one new Phantom Shitter incident. The nurse found it in one of the cubicles outside Doc Nessmith's in the Health Office. The second turd that Coach Boid reported in the Athletic Office turned out to be a baked apple that Buddy Ritchie forgot he bought in the teacher's cafeteria and left on his desk over the weekend."

"I love those apples." He inhaled.

* * *

"Doesn't look like it went well, Mario," Phyllis whispered when he came out of the office.

"Now he wants *me* to take the doors down. And he sent me to pick up a baked apple in the Teacher's Cafeteria."

"Dwayne Purvey was circling around your office. Said he wanted to talk to you. Something about Helen O'Dell. I didn't really understand him. He was babbling. I told him you were in a meeting and for him to come at the end of the period. He looks terrible. Nervous and like he hasn't slept in days. Reminded me of Willy in his final days. I think Purvey's losing it too."

"I don't have time for him and that union crap, Phyl. If he shows up again, send him to Noah Lewis. Right now I have a little job to do and I need to get some tools out of my desk."

"Hey, Mr. G," Virgil called from the detention chair. "I just–"

"No time for you, Loomis." He skirted around the counter and out of the office.

"Don't take it personally, Virgil dear." Phyllis was folding letters and stuffing envelopes. "These are very busy times, especially for Mr. Giovanni."

"I was just going to tell him that my attorney said it's looking good for two more varsity letters for the secret track and football teams."

"That's very good. I'll tell him, dear. I'm sure he will be very happy for you. Meanwhile, why don't you come give me a hand with some of these letters."

* * *

Jesse punched out at the end of the day. He stuck his hand into his mailbox and felt around. It was empty. A part of him was happy because that made having to decide easier. But it also meant everything he had done to be a good teacher during the past nine months, the preparation, those endless papers read and graded over weekends and vacations was for nothing. They didn't want him back. He was a failure.

"Get your letter yet?" Terry asked. He came into the Main Office smiling. He was always smiling, laughing, making jokes, doing silly things. Good for him that he could stroll through life and school with such indifference and nonchalance. It made Jesse angry. He was in no mood for more of his offhand remarks. Jesse shook his head. "I have other things on my mind. I really don't care."

"Of course you care. You care about *everything*!"

"I suppose I should be more like you and not care about anything."

It stopped Terry. He took him by the arm. "Come on, buddy, walk with me. We need to talk."

"I don't have the time. I have a long drive–"

"Just for a few minutes." He led him across the hall into an empty conference room. "What's going on with you?"

"I'm sick and tired of everything and I don't want to talk about it." Terry just looked at him and then it came out in a rush. "Since my first day here it's been every man for himself. Nobody told me anything about what I had to do or how I had to do it. Sure there were a lot of papers and memos and meetings. My mailbox is full every day, but there's no help. It's closed groups with long personal histories who sit in the same seats every day. And then they get mad when somebody doesn't know the rules. And believe me I've tried to figure everything out on my own. Nobody ever asks how things are going. Or offers advice with books, lessons… anything. Every day my senile grandfather asks me where I was all day and every day I tell him I was at school. Without fail he asks me, 'What did you learn today in school?' I tell him I'm the teacher and that I haven't learned anything and he says, 'Then why do you go?' That's the question I ask myself every morning, every Sunday night when I can't sleep."

"Welcome to the club. 'Blue Sunday' is some of the dues you pay for all those great benefits teaching provides, big salary, part-time job, summers off."

"I'm so naive. When I decided to become a teacher I thought I was going to change the world and I worried that I was going to teach them everything… the eight parts of speech and all the rules of punctuation… in two days, and run out of material for the rest of the year. Now I'm sure I I didn't teach them anything.

"The Seniors still don't know the parts of speech, And punctuation is something they ignore completely. Thank you, E. E. Cummings. Or they sprinkle it around like chicken feed," Terry said, but it didn't help.

"If I worked in construction I'd see results at the end of the day. Something I could measure. But teaching... I have no idea if I'm doing anything. I've been observed three times and all that does is tell me what I'm doing wrong. The desks aren't in even rows. The kids don't raise their hands. I talk too much. I don't talk enough. I don't use the board enough or use it too much. No wonder I didn't get a letter. I wasted my time every day commuting forty-two miles, spending hours marking papers, correcting the same mistakes over and over." He took a breath. "And I don't think I want to invest any more time trying to sell an abstract commodity to a distracted community."

"Hey, that's good," Terry said. "'Selling an abstract commodity to a distracted community.' Did you come up with that yourself? I'm going to steal it and use it and pass it off as mine... if you don't mind." He tried to make eye contact. "Listen... Teaching isn't desks in straight rows or kids raising their hands before they speak. It's starting a fire and getting them so excited they forget to raise their hand. It's an ongoing process, a continuum. Tests only measure memory, not what they learned. Real education comes from touching as many lives as you can and helping them to think. It takes years, a lifetime. And in the end you still may never see the results or know if you succeeded. If you're lucky years later you'll meet some kid you had, now all grown up, who recalls some insignificant thing you said or did that you don't remember. But he remembers it and he tells you how it changed his life. And that's why you come back day after day, year after year and try not to burn out."

"I didn't get my letter," he said.

"Don't worry about the letter. For everything they may do wrong here, they sometimes get it right. You'll get it. Now you can go home. No, wait." He pulled an index card and a pen from his pocket. "What was that you said before? I want to write it down so I don't forget it."

* * *

"Mr. Tietjen," Phyllis called to Jesse and smiled when he came back into the Main Office. "I was just about to put this in your mailbox." She handed him the sealed envelope.

Inside his car he looked at the envelope with just his name and the Superintendent's return address typed on the front. He opened it. "I, Jesse Tietjen, teacher at Rosencrantz and Guildenstern Memorial High School, will/will not be returning to the Farmington School District, UFSD 71 for the September 1972–1973 school year as a second-year English teacher (specific grade assignment to be determined) on Step 2–B.A. with a yearly salary of (subject to negotiations of a new teaching contract)." The second sheet instructed, "Return this Letter of Intent signed and dated to your building principal by the end of the last day of school on June 23, 1972. Failure to do so will result in a withdrawal of the offer and the possible loss of your position." It was signed Dr. Donald F. Flackett, Superintendent of Schools.

Jesse took a deep breath, folded the Letter of Intent in the envelope and put it in his attaché case where his letter of resignation had been.

"Well, hello stranger," Chuck LaFemina, the second librarian called from the doorway when he saw Rory Aaron in the Third Floor Faculty Men's Room. His voice echoed back off the tiles. "I thought it was you from down the hall. Long time no see. How are you? Where you been?"

"Chucky." The acting Guidance Chair smiled. He was meticulously scrubbing one hand while the other held the water open. His rings, watch and I.D. bracelet were resting on a sheet of brown paper towel on the metal shelf above the sinks. "Busy. Busy. Such a bitch of a day with all those college recommendations I still have to write. And everybody lining up for last-minute guidance because they are going to fail for the year. I've been pressuring teachers all week and I haven't had a minute to myself."

"Tell me about it." Chuck took the other sink and removed his jewelry.

"Paper towel?" Rory removed his private supply from his jacket pocket, unfolded a sheet and laid it on the metal shelf. "This place is a sty. Who knows what we might catch in here."

The librarian laid out his jewelry and twisted the faucet a little too hard and water splashed his pants. "Whatever are people going to think when they see me leave here with wet spots?"

"Probably what they already think. How's the Library? Is that Amazon still on your ass?"

"The bitch is relentless. She has no respect for my boundaries. But if I dare set one toe over the line. Sweet Jesus, she goes berserk!"

"Toothpaste?" He offered a squirt.

"I have my own, thank you."

They carried out their hygiene ritual, brushing and gargling.

"Spit or swallow?"

"You're so bad. Swallow, of course."

They finished off with a charge of breath spray.

"I miss you, Rory."

"Well it's that time of the year. All those meetings. I barely have time to pee." He removed a small flask from inside his jacket. "Cologne?"

"Aramis?"

"Of course. But not too much." They both applied a few drops.

"Now I feel revitalized, civilized again."

They helped each other with their jewelry.

"We still have fifteen minutes before the end of the period. Do you have the time?"

"Of course. I'm in no hurry to get back."

"But the doors are off again!"

"How barbaric. How... indecent! The working conditions in this hole are unbearable. So what are we going to do?"

"Time to file another complaint with the association and write more letters."

"I mean us."

"If you're free tonight for drinks and dinner at my place, Chucky, say sixish?"

"Of course, Rory."

He looked at his black-faced Movado. "Love the watch, but I hate that there aren't any numbers. If I leave early, I can pick up some things on my way home. Do you like artichokes? I have a great recipe I've been dying to try. You still eat pork?"

"I love pork. I'll bring the wine." He paused. "Rory?"

"Yes?"

"Without my wife, right?"

"Oh, Chucky, you are such a comedian."

Mr. Baltz watched them leave. It wasn't exactly the kind of information he had in mind, but every bit he learned about his staff could be very beneficial, if not immediately, at some point in his dealings with them. Joel Maxwell burst into the bathroom brandishing a roll of toilet paper and he lifted the opera glasses he had taken from his wife's drawer for a closer, unobstructed look.

He used to enjoy being early man. In the dead of winter he strolled around the building in the predawn listening to the rattle of the steam pipes. In the spring, the light was different, the building was cool and smelled almost sweet from whatever Eddie the night custodian used to sweep the floors, instead of old socks and the vomity parmesan cheese that always lingered in the background. But now that he was early man, late man and only man, it was a pain in the ass. Rita Reed was definitely no Helen O'Dell, may she rest in peace. He crossed himself. She became as useless as Noah Lewis in a remarkably short time, afraid to come in early when she would be alone, and she couldn't stay late because she had to get home in time to make dinner. She was intimidated by everything and everyone and he heard her constantly coughing, sneezing and blowing her nose doing busywork in her office, in *Helen's* office, may she rest in peace. He crossed himself again. Because Noah was senior AP, he never got early duty or late duty or any duty. And speaking of doody... He looked where he was stepping. The Phantom Shitter made walking through the dark halls almost as dangerous as walking through a minefield. It had already cost him one pair of shoes, those black Florsheim wingtips with the Cuban heels.

He climbed the stairway and circled each floor, checking locks and looking through door windows into the classrooms. On the third floor he routinely went into the faculty bathroom and did a cursory check of the walls. The stall doors were still down and so was the writing. He stepped out and into the women's bathroom. He knew no one would be in there, it was too early. He liked the women's bathroom and the little thrill he always got from being somewhere he shouldn't. It reminded him of the times his mother brought him into the Lady's Room with her when he was a boy. "I don't want anyone to steal you, so you come in with me, but cover your eyes." He always covered them at first, but he sneaked a peak if the opportunity presented itself. He followed his mother until he was twelve and the other women complained.

The women's bathroom on the third floor was bigger, cleaner and it smelled better than the men's room. There were toiletries and interesting things in the vending machine, and stall doors. He stepped into one and sat. He looked at his watch. He had plenty of time, at least twenty minutes, so he got comfortable. He looked at the door and he stopped. In red letters was a printed message: "Terry Scapelli is a great lay!"

"What the fuck!" He dipped the toilet paper he always carried into the water and rubbed at it until the paper went to mush. On his way to the Main Office the sound he heard coming from inside the (F)Utility closet slowed him down. He pressed his ear to the door and listened to the electric sound of a small motor. He turned the handle, but the door was locked. He found his passkey stamped "DO NOT DUPLICATE" and tried to insert it into the lock, but it didn't fit. Strange. That key opened all the other locks in the entire building. He tried another and another and another with the same results. When the electric sound stopped, he did too.

* * *

"I'm taking my break, Mario," Phyllis said when she saw him headed toward her desk, "and I'm coming back late… or maybe I'll just go home early. So don't you even think about asking me to do anything."

"I need a key."

"I already have too much stuff to do, rescheduling Guidance appointments and the final exam schedules have to be in for approval so they can be run off next week. All the new griping and complaining about the bathroom doors in the men's room has become my problem. I had a formal memo in my mailbox from Joel Maxwell demanding a meeting with his highness and of course he's nowhere to be found. Somebody left copies of a petition threatening legal action by the ACLU if the stall doors are not replaced immediately. It was signed by–" She looked at the names on the single sheet of paper. "–Dickie Hertz, Ivonna Etta Pussy and Claud Bawls. I'm too busy for this, Mario."

"You wouldn't happen to have another master key? Mine doesn't seem to work."

"Haven't you been listening, Mario? Keeping track of keys is the one thing in this place that isn't my job. Go ask Noah. He's in charge of keys. He's got them. He collects them. He hands them out."

"Yeah, right." He laughed. "Nobody's turned in their real keys to him for years. That pile of hardware he hands out in September and collects every June hasn't opened a lock in this place since the sixties!" He flashed her a special look. "Everybody here knows if they have a problem that you're the go-to person because you're so good at everything you do. *Everything*. I just thought you might be able to give me a hand sticking my key into a stubborn lock." He cracked his neck and did the lip thing.

"My, aren't you the silver-tongued orator," she said and patted his hand.

"What's that I hear?" Terry's voice called from the Administrative Alcove. "Who's got a silver tongue in there and what is he doing with it?"

"Come here, Scapelli. I have a few questions to ask. What were you doing in the third floor faculty bathroom?"

"When, Mario? I can't say for sure, but two possibilities come to mind. Although there are fewer choices now that the doors are off the stalls again."

"Someone reported that you wrote on the walls."

His expression changed. *"Moi?"*

"In the women's bathroom. Someone said that you went into the women's bathroom and wrote 'Terry Scapelli is a great lay' on the back of one of the stall doors."

He shook his head. "I swear I didn't write that, Mario."
"Bull!"

"Cross my heart and hope to die."

"Then if you didn't write it, who else would do such a thing?"

"I don't know. I really couldn't say for sure." He thought. "But if you include administrators, department chairs and secretaries"–he counted on his fingers–"it could be any of about twenty-five women."

Phyllis laughed out loud. "I'm going up there now and check. Maybe I'll recognize the handwriting."

"It's mostly gone. I–" he stumbled. "I had it removed."

"If you want, Mr. Scapelli, I can put it back."

"Would you, Phyl? It pays to advertise."

"My pleasure."

"That's what all twenty-five women said."

"That's not funny, you two. And don't you start writing things on the wall, Ms Lind–"

"Start?" she said and winked at Terry.

* * *

He removed the book from his locked drawer and laid it on the desk blotter. He folded back the cover. In five months, his *Memoirs of a Secondary Schoolmaster* was almost half filled. He turned the pages until he came to one that was blank. He twisted the cap off his fountain pen and wrote.

Project X–Eightieth Entry–May 5, 1972. The stall doors in the third floor bathroom have been off and on and off again, more times than Willy Zwill's been in South Oaks! Polakas wouldn't do it. Mario didn't want to do it, but of course I prevailed. He is so predictable and easy to manipulate, like a hand puppet. But he is still the best of the dwindling bunch. Rita Reed wasn't much of a Reading Teacher and less as an AP. If anything she makes Noah Lewis look good. I don't anticipate Zwill's eventual replacement, if there is one before the end of the year, to raise the caliber of the AP gene pool. [Aside–"caliber" is a very funny word choice considering how Zwill went out! Sometimes I amaze myself.] I've heard the faculty call Mario "Napoleon" and "Mini Mussolini," a reference to his lack of height as well as his "shortcomings." I've heard them refer to me as *El Exigenté,* The Demanding One, but I embrace it! Mario's insecurity combined with his ambition makes him malleable. He has his eye on my job. When I hinted to him I was considering my options including the possibility of retiring at end of the school year, his eyes got wide. "Are you sick? I hope it's nothing serious," he asked all concerned, but I could see his little *dago* mind calculating. I told him, "The job is taking a toll and my doctor is worried about my blood pressure and my heart." He couldn't keep his feet from swinging back and forth on the chair. I never realized just how short Mini Mussolini really is. "Edie wants me to retire while we are both young enough to enjoy it and travel. Maybe Noah has the right idea–get out and move someplace cheap and live like a king." But the icing on the cupcake was when I told him, "You could find yourself sitting in this chair very soon, Mario." That did it. He ran right up with the tools he keeps in his desk and took down the stall doors. If Mario hadn't gone to college he would have made a good garbageman, like the rest of his *goomba* family.

Of course I didn't mention that my wife won a "free" trip for two to Israel for making the biggest contribution to her Hadassah group. It only cost me a thousand dollars. Oy, Israel in June! It's Florida surrounded by Arabs! She hasn't stopped nagging me to take a leave from Memorial Day through the end of June. A charter flight, then a Mediterranean cruise and the rest of the time in Israel. "What good is being principal if you can't leave a little early?" When I said that Flackett would deny my request, considering we are so understaffed, she had an answer. "Take your sick days. God knows you have enough of them. You never stay home even when I'm sick!" I explained again that the unused sick days would go toward my final average salary and increase my pension in retirement. "Then retire," she said and gave me an ultimatum. "'You go with me or I go with someone else." I am still considering.

An increase in the personal information I am learning about the staff will be priceless and it's all on videotape. I told Dexter I needed more tape and I shut him down when he asked what I was doing with it. He's a spineless worm. Tempers are shorter and working relations between certain staff members have grown more strained. "The absence of privacy is power. Bowel control is people control!" Except maybe in the case of the "Phantom Shitter," who has been striking with greater regularity. [Aside –"greater regularity" is another gem. How do

I keep coming up with them?] Could it be that the Red Felt Phantom and the Phantom Shitter are one and the same and have I moved him from the toilet to the halls?

* * *

The teachers ranged around the Main Office like a conga line for their paychecks. It started at the mailboxes, wound around the front counter and ended at Phyllis Lind's desk, where she and Terry were engaged in deep conversation.

"Thank you for that 'vote of confidence' you added about me on the women's bathroom wall, Phyl."

She smiled and found his envelope. "I thought it was funny, but Mario didn't. Your comment that it could've been a secretary who left the first comment worried him. He takes things much too seriously. I told him he'd better lighten up or they'll cart him out of here like they did Willy Zwill. Or worse, like Helen O'Dell."

"That poor woman," Carolyn Butrum said without lifting her head from where she was eavesdropping and going through the teacher files. "May she rest in peace. Though I doubt poor Helen will have a minute's rest or peace until the full story comes out. Frozen mousse, my patootie, if you'll pardon my French. I know what I saw and it was a mouse. So did everyone else who was in that room. There's a coverup going on. The Sunshine Committee has been talking and you can bet that people have been listening with interest. You mark my words, everything will come out eventually." Dwayne Purvey heard Mrs. Butrum talking about Helen O'Dell and quietly slipped off the paycheck line.

"Tell me the truth, Terry," Phyllis asked lowering her voice. "you wrote that on the bathroom wall, right?"

He shook his head and crossed his heart. "I didn't. But I may have asked an unidentified someone to make me a legend in my own mind." He looked at Sue Wellen farther back in line. "Thank you for adding to it."

"Come on, Scapelli," Red Farley complain from the line. "Some of us want to get paid before President Nixon devalues the dollar again."

"You were in earlier than usual today, Mario. And you stayed late last night."

"I'm early man. Late man. Everyman. Every day. Every week, Phyl. And with the Founder's Day dinner and parade this is going to be an extra long week."

"You're going?"

"No choice. Baltz wants me to take pictures. At the dinner Friday night *and* the parade on Saturday. He hinted it might be his last Founder's Day."

"Why doesn't he tell Harry Dexter to do that? He's the AV guy."

"Have you seen Harry's work? Helen Keller could take better pictures."

She slipped into his office, shut the door and sat. "Test week schedule and proctoring assignments are done, and I'm not changing anything. I don't care who complains." She laid the stack of papers she was holding on his desk. "His last Founder's Day, huh?"

"Not for sure. But maybe with a little help he'll actually put in his papers."

She looked at the expression on his face. "That's a smug expression. Like the cat that swallowed the canary. Did you do something?"

He twisted his fingers over his lips. "There's an old Sicilian proverb. '*Cu è surdu, orbu e taci, campa cent'anni 'mpaci.*'" He translated. "'He who is deaf, blind, and silent will live a hundred years in peace.'" He cracked his neck.

"I heard him say that his cardiologist wants him to reduce his stress. And his wife has been nagging him about traveling before they need walkers," she said. "I'll keep my ears open. Meanwhile, am I going to see you at all this weekend?"

"Maybe after the parade. But if things go the way I hope, you soon just might be sleeping with the principal," he said with a John Garfield glint.

She shook her head. "I told Baltz I wasn't doing that again."

"Very funny. Very funny." The phone on his desk rang. He looked at the lighted button and his watch. Nine o'clock. "He's in. And so begins another day."

"Mario, get in here right away—"

The AP turned the receiver away from his ear. "He sounds more annoyed than usual," he whispered and grinned.

"And tell Miss Lind—"

"Ms," she called out.

"—to get back to work. Things are piling up on her desk." The phone clicked.

"That didn't sound good, did it?" he said almost cheerfully. "I wonder what's bothering him now?" He rubbed his hands together.

"Mario, what did you do?"

Again he twisted his fingers over his lips and he followed her through the alcove into the Main Office toward the buzzing door. He scooted around her and brushed a warm palm against her backside before he entered the office. The principal's face was gray and his mustache trembled slightly.

"You don't look good, Boss."

"I've been violated! In there, Mario." He pointed to the executive toilet.

He pushed open the door and looked in. "Break Baltz" was printed in large letters across the mirror in red lipstick.

"It was there when I came in." His face was a shade the assistant principal had not seen before. "That demented bastard was in here, in this office. In that toilet! My toilet! My private toilet! My sanctuary!" He took several deep breaths. The ashen gray was slowly turning his face a healthier looking shade of purple.

He stepped inside and looked behind the door. "Did you see this, Boss?"

"What is it Mario? There's more?"

Mr. Giovanni swung the door back and there was another message in the same red lipstick. "Eat shit and die!" Just below the words there was a brown turd on the tile floor.

Baltz squeezed himself into the bathroom. "Motherfucker! He shit on my floor!"

"I'm no expert, Boss, but that doesn't look like what I stepped in last week." He bent down with some difficulty in the tight space for a closer look. "I think that's dog shit."

"I don't care what it looks like, you idiot!" He tried to turn, but there wasn't enough room. "You know what this means?"

"That the Red Felt Phantom and the Phantom Shitter are the same person? And that he has a dog and maybe brought the dog in here–"

"God help me!" He was exasperated. "You were early man, Mario. Did you see any dogs wondering the halls?"

"The building was quiet and empty when I arrived, except for Eddie the tattooed night custodian."

"It means whoever did this has a passkey to this office and he had the opportunity. Who was late man last night?"

"Me."

"And I suppose you didn't see anything then either."

"Just Eddie the tattooed night custodian."

"Listen to me, Mario. This is what I want you to do now. First go down and see Polakas and ask him about that night custodian. Then I want you to take a ride to the hardware store at the plaza and get a new lock set. Something pick-proof, and tell Polakas I want him to put it on before the end of the day. If he tells you he's too busy, you do it. I want a new lock on my door!" He pulled a cigarette from his pack of Luckies and lit it. "You can't imagine how I feel, Mario. Violated, raped, unclean. I need to take a shower."

"You could go down to the Boy's Gym. Coach Boid and the other Phys Ed teachers shower there all the time. And what do you want to do about the dog shit?"

"Pick it up, Mario, and put it in a plastic bag. Save it in your office as evidence if I decide to call the police. Before you go for the lock, tell Marta to come here with *all* her cleaning stuff. I want that place sanitized and sterilized with bleach from top to bottom. Be sure you get a good lock, Mario. Maybe a Yale. And don't forget to bring me back the receipt."

Phyllis was at the door holding her steno pad. "Mario said you wanted me for dictation. Is there a problem?" He pointed to the bathroom and she leaned in for a closer inspection of the writing on the mirror. "Revlon's Brick Red," she said with certainty.

"Well, thank you very much for that makeup fashion lesson, Miss Lind–" he said sarcastically.

"Ms. And I was just saying because it's an old shade. Nobody wears red lipstick these days. I have a makeup drawer full of reds. Classic Rouge, Dark Plum, Cherry Red and that one, Revlon's Brick Red. I don't wear any of them. Today the look is more natural, pale pinks and corals." She pursed her lips for him.

"Have you seen anybody inside my office, Phyllis?"

"I hardly see you in here these days."

"Have you noticed anybody strange hanging around."

"No more so than the usual cast of characters. In fact, Joel Maxwell is out there right now waiting to see you. And Dwayne Purvey has been in and out of the office looking like he's about to burst. And Red Farley. Should I go on?"

He wasn't listening. "You can go. I'll write the memo myself and give it to you to type up."

When she opened the door, Joel Maxwell quickly inserted himself into the office.

"Get out, Maxwell! I don't have time for you."

But instead of leaving, Maxwell swung the door closed with a loud bang. "I am here as the duly elected president of the Farmington Teachers' Association, the sanctioned bargaining agent for the Farmington teachers and I will not leave until the issue of the stall doors in the faculty men's room is resolved and the doors are replaced permanently. I shall... I shall not be moved." He folded his arms in emphasis. But when the principal fixed him with an unwavering hate-filled stare it caused Maxwell to lose some of his resolve. He pulled folded sheets of paper from his pocket. "Here is a petition signed by the faculty and staff." He began to read. "Working conditions are deplorable and we, the teachers of Rosencrantz and Guildenstern, will no longer tolerate it. We demand to be treated like the professionals we are and we insist that the stall doors in the men's faculty toilet on the third floor be returned immediately. Furthermore, we demand the full use of teacher preparation periods again. Teachers will no longer give up valuable prep time to patrol the building, which is an administrative responsibility. In addition, teachers will not report to their duty assignments three minutes before or remain three minutes after their duty periods end. Teachers will not attend in-school meetings scheduled by administrators during their preps. This is also true of teacher lunch periods. And in the matter of lunches, we the entire faculty further demand the immediate and total elimination of all plastic utensils in the faculty cafeteria. They are inadequate and substandard." He refolded the paper. "I have been delegated by the teachers to present you with these demands and to warn you that failure to comply with all or any of them constitutes a violation of our contract agreement—"

"There is no contract agreement."

"Failure to comply with these demands," he started again, "constitutes a violation of the *old* contract that remains in effect until a new contract agreement is reached between the teachers and UFSD 71, and will result in a possible job action by the teachers." He took a deep breath when he finished. There was a trace of perspiration on his forehead and upper lip.

"Are you done, Maxwell?" The normal color was back in the principal's face.

"It's more like *you're* done." He played the signed petition on the desk like a trump card.

"The best thing you can do right now is take those papers and walk out of my office before this really gets ugly." Maxwell didn't move. "To be clear, I don't like you. I never liked you. I am not in the mood for your bullshit, so don't fuck with me, Maxwell."

He wasn't intimidated. "Don't *you* fuck with *me,* Baltz."

"I always thought I didn't like you because of your politics, your adversarial position," he said softening his tone, "but this year I really got to know you better and do you want to know what I learned about you?"

He hesitated. "What?"

"Besides being a phony and a fraud. and walking around with that air of superiority, like your shit doesn't stink." He paused. "Well, it turns out not only *does* your shit stink, but so do the women's underwear you're so fond of wearing."

"What are you talking—"

"Pink ones and yellow ones. Silky ones and lacy ones. The black ones you had on yesterday. But do you know the ones I like best? The bikinis you wore last week. Thursday I think it was."

He couldn't talk. His dry mouth just hung open and his shoulders drooped. When he was finally able to speak he said weakly, "I... um... er... The six minutes during the beginning and at the end of duty periods and the plastic utensils are negotiable."

"Pick up your papers, Maxwell, and get the fuck out of here! And don't slam the door on your way out."

When he was alone, the intercom on his desk buzzed. "What?"

"It's your dear wife. She's been trying to reach you and when she couldn't she decided to bother me. She said it's an emergency and insisted I put her through. I told her you were in a conference with the president of the teacher's association and would call her back as soon as you were free. You're free, so call her back so she stops interrupting me and so I can finish the work I get paid to do."

"Shit." He dialed his home number. "Jesus, Edie, what's your emergency this time? I'm really busy here and you can't keep bothering my secretary—"

"Don't use that tone of voice with me, Seymour. I'm not one of your teachers you boss around."

"I'm sorry. It's been a very trying day. You wouldn't believe the crap I've literally had to deal with from the minute I got here this morning."

"All the more reason to get away, Seymour. And *that's* the emergency. The trip is in two and a half weeks, so I have to book it or lose it and I don't plan on losing it. Have you put in for the leave?"

"Not yet. I told you, I've been a very busy man," he said and realized he sounded like his nephew. "What's the emergency?"

"Do I have to do this, Seymour? Do I have to do everything? I told you I'm going with or without you. Ask for the leave, take sick days, do whatever you have to do. That's simple enough. Mother invited Mr. Franks over for dinner tonight and I won't be in any mood to cook when I get back from the consciousness-raising session. I'm taking her with me to my women's group meeting, so you pick up something for dinner on your way home. Nothing fatty or salty. Maybe Chinese. And then swing over for Mr. Franks. He's expecting you."

"But I—"

"Tonight they are having an art raffle and we bought a hundred dollars worth. I took the money out of the cash bowl."

"Edie, since you started going to the girl thing—"

"Women's consciousness-raising group, Seymour. 'Girls' is a demeaning term men use to keep women down. Women are the new Negroes."

He sighed. "Are you done?"

"On second thought forget the Chinese. Get Mr. Franks first and take him with you to the butcher, not the supermarket, and get four nice steaks and have the butcher trim the fat. You'll need to make a salad and some vegetables. Corn and peas would be nice."

"Is that all?" he asked sarcastically.

"I'm not finished. You have to stop at Loehmann's to pick up my clothes for the air-sea cruise. Mr. Franks can sit in the car when you run in, just don't take too long and be sure to crack the car window so the steaks don't spoil and Mr. Franks doesn't pass out again. The Loehmann's receipt is pinned inside your jacket pocket."

He opened his suit jacket. Four pink slips were pinned to the inside pocket with a large safety pin. "Jesus, Edie, did you have to do that? Couldn't you just have handed them to me–"

"The barbecue is in the backyard behind the shed. But it has to be cleaned with Brillo. And then cover the grill with foil to keep down the drips and the smoke. You know how smoke can trigger Mother's asthma–"

"Don't I have *anything* to say about all this?"

"It's only going to get worse, Seymour, if you don't come on the trip. You'll be here alone taking care of Mother *and* Mr. Franks for at least a month. And you won't have me around to help. Before you prepare dinner, be sure to walk the dog as soon as you get home… and don't forget to feed him. We have to run."

The phone clicked and he put the receiver back in the cradle.

* * *

Mario Giovanni went directly to Baltz's office as ordered with the new lock. "It's a Yale like you asked for. I didn't know if you preferred chrome or polished brass, so. I went with the brass." He handed him the the receipt.

"I'm a little short on cash right now, Mario, so if you don't mind, I'll take care of it next payday." He lit a Lucky and bent to stash the receipt in the bottom desk drawer. When he looked up the AP was still standing there. "What are you waiting for, Mario? You have observations to do, but before you get back to them, go see Polakas and tell him I have the lock. I'm anxious to get it installed before the end of the day."

* * *

Stash Polakas was too busy so he sent Slow Charley. It took assistant custodian more than an hour to do the job. While he was busy studying the directions, Marta the cleaning lady arrived with her cart and immediately began a constant chatter with herself, Slow Charley and Mr. Baltz.

"Is nice toilet. Is clean already. Why is Marta cleaning more?"

"Just do it," Mr. Baltz told her, "and don't spare the bleach. And really scrub that spot in the corner of the floor. And when your done, do it again. I'm going to make the rounds of the building," he told Phyllis "I should be back before dismissal. If Charlie finishes before I return, make sure he gives you *both* keys and you hold on to them until I get them from you personally." He went through the halls toward the elevator.

"Mr. Baltz," Dwayne Purvey said falling into step next to him, "I need to talk to you–"

"Not now, Purvey," he said without slackening his pace. "I'm very busy. And I already settled the faculty bathroom thing with Maxwell." He opened the elevator door.

"It's not about that. It's important–"

"Then go talk to Mario. He handles all the important stuff." He pressed the button for the third floor and the elevator door closed.

"Hey. Mr. Purvey," Virgil said when he saw him standing inert in front of the closed elevator door. Virgil's sweater now had two varsity letters, a new one for not running track next to the old one for not wrestling. "You need the elevator? No problem." He produced a key and turned it in the panel. "Where you been? I haven't seen you around much. You been sick?"

The door opened and Dwayne Purvey stepped absently into the empty car. He turned and looked at Virgil as if he just realized he was there. "Did you ever have the feeling no one is listening?" he asked the smiling student.

"This is a high school, Mr. P. Nobody here listens to anything."

The door closed. Purvey didn't press a button so the elevator didn't move. In a minute the overhead light switched off and he remained there in the dark.

* * *

Slow Charley was still working on the new lock when Baltz returned to his office. "It's heavy-duty, so it took me longer. But it's finished."

It had only taken two hours, another outstanding accomplishment for Florence Sooter and the kids from CRMD. The principal tried both keys and they worked. That was a plus. One he put on his key ring and the other he would leave in his car for safekeeping. He inspected his bathroom and the smell of chlorine hurt his eyes. He walked through the deserted building without seeing Mario Giovanni. He was late man, but probably left early after he thought everyone else was gone. "Pick up Franks... rib steaks... dresses... feed the dog," he recited to himself like a mantra over and over. "Franks... steaks... dresses... dog."

He heard the blaring boombox on the custodian's cart. "Me and Julio down by the schoolyard..." and he saw Eddie the tattooed night custodian at the far end of the hall pushing his wide broom up the corridor in his direction. If he picked up his pace he could be out the door before Eddie passed and he wouldn't have to talk to him. The custodian raised his hand tacitly and he nodded back. "Just try to get into my office tonight, you bastard," he thought holding his key ring and the spare key.

His was the only car left in the courtyard. Actually it was his wife's Oldsmobile. He hated it, but she insisted on driving his Buick whenever her mother stayed with them. "It's bigger and nicer and more dependable and easier for Mother to get in and out of." And that was the end of his protests. "Franks... steaks... dresses... dog," he repeated.

He opened the door and squeezed into the driver's seat. It *was* a tight fit with the seat moved all the way forward. "Don't move the seat or change the mirrors," she warned him, "because I can never get them back where I like them." He had difficulty even fastening his seatbelt. He stuck the key into the ignition and turned it. Except for a series of clicks nothing happened. "Son of a bitch!" He moved the gearshift lever out of Park and back again, turned off the radio and the air conditioner and tried again. He turned the key again, again,

again. Clicks. Click. Then not even that. The old battery was dead.

"Fuck me!" He pounded the steering wheel with the palms of his hands. "You piece of shit!" he yelled at the car while he turned the ignition off and on one more time. The vein appeared in his forehead. He pounded the dashboard and when he recovered he struggled out of his seat and continued his attack on the exterior of the car. He banged the spotted car hood and hurt his toe when he kicked and dented the hub cap.

"Car trouble?" Eddie the tattooed night custodian was standing behind him.

"It won't start."

"Did you have it in Park?"

"No, I tried to start it in Drive."

The custodian ignored the sarcasm. He walked to the front of the car and reached inside the grill, feeling for the lever to pop the hood. "You need to get this greased. It sticks," he said. He opened the hood with some difficulty. "The hinges too." He stuck his head into the engine compartment. "Ah," he called. "I think I found your trouble. Your battery cable. It looks like somebody disconnected it and left you a message." Mr. Baltz went around to see. The night custodian handed him a sheet of ditto paper. "BOOM!" The one-word message was printed in Brick Red lipstick block letters.

"Fuck me!"

"Looks like somebody here doesn't like you," Eddie said with a grimace. Or was it a broad grin?

"I tell you, Mario, this was not meant as a joke." He nervously lit another cigarette. A smoke cloud lingered above his desk.

"But don't you think you might have overreacted, Boss, calling the bomb squad?" He fidgeted in the chair and kicked his feet.

"Overreacted?"

"It's not like it was a *real* bomb. It was only a piece of paper, a note. Probably some kid prank—"

"Even if it started out as one sick person's idea of a joke, Mario, it's gone too far. And well beyond just one person. They violated my bathroom and now they've threatened to blow me up. I shudder to think if it had been a real bomb and me all over the walls of the courtyard."

He pictured it in his mind and caught himself. "But involving the police? With all that's happened this year. Is it wise to call the cops again and draw more attention? Shouldn't we handle it in-house?"

"Handle it? You haven't handled anything and things have gotten progressively worse. The writing on the walls. The shitting in the halls. On *my* bathroom floor! O'Dell dead and Zwill as good as. And now I get another not-so-veiled death threat. Am I supposed to wait until some assassin actually does blow me up or shoots me?" He opened his desk drawer and handed over a sheet of ditto paper in a clear cellophane envelope. "I got this one last week."

The different size letters, black and white and color had been cut from newspapers and magazines and were pasted to form a single sentence: "Two down 2 to go – Whose next?" The AP removed the paper from the envelope.

"No, Mario, leave it in the cellophane," he yelled too late. "I want the police to check it for fingerprints, but now yours are all over it."

"Sorry, Boss. I just thought... Maybe I can get them off." He rubbed the paper with his fingertips.

"You're making it worse! Just give it back to me!" He grabbed it from him and stuffed it back into the plastic cover.

"Now your fingerprints are on it too, Boss."

"Fuck." He looked through the window and watched the single Nassau County police car pull into the courtyard without lights or siren. "They're here."

"Sergeant Sadowski to see you," Phyllis announced over the intercom. "He said you called the precinct? Is there something we need to know out here?"

"Just send him in, Miss Lind." He pressed the door buzzer.

"Ms."

"Seymour... Mario," Sgt. Sadowski greeted them familiarly. He adjusted his holster to the front and sat cheekily in the empty chair. "What is it this time? Anybody dead? Shot? Crazy? Dispatch said a bomb scare."

"In my car last night," he explained. "It wouldn't start. The battery was disconnected. And I found this in the engine compartment." He handed over the ditto paper. "The car's as dead as I might've been if the bomb was real. It's in the parking space in the courtyard where I left it. The grease stains on the paper are from the night custodian. You might want to check him out."

"BOOM! That's it? No bomb?"

"Not yet. But it's not the first threat." He handed over the cellophane envelope. "I was hoping you might be able to dust it for fingerprints, but unfortunately Mario got his all over it."

"Yours too," the AP reminded him.

"Yeah, well, you watch too much TV. We don't do that." He took it out and read it carefully. "Probably just one of your students. They used the wrong word. 'Whose' instead of 'Who's.'"

"Let me see." Mario Giovanni took it and nodded. "Good detective work. I didn't even notice it."

"And there's more," Baltz said. "When I came in yesterday, someone violated my office and left messages on my bathroom mirror and wall–'Break Baltz' and 'Eat shit and die.'"

Both, according to my secretary, were written in Revlon's Brick Red lipstick." The AP looked up, surprised. "And so is the 'BOOM!' You can smell the lipstick. And there have been similar messages in the bathrooms and other places around the building. But this was very personal because whoever broke into my bathroom also left something else. Mario?" The AP was still pondering the lipstick. "Mario! Go get it."

"It's in my desk in my office," he said.

"Go! Sergeant Sadowski doesn't have all day."

"How's my daughter Milly doing?" Sadowski asked while they waited. "She graduates next month and we're having a big party. So I hope there won't be any surprises, or summer school like last year that ruined our summer plans. She starts Nassau Community in September."

"Not a problem, Boris." He offered a cigarette that was declined and lit one for himself. "Milly's a very healthy young lady and we'll miss seeing her perky self around the building. Plan away. I'll take care of it if anything unexpected comes up."

The AP came in holding a sealed plastic bag and handed it over.

"Like I said, it was on the floor in my bathroom. We've also been having trouble with someone shitting around the building. But Mario thinks this looks like dog shit. You might be able to test it."

"Yeah, we don't do that either." He held up the bag. "Looks like dog shit to me too. Show me the writing you found."

"I had it removed and the bathroom thoroughly cleaned."

"Too bad. We do do handwriting analysis. And I just said doo-doo," he laughed. "Oh, oh, and one more thing before I go," he hesitated sounding like Columbo. "What can you tell me about Carolyn Butrum? Is she senile? She keeps bothering everybody at the precinct with calls and letters and her theories about Helen O'Dell being murdered. We told her the case is closed, but all the fuss she's making does have some people at Headquarters wondering."

"I'll take care of her too, Boris."

"If there isn't anything else, I'll see you at that the Founder's Day Parade on Saturday."

"About that. You think with all that's going on here it's safe for me in a crowd? Riding in a convertible with the top down if the weather's good?"

"No worries, Seymour. You'll be fine. Safer than Kennedy in Dallas. We'll have some uniforms there for crowd control. Not that there's ever a crowd to control. Louie Guitano can work the perimeter and I'll keep an eye on the book depository. So you just go and don't worry about a thing. Besides, if anything does happen, Mario will jump in front of you and take a bullet. Right, Mario?"

"I won't be in the car this year. I'm the designated photographer, so I'll be all over the place."

"Me and Louie will take a look at your car and reconnect the battery. I'll talk to the night custodian. When we're done Louie will write up a report and leave a copy with your secretary. If your car starts, you can drive it home later."

Carolyn Butrum was waiting at Phyllis's desk. "Sergeant? Mrs. Butrum the Chairlady of the Sunshine Committee," she introduced herself. "I've called your precinct a number of times with information about the Helen O'Dell case and they said someone would get back to me. Did you get my letters? Are you here to investigate? I have lots of information. The mouse–"

"Yes, it's going well," he cut her off before she got rolling. "Thank you for your ongoing concern. Everyone at Headquarters is on it and a special task force is following up on your leads. I'm sure it won't be long before they contact you and start hauling in some suspects for questioning."

Dwayne Purvey was listening intently at his mailbox. The color drained from his face and he slipped unnoticed out of the office and headed to his car.

"Now if you'll excuse me, Mrs. Butrum, I have a bomb in the courtyard to investigate."

"Bomb? What bomb? Is there a bomb in the building? Oh, Lordy," she fretted. "Do we have to evacuate the building?"

"Officer Guitano and I are on it, Mrs. Butrum. And I'm sure Miss Lind will keep everyone informed. Ladies." He tipped his cap.

"Ms," she said, but he was gone.

If D-day, June 6, was "The Longest Day," May 12, though the date changed from year to year, was the second longest. The second Friday in May every school year was Founder's Day, followed that night by the Founder's Day Dinner, a moveable feast, with the celebrations spilling over to the Founder's Day Parade Saturday morning, making Founder's Day a Founder's Day Weekend. The first Founder's Day was Friday, May 10, 1946, the year that Rosencrantz and Guildenstern Memorial High School opened its doors. The parade featured an open car ride for honoree, Board President Wilbur Vecht, leading Farmington's recently returned World War II veterans who marched through town. It immediately became an institution and each year thereafter one individual selected by the Farmington Board of Education was honored for "outstanding contributions to the education of Farmington's students."

In more recent times, the dinner had become an overpriced affair featuring mediocre food and a cash bar at Chez Antoine's. The owner, Gus Stopoulis, a personal friend of Dr. Flackett, had also been awarded the exclusive contract to supply lunch food for all of the school cafeterias in the district. Honorees were generally administrators. No teacher had been honored at the Founder's Day Dinner in modern memory. In keeping with that tradition, the Selection Committee's unanimous choice to receive the "1971-72 Founder's Day Award for Sacrifice and Service" was Helen O'Dell.

On the afternoon of May 12, the Chez Antoine's staff dragged the reusable artificial silk flowers out of storage and decorated the long dais where the district dignitaries were now assembled. At the center of the table, in the seat of honor, a black crepe-shrouded, larger-than-life photograph of a smiling Helen O'Dell, obviously taken in happier days, beamed out at the revelers.

Past Founder's Day Dinners were always sparsely attended by teachers unwilling to fork over forty dollars to eat bad chicken and pay for their own drinks while being ignored. This year, because Helen O'Dell was the honored guest, and because of all the renewed interest in the curious circumstances surrounding her demise, Chez Antoine's was filled to capacity, including a sizable representation from the various media. Local TV and radio commentators worked the room with questions about the honoree. The Mid-Island *Clarion-Herald-Sun-Times* always sent a reporter, but this year a photographer took pictures. Harriet Stegle and her one-armed son, Seth, were networking for the absent Willy Zwill's position. Education Writer Mike McQuinn from *Newsday* was there hoping for another scoop. When Mr. Baltz saw him buying Manhattans for Mario Giovanni, he left his place on the dais and sent his tipsy AP home.

The dinner always ran late and this year it set a record. Superintendent Flackett presented Helen O'Dell with the award, accepted on her behalf by Mr. Baltz, a plaque and a $100 non-transferrable gift certificate redeemable at Chez Antoin. The presentation was followed by speeches no one would remember, and when School Board President Lalo Adornau fell off the dais, the crowd began to thin. At the end of the evening, the Chez Antoine staff cleaned up, rearranged the furniture and put the flowers and the decorations back in the storage room. A very happy Gus Stopoulis counted the night's receipts at the bar with Dr. Flackett while Mr. Baltz collected Helen O'Dell and her award and drove them back to his house. They didn't get home until after midnight.

He hated Founder's Day more than he hated Parent's Night, except maybe this year's Parent's Night, and he hated most the Founder's Day Parade that followed. It meant giving up one of his precious Saturdays to watch Farmington slowly pass around him from the backseat of a slow-moving car. If it rained on his parade, he would be trapped inside the convertible with the top up between Flackett's residual alcohol fumes from dinner the night before, the numbing haze of Adornau's Aqua Velva cologne and their combined relentless farts. The honoree always sat up front next to the driver. If it didn't rain it was exactly the same with the convertible top down, with the addition pain of a blistering burn by a scorching May sun that would last for the entire week after.

It wasn't raining in the morning, so he sweltered between Flackett and Adornau in the open car as it crawled through the center of Farmington at fifteen miles an hour. He waved inanely like Queen Elizabeth to the onlookers. Flackett seemed to enjoy the attention and the hungover Adornau, with a black eye and a Band-Aid across his nose, napped behind the two-dimensional smiling Helen O'Dell propped up in the front seat. A nervous Mr. Baltz eyed the unenthusiastic assembly of people with nothing better to do on a sunny May Saturday than watch the dog and pony show roll past them like a funeral cortège. Despite the sunblock he'd applied generously, he knew he'd have a bad sunburn by the end of the day, and the muscles of his face, frozen in the forced smile he held throughout the route, would hurt him even more. He *really* hated the Founder's Day Parade!

The butter his mother-in-law tried to slather him with and the layer of Milk of Magnesia his wife insisted he put on had no effect. Sunday he walked around the house like an aging mime with a mustache. And he wasn't able to relax his face.

Monday morning his complexion was very red when he parked his Buick in his spot, dropped Helen off at Phyllis's desk and went directly to his office. He picked out the office key stamped DO NOT DUPLICATE, slipped it into the new lock and reveled in the inviolability of his sanctuary. He sniffed the faint aroma from the car fresheners he replaced regularly and switched on the window air conditioner before he removed his jacket and hung it on the back of his desk chair. He carried *Newsday* under his arm into his private and now again pristine bathroom, which was the best thing, he thought, to come out of this school year. Two women and only two bathrooms at home was one woman too many, especially when his mother-in-law laid claim to his. He looked at himself closely in the mirror and picked at some of the white specks of Milk of Magnesia that had survived his morning shower. His wife was right, the burn would turn into a deep tan. "A good foundation for our trip to Israel," he said out loud and sighed.

He smelled traces of Marta's chlorine bleach, another assurance of the level of sanitation, removed his pants, careful not to break the crease, doubled the legs and hung them on the wooden clothes hanger behind the door. He got comfortable on the bowl, opened *Newsday* and paged through Part I. A story about an eighteen-year-old high school dropout in neighboring Mineola elected to the School Board was another indication of the end of education as he knew it. He found Mike McQuinn's article about Founder's Day on page sixteen and read it, happy to see his name was spelled correctly.

"The night was filled with long speeches by Superintendent Dr. Donald Flackett and School Board President Elliot Adornau, who fell off the dais. But the keynote speaker was the beleaguered principal of Rosencrantz and Guildenstern Memorial High School, Seymour Baltz, who has lost two assistant principals so far this year, including the Founder's Day honoree, the late Helen O'Dell. And the school year isn't over yet. Mr. Baltz extolled the late Assistant Principal for her service to the district. He lamented her sacrifice in the name of education and mourned her 'untimely death in the saddle.' He presented the oversized photo of the honoree with the 1971-72 Founder's Day Award for Sacrifice and Service, a plaque and a gift certificate for dinner. Four months after Helen O'Dell's sudden and unexplained death in January, there are still many unanswered questions in the school district and among law enforcement authorities. Stay tuned because this story is to be continued!"

"Bastard," he said. He next turned to the comics. *Peanuts* had Charley Brown talking to the kid with the blanket. His dog Snoopy had moved into the college dorm and was somehow taking classes. And *Doonesbury* showed a dirty hippy making salad with unwashed lettuce while speaking a mixture of English and French. Neither made any sense. Then he did the Jumble.

Twenty minutes later he pressed a button on the intercom on his desk. "Phyllis, I'm ready for the mail now."

She came into the office with a stack of white envelopes and a number of large brown manilla Inter-school mail envelopes. "Another letter from Geraldo Rivera. This one is Registered Return Receipt. I had to sign for it. He's cuter than on TV, and he's relentless. One is marked 'Personal and Confidential,' but I recognize the return address as Harriet Stegle's, so I am guessing she's making another pitch for Seth getting Zwill's spot. And these." She laid them on his desk.

He opened the registered letter, read the first paragraph and handed it back to her. "Pull out the 'no time, too busy to see you, winding down the school year, wait until September' letter and send off a copy to that Rivera pain in the ass."

"How was Founder's Weekend? Did you have fun?"

"Does it look like I had fun?" He pointed to his face.

"Mario said you sent him home early."

"He was in no condition to talk to that McQuinn reporter, so I thought it best he go home," he said absently as he looked through some of the correspondence.

"He was in no condition to drive either, so I had to go pick him up." She was annoyed. "What do you want me to do with Helen O'Dell? She's where you dumped her. You should have seen Dwayne Purvey's face when he walked in and saw her there this morning. He freaked out. You'd have thought he saw a ghost."

"Put her in her old office. I'm sure Rita Reed won't mind sharing the space. And maybe Helen can help her actually get some work done. I'll figure out something later." He dismissed her.

The letter marked "Personal and Confidential" was from Harriet Stegle so he dumped it unread into the waste basket. Next he looked through the other inter-school mail manilla envelopes with lists of everyone who had used the same envelope throughout the district. Each recipient's name was crossed out when a new one and destination was added to the bottom, from the Music Department to Central Administration back to Willis Elementary and then the R & G Health Office. Only one envelope was unmarked, used for the first time with just his name, M. Seymour Baltz, High School in the destination column. He put the others down and carefully opened the metal clasp. He reached inside and pulled out the contents, a new tab file folder containing a single eight-by-ten sheet. He turned it over and saw a glossy color photograph taken at Saturday's Founder's Day Parade. "FUCK ME!" he said and dropped it on his desk.

Judging by the angle, it had been taken back and to the left of the car, from the vicinity of the flagpole on the grassy knoll between the Sweet Shop and Wetson's Hamburgers. The image was a little grainy because it had been taken with a telephoto lens, but it clearly showed Flackett and Adornau on either side of him in the back of the convertible. A red quarter-sized circle had been drawn around his head with cross hairs over his forced-smiling face.

"Hey, Mr. G," Virgil called down the third-floor corridor.

"What are you doing out in the halls this time, Loomis? Looking for something else to set fire to?"

"Another Lesson Stretcher." He handed over the official red Lesson Stretcher pass. "Mr. Farley again. You'd think by this time with a month until graduation we'd have come to some kind of an understanding. A *détente*. I mean, President Nixon did it with the Russians. It's not like Mr. Farley has to deal with me next year. I think it's this Varsity sweater that sets him off every time he sees me wearing it. Especially now that I have three varsity letters."

"Three? I thought you got one for wrestling."

"The first one, the one I value most. Then I figured I might as well try to become a four-letter man. It will look great on my résumé. This one's for track and this is for football. And after Memorial Day I have to pick up one for baseball at Central." He smiled. "I saw you taking pictures at the parade Saturday. Besides making movies I dabble in still photography too. Nice camera. Nikon?"

"Pentax," he said with pride. "A new Spotmatic with a single reflex fifty millimeter lens. It was a birthday gift."

"I use my father's old Canon. That's a great telephoto lens you were using."

"It's a two hundred millimeter zoom."

"I bet it put you right in the car with Mr. Baltz."

"You can see the whites of his eyes." He stopped. "It's great for bird-watching. Why do you care? And why are we talking about that here? You're out roaming the halls again and I'm late for a meeting."

"I like to think we're having a 'moment,' Mr. G. A human interaction. Something special and so rare these days. This is something I will take with me and remember and cherish long after I've forgotten quadratic equations."

"Yeah, well, take it with you and cherish it on your Lesson Stretcher. Maybe *if* you graduate we'll have another one at your tenth high school reunion." He handed back the pass and they set off in opposite directions.

At the elevator Virgil fished the key from his pocket and turned it in the slot. The elevator door slid open silently and the light went on. "Hey, Mr. Purvey!" he said to the figure crouching on the floor. "What are you doing in here in the dark? Are you okay?"

"Shut the door! Hurry!" He was covering his eyes.

"Are you hurt? Do you need a doctor?" Virgil stepped in and the door closed.

"A doctor? He can't do anything for me," he said enigmatically. "Can I trust you? Can I tell you a secret that's been eating away at me?"

"Of course."

He uncovered his eyes and looked directly at Virgil. "I'm the one, Virgil...*the one responsible for Helen O'Dell's death!*"

"Oh?" Virgil said matter-of-factly and nodded. His hand paused over the buttons. "Any particular floor you want me to press?"

* * *

"I wanted to talk to you alone before the others arrive, Mario." He took the last cigarette, crumpled the pack, tossed it at the wastebasket and missed. He waited for his AP to get up and retrieve it, but he didn't move. "Mario?" He nodded, indicating the paper ball that had rolled under a chair. The AP got up reluctantly with an audible sigh, knelt on the floor and fished out the cigarette pack. He straightened, dusted off the knees of his suit pants and dropped it into the basket before he sat. Mr. Baltz struck a match with some difficulty and held it to the tip of the Lucky. His hand shook visibly. He opened the desk drawer and removed the file folder he pushed across the desk.

"What's that?" His insides froze. He didn't touch the folder.

"Open it, Mario," he said.

Reluctantly he took it and held it in his hand. "I–I don't–" he stammered.

"Open it."

"A prank. A joke–"

"Just look. It stopped being funny, Mario, when it became a crime. The police call it menacing and assault."

"I don't know what to say–" He was beginning to perspire even in the air-conditioning.

"Don't say anything, Mario." He waited. "Tell me what you think I should do about this. What *you* would do," He crushed out his cigarette, opened a new pack and lit another one. "Look at me, Mario. Am I such a terrible person? A tyrant? An ogre?" He didn't answer or make eye contact. "I have feelings. I laugh at a good joke. I cry when I'm hurt and I bleed when someone stabs me."

"I'm sorry–" He took a deep breath. The perspiration ran down the back of his collar and he waited.

"I am too, Mario." He turned and looked away into the courtyard. "I got the message, Mario. Loud and clear. I called Flackett today. I'm done here, Mario."

"So–So what are you going to do–?"

"I arranged to take an extended sick leave, effective Monday, for the rest of the school year. That sick bastard on the grassy knoll was pointing a camera, but just as easily it could have been a high-powered rifle aimed at my head. Even though Noah Lewis has seniority, I proposed that Flackett appoint you to fill in during my absence."

The AP exhaled an audible rush of air, unaware that he had been holding his breath. "That's great... I thought...." And then he stopped himself. "For the rest of the year?"

"I'll use some of my sick days through the end of June. Of course there are a few things to be arranged. Loose ends to tie together."

He was relieved, but he stifled a smile. "How will we ever be able to get on without you?"

"Phyllis could run this place blindfolded. She'll be only too glad to tell you what to do."

"But you're not really sick?"

"Just between us, Mario, my wife got a free fly/cruise vacation to Israel. If I don't go with her, she threatened to go with someone else... or alone. You don't know how lucky you are being single. I really want to spend a month in a desert surrounded by Arabs like I want another hole in my head. But worse than Israel in June, if I don't go I'll be stuck taking care of her mother *and* her boyfriend."

"Edie has a boyfriend?" he asked incredulously.

"Not my wife's boyfriend, my mother-in-law's."

The intercom on his desk clicked. "Rita Reed is here," Phyllis announced.

He put the photo back in the folder and into his desk drawer. "No need to spread what I just said around, Mario." He stubbed out his cigarette and pressed the buzzer. Rita Reed stood in the doorway tentatively holding her balled handkerchief. "Come in, Rita." He indicated her place. "Is Noah with you?"

She started sniffing and dabbing her nose. "I haven't seen him very much. I thought he was out sick."

Immediately after she shut the door there was a soft knock and Noah Lewis came in. "I, auh, didn't know we met on Thursdays. Usually it's on Mondays. I, auh, was out of my office. Did I, auh, miss anything?"

"I'm taking a leave of absence, Noah."

"That's, auh, good news," he said and nodded. "Very good. So I, auh, can get back to the cafeteria? It's Taco Thursday, my favorite." He began backing out again.

"Come in, Noah. Sit down. We have things to discuss. Your tacos can wait."

He sighed, shut the door and took his seat next to Rita Reed. "Hello," he said. "You're the, auh, new woman, right?"

"I'm taking a leave of absence," he repeated. "It's a little health leave." He lit a cigarette and she coughed. "It will take effect as soon as I get things in order here."

"Lucky you. There are still, auh, five more weeks until school ends."

"It's nothing serious, I hope," Rita sniffed.

"Dr. Nessmith and my cardiologist concur that time away from the job will bring my blood pressure and the other numbers in line. I'll use the leave time to relax. Maybe travel a little. A change of scenery. Doctors' orders and all."

"Poland," Noah Lewis suggested. "Go to Poland. I, auh, plan to retire there and live like a king." The thought made him excited.

"I'll take it under consideration, Noah—"

"Who, auh, will have to do your job? I, auh, don't think I'll, auh, have time with the end of the school year and key collection and all that other stuff."

"No need to worry, Noah. Mr. Giovanni here"–the AP smiled modestly, stretched his neck and kicked his feet absently with excitement–"will be taking over the reins as interim acting principal while I'm gone. I'm sure he will be depending on both of you to help him make the transition. We're on the home stretch now and the finish line is in sight. Mario is capable. And while I am sure there will be no serious problems in the time remaining, with the two of you to back him up, I am confident that he will be able to handle any crisis that may come up. My absence will mean all of you will have to work a little harder, but there should be no hitches, no surprises, and the closing procedures will run smoothly." He put out his cigarette and stood. "Quite frankly, we all know that this place can pretty much run itself without us. But don't let the taxpayers know that or we'll all be out of a job," he added with a smile that still hurt his face. "I hope to see all of you right back here next school year in September." The smile on Mario Giovanni's face faltered for a second. "Noah." He shook his hand. "Rita, I hope you get over whatever it is that you have." She sniffed.

When they were gone he opened a side drawer in his desk. "Of course you'll want to use my office, Mario. This is where you can keep your stuff. I'll take what's essential and leave the rest of my things where they are. No need to bother with any of it. In fact, there's no need for you to even open another drawer." He selected a key from the ring he was holding and locked the other drawers. "This one"–he picked another key and held it between two fingers–"opens the new lock. You already have the rest of them. Elevator. Passkey. Keep my office clean and the bathroom cleaner." He looked around. "That should cover everything, Mario. Just remember what I told them, this building will run itself, so don't *do* anything, Mario, to fuck it up! Leave well enough alone and let everything wind down at its own pace. If you have *any* problems, if something comes up, just ask Miss Lind–"

"Ms," he corrected automatically.

"I'll pass the torch officially tomorrow with an announcement." He escorted him toward the door. "Don't fuck anything up, Mario."

Rosencrantz and Guildenstern
Memorial High School
AV/CM Department

To: All Teachers
From: Harry Dexter, Coordinator AV/CM Department
Subject: AV Equipment and Power Demand During Hot
            Weather

The Long Island Lighting Company has indicated that soaring temperatures created by the unseasonable heat wave have strained their ability to provide adequate power to meet the demand for electricity during peak hours of the day. LILCO is requesting its customers cut back their use of electrical equipment and the AV/CM Department will do its part to help.

Beginning immediately there will be a moratorium on issuing any AV equipment until the power emergency has eased. To further cut down on the consumption of electricity in the school, teachers are directed to return immediately any AV equipment in their possession.

LILCO is currently working on a solution to the problem. Construction of the proposed Shoreham Nuclear Power Plant is scheduled to begin in 1973 and when it is completed there will be sufficient electric power on Long Island even during times of peak demand. Teachers can look forward to when they will be able to use their AV equipment without interruption sometime in 1984.

The pledge, the National Anthem, the moment of silent prayer or meditation and the daily announcements ended and everyone was poised for the bell ending Homeroom to launch them into another school day, the next to last Friday of May. The PA clicked.

"Careful, Mr. Scapelli, Big Brother is listening," someone said.

A series of loud thumps on the microphone followed. Then the speaker on the wall squealed with feedback, followed by a flurry of unintelligible voices in the background. "–Damn it... useless piece of... Dexter... fix the fuh–" Finally Mr. Baltz's voice resounded throughout the school, "Stop all work. Stop all work. This is your principal, Mr. Baltz. Homeroom period will be extended for several important announcements–"

Teachers groaned. An extended Homeroom meant the rest of the day class periods would be off or some cut completely depending on the length of the extension. Lessons, reviews, quizzes–whatever was scheduled would have to be revised on the fly. Jesse went to his desk and opened his plan book. He needed thirty minutes for his test. Sue leafed through the New York *Times* waiting for whatever earthshaking announcements made it necessary to extend Homeroom. Red Farley had to pee. Guidance counselor John Hiller was in the teacher's cafeteria at a table with Noah Lewis dunking one of his semi-defrosted rolls, buttered and jellied thanks to the service cart, into the styrofoam coffee cup with his name printed on it. "Poland?" he asked. "Baltz's going to Poland?"

The principal began, "It has been quite some time since I've spoken to you over the PA from my office, where I have made so many decisions that affected you during your years here at Rosencrantz and Guildenstern. I have always tried to decide what was best for you, because a principal is like the father of a family. And during my years as principal all of you have become the children of my extended family."

Everyone stopped listening.

He cleared his throat and continued. "I have never been a quitter. But in the past few weeks something unexpected and very personal has come up and so it has become evident to me

587

that I can no longer be your father–" He paused to let the words sink in.

"What's he saying?"

"Is he getting divorced?"

"He's not *my* father. My father moved to California with his girlfriend."

"This is boring."

"Shhhhh!"

"–of course I would prefer to carry on through to the end of the school year, just weeks away, no matter the personal problems it would cause me. But your interests must always come before my personal considerations. Therefore, I have asked for and received from Superintendent Flackett an extended personal leave effective today at the end of the school day. And while the leave will, in all likelihood, be only temporary, I have every intention of returning to my post, my home and my school family sometime in the future. It saddens me that I will not be here with you to see this school year to the end. Assistant Principal Giovanni will take the reins as interim acting principal at the end of the school day today." He paused. "All of you have made me so proud always, and I know you will continue to do so for Mr. Giovanni. It is with more than a little sadness that I say good-bye–" He stopped. "No, not good-bye, but farewell, because in the words of General Douglas MacArthur, I shall return. And today I am the luckiest man on the face of the earth." He paused. "You may now resume all work. Resume all work." The PA clicked off.

There was silence.

"What was that all about, Mr. Scapelli? What did he just say?"

Terry had a strange expression on his face. "Holy shit!" They laughed. "Pardon my language. But the principal just said he's leaving! It's like Nixon's press conference in 1962, after he lost the election for governor of California and said he was getting out of politics. 'You won't have Dick Nixon to kick around anymore,'" he said doing a good impersonation.

"I don't understand. Isn't Nixon the president? He's not the governor of California too, is he?"

Terry was stunned. "Not since LBJ announced that he wouldn't run for a second term in 1968 have I heard anything so earthshaking."

A dull roar began on the third floor and built up in volume. It gathered momentum that spread from floor to floor until Rosencrantz and Guildenstern Memorial High School was filled with the resounding cheers from the teachers while the confused students watched them.

* * *

All day the building buzzed like a beehive on fire. Everyone speculated about Baltz's announcement that had come from nowhere. There was no lack of free-floating theories and opinions.

"Cancer," Mrs. Butrum said. "The man has lost weight and his complexion is so gray."

"He smokes like a chimney," Rita Reed said. "He told us APs he's taking time to travel, which doesn't sound very good. Like he sees the handwriting on the wall and wants to do the things he's always wanted to do before he kicks the bucket."

"Maybe Poland. I, auh, know for a fact that I, auh, plan to, auh, retire in Poland."

"Of course," Mrs. Butrum offered, "it could be that he's involved in the Helen O'Dell cover-up and wants to get out before it's too late. He was the one who said there was no mouse!"

"The rats are deserting a sinking ship."

* * *

At dismissal the teachers lined up in the Main Office, many with questions, the well-wishers waiting to shake hands and say good-bye. A smiling Mr. Baltz stood just outside his office with Mario Giovanni at his side greeted them all and tried not to look too pleased.

"It's not good-bye. That sounds so final. More like 'See you next September,'" he quipped. "Mr. Tejent," he said when

Jesse stepped up to shake hands, "I have to admit that first day I had my doubts you'd still be here by now."

"Not to worry, Mr. Baltz," Terry said. "He'll be in good hands while you're away. I'm personally taking him under my wing and I plan to teach him everything I know."

"What a wonderful idea, to cut off a promising career in education, Mr. Scapelli. Good luck, Mr. Tejent. you'll need it."

Later Jesse emptied his mailbox and found a hand-printed message in red felt marker: "Oh come all ye tired, ye poor, ye huddled masses yearning to breathe free, ye wretched refuse, homeless and tempest-tossed to the Hand Maid Inn today after dismissal to celebrate the end of an era. Break Baltz!"

23

Monday morning a whistling Mario Giovanni came in bright-eyed and early on his first day as Interim Acting Principal, or was it Acting Interim Principal? Either way it really didn't matter to him. He liked the title. The first thing he did after he arrived and was secure inside the office, *his* office, was pee in the executive toilet where the walls were graffiti-free. Everything was clean and the aroma was–he looked at the car freshener–Morning Dew. Then he spent a half hour moving everything around on the desktop and rearranging the furniture and the next fifteen minutes putting it back the way it was.

Baltz had locked the drawers and told him there was no need to open any of them other than the one designated for him to use, but he couldn't resist. The locks were no problem. He picked them all with a paperclip. He had a quick look through everything and resolved to do a more thorough investigation later on.

He wiggled his ass in the desk chair, the seat he had coveted for years. It was harder than he expected and he made a mental note to pick up one of those cushion seats with the springs inside, like the one he had in his car. He leaned back, careful not to tip over, clasped his hands behind his head and anchored his shoes in the open bottom drawer to hold the chair in its tilted position. He lit one of the celebratory De Nobile Cigars he had soaked in red wine and dried in the sun for the occasion. Its irregular shape, not unlike a dark turd, held his lips open slightly. He was careful not to drop ashes on his new double-breasted pinstripe suit. He removed the cigar and sniffed the fresh pink carnation in his lapel. He looked at his watch. It was only eight fifty-five. He still had the whole day ahead of him.

He hated golf, but to pass the time he removed Baltz's putter and nine iron from where they rested behind the flag stand, carefully lined up five golf balls and putted to an imagined spot on the rug. He was terrible, and golf was a stupid, boring game. On the last ball, he put the putter down and picked up the nine iron. He probably should have used the plastic ball with the holes in it, he thought too late, as he brought the club head back and swung. The ball shot up and out in a perfect arc, slammed into the wall and ricocheted off the ceiling before it knocked the hole-in-one trophy Baltz so proudly displayed off the shelf and broke into two irregular pieces.

Immediately the intercom on the desk made him jump. "What's going on in there, Mario? Did you break something?"

"No, I'm fine. I just knocked over the coatrack." He paused. "Could you please do me a favor, Phyl, call me Mr. Giovanni? I mean when we're here at work at least... to keep up appearances."

"Why of course, Mario," she said. "And to keep up appearances you can call me... not at all."

"Oh, come on, Phyl–"

"Ms Lind," she corrected and clicked off.

He surveyed the damage. There was a deep dent in the wood paneling near the door. He pressed his finger into it. A dark gouge marred the acoustical ceiling tile, and the little gold plastic golfer on top of the trophy was broken off. He would have to get everything fixed or replaced. "Fuck!"

At first the thought of having nothing to do seemed appealing, but now he was bored. How the hell did Noah Lewis do it day after day, year after year? He replaced the clubs and the balls and looked at his watch. It was going to be a long day; only six minutes past nine. He opened the office door. "Everything all right out here, Miss Lind?"

"Ms," she said curtly. "And everything is just the same as it was a half hour ago when you asked, *Mister* Giovanni." She didn't look up from repairing a chipped fingernail. "And by the way, you smell awful. Just like those awful cigars you started smoking."

He stopped at each of the other secretaries and watched them before he went through to archway into the alcove. Noah's office was empty, so he stopped to look in on Rita Reed. Mrs. Butrum was sitting in the chair in front of the photo of Helen O'Dell.

"Good morning, ladies. Just doing morning rounds."

"Congratulations on your temporary promotion." Mrs. Butrum turned back to Rita Reed and said in an audible whisper, "Such a terrible mistake."

"Excuse me!" he said.

"Oh, not you. I was just telling Rita about my neighbor across the street, the poor man. A volunteer fireman, bless him, up and down ladders all the time. And very handy. So when he needed to replace some shingles he lost over the winter he naturally thought to do the work himself." He looked furtively at his watch. "The man's roof has a steep slant." She indicated with her hands. "So he tied a length of rope to the back bumper of his car in the driveway and threw the other end up on the roof. Then he climbed the ladder on the other side and tied the rope around his waist for added safety so he couldn't fall off."

"Let me guess, the rope broke."

"If only it had." She shook her head sadly. "The poor man would have gotten off lucky. A half hour later his wife, who's very sweet but such a simple girl, took the car to pick up their daughter playing at a neighbor's house in the neighborhood. It was two blocks before she heard him yelling and looked into the rearview mirror. The poor man was being dragged along the pavement behind her. When she'd driven off he was still attached to the rope and she pulled him over the top of that slanted roof. But he grabbed the brick chimney, which didn't stop him and the chimney broke and he continued over the roof along with a bunch of the good shingles, through the shrubs, across the lawn and down the block. It's a wonder he wasn't killed."

"A miracle," Rita Reed said, dabbing her nose with her handkerchief.

"And now he also has to hire someone to come in to repair the roof and rebuild the chimney."

"That's terrible."

"But the worst part is that his wife served him with divorce papers in the hospital! She wasn't going to pick up their daughter at all. It turns out she was having an affair with the neighbor. Now their in a custody battle for their daughter."

"She could have avoided an expensive divorce by just stepping on the gas instead of the brake. Ladies." He nodded and left them.

His old office looked the same, but it felt strange being there, like taking a step backward in time. He pulled some things out of his desk drawers, some magazines, a copy of *The Godfather* and an Etch-a-Sketch he concealed in the folded magazines. He tucked everything under his arm and went back to his new office. "Everything still good?" he asked as he passed through. No one looked up or answered. "Well then just carry on and keep doing what you're doing. If anything comes up I'll be in my office."

Resettled behind the desk, he relit his cigar and took the Etch-a-Sketch in both hands. He was fascinated as he turned the horizontal and vertical knobs at the bottom and watched a tiny straight line trace across the screen. He tried turning both knobs at the same time to make curves, but they turned out more like steps. He flipped it over, shook it and the lines cleared. Then he had an idea and started by making a single straight horizontal line from edge to edge in the center. Almost on top of that he made another and another, repeating the process over and over. By eleven o'clock he had gradually scraped off enough of the gray coating on the inside of the screen to expose the internal mechanism, a nib attached to two rods controlled by the dials to make the lines when they were turned. He was still bored. He checked his watch to be sure it was working. "What time is it, Ms Lind?" he asked over the intercom.

"Time for my break."

Fifteen minutes later he went for another tour of the building. He watched Slow Charley replace some broken floor tiles in the Klaus Brinker Wing. He went out the side door and stopped by Helen O'Dell's grave. The bushes were starting to bloom. He surprised several students who were cutting class. They dropped their cigarettes, covered their faces and ran.

"Who'd a thought, Helen?" he said to her gravestone. "Baltz is gone. Maybe for good. And I made it to the top just like I always told you I would." He found a smooth rock nearby, cleaned off the dirt with his fingers and laid it on the gravestone. Then he went back slowly into the building through the open side door, where two more cutters passed him on their way out. "Hey," he called, but they didn't stop and he wasn't up for a chase, so he let them go. On the second floor he passed the Library and tried the door but it was locked. Next he headed down the science corridor, where it was always an adventure.

Dave Bowden was in front of his room in his lab coat and safety goggles amid beakers, bunsen burners and teeming tenth-graders. He opened the door and looked in.

Unflustered, the science teacher announced, "Hey, everybody, we have a surprise guest, our substitute principal, Mr. Giovanni. Come in, you're just in time for urine analyses." Happily he joined the crowd of students around the lab table that ran across the front of the classroom. "They all brought in urine specimens to test, Mr. Giovanni. I was just about to test mine." He held up a quarter-full Mason jar in his rubber-gloved hand. "Best to be careful everyone. But remember what I told you, urine is sterile... until it hits the floor. Still, you don't want to get it on you." He swirled the contents of the jar in front of him and held it up under the light. "Good color." He opened the lid and sniffed to the "Eeews" of his audience. "There's a slight aroma, but not too strong." Then he dipped his finger into the liquid and stirred it. They gasped. Mr. Giovanni winced as he watched the crazy science teacher tip up the jar and taste it. There were screams. "Nice bouquet. A little fruity with a strong flavor of–" There was chaos. Mr. Giovanni's mouth hung open in disbelief. "What's wrong with all of you?"

"You drank pee! You just drank your urine! You're insane!"

"Pee?" He looked at the jar before he tilted it and drained the rest, shaking the last drops onto his tongue. "Don't be absurd. That's my urine over there." He pointed to another jar. "This is apple juice. Or at least I think it is." He turned to Mr. Giovanni to wink, but he had already fled.

"Anything?" he asked Phyllis when he entered the Main Office. He was still shaken. "No calls?"

"Nothing."

"I just watched crazy Dave Bowden drink his pee!"

She laughed. "He must be doing his urine analysis lesson. It gets them every year."

He went into the office and took one of the magazines into the executive toilet so the day shouldn't be a total loss. He ran the water in the sink and sat. Steam billowed up and he was able to see faint traces of the red lipstick letters "re_ck_al_" that Marta hadn't been able to remove from the glass. He was still bored.

Rosencrantz and Guildenstern
Memorial High School
UFSD 71
Farmington, New York

TO: All Teachers and Staff
FROM: Mario Giovanni, Interim Acting Principal
SUBJECT: Building Problems and Suggestion Box
May 23, 1972

On one of my many rounds and in my official capacity as Interim Acting Principal, I have seen certain areas of weakness around the building. My goal during the remaining days of the school year is to correct all problems, major or minor, real or imagined, and shore up the areas of weakness that need shoring up. During my two days as Interim Acting Principal I have conducted a comprehensive study and compiled a list of those most critical issues that affect our working capabilities and in the next days and weeks I will introduce a program to correct all of them.

All teachers and professional staff will be issued a folder identifying the problems and outlining the steps you will perform to correct them. Be sure to read the information in the folder carefully and attach it securely to your Teacher Manual issued on the first day of school in September, as the folder will contain changes to some old practices and the new procedures that override what you have done in the past.

In addition, a Suggestion Box will be located in the Main Office at Phyllis Lind's desk to enable teachers and professional staff to voice their opinions regarding the smooth operation of the school in these our end of days.

Rosencrantz and Guildenstern
Memorial High School
UFSD 71
Farmington, New York

TO: All Teachers and Staff
FROM: Mario Giovanni, Interim Acting Principal
SUBJECT: Feet
May 24, 1972

On another of my continuing rounds of the building I noticed a blatant disregard for school property! Someone has been removing the rubber "feet" from the legs of student desks throughout the school. This has created the problem of unsteady desk surfaces, a distraction to the learning process of students that may hinder their performance on the upcoming final exams. It has also caused these "feetless" desk legs to scrape loudly across classroom floors, not only disturbing classes on the floors below, but also causing damage to floor tiles. Many tiles will have to be replaced and in some extreme cases the damage is un-reversible and un-repairable. Teachers should be on the lookout for anyone willfully removing desk feet and immediately count the number of desk feet presently present in your classrooms and the number of missing desk feet. Return the tear-off response section below with your tally tomorrow in a box located on Phyllis Lind's desk in the Main Office.

(Tear off and return)

- -

Teacher _____

Room _____

No. feet missing _____

No feet missing [ ]

Rosencrantz and Guildenstern
Memorial High School
UFSD 71
Farmington, New York

TO: All Teachers and Staff
FROM: Mario Giovanni, Interim Acting Principal
SUBJECT: Feet Clarification
May 24, 1972

For those who may have misunderstood my earlier memo regarding feet and the tear-off response section. "No. feet missing" with the period (.) refers to the number of feet missing from desks. "No feet missing" without the period (.) means there are no feet missing.

By way of further clarification, if you teach in more than one classroom, please list each room number and provide a separate tally of the missing feet in each room–unless there are no feet missing in one or more of the rooms you teach in.

**Rosencrantz and Guildenstern
Memorial High School
UFSD 71
Farmington, New York**

TO: All Teachers and Staff
FROM: Mario Giovanni, Interim Acting Principal
SUBJECT: Chalk and Chalkboards
May 25, 1972

Last year the New York State Department of Education conducted a study and determined that the color of chalk used on chalkboards has a direct impact on student learning. In their NYSDE Bulletin 447 they recommend using white chalk on standard black slate blackboards and yellow chalk on the newer green slate blackboards. A copy of that bulletin, along with all the others, can be found in your Teacher Manual.

During another of my rounds of the building I have noticed that teachers are not adhering to the policy of using proper colored chalk. Therefore, all teachers will check their chalk supply and see to it that they are using the right tool for the right job.

Red and blue chalk may NOT be used except in special instances such as Art class, but only with prior approval from my office.

**Rosencrantz and Guildenstern
Memorial High School
UFSD 71
Farmington, New York**

TO: All Teachers and Staff
FROM: Mario Giovanni, Interim Acting Principal
SUBJECT: Mold, Mildew and Other Toxic Waste
May 25, 1972

You will be happy to know that the incidents of unwanted "deposits" that had been left in various isolated locations around the school has fallen off dramatically since the first deposit was discovered by me on the second-floor landing. The last was deposited in one of the cubicles outside Doc Nessmith's in the Health Office.

But in the past week teachers in the Art Wing have reported a minor new reoccurrence of a problem that has caused some concern in the past. Once again traces of the black mold and mildew treated earlier this year in the Teacher's Cafeteria have begun to appear on the walls and ceilings of several classrooms adjoining the Teacher's Cafeteria in what is now the new Art Wing, formerly used by the Science Department. Steps are underway by Mr. Polakas and his crack custodial staff to clear up the condition before it gets worse. Be aware that in the next few days you may smell the strong odor of chlorine, but do not be alarmed!

Joseph E. Scalia

Rosencrantz and Guildenstern
Memorial High School
UFSD 71
Farmington, New York

TO: All Teachers and Staff
FROM: Mario Giovanni, Interim Acting Principal
SUBJECT: Fire and Emergency Drills
May 25, 1972

While the 1971-72 school year will soon be a fond memory, this is no time to become complacent. Emergencies can and will happen when you least expect them. Fires may strike at any time! A word to the wise. Be vigilant. Be prepared. And above all be ready!

The Principal's Office door burst open suddenly. "Ms Lind, it's time for a surprise fire drill!"

"But it's raining out, Mario. A lunch period and it's Friday before a three-day weekend. We never have fire drills on rainy days during lunch periods."

"Too bad," he said. "It's the dawn of a new day."

"You can't have a fire drill during a lunch period, Mario! It will be chaos!"

He removed the safety shield that covered the alarm box. "A real fire doesn't know what time it is."

"I just spent thirty-five dollars getting my hair done and if you think I'm going out there in the rain–"

"Too late... Real fires don't care about hair." He pressed the fire alarm button and clicked his stopwatch. The sound of the fire alarm bell reverberated throughout the building.

"But–"

"No buts, Phyl. It's done and can't be undone," he said reveling in his power. He listened to the alarm. "That should get an interesting response."

"Undoubtedly it *will* get a response, but not necessarily the one you were expecting. You forgot to disconnect the hookup to the Fire Department. You just turned in a false alarm, *Principal* Giovanni." She removed a plastic rain cap and a collapsible umbrella from her desk drawer and took her pocketbook. On her way around her desk she purposely banged into the Suggestion Box knocking it to the floor and spilling its contents. "Oops." The tip of her umbrella caught the tray with the missing feet tally and flipped it. "I have a suggestion. There's too much clutter around my desk. Find another place for your projects."

He was frantic. "How do I call them back? How do I stop it?" He tried to push the alarm back in place, but it was too late.

"Like you said, it's done and can't be undone." She walked out behind the other secretaries into the main hall where muttering teachers and students reluctantly exited the building into the late May rain.

The klaxon horn at the Farmington Fire Department was so loud the sound echoed and bounced off the facade of Rosencrantz and Guildenstern. It rolled across the wet lawn where people stood bunched together in the rain, girls in gym bloomers, teachers holding cups of coffee, secretaries huddled under umbrellas, all waiting for the fire trucks to arrive.

"It must be a real fire," Red Farley said. "Giovanni couldn't be dumb enough to pull a Friday fire drill on a rainy day in the middle of a lunch period."

"I hear sirens," Stanley Milnow said between bites of his sandwich.

"I don't see any smoke. Maybe it's a bomb scare again," John Hiller said. He covered his coffee cup so the rain wouldn't get in. "I just hope nobody takes the rolls I left on the table."

"Maybe it's not a fire at all. Maybe it's another toxic chemical spill like that chlorine gas attack back in '64. Remember? When that new science teacher mixed bleach and ammonia. He was a friend of yours, right, Red? What was his name? You know, the one who always wore a Goldwater button and almost killed us all from his own stupidity?" Terry said.

"Up yours, Scapelli!"

"Maybe it's a false alarm," Jesse offered and watched for the trucks. From the roar of horns and sirens they were getting closer.

"False alarms don't usually happen until test week," Sue said, her hair covered with a sodden New York *Times*.

"I told him," Phyllis said, "we never have fire drills in the rain, but he pulled the handle anyway. Now I'm going to be frizzy the rest of the day. I liked him so much better when he was just an assistant asshole and not the interim acting asshole in charge. The jerk."

Under the tree, Stanley Milnow laid out his briefcase. "Did you bring the cards, Buddy? We can finish the game while we wait."

"I know how I'd handle false alarms if I was in charge," Red said. "I'd make a voiceprint of everybody in the school, teachers and students. Every student gets recorded as soon as they come up from the junior high. Then just record every phone call that comes into the building. If there's a false alarm, a bomb scare, whatever, compare the tapes to the voiceprints."

"There may be a few wrinkles with that idea, Red. Boys' voices change in high school. What if they call in a false alarm when they're seniors? And what if they simply pull the alarm box handle? That's what I'd do."

"Just shut up and deal the cards, Stanley."

When the first fire pumper roared up to the school cheers erupted from the crowd. "Burn, baby, burn! Burn, baby, burn!" The volunteer firemen jumped down and began connecting their hoses to the fire hydrants while a small stream of students and teachers were still trickling from the exits. Other firemen with their axes in hand rushed past them to get inside the building.

Mario Giovanni was standing in the middle of the front lawn under the flagpole with his hands raised. "Go back! It's okay. It was a mistake! There's no fire!" But they didn't.

More trucks screamed around the side of the building, including the new hook and ladder. That brought another round of cheers from the crowd. One by one, the private cars of volunteer firemen called by the klaxon horn from their jobs in town swarmed in from every direction with their blue emergency lights flashing.

There was an audible moan from the dripping crowd when the all-clear sounded. Mr. Giovanni clicked his stopwatch and the firemen began rolling up their hoses and stowing their equipment on the trucks, disappointed there wasn't a real fire to fight. Some of the volunteers, recent high school graduates, paraded around with their boots rolled down and their raincoats open, posing and flirting with the girls, chatting with their friends and old teachers. When the trucks and cars pulled away, almost everyone else straggled back into the building out of the rain.

"I'm going to have to write this up, Mr. Giovanni," the fire marshal said in the Main Office. "I understand you made a mistake, but you turned in a false alarm, put lives in danger and cost the taxpayers of Farmington money. This is a citation." He signed the paper he was writing, tore it from the pad and handed it to him. "And this is an invoice for the cost. See you at the next School Board meeting. Have a nice day."

"Phyllis–" he said humbly when things settled down.

"*Ms Lind!* And don't say I didn't try to warn you."

He looked down at his stopwatch. "Twenty-two minutes to vacate the building.? We'll have to do better than that on the next fire drill."

**Rosencrantz and Guildenstern
Memorial High School
UFSD 71
Farmington, New York**

TO: All Teachers and Staff
FROM: Mario Giovanni, Acting Interim Principal
SUBJECT: Fire and Emergency Drills Follow-Up
May 31, 1972

The total elapsed time of last Friday's fire drill, twenty-two minutes and forty-two seconds to vacate the building, is not only NOT a record for fire drills, it is a DISGRACE! Your poor performance was made quite apparent to me as I watched you and your students slowly and haphazardly exit the building. You have forgotten the basic fundamentals of conduct during fire and other emergency drills. Absolute silence is to be maintained at all times during these drills.

Practice makes perfect. And once again I advise you to be vigilant, be prepared and be ready to redeem yourselves for your disgraceful performance!

To paraphrase Smokey the Bear, "Only you can prevent bad fire drills!"

Rosencrantz and Guildenstern
Memorial High School
UFSD 71
Farmington, New York

TO: All Teachers and Staff
FROM: Mario Giovanni, Acting Interim Principal
SUBJECT: Mold, Mildew and Doo-doo, Oh, My!

It has come to my attention, to the attention of TV News, *Newsday* and OSHA (Why aren't they out cleaning up the oceans like they are supposed to?) that there seems to be some question concerning the "state of health" inside the High School.

Oh, I'm not talking about the daily backups and overflows in the bathrooms adjacent to the cafeterias. That problem has been traced to the high-bulk, high-fiber menu formerly served by the food service. It has been corrected by offering more junk food and fillers. And I am not referring to the multiple deposits left at various locations around the building, perhaps another by-product of the now corrected high-bulk, high-fiber menu. And I don't mean when a first-year former science teacher who was not being invited to return to teach for a second year intentionally or accidentally (we'll never know for certain) mixed chlorine bleach and Drano in what came to be known as "The Science Disaster of 1964"! The resulting massive cloud of lethal chlorine gas caused the immediate evacuation of the building and kept it closed for two days until all traces of the toxic gas were gone. Those of you who were here will remember that the disaster resulted in the hospitalization of two teachers, several students and the arrest of that first-year teacher. The old Science Wing was abandoned and eventually turned over to the Art Department.

I am talking about complaints now emanating from unknown people in the New Art Wing eight years after the contamination was corrected! Disgruntled individuals, in an effort perhaps to interfere with my job as Interim Acting Principal, have reported "mysterious mold and mildew seepage stains" in several of the state-of-the-art Art classrooms. Although the dangers are no doubt grossly exaggerated and the health risk claims unsubstantiated, these complaints have once again brought unwanted attention to a problem that was resolved long ago.

As Interim Acting Principal, it is my duty to investigate the bogus claims and allay your fears. On my recent tour of the Art Wing earlier this week I made a thorough study of the classrooms in question. You likely didn't recognize me in my HAZMAT suit. After a thorough inspection I have come to the conclusion that the building, and particularly the Art Wing, is mold-free, nontoxic, perfectly safe and totally fit for most human habitation. As a further measure to placate all those "fraidy cats in artist smocks" who persist in "painting a worst-case scenario," I have come up with the following plan to be enacted immediately.

1. Anyone passing through the Art Wing should exhale only.

2. Art teachers and students required to spend more than 10 minutes at a time in the questionable Art area are directed to engage in the Shallow Breathing Technique (SBT) for the duration of time they are in the wing. For those who do not know how to perform SBT, a workshop will be conducted next week after school in one of the Art rooms. Date and time to be announced.

3. A decontamination center similar to the one that was used at the time of "The Science Disaster of 1964" will be reactivated and available to all the "nervous Nellies" who can't wait to go home to take a shower and decontaminate themselves.

4. An oxygen-rich environment, or "safe room," will be constructed within a brisk walking distance of the Art Wing for the exclusive use of Art teachers

between classes who *can't* or *won't* hold their breath for long periods of time.

5. Administrators have been directed to keep the "safe room" clear of non-Art teachers trying to use the room for recreational purposes.

6. Administrators will no longer patrol or do teacher observations in the Art Wing.

7. To avoid undue panic and concern, Art teachers will inform their students that the colorful stains and marks on the walls and ceilings in the Art rooms are ART and that they are perfectly safe and pose no health threat to them.

In the News
June 1972

June 17

Five burglars are arrested at 2:30 a.m. while breaking into the Democratic National Committee (DNC) Headquarters offices in Washington's Watergate Hotel where the DNC occupies the entire sixth floor. Frank Wills, the security guard, discovers the taped doors and alerts the DC police. At gunpoint three plainclothes officers seize James McCord, Frank Sturgis, and three Cubans. The five suspects, all wearing surgical gloves, have among them two sophisticated voice-activated surveillance devices that can monitor conversations and telephone calls alike; lock-picks, door jimmies, and an assortment of burglary tools; and $2,300 in cash, most of it in $100 bills in sequence. They also have a walkie-talkie, a shortwave receiver tuned to the police band, 40 rolls of unexposed film, two 35mm cameras, and three pen-sized teargas guns. Near to where the men are captured is a file cabinet with two open drawers. A DNC source speculates that the men might have been preparing to photograph the contents of the file drawers..

June 18

Washington Post reporter Bob Woodward learns that two of the Watergate burglars have the name E. Howard Hunt in their address books, both with notations that indicate Hunt has a post at the White House.

June 19

James McCord, one of the five Watergate burglars, is identified as the security director for the Committee to Re-elect the President (CREEP). McCord is also identified as a security consultant for the Republican National Committee (RNC), where he has maintained an office since January 1.

June 20

Pres. Nixon tells a gathering of reporters regarding the Watergate burglary, "The White House has no involvement in this particular incident."

June 21

Pres. Nixon tells his chief of staff H. R. Haldeman that the Watergate burglars "are going to need money."

June 22

Watergate burglar G. Gordon Liddy tells White House aides Frederick LaRue and Robert Mardian that he and his fellow burglars need money for bail, legal expenses and family support.

June 23

Pres. Nixon orders Chief of Staff H. R. Haldeman to tell the FBI not to go any further with its Watergate investigation. He justifies his actions on national security grounds.

Pres. Nixon signs the federal Title IX Education Amendment for nondiscrimination and affirmative action to insure equal rights for women's sports programs.

June 25

Alfred Baldwin, former FBI agent now working for CREEP, agrees to cooperate with the government's investigation of the Watergate burglary in order to avoid jail time.

June 26

White House counsel John Dean meets with Vernon Walters, the deputy director of the CIA, to ask if the agency can provide "financial assistance" to the five Watergate burglars.

June 28

Pres. Nixon announces that no new draftees will be sent to Vietnam as South Vietnamese troops begin a counteroffensive to retake Quang Tri Province, aided by U.S. Navy gunfire and B-52 bombardments.

Rosencrantz and Guildenstern
Memorial High School
UFSD 71
Farmington, New York

TO: All Teachers and Staff
FROM: Mario Giovanni, Acting Interim Principal
SUBJECT: Clarification Memo Re: Mold, Mildew and
                   Doo-doo, Oh, My!

June 1, 1972

The memo circulated yesterday, "Mold, Mildew and Doo-doo, Oh, My!" about the toxic mold and mildew problem in the Art Wing was not real and was not issued by me. So please disregard it. The bogus memo inaccurately referenced an event that took place in 1964 and offered a comprehensive strategy to prevent it from happening again. None of that was true.

To set the record straight, I did not make my rounds of the Art Wing or any other areas of the school in a HAZMAT suit and I do not have any comprehensive strategy for dealing with the mold and mildew problem. In fact, there is NO mold and mildew problem in the Art Wing... or, for that matter, in any other area of the school.

Joseph E. Scalia

Rosencrantz and Guildenstern
Memorial High School
AV/CM Department

To: All Teachers
From: Harry Dexter, Coordinator AV/CM Department
Subject: September Equipment Requisitions for the
              1972-73 School Year

June 1972

If you plan to use any AV/CM equipment in the 1972-73 school year, requisition forms must be completed and submitted to AV/CM by the end of test week. Since the office is closed for equipment inventory, maintenance and repair for the rest of the year, requisition forms may be picked up in a box in the Main Office as soon as they become available. All completed forms must include the equipment requested, the number of days and the specific dates it will be used. Forms must be returned to another box in the Main Office, NOT the AV/CM office.

Incomplete forms or those left in the wrong box will mean long delays, at best, in the delivery of the requested equipment next year. Your failure to plan ahead does not constitute an emergency for AV.

Happy summer from all of us in the AV/CM Department. We look forward to seeing you in the new school year in September.

UFSD 71

Camelot

Official Publication of the Partnership of Parents and Teachers in Association for better Farmington Public Schools

Harriet Stegle, President P-PTA

Vol. 10 Issue 10   June 1972

Well, it's June too soon and not soon enough! The school year is speeding to an end–and an interesting year it has been! We started another September on austerity, something that has become second nature, and everyone learned how to do without – without extracurricular activities, transportation, new books, ditto masters, ditto paper and toilet paper! The teachers worked another whole year without a contract and that turned out to be not so bad and they all survived. Well, except for the few we lost along the way. Some are dead, some have fled, but at least this year no one was arrested! There were some weddings and divorces, and at least one more wedding is planned... and maybe a baby on the way as well.

AROUND THE DISTRICT:

The Founder's Day Ceremonies were a great success. Helen O'Dell was this year's honoree. Helen received the customary plaque and a $100 gift certificate for Chez Antoine's. Too bad she won't be able to use it. And while I'm at it I'd like to say a special thank-you to Gus Stopoulis, owner of Chez Antoine's, for giving my son Seth an opportunity to work in his immaculate kitchen. Today Seth may be washing dishes, but tomorrow he dreams of being head chef! For those of you who aren't familiar with Chez Antoine's, the restaurant offers a large assortment of Greek and American cuisine. "Fine dining at moderate prices" is their motto, so be sure to make Chez Antoine's part of your summer dining plans. But Gus told me reservations are a must on the weekends.

The weather was just perfect for the Founder's Day Parade that featured its traditional open car ride through town. It was great seeing R&G's principal, Seymour Baltz, smiling between Supt.

Flackett and Board President Elliot "Lalo" Adornau. I bet the conversation in the backseat of that car was something to hear.

And speaking of Principal Baltz, May 19 was his last day of work. But it's not because he's "a rat deserting a sinking ship," as I heard around the building. Citing ill health, he asked for and got an extended leave through the end of the year. Get well soon, Seymour. I hope it's nothing *too* serious and that whatever has taken you from us will allow you to come back cured and well rested in September.

CONGRATULATIONS:

Best wishes to R&G's assistant principal, Mario Giovanni, who has been asked to fill the empty seat, and dare I say the empty suit, left behind by Mr. Baltz. If some of the rumors are true, Mr. Giovanni, who has ably taken the reins as Interim Acting Principal, just might be able to remove "Interim" from his title and someday act like a REAL high school principal.

Congratulations once more to the High School's typing teacher Phaedra Schwartz on two special occasions. Phay's hoping she's timed it right and will be able to tie the knot before her new husband-to-be Maurice cuts the umbilical cord. It will be her second trip down the aisle in less than a year! And yes, Phay's pregnant, and a little birdie stork told me she just might be carrying twins!

ON THE LIGHTER SIDE:

You may remember the brouhaha last year when Lois Weller at Old Dutch Mill Elementary School had some difficulty with the parents of her second-graders because of comments she made on their final report cards last June. In September, after all the dust and the threatened lawsuits settled, Lois was transferred to West Street Elementary, where she has taught Kindergarten without incident, at least so far. But final progress reports will be going home soon and Lois said she doesn't anticipate any problems this year because she has developed

"Teacher Speak," a way to say it without getting transferred to another school and a different grade next year.

WHAT I SAID LAST YEAR: "Your kid is a liar and can't be trusted when he tells you his name." TEACHER SPEAK: "Your daughter has a great imagination and the ability to integrate her imaginary concepts with factual material."

WHAT I SAID LAST YEAR: "He is a cheater, a sneak and he will probably end up in prison for stealing or worse." TEACHER SPEAK: "He's a free-thinker who adopts the rules and the standards of fair play and adapts them to his own advantage, a trait that will be useful when he interacts with others just like him in the institutions where he will likely find himself."

WHAT I SAID LAST YEAR: "Your son literally stinks and no one wants to sit next to him. Those who did sit next to him spent more time in the Health Office than in class. He needs a bath... maybe with bleach." TEACHER SPEAK: "He's a self-starter who works independently on a wide range of projects. He makes himself known to all of those around him and he can't be ignored. He lends a certain 'air' to the classroom and assists me in reviewing good health habits for personal hygiene every day with the class."

WHAT I SAID LAST YEAR: "Your daughter is a bully who picks on anybody smaller and weaker than she is. She has tortured to death a number of classroom pets and she is well on the path to becoming a serial killer." TEACHER SPEAK: "She definitely demonstrates the qualities of leadership. She shows specific interest in smaller and weaker members of the class. She is always the first to volunteer to feed, water and care for the gerbils and rabbits that we used to have in the classroom. I see lots of sick and dying animals in her future."

NEWS AND VIEWS:

The 1971-72 school year is almost in the history books. But as I see it, beyond our little school microcosm, there are so many wonderful things we all have to look forward to on the horizon. The 1972 Summer Olympics or the Games of the XX Olympiad, as they are officially known, will be held in

Munich, Germany, beginning on August 26 and run through September 11. The last time the Olympic Games were held in Germany was in 1936, and we all know what happened shortly after that. But this time it will be different. And what could be better than watching the world's greatest athletes competing for gold? I know my eyes will be glued to the TV to witness every minute. Like the rest of the world, I don't want to miss a single second of what will take place in Munich!

While there may be many other changes in the air, Americans can look forward to stability. The war is winding down. President Richard M. Nixon has opened China to the West. He has met with the Russians to reduce world tensions and make the world a safer, better place. And for all that our law and order president and his no-nonsense vice president, Spiro T. Agnew, have done for us, it looks like they are well on their way to a second term. All Americans can anticipate four more years of stability and bigger and better things for the world. But that isn't until November... and subject matter of a new *Camelot* in the upcoming new school year!

So, in the words of an American icon, Porky Pig, "That's all folks" for now! Wishing all of you a happy, healthy summer! See you next time with more news from the trenches!

He centered the nameplate on his desk. He asked Murray Fink have his boys make it in Wood Shop. Because it was a rush job it was not all he had hoped for and he had to settle for "Mario Giovanni, Principle." But at least they spelled his name right. He looked at the desk calendar.

There were only two weeks to go. Well, technically there were three weeks until graduation, but test week didn't really count. The week after finals and Regents exams and all that other crap was clean-up week and all classes would be over. Though official school policy was that students were expected to come to class, they didn't. A memo home told parents attendance would be taken, but it wasn't, and everybody knew it. Teachers couldn't actually tell their students to stay home, but most of them got the subliminal message. "All test papers will be graded and the final marks entered before the last official day of class, so... there wouldn't be anything for us to do–" Nudge nudge, wink wink. Those last days the school was virtually empty. The only kids in the building the week after finals were those who wanted to get their grades or to get their yearbooks signed. Ironically, the kids who cut classes all year always came in to hang around because they had no other place to go.

The week before finals was "Senior Prank Week," a recent school phenomenon that began years before with "Senior Cut Day" and grew in the following years into a weeklong event at R&G. To the acting interim principal it meant all he had to do was get through one week, next week, Senior Prank Week, without fucking it up.

He looked around his office for something to do. A line from some Shakespeare play, maybe *Julius Caesar,* he must have observed in an English class came to mind. "So," he said out loud, "what is now amiss that Giovanni and his staff must redress?" He wasn't exactly sure what it meant, but he remembered that the line came just before the only real action in the stupid play, a knife fight with Julius Caesar ending up on the wrong end of the knives. Thank God he didn't have to do any more observations this year, and maybe never if he got the permanent principal job. He paced around the office, peeked through the window into the courtyard and ambled over to the door.

"Miss Lind–"

"Ms." She sighed and didn't look up. She was whiting out a typo.

"–I was just looking out my window at the courtyard and I noticed that not all of the window shades in the classrooms are even. They're all at different heights."

"And I should be concerned with this because?"

"Because it looks terrible, Phyl–"

"Ms Lind," she said curtly.

"So I want you to stop whatever it is you're doing–" He backtracked. "I mean, when you've finished whatever it is you're doing, would you please get out a memo re 'Shade Height'? I'll approve it before you put it into all the mailboxes by the end of the day." He went to the window and readjusted the shade behind her desk to a height he liked, midway up from the bottom of the window. "Measure that and instruct all teachers to have their room shades in all their windows at this height."

"Will there be anything else? How about having them turn off alternating overhead lights to save electricity."

"Good idea." He missed her sarcasm. "Put that in the memo too."

"What are you doing, Mario? Why don't you just leave well enough alone and let people just do their jobs?"

He sighed, momentarily becoming his old self. "I don't know how long I'll be principal, Phyl. But while I am, I want to do something memorable. I want to leave my mark and be remembered. Will I see you this weekend?"

She patted his hand. "If I finish all that extra work you gave me."

He continued through the Main Office to his Suggestion Box in the Administrative Alcove. After she dumped it the day of the "fire drill," he asked Phyllis where he should put it. She gave him several suggestions and the alcove outside his office was the one he chose. Noah's door and Willy Zwill's were both closed. Rita Reed's was open, but her office was empty, except for the photo of Helen O'Dell still perched in the chair. He picked up the Suggestion Box, another woodworking project for Murray Fink's boys. It was a week since he checked it. It was heavy and he was delighted.

"I'll be busy for the next hour or so, so hold all my calls."

"There are no calls. And for the record, Mario, your *calls* may be the only things I'll be holding." She went back to typing his shades memo.

After a pee–how he loved having his own toilet–he went back to his desk and shook the Suggestion Box. His plan was to separate the contents into three piles–positive, negative and neutral. That would make more manageable what he judged to be by the weight the substantial contents. He picked up the remains of the De Nobili left in his ashtray and lit it. He fished into his vest pocket for the small key, opened the miniature padlock and spilled the contents of the Suggestion Box onto his desk. A math textbook, a paperback with the cover torn off, a wad of chewed pink bubble gum, three rubber desk feet and several sheets of folded paper of different sizes and colors. The books and the gum he dumped into the wastebasket, the desk feet went into his pocket. He pushed the papers together like a deck of cards and sorted through them. Most weren't even suggestions. Four were "missing feet" memo returns, three AV requisition forms for September, two cut slips and a partially torn detention referral form. He put them in a fourth pile. The next folded slip was actually a suggestion. "I suggest Acting Principal Giovanni STOP ACTING!" He recognized Phyllis's handwriting. He read the others–a demand that the stall doors be returned, old news, a shorter workday, larger portions in the teacher's cafeteria from John Hiller on a scrap of brown paper bag, better quality plastic utensils in the teacher's cafeteria, toilet paper of any quality in the faculty toilets, an end to the war in Vietnam. Three said "Fuck you," and there was one "Disregard previous suggestion!" He slowed down when he read, "I killed Helen

O'Dell." But it was the last one that he unfolded that stopped him cold. "i know what you did!"

"Shit."

* * *

Red Farley was out of breath when he came into the Third Floor Faculty Room. His face was flushed and he was sweating.

"Geez, Red," Terry called from the vending machine where he was waiting for his coffee cup to fill, "you'd better cut back on those french fries."

"Up yours, Scapelli. And in your face." He did a little dance and waved an envelope at him.

"What's that, Red? Proctoring schedule for the finals?"

"My ticket out of this place, Stan. My golden egg. I just won the lottery!"

Everyone looked up, suddenly interested.

"The lottery! How much?"

"Well, not the *real* lottery, but even better." He held up an envelope.

Terry stirred his coffee and drifted over nonchalantly for a closer look. "Did the new King Kullen weekly circular arrive already?"

Red ignored the quip. He opened the envelope, pulled out the letter and held it up for everyone. "I just got it in my mailbox downstairs. U.S. Mail, first-class postage, typed on premium stationery with a watermark." He unfolded the letter and read, "'Mr. Frederick R. Farley, Rosencrantz and Guildenstern Memorial High School. Dear Mr. Farley, The S. C. Rude Foundation of New York is a philanthropic organization that seeks out and rewards excellence in education wherever it exists. It is my pleasure to inform you that you have been selected from the thousands of educators considered by the Foundation as one of this year's recipients of the S. C. Rude Foundation Grant for Innovation and Achievements in Secondary School Mathematics.' Blah blah blah. It goes on with details about the selection process, but here's the best part. 'Enclosed is a check from the S. C. Rude Foundation made out to you in the amount of,'" he paused for effect, "'one million dollars tax-free!'" He held up the check. "Now what do you have to say, smartass?" He smirked at Terry, who was trying to read the check.

The room buzzed. "Whoa! A million bucks. You lucky bastard!"

"Let me see," Terry said.

"In your dreams, Scapelli. It's a real check. It's made out to me and it's signed." He held it out of reach. "But you can see the letter."

Terry took it. "It looks authentic," he said. "It feels authentic. Nice quality paper. Expensive with cotton fibers and a watermark." He read further. "But wait, Red, there's more. Did you see the last paragraph?" Terry read, "'There are two conditions related to your S. C. Rude Grant. First, the Foundation wishes to continue its good work anonymously, therefore under no circumstances are you to reveal the source of your good fortune. Second, you must never disclose the exact amount of the grant. Your failure to abide by either of these terms will necessitate your returning any unspent portion of the grant money to the Foundation. Good luck. S. C. Rude, President.'" He handed the letter back to Red. "Looks like you can kiss that million good-bye, Red."

"And you can kiss my ass, Scapelli. Because I'm holding the million-dollar check and you're holding squat. I'm out of here in two weeks, never to return. And you still have how many years to go?"

"But you just violated both conditions, Red," Stanley Milnow said. "You told everybody. You read us the letter. You showed us the check. One million dollars tax-free from the S. C. Rude Foundation."

"That's right," Terry said. "It looks like you just s-c-rewed yourself, Red!"

Everyone laughed and applauded.

"You did this, Scapelli! I know you did this. This whole thing has your stink on it! This joke isn't funny."

Stanley Milnow shook his head. "It's pretty funny, Scapelli." He turned to Red, who was rereading the letter. "So much for excellence in education."

* * *

It was 11:45 and he was still intensely focused on the note. He had run through in his mind anyone who might possibly have seen him and exactly what they might have seen. The building was always pretty empty whenever he was there early and stayed late. Except maybe for Eddie the tattooed night custodian, who occasionally appeared out of the shadows at unexpected times. But what could he have seen? And when?

The ringing phone on his desk made him jump. "Principal Giovanni," he said in a practiced tone.

"*Interim acting* principal," the distant voice at the other end said curtly.

"Who is this?"

"Have you forgotten so quickly? The *real* principal, Mario."

Involuntarily he sat up straight, slid the note he was holding into the desk drawer and closed it. "I was just thinking about you. I didn't recognize your voice. You sound so far away."

"That's because I am far away. I'm in fucking Israel in a hundred degrees surrounded by Arabs and by Jews holding machine guns. I might as well be in Miami. What's going on in my school, Mario?"

"Everything is fine, Boss. The weather is warm and sunny and–"

"I didn't call for a weather report. Is the building still standing? Have you done anything?"

"Of course not. How was your flight?" he asked casually. "You didn't have any problems, I hope."

"Funny you should ask. It was terrible. Somebody called in a bomb scare and we were delayed for three hours until they went through the entire plane and unloaded the luggage. They didn't find anything, but the whole time we were in the air I jumped whenever I heard a noise. And when

624

we boarded the ship in Naples there was another bomb scare. It kept us in port whole day. What are the chances of that happening?"

"Two bomb scares? Probably just a prank. You know how kids are always calling in bomb scares here."

"To tell the truth, Mario, I half expected there would be another bomb threat when we got here at the hotel."

"You didn't mention a hotel. Where are you staying, there in Israel?"

"The Tel Aviv Hilton. Israeli Security was on full alert, especially when they learned about the threats on the plane and the cruise ship. They take stuff like that very seriously. Interpol is all over the hotel and FBI agents from New York. These Jews don't fool around. They're looking into possible connections to the attack here a few days ago at the LOD Airport. They're still cleaning up the mess. Terrorists killed twenty-six people, Mario!"

"Interpol and the FBI?"

"I've been a wreck since we arrived. Security is everywhere. I haven't slept much at night and when I do I have terrible dreams. A recurring nightmare where everything is coming apart and falling down on top of my head, burying me alive. I'm in quicksand, I can't breathe... I'm drowning in... in a pile of... shit, Mario. When I wake up in a sweat." He paused. "Speaking of shit, have there been any more incidents?"

"Um, no, Boss." He was thinking about the FBI.

"My nightmares are filled with bombs... all around the school... in my desk!"

"It's probably because you're out of sync or from something you ate. How is the food?" He opened the desk drawer and saw the note. "i know what you did!"

"It's Jewish cuisine, Mario. How good could it be?"

"You just relax and enjoy. I'm in charge here and things couldn't be running any smoother. Finals start in a week. Like you said, Phyllis took care of everything. The test room assignments and proctoring schedules are done. They'll go out next Friday by the end of the day at the last minute, just like you always do, to keep the teacher complaints down. You have nothing to worry about."

"Hearing you say that worries me, Mario." He covered the receiver. His wife was talking in the background.

"Are you satisfied now? The world didn't end. Maybe now we can finally go out and see stuff and do a little shopping?"

"Okay, Mario. Just remember–"

"I know, Boss, don't fuck it up. And don't touch my stuff."

The phone clicked.

"Shit," he said staring at the receiver. "The FBI." When the phone rang again he snatched it up immediately.

"Mario, it's Harry Dexter in AV. I'm in the middle of the year-end inventory and I'm looking for some of my equipment."

"I don't have any AV equipment."

"Take a good look around, Mario. In February, Baltz checked out a bunch of equipment that hasn't been returned." He read from the invoice. "On February twenty-fifth, Polakas and Slow Charley picked up an Ampex-7000 one-inch reel-to-reel video recorder, an Ampex CC-452 black-and-white studio camera on a wheeled tripod, a remote control unit, one TV monitor, one reel of Ampex one-inch blank black-and-white videotape and two AV carts. I want them back."

"Well, it isn't here. Call Polakas and ask him where it is."

"I did. He said something about a job he did for Baltz. Project X? He told me to take it up with Baltz. He's on leave. So it falls on you. Do you know anything about Project X?"

"I know nothing. I see nothing. I can't help you. You'll just have to wait for your uncle to come back... if he comes back."

"Have you heard anything? Did he say he's not coming back?"

"Listen, Harry, I'm a very busy man. I have some principal stuff to do. I don't know anything about your equipment. You'll have to look somewhere else." He hung up the phone. Project X? He vaguely remembered talk about it, but nothing specific.

He reread the note before he tore it into small pieces. Then he went back for that closer look at the contents of Baltz's drawers. When he finished he wanted to talk to Polakas in the Custodial Annex to get some information about Eddie the night custodian.

Rosencrantz and Guildenstern
Memorial High School
AV/CM Department

To: All Teachers
From: Harry Dexter, Coordinator AV/CM Department
Subject: Missing AV/CM Equipment
June 5, 1972

The AV/CM Department is urgently trying to locate the following missing equipment for inventory:

3 10-foot three-prong grounded yellow extension cords

1 filmstrip "China the Communist Menace"

1 filmstrip projector, Decal # HD4070

2 boxes of clear transparencies for use with overhead projectors

1 overhead film projector, Decal # HD677P

1 Ampex 7000 one-inch reel-to-reel black-and-white video recorder, Decal # HD001AMP

1 Ampex CC-452 black-and-white studio camera, Decal # HD101AMP

1 wheeled camera tripod, Decal # HD347T

1 remote control unit for Ampex 7000 one-inch reel-to-reel video recorder, Decal # HD667R

1 21" TV monitor, Decal # HD007

1 reel of Ampex one-inch blank black-and-white videotape, Decal # HD8APM1

2 AV carts, Decal # HD707 and Decal # HD815

Check your classrooms, closets and storage areas. Return any items that may be in your possession to the AV/CM Center immediately. A thorough inspection of each classroom will be conducted over the summer and there will be severe consequences for any teacher found to be hoarding AV/CM equipment.

If these items, or any others not on the above list, are not recovered, sign-out procedures, distribution of summer checks and final dismissal on the last day will be delayed.

He stepped into the Main Office. "How's it going so far, Phyl? No emergencies? False alarms? Bomb scares?"

"The Second Precinct called to say they canceled all days off in anticipation of Senior Prank Week and they are massing equipment and police in riot gear on the border," she said sarcastically. "Just now a SWAT team in a show of force conducted a preemptive strike and rounded up the usual suspects and carted them off in a rented Hertz panel truck so they wouldn't attract attention." She checked her nail polish for chips. The in-house phone on her desk rang and she picked it up. "Yes, Mr. Farley, how can I help you?"

"I'm calling from the faculty room. There's nobody in my classroom!They *were* there at the beginning of the period. But I had to pee and when I came back they were all gone. The lights were off, the shades drawn, the door is locked and I can't get back inside. They all disappeared without a trace! I'm confused. Is there an assembly or something I don't know about? Did you move them to a different room?"

"I'll check the schedule." She ran her finger down the schedule master list. "No assembly. No changes. Second period, room 230. I'll ask, Mr. Giovanni."

"What's Red's problem, Phyl?"

She covered the receiver. "He says he lost his class. You know anything?" He shrugged and she spoke into the mouthpiece. "They should be there, Mr. Farley. Are you sure they aren't hiding? This is Senior Prank Week. Go back and have another look. Or maybe you went to the wrong room. Did you try the classroom next door. Call if you find them." She hung up the phone.

"I'm headed to see Polakas, Phyl. I'll be back after I finish my rounds. The pizza deliveries probably won't start until lunch. Let me know when they do. And save me a slice if I'm not back. I'm in the mood for a little Sicilian. How about you? You haven't had a little Sicilian in awhile." He winked.

* * *

Except for assorted broken stuff and a pile of student desks with missing feet, the front of the Custodian's Office was empty. "Anybody watching the store?" he called. There was no answer. He went through the beaded curtain into the dimly lit work area. Eddie the tattooed night custodian was sleeping on a cot in the corner.

"Whadda ya hear? Whadda ya say?" he asked sounding like James Cagney in *Public Enemy*. "And whadda ya *know*, Eddie?" he added. "How's it going? Anything interesting that I should know about?" He stretched his neck and postured. He didn't like Eddie. He didn't trust anybody who worked nights. He watched the night custodian's face to see if there was some reaction.

"It's going."

"I'm looking for Stash. You seen him?" He paused and added, "You seen *anything*, know *anything*, hear *anything* interesting?"

"Yeah, I seen some things. A lot a things. And I heard some too. How about you? You got a promotion. How's the new principal thing going for you?"

"It's going. While I'm here, Harry Dexter is looking for some AV equipment Baltz requisitioned back in February. You seen it or happen to know where it might have ended up?"

"I'm just the night man. I sweep the floors. Talk to Stash or Slow Charley. Stash is out sick today in Atlantic City, but Charley's in the back. Be careful, it's pretty dark. You might bump into something or trip and fall. You don't wanna get hurt, and your whole life blow up... Boom!" He snapped his fingers.

"What's that supposed to mean?"

He shrugged. "You could be gone... just like Baltz."

He went into the back area. "Hey, Charley," he called, "do you remember what you did with that AV equipment you and Stash picked up in February for Mr. Baltz?"

Charley was at the workbench eating a hero sandwich and tuning a staticky AM radio station. He shook his head. "Ask Stash when he comes back. He remembers everything."

"A TV set... a video camera... a recorder?"

"No, no," He shook his head. "Oh, yeah... yeah. I remember. We put it in the Utility Closet up on the third floor."

"Why'd you do that? Are you sure?"

He nodded. "It's in the office we made for Mr. Baltz before Christmas. Stash knows."

"Thanks, Charley. That will make Mr. Dexter happy. I'll check it out."

Eddie was back on the cot smoking a cigarette. "Be careful, Eddie. You don't want to get burned and go up in flames." He cracked his neck and grinned.

"You too, and watch your step. You never know what you might bump into or step in around this place." He grinned back.

*　*　*

He cut back through the Klaus Brinker, Jr. Temporary Wing and made his way past the Boys Gym heading toward the elevator and the third floor.

"Hey, Mr. G," Virgil called, coming out of the gym. "Or should I say, 'Hey, *Principal* G'? Sorry I haven't seen much of you recently, but I've been pretty busy with all the end of the year stuff, graduation… athletics…. yearbook pictures."

"And I don't have time for you now, Loomis."

"I can imagine, with your new principal duties, all those fire drills and stuff. New suit? Nice shoes. You look good."

"Why aren't you in class?"

"I had to pick up another Varsity letter from Coach Boid's office and now I have to decide where to put it. Here"– he pointed to a place on his sweater opposite the wrestling and track letters–"or here?" He indicated the other side. "What do you think?"

Buddy Ritchie's voice boomed out from the gym and into the corridor. "COME ON, YOU MARYS. THE SCHOOL YEAR ISN'T OVER YET. JUMPING JACKS. ONE TWO, ONE TWO. TOGETHER. LET'S GO, LADIES!"

"I know how Mr. Ritchie feels about you and all this letter stuff, but what did Coach Boid say?"

"Oh, he's very encouraging, actually. He wished me good luck and asked where I was going to college on a sports scholarship. I said I didn't get a sports scholarship and he was amazed. He said an athlete as good as me should have my pick of schools and that he had connections and would see what he could do. He was full of inspirational advice. I wrote some of it down." He opened a notepad. "'If you run… run fast. If you jump… jump high, unless you do the long jump, then jump long. And if you hurdle, run fast and then jump… run fast again and jump again… continuously!'"

"You're no athlete, Virgil. You're just taking advantage of an opportunity to exploit the System."

Virgil shrugged. "You're technically correct, Mr. G. But now I'm a four-letter man, and who can argue with that?" He thought for a second. "Do you know many people who really are what they say they are?"

"COME ON, LADIES… PUSH-UPS… ONE, TWO…"

He nodded his head and sighed. "I understand what you mean, Virgil."

"Well, good luck, Principal G. I'll see you at graduation. It's going to be exciting. Coach Boid said something about me getting some kind of athletic award." He turned and headed down the corridor.

Mr. Giovanni took the elevator up to the third floor and went directly to the (F)Utility Closet. It was locked and even though he knew none of his keys would fit, he tried each of them anyway, turning them carefully in the lock. Maybe Charley had the right key. And he wanted another go at Eddie the night custodian. The bastard thought he was a lot smarter than he really was. He opened the elevator door and stepped inside into the darkness. His foot slipped on something strange in the middle of the car. "Shit!" he yelled.

* * *

"Hello, dear secretaries, the force that keeps this building operating. Have the pizzas arrived yet? I asked my seniors to get one that was half anchovies when they order them." He sniffed. "Do I smell anchovies?"

"No pizzas yet, Mr. Scapelli," Phyllis said from her desk, "but the first lunch period starts in half an hour, so I imagine the pizzas are on the way. And that smell is definitely *not* anchovies. What *is* that smell?"

Mr. Giovanni burst into the Main Office hopping and dragging his foot behind him. "Jesus Christ!" he yelled. "Jesus H. Christ!"

"Are you hurt?"

"Jesus Christ! Quick. Hand me something, Phyl! Tissues! Something!"

"Are you bleeding, Mario?" She handed him the open box of tissues from her drawer. "What happened to you?"

He grabbed the box. "My shoes. My poor shoes. My brand new Florsheim wing-tipped featherweights!" He wiped the shoe with the tissues and took another handful. "Right inside the elevator." He wiped again and tossed the waded tissues into her pail.

"Don't leave them there," she protested.

"There are some very sick individuals in this building. Leather twenty-eight dollar shoes! Another pair of shoes ruined."

"I thought you were stabbed or shot or dying. It's only shoes."

He looked at her wounded. "Only shoes? This is the second pair, Phyl. Now it's personal. I want you to–"

"Put out another memo?"

"Call the custodian. Polakas is out, but have Slow Charley clean up that mess in the elevator and then come and empty the pail. And get Martha down there too." He stormed into his office.

Terry pulled his mail from his box. "Don't forget the anchovies, Phyl."

Mrs. Butrum strolled into the Main Office. "Oh, Lord," she held her nose. "Anchovies? Is that what smells so awful? Oh, Lord. No wonder people say hold the anchovies!" She fanned the air with her papers.

* * *

Fifteen minutes before the first lunch period a station wagon from Gino's Pizzeria pulled into the courtyard to the cheers of students and teachers leaning out of their classroom windows. The driver and his assistant struggled to carry a dozen stacked pizza boxes into the Main Office. Ten minutes after they were gone another van pulled in and a second dozen pizzas from Delmonico's across town arrived.

"Pizzas have arrived, Mario," Phyllis said over the intercom. "I took money out of petty cash. With delivery and tips it came to sixty-seven dollars, less than last year. But there still may be more on the way. I saved you two slices of Sicilian, one from each pizzeria."

"Thanks, Phyl," he said. "I'm sorry for that outburst before. I'll be out when I am done in here."

He went back to reading the book that he found in the bottom drawer, leafing through entries for references to Project X. "January 3, 1972: The tide has changed... It is regrettable that half a school year has been wasted... Giovanni... ineffective... he thinks with his little head... more interested in *schtupping* Phyllis... Giovanni... complaining ingrate. If it weren't for me he'd be picking up garbage with the rest of the *goombas*...." He skimmed on. to February 25, the date Dexter said was on the requisition slips. "The stall doors are back in place and I have to run in and out of the Observatory, it is exhausting... with great risk of being detected by someone. Despite all efforts the writing has increased... in colors and different handwriting... and now a rubber stamp..." He smiled when he read that. "Most of the offenses take place when I am not in the Observatory... the culprits are aware of my schedule. I will see Dexter about getting electronic surveillance equipment I'll callProject X." He jumped to May 5th. "Giovanni folded under pressure like a cheap suit and removed the stall doors under protest... He's not much of an administrator... but he knows his way around a screwdriver and he is ambitious. Mini Mussolini would step over my body to get my job. I saw his calculating little *dago* mind when I mentioned leaving before the end of the school year... Stash installed the camera and video recorder and they are working better than I anticipated."

"Camera? Video recorder? Observatory?" He had lots of questions... and he was angry. "Maybe the bastard needs just one more bomb scare at the Tel Aviv Hilton." He closed the book and a key fell out onto the rug. "Observatory" was printed on the tag.

* * *

The police response time grew longer and longer with each call. The Dispatch Code 3, reporting of a person or persons with a gun, had six Nassau County cars rolling into the courtyard in minutes with their blasting sirens amplified in the enclosed space and their lights bouncing around the walls. It turned out to be a water pistol fight on the front lawn that spread into the building. Answering the two bomb threats took longer, the first without sirens, the second without lights. and the third with a phone call to the school saying they weren't coming.

"Good afternoon. Rosencrantz and Guildenstern Memorial High School. Ms Lind speaking," she said mechanically. when the phone on her desk rang again.

"This is another bomb scare," the voice said. "Evacuate the building immediately."

"Mrs. Carton? You know there are no bombs in the building. You just want the boys and girls to march out again so you can see them from your window. When the police came to your house they told you that you can't do that, Mrs. Carton. It's against the law. They warned you if you did it again, they were going to arrest you, And they gave me very specific instructions to call the precinct if you did it again. The police are very busy, Mrs. Carton. They won't like it if they have to respond to another false alarm. I really don't want them to arrest you."

"But it's a beautiful day," Mrs. Carton said, "and the children all look so nice when they come outside.... And I'm so lonely."

"I know you are, Mrs. Carton," she said sympathetically. "If you give me your word that you won't call in any more bomb scares, I promise that I'll stop over and visit you this afternoon on my way home after school. We can have tea and chat." She paused. "Do you promise?"

"I promise," she said.

"Okay. Now you get yourself ready and then take a little nap. I'll see you in a few hours. And remember, no more phone calls." She replaced the receiver and she didn't notify the precinct.

* * *

Jesse surprised the girl standing on the landing of the back staircase, but he was more surprised when he recognized her. "Victoria? Is that you? I haven't seen much of you recently. Have you been out sick? You weren't in class this morning and we're reviewing for the final next week." She didn't answer and she avoided making eye contact. "You haven't been cutting?" He meant it as a joke, but her eyes welled with tears. "Are you okay?"

"I'm sorry, Mr Tietjen." A drop rolled down her face and exploded into a Rorschach design on the floor.

He stepped toward her, thought better and stepped back. "Maybe if you tell me what's wrong I can help." She lowered her head and leaned against him. Jesse's body stiffened. He didn't know what to do. Put his arm around her and comfort her? Could he? Was he allowed ? He hesitated and he pulled back.

"Everything is wrong. My mother's in the hospital. She's very sick–" She sobbed.

He handed her his handkerchief. "Use this. It's clean."

She wiped her eyes and blew her nose. "Sorry," she said. "I know I missed classes, but I wasn't cutting. I've been taking care of my little brother and sister so my father can be with my mom."

"I'm so sorry." He didn't know what else to say.

"I'll probably miss all my exams next week when my father takes my mother to the Cancer Hospital in Philadelphia–" It all came out in a rush. "That's going to lower my grade point average and mean I won't be able to apply to the colleges I want... if I'll even go to college... I sound so selfish. But I don't know what we're going to do, Mr. Tietjen... if my mother dies."

He put his arm around her and he felt her trembling. "You have more important things to worry about than finals. I can't speak for your other teachers, but I'll figure your final grade on what you did all year in my class. Did you tell Guidance what's going on? Who is your guidance counselor?"

"Mr. Hiller, but he's never in his office."

"I know where to find him. I'll fill him in and tell him you want an appointment to see him. He'll tell your other teachers what's going on, but you should talk to them too. Then you take care of the important things, and yourself. I hope your mom will be okay."

"Me too, Mr. Tietjen." She wiped her eyes, folded the handkerchief and handed it back to him. "Thank you."

"You keep that," he said. "I have a drawer full. My mother buys me new handkerchiefs every birthday and Christmas. And socks. I have a lot of those too. Handkerchiefs and socks. So if you ever need socks."

She smiled for the first time and he watched her continue up the stairs. "Hello, Mr. Scapelli," he heard her say when she passed him on his way down.

"Vicky Bower, you have turned into a beautiful flower!"

"Thank you, Mr. Scapelli. I really needed that."

When Terry reached Jesse on the landing he stopped. "I couldn't help overhearing. You did good."

"You mean 'well,' right?" Jesse corrected.

Terry smiled. "That too. Come on, let's go see if we can hunt down John Hiller in the Teacher's Cafeteria."

Rosencrantz and Guildenstern
Memorial High School
UFSD 71
Farmington, New York

TO: All Teachers and Staff
FROM: Mario Giovanni, Acting Interim Principal
SUBJECT: State of Affairs of the Affairs of the State
of the School

It is hard to believe that three weeks have passed since the peaceful transition of administrative power, acting and interim though it may be. The building is still mostly intact. Of course there have been a few hiccups along the way. Nobody told me that I had to disconnect the link the the Farmington Volunteer Fire Department when I pulled the alarm. And then there was a bomb scare or two. But I haven't done anything catastrophic since Baltz deserted the sinking ship, so far, and the *status* is pretty much *quo*–no contract, no raise and no change in the quality of the plastic utensils in the cafeteria!

The Phantom Shitter is still alive, though judging by our last encounter, not necessarily well, nothing that a change in diet couldn't help. Previous efforts to unmask, or more accurately, unpants the repeat offender, have so far turned out to be dead ends. So I have launched an investigation to explore my theory that this is "an outside job" and the deposits discovered around the building are being produced in another location and smuggled in. I have selected and assigned teachers to security duty at checkpoints at all entrances. They will stop anyone attempting to carry a package into the building. All packages are subject to search and/or seizure until the menace ends and the Phantom Shitter is caught holding the bag. Teachers, check your mailbox to see if you are on doody.

Rosencrantz and Guildenstern
Memorial High School
UFSD 71
Farmington, New York

TO: All Teachers and Staff
FROM: Mario Giovanni, Acting Interim Principal
SUBJECT: Another Clarification

This is to clarify any misunderstanding caused by a memo that was placed in your mailboxes on Friday, "State of Affairs of the Affairs of the State of the School." It was just another prank during a week full of pranks. The memo was completely bogus and so absurd that no right-thinking person could possibly have mistaken it for legitimate. As acting interim principal I have more important matters to waste my time. A comprehensive investigation is now underway to learn the identity of the guilty individual or individuals responsible for the bogus memo.

Rosencrantz and Guildenstern
Memorial High School
UFSD 71
Farmington, New York

TO: All Teachers and Staff
FROM: Mario Giovanni, Acting Interim Principal
SUBJECT: New Finals Week Procedures

I have implemented new procedures beginning today that will remain in effect during finals week.

In an effort to combat false alarms that have disrupted testing in previous years, all fire alarm boxes have been disconnected and will remain so until the end of test week.

To cut down on the volume of cutters from leaving the building illegally during final tests and to prevent unwanted visitors, all exit doors will be locked during Homeroom each morning and remain locked while tests are being administered.

In the event of a fire or other emergency, special duty teachers stationed around the building will alert their areas of the type and seriousness of the emergency. If the building has to be vacated, additional staff equipped with keys will be instructed to unlock the doors.

A list of special duty teachers will be in your mailboxes later today. Everyone assigned to unlock the doors be sure to see Mr. Lewis in his office as soon as possible to pick up keys.

IMPORTANT SPECIAL STUDENT ANNOUNCEMENT
FROM THE GUIDANCE OFFICE
FOR ALL SENIORS PLANNING TO GRADUATE
IMPORTANT
PLEASE READ BEFORE DISCARDING

June 1972

To All Graduating Seniors,

Your years here at R&G Memorial High School have passed quickly and will soon come to an end. Friday, June 23, as I am sure most of you know, is your graduation. Congratulations! We are all so proud of you.

For many of you in the Graduating Class of 1972, these will be your happiest four, or in some cases five years that you spent in high school, the high-water mark of your lives–the glory days. It's a fact and statistics prove it. Some of you won't live to graduate college! Some of you will overdose on drugs, some will drink and drive and die in car wrecks, and the lucky ones may make it a bit farther and die from disease.

So in an effort to make your graduation ceremony an event you will never forget, and so it runs smoothly, read and follow these guidelines. Dress appropriately. Girls, no overly revealing clothing and avoid using too much makeup because it looks cheap and slutty. Boys, jeans are never appropriate. No T-shirts, especially those with writing, particularly T-shirts with off-color or obscene writing. Even name brand sneakers are not suitable. No flip-flops. And be sure to shine your shoes.

At some point in the graduation ceremony you will be prompted by Mr. Gateway in singing the school's "Alma Mater" to the accompaniment of B Orchestra. How proud will your parents be when they hear your voices filling the Bernard H. Prahl Auditorium in unison and perfect harmony singing *all* the words and not just the few words everyone knows. Here is your personal copy of the words. Don't lose them and be sure to have them with you at the graduation ceremony. Better still, memorize them before the ceremony.

Alma Mater

Nestled in Long Island's valleys,
'Midst the mountains grand.
Proudly stands our Alma Mater,
To lead us by the hand.
Grateful are thy sons and daughters
Rising to our feet we stand,
Products of thee, Alma Mater,
Rosencrantz and Guildenstern Memorial
High School
To thee we raise our hand.

While singing the last line of the "Alma Mater" graduates will be directed to lift their right hand in salute. Be sure to raise your hand and not just your finger.

Graduation practice will be held in the Bernard H. Prahl Auditorium on Wednesday, June 21 at 1 PM sharp. You will have an opportunity to rehearse the song during the graduation walk-through. Caps and gowns will be available for pickup in the Boys' Gym beginning Monday, June 19. through graduation practice. All caps and gowns MUST be returned immediately after the graduation ceremony. If you do not return your cap and gown or if you damage it, you will not get your actual diploma until they are returned, repaired or replaced.

Let's work together to make this your best graduation ever. Seniors who are not graduating will be notified by their Guidance Counselors sometime before Graduation Day.

Sincerely,
Rory Aaron
Acting Guidance Chair

During test week, two one-and-a-half-hour tests were scheduled every day, with a fifteen-minute break between exams for students to get from one test room to the other. Subject teachers were not assigned proctoring duty during their tests so they could deliver test materials to each of the five proctors for their classes and to be available during testing time to deal with any problems. Because some exams took longer to correct and all grades had to be entered by the end of the week, English and History finals were on the first day.

The halls were quieter and emptier than usual. Hall teachers stationed on each floor relieved proctors who needed to run to the bathroom before their regular relief arrived. Outside the student bathrooms, one male and one female teacher escorted students into the bathroom one at a time and waited with them to lessen the chances of cheating.

Mr. Giovanni walked through the building, avoiding the elevator and using the stairs with caution. He looked in at each classroom as he passed, nodding to proctors, surprising a few who were reading instead of proctoring.

"How's the proctoring going, Mr. Milnow?"

He didn't stop doing the crossword puzzle. "I'm stuck," he said looking up. "What's a nine-letter word for 'annoyed'? Never mind–'perturbed.'"

Then he dropped into the Third Floor Faculty Room where English teachers were waiting for their tests to be over so they could immediately begin marking them. The Social Studies Department was counting and bundling their papers for distribution during the fifteen minutes between tests.

Mark Paulsen got the job as test coordinator when no one else in his department would take it. He was frantically trying to rally his department. "Does everyone have enough test papers? Be sure you put in at least one extra copy in each packet just in case. You don't want to be short. And composition paper, people. Everybody, listen up–Are you listening? Make sure you have the correct room numbers on each packet for the proctors."

"You're giving me a headache, Mark," Claire Hutton said. She was at the table playing Solitaire with a Pall Mall dangling from her lip. "It's not like we haven't done this a hundred times. Sit down, be quiet and leave us alone."

Sue was trying to recount her tests while Terry helped her. "Sixteen, thirteen... seven, twenty-five."

"Shit! Stop it! Now I have to start all over again."

Mr. Giovanni took it all in. "Aren't you supposed to be proctoring today, Mr. Purvey?" he asked, when he saw the math teacher sitting alone in the corner. "Math tests aren't until tomorrow."

Dwayne Purvey got up from his chair and left without answering..

"What the hell is his problem?" He shook his head and turned to the others. "The rest of you just carry on," he said. No one looked up.

Out of habit he went into the faculty men's room for a look around. He hadn't been there in almost three weeks and the writing on the walls was out of control. "Mini Mousse-a-lini sucks!" and "il Douchbag!" were lettered around on the walls between the old graffiti messages. Inside one of the stalls in red felt marker was the message "Jesus walked on water. Neil Armstrong walked on the Moon. Giovanni stepped in shit!"

He exited the bathroom and turned toward the (F)Utility closet. Except for the duty teacher sitting at the far end, the corridor was empty. He reached into his pocket and pulled out the Observatory key and slipped it into the lock. It fit. He turned it slowly. It turned. He took another look around to be sure no one was watching and opened the door.

When he was inside his jaw dropped. Through the one-way glass he had an unobstructed view into the men's bathroom. And there in the little room was all the missing AV equipment. "Holy... fucking... shit!" he said. "No wonder he was never in his office. No wonder he was nowhere to be found in the building. He was hanging out in the closet spying on everybody!" And then he had a thought. What had Baltz seen him do? What had he heard him say? He would have to go to the videotape. "Holy fucking shit!" he said again.

* * *

By Friday of test week, the building was almost completely empty of students, but the halls were full, mostly of the things dumped out of student lockers–unreturned textbooks, looseleaf paper, forgotten winter jackets, partially finished, unwanted Industrial Arts projects, makeup hair spray and aerosol paint cans. Except for a few teachers whose tests were later in the week and were still marking papers, most of the grades were already recorded. There was a stampede after the bell ending the last exam as students streamed for the doors. Teachers raced to collect their tests and get them graded by the deadline for the last-minute promotion meetings with Guidance that would decide if borderline seniors were graduating and who had to go to summer school.

John Hiller hovered in the faculty room with a cup of coffee and a roll, trying to cajole Red Farley to change a grade. "He just needs two points, Red, to get him to a 63 and then you can round that up to a circle 65. Pass him and he moves on. Otherwise he repeats the class."

"That makes four points, Hiller, not two. And when I fail him and he repeats the class, he'll be somebody else's problem next year."

"Not necessarily. With the way Guidance does the scheduling, you just might end up with him again next year."

"He's still not graduating," Herb Lupus said from the other side of the room. "He failed chemistry... again. I just marked his paper."

"–and social studies," Mark Paulsen added.

"Let's not be so hasty here, colleagues. We still have some wiggle room."

And so it went as the clock counted down slowly toward the finish line.

* * *

Reading all the essays had taken Jesse forever; it killed his eyes and his brain. He finally finished the last papers at home close to midnight. Though he knew they wouldn't be returned, he couldn't resist inking corrections and making comments on the pages. "Good job... You have to support your opinions... Off topic... Great!" When he arrived at school in the morning he combined the Part II essay scores with the Part I short answers.

He had learned a lot of things in a year, among them that grading wasn't always so cut-and-dry and just a matter of the numbers. Sometimes emotions got involved, sometimes he went back over a failing paper and agonized over it. Sure this kid was a pain in the ass all year, but he did try, eventually. Maybe his essays weren't really so terrible. He reread a batch, looking to find an extra point or two, especially for a kid who worked all year and fell just short of passing. It was a long and draining process. His class averages were calculated. Now all that remained for him to do was to enter the final grades on the Scantron sheets and turn them in by the end of the day. The Guidance secretaries would enter them onto the permanent records. He couldn't believe it. He was done.

"Hey, Mr. Teeg," Virgil had come into the room unnoticed while Jesse was staring out the window. "How'd I do?" He had a large watermelon under each arm.

"You did fine, Virgil. You went off a bit on your essay, but it, as always, was very creative." He looked in his marking book and traced his finger down the page. "Your final average was 92. How'd you do in your other classes?"

He tried to give him a thumbs-up and almost dropped a watermelon. "Mr. Farley was going to give me an incomplete for being out of his class so many days. But I told him most of the time I was out was because he kept sending me out. I didn't even have to play my ACLU lawyer card because in the end he decided he didn't want to spend his summer sitting around in a room for my appeal hearing."

"What are you doing with those watermelons?"

"I'm making another movie based on a dream I had. Hundreds of watermelons stacked in a giant pyramid and me dressed up like Evel Knievel or maybe Elvis Presley, I'm not sure which, and I drive my motorcycle off a ramp into the middle of them."

"And you're actually planning to do that?"

"Well, not exactly. I'd need a lot more watermelons and I don't have a motorcycle. So instead I'm planning to drop these off a roof and film that in slow motion. I'm headed up there now to do a test drop."

"What ever happened to that green Jello movie you were going to make."

"I've moved on, Mr. Teeg, after the Jello closed up over me in my test jump and I almost suffocated." He hiked up the watermelons under each arm. "This will be a lot easier and safer. I'll see you at graduation on Friday, right?"

"Absolutely. I wouldn't miss it."

Fifteen minutes later Jesse heard a liquid vuuuumph in the courtyard, followed a few seconds later by another. He went to his window and looked down at the two pink splashes in the center of the courtyard. One by one curious heads appeared in the surrounding windows. Jesse turned and looked up toward the roof. There was a smiling Virgil Loomis with both arms raised in a Richard Nixon double peace sign.

**Union Free School District 71
Department of Building and Grounds
Central Administration Building
Farmington, New York**

To: All Faculty and Staff
Subject: End of Year Procedures
June 19, 1972

Teachers and staff are directed to take home all personal items from desks, closets and classrooms by the end of the school day Friday. Building and Grounds will do necessary maintenance and repairs throughout the district during the summer. All classroom materials, books, etc., must be packed in cardboard cartons, sealed and labeled with the teacher's name and room number clearly marked and visible on each carton. Teacher desks, desk chairs and file cabinets must also be labeled with names and room numbers if you want to see them again. Teachers who will be in a different classroom in September and want their things moved to the new room must label each item to be moved with name, old room number and destination room number. While you are away on vacation, traveling to exotic places and keeping cool in your pools, Buildings and Grounds, the Custodial Corps and Maintenance will be sweating and working hard to make your return in September easier. But there are no guarantees and Building and Grounds is not responsible for any loss.

Joseph E. Scalia

Union Free School District 71
Office of the Superintendent
Central Administration Building
Farmington, New York

From: Donald F. Flackett, Superintendent
To: All Faculty
Subject: Letters of Intent
June 20, 1972

Letters of Intent were distributed in May to all tenured teachers and nontenured teachers invited to return for another year. If you are planning to remain employed in the Farmington Schools in the 1972-73 school year, all signed and dated Letters of Intent must be in the hands of your building principal by the end of the last day of school on June 23. A nontenured teacher failing to return his letter in a timely fashion will have his job offer rescinded and lose his position. Tenured teachers who return in September without submitting their letters may be reassigned to a different grade level and/or school.

Have a great summer. I look forward to seeing most of you in September.

TheThird Floor Faculty Room was decorated for the double shower. Pink and blue helium balloons covered both baby possibilities and white balloons, a few of which were beginning to sag, were for the upcoming wedding. Mary Jane Orlando in the Art Department hand-lettered the long banner on brown butcher paper that hung from the far wall. She put it up before it had been proofread.

"CONGRADULATIONS ON YOUR NEW BABY! CONGRADULATIONS ON THE NEWEST HUSBAND!"

An iced sheet cake baked by Sylvia Berkowsky's Home Ec Department rested in the center of the table next to a tray of stacked Italian cookies from the Allied Supermarket bakery, a coffee urn, leftover "Happy Birthday" hot cups and matching napkins and assorted plastic utensils.

John Hiller was dunking and drinking and watching the bridge game. Claire Hutton took a puff of her Pall Mall and laid down a card. Elsie Bergin followed suit and Rita Reed shook her head and sneezed. Carolyn Butrum was the dummy.

"So, Rita," Elsie Bergin asked, "have you decided if you're coming back to the classroom or going to continue as AP next year?"

"In the beginning it was so stressful I couldn't wait to get back to Reading. I begged and pleaded. But now it's not so bad. And the extra money is nice." She picked up the played cards and stacked them in a neat pile next to her. "If I ever get my own office–"

"I thought you had your own office?"

"I'm still sharing it with Helen O'Dell. She's been looking over my shoulder since Founder's Day. No one seems to know what to do with her. And honestly, it's getting to be very creepy."

"I wonder what she's going to have?" Mrs. Butrum said, changing the subject, "Phay whatever her last name is now. I've changed it so many times on her Sunshine Committee file I'm running out of room."

"A girl," Elsie Bergin said. "Her face changed and whenever your face changes during the pregnancy you can bet you're having a girl."

"Take a look at her rear end," Claire Hutton said. She laid her cards down, put her cigarette between her lips and demonstrated with both hands. "A fat ass is definitely a boy. I'd bet money."

"Does anybody really know whose child it is?" Mrs Butrum asked casually.

"Does anybody really care?" Terry answered and then broke into song, his version of the Chicago hit. "As I was walking down the street one day a man came up to me and asked whose child it is, yeah, and I said does anybody really know who his father is? Do you know, Red?"

"Nice voice, Scapelli. You should sing solo... so low we can't hear you," Red Farley said, delighted by his cleverness. "Or maybe you could sing far, far away!"

"Why don't you ever say anything nice to me, Red?"

"Why don't you go shit in your hat and squeeze it, Scapelli?" He was still mad about losing all that money.

"That's nice?" Stanley Milnow asked.

"My mother was nice and she used to say that to me all the time."

"Nice and classy. Your mother had it all."

"Up yours, Scapelli."

"I guess the father could be either of them," Mrs. Butrum said, counting on her fingers. "Lord knows she got rid of that first husband in a hurry. And she found this new one before the ink on her divorce papers was dry."

The door opened and the conversations stopped. All heads turned expecting to see the obviously pregnant Phaedra Schwartz, but it was Phyllis Lind.

"She's not coming," she announced. "She wasn't feeling well and went home this morning. And I just got word. She gave birth fifteen minutes ago!"

"What did she have?"

"A boy, right?"

"A girl?"

She looked at the paper where she had written the specific information. "Both," she said. "Twins–a boy, Evan, six pounds three ounces, fourteen inches long. Followed six minutes later by a girl–Yvette, weighing in at seven pounds even and fifteen inches long. Mother and children are all doing well."

"I guess they weren't premature," Rita Reed said and blew her nose in her handkerchief.

"Who's the father? Did she say?" somebody asked.

"Well, they are fraternal twins," Mrs. Butrum said, "so I suppose it is conceivable they both might be the fathers!"

"Conceivable," Terry said. "Good one, Mrs. Butrum."

"Oh, my goodness, I don't even want to think about that."

"I had a cat that got pregnant," Stanley Milnow added. "Every night the male cats lined up and took turns. When she had her litter not one of those seven kittens looked like the other."

"Oh, Lord. I really don't want to think about *that!*"

"That leaves only one unanswered question," John Hiller said. He refilled his coffee cup from the urn and wiped his fingers on the inside of his tie. "When are we going to eat?"

* * *

The best prank of Senior Prank Week actually happened the week after, on Wednesday at graduation practice.

"It looks like you're up, Rita," Phyllis said. "I can't locate Noah Lewis, And Mario's not around, so you're going to have to do graduation practice." She looked at her watch. "It starts at one."

"But–" she stammered, "I can't. I don't know what I'm doing." She began to sweat and fanned herself with her handkerchief.

"Not knowing what you're doing never stopped anyone else around here. There's nobody else, Rita. Helen O'Dell did it every year." She looked over at the photo propped up on the chair. "She had it down to a science and could get them in and out in twenty minutes–even when Mario helped her."

"Then couldn't he do it?"

"He might *if* I could find him, but I can't. He hasn't been in his office much smelling it up with his guinea stinker cigars since Friday." She handed her the folder. "Everything you need is in here, including the names of all the graduates in alphabetical order."

"I don't have to read them, do I?" She panicked.

"Not today, but at the actual graduation you will. You remember what happened when Noah did it last year. If he does it again this year we won't get out of graduation and pick up our checks until midnight. You have two days to practice. Today you just have to get them in alphabetical order. Show them how they have to march down the center aisle, fill in all the seats front to back, A to M on the right, N to Z on the left. When you call each name they go up on the stage one at a time, always on the right, cross to the middle, take the fake diploma from Mario with the left hand, shake with the right, sidestep to Flackett, shake, all the way across the stage, exit on the left and go back to their seat. It's easy. Just remind them today that there should be no signs or displays at the ceremony and no beachballs. And be sure to emphasize that they have to return their caps and gowns if they want their real diplomas. You'll be fine."

"That's so much to remember." She looked over the list. "And so many foreign names."

"There will be teachers on duty today to help herd them in and out, distribute the packets with detailed instructions and maintain some semblance of order. All the dittos aren't run off yet, but they should be ready before the practice even if they aren't stapled. You'll be fine," she repeated. "And if Mario shows up I'll send him down to the auditorium."

The Bernard H. Prahl Memorial Auditorium was packed to capacity. The custodians forgot to open the windows, so two large oscillating fans that were set up for graduation just blew the hot air over the heads of seniors hoping to get out fast and head to Jones Beach.

"People... Everyone..." Rita Reed's reedy voice was lost in all the graduation party conversations. "People... listen up... We have a lot to do and the sooner we do it the sooner you'll get out of here." She looked over at the bored duty teachers, who weren't much help. They were talking among themselves at the back of the auditorium.

Mr. Gateway arrived twenty minutes late and announced it was time to rehearse the "Alma Mater." He indicated the pit area in front of the stage. "At the ceremony B Orchestra will be here to help. But today we'll just use the piano. Please take out your copy of the words. Ready?" He opened the top of the keyboard. His hands rose and paused in the air. "Begin." He brought them down hitting a major chord.

That was the signal. Thousands of crickets were released simultaneously from both sides of the auditorium. There was an explosion of darkness from the balcony as more crickets were hurled into the air. Propelled by the blowing fans they rained down and filled the auditorium. They landed on the screaming crowd rushing for the exits. In minutes the auditorium was empty, except for the scattered unstapled papers that littered the floor and the swarming, chirping crickets that were everywhere.

"Mr. Polakas," Phyllis's calm voice echoed over the PA through the empty building, "please report to the auditorium immediately with a shop vac."

* * *

"Take a ride up to Sears, Charley," Stash Polakas said when he saw the auditorium. "It's Biblical! Like the plague of locusts in the Old Testament."

"I think these are crickets," Charley said.

"It doesn't matter. We're going to need a case of bug spray at least. And get some painter's masks and trash bags too. Big heavy-duty ones that we can wear. I'll suck up as many as I can until you get back with the spray. Then we'll get the rest of the dead fuckers. And be sure to pick up a new filter for the shop vac. Two of them. We're gonna need 'em."

1

The auditorium cleanup was a bigger job and took them much longer than expected. They worked for hours wrapped in plastic bags, spraying and vacuuming well into evening, when Eddie the night custodian joined them. On Thursday, most of the crickets were gone, but the smell of bug spray was overpowering even with all the windows open and the fans blowing nonstop.

"I think it will work, Phyl. Maybe we can skip reading the names and get them in and done in half an hour."

"The place will be filled to capacity with parents and grandparents, Mario. Just finding their seats will take longer than that. Imagine the lawsuits when somebody gets sick… or dies. Be the man, Mario. You're the principal. Make a decision. You have to move it outside," Phyllis reasoned.

And with her help, the acting interim principal made a firm decision. "We'll move the ceremony outdoors to the football field and hope for the best."

"We got some overtime," Stash said to his Custodial Corps. "Now start lining up all those folding chairs on either side of the fifty-yard line!"

Friday began warm and muggy and overcast. Tex Antoine put the chance of rain at sixty percent. "The first thunderstorms of summer, folks, with damaging winds and dangerous lightning." An hour before the ceremony it started–a teasing shower at first, that grew in intensity.

"What do we do now, Mario?" Herb Gateway asked.

"Fucking Tex Antoine!" He looked out his window. "I think it's going to stop and blow over, Herb. Doesn't it look like it's letting up, Phyl?" He looked over at her shaking her head.

"But even if it does, Mario, everything is drenched. Maybe Marching Band could slog around on the football field in the rain, but not my B Orchestra. And I won't ask them to. And then there's all that wet electrical equipment–"

"We'll just move it back into the auditorium," Phyllis said, making an executive decision.

"But what you said before about the crickets and the smell, Phyl, and the lawsuits–"

"We'll take our chances. At least it'll be dry and there's less of a chance anyone will be electrocuted. I'll tell Stash to get the fans going again and spray some air freshener. It'll still smell, but a little better." She was in motion. "I have to make up a new duty list and get the teachers to redirect everyone who shows up outside inside, parents to the auditorium, graduates to line up in the Boys' Gym." She went back to her desk and started typing.

Several minutes later the PA system crackled and Phyllis's calm voice filled the building. "Will the following teachers please report immediately to the football field for special duty–with your umbrellas if you have them." She read a list of names including Jesse's and Sue's. "That was the easy part, Mario. Now you go and make sure they show up!"

* * *

They began arriving at eleven. The confused parents and grandparents were redirected to the Bernard H. Prahl Memorial Auditorium, the prospective graduates to the Boys' Gym to line up for last-minute instructions. At eleven forty-five, B Orchestra, under the direction of Herbert Gateway, began almost in unison playing "Pomp and Circumstance." The sound boomed through the first-floor corridor, signaling the official beginning to the ceremonies and the procession of R&G soon-to-be alums marched into the sweltering auditorium. Their proud families and friends held handkerchiefs pressed to their faces, waving them to disperse the smell and fan the hot air, signaling their sons and daughters straggling down the aisle to the empty seats.

Despite several announcements asking everyone to hold their applause until the end, the audience cheered as each of the 1972 class of Rosencrantz and Guildenstern Memorial High School marched one at a time from their seats to receive an empty vinyl folder and shake hands with their acting interim principal, the superintendent of schools, the president of the school board across the entire stage. Actual diplomas would be handed out after caps and gowns and any outstanding textbooks were returned, paid for or replaced. Some diplomas would go unclaimed for years, some would never get picked up.

For an hour and a half, in heat and smell, amid chirps of super crickets who had survived the insecticide holocaust, Rita Reed hacked and coughed, wheezed and sneezed her way through the list, attempting to pronounce the names of four hundred and eleven graduates. Finally, the newly nearly-graduated garbled most of the words of the "Alma Mater," raised their hands and their fingers, moved their tassels from the right side of their mortarboards to the left and everyone cheered. When the fire alarm bell resounded throughout the building, the only ones stampeding up the aisles faster than the grads and their families were the teachers.

A minute later, Phyllis Lind's voice announced calmly over the PA, "Please disregard the bell. It's a false alarm." The klaxon horn at the firehouse across town sounded. And commencement officially ended.

* * *

After the fire trucks left, the teachers went back inside, some to their classrooms, others to the faculty room to wait for the end of the year checkout with Phyllis Lind before collecting their summer checks from Mr. Giovanni.

Jesse was having a final look around in his room. His books were boxed and labeled. His desk, chair and filing cabinet were marked with his name and room number and his final test papers were bundled into two piles, "Passing" and "Failing," that he had to drop off in the Main Office. He had gone out of his way and given all his students every opportunity to pass, but still there were a few who didn't make it. He finally understood what his teachers meant when they told a failing student, "I didn't fail you. You failed yourself." But still he was sorry they would have to go to summer school or double up and take two English classes in September. But he didn't feel guilty, well, not very guilty. He had been counting down the days all year to today, but surprisingly he felt no elation. He was vaguely depressed.

"Hey, Mr. Teeg," Virgil said. "I'm glad you're still here. I wanted to say good-bye and thank you and ask you to sign my yearbook." He was wearing his letter sweater over his gown and his cap was nestled into his hair.

"Thank *you,* Virgil. And congratulations for your award."

He held up the plaque. "Who knew? Coach Boid can really deliver. 'Rosencrantz and Guildenstern Memorial High School Athlete of the Year 1971-72.'" He handed Jesse his yearbook. "You can sign anywhere on my team pages." He waved his hands. "But I'm kind of partial to wrestling because it was my first letter and I was the secret team captain." He looked around. "I see you got everything packed away."

"Yeah, it's over. I can hardly believe it. And I survived. I just thought I'd be a lot happier."

"Me too and I just graduated. But I guess that's life. Never really satisfied… always wanting more." He shook Jesse's hand.

"I hope I'll see you again, Virgil."

"Oh, you will, Mr. Teeg. I've decided to run for the School Board in the fall. I already started collecting the necessary signatures today. I just have to file them." He grinned. "If I win, you'll be working for *me* in September."

Jesse laughed. "Good luck." He gave him a hug. "Congratulations and thank you for teaching me, Virgil. Don't ever let the world change you."

* * *

The rain had stopped and he was hot and sweating when he locked his classroom door and he was on his way to the Main Office.

"Have a great summer, Mr. Tietjen," Mrs. Butrum called when he passed her classroom. "And do be careful. Statistically most serious and fatal accidents occur during summer."

He nodded. "I will, Mrs. Butrum. But at least we don't have polio to worry about anymore."

"If you're going to be around, call my daughter. She's been asking for you–"

He smiled and waved.

"Everything in, Mr. Tietjen?" Phyllis asked. "Class book? Plan book? IBM green bars? IBM brown bars? Attendance cards? Keys with Mr. Lewis?" He nodded and she mechanically checked the boxes on her list. "Your Letter of Intent?"

"Almost forgot." He pulled the envelope from his jacket pocket. It was warm and damp. He handed it to her.

She opened it, read through to his signature. She smiled and touched his hand. "So glad that you decided to be back with us next year, Jesse." It was the first time she called him by his first name. "If you get in that line," she pointed, "Mr. Giovanni has the checks in his office. Have a wonderful summer."

"Well, that's one down and only twenty-four more to go," Red Farley said when he joined the back of the line. "Just another five for me. Maybe by the time you're ready to retire it'll only be twenty years."

"And maybe we'll even have a contract by then," Stanley Milnow added.

"What are your plans for summer vacation? Are you traveling?" Jesse asked.

"Vacation? Tomorrow I'll be in the South Bronx selling shoes."

"Teaching summer school. All the losers. But it's worth it because the extra money I make will pad my final average salary when I retire."

They all inched up. Terry came out holding his check. "Have a nice summer, Mario. I guess it's going to be tough having to give up that air-conditioned office when Baltz comes back."

"*If* he comes back." He winked. "Have a good time in Florida."

"Florida? Who goes to Florida in the summer?" Phyllis asked.

"Me. I'm driving down with a friend and camping in Flamingo Park. The Democrat and Republican Conventions are both in Miami Beach just a few weeks apart."

"That sounds very appealing. A week in Miami surrounded by unwashed hippies in tents."

"There's room, Red. It's a perfect opportunity for you to actually participate in the presidential selection process instead of just bitching. A chance to be a part of history and maybe even change history."

"No thanks. I'll watch it on TV in my air-conditioned living room. "Besides, it'll be four more years for President Nixon."

"Look for me on TV."

"I'm looking forward to seeing you getting arrested with all the rest of the great unwashed!"

Terry turned to Jesse. "Will we see you next year?"

Jesse nodded. "Now I have the whole summer to worry about September."

"*Tempus fugit.* Not to be pessimistic, but the days have already started getting shorter, since yesterday. And summer will be over before you know it." He waved good-bye. "See you at the Alibi for a drink. Red said he's buying the first round. Have a great summer everybody."

"Bullshit, Scapelli!" Red called after him. "I hope you get your head busted in Florida. The police have dogs there too."

Jesse got his check, said his good-byes and stopped at his mailbox. He was surprised to see a small wrapped package inside. He read the note card that was attached. "Dear Mr. Tietjen, thank you for caring. I hope you will carry this with you and remember me. Love, Vicky." Inside the wrapping paper was a folded red bandanna. He smiled and put it into his pocket.

"Hey," Sue said. "Just heard you're coming back!" She was carrying two shopping bags filled with gifts. "What did you do with that resignation letter?" He laid his attaché case on the counter, opened it and took the envelope from where he'd put it. He was about to rip it in half. "You sure you want to do that? You know you still have two more long years before you get tenure."

He smiled and replaced it in his case. "Thanks to you."

"You're going to the Alibi for a welcome summer bon voyage drink. Terry's driving down to Miami with a friend and they're camping out in a tent to be there for *both* presidential conventions."

"I heard. No, I'm heading home. I have a long drive, and my parents are taking me out for dinner to celebrate."

"Then would you mind giving me a hand with these?" She handed him a bag and they walked together through the hall, under the plywood "Silence Area" sign, past the trophy cases and out the front exit to their cars.

"Sure you won't stop? Just one drink?"

"Maybe another time… if you're going to be around this summer?" he asked timidly.

"Sure. Give me a call. My number's in the directory. We can go to the beach." She loaded her car and kissed him on the cheek. "Have a great summer."

He felt the place where she had kissed him and watched her drive away. He walked toward his car. Then he remembered something and he turned up the cement walk back toward the building. The sound of his leather heels reverberated over the lawn. He stopped at the entrance. "THIS SCHOOL SUKS BIG DICK." He reached inside his jacket and took out a red felt marker and carefully inserted the missing letter. He turned and cut across the grass to his car. The rain was gone and the June sun was warm on his face. His first teaching year was behind him and it was a definite eight, maybe even an eight and a half. Now he had the whole summer, seventy-three days, ahead of him before the first day of the next school year.

THE END

Aftermath
In the News
Summer 1972

July 10-13

The Democratic National Convention is held in Florida at the Miami Beach Convention Center. Sen. George McGovern of South Dakota is nominated for President. He selects Sen. Thomas Eagleton of Missouri as his Vice President. Eagleton later withdraws from the race when it is disclosed that he had undergone mental health treatment, including electroshock therapy, in the past Sen. Eagleton is replaced on the ballot by Sargent Shriver of Maryland, the brother-in-law of Pres. John Kennedy and Sen. Robert Kennedy.

August 21-23

The Republican National Convention is held at the same Miami Beach Convention Center. Richard M. Nixon and Spiro T. Agnew are nominated for reelection. Delegates entering the Republican National Convention are harassed by 3,000 antiwar demonstrators, many painted with death masks. The rest of the convention is marked by demonstrations outside the meeting hall. Hundreds of protestors are arrested and many are injured when police use riot-control agents including tear gas.

September 5-6

On Tuesday evening September 5, two weeks into the 1972 Olympic Games in Munich, Germany, eight tracksuit-clad members of the Black September faction of the Palestine Liberation Organization carry duffel bags loaded with AKM assault rifles, Tokarev pistols, and grenades into the compound. They scale a chain-link fence in the Olympic Village and take nine Israeli Olympic athletes hostage in their apartments. When negotiations between the German police and the terrorists fail, a botched rescue attempt results in the deaths of all the Israeli hostages. Four of them are shot, then incinerated when one of the terrorists detonates a grenade inside the helicopter where the hostages are sitting. The five remaining hostages are then machine-gunned to death. All but three of the terrorists are killed as the world watches the events on international TV.

Made in the USA
Columbia, SC
01 June 2018